GLENN MEADE

Resurrection Day

Hodder & Stoughton

First published in Great Britain in 2002 by Hodder and Stoughton
A division of Hodder Headline

2 4 6 8 10 9 7 5 3 1

A CIP catalogue record for this title is available from the British Library

ISBN 0 340 65747 2 (hardback)
ISBN 0 340 824514 (trade paperback)

Typeset in Plantin Light by Palimpsest Book Production Limited,
Polmont, Stirlingshire
Printed and bound in Great Britain by
Mackays of Chatham plc, Chatham, Kent

Hodder and Stoughton
A division of Hodder Headline
338 Euston Road
London NW1 3BH

This book is dedicated to the memory of my father,
Thomas P. Meade,
a wonderful man, much missed . . .

PROLOGUE

1 October – 10 November

'Seven days that will change the world'

I

Istanbul
1 October
6.15 p.m.

It wasn't the Istanbul of golden minarets and crowded alleyways, of teeming bazaars and the Telli Baba, the tiny cemetery where only one person was buried and to whom the people came to pray, but a wooden hut in a peaceful birch forest twenty kilometres from the city.

The location of the hut was secluded, the nearest neighbouring farm four kilometres away, and the site had been well chosen. The two cars drove slowly along the dirt track. Their passengers had arrived separately for the meeting and, as they moved into the hut, the bodyguards fanned out to take up defensive positions in the surrounding forest, joining the advance party of guards already hidden there since early morning, each armed with assault rifles and automatic pistols. These were hard men, watchful and ruthless, their senses honed in many bloody battles, and they were prepared to react brutally to the slightest hint of danger. In less than five minutes, they had taken up their positions.

At exactly 6.15 the meeting began.

The hut was threadbare. One room with only a wooden table, two chairs and thick curtains on the windows. The two men faced each other. One was a tall, bearded Arab wearing a linen suit and overcoat. He had the quiet stillness of a man in control of his body and his emotions. He greeted the American like an old friend, kissing him on both cheeks.

'My brother, it is good to see you again.'

'And you.'

The American was one of the US President's closest advisers. To ensure the secrecy of his visitor's identity, the Arab had been careful to use only his most trusted men. 'You managed to get away safely, without being observed?'

'It wasn't a problem.' The American had kept to his instructions, met his pick-up in the crowded back streets of the bazaar at the appointed time, before being bundled into a car and driven here. 'But I'll need to be back at my hotel within the hour. Otherwise, my Secret Service detail could get suspicious. I've taken a big enough risk as it is.'

The Arab pulled up a chair, laid a leather briefcase on the table. 'Then let us not waste any time.'

The American took a seat opposite. The Arab flicked the briefcase locks, removed a sheet of paper, handed it across. 'This is what we intend, my brother.'

The American read the contents of the paper with disbelief. 'You're not serious? You know what something like this can do? The enormous power it can wield? Its potential for devastation?'

'Of course.'

'The lives of hundreds of thousands, perhaps even millions, of my countrymen will be threatened.'

'We have known each other a long time. You must believe me when I tell you it is the only way.'

The American was pale, licked his lips with fear, put aside the paper. 'What if it goes wrong and I've helped devastate my own country?'

'How can it go wrong, my brother? Our strategy is foolproof. You are a man the American President trusts. Someone he would never suspect. With you on our side and your President caught in a dilemma from which there is no escape, he will have no choice but to give in to our demands.'

The American was grim. 'You're playing a dangerous game. And if it goes wrong it has the potential to cause terrible human tragedy. It'd be nothing less than Armageddon.'

'Think of the alternative. Many more years of bloody struggle that could end in even worse tragedy. Without your help, there would be many more deaths. You know the steel of our determination. We will do whatever we must to achieve our ends.

This way, it is over and done with quickly, and all our aims will have been accomplished. The injustices that have angered both our hearts for so long . . .' The Arab held up his thumb and forefinger, clicked them. '. . . finally ended. Just like that. Isn't that what we both wish?'

He saw that his words had hit their target. The American nodded his agreement.

The Arab replaced the sheet of paper in his briefcase. 'Trust me. There is no other way. And if we play this game with cool heads and strong hearts, we cannot lose.' He shut the case, locked it, regarded the American with an unflinching stare. 'Now you know what we intend, only one question remains. Are you with us?'

Outside, it was growing cold and dark. The American had gone, the car disappearing down the wooded track. The Arab pulled up his coat collar, looked out beyond the forested slopes, saw the pin-prick lights of ferry boats that moved across the black waters of the broad Bosphorus. Istanbul sparkled in the twilight. The colossal illuminated dome of the Blue Mosque was clearly visible, and the magnificent Topkapi, the ancient walled palace built by Suleman the Great, where pilgrims came to visit each day before the preserved relic of a finger bone of the Prophet Mohammad.

The venerable Turkish citadel, straddling Europe and Asia across the wide Bosphorus, has a blood-soaked history, its inhabitants ravaged by conquering armies that have come and gone over countless centuries. First the savage Mongol horsemen of Tamerlane, then the Romans, and later the Crusader knights, eager to defend the boundary which for them had marked where Christian civilisation ended and Judaism and Islam began. The Arab was conscious of this, and conscious too that the choice of Istanbul seemed entirely appropriate for a meeting that could have consequences far more dire than the deadliest of this fortress city's historic wars.

His men filed out into the cold evening, towards the cars, as the armed bodyguards retreated from their forest positions, silent as phantoms. The entire meeting had lasted no more than ten minutes. The Arab was the last to leave. His vehicle started up, prepared to follow the others down the dirt track, their headlights doused despite the growing twilight. As he climbed into the back of the car, he nodded to one of the bodyguards, a bearded, heavily built man, an AK47 slung over his shoulder. 'You know what to do.'

The bodyguard moved to the hut, tossed in the incendiary, shut the door, and moved into the rear of the car.

Five minutes later, as it drove back along the track towards the distant lights of the city, the Arab turned round in his seat, stared back at the hut. A flare of light suddenly glowed in the window as the incendiary ignited. The wood was bone dry, caught easily, and flames licked at the hut within seconds. No fingerprints would be found among ashes, no microscopic shred of evidence of the meeting would remain. Not that he imagined anyone would think of looking, but it was a precaution he deemed necessary. The American's treachery must never be discovered.

The Arab stared at the fire through the rear window, as if mesmerised, until it faded from view as the car drew away towards Istanbul. Beside him, one of his trusted aides said, 'Will the American do it? Will he betray his own countrymen?'

The Arab turned back. He nodded, and without speaking listed in his mind the sequence of events he had planned to the last detail, and which were about to unfold. A plan that would bring America to its knees, and change the world for ever. 'Now, *inshallah*,' he told himself, 'the final battle can begin.'

The shepherd saw the smoke from the hill three miles away, and trekked towards the forest clearing, as fast as his legs could carry him. When he saw the hut and the flames devouring the crackling wood, he ran another two miles to the nearest telephone.

It took almost an hour for the local police to arrive in a battered blue-and-white Renault, and by then it was completely dark and the hut had been reduced to a crumpled, smouldering mess of blackened embers. The twin beams of the car's headlights knifed the darkness, their harsh cones of light swamping the forest in the background, shining on the coiled wisps of smoke that rose eerily from the charred remains, like ghostly souls seeking heaven. When two of the policemen had picked carefully among the debris and determined that there were no bodies, the local police chief took off his cap, scratched his head and said to the shepherd, 'Who owned the hut?'

'I don't know.'

The police chief frowned. 'You don't know? How long have you lived around here?'

'Thirty years. That's why it's so odd.'

'What do you mean?'

The shepherd was baffled. 'I came this way only the other day.'

'And?'

'The hut wasn't there.'

2

Azerbaijan
31 October
12.05 p.m.

Through the dusty windscreen of his car Police Chief Ulan Fawzi watched as the shabby buildings and cheap hotels of downtown Baku collapsed in a slow dance of disintegration, one after another like rows of massive skittles being demolished in some gigantic bowling alley.

'Ten minutes,' the uniformed policeman at the wheel promised. 'Perhaps even less.'

Fawzi nodded absently and stared at the buildings. The illusion of their collapse never ceased to fascinate him. The glaring heat from the midday sun reflecting on the windscreen caused the mirage – made the buildings seem to cascade down into the streets in a dazzling waterfall of brick and glass.

It was five minutes past noon and the streets and markets of Baku thronged with people, but very few of them noticed the police car, two covered trucks and the grey single-deck bus speeding towards Bina Airport, ten miles from the capital. Chief Fawzi was riding in the first car, ahead of the other three vehicles. Under ordinary circumstances, he would have stayed in his office and left the job to his second-in-command, but these circumstances were far from ordinary and Chief Fawzi had a twofold reason for being here personally.

First, the airport was a den of corrupt, bribe-seeking officials and pick-pockets, so it was necessary to ensure that when the dozen VIPs arrived they were whisked through the terminal without any bother. Second, and more important, he had to ensure the VIPs' protection. If Fawzi handled it well, he figured he could count on the personal thanks of the Prime Minister and perhaps, God willing, even a raise in his salary.

The police chief turned his thoughts to what lay ahead. He was bringing with him thirty of his best men, all heavily armed. Another two dozen had already taken up positions at the airport since early morning. His main problem would come later that afternoon when he had to ensure the VIPs' safety as they travelled through the badlands of south-west Azerbaijan to their destination at Shusha, over two hundred kilometres from Baku. The region had lousy dirt-track roads, was pretty much lawless, and the mountains were often controlled by warlord bandits, army deserters and gangsters. Fawzi was no fool. He knew that the job he had been entrusted with could turn out to be a poisoned chalice. If any harm befell the men he was to protect, it would not be good for his career.

He would have to make certain that everything went smoothly, that his visitors' trip was comfortable, and that the convoy moved speedily. But his major objective was to ensure that security remained tight throughout the entire journey, and he couldn't afford any mistakes.

As the car sped down Izmir Street and swung left towards the airport, Fawzi felt a tightening in his stomach. He mentally checked over the list of precautions he would have to take if the convoy was to reach Shusha safely before nightfall.

12.55 p.m.

The wheels of the Boeing 757 bit the runway with a squeal as they touched down at Bina International Airport. The aircraft taxied to the apron, the engines died, and a mobile passenger staircase was quickly wheeled into place. On board the specially chartered 757 that afternoon were only fourteen passengers. They were Americans who had flown in late the previous afternoon to London's Heathrow from New York's Kennedy Airport, before their onward journey to Baku.

When the tired-looking passengers came down the steps, Chief Fawzi introduced himself to the American in charge of the US delegation, then shook the hands of each of the passengers in turn, welcoming them to Azerbaijan. All were male and ranged in ages from their middle twenties to early fifties. Casually dressed, some of them carried video cameras over their shoulders or clutched plastic bags of duty-free. Fawzi knew from his briefing that two of the delegation were with the CIA, there to ensure the protection of their American countrymen, and his practised policeman's eye could spot them easily: two burly men with restless eyes and weapon bulges under their jackets. One of the two CIA men presented his ID. 'Sir, I'm Greg Baktarin, with the Central Intelligence Agency of the United States. And this is my colleague, Joe Calverton.'

'Pleased to meet you, sir,' Calverton told the police chief.

The two men were in their early thirties, clean cut and ultra-polite. Fawzi thought the man named Baktarin had the look of someone with Azerbaijani blood in his veins, as his surname suggested. He was darkly handsome and tall, but unlike a typical Azerbaijani the CIA man was well fed, with perfect teeth, not a gold crown in sight. A lucky bastard whose parents had had the good fortune to emigrate.

'You have no need to worry.' The police chief offered his best smile. 'Everything is under control.'

'Sure, but if we could just take a minute to go through the security you've got in place,' Baktarin said in perfect Azerbaijani. 'We'd very much appreciate it.'

Fawzi produced a map, patiently explained the route, and the fact that thirty of his men, well trained and heavily armed, would be guarding the delegates during the trip. 'The roads are bad, but apart from that I expect no problems,' Fawzi offered.

The CIA men studied the map, cautiously assessing the information, until finally Baktarin gave a grudging nod. 'I guess we're in your hands. Are you ready to proceed?'

'At once. The convoy is waiting.' Fawzi couldn't tell whether the CIA men were entirely happy, but he himself was reasonably positive that the journey would go without any major hitch, despite his earlier anxiety. It was a straightforward operation, no more than a baby-sitting job, and he had every confidence in his men. There was no *real* danger likely on the trip. He had taken all the right precautions – alerted every police and militia station en route to ensure that their sector was vigorously patrolled, and be on the lookout for any trouble from bandits or brigands. But it had done no harm for Fawzi to strike the fear of God into the police commissioner by pointing out the *possibility* of danger from bandits attacking the convoy. Therefore, once the job was successfully done, the commissioner would be all the more grateful. 'This way, gentlemen, please.'

Fawzi escorted the Americans to the terminal through a private entrance used for visiting VIPs and government ministers. Two senior customs officials and an immigration officer, under Fawzi's withering stare, processed the visitors in record time. The British air-crew had remained on board the aircraft. When the Boeing had refuelled they would fly back to London, returning to Baku in three days' time to pick up the passengers, their business completed. Fawzi led the Americans out through the terminal into the cloudless, sunny afternoon, the temperature still a warm twenty-three degrees, hot for November. The route was lined at intervals with his men, all the way out to the convoy and the waiting single-deck grey bus.

The Americans filed on to the bus and, when Fawzi had made sure they were comfortable and that their luggage was safely aboard, he moved to his car at the head of the convoy, feeling pleased with himself. Everything so far had gone like clockwork. He gave the order and his men clambered into the two covered trucks. Then Fawzi raised his hand, blew a whistle, and proudly led the convoy out of the airport.

Bina Airport wasn't busy that afternoon, only three arrivals since midday, but the elderly cleaner noticed the armed police everywhere. He tried his best to look busy, sweeping the dust in his path with a heavy broom. He whisked the refuse into a long-handled metal dust-pan.

He counted the number of passengers who had come down the Boeing's steps, remembered the descriptions of the vehicles they had climbed into, the number of policemen who guarded them, the kind of weapons they carried – Kalashnikovs and sidearms – and the exact time the convoy left the airport. Then he made his way up the stairs to one of the public telephones at the rear of the departures terminal. He inserted a coin in the slot, dialled the number, and heard it ring over two hundred kilometres away in Shusha.

4.30 p.m.

Fawzi's windscreen was streaked with dust and dead flies. The road ahead wasn't up to much, a ribbon of cracked, potholed asphalt. It cut its way through a harsh, deserted landscape of parched, boulder-strewn fields and shale mountains. When the Russians had occupied Azerbaijan the road had been reasonable. Now the country had its autonomy there was no money for repairs.

Three hours into his journey, Fawzi was well pleased. Hardly any traffic – a few lorries heading east towards Baku, weighed down with farm produce, and the odd few country peasants on mule carts. With luck, the convoy would make Shusha in less than another two hours. Fawzi rolled down his window and looked back at the bus-load of Americans, sandwiched between the two police trucks. The convoy was approaching a dangerous gully on his left, the ground falling off to loose rock, boulders and rough brush. He saw the driver swerve to avoid a deep pothole before he righted the bus, narrowly missing the gully. Fawzi sighed with relief.

BOOM!

The sound of a massive explosion fifty yards behind him made Fawzi jump. *Missile*, something in his mind told him. He sensed the whispering sounds of fragments in the air, and a split second later there was a second explosion, the crack of a fuel tank erupting. Fawzi jerked round, saw the first police truck completely disintegrate in a blaze of red-and-orange flame. Suddenly debris rained down, twisted clumps of metal hammering on the roof and bonnet of his car. A wheel crashed into the road ten feet in front of him, the rubber tyre in flames as it bounced away.

'Stop the car!' Fawzi roared at his driver. 'Stop the fucking car!'

The man slammed on the brakes. With a surge of adrenalin Fawzi yanked open the door and jumped out, pulling out his pistol, his driver following. Fawzi saw that the bus was blocked by the blazing truck. The second truck at the rear had already halted and his men were jumping down, cocking their weapons. Fawzi tried to determine the source of the missile, turned to look up at the mountains. His blood ran cold. Another missile came streaking down from the hills, zooming through the air with white smoke pluming from its tail.

'*Oh my God! No!*' Fawzi pleaded, the missile hurtling towards him like a deadly comet. 'Get down!' he roared at his driver, and threw himself to the ground.

The missile screamed over their heads and exploded. The second truck disintegrated with an almighty detonation, sending a ball of flame and oily black smoke fifty feet into the air. Those of Fawzi's men who were still in the truck, and the others who had clambered off the back, were vaporised or blown out of the vehicle with incredible force, their bodies hurled into the air, then raining down in a shower of smouldering debris and flesh. The few survivors, some on fire or badly wounded by shrapnel, screamed and writhed in agony.

'*Bastards!*' Fawzi snarled at his unseen attackers, but he didn't move, waiting for yet another missile to strike the bus or his car. With the two trucks in flames, the bus was trapped and vulnerable. He saw the desperate Americans inside, terror etched on their faces as the driver tried to steer the bus off the road and manoeuvre it free.

Then it happened.

Fawzi heard the angry roar of engines. Looking to his right, he saw three vehicles race towards the blazing convoy from below some hills two hundred metres away, kicking up trails of dust in their wake.

As they came closer, Fawzi saw they were half-top Japanese four-wheel-drives, groups of men standing up in the back. When they were a hundred metres away the occupants opened fire. Weapons stuttered, sparks flew off torn metal, and the front windscreen of the bus was raked with gunshot. It shattered into a thousand fragments, and a slash of crimson was stitched across the driver's chest, his body convulsing behind the wheel.

Then Fawzi saw his car punctured by rapid volleys of machinegun fire.

The surge of adrenalin left him as quickly as it had come, replaced by fear. There was nothing he could do to save anyone. 'Get back to the car!' he roared at the driver. 'Run!'

Fawzi ran. The men in the vehicles continued firing. A round struck his driver in the back. The man yelped like an injured animal, spun to the ground and was struck again. A round punched Fawzi in the right arm, like a hammer blow, but he kept running.

'*Please, God . . . Please . . . save me.*'

Reaching the car, he clambered into the driver's seat, started the engine. As the car jerked forward, a burst of machinegun fire raked the bodywork. Fawzi was struck in the right shoulder. He lost his grip on the steering wheel and skidded off the road's edge. The car bounced down into the gully in an avalanche of dirt, rock, torn brush and shredded metal, crashed into a boulder with a sickening thud, and flipped over. Fawzi's head bounced hard off the roof, knocking him unconscious.

When he came to seconds later he was upside down in the driver's seat, in excruciating pain from his wounds, astonished still to be alive and that the petrol tank hadn't ignited. He cried out in agony, tried to crawl out of the wreckage but froze when he heard rocks tumbling down. He tried to see back up the gully. What he saw struck fear in his heart. Four tough-looking men with Kalashnikovs were clambering down, dressed in camouflaged army fatigues and menacing black woollen balaclavas, only their eyes visible through the slits. The men halted halfway down, studied the crashed, bullet-punctured wreck until

Fawzi heard one of them say, 'Forget it. He's dead. Get back to the bus.'

The men climbed back up to the road. Fawzi's relief didn't last. Seconds later he heard the deafening crackle of sustained gunfire, the terrifying screams of men being executed. Fawzi's blood turned to ice and he wanted to throw up. Moments later he heard engines start up and a convoy of vehicles drive away. Fawzi was still in shock, the gunshot wounds in his arm and shoulder throbbing mercilessly. His shirt was drenched in blood and his mind tortured by questions. What had happened up on the road? Had the Americans been executed along with his injured men? And *why*? Why had his convoy been attacked and massacred? And who were the attackers?

A swarm of flies buzzed around him, scenting blood. Fawzi closed his eyes, cried with pain, cursed the day he had become a policeman. His mother had been gone fifteen years, buried in the chalk hills above Baku, but he called for her now, called her name as he lay there in the bullet-ridden car, praying to God that someone would find him soon before he bled to death.

3

Montreal, Canada
9 November
9 p.m.

A ghostly flurry of icy sleet drifted across the bridge of the Estonian freighter *Tartu*. Captain Viktor Kalugin, smoking a half-finished cigarette, snug behind the warmth of the ship's plate-glass window, lifted his binoculars and scanned Montreal harbour, looming less than a mile away in the freezing darkness of the St Lawrence river.

The metal plates of the rusting, sixteen-thousand-tonne vessel he mastered shuddered and creaked beneath his feet as he stared at the blaze of lights from the towering skyscrapers filling the city skyline, their mammoth shapes reflected in the river. The same river French settlers led by Maisonneuve had sailed down from Quebec to found Montreal in 1642, and as fine a natural harbour as you would find anywhere.

'Fifteen minutes to dock,' called the first officer.

Kalugin judged the estimate to be about right. There was a slight swell, an eight-knot wind, nothing for him to worry about. The first officer was a trusted and experienced man who knew the St Lawrence seaway as well as his captain did. Kalugin put down his binoculars, took a nervous drag on his cigarette, crushed it in the ashtray at his elbow. 'Take her in the rest of the way. I'll be below in my quarters if you need me.'

Kalugin went down the metal steps to his private quarters. For eight months of the year the cabin served as his home, the photographs on his desk of his wife and two sons reminders of his other life back in Estonia. After fifteen years serving in the Soviet navy, he had resigned and taken a master's job with a private shipping line operating out of Tallinn. These days, you had to go wherever the money was.

And it was money that made Kalugin risk his career that cold November evening as he unlocked his desk drawer with a key he took from his trouser pocket. Inside, underneath a thick sheaf of paperwork, was another key, this one secured by some thin metal wire to a three-inch chunk of brass, so Kalugin wouldn't mislay it. Slipping the key into his pocket, he relocked the drawer. Then he stepped out of his cabin, shut the door after him, and anxiously made his way along the corridor to the port cabin.

Kalugin rapped twice on the metal door, and twice again, before he slipped the key into the lock. When he stepped inside, the cramped, twin-bunked cabin was in darkness. The light flicked on as the *Tartu*'s only passenger sat up listlessly and Kalugin closed the door behind him.

The Russian wasn't tall but he was reasonably well built, his body taut and fit. He was a handsome, lean-faced man. Where exactly in Russia he was from Kalugin couldn't tell, because the passenger had barely spoken a single word to him during the entire ten-day crossing. The cabin had been his home for the journey, an electronic chessboard his only companion to help take his mind off the angry waves of the harsh Atlantic. 'Better prepare yourself. We'll be docking in fifteen minutes.'

The Russian nodded. Already he was pulling on a dark blue windcheater, impatient to quit the stuffy confines of the cabin.

'You know the drill,' Kalugin advised. 'You don't move until the harbour officials and the crew have disembarked. You don't speak to anyone as you leave the ship, keep your head down and trail behind the crew. Your papers all look in order, so you shouldn't have any trouble. After that, you're on your own.'

'My thanks for your hospitality, Captain.'

It was the first complete sentence the man had spoken to Kalugin since he'd boarded. The captain still couldn't place the Russian's accent, but couldn't have cared less. He grunted, put his hand on the doorknob. 'I'll be back when it's time for you to leave. Until then, it would be wise if you remained locked in the cabin.'

Twenty minutes after the *Tartu* had moored, an inspector from the Canadian Customs Office, accompanied by an officer from the Immigration Department, strode up the gangplank. Kalugin knew both men from previous visits and led them down for mugs of steaming coffee in the mess-room, where he signed the four copies of the ship's manifest, the declaration listing his vessel's cargo, the port of origin and the cargo's final destination. The crew had been assembled, and they waited to present their crewman's papers to the immigration officer for inspection, before each was issued with a seaman's shore permit, allowing him freely to enter and leave the port while the *Tartu* was docked. Finally, the immigration officer handed the list to Kalugin for signature. Because the captain or his shipping company had no known record of violation, the visit was no more than a necessary formality. No search of the ship was conducted, nor was the cargo examined.

Ten minutes after the two officials had left the *Tartu*, Kalugin, smoking anxiously, stood hunched over the starboard rail, watching as most of his crew left the ship, intent on a night of whoring and drinking in downtown Montreal. Kalugin would have his own fun ashore, but later, when his business was done. Timing it until the last crew member had gone down the gangplank, he tossed away his cigarette and retreated back down to the cabin.

His passenger was already waiting, wearing his windcheater, the hood covering his head and most of his face, a thick woollen hat and scarf concealing his features. He carried no luggage, but clutched in his hand were his forged passport, crew papers and shore permit. 'Ready?' Kalugin asked.

The man nodded.

On the starboard deck, Kalugin pulled up his collar and watched from the rail as the passenger went down the gangplank. The engineer's mate, busy checking a hoist on the far side of the freezing deck, barely gave him a glance. The Russian headed towards the harbour exit, trailing behind the crew. The customs and immigration officers on duty made no attempt to check the identities of any of the *Tartu*'s crew leaving the docks, preferring to remain in the warmth of their offices, and the Russian passed out of the port unchallenged and disappeared into the bitterly cold Montreal night. Kalugin had no idea who he really was, nor did he care. An illegal immigrant, he had been told by the Chechen who had brought him on board, after midnight, in Tallinn, the day before his crew had joined ship, an explanation he didn't question. Kalugin's reward had already been deposited in a Helsinki bank account under a false name.

The captain spat over the rail and smiled to himself, happy in the knowledge that he was twenty thousand US dollars the richer. 'Good luck to you, whoever you are.'

By midnight, the passenger had reached the small town of Dunstan, a mile from the Canadian–US border. The Egyptian-born cab-driver who picked him up outside Montreal's Catherine Street underground station had simple instructions: take his passenger to the back road half a mile outside Dunstan and leave him there. Don't speak unless spoken to and don't look at the passenger's face. Less than ninety minutes later, the driver dropped his passenger exactly where he had been instructed, then turned his cab round and headed back to Montreal.

The back road outside Dunstan was heavily forested on either side with pine and birch trees. US Immigration had installed remote infrared cameras on many of the minor crossings in isolated and wooded countryside where no border posts existed, but across a vast, 3,500-mile frontier, there were still thousands left unguarded, and this was one of them, protected only by sporadic Canadian and US patrols.

The man left the road and trekked through the forest darkness for half a mile until he came to a narrow dirt track that cut through the woods into upstate New York. A blue Explorer four-wheel-drive was parked on the track, its lights extinguished.

A young woman sat in the driver's seat. When she saw him come out of the woods she stepped out of the vehicle. Even in the watery lunar light it was obvious that the woman was very pretty. Mediterranean looking, with dark hair and high cheekbones, she wore a brown suede jacket over a pale grey sweatshirt, blue jeans tucked into ankle boots, a scarf and gloves to keep out the chill. When the Russian reached her, the woman hugged him, kissed him on both cheeks. 'It's good to see you, Nikolai. I'm so glad you're safe.'

The man smiled back. 'And I you. Did you miss me, Karla?'

She smiled up at him. 'You know I did.' She touched his face, kissed him again, gently pulled away. 'Come, we'd better move, Nikolai. We've a long drive ahead of us.'

Fifteen hours later they reached Washington, DC. The apartment was in Alexandria, Virginia, seven miles from the capital.

The block was four floors, built of red brick, and surrounded by pleasant, well-kept gardens dotted with maple and oak trees, the branches already bared by the windy rigours of autumn. Karla Sharif pulled into one of the parking spaces in the grounds. She locked the Explorer's doors, led the way in through the main entrance lobby, and they took the elevator to the third floor.

The apartment was large, built when space near the capital wasn't at a premium. It had been renovated in a modern style: mushroom-coloured walls and beige curtains and inexpensive Scandinavian-style beech furniture. The Russian stepped into the large living room with its wide window looking down on to the gardens. There was a separate kitchen, and the two bedrooms had views towards Washington. For the next week the apartment would be his home.

'You've got the smaller bedroom. It should be comfortable and private enough. The bathroom's right beside you. Would you like coffee? I've got freshly roasted beans.'

'Coffee would be good, Karla.'

She led him into the kitchen, filled a small aluminium percolator, and when she poured their coffee they went to sit in the living room. The Russian took one of the easy chairs. Karla Sharif sat on the couch facing him.

'There are some things I need to explain.' She took a set of keys from her handbag, handed them across. 'There are two locks on the door. Always make sure you lock the dead-bolt if you have to leave. We use an agreed procedure before entering the apartment – a certain way of knocking and using the buzzer – just to be safe.' She told him the procedure. 'Use it every time you need to come in. There's a store near by, a 7–11, and I've written down the directions on the note in your bedroom. If you need to go out unexpectedly, tell me, or leave a note saying you've gone, so I don't get worried.'

'Who are your neighbours?'

'The apartment on our left is occupied by two Spaniards. They're both musicians. You may hear a piano playing now and then. That's José, he's with the Washington Philharmonic, and the boyfriend he shares with is Jaime. The other apartment on the right is owned by a middle-aged woman. She was an executive with an advertising company but isn't working right now. She's divorced, drinks a lot and stays at home most of the day. She likes to talk, so be careful if you bump into her and she gets inquisitive. I made it my business to mention casually that my boyfriend would be coming for a week, so that should put her mind at rest if she sees you coming and going. Two other things Rashid said to remind you of. You leave nothing in the apartment that might incriminate you, and always have your personal belongings packed, ready to leave at a moment's notice, in case of any danger. Do you have any questions, Nikolai?'

'Where's Rashid?'

'He said to tell you he'd meet you later. You won't recognise him. He no longer has a beard. He cut his hair short, dyed it blond, and wears an earring and American clothes.'

The Russian looked amused. 'How have you two been getting on?'

Karla Sharif flushed with a hint of anger. 'I do as he tells me. That way, there are no arguments.'

She went into her bedroom, came back with a brown paper

bag. The Russian opened the bag. Inside was a Beretta automatic pistol and three spare clips of ammunition. He checked the pistol's action and the spare magazines.

'It's been a long journey, Nikolai. Perhaps you should try and get some rest?' Karla went to go, but hesitated. 'One last thing. When do we deliver the package?'

'Tonight,' he replied. 'We deliver it to the White House tonight.'

He sat on the bed, smoking a cigarette, looking at his face in the mirror. It was the face of a man in his late thirties, boyish looking, with dark hair and high Slavic cheekbones. His passport said he was Dimitri Pavlov, a Ukrainian from Belarus, and he had apparently lived in America for over four years and possessed a legitimate work visa. But in truth he had been born in Moscow and he was wanted by Russia for murder, bombing and assassination, all committed in the name of the Chechen cause. He had even been given the ultimate accolade by Russia's Federal Security Service, the FSB. A code-name had been assigned to him – the Cobra.

These cold facts didn't even enter his mind as he looked out of the bedroom window towards Washington. The afternoon sun had started to give way to twilight, lights coming on all over the American capital. For a while he was a boy again, seventeen years old, lying in the long grass in the Sparrow Hills above Moscow, the city stretched far below him, a girl beside him in the long grass whose name he couldn't even remember. Life seemed to hold infinite possibilities. He felt an aching, a longing to be back, as if everything in between was just a dream.

But it wasn't a dream and he wasn't Dimitri Pavlov. Tonight, his mission began. It would be the longest seven days of his life, and infinitely dangerous. He looked back at his face in the mirror. The name on his passport was a lie, of course. He was Nikolai Gorev.

And he was going to change the world.

PART ONE
11 November

'Let this serve as a warning'

4

Washington, DC
Sunday, 11 November
3.15 a.m.

Forked lightning lit up the darkness as the uniformed Secret Service guards waved the black Buick sedan through the south-west gates of the White House. The car glided up the avenue and halted outside the West Wing entrance. The driver climbed out, held open the front passenger door, and an elegantly dressed man with strained features – a pursed mouth and troubled eyes – stepped out of the car into the sheeting rain. Two plainclothes Secret Service agents came forward immediately and escorted the man under the off-white canopied entrance.

A White House aide, who looked as if he'd just been roused from his sleep, waited in the hallway. He helped the man remove his overcoat. 'Good morning, sir.'

There's not one solitary thing good about it, the man thought. *Certainly not the lousy weather, and least of all the news I'm about to deliver.* 'Has the President been woken yet?'

'I believe so, sir. Let me take you on in.'

He followed the aide along a warren of hallways until they came to an oak-panelled door. The aide stepped inside, flicked on a table light, gestured the man to a nearby armchair. 'I hope you'll be comfortable, sir. I'm sure the President won't be long.'

The aide withdrew, closing the door. The man sat uneasily in the armchair and sighed heavily, as if carrying a terrible burden. He was in one of the anterooms to the Oval Office, heavy with period furniture and solemn oil paintings of early American native scenes.

Next to it was another anteroom, one that led directly to the Oval Office, the polished oak door open to reveal a chest-high plinth topped with a bronze bust of granite-faced Abraham

Lincoln, and yet more oil paintings: of Quincy Adams, and Jefferson, historic men looking down from historic walls, their portraits adding emphasis to the dignity of the presidential office just a few feet away, which the now-waiting visitor was soon to enter.

He had waited here on many previous occasions to see his President. But this cold, stormy November morning, he solemnly wished he was someplace else. Douglas Stevens, the head of the FBI, was besieged with anxiety. In a career in the service of his country that had spanned almost thirty years, it had sometimes been his duty to deliver bad tidings to his President. But of one thing he was absolutely certain. No other president in the history of the United States had ever been presented with such devastating information as he was about to deliver.

Outside, he heard the faint noise of approaching footsteps. He stood, checked himself in one of the wall mirrors. As always, his clothes were immaculate, and his body smelled faintly of fresh soap after the steaming-hot shower he'd taken at his home in Arlington almost two hours ago, after being woken by the ringing of his cellphone.

But his face was another matter. Raw fear had carved deep worry lines into his skin and added at least ten years to his appearance. He looked down at the briefcase in his right hand which contained the source of his distress. Thinking about the contents, he noticed his hands tremble, felt cold beads of sweat rising on his forehead. Normally he was a calm man, totally in control of his emotions. But he wasn't calm now. This morning, America's worst fear had finally come true.

Glancing at the bronze bust through the open door, Stevens saw Abraham Lincoln stare down with his usual sorrowful expression, as if to say: *I understand the weight of your burden. You have my sympathy*.

Stevens thought: *Thanks, Abe. But I'm afraid it doesn't help any.*

The door opened, the aide reappeared. 'The President will see you now, sir.'

* * *

They were seated in the Oval Office, the President at his desk with the American flag behind him. He wore a dressing gown over his pyjamas. His hair was rumpled, his eyes puffy after being woken from his sleep. Still a relatively fresh-looking man, and barely into his middle fifties, President Andrew W. Booth had fought his way up through the ranks of politics with gritty Texan determination, and a willingness to face up to any obstacle or crisis. But Stevens knew that this morning the man was going to be tested by a crisis far greater than any he'd ever had to deal with.

One of the night staff had left a pot of fresh coffee on the desk. Booth glanced beyond the window at the pouring rain. Tentacles of forked lightning lit up the White House lawns. He smiled slightly, indicating a chair. 'It seems quite a morning out there, Doug. Coffee?'

'No thank you, Mr President.'

'Your call said it was extremely urgent.'

Stevens nodded. 'My apologies for waking you, sir, but it's a matter that demands your immediate attention.'

'Then I guess we better begin.' The President finished pouring coffee for himself, barely awake as he sipped tiredly from his cup.

Stevens's voice was hoarse, braided with fear. 'A package was delivered to the Georgetown home of a Saudi Arabian diplomat at approximately twelve-fifteen this morning. The package was addressed not to him but to you, sir – the President of the United States. As to why the particular man was chosen as an intermediary we've no idea. But the circumstances of the delivery are pretty simple. The man's doorbell rang. When he got out of bed to answer, he found the package waiting for him on the doorstep, addressed to you. That's when he decided to call the FBI's Washington field office for advice. I was contacted about the matter at one forty-five a.m. by my Assistant Director, who requested to see me urgently. We met in my office forty-five minutes later, and once I was made aware of the package contents, I knew I had to see you immediately, sir. So I headed straight here and called you on the way.'

The President frowned. 'You have this package with you?'

'Yes, sir, I do.' Stevens flicked open his briefcase, withdrew an A4-size Jiffy bag.

'Naturally, standard procedure was followed. The package was examined for any dangerous or explosive material.'

At least one hundred thousand letters and seven thousand parcels were delivered unsolicited each year to the White House. Most of the letters addressed to the American President were from well-wishers, or citizens with an axe to grind about his policies. But about five per cent were from nutcases, abusive missives or blatant *'I'm going to kill you'* threats that would promptly be investigated by the Secret Service and FBI.

As for the parcels, most contained simple gifts – baked pies or cookies posted by concerned matronly citizens, anxious to nourish their President's health with home-cooked food. But a small percentage of the packages – less than three per cent – contained anything from human excrement posted anonymously to sexy underwear dispatched by female admirers. It was one of the trials of being elected to the most powerful office in the land that you were the subject of reverence, revile and sexual attraction all at once.

'The package was declared safe,' Stevens added, 'but these are the exact details of the contents and the delivery. I thought you might like to see them before we get down to specifics.'

The President took the single page that Stevens offered, and read.

FBI REPORT on package delivered to Saudi diplomat Mohammed Faud, at Georgetown, November 11th.

PACKAGE:

One (1) standard A4 size Jiffy bag, addressed to the President of the United States.

CONTENTS:

One (1) standard 60-minute magnetic videocassette, of possible Far East manufacture, contained in a clear, hard plastic wallet. Recorded contents: an eight minute thirty-two second (8:32) recording.

Two (2) typed pages, all on A4 size sheet paper. The pages contain a list of Arab names.
One (1) written page, which pinpoints the location of a left luggage box – number 02-08 at Gate C, in Washington's Union Station.
PRELIMINARY FORENSIC ANALYSIS OF CONTENTS:
None of the three pages showed up any fingerprints during tests. The cassette also appears to contain no fingerprints or other identifiable forensic marks, internally or externally, nor have the internal mechanics of the cassette been interfered/tampered with.
According to the date stamp on the visual contents, the recording on the tape was made on November 1st, at 9 p.m.
NOTE: The cassette was discovered by Saudi Arabian diplomat Mohammed Faud when the package it contained was left outside on his porch at his home in Georgetown at approximately 12.15 a.m. on the morning of November 11th, having answered a ring to his doorbell. There was no trace of the person(s) who delivered the videotape, but Faud reported that he thought he heard a car start up and drive away shortly after his doorbell rang. Investigation is continuing.

The President considered the report, then sat back in his chair. 'And what exactly does this tape contain?'

Stevens gestured to a TV/video recorder in a corner, for the President's personal use. 'If I may show you, sir?'

'I take it that's the primary reason you're here, Doug.'

'Yes, sir. But a word of warning, Mr President. You better prepare yourself for a shock.' Stevens crossed the room, switched on the TV and video, and slid in the cassette. He stepped back, holding the remote control, pressing several of the buttons until the screen flickered to blue. Seconds later, it dissolved to black lines, and then the figure of an Arab man emerged, only his head and chest visible. He appeared to be in his middle forties, his face soft, gentle looking. He wore typical Islamic dress: a grey half-turban and a white *kafiya*. At first, the man's dominant feature appeared to be his dark, bushy beard, streaked with grey. But on closer study it was his eyes which held the attention. Dark brown, hinting at compassion, but with the diamond-hard glint of the fanatic. It was a face President Andrew Booth was familiar with. A face that promptly caused him to clench his teeth in anger.

He directed a meaningful glance at Douglas Stevens, as if to say something, but the FBI director cut in, removing two pages from an envelope he took from his pocket. 'The words you're about to hear spoken on the tape are in Arabic, sir. I've had them interpreted by our top Arab translator, Mr Edwin Marshall. This is his translated copy, if you'd care to read it.'

Stevens handed over the pages. Almost immediately the Arab spoke directly to camera, his voice soft, almost courteous, and as he spoke the President read the translation:

> With the copious blessings of Allah the all powerful and compassionate, I, Abu Hasim, address myself to the President of the United States.
>
> I speak to you as a man of God, concerned with the suffering and oppression of the Arab peoples. For centuries now, we have been subjugated by the West, first the British and Europeans, and now by the Americans. It is my opinion, however, that America represents the most oppressive of all these occupiers, and the worst evil in mankind's history. I believe this for many reasons. Your corrupting influence extends everywhere in the Middle East. In the Arab Emirates, in Egypt, and in the lands of Jordan, Israel and Palestine. Countries in which you Americans should have no rightful place, but in which you continue to interfere, by force or influence. Most importantly, your armed forces are present in Saudi Arabia, my homeland, the land of the two holy shrines – Jiddah and Mecca, the most sacred of Islamic cities.
>
> This occupation is unacceptable to all God-fearing followers of Islam. In Saudi, you support a regime in which the royal family – the King and his princes – corrupt themselves materially and spiritually, flouting the laws of God the Almighty, while you Americans openly rape the country of its most precious natural resource, oil. This resource, bestowed by Allah, blessed be his name, rightfully belongs to the Arab peoples, yet you Americans

use it to fuel the corrupt and evil power of your economy. You do this in many other Arab lands – in Kuwait, in the Arab Emirates – where your presence was not sought or desired by the God-fearing Islamic population.

On occasions, President Booth, you and your predecessors have said you maintain your presence in these lands because you wish to establish peace in the Middle East. I say that this is a lie. Instead of helping to bring about peace you continue to aid Israel, while you murder or imprison Islamic warriors who battle for the freedom and self-determination of the Arab peoples, warriors who take up a just and rightful armed struggle against American oppression. You have even tried to kill me. But by the Grace of God the all powerful, blessed be his name, I was spared to continue his good works. Spared to honour the pledge I made long ago that I would offer myself to God's blessed cause and be a saviour of Islam.

In response to your aggression, I, and others like me, have sought to defend ourselves by attacking your military bases, your countrymen, and your interests throughout the world. This has proved ineffective. Our numbers may be large and blessed by God, but you possess the modern technology of warfare that we do not. You have also kept this same technology from the Arab world. No Arab country wields nuclear weapons or other weapons of mass destruction for their defence, and yet Israel, the mortal enemy of all true followers of Islam, is allowed to maintain such an arsenal. Why should this inequality be so? It is only so because you and your predecessors have wished it, Mr President, in order to maintain an imbalance of power in the Middle East in your country's favour. In this way, you play jailer with us. We remain prisoners to America's cause, a people in chains, without control of our own destiny. This is a situation that cannot be allowed to continue. Accordingly, it falls to me, Abu Hasim, to counter the oppression and corrupt power of America with force.

Therefore, by the Grace of God, and to honour my pledge to Allah and the Arab peoples, I send you this recording to inform you that I now possess a weapon truly powerful enough to change this unacceptable state of affairs. It is no ordinary weapon, but one that can and will cause untold devastation, and bring America to its knees. I have ordered this weapon placed in Washington, DC, the very heart of American evil. It is timed to unleash its devastation in seven days from midday today, Greenwich Mean Time, 7 a.m. Eastern Standard Time, November 18th, unless the following conditions are met:

One – the US withdraws all its troops and military support from the entire Arab Middle East region within those seven days.

Two – within the same period, the US releases all Islamic prisoners, of which I have supplied a list of names. Others on the list are held in foreign prisons. America will use its power and influence to guarantee their release.

Three – Washington must not, I repeat not, be evacuated, nor this threat made public.

Four – you, President Booth, must not attempt to leave the capital, but must remain within its confines.

I would also strongly suggest that your forces of law and order, your police and FBI, do not seek to find my weapon. If they do – if they attempt to hunt down my followers in your capital – then they risk the consequences. My people have been ordered to detonate the weapon if they are under dire threat from your forces of law.

Also, if any of these demands are not met, or if any of the conditions are ignored, the blame will fall on your head, President Booth, and I, personally, will immediately trigger the weapon. If proof is needed that my threat is real, then you will find this proof at the location details of which you have been provided with.

I earnestly pray that God will deliver on you the blessings of his compassion and wisdom at this difficult hour.

The image faded to a dazzling blue, then flickered to black lines again. There was total silence in the Oval Office, and then the President, having read the translation, and completely awake now, looked at Stevens with amazement and consternation on his face. 'What in God's name was that all about?'

'At this moment I'm as wise as you are, sir. We haven't had time to determine if it's a hoax. But it certainly looks like Abu Hasim, and sounds like him.'

The President's mouth tightened as he put down the pages he had read. Stevens couldn't fail to notice the repressed anger in his expression. As far as the United States was concerned the man in question, Abu Hasim, was the most wanted terrorist in the world. Al-Qaeda, the Islamic terror group he led, had been responsible for the savage deaths of hundreds of American troops and citizens in suicide bombings in the US, Africa and the Middle East. The President spoke, barely able to conceal his angry contempt. 'Has anyone run a voice analysis on the tape?'

'It's being done as we speak, Mr President. We've got recordings of his voice from journalists' taped interviews and from a number of Hasim's telephone conversations we intercepted. We can use them to verify if it's definitely him.' Stevens paused. 'I should point out that so far I've limited our operation to no more than a dozen FBI personnel. They've each been advised of the need for absolute secrecy until we get to the bottom of this.'

'What about this proof that he spoke about?'

'I dispatched a team of agents to the Union Station. They'll phone me as soon they've located and opened the locker.'

The President ran a hand over his face, stared over at the blank TV screen, then looked back at Stevens. 'You think Hasim's threat is for real, Doug?'

'I think so, Mr President. I doubt it's a completely empty threat. Why go to the effort of recording and delivering the tape if he can't back up what he says? But I guess it all depends on what we find in the locker.'

'What do you think this weapon he spoke about might be?'

'God knows, sir.'

'Who are the prisoners he mentioned?'

Stevens offered two of the pages from the package, watched as the President studied the list.

'Three hundred and eighty-five names, all males,' Stevens explained. 'I've had each of the names checked on our databases. Fourteen are Arabs being held in US penitentiaries. At least two hundred and fifty appear to be Islamic guerrillas captured during the Chechen wars by Russian forces and mostly incarcerated in Moscow. The remainder are imprisoned in Israel, except for three names on the list – two are in British jails, the other's in Moabit Prison in Germany. They're pretty much all serving long-term sentences for serious terror crimes. Bombings, assassinations, conspiracy to maim and murder. In the case of the prisoners held in the US, almost half were convicted of involvement in the embassy bombings in Africa.'

The President's face darkened. He got to his feet. 'And he wants all of them released? That's a grave demand in itself. But this business of us withdrawing from the Gulf – Hasim can't be serious?'

'He sounded pretty serious to me, sir.'

The President began to pace the room, strain on his face. 'We're talking about a withdrawal from a region of *vital* military and economic importance, not only to us, but to the entire Western world. Have you *any* idea the kind of nightmare scenarios that could materialise if we no longer had a military presence in the Gulf? Oil flow to the West would be jeopardised, and devastating economic crises could result. Not to mention the danger of Islamic fundamentalists taking over the region, and the position Israel would find herself in. We're not only talking about a change in the balance of power in the Gulf, but in the *world*. If Hasim thinks we can just walk out of the region, he has to be totally crazy.'

'That may be, sir, but the man's obviously got something pretty serious up his sleeve. Otherwise he wouldn't have made such earnest demands or so grave a threat. From the way he's talking, the entire Washington district may be in danger. And it's not as if we can retaliate effectively against someone like Hasim. We've learned that in the past. It's not a foreign country we're talking about here, but a stateless individual, someone whom we can't make a meaningful countermove against. We can't threaten him with sending in the Marines, or deploying our missiles or nuclear arsenal. Least of all now, if he's holding a gun to our heads.' Stevens paused, his voice tense. 'There's always the possibility this whole thing could turn out to be a hoax, Mr President, but I really wouldn't like to bet my bottom dollar on it.'

The President returned to his leather chair, reached for his phone. 'I'll call a crisis meeting of the National Security Council for eight-thirty a.m.'

'Can't we make it earlier, sir?'

'The Vice-President's in Colorado, attending a party convention, and the Defence Secretary's overnighting in Kansas, visiting family. I'd like both of them to be present, in person, for the meeting, and I reckon we can get them back in the White House by eight-thirty.'

Stevens's cellphone vibrated and he reached in his jacket. 'Excuse me, sir.' He switched on the phone, identified himself, and listened for several moments before replying. 'You're sure?' He paused, listened again, said urgently, 'I'll keep the line open. Get back to me as soon as you can.'

The President raised his eyebrows. 'Well?'

'Two things, sir.' Stevens kept his cellphone cradled at his neck as he spoke. 'One, the voice analysis was positive – it's definitely Hasim on the tape. Two, my men are at the Union Station. They're about to open the locker.'

5

Fifteen minutes earlier, at precisely 3.45 a.m., Washington's Union Station was almost deserted. A heavy downpour hammered the pavement outside, and the night-shift cleaners were working away with their vacuums and polishing machines, getting ready for the busy day ahead, which would see at least one hundred thousand passengers pour through the station's doors. Dating from 1907, a magnificent neoclassical structure with graceful fifty-foot ceiling arches, soaring pillars and marble walls and floors, it was once the largest train station in the world.

A handful of vagrants had taken refuge from the miserable, stormy night, joined by a half-dozen disgruntled passengers who had missed late-night trains, destined to wait until the early morning to make their connections to Virginia or Maryland, Philadelphia or New York. Curled up in sleeping bags or wandering the tiled floors, hands stuffed in their pockets to keep warm, the night-time refugees had their peace interrupted by the heavily armed FBI teams, a six-man bomb squad detail, and at least twenty District police wearing rain capes who swarmed into the Union like a force. Within seconds, the station walls rang with voices and footfalls, as uniformed officers sealed off the terminal and secured every single one of its exits and entrances.

Jack Collins, a thickset man of forty-three, his dark hair flecked with grey, was the senior FBI agent in charge. He had a walkie-talkie clipped to his chest, and like his men wore a navy blue zip-up nylon jacket, the FBI logo on the back in prominent gold lettering. His hair was drenched from the short dash through the rain from the Dodge Intrepid parked outside, and he assembled his men with a commanding tone of controlled urgency.

'I want everyone out of the station, except our people. And I mean *everyone*. Amtrak staff included. Check the platforms and toilets – every damned nook and cranny. I want no civilians on the premises.' He pointed to one of his men. 'Find out where the lockers are at Gate C and if someone here's got a set of master keys.'

A young FBI agent said, 'Sir, where do we move the people from the station?'

'Where the hell do you think, Grimes? Outside.'

The agent glanced out at the sheeting downpour. 'Sir, it's teeming out there.'

'I don't give a damn if there's a blizzard and five feet of snow – get this place cleared. *Pronto!*'

Minutes later a procession of puzzled vagrants, surly teenagers, waiting passengers and station staff were briskly escorted out into the wet night, all looking unhappy as hell. 'Gonna see my fucking Congressman!' an elderly homeless black man wearing a pair of shabby earmuffs, a tattered overcoat and filthy sneakers shouted at Collins as he went past. 'You mo'fuckers always harassin' a black man down on his luck.'

'Sorry, sir, but we've got to clear the area.' Collins smartly ushered the man along, then turned away from the protest as one of his agents hurried up, accompanied by a uniformed Amtrak police officer. The agent pointed towards an archway that led to the arrivals/departures concourse. 'The Gate C lockers are over there by the wall, sir. This is Duty Officer Vincenti, he's with Amtrak. He's got a master key that opens all the lockers.'

'Let me see it,' said Collins.

The man produced a single key attached on a ring to a chunk of grubby, heavy steel, and handed it to Collins. 'You mind me asking what in the hell's going on here?' the Amtrak officer asked.

Collins palmed the key, ignored the question. 'Come with me.'

He strode towards the left-luggage area at Gate C. Several rows of beige-painted metal lockers were set against the wall. Collins located box number 02–08. It measured about eighteen inches by twelve, and like all the others was electronically operated. He stared at the locker for a time, then turned instinctively, his practised eye noticing a security camera high up in the ceiling, aimed at the lockers. He looked round and spotted another two cameras near by, trained on the same area. 'Those cameras work?' he asked the Amtrak officer.

'Yes, sir. They're on twenty-four hours a day.'

'You mean anyone using these lockers is caught on tape?'

The Amtrak man nodded. 'We use thirty-day tapes. There's a camera room back at my office. The lockers themselves have a twenty-four-hour timer. If they're not opened within that period, we open them with the master and remove the contents. It's a security measure.'

'You're saying if someone left something in any of these lockers it would have to be within the last twenty-four hours?'

'Yes, sir.'

'I want the tapes. Every last one you've got,' Collins said urgently, and turned to the agent who had accompanied the Amtrak man. 'Take him back to the office. When you have the tapes, take them out of the station and back to your car. And take this officer outside. Let me know when you're done.'

The Amtrak officer went to protest, but the FBI agent promptly led him away. Collins turned to another of his men. 'OK, let's get the bomb squad in here, open up the locker, and get this thing over and done with.'

Collins heard a commotion behind him and turned. Striding towards him was Tom Murphy, the head of the FBI's Counter-Terrorism Division. At six foot four, he was a big-boned man of fifty-three with a bushy grey moustache, and Collins's boss. Behind him came two senior agents from FBI headquarters whom Collins recognised. 'Jack, I see you've got everything under control.'

'We're just about ready to open the locker.' Collins explained about the Amtrak security tapes and Murphy looked hopeful.

'Let's keep our fingers crossed they turn up something.'

'You mind telling me what the devil's going on, Tom? All I got was a call telling me to get a team down here fast, that someone may have left a dangerous package in the locker. I was to secure the station, liaise with Amtrak security about the locker, and have the bomb squad standing by to open it up.'

Murphy nodded. 'That's all you need to do for now, Jack. I'll take it from here on in.'

'What do you mean?'

'Just do as I say, Jack. Get the bomb guys over here, then get your men together, stay on the periphery and make sure the cops keep well back out of the way. When we're done here, stand your men down. Then you go home, get some sleep.'

Collins frowned, puzzled, as he stared at Murphy and the senior agents accompanying him.

'What's the story here, Tom?'

Murphy was grim, shook his head. 'Sorry, Jack. Orders from above. From here on, it's my baby.'

An Arab man stood in the teeming rain, smoking a cigarette, watching the activity outside the Union Station from across Columbus Circle, two hundred yards away. Mohamed Rashid was in his late thirties, a tough-looking stocky figure with olive skin. His hair was cropped short, dyed blond. He wore a gold earring and a leather baseball jacket with 'Yankees' emblazoned on the back. He walked back to the blue Explorer parked twenty yards away at the kerb, yanked open the passenger door and climbed in. Nikolai Gorev sat in the driver's seat. 'Well?'

Rashid grunted. 'They've found it. Now let's finish what we have to do.'

Half an hour later, in heavy rain, the Explorer pulled off the main Baltimore highway and turned east, down a minor country road. There was no traffic at that hour of the morning. The road was deserted and badly lit, and in the rain and pitch darkness Nikolai Gorev carefully watched his speed. Five minutes later, on Rashid's instructions, he pulled in and halted beside a pair of chest-high wrought-iron gates with a low stone wall on either side. A plaque was fixed to one of the padlocked gates: *Floraville Cemetery.*

'Wait here,' Rashid told him. He slipped on a pair of thin black leather gloves, took a bulky package a little bigger than a brick from under his seat, and stepped out into the downpour. Vaulting the cemetery's stone wall, he landed on a gravel path. He walked for over fifty yards across the crunching stones, passing dark legions of headstones, until he came to a polished granite slab. Inscribed on the stone was a name: *Margaret Coombs.* Taking a notebook from his pocket, Rashid recorded the woman's name, her date of death, and the exact location of her burial. The grave was neatly kept, with a granite border, limestone chips covering the ground inside, and several bunches of dead flowers lying withered on the tomb, the falling rain drenching the crisp cellophane. Rashid took a pearl-handled flick-knife from his pocket and clicked the button. The blade flashed. He knelt and scraped away a section of the limestone chips until the wet earth beneath was exposed.

Then he began to dig with the knife, scooping out the moist topsoil, making a recessed hole no more than a foot square. When he had finished, he placed the package neatly in the hole, replaced the earth on top, tamped it down with his gloved hands, then covered it again with the limestone. Removing a pencil torch from his pocket, he briefly flicked it on, making sure there was no evidence of the grave having been disturbed. His task completed, he stood, his body drenched, then trudged back, vaulted the wall and climbed into the waiting Explorer. He tugged off his gloves. 'It's done. Let's get out of here.'

Without a word, Nikolai Gorev started the engine and turned back towards the Baltimore highway.

6.15 a.m.

The man came awake to the sound of his bedside telephone ringing. He switched on the nightstand lamp, plucked the receiver from its cradle and listened to the caller's terse message. 'Thank you. Please tell the President I'll be there,' the man answered, and replaced the receiver.

Climbing out of bed, he pulled on a dressing gown and anxiously crossed to his bedroom window. He was wide awake, had barely slept all night. Drawing back the curtains, he stared out at the rain-washed darkness. The call he'd just taken over a secure line had come from the White House communications room, which had conveyed the very same message to sixteen important men and women scattered across the country, members of America's prestigious National Security Council, summoning them to an unscheduled 8.30 a.m. meeting with the US President in Washington.

Roused from their beds, they would, at this very moment, be making urgent plans to travel to the US capital. As one of the President's closest advisers, and a respected Council member, the man was expected to be there. He was used to urgent calls from the White House in the middle of the night. But this one was very different. Unlike the other men and women contacted by the communications room that morning, who were totally unaware of the dire emergency that required their presence in the White House, he already knew the reason for his summons.

A dangerous journey was about to begin, and he knew that had any of his White House colleagues been aware of his remarkable secret, they'd have judged him guilty of the worst treachery, a traitor to his country. But the man thought differently. He had been guided by his principles, his hopes, his dreams, his vision, and he was totally committed to the role he was about to play. Yet he still shuddered, thinking of the days ahead, knowing they'd be fraught with hazards, would endanger the lives of hundreds of thousands of Americans.

The next seven days would decide the future course of his country. And with it the fate of the entire world. He looked back at the clock on his nightstand.

6.20.

Resurrection Day had begun.

6

Georgetown, Washington, DC
Sunday, 11 November
9.50 a.m.

Jack Collins saw the milk start to bubble in the pan, added a sliver of butter, then cracked a brown free-range egg with a fork and whisked it into the milk. He turned back to smile at Daniel, seated at the kitchen table, dressed in a Barney sweater and busily munching sugared Cheerios. 'How we doin' there, partner?'

'OK, Jack.'

'Better eat up your cereal, your scrambled egg's going to be ready pretty soon.'

'What 'bout my toast?'

'It's on the way, cowboy.' In truth, Collins had forgotten the toast. He popped four slices of wholemeal bread in the toaster and pressed down on the slide switch. 'Happy now?'

'I *is* happy, Jack.'

As Daniel avidly returned his attention to his Cheerios, Collins couldn't suppress another smile. No matter how often Nikki corrected her son, *am* always became *is*. I *is* happy. I *is* going to the toilet. And on bad days, when Collins witnessed the occasional argument between Nikki and Daniel, when the normally angel-faced boy got huffy and sulked in a corner, narrowing his eyes defiantly like the Devil's child out of *Damien*, it was '*I* is *not going to be a good boy, Mommy*.'

Collins knew that Nikki had given up trying to correct the grammatical error months ago; Daniel would grow out of it eventually. Besides, she had admitted, it was even cute, and if grown-ups were honest with themselves, they pretty much all wanted their children to stay infants for ever. He knew from his own experience of parenthood that the months and years passed so quickly; before you knew it kids were teenagers, and that wonderful, magic experience of sharing in their childhood was too abruptly gone. In Daniel's case, he was long out of the baby stage. At night, the little boy still wore a diaper, but even that habit was coming to an end, and he was starting to insist that he shouldn't have to wear one. Collins turned down the heat on the pan, poured himself a cup of hot coffee, added a spoonful of sugar, then swallowed a mouthful. He could hear Nikki's voice out in the living room, busy on the phone, making the call she said she needed to make, but he couldn't hear the conversation. She'd arrived at his apartment ten minutes ago, looking cheerful. No matter what troubles afflicted her, or others, Nikki always tried to be upbeat. That was her way. It was part of what attracted him to her when he met her eight months ago. He remembered their second outing together, dinner at Old Ebbitt's Grill, when he had got to know her a little better, and she had told him of the funny incident from when Daniel was two, the first time her son had really seen her completely naked.

He had surprised her in the shower, pulled back the curtain, and on seeing the dark V patch between her legs, he'd exclaimed innocently, 'What's *that* thing, Mommy?'

'Never you mind. What are you doing in here, Daniel? Come on, close the curtain, that's a good boy, and let Mommy finish in the shower. We've got to get to the store.'

And Daniel pointed to the V again. 'Are you taking *that* with you, Mommy?'

Nikki had told him the story in that earthy way of hers that had made him crack up with laughter. He always felt good knowing she and Daniel were here. In the last two years he had been tossed through some rough seas, but with Nikki's help and friendship had come a stable sense of reality. And for company he also had the added distraction of a three-year-old – soon to be four – endlessly active and inquisitive boy. Even the simple practicality of feeding Daniel his breakfast somehow gave him much-appreciated comfort.

The apartment in Georgetown was one-bed, with a tiny living room, a kitchenette and a bathroom the size of a closet. After he'd sold the house in Alexandria, Collins had moved here, hoping to make a fresh start, unable to live in the house any more because it haunted him, had such consecrated memories, but sometimes he felt he hadn't made any kind of start at all. He was forever trapped in his past, bound by its chains. The dreams still came. The memories still haunted. No matter what he did to try to forget, they still came back. And he knew why. They were all he had. All he had to remember the sacredness of their lives together, the life he had shared and lost with his wife and son.

Strong sunlight poured into the kitchen, which was close to a mess as always. Cooking was not one of Collins's favourite pastimes, not something he excelled at, but he did it out of sheer necessity. For a long time after Annie's death, even eating had been difficult. He'd had a double loss to deal with, and he'd rarely cooked, just ate fast food when he felt hungry, which wasn't very often. He'd shed thirty pounds and hadn't put them back on. But now, cooking occasionally for Daniel and Nikki had become, at least, a small pleasure. The toast popped. He finished his coffee, whisked the scrambled egg some more, and when it was done he spooned it onto a plate and buttered some toast and cut off the crusts. Important that, otherwise Daniel bitched like hell. 'There you go, cowboy.'

'You not having *a* egg, Jack?'

'Not this morning, Daniel.'

'Why?'

'Too many eggs are bad for you. And I try not to eat too many.'

'*Oh.*' Daniel frowned, tried to fathom that one out, his face crinkled with concentrated puzzlement, before he obviously decided that the intensity of thought wasn't worth the effort, relaxed and went back to his food.

Collins heard a tiny laugh and looked round. Nikki was leaning against the door frame, her arms folded. Her hair was tied back, emphasising her oval face, a smile lingering on her lips. She wore a pale grey sweater under a dark leather jacket, dark woollen pants and black ankle boots, her only jewellery a pair of tiny diamond-studded earrings. She was not quite medium height, but her figure was well proportioned, petite but athletic looking, and she had an immediate impact far greater than her size or appearance could explain. But more than anything she radiated vitality and a youthful spirit, which both belied the fact that Nikki Dean was thirty-six, a divorced hard-working mother with a lively three-year-old boy to contend with and a busy career as a news reporter for the *Washington Post*. 'How are you guys doing?'

'We're doing OK.'

'I overheard the egg business. You got off lightly, you know. Count yourself lucky you didn't have to get into a detailed medical explanation of how egg yolk can raise your cholesterol and narrow your arteries. Daniel's a reporter's son, remember. Most times, he wants all the facts.'

'I think maybe you're right there.' Collins smiled.

Nikki laughed again, came over. 'He already had a muffin, juice and cereal before we left the house, you know.'

'Think yourself lucky. Some kids you've got to force-feed. I remember we used to have trouble with Sean the first couple of years. All he wanted was cookies and candy. Anything else you had to struggle to get down him.'

'Well, there's no chance of that with Daniel. That boy would eat out of your mouth.' She stood beside him, reached out her hand, gently rubbed his back. 'You get enough sleep after your call-out last night?'

'Five hours.'

Collins had returned to his apartment at 4.30 a.m. after the incident at the Union Station. He'd told Nikki he'd been called out but didn't explain the reason why. That was FBI business, and they rarely if ever discussed his work. But Collins was still none the wiser about the incident, and it rankled him that Murphy hadn't told him what the hell was going on. And the more he thought about it, the more odd it seemed. What the hell was in the locker? If it had been a bomb it would have been plastered all over the TV news this morning, but he'd watched the news and there had been nothing.

He'd thought about calling headquarters and speaking to Murphy again, or some of his colleagues, to find out if they knew anything, but he put that thought from his mind. He had the day off today, and he and Nikki had planned to spend it together. The talk with Murphy could wait.

'You sure you're not too tired?'

'Sure.'

'Mom? You not having *a* egg too?'

'Not this morning, Daniel. Just toast and coffee for Mom.'

Daniel looked back down at the table, engrossed again in his second breakfast. Collins poured Nikki some coffee and buttered her a slice of toast. 'You're sure that's all you want? No jelly?'

'Sure. No jelly.'

'You're not on a diet, are you?'

She leaned over, wiped a smudge of hot butter from his mouth, put a finger to his lips, winked at him. 'No way. Unfortunately, what you see is what you get, like it or not.'

'Did you get your call made?'

'Sure. I called Mom. I'm leaving Daniel over at her place for the day. Would you believe she's actually looking forward to it?' Nikki giggled, raised her eyes. 'Just wait until he gets started on her walls with his crayons. That ought to take the edge off her enthusiasm.'

'You've got something to do?'

'To tell the truth I thought I'd take you for a drive before you visit the cemetery this afternoon. But there's an ulterior motive. I got some news yesterday I'd like to tell you.'

'Yeah? What kind of news?'

Nikki was usually always upbeat, but this morning Collins thought she seemed even more perky than usual. He began to wonder whether she was just trying hard to uplift him, because of what day it was, the anniversary of Annie's death, or whether it was something else. There seemed to be an almost nervous excitement about her. 'You want to tell me what it's about?'

She smiled, shook her head. 'You FBI guys hate a mystery, don't you? No explaining, not until later. I'm not on duty again for the *Post* until tomorrow. And you've still got a couple of days off work. So we've got the entire afternoon and evening together. We can take a drive, maybe have some lunch. In fact, there's somewhere special I'd like to take you – it's kind of a surprise. And then I can tell you my news.'

7

Sunday, 11 November
8.55 a.m.

In the confines of the underground laboratory in Maryland, Tom Murphy, the head of the FBI's Counter-Terrorism Division, felt like shit.

In fact, he'd just spent one of the worst nights of his life, staying awake through the early hours, drinking coffee by the barrel-load and trying to fend off the crushing need for sleep that threatened to take him to the edge of collapse. Before the business at the Union Station that morning he'd worked a straight fourteen hours at the FBI's Washington headquarters and hadn't seen his wife in almost two days. Shit happens, he told himself, but somehow it always seemed to happen to him.

As he stood in the glass-fronted office, sipping coffee, the door opened behind him and an FBI agent from the HMRU – Hazardous Materials Response Unit – poked his head round.

'They're almost done, Tom.'

'How much more time?'

'A couple of minutes, according to Professor Fredericks. Says he'll be right with you as soon as he's got the final result. Then I guess we can all go home and get some rest.'

'Let's hope so. Right this minute, I'd sleep in a kid's stroller.'

The agent smiled and left, closing the door. Murphy poured another cup of coffee from the percolator beside him, spooned in two sugars, and took a long sip, hoping the caffeine would keep him awake. He had passed the pain barrier about 7 a.m. and right now it seemed he was operating on autopilot, feeling a little woozy and barely hanging in there. His eyelids drooped, and his aching body felt as if a couple of toughs had worked him over.

The source of his sleeplessness and irritation was out there in the laboratory beyond the glass-fronted office: the package found in locker number 02–08 at Gate C, Union Station. Bright light flooded the lab area; it looked like a scene out of a sci-fi movie. Technicians walked around in white biohazard suits wearing glass-bubble helmets with airlines attached to them. The Biological and Chemical Research Laboratory in Maryland was one of the most frightening places in the world, Murphy reckoned.

Samples of every bacteriological strain, every gas or poisonous substance known to man, were contained there in platinum-sealed containers, kept a hundred feet below ground in pressurised vaults. And it didn't end there. The entire structure was built on spring-loaded piles, to protect the building from nuclear shock. Which wasn't really surprising when you considered that there were enough deadly samples stored in the vaults to wipe America off the map.

Murphy rubbed his eyes to stay awake. The package from the station had been X-rayed, revealing a sealed vial inside. Shaped like a laboratory test tube, four inches long, it looked as if it had nothing inside. But whatever it was, his superiors had decided that this was one for the experts. Within half an hour, a team from the FBI's Hazardous Materials Response Unit had arrived in a special transporter and taken the package away in a sealed, cushioned container. Murphy had followed in his car with two of his senior men, and almost five hours later he was still at the laboratory, patiently awaiting the analysis results. Professor Fredericks, the lab director, had told him that on visual inspection the sealed vial was made of thick shatterproof glass and appeared to contain a minute trace of brown, viscous liquid. That was all the information Murphy had so far.

The door opened and a small, gnome-like man with a heavily stooped back entered, wearing a white lab coat and carrying a sheaf of papers. Murphy drained his paper cup, crushed it in his palm and tossed it in the bin. 'What have you got for me, Professor?'

Professor Elliot Johnson Fredericks wore half-rim glasses, and his sober expression made him look like Mr Serious. When Murphy had first met him earlier that morning he knew immediately that the professor wasn't the kind of guy to linger over a beer or pass a fun evening of stud poker with. But then he guessed that anyone who was a key-holder to a Pandora's box that could wipe out half the planet wouldn't exactly have been comedian material either.

Fredericks removed his glasses and looked troubled as he held up the sheaf of pages. 'I've got the results. But first, I'd like to clarify something.'

'What?'

'You said this entire matter was to be kept absolutely secret?'

'Correct.'

'Even so, if only for the sake of *my* curiosity, as director of this laboratory, do you mind telling me what the hell's going on? Where did you get this vial?'

'Sorry, Professor. This goes a lot higher than me. The bottom line is everyone here keeps their mouths zipped – and I mean airtight – until you get the say-so to do otherwise. I've no doubt you and your colleagues are used to that kind of injunction. You work for a government establishment.'

Fredericks looked affronted, handed over the sheaf of stapled pages. 'Look at the last page of the report, please. It identifies the contents of the vial.'

Murphy accepted the pages. Most of the report was written in technical jargon he couldn't understand, complete with tables of analysis figures. He quickly flicked to the last page, which read like a summary of results, but written in reasonably plain English. He took several minutes to digest the lines, then looked up, open mouthed. 'You've just *got* to be kidding me, Professor.'

'We did three individual tests, to be absolutely certain. There isn't a shred of doubt.'

9.45 a.m.

Nikolai Gorev sat forward on the couch and flicked the TV remote to NBC news, keeping the volume low. A newsman was giving his report at the scene of a bungled filling-station robbery in Georgetown, where two youths had been shot dead by police. Gorev flicked through the other news channels, national and local, and sampled the bulletins.

Violent robberies, shootings, race-related crimes and murder: a killing spree by two students at a high school in Idaho which had left three students dead and four wounded; two white men in Alabama had knifed a homeless black man to death because he'd asked them for money. Life was going on normally, or as normally as it could in America. No panic in the streets since the taped message had been delivered, or dire warnings to Washington's citizens about an imminent threat to their capital. Which meant the people in the White House were obeying their instructions.

Gorev flicked off the set. He'd slept for barely four hours after he had returned with Mohamed Rashid from the cemetery in Floraville, but he was wide awake now, his adrenalin flowing. He heard the shower running in the bathroom. After a few minutes it stopped and Karla Sharif appeared wearing a bathrobe, the flimsy cotton straining against her hips and buttocks. 'Did you keep watch on the news?'

Gorev tossed the remote on the coffee table. 'There were no warnings.'

Karla sat down beside him. She had a face that changed from interesting to beautiful, depending on her mood, and the kind of figure that could make other women envious. Gorev knew that with its high model's cheekbones and almond-shaped brown eyes it was a face that could stop men in their tracks. But that wasn't why he loved this woman; there were countless other reasons. 'By now the Americans will have had time to digest the contents of the tape. And most probably they'll have analysed the vial.'

'What if they make the threat public, or try to evacuate the city?'

'According to Rashid, they won't, not if they've any sense. How could they empty a city under our noses, Karla? We'd see it happening. Believe me, the Americans will play this game exactly as they're told to.'

'And if they look for us?'

Gorev saw the sudden strain on her face, looked into her eyes, touched her cheek. 'No doubt they will. But Rashid's plan is foolproof. And if we follow it we'll all come out of this alive.' He let his hand fall away, looked at his watch. 'You better go, or you'll be late and Rashid will get worried.'

Karla stood. 'You don't want to come with me?'

Gorev shook his head, got to his feet. He reached across the couch, retrieved his jacket, made sure the Beretta pistol was tucked inside the pocket. 'It's better we go separately. You can bet that by now the Americans will be trying to find us. What time do we meet?'

'Noon,' Karla said, and kissed him on the cheek. 'Rashid and I will pick you up at Dupont Circle at noon.'

8

Washington, DC
Sunday, 11 November
8.30 a.m.

The National Security Council meeting got under way on schedule in the White House situation room. It was a solemn-looking President, dressed in a suit and tie, who entered the chamber. Among those round the table were Alex Havers, the Vice-President, along with the Chairman of the Joint Chiefs of Staff, the heads of the FBI and CIA, the Secretary of State, and the Defence Secretary. The fourteen men and two women waiting in the situation room that morning were the President's closest advisers and confidants – several among them were the heads of executive departments or senior military officers – and they all got to their feet out of respect.

President Andrew W. Booth spoke in the homely tone he sometimes liked to employ. 'First of all, I'd just like to thank you all for being here.' He paused briefly for effect. 'I'd also like to say that I earnestly hope that the crisis that has brought us all here this morning is nothing more than a madman's bluff. Because if it's not, then we've all got a very difficult and trying time ahead of us.'

The situation room itself – known as the sit-room to those working in the White House – was unremarkable: cream-painted walls and a large rectangular table with inexpensive chairs. Yet it was the core of breathtaking power. Here, plans to crush Iraqi dictator Saddam Hussein's occupation troops in Kuwait with operations Desert Shield and Desert Storm had been deliberated upon. At the touch of a button a massive screen came down from one wall. Another button swept aside two huge curtains, to reveal an electronic map board. Beside each seat was a secure telephone, routed through the nearby Communications Unit, where banks of electronic telecommunications consoles and television screens linked the White House to Strategic Air Command, the Pentagon, the CIA, the FBI, and every nerve centre of government that came under the President's control.

If the Council members so wished, the Communications Unit could relay images from any US military or civilian satellite hovering in the earth's stratosphere. They could discern the face of a peasant farm-worker toiling in the fields of a remote Chinese province, or study the progress of the new villa that a senior Iraqi commander was having constructed on the outskirts of Baghdad.

A call from the sit-room could dispatch lethal firepower from any US military aircraft, army base or naval vessel anywhere in the world – from instructing the watch commander of a nuclear warhead site hidden in a Midwest silo that he was to dispatch his deadly salvo to ordering the captain on board a destroyer in the South China Seas to fire a cruise missile, and at any chosen target within striking distance.

The men and women present that morning wielded enormous collective power. But less than twenty minutes after the meeting began – once the crisis had been outlined and they had viewed Abu Hasim's video on the large screen behind the President – their reactions said it all: shock, fear, dread, emphasising a dilemma of truly serious proportions, one they had never faced before.

The President turned to FBI Director Douglas Stevens, the man whose Bureau was responsible for protecting America from terrorist threats. 'Doug, perhaps you can fill everybody in on what's been happening since we received the package this morning.'

'Yes, Mr President.' Stevens cleared his throat, addressed everyone at the table. 'We've determined that the videocassette is of German manufacture, part of a large batch exported to at least a dozen countries in the Middle East. According to our lab, the recording itself was made under non-professional conditions. There's a lot of hum and noise in the background which wouldn't have been present had it been made in a soundproofed studio. Unfortunately the background noise is of indeterminate source. And there are no fingerprints on any of the material – it's completely clean. The handwritten note and the two typed pages containing the prisoner names are being examined by the Secret Service, at their behest – their paper and ink experts are among the best this country has, so if there's any evidence to be gleaned, they'll find it. We've also no indications yet as to why the Saudi diplomat should have been chosen as a conduit for Hasim's message. We're still working on the contents of the package found at the Union Station, Mr President. But I expect results within the next hour. I've given an instruction that as soon as they come through, I'm to be contacted here.'

'Have we any idea who left it at the station?'

'We got hold of Amtrak security's videotape that recorded someone depositing a package in box 02–08 at Gate C, at about eight p.m. last night.' Stevens saw he had the complete attention of everyone present. 'Unfortunately, the person in question wore a dark blue parka with the hood up, and a scarf over their face, so identification was impossible. They also wore gloves, so we couldn't get any prints.'

'Could you tell if it was a man or woman?' Rebecca Joyce, a tall, striking black woman, and one of the two female NSC members, spoke up. The product of a working-class family from Detroit, Joyce was a brilliant Harvard graduate who had a reputation for being one of Booth's most ardent supporters.

'We think it was a man, but we're not a hundred per cent certain.'

The President sighed and addressed his next question to a tall, thin man with a shock of grey hair. In his late fifties, clean shaven, with the slim build of an athlete, Richard 'Dick' Faulks was a Princeton-educated lawyer and the Director of the CIA, responsible for gathering intelligence on foreign terrorist groups which threathened the USA. 'Dick, do we have any intelligence to suggest that Abu Hasim might have been ready to try something like this?'

'Mr President, as we're all well aware, al-Qaeda has carried out serious crimes against America in the past,' replied Faulks. 'The bombings of our embassies in Nairobi and Tanzania, and the attack on the USS *Cole*, have been the worst so far. And al-Qaeda has made it pretty much publicly known that they intended further attacks against the US. But we've had no firm intelligence to suggest that they might try and carry out something quite as big as this.'

'What about the Saudis,' the President queried. 'Have you been in touch with them yet?'

'No, sir. In my opinion, it's a little bit early for that. Granted, they really should be in on this, as well as the other countries that are holding imprisoned terrorists on the list. But just for now, I'd like to keep it as close to our chests as possible.'

The President paused to reflect, tapping his palm on the table. 'Tell me, Dick, do we know if al-Qaeda is capable of producing a weapon powerful enough to destroy Washington?'

'No, sir, we've no evidence. We know they've tried to get their hands on nuclear material in the past, if that's what you mean, sir. And we know they've attempted to secure supplies of deadly biological and chemical agents. But then so have a lot of other A-category terror groups. We've been doing our best to monitor the situation and up to now we believe they haven't been successful. We've also kept a close watch on their bank accounts, at least the ones we know about, in Switzerland and the Far East. So far as we can tell, there've been no significant movements of funds from any of these accounts which might indicate a payment for materials to manufacture a weapon of mass destruction, or even to purchase such a weapon, ready made.'

The President turned to his right. Two seats away sat his old friend, Charles Rivermount, an adviser to the President on economic policy. A broad, bull-shouldered Mississippian who had made a fortune in private banking, mining and gas exploration, he leaned his solid frame forward in his seat, resting his arms on the table.

'Mr President, I don't mean to speak out of turn, but if you ask me, ain't we wasting our time here? We spend billions of dollars a year on defence. If we want, we can tune into one of our satellites right here and now. See anything we care to on that screen behind you. The rouge on the cheeks of a ten-dollar hooker loitering in the red-light district of Moscow. Or some Burmese peasant wiping his ass in a corner of some paddy field. Surely we can pinpoint Hasim with one of our satellites? Pinpoint him and blow the sonofabitch to hell. Or tell me that isn't possible?'

The President listened to the blunt-speaking Southerner, then nodded at the CIA Director. 'Perhaps you'd care to answer the question, Dick?'

'It isn't quite as simple as that, Mr Rivermount,' Faulks replied. 'Sure, we've got the technology. Satellites that can view a terrorist base from a hundred miles up in the stratosphere. Powerful missiles that can be launched from aircraft or naval vessels. But we've pinpointed Hasim's terrorist bases before, tried to destroy him, and failed. The reasons are simple. Air power and missiles are a blunt weapon, wholly inappropriate for use by themselves in this form of conflict. It's not easy for pilots flying low at five hundred miles an hour over terrain, or a commander on board a destroyer in the Gulf, to identify a target with exactness. Without military personnel or agents on the ground to "paint" the target – by that I mean to verify it – we can make mistakes.

'The core of it is, we'd almost need somebody within Hasim's close circle to paint the target for us, and confirm we'd got him in our sights before we launched an attack. And believe me, we've tried to recruit such people in the past. But Hasim surrounds himself with a tight circle of fanatical followers. Finding someone among his men to betray him has proven impossible. One approach we tried was to a relative of one of his followers. It ended in the Afghan agent we used being tortured to death, decapitated, and his head left in a box outside the American embassy in Islamabad.'

Rivermount's face flushed with subdued anger. 'You ask me, I'd still take the damned chance, find his camps and blow them to hell—'

The President interrupted. 'Charlie, we can't take that risk.

We're responsible for the lives of the citizens of this capital, our own included. Until we learn otherwise, we have to assume Hasim has the ability to trigger his weapon remotely. Even if we did manage to destroy him, there's a chance this device of his, whatever it is, would go off in the process, causing massive numbers of deaths.'

Fury got the better of the man from Mississippi. 'But what if Hasim's bluffing, Mr President? What if he's got nothing up his sleeve but a dirty arm and we give in to his crazy demands? You ask me, a situation like this requires only one kind of response. We've got to annihilate the man – put him out of the picture for good.'

Across the table, neither man had noticed the red light flashing on Douglas Stevens's telephone, indicating an incoming call. Stevens picked it up, listened, suddenly raised his hand. 'Mr Secretary, if you could hold a moment. Mr President, sorry to interrupt—'

'Yes, Doug.'

'It's about the vial, sir. We've got the results.'

Fifteen miles away, at the Biological and Chemical Research Laboratory, Tom Murphy had moved to the privacy of Professor Fredericks' office, two floors underground and swamped in harsh neon light.

Murphy put through the call to the White House at 9.05. Within moments he was connected to Douglas Stevens in the situation room. Now Murphy turned to the bemused Fredericks, held out the phone. 'My boss would like you to explain your findings to someone, Professor.'

'Explain to whom?'

'The President of the United States.'

The call had been switched to the speakerphone on the centre of the table, so that everyone could hear the conversation. The President addressed Fredericks. 'Professor, I believe you have completed your tests?'

The voice filtering through the speaker had an unreal, metallic quality, and seemed awed. 'Yes . . . yes, sir, Mr President.'

'Would you care to tell us what the vial contains?'

'A minute trace of liquid chemical. Quite an incredible solution really. We examined the component parts to determine—'

'Excuse me, Professor Fredericks, I don't mean to be rude, but we're all laymen here, not chemists. In simple terms, what is the liquid?'

'A variation of a deadly chemical agent known as VX, sir. As I'm sure you're well aware, VX is a nerve gas. One of the most lethal known to man. But this sample we've analysed is even deadlier.'

'How so?'

'The basic VX chemical formula has been altered to greatly enhance the toxicity of the nerve agent.' Fredericks sighed in frustration. 'It's kind of difficult to explain in layman's terms, Mr President, without going into technical details. But if I were to try to put it simply, think of our sample as a kind of concentrated form of VX nerve gas. Which means you get a far more fatal effect for a smaller amount of the nerve gas. More death for your dollar, if you like. It's really quite amazing. A brilliant feat of chemistry.'

The President paused, couldn't fail to discern the hint of professional excitement in Fredericks' voice. 'I'd like to ask you a question, Professor. Could a chemical like this wipe out the population of a city the size of Washington?'

Before Fredericks' voice replied he paused for a moment, as if to register his alarm at the question. 'Mr President, the power of this chemical is simply way beyond anything you can imagine. To give an example, the amount of VX you could fit on a pinhead is enough to kill a human being. The chemical we've analysed, in my estimate, could do the same job with *one tenth* of that amount. But to answer your question I'd have to assume there's a very large quantity of this nerve gas and it could be effectively dispersed over the capital.'

'Then assume both if you must.'

There was another pause, then Fredericks' voice came back,

tainted with fear. 'Sir, if that's the case, then I'd have to say yes, it could easily wipe out Washington's entire population.'

'Where to, lady?'

'Dupont Circle.'

Two blocks from the apartment building, Karla Sharif hailed a passing cab. The middle-aged driver smiled, shot her an appraising look. 'For you, lady, anywhere.'

As the cab merged with the traffic, Karla saw the driver glance at her appreciatively in the rear-view mirror. She avoided meeting his eyes, turned her face away, stared out of the window. They drove past the Pentagon and across the Roosevelt Bridge, heading towards DC and New Hampshire Avenue. Washington had been her home for the last ten weeks, and she had been surprised by its beauty.

When she'd arrived it was September, and still hot, the white stone buildings shimmering in the sweltering heat. In the following weeks she had helped Rashid set up the safe houses, assemble the equipment, and scour the city looking for suitable warehouses and storage facilities where they could stash the deadly cargo. But that first week, Rashid had made her take him on a guided tour in her car to familiarise him with the city, pointing out places and buildings of interest: Washington Harbour, the White House, the Smithsonian Institute, the homes of the rich and famous who inhabited Georgetown's chic seventeenth- and eighteenth-century town houses. At the Lincoln Memorial they had climbed the steps to look out over the reflecting pool, then visited the rooftop bar of the Hilton with its stunning views of the capital. Washington, she had always thought, was the least American-looking of US cities, with its absence of skyscrapers, and she had told Rashid that the law forbade any structure higher than Capitol Hill.

Karla looked out at the crowded streets, at the faces passing beyond the cab window. *Don't think about anything other than your mission*, they had told her. *Force yourself to focus on nothing but your cause.* But how could she not think of the sea of faces she saw every day? The mothers and fathers and their children in the neighbourhood where she lived. The people in her apartment block, the faces she saw in the streets: old faces, young faces, black faces, white faces, and every colour in between, all living in this multicultured city. The little boys and girls playing in the parks. The penniless black men she passed on 14th Street; the polite young policeman who gave her directions for the subway. How could she not see the lives she would help destroy if everything went wrong?

And how could she not think of her own beloved Josef? He was the sole reason she was here, prepared to risk her own life, so that he would live. She sank back in her seat, tried to focus on her mission. She was Karla Sharif, thirty-eight years old, a Palestinian. As Safa Yassin, a Lebanese-born émigrée, she had illegally entered New York's Kennedy Airport in early September and travelled by train to Washington, DC. The false American passport, green card and social security number had been acquired for her by the mujahidin. Even her car and driving licence had been prearranged – the licence was a genuine document, but with a false address.

'We're here, lady.'

The driver's voice cut off her thoughts. Karla Sharif paid the fare, added a dollar tip and climbed out. Crossing the pavement, she lingered in front of a bookstore window. When she was certain the cab had driven off, she turned away from the window and walked east, checking every now and then to make sure she hadn't been followed. Two blocks farther on, she hailed another taxi and told the driver to take her back to Alexandria. When she stepped out of the second cab, she walked the short distance to the apartment.

The complex was in one of the less desirable parts of Alexandria, near the old docks. The sign on the wall outside said: Wentworth Apartments. They were discreetly set back between two rows of red-bricked two-storey town houses, and Mohamed Rashid had rented a one-bed unit on the second floor. She noticed his blue Explorer parked outside in the lot and stepped up to the apartment entrance. The lobby door was unlocked, and she could have stepped inside, but instead she jabbed her finger at the intercom buzzer to her left. Almost instantly, a man answered. 'Who is it?'

'It's me, Karla.'

'Come up,' the man ordered. For a second, Karla hesitated at the lobby entrance. It seemed like the mouth of a menacing cave she didn't want to enter, knowing what lay ahead, knowing what she and the others had to do that day.

But there was no going back now.

She stepped inside the Wentworth's open lobby door and closed it behind her.

8.55 a.m.

A silence had descended on the situation room after Professor Fredericks had made his terrifying statement. The President was the first to speak, his voice hoarse, almost a whisper. He addressed Fredericks again. 'Professor, I'd like to ask you another question.'

'Yes, sir.'

'Where could someone get a chemical like this from? And by that I also mean what's its origin?'

'Difficult to say. But its extreme toxicity suggests to me it could be one of the newer Russian Novichok gases you may have heard about, or something similar.'

'Novichok?'

'Literally, it means newcomer. Mustard gas was a first-generation gas. Those like Zyklon B second. VX is third-generation – a class of incredibly powerful chemical weapons that take toxicity to a whole new level, and to which Novichok belongs.'

'You're saying it could it have come from Russia?'

'It's possible. Russian VX, more commonly known as R-VX, is similar to US-manufactured VX, but has some structural differences in formula. I'm seeing those same kinds of structural differences in the sample we analysed. But it's just as possible it could have been manufactured somewhere else, other than Russia. Saddam Hussein is known to have experimented with Novichok gases. As have the Chinese and the Iranians. Or it could have been manufactured independently, in secret. But that would take a lot of money and research. You're talking about employing the services of top scientists.'

'So you can't tell the exact source?'

'Not as yet, sir, no.'

'How difficult would it be for a terrorist organisation to acquire the component parts to manufacture this chemical?'

'To produce what kind of quantity, Mr President?'

'Say the amount it would take to kill every citizen in Washington.'

The silence from Fredericks' end of the line was noted in the hushed situation room. 'Are you still there, Professor Fredericks?'

'Yes . . . yes, sir, I'm still here.' Fredericks sighed. 'It wouldn't be at all difficult. The hardest part would be coming up with the formula. As for the actual chemical ingredients, they're fairly commonly available and easily purchased – most are derived from agricultural pesticides, pretty much like most deadly nerve gases. Even ballpoint pen ink is only one step removed from Sarin gas. Certain of the formulas aren't difficult to acquire either. The British invented VX, for example, and the method of preparation was first published by the British Patents Office over thirty years ago, and is still publicly available. With some simple lab equipment, almost anyone with a basic knowledge of chemistry could produce VX, or almost any other nerve gas. Many of them form part of a class of industrial chemicals known as organophosphates, commonly used as insecticides, but for military purposes they are manufactured to a much higher level of toxicity. For a long time now my colleagues and I have been warning about this same danger, Mr President.'

'I'm well aware of that, Professor, but to get back to the question of quantity . . .'

'If I were to give a rough estimate, a liquid ton of this chemical, correctly dispersed, might do it. That's about a thousand litres. The amount you'd fit in a typically small, suburban home heating tank. It would be more than enough to cause massive numbers of deaths.'

'And how does it work?'

'Just like VX itself, and pretty much like all other nerve gases, which are probably the most barbaric weapons ever devised. It affects the nerve motor receptors in the human brain and body. The synapses that carry brain signals between nerve cells shut down. A victim of a nerve gas attack would go into uncontrolled physical and mental spasm. The chemicals affect the respiratory tract and lung function, and the victim can't breathe. It feels like their lungs are on fire. The blood vessels often rupture. It causes an extremely ugly, violent death.'

'Are there antidotes?'

'Well, yes and no. There is an antidote called atropine. Victims exposed to VX, for example, would have to be immediately removed from the contaminated area and injected – which might not be possible if the gas has been dispersed pretty much everywhere. Coupled with that, you have to deliver atropine fast, and the method of injection isn't pleasant. It's usually delivered with a six-inch needle into the thigh muscle, or even straight into the heart. But atropine isn't always successful. It depends on how much of the toxic chemical a victim has been exposed to, and for how long. And remember, we're dealing here with something far more toxic than VX, so it's questionable whether the antidote would work at all in this case.'

'But if it did, could people be given the antidote *before* an attack?'

'In theory, if you had a proven antidote, yes.'

'How do we get one?'

'Whoever manufactured the gas may have one. They may not. If they don't we'd have to try to manufacture one ourselves.'

'How long would that take?'

'Impossible to say. Three months, six months, or maybe never.'

'*Never?*'

'All nerve gases attack the body very rapidly through the lung and/or skin tissue. They're absorbed almost immediately into the bloodstream and act aggressively. Gas agents are not like bacteria or viruses. They're highly toxic, lethal within a very short time – seconds and minutes rather than days and weeks. And this one's the most aggressive I've ever come across. It would kill *instantly*. It's so highly toxic that any antidote you come up with may prove completely ineffective.'

The President sighed. 'But surely it would be difficult to store?'

'Not at all. That's the great advantage of this kind of Novichok – it's usually held in binary form. By that I mean it consists principally of two benign chemicals that become lethal only when mixed together. The two chemicals can be contained in separate compartments within an artillery shell housing, or in separate chambers inside a missile, or some kind of protective container, even a sealed oil drum, for example. When the shell or missile – or whatever container is used – explodes, the chemicals combine to produce the toxic gas. I should point out that one of the reasons the Russians held Novichok in binary form was to circumvent future bans on chemical weapons. Stored as separate chemicals, they're mostly harmless. Combined, they're incredibly deadly. Another advantage is that binary form also makes it hard to monitor or detect.'

'How would this nerve gas be dispersed?'

'Several ways. By aerosol. By explosion – using a missile containing the liquid, say, or some kind of bomb, or even a cropduster aircraft. If a cropduster were used, the pilot would obviously have to wear a protective suit, otherwise he'd be a victim too, rapidly, though I think such a method is unlikely – it's far too difficult and unsafe. Or it might be dispersed naturally, by the wind, but that's an ineffective means also, unless the weather conditions are favourable. And by that I mean reasonably mellow winds blowing in the right direction. If they're too strong, they disperse the gas and reduce its effectiveness.'

'You mean it wouldn't have any harmful effect?'

'No, sir, that's not what I mean. The nerve gas would still kill its victims, but it just wouldn't kill as many. And there would still be long-term effects you'd have to deal with, people invalided with permanent nerve-receptor, lung or brain damage. Many would still die, but more slowly. Another problem – with VX, but the same should apply in the case of this derivative – is that it remains active for anything from three to sixteen weeks. So anyone in the vicinity up to three months after the dispersal would still run the risk of being contaminated. My guess is the sample we've got could remain active for even longer.'

The President took a moment to reflect before asking his next question. 'Professor, is there any possibility of error in the tests you carried out?'

'Mr President, you're at liberty to seek another opinion . . .'

'I'm not doubting your learned judgment, Professor. And I'll certainly seek other expert opinion, the very best this nation has. But for now, are you absolutely certain about the kind of damage this gas could inflict?'

Fredericks came back with a forceful reply. 'Mr President, let me be perfectly honest with you and put this thing in perspective, just in case you don't realise the truly lethal, awesome power of this chemical. You've got to think of it as kind of a poor man's atom bomb. With just ten ccs, that's a mere two tablespoonfuls of the stuff, I'd estimate it could easily kill tens of thousands of people in a confined space. And I do mean *easily*. Let's extrapolate that a little further for effect. If a terrorist had a large enough quantity of this chemical, say five or six of those thousand-litre oil tanks I mentioned, and they were strategically placed in major cities on the East Coast and about to explode, then I wouldn't just be worrying about Washington, DC. Me, I'd be worrying about most of the eastern seaboard – close to a quarter of the citizens of this entire country.'

9

Maryland
11 November
11.45 a.m.

Collins rubbed condensation from the windscreen of Nikki's dark green six-year-old Toyota Camry to get a better view. 'So what's the big secret? Where are we headed?'

They were on Route 4, heading towards Chesapeake Bay, that long inlet of seawater that stretches for almost a hundred miles, all the way from north Maryland to the Atlantic seaboard. Chesapeake in the sunshine was a beautiful expanse of water, the inlet coves dotted with pretty marinas and attractive bay properties that ran all the way along the length of the coast.

'Who says it's a *big* secret?' Nikki smiled. 'You know something, Jack Collins, you're worse than Neal for fishing for clues. Didn't they teach you FBI guys at Quantico not to pry into highly classified stuff?'

'What did you do? Steal military secrets you want to show me?'

Nikki giggled. 'You'll have to be patient. So stop prying, and just enjoy the ride.'

They had dropped Daniel off at his grandmother's. A spry, attractive widow, Susan Dean had met them at the door of her town house in Arlington. She was a little more reserved than her daughter, but there was warmth there, and a streak of independence that saw her, at sixty-four and a widow, still working as a part-time legal secretary. 'Don't you worry about this little man. He and I are going to have a terrific time, aren't we, Daniel?'

Daniel had become instantly tearful. 'I wanna go with Mom and Jack.'

'But we're going to have much more fun,' his grandmother told him. 'You'll have Mitzi to play with.'

Daniel loved playing with his grandmother's dog, Collins knew, but the boy wasn't won over yet. 'And don't you want to see the surprise present I've got for you?' Susan said enticingly. 'I picked it up yesterday at the toy store.'

Daniel's eyes lit up. 'Can I see the surprise *now*, Nanna?'

'Sure. It's all wrapped up in the front room. Why don't you go take a look?'

Daniel gave his mother a quick hug as his priorities suddenly shifted and he darted inside the house. Susan laughed. 'Works every time. Promise a surprise and they'll forget about everything else.' She gave them the assured look of someone who'd had the experience of raising four children and knew well how the diversion game was played. 'He'll be fine. You two run along. I've got your cell number if I need you, or in case he pulls Mitzi's tail off.'

An hour later and Nikki had passed Plum Point and turned off Route 4 on to a solitary track that ran parallel to the Chesapeake shoreline. It cut inland for almost half a mile until they came to a cluster of wood-and-brick two-storey cottages. Each had its own large plot, half a dozen of them lining the right-hand side of a private road. They looked neatly kept, except the one Nikki pulled up outside, which appeared neglected, the whitewash peeling, the picket fence rotted in places.

'You going to tell me where we are?'

'It's called Buff End.' Nikki switched off the Camry's engine. 'Don't you think it's pretty?' Collins saw that the cottage was protected from the harsh Atlantic winds by a semicircle of pine trees. About a mile away, across some fields, was a promontory that sloped out to sea. He knew Chesapeake Bay, and that the nearby coast was the habitat of several dozen species of seabirds. A few hundred yards farther along the shoreline there was a long stretch of sandy beach. The cliffs were forty feet high on some parts of the bay, made of crumbly sandstone, but those farther south reached a little higher. Erosion had eaten deep into the cliff face but the cottage was far enough back for it not to matter.

'Mom and Dad used to bring the family here for most of the summer when I was a little girl. Even when Dad wasn't on vacation he'd stay with us, and drive to work in Washington. We all loved the place. With the sea so close, farms near by, and lots of places to explore, it was a really happy time.'

'Your dad owned the cottage?'

'Part owned, with Frank, his brother.' Nikki smiled. 'Uncle Frankie to us kids, but Mom used to call him Flash. According to her, he was something of a guy about town in his day. He'd never married, and used the cottage as a hideaway, somewhere to bring his girlfriends and romance the pants off them. He passed away last year and left his share of the property to Mom. The past few months I've been coming by the odd free day I've had, trying to get it into shape.'

'How come you never told me?'

'A girl's got to keep some secrets. Come on, I'll show you around.'

She led the way up a loose gravel path on to the veranda and unlocked the front door. They stepped through a short hallway into a cosy front room that smelled of fresh paint. There was a blackstone fireplace, and a big old Zeiss telescope on a tripod, pointed seaward. Marine bric-a-brac garnished the walls – old conch shells, sculpted carvings made from shark bones, and mounted paintings of old schooners and frigates – which gave the place the look of a quaint mariner's cottage.

The kitchen was painted a straw yellow, creating a warm effect, and the paint cans and brushes that Nikki had used were piled on some old newspapers in a corner. She opened the windows downstairs, letting the salt air invade the rooms, then they went upstairs and Collins helped her open out the rest of the windows. The master bedroom had been cleared of furniture, and Nikki had rag-washed the walls in pale apricot, giving the room a feminine touch. The view from out over the water was stunning, sunshine sparkling on the calm bay waters.

'Another few weeks and I should be through with most of the decorating. I have to leave Daniel with Mom every time, otherwise he'd have us both covered in paint and I'd never get anything done.' Nikki took in the view with a deep breath, exhaled. 'Well, what do you think?'

'You did good work. And I can see how you'd like it here. Mind you, downstairs looks like somewhere Captain Ahab might have bided his time before he went in search of Moby-Dick.'

She smiled, gently punched his arm. 'Come on, it's not that bad. I'm looking forward to getting it finished. A little more paint and it'll be fixed up like it was when we were kids.' She turned towards the window, crossed her arms as if to protect herself against the faint chill in the sea air. 'Every time I come here, I find myself wishing for those days back. It's such a wonderful old house, Jack. Full of the warmest memories. I wish you could have known it back then.'

Collins saw the genuine yearning in her face, heard the trace of excitement her memories engraved in her voice. He looked out towards Chesapeake Bay. There were memories out there on the bay for him, too. When Sean was a child he'd often taken him there, sometimes with Annie, sometimes just the two of them, and that part of the beach where the sand dunes rose high had always been a favourite place for them all.

That terrible day, the day he'd received word that Sean had been killed on the USS *Cole*, he had driven alone out to Chesapeake, his mind numbed by an unfathomable grief. He had parked the car, taken a path along the cliff and followed a worn track down for two miles until he came to the beach, the one that he and Sean used sometimes to walk and play together on. It was deserted. An avalanche of heavy fog had rolled in off the bay, and he had walked along the shore as if in a daze. At every rise in the sand he could see Sean again as a small boy, his tiny face thrilled by some small discovery he'd made: a sand crab or a seashell – something trivial, but infinitely important to a child of four.

For hours that day, tortured by his precious memories, he had pushed on for mile after mile along the sand, like a man demented, driven on by his intense sorrow, completely lost in the past. It was as if Sean was still there and he could hear him again in the fog, giggling as he scurried on ahead playing hide-and-seek, then shaking with a fit of excited laughter when he was discovered.

Nikki touched his arm. 'Jack, are you OK?'

'Sure,' Collins lied, feeling a jolt of grief in his chest so sharp it felt as if someone had stuck a hypodermic in his heart. Looking into Nikki's face, seeing her concern, he wanted genuinely to share his memories with her, but knew they were too precious ever to be shared.

'You seemed distracted.'

He offered her a half-smile, spoke as gently as he could. 'Can I say something? I sort of get the feeling there's something more to this, Nikki. Unless you want a hand with the decorating?'

She blushed a little. 'They teach you that at Quantico, too? How to mind-read?'

'A woman's? Never. That's up there with the big, unfathomable mysteries of life.'

She laughed, slipped her arm into his, kissed him on the cheek. 'There's a restaurant over at Chesapeake Beach that serves great food. How about we lock up the cottage and talk there?'

Washington, DC
12.50 p.m.

The two storey red-bricked house was in the South-East, off the Suitland Parkway, and less than five miles from the centre of DC. The property looked like a real-estate agent's worst nightmare. Several of the windows were shattered and nailed up with wooden planking, the lawn was overgrown, the roof leaked, the exterior badly needed a paint job, and to top it all, the house was located in a lousy part of town, infested with drug peddlers and scoured by crime.

It was just before one that afternoon when Mohamed Rashid turned his muddied six-year-old Explorer into the weed-covered driveway. He wore a dark blue windcheater, grey sweatshirt and pants, and as he switched off the engine he turned to his two passengers, Nikolai Gorev and Karla Sharif. 'The two men came highly recommended. They're loyal supporters of the Islamic cause.'

'You trust them?' Gorev asked.

'Yes, I trust them,' Rashid replied. 'You can be certain the Americans are going to concentrate their attention on anyone with a Middle East background once they start to look for us. It wouldn't be safe using people from our own cells. They may be under surveillance. But these men have no criminal records, or connection to any of the cells.'

Rashid locked the car and activated the alarm before he led the way up the front steps and rang the bell – twice, then a three-second pause, then twice again. As they waited for an answer, Rashid looked back across the street they had just driven into.

A long row of run-down stores stood opposite, among them a grocery and a liquor store, the pavement in front spattered with litter. A half-dozen black teenagers loitered in a group, wearing baseball caps back to front, baggy clothes and chunky sneakers. They drank from beer cans, a noisy ghetto-blaster at their feet, and didn't seem to pay the slightest attention to Rashid. Still, he guessed they hadn't failed to notice the blue Explorer and its occupants, no more than they failed to notice anything within their orbit. It was the kind of neighbourhood the police avoided venturing into unless they had a death wish, or it was absolutely necessary.

He turned back as a big, rugged black man opened the door. His name was Moses Lee and he wore a grey T-shirt, muscles bulging beneath the stretched cotton. He quickly ushered them into a hallway lit by a single naked bulb, then glanced out at the street before closing the door. 'Been expecting you brothers half an hour ago.'

'The traffic was heavy,' Rashid explained. He noticed the man take a Beretta automatic that he'd been holding behind his back and slip it into his trouser pocket. 'Why, is everything all right?'

'Sure, everything's real fucking sweet. Apart from the assholes living in this motherfucking neighbourhood. You lock the car?'

'Of course.'

'Assholes round here would steal fucking anything that ain't guarded, nailed down or securely locked.'

Moses led them into the front living room. It was a mess. The curtains were closed, the light on, and the room was scattered with magazines, newspapers and empty takeaway food containers. A portable TV flickered in a corner, a news channel on, the sound turned down, and on a sofa chair was a Heckler and Koch MP-5 machine-pistol.

Rashid said, 'Where's Abdullah?'

Moses picked up the Heckler, rested the barrel in the crook of his shoulder, nodded towards a door across the hall. 'Man's in the garage, doin' the baby-sitting.'

The garage was an integral part of the house, reached from the kitchen, and just as neglected. It smelled of oil and grease, the bare concrete walls daubed with paint splashes. A dirty neon tube was lit overhead, and parked in the middle of the floor was a muddied, dark grey Nissan van.

Gorev, Karla and Rashid followed Moses Lee over to where a clean-shaven young Arab man with designer glasses and wearing Western clothes – sneakers, jeans, a pale grey Virginia University sweater – sat on a packing crate, a pump-action shotgun resting on his lap, the breech open, exposing two live cartridges. 'Abdullah's been making sure the property is kept safe, ain't you, man?'

'Yes.'

'Any dude tries to come through that garage door without a formal invitation is gonna get some twelve-gauge buckshot up his ass.'

'You've kept the van locked and the alarm on?' Rashid asked.

'Just like you said. Been watching over the merchandise, but didn't touch nothin'.'

'We need a few minutes alone.'

Abdullah stood, cradled the shotgun over his arm. 'Of course.'

'We'll be inside when you're finished,' Moses said. 'You want me to make some coffee for you guys?'

'Thank you. That would be excellent,' Rashid replied.

Moses led Abdullah towards the kitchen and the door closed behind them. When they had gone, Rashid said, 'Moses served with the American special forces. He's an excellent shot with any kind of weapon, and much brighter than he looks. He'll protect the cargo with his life, if necessary.'

'And the other one?' Gorev asked.

'Abdullah will do exactly as he is told.'

'How much do they know?'

'Only Abdullah knows the truth. But they will both follow my orders, without question.' Rashid removed his jacket, nodded towards the Nissan. 'We'll need to test the detonation program. Make sure it's working.'

Karla Sharif looked fearful. 'Isn't that dangerous?'

Rashid ignored her as he moved towards the van. 'Let's do it.'

10

Washington, DC
11 November
11.30 a.m.

Seven blocks from the White House, between Tenth Street and Pennsylvania Avenue, is the J. Edgar Hoover building, the headquarters of the FBI. A bland concrete structure that looks like a modern fortress, crammed with over five thousand employees, it serves as the command centre for fifty-seven of the Bureau's field offices and more than seventy thousand Special Agents in towns and cities across the United States.

On the sixth floor is the Counter-Terrorism Division. Under its umbrella is the WMD (Weapons of Mass Destruction) Unit, with responsibility for nuclear, bacteriological and chemical weapons attacks on American soil. It is manned twenty-four hours a day, 365 days a year by teams of specially trained agents.

By 3.15 a.m., when Director Douglas Stevens had made his emergency visit to the White House, the Counter-Terrorism Division and its WMD Unit had already got their investigation under way. A team of agents had been dispatched to Washington's airports and were checking arrival and entry lists for possible terrorist subjects. The same was happening in every US city, from Los Angeles and San Francisco on the West Coast to New York and Boston in the East and all points in between. Legions of agents roused from their beds in the middle of the night by the Bureau's field offices scattered across the country were poring over passenger lists in ports and airports, examining cargo manifests to see whether any suspect materials had recently been shipped in by air freight or in ships' containers from Afghanistan, its neighbour, Pakistan, or from any Arab country deemed suspect.

Another squad of agents had been ordered to compile inventories of any US company or chemist who had ever manufactured or worked with nerve gases, and yet another was gathering lists of suspects of Middle Eastern origin living in the US. By noon, over eight hundred agents would already be involved.

In charge of the WMD Unit was Carl J. Everly. At fifty-one, he had thinning grey hair and a badly shaped nose, a relic of his boxing days in a Boston youth club, giving him the air of a tough-looking street fighter. Which was deceptive, because it concealed one of the sharpest minds in the Division. That morning at 11.30 his office was a frenzy of activity as a half-dozen people crowded into the room. They included three FBI senior investigating officers and two chemists attached to the section. Everly fired off a question to one of the seniors. 'What's happening with our second expert opinion the Director asked for?'

'We've got three top nerve gas scientists with the US military being flown in to reassess Professor Fredericks' analysis, sir.'

Everly turned to another agent. 'What about the cargo lists, Bobby?'

'We're making slow progress. The US imports a lot of raw materials. In excess of twenty-five billion tonnes a year. We'll have to narrow it down, otherwise we're going to get swamped.'

Everly sighed. The mound of cargo manifests that would have to be thoroughly checked through was awesome. He needed to reduce the pile, at least for now. 'Go back only three months, and ignore everything else for the moment. If we find nothing interesting, go back another month, then keep going back by a month each time, right back for a year. Ray, what about the passenger lists?'

'All we've got so far is a suspected Palestinian militant who arrived at JFK three weeks ago. But it turns out the charges against him go back over fifteen years. Even the Israelis reckon he's been out of the game for at least a decade.'

'What extra help's been assigned to us?'

'Every available man the Division's got.'

'You better get in touch with any of our guys on leave. The

order is all leave's been cancelled, in every department and every field office. Unless someone's ill or dealing with a dire personal emergency, they're back on duty as of today.'

Everly paused to draw breath, felt acid pains in his stomach. He hadn't eaten since the previous night, but had drunk at least a dozen cups of strong coffee. 'As soon as our boys get through talking with these nerve-gas experts, I want their report *immediately*. The same applies if any one of you turns up anything interesting – get in touch with me, *pronto*. If I'm not at my desk, you all have my cellphone number. In the meantime, everyone back to work.'

Washington, DC
12.55 p.m.

Mohamed Rashid stepped over to the van and took a set of keys from his pocket. There was an alarm keypad on the ring and he pressed the button. The Nissan's lights flashed, and the central locking disengaged. He swung open the rear doors. Inside were two sealed oil drums, their tops locked securely with metal bands. He knew that inside those drums, securely placed in layers of shock-resistant foam, were three hundred toughened-glass balls, each not much bigger than the size of a tennis ball, and individually filled with a colourless liquid chemical.

On the floor, next to the drums, was a laptop computer. It was hooked up to a satellite dish receiver, which was placed near the front of the van. The laptop was also connected to the drums by slim electric cables. Farther back in the van was a black leather briefcase with sturdy brass combination locks. Only Rashid knew the secret of what was contained in the briefcase, but for now he was interested only in the laptop computer. He rolled up his sleeves and climbed into the van. Gorev and Karla joined him, hunched in the back.

Rashid detached two of the leads that ran from a connector on the back of the computer, one to each of the drums. 'I've disconnected the detonators. Now for the disk.'

Sweat sparkled on his temples as he removed a square, hard plastic wallet from the breast pocket of his shirt, opened the laptop and switched it on. After a few moments, the screen flickered to life and the boot program started to load. It took about a minute, and when it had finished Rashid opened the plastic wallet, slid out the disk, inserted it into the slit at the side of the laptop, and hit the enter key. Within another couple of minutes the computer had loaded the contents of the disk, and then a prompt appeared at the top left of the screen: 'ACTIVE. TO PROCEED, ENTER PASSWORD.' Rashid tapped in the Arab word *al-Wakia*; the screen cleared, and another line appeared, replacing the first one: 'ENTER COUNTDOWN PERIOD'.

Rashid entered the figures 00.00.05 and hit enter again.

Another line appeared on screen: 'COMMENCING COUNT-DOWN. FIVE SECONDS BEFORE DETONATION.'

The figure 5 he had entered started to count down: 4. 3. 2. 1. 0.

Then the screen flashed a message: 'DETONATION CODE FIRED.'

Seconds later, another message flashed below it. 'PROGRAM WORKING. DETONATION CODE NOW RESET. TEST RUN COMPLETE.'

'It works.' Rashid smiled. 'Thanks be to Allah.'

Gorev noticed fine beads of sweat on the Arab's upper lip. 'What's the matter? You look worried.'

'I'm not. But I know the power of this chemical, what it can do. If the detonators were connected when the code was fired, we'd all be dead by now.'

'You're sure it's safe?' Gorev asked.

Rashid nodded. 'Until we're ready to teach the Americans a lesson, if we must. And when that happens, we program in whatever time period we want – be it five seconds or five hours, or however long we need to get far enough away from Washington. The computer will do the rest, and detonate the drums once the exact amount of time has elapsed. And there's the other alternative. That Abu Hasim will decide to detonate it himself, remotely, with a satellite signal.'

'And what if the computer goes haywire?' Gorev asked grimly. 'Or generates a spurious signal to trigger the drums?'

'I've been assured that can't happen, Gorev. There are safety circuits built into the detonators that require them to be addressed by a specific code from the computer. Otherwise they won't explode the chemical. And there are only two ways they can be addressed. Either by us, with our program.' Rashid gestured to the satellite dish. 'Or by Abu Hasim over the airwaves, if he remotely accesses the computer with a satellite signal. At all times, the laptop remains in a stand-by mode, ready to receive his signal, even while it's switched off. And it has a long-life battery pack that will last for weeks once it's in a stand-by mode.'

'We better pray you're right and it's safe.'

Rashid wiped the sweat from his face with the back of his hand, removed the disk, replaced it in the plastic wallet. Then he turned off the computer, gingerly reconnected the detonator leads and climbed down out of the van. When the others had joined him, he locked the rear doors and flicked on the alarm again. He heard the electronic 'beep', the clunk of the front doors locking, and consulted his watch. 'It's time the Americans realised what's in store for them. Time to let them see the power of our weapon.' He pulled on his jacket, said to Karla, 'You can drop me off back in Washington. I'll meet you both later.'

'You don't need company?' Gorev asked.

Rashid shook his head. 'No, I'll do this alone.'

The White House
9.55 a.m.

The President stared at his advisers. Silence had descended on the situation room once again. This time, total shock had stalled the proceedings. Those around the table had had to face many crises in the past. But never a situation in which the entire population of the nation's capital was being held hostage, including, for many present, their own families.

The President addressed Douglas Stevens, the FBI Director.

'Assuming al-Qaeda's got a large quantity of this chemical hidden somewhere in Washington, ready to be dispersed by some kind of explosive device – a bomb, a missile, whatever. And – again assuming – Abu Hasim's got the will to carry out his threat, what are our chances of finding the nerve gas and disarming the device?'

The FBI Director was dreading the question. Ultimately, the job of trying to locate and neutralise the threat would be down to him and his men. 'Washington might not seem like a big city, sir. But we're talking about sixty-seven square miles. Searching an area of that magnitude would require many, many thousands of men. And we're assuming the nerve gas is already in Washington. There's always the possibility al-Queda's people may be hiding it in a surrounding state – Maryland, or Virginia, or even Pennsylvania. Which means an even greater search area – many thousands of square miles. That would take a mammoth amount of manpower.'

'Don't worry about the manpower. Can it be done, discreetly?'

'That's the problem, sir. I don't see how it could. That kind of massive activity is going to get noticed by the press and the public. The chemical could be stored almost anywhere. In a warehouse, a derelict building, in the basement or garage of a private home. We're talking about a huge, intrusive search that's going to get noticed, and people are going to ask questions.'

The last prospect sent a shiver down the President's spine. If the press got the slightest inkling of what was going on, there would be pandemonium on the streets. People would try to flee the capital, which in turn could cause the terrorists themselves to panic and carry out their threat.

'I want a blanket thrown over this – not a word gets out, not a damned whisper. You all realise the implications if it does. We'll need to think of a plausible excuse for the search, so I want you all to try and come up with something. And I don't want anyone moving their families out of the District, either, if they're already here. Life should go on as normal on the surface. You all attend whatever civil functions you're scheduled to attend, and carry out your usual duties with absolutely no hint of a crisis. I want to stress those points. Is that understood?'

The faces around the table nodded. Katherine Ashmore, a slim, blonde, middle-aged Kansas-born attorney, who was the Counsel to the President – and the second woman on the NSC along with Rebecca Joyce – spoke up. 'What about Abu Hasim's warning that our police and FBI don't try to hunt down his followers or find the weapon? What about the consequences if we do that? Hasim says he's ordered his people to detonate the device if they're under dire threat.'

'I take that on board, Kathy. And it's a grave risk, but it's one we've got to take.'

'But what if these people are cornered and set off their device?'

'I know, Kathy. We're caught between a rock and a hard place. But just to stand by and do nothing would be absolutely unthinkable. So we've got to try and find these people and their weapon stealthily.' The President turned to Stevens again. 'I presume you have lists of Arab terrorist suspects?'

'Of course, sir. But the terrorists behind this may not even be on our lists – they may be sleepers who have never been active before now, or specially brought in for the job. Hasim has recruits and trained followers from pretty much every country you'd care to mention that's got an Islamic following, and that includes America. The Muslim provinces of the Russian Federation, like Chechnya, for example. Countries like Bosnia, Somalia, Sudan, the Yemen, as well as Libya, the Philippines, Egypt and the Lebanon. Our culprits could be among any one or more of those nationalities. And for many years Arab terrorist cells, including the al-Qaeda network, have been using American-born recruits with Middle Eastern family backgrounds. Without solid clues, we'd really be working blind.'

'Then look for clues, fast. Manpower or cost is no object.' The President addressed the head of the CIA. 'We'll need your help, Dick. Scour your files, see what you can come up with. Again, I want it done discreetly. And try to find where Hasim might be hiding out. What he's been up to recently. Who's been helping him. The names of anybody who can get to him.'

Faulks raised his eyes. 'You mean kill him, sir?'

'No, I mean anyone who can communicate with him directly.' The President turned to the Chairman of the Joint Chiefs of Staff, General 'Bud' Horton, a tall, ruggedly built, fit-looking man in his late fifties with cropped, steel-grey hair. 'General Horton, I want a feasibility study on how long it would take to withdraw our troops and military personnel from the Arab region.'

'Sir?'

'Every serviceman, every US citizen who works for the military, every weapon, tank, aircraft and base we've got in that part of the world – lock, stock, and barrel.'

Horton, a man known for his diplomacy but one who was equally capable of speaking his mind, looked horrified. 'Surely we can't contemplate *that*, Mr President?'

'We'll contemplate it if we have to.' The President turned to Stevens. 'The same applies for evacuating Washington. I want to know how long it would take to empty the city and get people a safe distance away. I presume we've got disaster-scenario studies or people who can carry them out, rapidly?'

'Yes, sir. I'll get on to it immediately.'

'And find the best brains you can in the field of terrorist behaviour, people we can trust – we may have need of their expertise. All the better if they're familiar with Abu Hasim.' The President stood. 'I want our search under way as soon as possible, so get to work, gentlemen. I'd like you all back here in just under three hours – one p.m. exactly.' He looked down at Paul Burton, a darkly handsome and neatly dressed man in his early forties, a former Marine officer who was the Assistant to the President for National Security Affairs. 'Paul, get back to me even sooner if you have anything important to discuss. And once again, everyone, this remains watertight. Whoever else you need to be involved within your departments are to be made thoroughly aware of that fact.'

The President waited as the assembly stood and began to move out of the room. He gestured to the Vice-President. Alex Havers was a rotund, soft-spoken man touching sixty, who tended to wield his power quietly but effectively in the background. 'Alex, can you stay a moment?'

'Of course.'

When the others had left, the room was eerily silent. 'Walk with me to the Oval Office, Alex.'

'Yes, sir.'

They strolled through the corridors, past the Secret Service agents, and when they reached the Oval Office the President slumped into his leather chair and stared out towards the Washington Monument.

When Pierre L'Enfant came up with the 'Plan of the City of Washington' in 1792 he had a surveyor divide the city into four compass quadrants, with the Capitol Building at the epicentre, and those same quadrants exist today. But over two hundred years ago the population had been less than fifty thousand. Now it was over six hundred thousand. But it didn't end there. Another two million people flooded into the capital each working day, employed in factories, stores and schools, offices and government departments. And the greater metropolitan area, which encompassed the District and the towns and boroughs of the surrounding states, contained a population of over six million.

'My God, what's the world coming to? A madman wants to wipe out an entire city. What if something goes horribly wrong in the meantime – what if Hasim's people mess up by mistake and that device of their goes off and Washington's a graveyard?'

'I've no answer to that, sir.'

'We'll need to talk with the mayor.'

'I believe Al Brown's in London, sir. Attending a conference on city planning.'

'Get him back. Think of some excuse. Don't tell him why just yet, I'd prefer you left that to me. But get him back just as soon as you can and make sure nobody gets suspicious. I don't want the press asking questions.'

'Yes, Mr President.'

'Then try and find yourself someplace quiet. Have a long hard think about this, Alex. See if there's anything you can come up with, any angle we haven't considered. Then we better make the necessary precautionary arrangements to get you well out of harm's way, a long way from DC. God forbid, if this thing turns bad, we want to make sure you're alive to assume presidential authority, if need be.'

'Yes, sir. What if you're confined to the White House? How do we cover that with the press?'

'We'll think of something. A flu bug, some minor ailment, or whatever. But we'll worry about that later, Alex. Meet me back here a quarter before one.'

When Havers had gone, the President swung his leather chair to face the window behind him. He put a hand to his cheek in meditation, stared out beyond the bullet-proof, green-tinted windows. His worst dread and that of his administration had come true: an attack on American soil by a terrorist group with a powerful weapon of mass destruction. And worse, a terrorist group led by a mad religious zealot who had already proved in the past that he meant serious and deadly business.

As President, ultimately it was his problem to try to solve. The words on Truman's plaque were as true as ever: The buck stops here. The thought chilled him to the bone. *The lives of hundreds of thousands of people are in my hands. If I fail, many of them may die.*

He reflected on his awesome responsibility, then shook his head, bewildered. What kind of man would sentence hundreds of thousands of innocent men, women and children to death in the name of religious fanaticism? What kind of man could hate America with such vehemence that he was prepared try to wipe out the citizens of an entire city for the sake of his cause? What kind of man would do that?

The President had no answer. He closed his eyes. Very slowly, and with sincere conviction, he began to recite the Lord's Prayer.

11

Chesapeake Beach
11 November
12.15 p.m.

Davito's restaurant was busy that Saturday afternoon, but Nikki managed to get them a table in the conservatory which overlooked the marina. Sitting in the warm sunshine, they had a clear view of the boats, the long curving beach and coastline, the gulls hovering in the cold autumn jetstreams. She ordered a chicken salad for her and Jack had *saltimbocca*, both excellent, accompanied by a half-bottle of house Chianti. She poured barely half a glass for herself, but filled Jack's. 'Seeing as I'm driving, you have my permission to get as laced as you like. Want me to book the ambulance now?'

'What are you trying to do, get me plastered?'

'Would I ever?' She smiled, looked into Jack Collins' face. It wasn't handsome, by any means. It had a craggy, weathered look, and with his slightly husky voice, hair combed back off his face, and faded-denim eyes, it made her think of a much younger-looking George C. Scott. There was a solidness about him, a promise of strength like that of an old dray-horse you know can pull the load and go the distance.

They had met eight months previously at a house-warming in Georgetown given by Kelly Tuturo, who she had once worked with at Channel 5, many years ago. He had arrived late and sat nursing a beer at the kitchen table with Kelly's husband, Dave, who worked for the FBI. Kelly had tried to make the introduction. 'Come and talk with Jack. You'll like him, Nikki. He's an interesting guy.'

Nikki had balked. When Mark and she had broken up eighteen months after Daniel was born, and her husband just walked out, telling her he had met a twenty-two-year-old nurse and was moving to Chicago, she didn't want a man to come near her. To make it worse, after Mark left he never rang, never wanted to see Daniel. She was confused, angry, mystified. How could a man do that to an infant son? How could a husband she had trusted and fallen in love with so hopelessly just walk away from his own flesh and blood, and a beautiful baby boy at that? A boy who needed him, who missed him, a tiny human being who sensed the loss of his father, especially in those first empty months when Daniel would innocently look up into her face, his lips trembling as he asked, 'Where Daddy, Mom? I want see Daddy.' That was the part that always broke her heart, reduced her to the verge of tears, made her hurt seem scalpel sharp.

For whenever she had hugged Daniel and told him, 'Daddy's gone, pumpkin,' he would break into floods of tears. She had learned to deflect the question, to distract her son until he had learned to forget, to accept that the man who had been his daddy wasn't there any more. Later, when she discovered that Mark had been having a string of affairs behind her back for years, her pain was all the worse. For a long time afterwards even the very thought of being in a man's company, married or otherwise, let alone trusting him, made Nikki quail. She still went through days like that every now and then, when all the bitterness and anger returned, and that day at Kelly Tuturo's party had been one of them. 'I really don't think I'm in the mood for meeting men, Kelly.'

'Hey, don't get me wrong, I'm not trying to match-make. It's just to make conversation.' Then she heard the slight reproach in Kelly's voice. 'Honey, I know your divorce just came through, and men aren't exactly high in your estimation. Sure, there are a lot of bastards out there, but in Jack Collins' case, you'd be way off the mark. And he's had a pretty rough time, Nikki. So go easy on him, OK?'

Kelly had a compassionate, almost protective, attitude towards her husband's friend. Nikki let the reproach pass. Kelly, a warm-hearted girl with perfect hair and exquisitely manicured nails, had always had a liking for men, good or bad. 'Why, what happened to him?'

Kelly glanced towards where her husband and Collins were still taking, and whispered, 'Not now, Nikki. It's not the time. Now how about you help me freshen up the drinks?'

Later, sitting in the garden sunshine, the two of them alone, Nikki had said, 'So what's the story with Dave's friend Jack? Does he work for the Feds, too?'

Kelly nodded, lit a cigarette. 'CT Division – that's counter-terrorism to you and me, Nikki.'

'What happened to him?'

A shadow crossed Kelly's face. 'Remember the attack on the USS *Cole*?'

Nikki couldn't but remember. Every newspaper and TV station in the country had covered the story. Seventeen young American sailors had been killed when suicide terrorist bombers had tried to blow up their ship while it was berthed in Aden harbour. 'Sure.'

'One of the sailors killed was Jack's son.' Kelly shook her head in dismay. 'He was just nineteen, Nikki. A boy, barely out of high school. It was his first tour of duty overseas. Sean was Jack's only child. You've no idea how much it broke him up.'

'I . . . I'm so sorry to hear that.' Nikki felt a pang of guilt for her testy mood and shuddered. As with most parents, the fear of losing her child preoccupied her now and then, but the thought was too heart wrenching to contemplate, and it was something she tried hard not to dwell on. 'I guess he and his wife must have found it pretty difficult to cope?'

'That's what made it all the worse.'

'What do you mean?'

'His wife Annie loved Sean like there was no tomorrow. They both had a pretty rough time of coming to terms with his death, but Annie seemed to take it worst of all. She was in a private hospital over in Bethesda for a time, living on medication, trying to cope. Jack used to drive over there every single day, meet her out on the lawn, at a bench where she'd like to wait for him. Then one day she wasn't there. The doctors said she'd lost the will to live. It happens to some people, you know. The stress of losing someone close, someone they love dearly, it gets to them and they don't have the strength to go on. I guess you just don't believe that kind of thing can happen, until you have kids of your own and you know what love really means and you realise how it might affect you, losing a son or daughter like that.'

Nikki shuddered again. She couldn't imagine how *she'd* cope if Daniel was gone, how she'd have the will to go on living. Suicide would probably figure in her thoughts; as it would with most mothers who lost a beloved child, especially the only one you had. 'You make me feel like divorce isn't the worst thing a girl can go through.'

Kelly brightened, said in her warm Tennessee accent, 'Hey, isn't that what I've been trying to tell you for months? And you're talking to someone who's been down that road once already. There's a lot worse in life, believe me. So maybe that ought to perk you up.'

Nikki looked back towards the kitchen, where Jack Collins stood beside a circle of guys discussing a football game. Even to her he seemed slightly lost, nursing a beer, on the edge of the conversation.

Later, Kelly had introduced them. It was his denim eyes that first struck her, eyes that looked as if they had prowled the bleakest chambers of the human heart. A tough guy, but gentle too, with a sentimental streak a mile wide. Nikki had found him appealing in a vague sort of way, and when they had met again at Kelly's house two months later, whatever slight attraction had passed between them was to become a friendship. And for almost six months afterwards they had met for dinner now and then, nothing more than that, until one night in August it had happened.

Nikki had asked him to her apartment for dinner. He had stayed over, sleeping in the spare bedroom, and when she had gone in to say goodnight she had lain beside him, wanting to be held, cherished again. A hug had become an embrace, an embrace a prelude to lovemaking. Afterwards he had told her she was the first woman he'd slept with since his wife had died. She believed him. She also knew that it was the first time in a long while that she had believed anything remotely intimate a man had told her.

'So, do I get to hear the real reason why a good-looking woman buys me lunch?'

Nikki came out of her reverie. Jack was staring at her – not intently, just inquisitively. She slowly put down her napkin, reached for her glass, took a measured sip before setting it down again. 'I had some news I wanted to tell you. The *Capitol Gazette* in Annapolis has offered me an editorial position. I've been thinking of taking the job and moving out here to the cottage.'

'How come you never told me before now?'

'I only got the offer yesterday. My interview was the day before, so I didn't want to mention it in case it came to nothing. But it has, and now I've got a decision to make. That's why I thought I'd ask your opinion.'

She studied his face for a reaction. It was hard to tell whether his expression was one of disappointment or surprise. 'I didn't know you wanted to leave Washington, Nikki.'

'To be honest, it's more for Daniel. I mean, Washington's wonderful, Jack, don't get me wrong, but it's a big, impersonal city with all the big-city problems that go with it. A crime rate that's still off the clock, a drugs problem that's not going to go away. I did a story for the *Post* last week. A seven-year-old kid got caught with an automatic pistol in a school in the south-east district. A *seven-year-old*, Jack. Jesus, that frightens me. I don't want to continue to raise my son in conditions like that. Down here, there's no crime worth talking of, good neighbours, a beach near by. It would be wonderful for Daniel. And the job's nine-to-five, which would be perfect. It's only half an hour to Annapolis from the cottage, and there's a day care centre right by the office. I could check on him any time I like.'

She waited for a response, a word, but nothing came. She twisted her napkin. 'So what do you think?'

'How does your mom feel? She'd miss seeing Daniel so often. As it is, she gets to see him pretty much every day.'

'I didn't tell her.'

'Why not?'

'I wanted to run something by you first.' Nikki stopped twisting her napkin. She felt her face flush beneath her make-up. 'Maybe I should put all my cards on the table?'

This time Jack raised his eyes. 'There's more?'

She nodded. 'That was the easy part. At least, I think it was. And I don't know why I feel embarrassed saying this, but . . .' She hesitated, stretched her fingers out to the napkin again, but toyed with a dessert spoon instead, said it as frankly as she could. 'I just thought, well . . . I thought maybe you might like to stay here for a while with Daniel and me.'

'You mean move in? Commute to Washington from here?'

'Yes, I mean move in.' She felt herself blushing again. 'Kind of see how it goes.'

'What brought all this on?'

Nikki hesitated. She knew she desperately wanted to be more honest. But she couldn't, not completely, not right now. She had wanted to tell him about what had been bothering her for months, since they'd slept together. That she suddenly hankered for a man in her life again, that she realised Daniel needed a father. That maybe she even wanted more family. She wasn't getting any younger, and in another few years the risks involved in getting pregnant would become too great. She wanted to tell him all those things, but instead her hand reached over, lay on top of his. 'I want to help you heal the wounds, I really do, Jack.'

He took her hand in his warmly. 'I know you do, Nikki. And I'm grateful. More grateful than you can ever know.'

'Maybe . . . it's just that today, of all days, I wanted you to know that I'm there for you. It's not a marriage proposal, the offer for you to move in. But maybe it's a step towards something. A trial run, if you like. You need someone in your life. So do I.'

Jack Collins looked out towards the marina, to where an elderly man was coiling up some rope on the deck of one of the boats in the autumn sunshine, looked out to where the sea shimmered under the blind stare of the blue sky. Nikki saw that he seemed in some kind of turmoil, or maybe discomfort. Had she said too much, too soon? At once a part of her regretted having said what she had. But she had wanted to say it, needed to.

When he looked back at her face, he spoke gently. 'I know what you're trying to say, Nikki. And I'm touched, honestly I am. Apart from everything else this has been a great friendship. And everything else has been good too. I'm sure any other guy would jump at the chance. And I'm pretty sure that this is the last opportunity in my life I'm ever going to get to meet someone like you . . .'

Her heart sank a little. Jack's voice had barely changed, but a new alertness coloured it, a shade of wariness. The pale blue fabric of his eyes flushed now with caution.

'I sense a *but* there somewhere.'

'Nikki, I just don't know that I'm ready for that kind of commitment. Not . . . not just yet.'

She let his reply sit there a moment, feeling rebuffed but trying to hide it. 'You're sure there's no other reason?'

'What reason could there be?'

'Sometimes men find it difficult to be a father to another man's child.'

He shook his head. 'I like Daniel very much, Nikki, you know that. Maybe it's even more than like. He's such a great little boy. And there's times I'll admit when I've wondered what it might be like being a father to him.' He paused. 'But in a little while, maybe, not right now. Can you understand, Nikki?'

For a moment she was silent. She wanted to tell him that she couldn't wait for ever, that she was suddenly so aware of time and life racing on, that she needed to grasp something solid now, a good relationship, as much for Daniel's sake as her own. That she didn't want herself and her son to be alone. But still she couldn't tell him. 'I understand.'

'Do you, Nikki?'

'Sure.' She tried to hide her disappointment. 'Forget I ever mentioned it, at least for now. So let's not talk about it any more. Today's probably the wrong time for me to even bring up the subject, anyway. I'm sorry, my love.'

'What about the job offer?'

Nikki shook her head. 'There's lots of time to discuss it. The *Gazette*'s given me a week to think about their offer.'

He kissed her palm. 'You're not sore, are you, Nikki?'

'No, I'm not sore.' She smiled, leaned over, pecked his cheek, said the words softly, to his face. 'But I wanted you to know what I felt.'

Nikki parked outside the cemetery. Collins walked alone through the gates in the cold sunshine, while she waited back in the car, knowing that this was a private moment, a moment when he needed to be alone. This day, of all days, he had an obligation to the dead. To stand upon the earth that covered his wife and son, to touch the stone that bore their names.

Collins moved past the tombs of granite and bronze, past the uprooted earth of freshly dug graves and mourners hunched in their own private grief. Some people preferred to inter their loved ones in elaborate crypts, or behind brass plaques in a wall of remembrance, but he had placed his wife and son to rest on a small hill shaded by some pines and a gnarled old arcadia tree. He laid the flowers on the grave, said the prayers and the words he wanted to say, the same words he always said, that he missed them so much, that he longed for them back, that their passing had left such a terrible sorrow, an unending ache.

That nothing could replace them, *nothing*, not ever. Standing there, out of the sun, in the shadow of the pines, his eyes swept over the smooth granite, stared at the gold-leaf paint in the cold-chiselled words and numbers that inscribed his pain.

Here lie the bodies of Annie Collins,
born 1960, died November 19th 2000,
and Sean Collins, born June 1981, died October 12th, 2000.
Beloved wife and son of John Collins.
'Until we're together again, I'll miss you, always.'

He still missed them. Of course, he had dreams and he had photographs. But his dreams were sometimes disturbed, and photographs were always so inadequate, never captured the real truth; the soul behind the image, the beauty behind the smile, the happiness behind the laughter. They had never captured the real Annie that he had known since they had met in high school when he was sixteen: warm hearted, fun loving, sensual, a good, kind friend, a loving mother. Or the *real* Sean behind the photograph taken on his third birthday. Not a sullen crying child, unhappy because one of the other children had seized one of his presents, but a beautiful, blond-haired little boy with a lopsided smile, always ready to make mischief, who loved to run to his father's arms, be held and tickled, smothered in kisses. And the other photographs, the ones of Sean in his naval uniform, looking like a man, though not yet a man, just a shy, uncertain youth trying to forge his manhood, find his way into the adult world.

It was Sean's death, and the manner of it, which had troubled him most. Collins had learned from one of the naval medics who attended the dead and injured that after the explosion Sean was still alive and conscious, even though his body had been shattered by the blast. Death had come not in seconds but in a gradual diminution of his senses as he slowly, agonisingly, bled to death. Every time Collins visualised that image of his son, his beautiful boy, in such horrendous pain, it broke his heart, cut him to pieces.

He knew that the loss of a child at any stage of life was unnatural, so wrong that purpose was difficult to reclaim. It compressed the heart into a small stone, turned the mind into a graveyard. Collins knew that the experience had carved his face and painted a dull sheen of desolation over his eyes. He had read somewhere that after the death of a child parents often reported a disturbing inability to care about the suffering of others. Music that had once stirred the heart no longer moved you, and you became numb, unaffected. It had been that way with him. After Sean's death, and then Annie's, the hardness of his own heart had truly frightened him.

And for a long time afterwards, haunted by absence, he had come here, visiting the cemetery at all hours of day and night, to lie down on the ground beside them, stretch himself out on the cold earth, feel it seep into his bones as it seeped into theirs, as if by lying beside them he could somehow connect to them again. People visiting the cemetery who saw him then must have thought he was crazy. And for a time he was. He had seen a therapist. The counselling had not helped. His doctor had recommended anti-anxiety medication. He rejected the prescription. He had wanted to feel the pain. It was all he had, all that allowed him vividly to recall the happiness of his past life. And now, though his dreams still reclaimed him briefly, especially on anniversaries, they came less often.

Nikki had been responsible for that. Nikki, with her soft touch and her caring eyes and maternal instinct, had been a rock, had helped bring him out of himself, bring him into the world again. With her, he had found a reconnection to life that had eluded him for so long. And being around Daniel had made him feel what it was like to be a father again, and he cherished that feeling. But Nikki's offer was too much, too soon, something he knew he wasn't ready for, and he didn't know how else to tell her, except by being honest. To move on, to make another life for himself, to let go completely of his wife and son was too much right now, almost like forsaking them.

I miss you, Annie. I miss you, Sean.

For a fleeting moment an image flashed before his eyes: the grainy photograph he kept hidden in his desk, of the cold, hard face of the man who had helped take his son's life. The terrorist who had helped mastermind and execute the *Cole* bombing and had escaped the FBI's intensive international efforts to apprehend those responsible.

Mohamed Rashid.

The name came to Collins' lips with such hatred, such vehemence, that he trembled, felt his rage marrow deep. The kind of anger that made him fear his own potential for human savagery, know the ease with which he might embrace vengeance, and with reason call it justice. A molten anger, which despite the passage of time was still so overwhelming it nearly broke his self-control, took him almost to the verge of tears.

He fought the rage. Forced the image of Mohamed Rashid from his mind.

It wasn't the time or place. On this of all days, he didn't want his anger to intrude, wanted simply to remember the sacredness of his memories of his wife and son.

When he had finished talking, when he had finished his whispered words to the dead, he took a deep breath, touched the stone, felt its glacial coldness seep into his fingers, exhaled, and slowly let the stone go.

Then he turned and walked down the hill, slowly back towards the gates behind which Nikki waited.

Washington, DC
1.28 p.m.

Seven miles away Mohamed Rashid was stepping out of the subway from the Gallery Place metro station, in Washington's Chinatown. He walked for two blocks towards the busy shopping area on Gallery Row. He found the phone booth he had chosen, on a quiet side street round the corner from a Borders bookstore. Wearing soft leather gloves, he stepped into the booth, removed his metal-banded wristwatch and placed it on top of the call-box, the face towards him. As the second hand swept round, he fiddled with his gold earring as he made sure no one had stopped outside, waiting to use the booth. To his relief no one had. Preparing himself, he cleared his throat, then put a coin in the slot and dialled the number from memory. There were half a dozen rings before the call was answered by a polite female voice and the coin clanked home. 'The White House. How may I help you?'

Rashid cupped the receiver in both his hands, holding it close to his mouth, and paused a moment before speaking, still keeping his eye on the watch's sweeping second hand. 'Can you hear me clearly?'

'Yes, sir, I can hear you. How may I help you?'

'By listening carefully. Because I will not repeat what I have to say. This is an important message for your President.'

There was a noticeable hesitation at the other end. 'I – I hear you, sir.'

'Good. Don't interrupt. Just listen, and take note.'

Rashid guessed that at that very moment the female switchboard operator was frantically signalling to her supervisor that she had a potentially threatening or abusive call, alerting the attention of the Secret Service, but that didn't matter to him right now. He delivered the message slowly, carefully enunciating what he had to say, but all the time observing the watch dial, making sure that he did not exceed his allotted time. When he had finished, he abruptly hung up the receiver.

A drop of sweat dripped from his brow on to the arm of his windcheater. He checked the time. Forty-six seconds had elapsed from the moment he had got through to the White House switchboard. Not that it really mattered all that much, but he had kept his call so brief to ensure that it couldn't be traced. He slipped on his watch, stepped out of the booth, and walked south-east for three blocks, until the streets became busier and dirtier and he found himself on 14th. The street was filled with cheap bars, fast-food restaurants, and prostitutes loitering on street corners. As Rashid walked past, a girl said, 'Like a date, honey? You'll have the best time of your life.'

Mohamed Rashid ignored the request and strolled on, catching a distant glimpse between streets of the soaring marble columns of Capitol Hill, and the massive granite fronts of US government buildings. He thought: *How I hate this country. Hate it with a crushing intensity. Its streets, its people, its incredible arrogance, its corrupt power.*

A power he would soon destroy.

A block away, he found the bar he'd been told about, a seedy, run-down place with a flashing Budweiser neon light in the window. When he stepped inside he found himself in a dark cavern that stank of stale beer and marijuana smoke. No more than six customers, all watching a blaring TV set above the bar, showing a basketball game.

One customer, a small black man wearing a black leather jacket and a blue baseball cap – the man Rashid was seeking – sat nursing a beer near the wall phone. Rashid approached him, and the man said, 'Hey, brother, how you doing?'

His eyes looked glazed, as if he'd been sampling too much of his own merchandise.

'I need some pills,' Rashid said quietly.

'Don't we all, brother.' The man's eyes narrowed, suddenly no longer looking glazed as they studied his potential customer, his well-practised streetwise instinct for danger telling him in an instant that this one wasn't a threat. 'What you need?'

'Amphetamines.'

'Crystal meth do?'

Rashid nodded. The black man smiled, but the deal with the stranger was far from done. 'You come back here, say, in ten minutes, maybe I might know where you can get some, understand what I'm saying?'

Rashid nodded again, knowing how the game was to be played. 'Ten minutes. I will come back.'

'You do that.'

Rashid left, stepped out onto the street again. In the days ahead, with the tension, stress and sleeplessness he'd endure, he would have need of the drug to keep him awake and alert. He would return to the bar in ten minutes, but now he had one more thing to do. A block farther one, he found another phone booth and stepped inside. This time he used a twenty-dollar phone card and dialled an overseas number in Montmartre, Paris.

12

Washington, DC
Sunday, 11 November
1 p.m.

As the clock swept past one o'clock, there was a growing air of panic in the White House situation room. The President had entered the chamber at exactly three minutes before one. The members of the Security Council immediately got to their feet when he appeared, but with a wave of his hand he indicated that they remain in their seats.

'Ladies and gentlemen, we now have three other expert opinions on the vial contents and I have to tell you that they confirm the awesome human devastation a device loaded with such a chemical could cause were it detonated in Washington.' The President looked at Douglas Stevens. 'Doug, perhaps you'd hand out the draft report of the experts' analyses.'

'Yes, sir.' Stevens took several photocopied, stapled sheets from his briefcase and handed them around the table.

'You'll also see that our experts suggest that a likely source for the nerve gas could be Russia, which is a leader in the field of chemical warfare, way ahead of the US, or any other country. Does anyone have any questions?'

Heads went down to study the transcript, and after several minutes the Defence Secretary, John Feldmeyer, looked up. 'If the source is Russia, what are we going to do about it, Mr President?'

'I'm going to make a personal call to President Kuzmin to discuss the matter.'

Mitch Gains, a barrel-chested former Boston judge and one of President Booth's advisers, spoke up. 'You're going to tell him about the threat to Washington?'

'I see no other way, Mitch. We may need his co-operation

to find out where al-Qaeda got the gas. We've all heard of rogue Russian scientists working for terrorist organisations in return for a big pay cheque, and the Russian mafia supplying terrorists with the materials for weapons of mass destruction for the same reasons. That may be the case here. Naturally, I'll insist on Kuzmin's absolute discretion, and that he makes sure any investigations he orders are kept top secret.'

'What about the issue of the prisoners in Russian jails, sir?' Bob Rapp, a bearded Californian – and a much-respected one-time journalist who was one of the President's key special advisers – addressed him. A veteran journalist in his early fifties, he was a tall, sober-faced man who rarely smiled.

'Naturally, I'll also be bringing that up with Kuzmin. But if it does go to the wire, it may be a question of us having to use leverage to convince the Russians, Germans, Israelis and British to help us. Exactly what leverage we may have to use is another matter.'

'With due respect, Mr President,' Rapp replied, 'you have enormous power at your disposal, both military and financial, to influence these other states. You can use that power to its ultimate to ensure that all the remaining prisoners are released.'

'Bob, let's just hope it doesn't ever go that far. And let's get this thing in perspective – the question of the prisoners is the least of our concerns right now.' President Booth turned to another of the generals present, the Army Chief of Staff. 'General Croft, as a former head of army communications, I believe you can explain how a terrorist like Hasim might remotely trigger this chemical weapon of his. Be it a bomb, or whatever.'

'Yes, sir.' The general readied some notes in front of him before looking up. 'My experts tell me there are really only two ways, by radio wave or by telephone. But I believe there is, in fact, a third option, which I'll come back to in a moment. First, let's consider radio. Basically what happens is that the terrorist attaches his bomb to a radio receiver. In this case, let's say he's placed both the receiver and the bomb somewhere in Washington. Then the terrorist can walk away and either himself or one of his buddies can set off the bomb remotely, pretty much from anywhere in the world. All that's needed to detonate the device is a transmitter tuned to the same frequency as the receiver, and a little bit of simple electronic circuitry. To stop the bomb going off inadvertantly the signal will be modulated with another frequency. But simply what would happen is this: the terrorist transmits his signal from somewhere a distance away, and the receiver picks it up. It would then make a circuit inside the receiver, which in turn energies a relay of some kind, and detonates the bomb. For a long distance, he'd have to use short-wave transmission, which bounces off the ionosphere. For a shorter distance, VHF.'

'How many frequencies could he possibly use for something like this?'

'Hard to say, sir. It depends on the transmitter's power, where it's situated, and how far a distance you need to send the signal.'

'Could we jam all the possible frequencies?'

'Impossible, sir. We wouldn't have the transmitter capacity to block such a broad spectrum of radio waves. And besides, even if we did, we'd be shooting ourselves in the foot.'

'Explain.'

'Because we'd end up incapacitating our own frequencies, those vital to the police and FBI, even the fire departments and emergency services. There'd be chaos on the airwaves, or more likely there would be no airwaves at all.'

'What about the telephone system?'

'Again, it's pretty simple. You attach the bell wires of a telephone to a digital decoder box. When an incoming call is detected, the decoder comes alive and sits there waiting for another signal to activate it. When the digital activating code comes in over the phone line, and the decoder verifies it's the right one – that is, they match – then it triggers the bomb. It also means a wrong number can't set it off. All a terrorist has to do is dial the number in Washington, or wherever the device is, and when it answers, he transmits his code over the line. The code could be aural – like the fast digital codes you hear when you punch a number on a phone keypad – or something in a higher frequency range that can't be heard. Either way, it's simple stuff technically, but deadly effective.'

'Could Washington's phone communications be totally sealed off from the outside world?'

'Again, that's impossible, Mr President. Besides, there's another possibility, a combination of both methods I've outlined. The phone in question could be a cellphone, which uses a satellite. But again, if we tried to shut down all cellphone communications, we could be shooting ourselves in the foot. The same applies with ordinary land-line telephone communications. All 911 and military phone traffic in and out of DC would be affected. You may not be aware of it, sir, but ninety-eight per cent of all Department of Defence and emergency response communications are transmitted down public phone lines.'

The President sighed. 'It's at times like this you realise how vulnerable we all are in this technological age of ours.'

'That's a fact, Mr President.'

'You mentioned a third method.'

'Again, it could be part of a combination. A suicide volunteer baby-sits the device until he gets a verbal call to detonate. And in the case of Islamic fanatics, that's entirely feasible.'

'So we're pretty much at the mercy of Hasim's method, whichever he uses?'

'It looks that way, sir. Hasim would probably go for a combination of both methods, radio and telephone. Or he could also simply control the operation entirely by himself, using a satellite radio link – with the bomb hooked up to a satellite dish receiver, instead of using a telephone line or a conventional radio transmission over the airwaves. That's a possibility too. It's the sort of communication we know he uses frequently.'

'Surely we can control those links?' Paul Burton, the Assistant to the President on National Security Affairs, suggested.

'To an extent. We can definitely control any non-terrestrial communications under our influence – by that I mean US military and commercial satellites. We could probably even get the co-operation of our European allies and perhaps the Japanese to allow us to monitor their satellite signals traffic, or agree to shut them down altogether. But the Russians and the Chinese have satellites, too, most of them for military use, that are totally independent of us. There's no way they'd allow us to control their sat-com signals. We could try to jam them electronically to shut them down, sure, but if we do that we'd be wading into dangerous waters. And there's still no guarantee we'd stop Hasim.'

The President sighed again. 'It seems we're stuck up a creek.'

There was a deep silence, and then the man from Mississippi and adviser to the President on economic policy, Charles Rivermount, said, 'Be that as it may, Mr President, we still haven't got a valid excuse for our search.'

'I'm about to come to that. The Vice-President has come up with a suggestion. Alex, would you care to explain?'

Alex Havers put down the copy of the experts' report he had been mulling over. 'All FBI agents and Secret Service agents directly involved will be told the truth. There's no other way we can carry out the search effectively, and with such a direct threat to the President's life by Hasim's stipulation that he remain in the White House the Secret Service will obviously have to be on board. However, anyone else, and by that I mean the police, the National Guard, the military – apart from their specialist chemical units, which we'll need – or whoever else we bring in to help with the search, we simply tell them that we're looking for a number of barrels of potentially hazardous chemicals that went missing. By that I mean chloric acid. It's an industrial chemical used in the etching process. It can also cause serious pollution, severe skin burns if anyone's physically exposed to it, and even death if the fumes are inhaled. If need be, and the army's brought in at a later stage, we could admit the consignment went missing from an army base, which gives us good cause to involve the military. But that's only if our backs are absolutely to the wall. Instructions will be given to everyone involved not to talk to the press for any reason. And that includes all of us here, gentlemen. No matter how well we know the reporter – and we all know reporters – no one breathes a word.'

One of the generals raised a dubious eyebrow. 'You really think that can work, Mr Vice-President?'

'Right now, it's about the best excuse we can come up with. And it's simple enough to be effective. Unless anyone can think of anything better? And in this case, I'd be more than happy to submit to any superior advice or opinion.'

There was nervous laughter and then the men around the table fell silent again. The President said, 'OK, it's what we go with for now. If anyone in the press starts asking questions, we know what to tell them. But if we do this right, that problem shouldn't arise. I want the search under way immediately. Doug, it'll be your job to liaise with the Police Commissioner, after I speak with him personally. It's obvious he'll have to know the truth if this is to work, as will a number of key officials. Are you confident we can rely on his discretion?'

'Absolutely, Mr President.'

'Now, have any of you any questions, or anything to report? Yes, General Horton?'

'Don't you think the military ought to be involved in the search right away, sir? The extra manpower could help move things along a lot faster.'

'I think the less uniforms seen on the streets for now, the better. But if the situation changes, obviously we may have to draft in the army and National Guard.'

'Mr President, I have a question.'

It was Rivermount. 'Yes, Charlie?'

'What if we rattle Hasim's chain by trying to find this nerve gas? What if these terrorists notice extra police activity on the streets, figure out what we're after, and decide to explode their device? Or if we stumble on their hideout during the search and cause them to set it off deliberately, or by accident?'

'There's no answer to that, is there? Except that we've got to try.'

The President's phone flashed. He grabbed the receiver, listened and said, 'Send it in at once.'

The door opened and an aide appeared, handed the President

a sealed envelope and retreated. The President opened the envelope, read the slip of paper inside, looked up. 'It seems al-Qaeda may have another message for us. There was a phone call to the White House switchboard a couple of minutes ago. The caller claimed there was another package left at a specified location near Washington. A team of Secret Service and FBI are on their way there as we speak.'

2.10 p.m.

Within thirty-five minutes of the phone call to the White House, a flurry of cars, a blue Dodge van and two jet-black four-wheel-drives with tinted windows braked to a halt outside a cemetery in Floraville, eight miles from Washington. The small graveyard was empty of visitors and mourners that afternoon as the two dozen burly Secret Servicemen and FBI agents scrambled out of the cavalcade in a burst of activity. They immediately cordoned off the entrance, much to the puzzlement of a solitary elderly man weeding the grass verge just inside the gates. He came over to investigate, carrying a hoe. 'Hey, you fellas mind telling me what in tarnation you're doing?'

'You the caretaker, sir?' one of the men asked.

'Yep, I am.'

'A woman named Margaret Coombs. Where's she buried?'

'You talking about Maggie Coombs?'

'Maybe.'

'Guess you must be. 'Cause she's the only Margaret Coombs we got buried here. Passed away last fall.' The man pointed behind him, past the rows of headstones, towards several of the graveyard's more recent interments. 'You'll find her plot over there. Nice granite slab, if I do say so myself. Hey, who are you boys?'

One of the federal agents flashed his ID. The old man's eyes popped with interest. 'Say, what did poor old Maggie do afore she died?'

'Nothing, sir, not that I know of. Now, if you could just lead us to the exact spot we'd appreciate it. And please, don't go any closer than about twenty feet from the grave.'

The caretaker frowned. 'Sure, whatever you say. You fellas follow me. Just stay on the gravel.' He led the way along a path, keenly followed by a dozen of the FBI agents and Secret Servicemen, their feet crunching on the gravel chips. When he reached the area he had indicated, he pointed to a polished, granite-bordered headstone, almost a respectful twenty feet away, the name *Margaret Coombs* inscribed on it. 'That's Maggie. Never thought she might have been one for getting herself in trouble. Saw out her last days in an old folks' home outside town. Good lady. Sharp poker-player. What she do wrong?'

Very carefully, one of the Secret Servicemen took a few steps closer to the grave. Kneeling, he visually examined the bordered site, took out a notebook and cross-checked his notes with the details on the headstone. He stood, stepped away and addressed his colleagues. 'This is it. Better tell the guys back in the van to get their equipment up here.'

An FBI agent hurried back towards the entrance gates and the cavalcade, where the Dodge was parked. A Secret Serviceman turned his attention to the caretaker. 'The lady didn't get herself in any trouble, sir. Are you the only one working here?'

'Nope. Henry works here, too, but part time. Henry Folson. Lives local. He's the gravedigger. What's the trouble that the Feds are so interested in old Maggie?'

'Sir, this agent here will take you back down to the gate.'

'What in the hell for?'

'If you could just go with the agent, sir, I'd really appreciate it.'

One of the men took hold of the caretaker's arm. 'This way, sir.'

'Hey, I know the damned way! Say, what the devil's going on here?'

As the man was led away, out of earshot, the FBI agent addressed his colleagues again.

'OK, no one touch anything. I want the gravestone and border cordoned off, the surface area thoroughly inspected, and every part of the grave that can be dusted checked for prints. The same for those in the immediate vicinity. I don't care if you find a million prints on there, I want every one of them. We'll need to question the caretaker, and anyone else who's been working here in the last couple of weeks. And find out if any burials took place during the same period. I want to know if anyone's been seen around this site in particular, or behaving suspiciously in the cemetery area. Get sketch artists if you need them.' He paused, took off his jacket and rolled up his sleeves. 'Now, let's go help the boys get their equipment set up, find some shovels, and get this business over with.'

The White House
3.17 p.m.

'One videocassette, like the last time.' Doug Stevens held up the cassette for everyone in the situation room to see.

'There was no message with it?'

'No, Mr President. Just the cassette. Found inside a protective waterproof plastic wrapper, exactly where the caller said it would be, buried near the top of the grave. The area's still being checked out by a forensic team. There was a caretaker on the site, but he claims he saw no one disturb the grave, or anyone suspicious hanging around the vicinity of the cemetery recently.'

'This caller – what have we got on him?' Mitch Gains said. 'I presume his voice was taped?'

'Yes, sir. The switchboard initiated a recording moments after his call was received.'

'And?'

'The voice is being analysed as we speak.'

'How did the caller sound?' asked Rebecca Joyce.

'Well spoken. No trace of nervousness. His accent certainly wasn't American, but he didn't sound particularly Arab, either. We'll try to get a fix on his ethnic origins, approximate age and likely social status, using our computers and experts in vocal analysis. We have recordings of known Islamic and Arab terrorists and supporters in our voice databanks, from interviews they gave to journalists, or from intercepted phone calls. We can try to find a match.'

'And the origin of the call itself?' Katherine Ashmore addressed the FBI Director.

'Internal in the USA. That's all we know for certain. The man stayed on the line for less than a minute. Just said what he had to say and hung up. The supervisor on duty tried to get a trace, but had insufficient time.'

'So we've got nothing, really?'

'No, Kathy. Apart from the fact that the call was made in this country.'

The President grimaced. 'Then let's concentrate on what we *have* got. The cassette.'

'There were no prints, just like the other package,' Stevens offered. 'The video mechanism was also X-rayed. It was totally safe – completely harmless.'

'That remains to be seen. I'm assuming if it's Hasim again he'll be speaking in Arabic. What about a translator?'

'I've got Ed Marshall, our Arabic expert, waiting outside. He's ready to interpret, sir.'

'OK, bring him in, and let's take a look at what's on there.'

Stevens summoned the FBI translator, and a silver-haired, distinguished-looking man entered the room. The President greeted him, and Marshall was directed to a chair near the TV to prepare himself, opening a pad and readying his pen, while Stevens turned on the TV, slid in the cassette and flicked some buttons on the remote.

The room had fallen completely still, every face mirroring the President's anxious curiosity. The TV screen turned to vivid blue, and after about twenty seconds the colour image of Abu Hasim appeared. As before, he wore a grey half-turban, a white *kafiya.* He sat cross-legged on the floor, staring into the camera. The tension in the situation room rose as Hasim began to speak, but

Stevens hit the hold button. 'When you're ready, Ed. Just give it to us word for word.'

'Yes, sir. I'm ready.' Marshall leaned forward, Stevens cancelled the hold button, the tape rolled again, and Marshall translated the Arab's words:

> Once more, I address myself to the President of America. By now, you will have had time to reflect upon my first message. Naturally, you will be considering your options and the grave decisions that you will have to make in the coming hours and days. However, you may also be questioning my determination to carry out my threat. Therefore, I wish to take this opportunity to assure you again that my threat is a very real one.
>
> You may also be tempted to assume that I or my followers do not have the resolve to carry out our strike against America, and inflict large numbers of deaths. In that assumption, you would be very wrong. We of al-Qaeda are possessed of a terrible fury for the wrongs that have been done by your country against the Arab peoples, and I can promise that our wrath, if it must be unleashed, will be vengeful, ruthless, and decisive.
>
> So that you may believe this pledge, and thus hasten those pressing matters that you have to attend to with all your vigour, I must therefore ask you to witness an example of the fate that lies in store for the millions of citizens living in your capital, if my demands are not fully met. To again remind you, if my deadline is passed without total compliance on your part, of the terrible calamity that will befall America.
>
> This world in which we live is often cursed by tragedy. I see no other way to reinforce my threat than to add to that tragedy. I shall do this by showing you a vivid example of the powerful weapon which you now know we possess. But first, let me explain. Ten days ago my followers abducted fourteen American citizens in Azerbaijan. No doubt you have heard of their disappearance. Your intelligence organisations may even have told you of their fears for the men's safety. Their safety is no longer of concern.

What should be of concern is what you are about to witness. So let this serve as a warning. If you do not heed it, then the entire citizenship of Washington will be forced to suffer exactly the same fate as that which you are about to behold. Therefore, I will pray most earnestly to Allah that the President of America will have the wisdom and intelligence to see that the only course of action open to him is to comply with my wishes. And that he pursue this necessary course vigorously, before the time runs out to save his people from a terrible misfortune.

Abu Hasim fell silent. Marshall finished his translation moments later, and suddenly the Arab's image disappeared. The screen went blank, cut by rolling white lines. The CIA Director, seated directly across from the President, said urgently, 'Sir, you received my report about the Azerbaijan incident ten days ago. You'll recall that twelve American mining engineers and their two-man CIA escort were abducted in a remote mountain area in south-west Azerbaijan. We sent a team to help the Azerbaijanis find them, but so far there's been no ransom demand, no leads, nothing.' The Director was ashen. 'But that crazy sonofabitch Hasim must have kidnapped—'

'Dick, please . . .' the President interrupted, grim faced.

Everyone in the situation room stared at the TV as the rolling lines suddenly cleared and the video came to life again. A room appeared on the screen. It looked like some kind of laboratory chamber, but starkly empty, the pale-coloured walls bare. Half of the nearest wall was glass fronted, stretching from approximately waist height to the ceiling. In the farthest back wall was a closed door. Slowly, without a noise, the door opened. As if in a daze, a line of men began to file in.

Their casual attire was filthy and dishevelled. Pathetic-looking creatures, the men appeared exhausted and disoriented. Some of their faces were badly bruised and their eyes swollen, as if they had been beaten. The youngest looked barely in his twenties, the oldest perhaps fifty.

The door closed behind the men. The fourteen Americans

stood silent, huddled in the centre of the chamber like a group of frightened schoolchildren, some with their heads bowed, others staring dazedly at the walls, or through the glass window towards whoever, if anyone, was on the other side of the camera. There was still no sound. Deliberately or otherwise, the event wasn't being audibly recorded. Most of the men looked fearful, bewildered as to why they had been ushered into the room. Two of the captives, whose faces appeared more heavily bruised and battered than the others, could barely stand.

The CIA Director suddenly recognised them, jabbed a finger at the TV. 'Sir, those are my two men. Greg Baktarin and Joe Calverton.' Anguish flared in Faulk's voice. 'I can't believe this. If Abu Hasim intends to kill—'

'Quiet please, Dick!' the President interrupted again, and continued to focus on the screen, his jaw tightening in barely controlled fury.

Quite suddenly, the stocky figure of what appeared to be a man crossed in front of the camera, moving slowly towards the glass window. He wore a white biohazard suit, thick white rubber gloves, and a gas mask shielded his face. In his left hand, slightly outstretched, he carried what appeared to be some kind of laboratory apparatus, no more than the size of a small lunch box. The confused men could only stare as the figure in the biohazard suit halted, and pulled open a chute-like metal drawer positioned just below the window. Very delicately, he placed the apparatus in the chute. For a few moments he lingered, his gloved hands remaining inside the metal drawer, working cautiously, as if he was adjusting some critical mechanism. When he had finished, he gingerly shut the drawer and promptly retreated out of the frame.

Around the situation-room table, the President and his advisers stared in silence, each dreading in their hearts what was to come. Seconds passed, stretched into what seemed an eternity, but nothing happened. Then, suddenly, it seemed as if a furious, malevolent force invaded the chamber.

The men inside began to twitch and jerk, their bodies convulsing like crazed marionettes in some obscene dance. Mouths yawned in silent screams of terror. They no longer looked or behaved like humans but like rabid animals, features distorted, racked by expressions of deranged agony. Within seconds, their eyes bulged grotesquely, their lips and nostrils bubbled a milky froth. Victims staggered or rolled on the floor, clawed and scratched their bodies until they drew blood.

'Oh my God . . . those poor bastards,' breathed John Feldmeyer, the Defence Secretary.

This time the President didn't suppress comment but watched in mute horror while fourteen innocent men were gassed to death in front of his eyes. In less than two minutes, it was over. Twisted bodies lay where they had fallen. Alone, in corners, or slumped together, a twisted matrix of corpses.

The tape clicked. The screen went blue.

Everyone in the situation room turned to stare at the President, as much in confusion as seeking from him some kind of guidance. They saw tears fill his eyes for the fourteen lives he had witnessed being extinguished. He didn't speak. It was Katherine Ashmore, his Counsel, who seemed to echo his thoughts, her voice trembling unashamedly. 'May God have mercy on their souls.'

There was a long, unbroken silence, and then a visibly shocked Mitch Gains regarded the others round the table. 'If Hasim carries out his threat, it'll be nothing less than the worst devastation to befall this nation. On the same scale as Hiroshima or Nagasaki.'

The President, his fingers bone white as they gripped the table in front of him, seemed totally overwhelmed. Very slowly, he turned to stare at the circle of shocked faces. And when his question was finally uttered, it was in a dismayed, agonised voice, addressed to them all. '*How?* How in God's name could he get his hands on such a murderous weapon?'

PART TWO

21 July – 9 November

Beginnings

13

Lebanon
21 July

Some sixty miles south of Beirut and less than twelve from the Israeli border lies the island city of Tyr, once one of the busiest maritime ports in the Mediterranean.

From its earliest recorded history, the wealthy settlement had attracted jealous invaders: the Phoenicians and the Pharaohs, the Romans and the armies of Alexander the Great and Constantine, all eager to exploit the trade in dye and glass for which the port was famous. Tyr would eventually become a bustling melting-pot, Muslim and Druze, Christian and Maronite all coexisting within its prosperous walls. Over the centuries, its merchants amassed fortunes trading with Egypt and the North African coast, and as far away as Spain and France, and French architects were brought in to build large villas in the hills overlooking the port, many of which may still be seen today in this most beautiful of Mediterranean ports.

Later, when Lebanon's savage civil war erupted, it was Tyr's inhabitants who were to suffer most from relentless attacks by Israel's armed forces, who finally invaded and occupied the city, intent on destroying the Islamic-backed rebel groups operating in southern Lebanon which threatened its security. Men and women, young and old, regardless of whether they were Muslim, Christian or Druze, if suspected of being terrorists or their sympathisers, were rounded up by Israeli army snatch squads. Innocent or guilty, some as young as fourteen, they were jailed without trial in Israeli-controlled prisons like the infamous camp at Khyam, in southern Lebanon. Hundreds more Arab prisoners still languish in other Israeli prisons to this day, in some cases hostages for almost fifteen years, forgotten captives in the timeless war of Arab versus Jew.

But it was to a peaceful city of Tyr that the visitor arrived that sunny afternoon in late July, almost four months before Abu Hasim's threat was delivered to the White House. He was in his late thirties, a handsome, lean-faced man with fair hair and Slavic cheekbones, one side of his mouth hooked into a slight, perpetual half-smile, as if permanently amused by the world and its inhabitants. He drove up into the hills until he eventually found the villa, an old grey Renault parked outside. It was a pleasant-looking house, a homely place that had once been owned by a French colonial doctor, with splendid views out over the blue Mediterranean, the sweeping gardens planted with jasmine and olive trees.

The man went up the path carrying a bunch of yellow roses. He knocked on the blue-painted front door, and when it opened he smiled. 'Hello, Karla.'

The woman was strikingly pretty, about his own age. Dark haired, with almond-brown eyes and Mediterranean looks, she wore jeans and a pale blue sweater. She gave a tiny gasp when she saw her visitor, her hand going to her mouth in disbelief, a look of total shock on her face, as if she had just seen a ghost. For a few moments she stared back at the man, until finally she tried to speak.

And then she fainted.

Nikolai Gorev dabbed a wet towel on Karla Sharif's face. They were in the kitchen at the back of the house. There were flower boxes in the windows, shelves of glass jars, tea and coffee and spices. He had helped her inside, sat her on a chair. 'Did I really frighten you that much?'

'I . . . I thought you were dead.'

Gorev smiled. 'I can think of a few people who'd be more than happy if it were true. Are you all right, Karla?'

She got to her feet, reached out a hand to touch his cheek, as if to make sure she really wasn't seeing a ghost, and then her arms went around his neck to hug him, her eyes wet.

'Oh, Nikolai, it's so good to see you again. So very good.'

'And you.'

When she drew back, she looked into Gorev's face. 'But what are you doing in Tyr? Why are you here?'

'It's not a social visit, Karla, much as I'd like it to be.'

'Then why?'

Gorev smiled again, picked up the flowers he'd brought. 'How about I put these in some water and make us some coffee – Russian style, like the old days in Moscow – and then we can talk.'

Karla found a vase and Gorev filled it with water from the kitchen tap. He placed the vase of roses in the centre of the table, took the coffee jar from one of the shelves, heaped four spoonfuls of the aromatic coffee into the aluminium percolator, and turned on the stove. He came to join her at the table, took out a cigarette and tapped it on the pack.

'How long has it been?'

'Over seventeen years. The last time I saw you was on the platform at the station in Moscow, waving goodbye.'

Gorev nodded. 'A long time ago. So much has happened to us all since then. You really thought I was dead?'

'A Palestinian I knew at Patrice Lumumba told me he'd heard it from someone in Moscow. That was over a year ago. I cried for days.'

'At least I'd have had someone to mourn my passing. And how was I supposed to have died?'

'In a shoot-out near Grozny. You and your Chechen comrades against the Russian special forces.'

Gorev threw back his head and laughed. 'That's a good one. The Russians would have had their work cut out.'

'All the things I've heard about you, are they true?'

'That depends on what you've heard.'

'That you had become a maverick terrorist, someone who killed without compunction for the Chechen cause.'

'What do you think?'

'If you are, you're not the man I used to know. The Nikolai Gorev I loved in Moscow was kind, sincere. One of the finest people I ever knew.'

Gorev reached across, touched her hand in a gesture of friendship. 'Then you should know better than to believe all you hear. And what about you?'

'I work as a secretary in a lawyer's office in Tyr, four days a week. It pays badly but I love the work.'

Gorev shook his head. 'Someone as brilliant as you, I would have thought you'd have left here a long time ago. A masters from the American University in Beirut, your fluency in languages. You could have gone anywhere, Karla. Had a glittering career.'

She brushed a strand of hair from her face. 'Now you're flattering me. But my life is here in Tyr.'

'You mean because of Josef?'

Karla Sharif's face suddenly darkened. 'How did you know?'

'Like you, I have friends who keep me informed.'

'And what did you hear?'

'Your husband Michael died in a car-bomb blast in Beiruit, ten years ago. That a year ago your son was stopped at an Israeli checkpoint near Hedera, in a car driven by a member of Hamas, ferrying weapons and explosives. That he was shot and badly wounded and he'll be lucky to walk again. But unlike his Hamas accomplice, he was lucky to escape with his life. Though not so lucky that he wasn't sent to prison. For a teenager, he's plucky, I'll give him that.'

'What else did you hear?'

'That he had the same hatred of injustice as his father. The same hunger to fight oppression.'

A pink blush stained Karla's face and neck. 'Go on.'

'That he wanted to walk in his footsteps and strive for the same cause. That the Israelis haven't sentenced him yet, but we both know that doesn't really matter, does it? They can hold him in detention without trial for the rest of his life if they want. Either way, he'll never get out. He'll serve thirty years if he serves a day.'

'He's only sixteen.'

'Do you think the Israelis care a whit? There are boys as young as fourteen languishing in their prisons. Even younger in their detention centres – eight-year-olds from Gaza and the West Bank. And for what? Throwing stones at Israeli patrols. Children have been shot dead by them on the streets for the same reason. Where's the justice in that?'

She almost broke down then, and Gorev saw the despair in her face, the tears at the edges of her eyes. He touched her arm. 'I'm sorry, Karla. I can imagine how much you love your son. He's all you have. It must be hard to bear.'

Karla wiped her eyes. 'You've no idea.'

'Don't I? You're allowed four visits a year, ten minutes each visit. You cannot touch your son, cannot embrace him, can only talk through a metal grille in the company of two Israeli guards who listen to your every word. You're searched before entering the prison room and searched after leaving. Every word, every whisper, every loving word between you both is overheard and recorded . . .'

The percolator bubbled. Gorev let go of her arm, crossed to the stove, poured a cup for each of them, heaped sugar in each. Standing at the window, looking towards the sea, he noticed dark summer clouds drifting in, heavy with rain. Karla said quietly, 'How did you know all this?'

He came back to the table. 'The same friends who told me where to find you.'

'So why did you come here? Why did you want to see me after all this time?'

Nikolai Gorev put down his cup, said earnestly, 'Because the Brotherhood needs your help.'

She frowned. 'I don't understand. Why would they send *you*?'

'A long story. Too long to go into now. Let's just say that certain Arab acquaintances of mine have engaged my services.'

'To do what?'

Gorev smiled. 'Something highly dangerous but infinitely rewarding.'

Karla shook her head. 'I'm no longer involved, Nikolai. Not any more. Not for many years. I'm not a Kalashnikov-wielding PLO freedom fighter any more, manning the barricades at Chatila, or training recruits to fight the Israelis. The Brotherhood knows I left that life behind me. I'm a woman who wants a quiet existence, a peaceful life. One that I've worked hard to build.'

'But you're still a Muslim.'

'Who never goes to the mosque, and hasn't in years. I was never one for religion, you know that.'

Gorev smiled again. 'OK, so you're a modern woman. But the Arab cause was always dear to your heart, as it was to your husband's. You can't escape your past, Karla. It's in your blood.'

'You're wasting your time, Nikolai. Whatever it is. The answer's no.' She balled her fist, beat it against her breast. 'Of course my heart rages against what has happened to the Arab people. But it's no longer the only thing it rages against. I couldn't get involved again, not ever. Not for you, not for the Brotherhood. Not for anyone. For me, the war and the killing and the struggle are over.'

'Even if there was a reward?'

'Money doesn't interest me.'

'Not that sort of reward. A different kind.'

'Then what?'

'Remember Moscow? You and your Palestinian friends believed you were different, believed you were special. And you were. Anyone destined to graduate from Patrice Lumumba, the most infamous university in the world, was bound to be. You were being groomed to spread terrorism and anarchy. Remember the radical ideals you all had, how you dreamed you were going to change the world? Well, what if I told you of a way you could?'

'Change it how? For whom?'

'For the Arab peoples. Give them control of their own destiny. Free them once and for all from the Western yoke, change the world irrevocably. And for you, personally, there would be another reward, one just as important.'

'What?'

'Your son's freedom.'

Karla Sharif looked back at her visitor, totally stunned. 'Tell me how.'

And Gorev told her.

The dark clouds had drifted in from the Mediterranean, bringing heavy rain, and it came in a sudden downpour, drenching the windows. The room was very silent when Gorev finished, the only sound the rain flailing the glass with its silken lash. Karla Sharif looked back at him, incredulous, shaking her head. 'What you're suggesting is madness. Completely crazy. Something like that could take the world to the brink.'

'Crazy or not, it can work, Karla. And free Josef and many others like him. And it's not going to fail. Too much work has gone into the plan, too much is at stake.'

'Who put you up to this? Who are you working for?'

'You don't need to know. Not yet. Not until I know where you stand.'

'Then why me?'

'There aren't many Arab women with your experience or qualifications. It might surprise you to know that there are still people who talk about Karla Sharif with nothing short of awe. How she ran the women's training camps with a fierce discipline, turned out some of the best, most highly trained and committed recruits for the Palestinian and Arab cause. But there's another reason. You're someone I'd trust with my life. Which is probably the most important qualification of all.'

Karla stood, again shook her head. 'I still can't believe what you're proposing. It's deranged.'

'But exactly what's needed if the world is to be changed,' Gorev answered. 'The war between Arab and Jew has lasted thousands of years. Do you really think it will end tomorrow with some peace agreement the Americans might broker? That the Israelis or the Americans won't stop trying to kill your people, to crush their aspirations, make martyrs of their sons and daughters? Or that the West will stop treating the Arab peoples everywhere like serfs, or cease controlling their destiny? Power is the only thing the West understands. This plan will take away their power. Force them to give in to every demand we make of them.'

'It's too daring, Nikolai. Far too dangerous. Surely you must see that?'

'What I see is the decisive moment the Arab people have been waiting for. Not to seize the opportunity would make a mockery of everything they've fought for.'

'And what happens afterwards? Have you thought of that? Do you think the Americans would allow you and your friends to walk away without punishment? They'd destroy you, Nikolai. And me if I helped you.'

Gorev offered her another smile. 'That's the beauty of the plan. Once we achieved what we set out to, it would be a fait accompli. There'd be no way the Americans could turn back the clock. They'd have been defeated. And if everything goes the way it is planned our safety won't be an issue. We simply do the job and walk away, with no one the wiser.'

Karla Sharif shook her head. 'I can't be part of this, Nikolai. I'm sorry. You're asking too much.'

Slowly, Gorev stood. He crossed to the door, opened it. The rain still fell outside, a cool wind brushed his face. He shivered, came back, Karla Sharif's brown eyes rising to meet his stare. 'Can I tell you something? Something I've always wanted to tell you?'

'What?'

'Eighteen years ago in Moscow, when we first met, I fell in love with you. Of course, it wasn't to be. It was all too complex. I couldn't commit myself to you, much as I loved you. And besides, you were engaged to another . . .'

Karla blushed, saw something close to pain in Gorev's face. 'Nikolai . . . there's no need . . .'

'I know. I shouldn't rake over old coals. Moscow was such a long time ago. But it was a happy time. I think of it often.'

'So do I.'

'Perhaps I just wanted you to know that. And know that I still care, and have never forgotten you, Karla. If there's ever anything I can do . . .'

'Thank you.' Karla Sharif looked away, smelled the roses, as if to avoid the thrust of Gorev's conversation. 'I never thanked you for the flowers. It was very kind of you, Nikolai.'

'The least I could do for an old friend.' Gorev paused. 'Do something for me, Karla? Just think about all I've said. Think about how Josef can have his freedom and you can have your son back. Think about how he wouldn't have to martyr his life to a cause any more, because there wouldn't be a cause. The war would be over, the Arab world liberated.'

'Nikolai . . . I can't . . .'

Gorev gently put a finger to her lips. 'Don't decide. Not yet. Sleep on it. Consider all I've said. But just remember, everything you've heard is for your ears only. I'm staying in Tyr tonight. I'll come by in the morning. You can give me your final decision then.'

That same day, in the early afternoon, Karla Sharif made a journey, a pilgrimage of fifty miles over the border to Israel, to a high-security prison outside Tel Aviv.

The border between Lebanon and Israel was a no man's land, a danger zone that she had to negotiate with every visit to her son. Patrolled by fanatical, gun-toting Islamics on one side and vigilant Israeli troops on the other, it was buffered by the UN area in between, a perilous mission for the peacekeepers, who often had to suffer lethal shelling from both sides. At Hezbollah checkpoints on the Lebanese flank her papers would be scrutinised and her business questioned. But once they learned the reasons for Karla's need to cross into Israel, they were always immediately sympathetic, almost reverential.

'Pass, *emraa*. And may Allah protect your son. He is a martyr to the cause.'

Once she had left the safety of the UN area behind her and crossed the 'rat-line' – a dusty road into Israeli territory protected by heavy barbed-wire runs and minefields on either side, helicopter gunships patrolling overhead – it was a different matter. She and her car were thoroughly searched, her papers examined and re-examined at dozens of checkpoints for the first ten miles inside the Jewish border, and with every trip she had to run a gauntlet of nervous young soldiers and trigger-happy Orthodox settlers who regarded her with a mixture of suspicion and contempt.

Throughout her journey her mind was preoccupied. Not only by the thought of seeing her son again for the first time in three months, but by Nikolai Gorev's visit. Seeing him alive and after so many years had stunned her completely, and she was still trying to get over the shock. She remembered the day they had met, when she had arrived in Moscow with over thirty other Palestinian and Arab students to study at Patrice Lumumba University. She remembered the wonderful times she had spent in Moscow, and the love she had felt for Nikolai – a glorious, tender passion they had shared and which she had never forgotten – and it made her think of a life that she had long ago put behind her, and about the secret she had kept, a secret that no one could ever know but herself, which would go with her to the grave.

It disturbed her almost as much as the distressing shock of the plan Nikolai had outlined, and his appeal for her help, but difficult as it was she tried to put such troubled thoughts from her mind. This was a day she had been looking forward to for three long months. It was almost two when she reached the prison. Set on a hill, it was a grim and daunting place, a vast security complex built of breeze blocks, protected by razor wire and concrete watchtowers. She parked her car in a dirt lot outside and walked up the hill to the first barrier, where her business was queried, her papers examined and her name checked against a list of permitted visitors before she was ordered to step through a metal detector and was frisked for weapons. Once inside the steel prison gates she was led into a room where she was strip-searched by two uniformed female Israeli wardens wearing surgical gloves who probed every intimate part of her body, before she was escorted by two male wardens through an underground passageway to the visitors' room.

It was a bare white-walled chamber, twelve feet by twelve.

A barren, sterile place divided in two by a brick wall, with a small window in the centre, fitted with bullet-proof glass. Communication was through microphones, one on each side of the divide.

As the two wardens took up their positions directly behind her, Karla sat on the single wooden chair in front of the window, and waited for her beloved Josef to appear.

Her heart was beating as the steel door opened on the far side of the glass. She gave a tiny cry of recognition as Josef was led in. His hands were shackled by loose steel chains and he shuffled to his seat with the aid of crutches. He was sixteen, a slim, handsome youth with dark tousled hair and pale olive skin. In the last year his attempt at growing a beard had produced a few fuzzy hairs, but Karla knew that the effort at manliness was wasted. The moment her son smiled he looked such a child. 'Hello, Mama.'

'How are you, my love?'

'Well, Mama. And you?'

'I've missed you.'

Josef nodded, flicked a look at the guards behind her, and his smile faded. Karla had become used to the fact that her son never admitted to missing her. It was almost as if the disclosure would make him less manful in the eyes of the Israeli guards, whom she knew he despised. She would have loved him to say it, even once, just for her sake, but she knew that was asking too much. 'Tell me what you've been doing, Mama.'

It was Josef's usual query, every time she visited. Forbidden from discussing events in the prison, or any aspect of his internment, it was all he could really ask. Those were the rules and they were strictly enforced: the guards spoke fluent Arabic. She knew that her conversations with her son were recorded, every nuance pored over afterwards by the prison authorities, just in case their words might somehow be coded to convey secret messages. Breaking the rules would mean an end to the visits, and so she stuck to them, just as Josef did, even if it meant their conversation was severely limited.

Karla always lived for these few fleeting minutes in her son's company. But as always the experience was traumatic. Not being allowed to hold him in her arms, embrace the flesh she loved so much, broke her heart every time she saw him. And as always she forced herself to hide her trauma, told her son the mundane, harmless things that she always told him: about her work in the office in Tyr, how she had tended his father's grave and left flowers from them both, how the villa's gardens were overgrown and needed attention, or how she had had to endure some minor problem with her car that no doubt Josef could have helped her fix.

The important things, the intimate things that she longed to tell him, were as always left unsaid: that sometimes when she looked into his childish face she remembered him as a baby, suckling at her breast, or vainly attempting his first steps, or suffering his first tiny teeth, and that more than anything in the world she desperately wanted him to be free. That the thought of her beloved child being locked up like a caged animal was becoming too much to bear. The unsaid things, the things she couldn't express because of Josef's bravado or prison rules, always broke her heart, took her to the edge of despair. 'You're eating, Josef? You're sleeping OK?'

'Yes, Mama.'

'How are your wounds? Are you in any pain?'

'No, they're fine, Mama. There's no pain.'

It was a lie, Karla guessed. The bullets that had ripped into Josef's body had wounded his right arm and completely shattered his right thighbone and knee. His arm had healed, and only a rutted scar remained, but despite three operations by Israeli surgeons he still couldn't walk without the aid of crutches. But at least her son was alive. 'Do you need anything? Extra clothes? Food?'

'No, nothing.'

Karla could hear the stubborn defiance in her son's voice. Prison had not lessened his rebellious streak. His answers to such queries were always the same: Josef would never admit to needing anything in the face of an enemy. One of the guards touched her arm. 'A minute more, please?' Karla begged.

'I'm sorry. Time's up, lady. That's the rule.'

The Israeli guard wasn't an unkind man, he wasn't a beast, and she saw a hint of compassion in his eyes, but he was determined to do his job, and at that moment Karla could easily have hated him. She touched the glass with her palm. Josef did the same. The guard gripped her arm. 'Please, lady.'

She stood, scraping back her chair, the remains of her handprint engraved fleetingly on the glass, mirroring Josef's. She blew her son a kiss. He waved back. 'Goodbye, Mama.'

Moments later he was shuffled out of the room, his chains rattling, and Karla was led out by the guards.

On the drive back to Tyr, Karla Sharif's mind was in turmoil. After her visits to the prison she felt fragile, emotionally drained, and it was an effort not to be overwhelmed by despair. The thought of Josef being imprisoned for many more years, the agonised frustration of not being able to see him when she wished, tore at her heart.

Not a day or night went by when she didn't picture him huddled alone in his tiny cell, or fret about his health, his loneliness and despair, or wonder whether he was in pain. She was fearful, like any mother, that her child could not possibly remain sane, locked up for twenty-three hours a day. She had heard of Arab prisoners in Israeli jails committing suicide because they couldn't endure the distress of harsh confinement, and the image of Josef being found hanged in his cell tormented her with worry.

Her mind was distraught as she drove back over the Lebanese border. Two miles inside the Hezbollah-controlled zone she came round a bend in the road with chalky white hills on either side. She saw the roadblock up ahead, guarded by half a dozen black-masked men armed with Kalashnikovs, a couple of dusty four-wheel-drive jeeps blocking the road. She had no doubt the men were Hezbollah; they controlled the area. One of the guards waved her down. Karla halted, rolled down her window.

'Step out of the car,' the guard ordered.

'Why? What's the matter?'

'Do as I say, *emraa*. No arguments.'

Karla stepped out, puzzled. As soon as she did one of the men jumped into her Renault and moved it off the road. 'What do you think you're doing?' Karla protested.

'Shut up.' The guard brandished his weapon. 'Just do as you're told. Move this way.'

With one of his armed companions he marched Karla up the hill on the opposite side of the road. They came to a clearing at the top. A man sat on a boulder, under the shade of some cedar trees. He was peeling an orange with a deadly-looking pearl-handled flick-knife. He appeared to be in his late thirties, stockily built, with a thin, cruel mouth and murderous dark eyes. A flash of malice in them that suggested he was capable of extreme brutality. He wore a crumpled linen suit, and with his hooked nose, jet-black beard and hair and olive skin was obviously Arab. He pointed to another boulder opposite. 'Sit down.'

'Who are you? Why was I stopped?'

'Sit.' The bearded man's tone was arrogant. Karla sat on the rock. The guards moved back down the hill and out of view. The man stopped peeling the orange, studied her face. 'You don't recognise me?'

'No.'

'We met once before, a long time ago. My name is Mohamed Rashid. Does that jog your memory?'

The moment Karla heard the name, she remembered. A fleeting encounter in Beirut many years ago. He was Egyptian, an Islamic terrorist with a fierce reputation for savagery who had once helped run the PLO training camps in Libya. 'Yes. I remember.'

'You haven't changed much. The years have been good to you.'

'What do you want?'

The Egyptian ignored her question, sucked at a fleshy segment of orange, the juice running down his beard. 'You're a remarkable and interesting woman, Karla Sharif. Born in America of

Palestinian parents, you returned with them to Lebanon when you were twelve. You're a graduate of the American University of Beirut, you speak fluent English, French and Arabic.'

'I asked you a question—'

'I haven't finished. At nineteen, if I recall rightly, outraged by the plight of your people, you joined the PLO and later became one of the few volunteers privileged to be sent to Moscow's Patrice Lumumba University to receive a terrorist education by the Soviets. There, you earned the reputation of being one of their finest pupils. First in your class in weapons training, bomb-making and intelligence-gathering. You outshone even the PLO's very best male recruits. I hear Carlos the Jackal was so impressed he offered you a place within his terrorist cell, an offer you declined, much to his disappointment. Yes, you're a very remarkable woman.'

'What is this? Why am I being held against my will?'

The Egyptian tossed away the remains of the orange, wiped his beard and, retracting the blade by pressing a button on the pearl handle, slipped the knife into his pocket. 'Once you had a fire in your belly for the Arab cause. Not any more, it seems. No doubt the Israelis know that too. Which is why they allow you to visit your son. What happened to you, Karla Sharif? Did you grow tired of the cause? Have you become a coward?'

Karla stared back at the man's face, suddenly aware of why he was here. 'This has to do with Nikolai Gorev's visit, doesn't it?'

The Egyptian nodded.

'What do you want of me?'

'Your commitment.'

'I told Nikolai. I live a different life now. I haven't wanted to be a part of your fight for many years. The answer's no.'

'None of us want to fight. We do it because we must, and in the name of Islam. Just as you must. Once, you took a solemn vow . . .'

'A long time ago.'

The Egyptian's dark eyes flashed dangerously. 'That's of no consequence to the Brotherhood. Do you remember the words of the Koran? "And if they turn back from their vow, take them and kill them, wherever ye find them."'

Karla said quietly, 'Are you threatening me?'

'The logic of your vow is simple. Those not with us are against us. And if they are against us, they will die. Besides, you know too much already about our plans.'

'Killing me would achieve nothing.'

'Perhaps.' The Egyptian stood. 'But there is another consideration. Your son Josef. Some of the men you met below have friends or brothers in the same prison.'

Karla was suddenly pale. 'What are you implying?'

'It would be easy to arrange an accident. Your son might be found hanging in his cell, or have a knife slipped between his ribs.' The Egyptian shrugged, gave a malicious grin. 'Sadly, such unfortunate things happen all the time in prisons.'

'You bastard.' Livid anger erupted in Karla Sharif's eyes. She moved to claw at the man's face but his hand came up, gripped her arm, and with his other hand he slapped her across the face. With one swift movement Karla twisted free and punched him hard in the mouth. The Egyptian staggered back and hit the ground, blood on his lips. In an instant he had scrambled back up, his hand dipping into his pocket, bringing out the flick-knife, clicking the button. The blade flashed. 'That was very stupid. Why don't we see how good you really are, Karla Sharif?'

The Egyptian lunged towards her like a raging bull, his arms wide open, but instead of moving back, Karla sidestepped, brought her hand down in a swift chopping movement, knocking the blade from the Egyptian's grasp. Another swift blow struck him on the back of the neck and he went down again, harder this time. Karla moved in, grabbed the knife, stamped a foot on the man's neck and stood over him, the blade pointed at his face. 'Does that answer your question?'

Suddenly the guards appeared, scrambling up the hill, cocking their weapons. The Egyptian raised his hand. 'No. Don't harm her.'

The men lowered their weapons. Karla stepped back and threw

the blade, which stuck point first in the dirt next to the Egyptian. He pushed himself up, dusted his clothes. 'Leave us,' he ordered the guards. 'Wait below.'

The men left. The Egyptian took out a handkerchief, dabbed his mouth, gave a pained grin. 'You're still good, Palestinian. I like a woman who's capable. In different circumstances, someone such as you might even excite me.' He looked at the blood on his handkerchief, glared up at her. 'At least your training wasn't in vain.'

'Harm my son and I'll kill you, I swear.'

The Egyptian felt his jaw for loose teeth, put away his handkerchief. 'If I have to, I assure you I will do what I must.'

Karla stepped forward threateningly.

The Egyptian said, 'Don't be a fool. If you value your son's life you'll do exactly as I say. When Gorev calls tomorrow, you will pack what belongings you need and go with him. False papers have been arranged, everything you will need.'

Anger raged on Karla's face. 'Who's behind this? Who are you really working for, Mohamed Rashid?'

'You'll find out in good time. For now, it's enough to know that there will be three of us taking part in the operation – me, you and Gorev. And that there are difficult journeys ahead and much hard work. First, two weeks of training and planning, so that you'll know what's expected of you. Your friend Gorev is a first-class terrorist with no equal. We are fortunate to have his services.'

'And what then?'

'Gorev and I have some business to attend to in Moscow. Then you and I travel to America, to do the groundwork. Gorev will join us later, when our mission begins in earnest.' The Egyptian grinned. 'You should feel honoured, Karla Sharif. You're about to be part of the most daring terrorist attack ever committed, more audacious than anything the world has ever seen. And it happens in the land of your birth, on American soil. Ironic, don't you think?'

Karla was silent, tried hard to control her hostility as she stared back at the Egyptian. He bent to pick up the knife, retracted the blade, slipped it into his pocket. 'One other thing. You don't ever mention our conversation to Gorev. It would be better if he thought this decision was entirely your own.'

The look on Karla Sharif's face was nothing short of furious contempt. 'Anything else?'

'You may go now.'

14

Moscow
31 August
9 p.m.

It was raining hard at just after nine that evening as Boris Novikov's chauffeured black E-class Mercedes was waved through the wrought-iron entrance gates by the security guards. It glided up the gravel driveway and halted outside the imposing entrance to a luxurious dacha in Kuntsevo, on Moscow's outskirts. A bodyguard climbed out and held open the rear passenger door. Novikov, a rugged, elegantly dressed man with blunt features – a wide mouth, broad face and hard, deep-set eyes – stepped out of the car into the sheeting rain.

He was no longer smiling, but the source of his delight, an arousing sexual cocktail of pain and pleasure that he soon intended to enjoy, was still foremost in his mind. Another bodyguard immediately scurried forward with an umbrella and escorted him towards the entrance hall. The dacha was large even by Kuntsevo standards, eight bedrooms in all, exquisitely furnished and surrounded by walled gardens. An attentive young aide was waiting in the hallway. He helped Novikov remove his overcoat. 'Good evening, sir. Your business with the President went well?'

'No better than expected,' Novikov replied curtly. 'Has the woman arrived yet?'

'She's in your room, sir. The same lady as the last time, I believe.'

'Make sure I'm not disturbed. No telephone calls, nothing. Understand?'

The aide inclined his head. 'Of course, sir. As you wish.'

Boris Novikov checked himself in one of the gilded mirrors in the hallway. He wore an elegant dark suit, complemented by a hand-painted Louis Feraud silk tie, his ox-blood Italian leather shoes buffed like polished ceramic. His face was another matter. Brash, ugly almost, his skin pitted by old scars, an aggressive countenance that suggested he was no stranger to extreme violence. Novikov had formerly held the rank of colonel in the FSB, Russia's domestic intelligence organisation – which, along with its sister organisation, the Foreign Intelligence Service, SVR, had replaced the KGB. Four years ago he had taken early retirement and launched himself vigorously into a number of private business ventures, some of which had won lucrative government contracts and had helped make him a wealthy man. But tonight his mind was on more personal matters as he eagerly climbed a sweeping staircase that led up to his private bedroom suite. Stepping inside, he locked the door behind him.

The room was large and luxurious – silver and brass Russian vases, richly coloured carpets made from the finest Astrakhan wool, a hand-carved oak writing bureau, an original eighteenth-century Stavinsky oil painting of the Kremlin on one wall. The rain hissed outside, and Novikov noticed that one of the windows was open, the curtains gently ruffled by a cold breeze. Light from a table lamp flooded through the open doorway that led into his en suite, the bedroom in near-darkness. He grinned, moved to close the open window but changed his mind, enjoying the draught of cool, autumn-scented air, then strolled over to the bedroom and looked in.

The queen-size bed was draped with silk sheets and a young woman lay there on her side. Blonde, with a ravishing figure. The flimsiest pair of lace panties and matching bra adorned her slim, tanned body. Silk stockings, suspenders and glossy, knee-high, jet-black PVC boots added an erotic touch, as did the coiled, burred leather whip lying beside her on the bed. The woman worked for one of Moscow's finest escort agencies, a beauty who could be relied on to be completely discreet.

Novikov, a bachelor, liked to indulge himself in the company of young women, if necessary the finest money could buy. The young woman he had chosen tonight had the body of a goddess, and like Novikov enjoyed sex that was extremely rough, almost bordering on the sadistic, a weakness he could afford to indulge discreetly. He licked his lips, stepped over to the bed, sat on the edge. For a moment he admired the woman's beautiful curves, smiled as he ran a hand over her bronzed silky flanks, attempting to rouse her.

'Time to pleasure me, my sweet. And tonight, I'd like to be very rough indeed. But I'm sure you'll enjoy it immensely.'

The woman didn't reply. Novikov saw that her eyes were closed. She had appeared to be resting, but he realised now that she was totally unconscious. He frowned, felt her pulse. She was alive, of that he was certain, but it seemed she was drugged.

If the stupid bitch has taken narcotics, she's ruined my fucking evening.

For some odd reason Novikov remembered the open window. He turned and his blood froze. An intruder, dressed completely in dark clothes, stood before him. He wore a black windcheater, black pants and leather gloves; a black woollen ski mask covered his entire face, except the eyes. The intruder held a silenced Beretta automatic. It was pointed at Novikov's head. 'What . . . what's going on?'

The intruder spoke softly, almost in a whisper. 'Be silent. Scream, or call for help, and I'll see you in hell.'

Novikov glanced slyly at the bedside locker nearest him. For his personal protection, he always kept a Tokarev pistol in the locker recess, the magazine loaded and the safety off. 'Kill me and you'll never get out of here alive. The police will be immediately alerted. And there are bodyguards, electronic security—'

'Your security is ineffective.'

'What do you want?' Novikov demanded.

The man gestured at the Kremlin oil painting. 'The safe behind. Open it.'

Novikov paled, realising what the intruder was after. 'You'll never get away with such a theft. *Never.* For a crime like this, you'll be hunted down like an animal. No matter where you run to. You'd be a dead man walking.'

'Do as I say,' the intruder ordered.

Novikov crossed to the painting, flicked a catch, and the frame swung back to reveal a big steel wall safe with an electronic keypad. He entered the code. The safe clicked open.

'Hand me the papers inside. Then go lie on the bed, face down, and keep your mouth shut.'

Novikov did as ordered, removing a red folder from the safe and handing it to the man, then he crossed to the bed and lay face down. The man opened the folder, studied the papers inside, and smiled behind the mask. 'It seems I'm in luck, Colonel.'

Crossing to the writing bureau, the intruder switched on the desk lamp, took a miniature Japanese camera from his pocket and photographed the papers. It was all over in less than two minutes, then he replaced the folder in the safe, locked it, and swung back the painting.

There was a sharp noise from somewhere downstairs in the residence, like a door slamming. The intruder glanced behind him, and in that brief moment of distraction Novikov, still lying on the bed, looked over and saw his chance. He reached into the locker recess, managed to grab the Tokarev, brought it up smartly. 'You fucking bastard. It's you who'll go to hell!'

He managed to get off one shot, but missed his target and hit the wall, as the intruder's pistol coughed once in reply. Novikov screamed, the slug chipped his fingers, and he dropped the Tokarev, clutched his bloodied hand.

The intruder stepped over and pressed the tip of the silencer into the centre of Novikov's forehead. From below came the sound of raised voices, then heavy footsteps climbing the stairs, responding to Novikov's gunshot. He suddenly remembered he'd locked the door. There wasn't enough time to save him. He trembled. 'Who . . . who are you?'

The intruder lifted his ski mask. 'Remember me, Colonel?'

A horrified Novikov stared into Nikolai Gorev's face. 'You! Oh my God!'

Gorev squeezed the trigger.

Major Alexei Kursk stood in the centre of the bedroom. In front of him, Boris Novikov's body lay partly covered with a bloodied white sheet, one end of which was held up by a lieutenant from the FSB's Investigation Directorate. Kursk studied the corpse, examined the single bullet hole drilled into the victim's forehead, noticed the bloodied fingers, then looked away to take in a discarded Tokarev pistol on the floor, the open bedroom window, and a rutted bullet mark on the wall. 'I've seen enough. So what's the story?'

The lieutenant replaced the sheet. 'The bodyguards heard the shooting just after nine p.m. When they broke down the bedroom door they discovered Novikov dead. The gun we found on the carpet is Novikov's own, licensed in his name. It's been fired once.'

Kursk, a small, stocky man with a penetrating stare, examined the bullet hole in the wall, touched it with his fingertip. 'Clues or witnesses?'

'We found three shell casings on the floor. Two of them are nine-mil. Most likely from the gun that killed Novikov.'

'What about this call-girl?'

The lieutenant suppressed a smile. 'She had a regular thing going with Novikov, playing naughty bedroom games. But she saw or heard nothing. Claims someone came up behind her and jabbed a hypodermic in her arm. The next thing she knows she comes to, sees police swarming all over the bedroom, Novikov's brains on the floor, and she's screaming her head off.'

'Where is she now?'

'At Moscow General, being treated for shock.'

Kursk moved over to the window, held back the curtain, peered out on to expansive dark lawns, ringed by high walls. 'She's quite sure she saw nothing?'

'She seems to be telling the truth. But we'll have her checked out. Find out if she played any part in this.'

'And the bodyguards?'

'One of them caught a glimpse of an intruder dressed in black, running across the lawns just after the shooting, and climbing over the wall. After that, he heard what sounded like a motorcycle start up and roar away.'

'Have the bodyguards checked out too. Anything else I should know?'

The lieutenant indicated the Kremlin painting on the wall. 'Novikov has a safe behind there. Not unusual for a businessman of his standing who might have to work on important documents at home. But it's locked, doesn't appear to have been touched, and according to Novikov's aide, only Novikov himself knew the combination.'

Kursk crossed to the painting, pulled it back on its hinge, studied the locked safe. 'Any idea what might be in there?'

'No, sir. We also set up checkpoints all the way to Moscow, in the hope we might catch the intruder. But so far we've drawn a complete blank.'

There was a commotion at the bedroom door and the guards stepped back to allow a visitor through. Igor Verbatin, the bullish head of the FSB, looked in a foul mood. He glanced at the covered body with distaste. 'Well, Kursk, what can you tell me?'

'There's been a murder.'

'Don't be smart with me, Major. I've known that much this last hour.'

'I've just arrived.' Kursk was surprised that the head of the FSB himself should take such a keen personal interest in the homicide. 'But from the sounds of it, Novikov was killed by a masked intruder who managed to evade the colonel's tight security.'

'Novikov's safe. Was it touched?'

'It doesn't appear so. Why?'

Verbatin's face darkened. 'We'll discuss that later, Kursk, in private. Any idea who might have done this?'

Kursk shrugged. 'A man like Novikov, a former FSB colonel and a successful businessman, is bound to have had enemies. But it's early days yet.'

The FSB head fumed, then took Kursk's arm and led him aside. 'You're aware this is to be kept out of the press? That it's imperative it be kept secret for now, that the investigation is to be conducted solely by the FSB, and the police are not to be involved?'

'So I was informed. Why all the secrecy?'

'That's a matter you may learn in good time. For now, you ought to know that the President himself, Vasily Kuzmin, has taken a very personal interest in the case. You're one of the FSB's best investigators. So find the culprit, and fast. It's got top priority. You have my personal authority to use any means you have to. And I mean *any*, Kursk. Whoever's behind this crime simply has to be caught.'

15

Kandahar province, Afghanistan
3 September

As the sun dropped towards the horizon, a solitary man climbed up a rocky slope, his lonely figure silhouetted against the dying orange light. He was tall, six foot five, with an olive complexion and brown eyes, and wore a loose grey-coloured Arab gown and a white mini-turban. Carrying a cane to aid his climb, he looked pale and sickly, his bearded face covered in sweat from his exertion.

Abu Hasim reached the top of the slope, then paused to get his breath and take in his surroundings. The landscape below was a desolate place: rust-coloured rock, parched stony mountains, craggy hills. Despite the dying sun, the air was still hot, completely windless, and the only sound was of Hasim's own laboured breathing.

Under his arm he carried a prayer rug. He unrolled it slowly. Facing south-west to Mecca, he invoked the name of Allah, the Master of the World, the All Merciful and All Compassionate, the Supreme Sovereign of the Last Judgment. Then he knelt, prostrating his body three times, touching his forehead to the ground each time, glorifying the name of God and his Prophet with each incantation. When his ritual was over, Abu Hasim sat back on his rug, breathing slowly, immersing himself in the peace and solitude of his surroundings.

At this time of evening, sundown, the mountains were a tranquil place. In the desolate landscape of his beloved Afghanistan, nature at its harshest but most beautiful, he always felt closest to God. Once, he had been accustomed to a privileged upbringing. He recalled his father's palatial villas with marble floors, gilded bathrooms, palm-fringed gardens and dozens of servants. But for almost twenty years he had chosen a spartan life, had shunned vain comforts for the glory of Allah. That same life had led him to become, in the eyes of America's intelligence agencies, the most wanted and dangerous terrorist in the world.

He turned as he heard a noise below him, a clatter of stones tumbling away. In the fading light he saw a man hurrying up the slope from the camp below, clutching the hem of his gown as he manoeuvred his legs into secure footholds. When he reached the top, Hasim smiled and called out, '*Salaam alaïkum!*'

'*Alaikum salaam*,' the visitor replied, his face flushed with exhilaration. 'I hope I did not disturb your evening prayers, Abu?'

Hasim stood. They embraced, kissed each other's cheeks, like old friends. 'My prayers are completed. It is good to see you have returned safely from Moscow, Mohamed, dear brother. When did you arrive?'

'Just now. The men told me where to find you. I have great news, Abu . . .'

Hasim raised a hand to silence his visitor and sat back down on his rug, cross-legged. 'Come, join me. Rest after your climb. Then we will talk.'

Mohamed Rashid sat. The two men, seated together, looked total opposites – Hasim tall and bearded, calm, his appearance almost monk-like; Rashid stocky, of medium height, fiery, quintessentially Arab. Rashid took a deep breath and trapped it in his lungs, as though trying to hold back the rush of words ready to spill from his mouth, the news that he could barely contain.

'Now, tell me the news I have been waiting for, Mohamed.'

'It worked, Abu. We have the formula.' An exultant Rashid took the photographed papers from inside his gown, handed them across eagerly. 'The details are all here.'

Hasim took the papers, held them in awe. He did not understand the figures and chemical symbols the pages contained, but he understood their potency. His first reaction was to bow his head in silent prayer, a prayer of gratitude for the power that now lay in his hands. 'I thank Allah that you have done his work, Mohamed. I thank Him that our day has finally come. This is a great moment. How soon before we can test the formula?'

'Within days, *inshallah*. We will begin our work straight away. Our chemists are outstanding scientists. They will have little problem once they have the formula.' Rashid was still overcome, his face lit up. 'I still cannot believe it, Abu. Our day has finally come. Now we can challenge the Americans as equals.'

Abu Hasim said calmly, 'Let us keep our heads, Mohamed. There is still much work to be done. It is hardly over yet.' He put down the papers, folded them neatly. 'Now, tell me everything. Did all go as planned in Moscow?'

As Rashid explained, Hasim listened in silence to every detail. He didn't comment until his visitor had finished. 'The Russian has lived up to my expectations. Where is he now?'

'Below in the camp.'

Hasim paused, searched Rashid's face. 'You still don't approve of him, do you, Mohamed? His obvious talent hasn't changed your opinion?'

'He is a capable man. An adept terrorist,' Rashid began, and then a bitter tone crept into his voice. 'But his attitude and manner are irreverent. And his motives worry me, Abu. His concern is solely for the Chechen people, and the release of his men. He is not a true follower of our cause. In that regard, he is no more than a hired mercenary, and I despise such men.'

'But you forget, it was we who sought his help,' Hasim answered. 'He owes us a debt on behalf of his Chechen brothers, which he will repay. And such men as he have their uses.' He held up the papers. 'He has proved himself by bringing us these. As he will prove himself again in Washington.'

'If you say so, Abu.'

'What about the woman?'

'She has proved satisfactory, and her training is complete. Now that we have the formula and our chemists can finish their work, she will travel with me to Washington. We will leave within a week, perhaps less.'

'You trust her?'

Rashid nodded again. 'She will do exactly as we tell her. She has no choice.'

'Good. But for the sake of our cause, you must learn to put your differences aside. Now that our plan is under way, your co-operation with each other is important. You will do this for me?'

Reluctantly, Rashid nodded, bit back his discord. 'Yes, Abu. If you wish it.'

'I wish it.' Hasim stood, tucked the papers inside his gown, rolled up his prayer mat. 'Come, let us return to the camp. There are matters we need to discuss with our Russian.'

The camp was a rabbit-warren of caves in the rocks, a hundred feet below the hilltop, their entrances shaded by camouflaged canopies the same colour as the russet earth. Thousands of years before, a few dozen prehistoric families had lived in these caves. Now they were home to over three hundred well-armed, highly trained Islamic mujahidin fighters. Natural channels that tunnelled deep into the limestone rock had been drilled out at strategic places to provide underground bunkers, a garage workshop, and emergency escape routes. Cool in daytime, warm at night, the caverns offered basic quarters, with ample room for the camp recruits' stores and equipment. Among them was a doctor, a dentist, several good cooks who could work wonders with lamb and herbs, and a Muslim cleric. Sentries were posted up to five miles away, linked by radio to the camp, and dotted around the hills were machinegun emplacements, a mini-arsenal of anti-tank rockets and mortars, and Russian-made anti-aircraft guns.

Hasim and his visitor descended the hill until they came to the mouth of one of the caves. Two bearded sentries stood guard outside, brandishing assault rifles. Hasim went past them, his visitor behind. The cave they entered was large, fifteen feet by twenty. This was Hasim's headquarters.

In one corner were several wooden bookshelves containing dozens of hefty Islamic religious tomes, among them a well-worn copy of the Koran. In another was a tattered reed mat that served as a bed, and a scratched metal chest that contained Hasim's sparse wardrobe of clothes and personal belongings. A

Kalashnikov assault rifle, spare ammunition clips and a holstered Soviet pistol lay on top.

Cushions were placed neatly around a worn Bokkara rug in the centre of the floor. The lair could have resembled the home of a nomadic Bedouin tribesman, except for the ultra-modern technology displayed on the desk: a short-wave radio transmitter with a heavy-duty back-up battery, a Japanese laptop computer, and an Inmarsat satellite communications unit in an aluminium carrying case.

Gorev was seated cross-legged on the rug, drinking coffee from a tiny glass cup. He stood when Hasim entered, and said to Rashid, 'About time. I was beginning to think you'd forgotten about me.'

Hasim greeted him in the Arab fashion, touching his head, then his heart. 'Forgive me. But Rashid and I had matters to discuss. Please, be seated.'

They all sat. On a low wooden table was a small primus stove with a silver Arab teapot and some glass cups, and Hasim filled two more tiny cups, topping up Gorev's. 'You have had great success in Moscow. For this you have our heartfelt gratitude.' Hasim's voice was almost reverent. 'You are a remarkable man, Nikolai Gorev. A truly remarkable man.'

'You have the formula, that's all that matters,' Gorev said dimissively. 'So let's stick to what's important. The next stage of the operation.'

Rashid, sipping thick, dark coffee from his cup, set it down before answering. 'Nine weeks after the woman and I have arrived in America, you will join us. By that time the nerve-gas device and other equipment will have been transported secretly to Washington by a safe route. Your Chechen friends will help with the rest of the things we need.'

'You're certain you can do what's expected of you?' Hasim asked.

'Don't worry,' Gorev answered. 'You'll get your pound of flesh. What about safe houses?'

Rashid glared at him, registering the insolence in Gorev's tone, but continued, 'Everything has been well planned. By the time you arrive we will have set up the safe houses we need. One for you and the woman, another for me, both near the American capital. There will be a third, a back-up outside the city, a cottage at a place called Chesapeake, Maryland, should we have need of it and things go wrong. But let's hope not.'

'Where will the chemical be stored?'

'At first, it will be kept a safe distance from the centre of Washington. The Americans will be searching everywhere, of that you can be sure. But it seems logical that at first they will concentrate their search in the city. Later, when it's safe to do so, we will move the chemical near the centre of the capital.'

'I assume we'll have local help?'

Rashid nodded. 'That will be arranged. But for the moment, it is of no concern to you.'

'How do you maintain contact between Washington and here?'

'Two ways,' Rashid answered. 'One is by phone, using simple coded messages, which will be relayed through a special contact phone number in Paris, manned twenty-four hours. The other is by computer, which has a satellite dish, for more urgent signals.'

Rashid explained that he would have a transmitter-receiver which had been expertly built into a harmless-looking laptop computer. A message could be typed into the laptop, then the integrated circuits would work their magic, encrypting the message. When transmitted via a satellite dish, the signal was compressed into a 'burst' lasting no more than a few seconds, or even milliseconds. Once received, the message would be electronically 'slowed' to its normal speed, and decrypted. The transmitting and receiving would only be carried out at certain 'window' times, predetermined periods of the day and night, but varied daily so as not to reveal a pattern.

'Very well.' Gorev stood. 'If that's all, I'll turn in.'

'Of course,' Hasim said. 'You've had a long and difficult trip.'

Gorev stopped at the mouth of the cave. 'One more thing. I presume the operation will need a name, a code word?'

'It will have one, and most suitable. You know the Koran, Nikolai?'

'In the days when I fought against your mujahidin in Afghanistan, I made it my business to acquire more than a passing knowledge. Why?'

'Then perhaps you will know that the Prophet made reference to a day called *al-Wakia*?'

Gorev nodded. 'The Last Day. The Day of Resurrection, when the evil of this world will come before God and be judged and punished for their sins, and the good and holy will be rewarded. It's a common theme among most religions. Not that I'd put much store by it. I've always had more faith in the kind of judgment that comes from the barrel of a gun.'

'A weapon has its uses, especially one as powerful as ours. It will bring a day of judgment for the Americans, and a day of revival for Islam. And that, Nikolai, is what we will call our plan. *al-Wakia*. Resurrection Day.'

Darkness had long fallen and the moon was out. Gorev stood outside the cave assigned for his sleeping quarters, idly smoking a cigarette. He heard a noise below him on the rocks and turned. Karla stood ten feet away, her arms folded, staring at him. 'Do you always like to break rules?'

'And what rules are they?'

'Smoking is forbidden in the camp.'

An amused smile crossed Gorev's lips. 'For the mujahidin, maybe. Not for me. I do as I please. Besides, a decent smoke is about the only pleasure that keeps me going these days. So what kept you?'

'I was asleep when the guard woke me and told me you were here.' She smiled, came over, kissed him on the cheek. 'It's good to see you back safely, Nikolai.'

'How have they been treating you while I've been away?'

'Well enough. How did Moscow go?'

He told her everything, and Karla's face darkened. 'Did it trouble you having to kill this man, Novikov?'

'How could it? I had first-hand experience of Novikov when he served in Chechnya. But long before that, we'd crossed paths when I was a fellow officer in Moscow. The colonel was a beast, with a reputation for savagery. He and his men tortured boys as young as thirteen and destroyed more villages than he had cause to, most of them occupied not by rebels but innocent civilians. As for any of my comrades who fell into Novikov's hands, they fared even worse. A bullet was far more humane than the treatment he meted out to most of his victims.' Gorev tapped ash from his cigarette. 'So, the job's done, and everything goes ahead. Another week at most and you and Rashid will be on your way to get everything set up. He's not the best of company to have to endure, but I'll be joining you both later, by a different route.'

Karla Sharif was silent. She went to sit on a rock.

Gorev said, 'What's wrong, Karla?'

She looked over at him. 'That day you came to see me in Tyr. You never told me why you agreed to be part of all this. Perhaps it's time you told me now.'

Gorev shrugged. 'Lots of reasons. But most of all, I have a debt to repay.'

'What kind of debt?'

'Three years ago, after the Russians invaded Grozny, the Chechens had little to fight back with. A few meagre supplies, some stolen Russian weapons. You've no idea what it was like. We were bombarded day and night, hounded through the hills, hunted down like wild dogs. We were desperate. And then Mohamed Rashid and his friends came and offered us everything we needed. Weapons, supplies, the best equipment and training anyone could offer. And we took it.'

'And now the debt is being called in?'

'Something like that.'

'But why you? Why not one of your comrades?'

'Several reasons. I speak reasonable English and don't look Arab, both advantages on a mission like ours.' Gorev tossed away his cigarette. 'And you, Karla. That day in Tyr you seemed so adamant you wanted nothing to do with all this. Why did you change your mind? Was it because of Josef?'

Karla hesitated. 'Yes, it was because of Josef.'

'You must love him very much.'

'More than you could ever know.' She felt close to tears at that moment, but she hid the pain as she looked back at Gorev. 'You never married, did you, Nikolai?'

Gorev shook his head, smiled. 'Who'd have me? But it must be wonderful to have a son.'

She moved off the rock, tried to overcome her emotion. 'And now I'd better get some sleep.'

Gorev gently touched her arm. 'I just want you to know something, Karla. I never asked for you to be part of all this. In case you think it was I who chose you.'

'Then who?'

'Rashid and his friends. And it's obvious why. There are few Arab women with your qualifications capable of taking part in something as daring as this. Your name was at the top of a very short list. I want you to know that, if it had been up to me, I wouldn't have put you through it all. You understand? It's important to me you know that.'

She nodded, began to turn away, but suddenly looked back. 'Do something for me? Come with me to the airport when I leave, Nikolai.'

'Any particular reason why?'

'None, except I'd like a friend with me to say goodbye. And wish me luck.'

'Are you afraid, Karla?'

'More than I've ever been.' She hesitated, bit her lip. 'And I want you to promise me something. If anything happens to me, if I don't come through, promise me you'll make sure that somehow Josef is looked after.'

'Of course.' Gorev studied her face. 'But is that really why you're afraid?'

She nodded. 'It's troubled me so much lately. The thought

that Josef would have no one if I were to die. And I can't bear the thought of that.'

'I told you. We'll walk away from this with no one the wiser. You'll survive, Karla. We both will. And Josef will be free.'

She looked back at him, close to tears. 'I hope you're right, Nikolai. I so hope you're right.'

Gorev smiled, reached out, touched her face to reassure her. 'That I promise you.'

He watched her go down the hill to her quarters, her figure retreating into the darkness until she had disappeared from sight. He lit another cigarette, heard a noise behind him, the sound of feet on rocks. 'It must be true, the rumours I heard.'

Gorev turned. Mohamed Rashid stood ten feet away, a smirk on his face. 'And what rumours are they?'

'She loved you, but you spurned her, the time you both knew each other in Moscow. But then it was more complex than that, wasn't it? She was engaged to marry her future husband, though from what I heard she was prepared to forsake him for you. All a long time ago, of course. But don't tell me you still have feelings for her, Gorev? Because if you do, that might complicate things. Especially on a mission as important as this.'

Gorev looked at the Arab with distaste. 'Do you always make a habit of listening to other people's conversations?'

'Only if it concerns me. And in this instance it certainly does. If either of you are tempted to renew your old relationship, it might be better to wait until after our mission is over. Don't you think?'

'You know something, Rashid? You're beginning to grate on my nerves. So why don't you keep your nose out of my business.'

Rashid stepped closer, the smirk gone, suddenly replaced by a threatening look. 'You know what your problem is, Gorev? You have no respect. Personally, I thought picking you was a mistake. A decision, unfortunately, out of my hands.' The Egyptian stared at him unflinchingly. 'So for your sake, I hope you don't disappoint those who have put their faith in you, including your Chechen friends. They can only continue their struggle with our support. And the only hope those comrades of yours locked away in Russian cells have of being set free is with our help. Don't ever forget that.'

'I told you, you'll get your pound of flesh.' Gorev glared back, tossed away his cigarette, moved to go, but Rashid grabbed him by the arm, stared into his face. 'What's eating you, Gorev?'

Gorev jerked his arm free of the Arab's grasp. 'Let's just say I have a niggling feeling you've been up to no good.'

'What do you mean?'

'After I spoke with Karla in Tyr, you're sure you didn't have a quiet word? Threaten her, to help change her mind? You know the kind of threat I'm talking about. Embrace the cause or face your wrath. That'd be just up your street, Rashid. The same kind of persuasion you used on me. Except in my case, you'd hang my Chechen comrades out to dry.'

Rashid frowned. 'I don't know what you're talking about.'

'Odd, but I've got a feeling it might be otherwise. However, you'd better be right. Because if I find out differently, you'll have me to answer to, Rashid. Remember that.'

The Arab's face tightened with malice. 'Don't be insolent, Gorev. Remember who helped your comrades when your backs were to the wall. Now it's time to repay that help. And remember, too, who's in charge of this operation. You'll talk to me with respect.'

'You can be sure I will.' Gorev tipped his forehead in a mock salute. 'The moment I think you deserve it.' He began to turn away dismissively. Rashid grabbed his arm once more, and Gorev stared back at the Arab with an infinitely dangerous look. 'I really wouldn't do that again. Or someone's liable to get badly hurt.'

There was a moment of stand-off as both men faced each other, then Rashid's grip relaxed and his face twisted with a look close to hatred. 'Remember something else, Gorev. We have our duty. *All* of us. I intend doing mine. So see that you do yours. Or I promise you, al-Qaeda's wrath will be unforgiving.'

16

Moscow
9 November

The Lada sedan carrying Major Alexei Kursk deposited him outside the private house in the Ramenka district just before eleven that evening. The property was impressive, a wood-and-brick dacha in its own grounds, with a double garage and a sentry box outside.

'Wait here,' he told the driver, and strode up the walkway to the entrance, where a couple of armed militiamen stood guard either side of the front door.

Kursk showed his ID and moments later found himself being escorted into a wood-panelled study by a squat, bullish-looking man whose suit jacket strained with steroid-induced muscle, one of the team of personal bodyguards who protected the head of the FSB twenty-four hours a day.

Igor Verbatin stood at a French window, wearing a dressing gown, a glass of vodka in one hand, staring absent-mindedly out at the dark gardens. He turned as Kursk was led in. 'Thank you, Georgi. You may leave us.'

The bodyguard withdrew, softly closing the door. 'Major, take a seat.' Verbatin raised his glass. 'Forgive me if I indulge myself in a nightcap. And for wondering what's so important that you asked to see me here at such an ungodly hour.'

'There's been a development in the Novikov case, sir.'

Verbatin raised an eyebrow again as he came to sit behind his study desk. 'Really? And I thought your investigations into the affair had led nowhere in over two months? It amazes me, Kursk. You have a reputation as one of our finest investigators, relentless in your work. Yet you and your men hit a brick wall, and a very thick one at that.'

'It's been a difficult case.'

'Explain this development.'

Kursk looked uncomfortable as he snapped open his briefcase. 'Whoever killed Boris Novikov is a professional, that much is obvious. Not a fingerprint was found, not a single clue, no crystal-clear motive. Novikov's security cameras weren't much use, either – a few shots of a man in black, his face covered by a mask.'

'We know all this. Go on.'

'Whatever his motive was, it stands to reason the intruder must have been observing Novikov before he struck. For days, weeks, months perhaps. So I had my men go back over the colonel's movements. Where he went, who he visited, official business or not. Visits to his bank, his businesses, government departments.'

'Get to the point, Kursk.'

'These places have security cameras and most keep the videos for months. I checked back through hundreds of cassettes, examined them diligently, frame by frame, going back over three months. It's been painstaking work, which I only completed this evening. The good news is we got lucky. Almost three months ago, at the same time Novikov was visiting his bank, a man was caught on camera, outside the building, looking like he might be observing Novikov. A week later, when Novikov's visiting the Defence Ministry, the same man turns up in footage from a street camera positioned on top of the Ministry's roof.' From his briefcase Kursk plucked two photographs and placed them on the desk. 'The really bad news is it looks to me like Nikolai Gorev.'

A stunned Verbatin examined the grainy black-and-white photographs of a man whose features were barely distinguishable, and looked instantly worried. 'Oh, my.' His voice softened to almost a whisper, hoarse with sudden anxiety. 'You're sure?'

Kursk blushed, his discomfort even more obvious. 'Very sure. I'd swear it on my mother's life. I had the photographs electronically enhanced and had several experts give their opinion. I've no doubt it's Nikolai Gorev.'

Verbatin looked up, studied his visitor's face intently. 'Of course. I completely forgot. You once knew Gorev. You and he even served together in Moscow, am I correct?'

'Yes, sir.'

A terrible thought occurred to Verbatin. His mouth twitched nervously. 'Do you now think there's a chance Novikov's safe was touched?'

'That's what worries me, considering you said it contained important papers, though nothing appeared to have been taken. But a camera could have been used to photograph the contents. And on that score my nose would be twitching if Nikolai Gorev's involved.'

Verbatin went suddenly pale. 'This is even worse than I thought. The President must be informed at once.'

A coal fire blazed in the Kremlin private office and Vasily Kuzmin, the third President of Russia, stood over it, in a sour mood, warming his hands.

It was the office he had moved into after Boris Yeltsin had vacated the presidency, and one that Kuzmin had quickly made his own. Gone were Yeltsin's personal photographs, his drinks cabinets, the jumble of personal knick-knacks with which the blustering, larger-than-life former President had garnished his desk in over eight years in office. Now the room was scrupulously neat, a place of order and sober industry, virtues for which Vasily Kuzmin had a solid reputation. The only hint of a more private life was an array of personal photographs, one of which graced his desk, of himself and his wife, Irena, and their two daughters, Zoya and Tatiana.

As FSB head Igor Verbatin was led in, Kuzmin dismissed his secretary, and said to Verbatin, 'So, you believe it's Nikolai Gorev in these security videos you spoke about? The man they call the Cobra. And that he was tailing Boris Novikov?'

'Yes, sir. We think it's him, all right.'

'And that he was behind Colonel Novikov's death?'

'Considering Gorev's terrorist background, Mr President, I'd say it's quite likely.'

Kuzmin sighed heavily. 'I've heard of Gorev, of course. But refresh my memory. What's his background?'

'He's Russian by birth. His father was from Moscow, but his mother was Chechen,' Verbatin began. 'He's a graduate of Moscow University who speaks several languages fluently, English and Arabic included. He joined the KGB immediately after graduation and spent four years as an intelligence officer, two of which were spent as a lecturer at Patrice Lumumba University, where he specialised in teaching the KGB's Arab students. But Gorev appears to have been restless for action. He resigned from the KGB and later joined the army, then he took up a commission in the Hundred-and-fifth Airborne Division, reaching the rank of captain, and saw service in eastern Europe, Afghanistan and Chechnya.'

'This gets more curious by the second. What else can you tell me?'

'He's the only son of General Yuri Gorev. He passed away many years ago, but no doubt you've heard of him, sir?'

'*The* General Yuri Gorev?'

'Yes, sir.'

'I can't think of any Russian citizen who hasn't. A courageous military hero of the former Soviet Union. An officer of the highest calibre who commanded the utmost respect of everyone he served with.' Kuzmin shook his head in near-disbelief. 'So, this man is the general's son.'

'And he seems to have been cut from the same cloth,' Verbatin offered. 'In Afghanistan, Nikolai Gorev showed uncommon bravery and earned at least half a dozen medals for valour, often under withering enemy fire. Until the Markov incident when he served in Chechnya in 1994 and Gorev shot dead his commanding officer. That was the start of the slide.'

'Yes, I know all about the Markov incident,' Kuzmin said uncomfortably, as if the subject was a dark one that he didn't wish to discuss. 'Such a terrible tragedy. But go on.'

'For the part he played in the affair, Gorev was arrested and sent to a high-security military penal camp in Siberia to await trial. To make matters worse, he learned he was being charged with the murder of a fellow officer and seems to have completely flipped. Then a week later Gorev escaped from the penal camp. The military scoured the area but he'd simply vanished, and gone on the run.'

'You're telling me he broke out of a heavily guarded Siberian camp at the height of winter? Those camps are in the middle of nowhere, in the worst terrain imaginable. They're impossible to escape from.'

'Gorev's no ordinary man, sir. He not only escaped, but went on to carve out a new career for himself working for the Chechen cause. Given that he's half Chechen, the Markov incident obviously incited him to switch his allegiance. Within three years, he had to our certain knowledge been responsible for at least a dozen assassinations and bombings on the Chechens' behalf. The murder of a Moscow businessman, the car-bombing of a senior Russian army officer, the assassination of a government official in Grozny . . .' The head of the FSB took a sheet from his briefcase and handed it across. 'A list of jobs we think he was involved in. As you can see, his victims have been from every part of the political and military scene. But with one thing in common. They were all, in Gorev's eyes at least, enemies of the Chechen people.'

The President read the sheet slowly, looked up. 'So, Gorev's still allied to the Chechens.'

'Yes, sir. And on their behalf his sole intention is to spread chaos, fear and unrest in Russia, and to maximum effect. We also discovered some disturbing links to other terror groups, if you'd care to study the list.'

Kuzmin regarded the sheet, then looked up, his face bleak. 'You mention here his possible involvement with Mohamed Rashid, an accomplice of Abu Hasim's?'

'Rashid is Egyptian born, one of al-Qaeda's top terrorist commanders. He's had a chequered past, working for various Islamic causes. He's advised the PLO, fought in Algeria, and later joined the al-Qaeda cause. He's an arch-terrorist, a raving Islamicist, who two years ago was sent by al-Qaeda to help train and arm the Chechen rebels.'

'You say here that Rashid was involved in the Moscow terror bombings, the al-Qaeda bombings in Nairobi and Dar es Salaam, and the attack on the USS *Cole*?'

'We've the best of reasons for believing Rashid was involved in both the planning and the execution in each of those incidents. It's hardly surprising. What we know of him suggests the man has a pathological hatred of America and the West.'

'Why is that?'

'The man's insane, totally unstable, and sees any non-Islamic state as a target. And you can include Russia among his list of enemies – the Moscow bombings testify to that. I also heard of one incident in Afghanistan where Rashid personally executed at least a dozen wounded Russian troops who had surrendered when their field hospital was overrun. He lined them up on their stretchers and machine gunned them to death. There's evidence Rashid was also responsible for organising these lunatic suicide squads in Chechnya that continue to massacre our troops.'

Kuzmin's jaw tightened with unconcealed anger. 'Go on.'

'To add fuel to his hatred, several years ago, when the Americans rained their missiles on al-Qaeda's camps in retaliation for terrorist acts, Rashid lost a number of comrades, including a brother. He swore revenge on the Americans, and saw it through with the savage bombings he helped mastermind. Gorev may be bad enough, but Rashid's the Devil's handyman. Capable of any insanity. Men, women, children, he'd kill them all without a shred of remorse if he thought it might advance the Islamic cause a single inch.'

'So what's his relationship to Gorev and the Chechens?'

Verbatin shrugged. 'The rebels had their backs to the wall when our troops invaded. They needed help, arms and supplies. Al-Qaeda offered it, and the Chechens accepted. Gorev was instructed to act as their middleman and had to deal through Rashid.'

'But Gorev's not a Muslim, is he?'

'No, sir, he's not, but then not all the Chechen rebels who defy us are Muslims. But that's not the point. I'm sure the psychiatrists would have fancy terms to describe Gorev's mental condition. They might even paint him as a tragic victim, or suggest that what happened to him because of the Markov incident turned him into a vengeful turncoat. But I'm not really interested. I just want to see him caught.'

Kuzmin tossed aside the list and sighed. 'You haven't had much success in that arena, have you? So where's Gorev now?'

'God only knows. We'll need to put out feelers, at home and abroad, investigate this thoroughly before we jump to any rash conclusions.'

Kuzmin looked troubled. 'This worries me. Especially if Gorev's motive was to photograph Novikov's papers. The man's already guilty of treason. This only adds fuel to the fire with another treasonable offence.'

'There's no other strong motive we can come up with, sir. We've considered every one.'

'Then there's no telling where this might lead. But not a word gets out about this, you hear me?' Kuzmin was adamant.

'But sir,' Verbatin protested, 'the Western intelligence agencies will need to know. In the wrong hands, the formula's a time bomb waiting to go off.'

'Not a word, I said. It couldn't be worse from our point of view. A former Russian army officer, turned traitor, stealing a deadly nerve gas formula from under our noses. Imagine the adverse publicity if the press got hold of that? The government would be seen as a laughing-stock, totally incompetent, unable to guard its military secrets. No, we handle it ourselves for now. Which means finding Gorev and finding him fast. We need to know what he's up to and who he's really working for. Tell me about this officer of yours you mentioned, Major Kursk.'

'He's one of our best intelligence officers. In the past, he and Gorev were close, almost like brothers. They worked together as KGB staff, even grew up together.'

'How is that?'

'Nikolai Gorev was twelve years old when his father died. His mother had already passed away. Major Kursk's father served under the general – he was a devoted personal friend, and took it upon himself to foster the boy.'

'So where's Kursk now?'

'Waiting outside, sir.'

'Does he know what we intend?'

'Not yet, sir. He's been told some of the facts, but nothing about our plans.'

'Then bring him in.'

Alexei Kursk was led into the room and crossed to where Kuzmin sat. Verbatin made the introductions. 'Mr President, this is Major Kursk.'

Kursk stood there, slightly awed by his surroundings. 'You sent for me, Mr President.'

'Major,' Kuzmin began, 'I've just been hearing about your rather special relationship with this terrorist, Nikolai Gorev.'

'It's been a number of years since I last saw Nikolai Gorev, sir.' Kursk looked uncomfortable. 'Our paths have long gone different ways.'

'Nevertheless, you've confirmed it was he in the photographs.'

'Yes, sir. It looks that way.'

'We also suspect Gorev's motive may have been to steal a valuable state secret in Boris Novikov's possession. But first, I must caution you. What you are about to hear is a matter of the utmost secrecy.' Kuzmin turned to Verbatin. 'Proceed.'

Verbatin addressed Kursk. 'As you know, Major, a nation's defence depends heavily upon its arsenal of weapons and their efficacy. Limited as Russia is by the various weapons treaties with the US, we have little scope for pursuing new defence strategies to protect our country, except in secret. There is also the matter of expense and benefit – new weapons can cost a fortune in terms of expenditure on research and development. The exception is chemical weapons. They're probably one of the cheapest to manufacture. You may already have heard of some of the nerve gases already in our arsenal, such as VX and Sarin, which are incredibly deadly. But let me give you an example.'

Verbatin picked up a carafe of water from Kuzmin's desk. He poured a drop into a glass, then held up the glass, swirling the meagre amount of liquid. 'Imagine if this were VX. The cost of manufacturing such a quantity would be in the region of six thousand roubles – two hundred US dollars. Not a huge sum. Especially if I were to tell you that this amount of VX, properly dispersed, could wipe out a thousand enemy troops. However, our military scientists, working with a private chemical research company that was run by Boris Novikov, have gone a step farther. Recently they developed a new, top-secret chemical weapon, one that far surpasses the potency of any other in our arsenal. Code-named Substance A232X, its potency is truly devastating. With this same amount of liquid – this small drop – the capacity for human destruction would increase *tenfold*.'

Verbatin paused to let his information sink in. Kursk was astounded. 'And you're telling me Boris Novikov had the formula in his safe?'

'He had been attending a series of meetings at the Defence Ministry to discuss research matters, and on the night he was killed had just returned from a meeting with the President on the same subject. His possession of the formula was entirely appropriate in this case – his company had helped enormously in the research, and Novikov himself was a graduate chemist long before he joined the FSB, and was thoroughly involved in the project.'

Verbatin put down the carafe and glass. 'Nothing as potent as this nerve gas has yet been developed by any other country, including the US. Which means that Russia possesses the supreme chemical weapon of mass destruction in the world. What's more, the manufacturing process is relatively simple and uses mostly easily available chemicals. So much so that were the formula to fall into the wrong hands – and by that principally I mean terrorists – I dread to think of the consequences.'

'Which brings us to why you're here, Major,' Vasily Kuzmin said. 'Since we strongly suspect Gorev may have stolen the formula, we want him found. Your special relationship will no doubt give you an insight into this man's mind, deranged as it is. That's an advantage to be exploited. The head of the FSB will co-ordinate a specialist intelligence team, in conjunction with the SVR, whose purpose will be to hunt down this criminal terrorist, be it at home or abroad. We'll have our Muslim agents in Chechnya and abroad on full alert to be on the lookout for Gorev. You, Kursk, will be part of that team, and your task will be to pursue him with the utmost vigour. Find him, no matter where he is. And ascertain what he's done with the formula.'

'And then, sir?' Kursk looked ill at ease.

Kuzmin fixed both his visitors with a cold stare. 'I should think that's obvious. This man is a menace and a traitor. He must be eliminated.'

Alexei Kursk arrived at his home in Mazilovo on the western outskirts of Moscow just after two that morning. It was a small, two-storey brick-built house on a bend near the Moscow river. Compact, simply furnished, with a living room and tiny kitchen, the two-bedroomed property had been the family home, and after his parents had passed away he'd simply continued living there, preferring it to the soulless breeze-block apartments that blighted Moscow's suburbs. Kursk had the place to himself for a week; his wife Lydia was in St Petersburg, visiting her sister, and had taken their eight-year-old daughter Nadia with her.

Nadia's farewell note to him was still on the coffee table: 'Mama and I will miss you, Papa. She says not to forget to fix the tap in the kitchen! We love you, Papa! Nadia.' Around the page, in pink marker, she'd drawn tiny hearts and flowers, and dozens of kisses. Kursk smiled. He loved his daughter to distraction, as much as he did Lydia, even after ten years of marriage. For some reason, he wanted to phone Lydia now, tell her of his dilemma, though he knew that was out of the question. He was still reeling, his mind racked by memories. He looked around the walls. There were family photographs of himself and Lydia and Nadia, and one of his parents that took pride of place above the mantelpiece. But there were others.

He went into his bedroom, found the worn, leather-bound photo album. He flicked through the cellophaned pages. There were photographs here he treasured, and one stood out, taken many years ago on the steps of Moscow's St Basil's Cathedral: Nikolai Gorev and himself, smiling for the camera, both of them eighteen, the day they graduated from high school. Kursk felt a twinge of sadness as he looked down at the image, a sadness so intense that he quickly flicked over the pages.

When he came to the photograph he was looking for he removed it from the sleeve. It was a photograph of two small boys, sitting on the winter banks of the Moscow river. Nikolai and himself, both twelve years old, their arms around each other's shoulders, looking earnest for the camera. He remembered a time six months before it was taken. It was a hot July day, the morning Nikolai Gorev's father had been cremated, the ashes contained in a small plaster urn, and Nikolai had been inconsolable. Kursk remembered walking across cornfields, led by his father, Nikolai following behind, desolate, until the three of them came to a small rise where a willow tree overhung the Moscow river. His father had handed Nikolai the urn. 'You must lay your dead to rest. Be a brave boy, now. Do your duty.'

Crying, Nikolai had scattered the ashes on the water.

Kursk's father had said a short prayer. 'It's done. Your papa's at peace.' He pulled the grieving boy towards him, gave him a solid hug. 'No more sorrow now. It's over.'

But it wasn't. Afterwards, Nikolai Gorev had built walls around himself, and in the small bedroom they shared Kursk would be woken at night by his sobs in the darkness, calling out for his father. It took a long time for the walls to come down, for Kursk to win the trust of the new addition to the family. It happened slowly, in small ways, by telling confidences, sharing a few meagre toys, standing up for each other in the school fights that plague all children, until the wary acquaintance between them became camaraderie, the camaraderie became friendship, and the friendship strengthened into a childhood bond that made them almost inseparable. Kursk had treasured those days.

'We're blood brothers, remember?'

Kursk remembered. It was the day the photograph had been taken. Nikolai had pricked his forefinger on a thorn bush and Kursk had done the same. They mingled their blood as a sign of fraternity, and for the first time in months Nikolai had forgotten his grief, his face alight with childish *naïveté*. *'Now we're not just best friends, we're blood brothers, Alexei. That's as good as real brothers, you know? We're united for ever. Nothing can ever change that.'*

Those childhood years had disappeared. He and Nikolai had long gone their separate ways. They hadn't seen each other since before the Markov affair, the tragedy of which had changed everything. Kursk knew the details, had seen the report.

In that first bitter campaign against the Chechens in '94, the Russian army had gone in hard. Atrocities were committed, innocent Chechen civilians killed, but the Markov affair had been savage in the extreme. Boris Markov was a much-decorated paratroop commander, but a man known for his brutality. A Chechen border village suspected of harbouring rebels was surrounded by Markov's troops. A shot rang out, fired by a young rebel sniper, fatally wounding one of Markov's men. Enraged, the commander had ordered a dozen men and young boys from the village rounded up – three of them as young as twelve. Unless the sniper was handed over, every one of the hostages would be executed. The sniper wasn't handed over. Markov, in a fit of rage, set up a light machinegun on its tripod and began to mow down the hostages.

One of his officers – Nikolai Gorev – arrived and intervened. By the time he managed to overpower Markov, most of the hostages were dead or dying. But it didn't end there. Markov still wanted blood. Drawing his pistol, he moved to finish a wounded, frightened young boy who had somehow survived. When Markov raised his pistol to execute him, a furious Gorev almost cut his commander in two with a burst from his Kalashnikov. The rest – Gorev's arrest and imprisonment, his escape, his defection to the Chechen cause – was history.

But now Kursk had to find Nikolai Gorev, kill him if necessary. Could he do it? Could he kill someone who had been almost like a brother to him? Kursk was suddenly afraid. For the first time since childhood he was really and truly afraid.

'You damned fool, Nikolai,' he said aloud, staring down at the photograph. 'What the hell have you gone and done?'

PART THREE

11 November

'Destroy Abu Hasim!'

17

Washington, DC
11 November
4.06 p.m.

The President of the United States sat motionless, his hands clasped tightly together, his index fingers touching his mouth as he stared blankly at the polished table in front of him. Everyone was back in the situation room.

They had taken a fifteen-minute break – for 'reflection', as Alex Havers put it. The President had walked alone in the Rose Garden, brooding, unable to shake off the disturbing images of fourteen of his countrymen being massacred. To see death inflicted so cold-bloodedly, simply to underline a madman's point, was revolting, and he'd fought hard not to throw up. The others in the room were equally affected. Since they'd reconvened, there had been an air of helplessness that had proved difficult to break.

Finally the President spoke. 'I think we can assume first that al-Qaeda is deadly serious. Second, that they've got a significant quantity of nerve gas hidden in or near Washington. The third assumption we can make is that this threat to disperse the gas if any word of this gets out to the press is real. On that point, obscene as it sounds, I believe Abu Hasim's done us a favour. If word did get out, this city would be in chaos. Our job's going to be hard enough without having to worry about that.'

The President paused. 'I know witnessing the deaths of those innocent men has been hard to stomach. I know many of you are angry about what you saw. I share your revulsion and anger. Our prayers will go out to the dead and the bereaved. But let me make one thing perfectly clear. What we saw must be kept secret until this crisis has been resolved. Cruel as that might seem to the victims' next of kin, there's something far more important at stake here – our obligation not to jeopardise the lives of Washington's citizens. Secrecy is absolutely paramount. Do you have any advice for us in that area, Dick?'

'The obvious things come to mind, sir,' the CIA Director replied. 'Nobody leaves anything written down on paper, or stored on their personal computers. No scraps left around for nosy secretaries or aides to read. No bedroom confessionals to loved ones, no matter how much we think they can be trusted. And if we need to talk about it outside of this office, we use secure lines. Equally important, difficult as it might seem, is that everyone tries to behave normally.' Faulks paused. 'For me, sir, the big problem is how the hell are we going to keep this from the press?'

Over a thousand American and foreign journalists were accredited to the White House. Dozens were in constant attendance there during the day, haunting the press office. The more seasoned correspondents, like skilled bloodhounds, could tell that something was amiss in the White House simply by scenting the air. And Washington was a city that thrived on scandal and rumour. Gossip about government secrets was discussed at Old Ebbitt's or the Willard, or the favoured watering holes near Pennsylvania Avenue. Everyone in the room knew that secrecy was going to be a major problem.

'What if the press secretary somehow gets hit with a question about this?' Paul Burton, the National Security Affairs Assistant, asked. 'Should we tell him, so we'll get to know of any press queries?'

'If we do he'd have a hard time trying to lie barefaced about something as big as this,' the President replied. 'If we don't tell him, his reply will come across as honest, and we'll get to hear about the query anyhow. No, I think it best we keep him in the dark. Has anyone made a list of the people outside this room who know about this?'

'Yes, sir,' the FBI Director answered. 'I've compiled a list of the names of everyone who's involved.'

'Speak to them all again. Make plain the consequences if they don't keep their mouths shut – that they may as well detonate the nerve gas themselves. If you have the slightest doubts about any one of them, lock them up, incommunicado, until this thing's over. Also, you should be aware that within the next hour the Vice-President will be moved to a secret location, to ensure his safety and the continuance of government.' The President paused. 'General Croft, I believe you have some facts to hand regarding withdrawing our forces from the Gulf?'

'Yes, Mr President. They're part of a study carried out by the Defence Department. The report was updated six months ago, so it should be reasonably valid.'

'Proceed, General.'

The general stepped in front of the lectern and dimmed the room lights. Behind him a back-lit map projection of the Middle East snapped on. The general picked up a laser pointer, circled the map with the red dot. 'At this moment, we have approximately twenty-six thousand military personnel based in the entire Middle Eastern region. That comprises navy, air force and army. Most of our forces are concentrated in Saudi and the Emirate states.' The red laser dot settled on each country in turn. 'We've also got several hundred civilian support staff in each of these countries, and added to the figures, of course, will be State Department embassy officials and staff, and CIA personnel.'

'How long would it take to disengage all those forces, personnel and their equipment?'

'That really depends, Mr President.'

'I'm not interested in depends, General. I want hard answers.'

'At absolute minimum, assuming we muster civilian transport to help carry out a smooth and orderly withdrawal, I'd say three weeks.'

'We haven't got three weeks. We've got less than seven days.'

'Sir, that kind of timeframe would be absolutely impossible. We've got a hell of a lot of military hardware in the region. We'd be talking about one of the biggest air and sea lifts since the Gulf War.'

'Then how fast can we get just our troops and personnel out of there? Does the study tell you that?'

'Sir, we couldn't just walk away and leave behind billions of dollars' worth of valuable military hardware. Some of it's highly classified equipment . . .'

'I'm not concerned about the costs, General. I'm concerned about lives. Please answer the question.'

'The study has a scenario in which all personnel and a minimum amount of vital equipment are evacuated.'

'How long, General?'

'Ten days, minimum. But there's a problem, sir.'

'Which is?'

'We start a pull-out that big, the world's going to know about it. Airspace in the region's going to get clogged. Sea lanes are going to fill up. I've no doubt, sir, that if we really had to get out of the Gulf hell for leather we could move every single soldier, airman and sailor from the region within seven days. Maybe even a lot faster if we hired in extra civilian aircraft to help ferry them out in a hurry. But I guarantee that after a couple of days or even less, it's no longer going to be a secret.'

'And the markets will smell trouble,' Mitch Gains added. 'Wall Street will go crazy.'

'To hell with the markets. Could we start a withdrawal right now? Move out, say, a percentage of our troops without too much notice being taken?'

'What kind of percentage, Mr President?'

'Twenty.'

'That kind of movement's going to get noticed. Not only in the press, but in Congress. People will want to know why.'

'Then what percentage, in your estimation, could we safely pull out without attracting much attention?'

'Perhaps ten, maybe fifteen per cent, tops. But even then I couldn't guarantee it wouldn't get noticed.'

'Is there any way we can mask it and avoid questions being asked?'

The Defence Secretary, John Feldmeyer, interrupted. 'The Christmas season's less than six weeks away. The army could say it's trying to facilitate troops who want to spend time with their families. It's a reasonably plausible excuse.'

'Then do it,' the President ordered. 'Commence the removal of fifteen per cent of our forces.'

'But, sir . . .' The general flushed.

'You heard me. Get them out, General. Starting as soon as this meeting's over. But leave our listening posts intact for now. We're going to need as much intelligence as we can get.'

'Should we really be going this way so soon, sir? Shouldn't we give it more time before making that final a decision?'

'Time's what we don't have. Issue the necessary orders. But they'll be your orders, not mine. Don't make a big deal of it. But get things moving.' The President looked at the others. 'General Croft made an important point. If we have to pull out all our forces, we can't keep it a secret for very long. That's something we'll have to try to relay to Abu Hasim. He can't expect our troops just to disappear from the Middle East. There's going to be questions asked. The media will want answers.'

'Why the hell don't we just nuke the bastards?' Rivermount's livid voice interrupted. 'That'd stop those sons of bitches in Afghanistan setting off their device.'

'General Horton, I believe you can best answer that question.'

Horton, Chairman of the Joint Chiefs, stepped towards the podium. He hit the remote and a map of Afghanistan appeared on the screen. Outlined in black were the surrounding borders: with Pakistan, Iran, Kashmir, the Russian Federation's independent republics of Turkmenistan and Uzbekistan, and a narrow strip in the north-east that adjoined China. Beyond those were the greyed-out border areas of India. 'All our latest intelligence suggests that Abu Hasim is somewhere in Kandahar province, Afghanistan.'

The general directed the laser dot to Kandahar, almost three hundred miles south-west of Kabul. 'However, to verify it, we'd have to send people in on the ground, which would take a couple of days at least, and that's being optimistic in the extreme. But let's say we located him in one of his camps and to be certain of annihilating him we dropped a nuclear warhead. We could destroy Hasim and his camps, wipe them off the map, no question. But the radioactive fallout wouldn't be contained. It could drift with winds, to Kabul, the capital, and over the border to Pakistan. We'd put the lives and health of millions of people at risk. And remember, it's a volatile region. Third World by Western standards, but countries like Pakistan and India are bitter enemies with nuclear weapons of their own. If we nuke, they're going to be less inclined not to use their own atomic weapons in any future regional conflict that arises. God knows what we could start. The whole thing could snowball and the lives of billions of people be put in jeopardy.'

'You're telling me we can't hit Abu Hasim?' Rivermount asked.

'We could, but the risks far outweigh the likely results. We've no real friends in the region. If we nuked, we'd have even less. Every Muslim country in the world would be out for our blood. Every American citizen a target.'

Rivermount fell silent, his question answered.

Rebecca Joyce spoke up. 'Mr President, I'd suggest that every one of the countries that holds terrorists on the list be informed. They may have ideas on which of Hasim's people are involved.'

'Isn't that taking a risk?'

'But a calculated one, if we send it eyes-only to the Russian President, and the others. The Germans, the Israelis, the British. They may be able to come up with something.'

The President considered. 'Very well, we'll do it. In regard to the Russians, I'll speak to Kuzmin personally, just as soon as our meeting's over, and fill him in. But we'll keep the Israelis out of the picture for now. They're likely to go apeshit if they get an inkling of this. And we'll need someone who can get a message to Hasim. Tell him our problem regarding keeping a complete withdrawal secret and out of the press.'

'What if he won't agree to talk?' Paul Burton asked.

'Once we tell him we want to discuss ways of accommodating his demands, but that we need more time to work out the details, my guess is he'll have to. If nothing else, it may buy us time.'

The men around the room looked mentally fatigued. The President stood. 'We meet back here at eleven p.m. Until then, we better all pray we can find answers. Because right now, it looks to me like Abu Hasim's got us by the balls.'

18

Moscow
12 November
12.47 a.m.

A flurry of icy snowflakes gusted across the cobblestones on Red Square, a bitter taste of the harsh winter soon to come, and as the clock in the Kremlin watchtower chimed out the hour, Vasily Kuzmin rose moodily from behind his office desk.

Crossing to the window, he stared out blankly at the snow falling in the courtyard below. The magnificent candy-whorl domes of St Basil's Cathedral poked their heads above the Kremlin's walls, but Kuzmin, immersed in his own thoughts, paid no attention to their splendid beauty.

An athletic, youthful man in his late forties, he wore a dark blue business suit, crisp white shirt and grey silk tie. His expressionless face and reputation as someone who rarely smiled had earned him a nickname, the 'Grey Cardinal'. But Kuzmin's mild manner hid a ruthless streak. The more unkind among his political enemies compared him to a latter-day Stalin. Those who had worked closely with him attested to their President being simply an ambitious man who wielded power quietly but decisively behind the scenes. A tough, resourceful leader who had a firm grip on Russia's parliament, the Duma. Above all, a man with a passion for the security of his motherland, which was hardly surprising considering his past.

For fifteen years Vasily Kuzmin had served in the KGB's First Directorate, much of it spent in the Stasi headquarters in Dresden, and had proved himself a loyal, trustworthy and hard-working state servant. Those same qualities had led to his rapid rise to power. It was Yeltsin, his former boss, who had introduced Kuzmin to the Russian people as his chosen successor, with the praise that he was the only man who would be able to help revive a

Great Russia in the twenty-first century. For once, Yeltsin wasn't bluffing. It was Kuzmin's vision that one day he would return his motherland to its former military glory.

Behind him on the wall, among the photographs of handshakes with Western leaders, were shots of Kuzmin in his KGB uniform, visiting Russian troops on the Chechen front, sitting on the turret of a T-80 tank and in the cockpit of an SU jet fighter. Kuzmin dressed in the judo-style kit of sambo, the Russian form of self-defence, a sport in which he had won the St Petersburg championship three times. The image of an aggressive sportsman helped portray him as a tough, no-nonsense leader, a man who believed that the only way to maintain the might and unity of Russia's vast nation was with a steel rod in a firm hand.

When Chechen Islamic militants ventured into neighbouring Dagestan and attacked Russian Federation troops, it was Kuzmin who had them expelled with brute force. Later, when the Chechen problem deepened into all-out war, he had ordered the army to invade, and began a remorseless air bombardment of Grozny to crush the Islamic rebels, until hardly a brick was left standing.

Fifteen minutes earlier Kuzmin had been given yet another reminder of the danger the Islamics could pose. At exactly 12.32 a.m. he had taken the private call from the President of the United States. It had both disturbed and surprised him. Disturbed him because of the terrifying nature of al-Qaeda's threat. Surprised him because President Booth had perceived the threat as being solely against Washington and the United States. But Kuzmin's sharp mind saw something else. The menacing hand of a fanatic whose mujahidin supporters had helped to bloody his army in Chechnya and Afghanistan, slaughtering thousands of Russian troops.

And then there was the question of the source of the nerve gas at the heart of Hasim's threat, which distressed Kuzmin just as much.

Moving away from the window, he crossed back to his desk and reviewed the notes he had scribbled during the conversation with the American President, and then gave a troubled sigh. There were aspects to the frightening scenario that could directly affect Russia. The next morning at 10.30 a.m. he was due to depart for London with his wife, an important diplomatic visit that had been planned for months. He knew he needed time to assess the alarming information the American president had passed to him. The matter of complete secrecy had been stressed, but Kuzmin had informed the President that before he could even contemplate an answer to the difficult question of prisoner releases he would have to discuss it with his Security Council. Only the specially appointed council, members of the Russian government, judiciary and military, could decide on such a high-level issue which affected state security.

In the courtyard outside, he heard the throb of a motorcycle engine. His messenger had arrived. A few minutes later there was knock on the double oak doors and a presidential aide stepped in and handed him a large envelope. It was wax sealed and bore the words '*Sovershenno Sekretno* – Ultra Confidential'. Prepared in an anonymous FSB office at Dzerzhinsky Square, the envelope contained two sets of pages. One was the latest intelligence report on Islamic terrorist movements in Russia, which Kuzmin had requested as soon as he had put down the phone to the American President. The second was a list of Chechen prisoners held in Russian jails.

The aide withdrew and Kuzmin broke the wax seal and scanned through the four-page list of prisoners. Then he studied the main points of the intelligence report, six pages long. His jaw tightened as he read, an almost greyish pallor discolouring his features. He put down the envelope and pressed the intercom on his desk. 'Leonid. My office, now.'

Almost as soon as Kuzmin released his finger from the buzzer the double oak doors opened. Leonid Tushin, his trusted private secretary, entered. 'Mr President?'

'My visit to London is cancelled.'

'But, sir,' Tushin wailed, 'the British have everything arranged. And their Prime Minister has important matters to discuss.'

'Send my regrets. Inform him that pressing business has arisen. Then arrange to have my car ready in fifteen minutes.'

The private secretary frowned. 'What pressing business, sir?'

'Have the members of the Security Council meet me at the Kuntsevo dacha within the hour, at no later than one-forty-five a.m. No excuses. Tell them it's a matter of the gravest urgency.' Kuzmin's mouth twisted with scorn. 'Tell them it has to do with Abu Hasim.'

Afghanistan
11 November
6 p.m.

Over two thousand miles away, the man whose name Vasily Kuzmin had uttered with such contempt was standing anxiously outside his command post, awaiting a visitor.

The dying evening sun tinted the desolate mountain landscape with amber light, and Abu Hasim, with the aid of his walking cane, stood in the cavern mouth and saw the dented, dust-covered Nissan jeep pull up below and the man climb out. Hasim waved as the visitor climbed up the slope, and when he waved back Hasim turned away and entered his lair. Moments later, the visitor moved past the armed guards and followed him in. He found Hasim seated on the floor, cross-legged on the Bokkara rug. 'Wassef, old friend.'

'Abu . . .' The man was breathless.

'Sit, Wassef. Tell me your news.'

Wassef Mazloum sat. He was a senior mujahidin commander, a tough-looking specimen with a heavily scarred face that looked as if he'd been clawed by a wild animal. His disfigurement had been inflicted by a Soviet grenade, and the metal fragments had been removed by a surgeon, but he'd sewn up the wound so badly it had left the commander with a ravaged appearance. Exultant, he took a slip of paper from inside his gown and handed it across eagerly. 'The report came from Washington, Abu. Our messages have been delivered. Mohamed says that everything goes as planned.'

Hasim took the slip of paper and read. His face barely showed a reaction, except for a spark that flickered in his soft brown eyes as he lifted his head. 'I thank Allah. This day, He has looked with goodness on the Arab peoples.'

Wassef Mazloum was still overcome, his face lit up. 'It is wonderful news, Abu. From now on, the Americans must do exactly as we say, or we have it within our power to teach them a terrible lesson.'

Abu Hasim said calmly, 'Let us not be foolhardy, Wassef.' He put down the paper, folded it neatly. 'Six long days remain. And in that time, anything is possible. But we must continue to pray for our success.'

'Of course, Abu.'

Hasim calmly turned to the wooden table and the primus stove with its silver Arab teapot. He poured thick coffee into two glass cups. Wassef Mazloum reached for his. 'I have a question, Abu.'

'You only have to ask.'

Mazloum gestured to the satellite transceiver in the aluminium case. 'I know that at the first sign of any American aggression against us, or if they fail to comply with our demands, we can detonate the nerve gas by remote control. But I am not an expert when it comes to technical matters. What happens if the satellite we use fails at the critical time we send the signal?'

Hasim sipped coffee from his cup, set it down. 'If that should happen, a simple telephone call relayed to America, and using a code word, will instruct Mohamed in Washington to detonate. Believe me, Wassef, the Americans cannot win this battle. And if they are foolish enough to attack us, they will pay the price of their folly.'

'But if we are forced to carry out our threat, they will seek revenge.'

'Of course they will. But what will it profit them, even if they kill us, and we have sacrificed our lives? By then we will have caused the Americans the greatest destruction in their history.'

Wassef Mazloum nodded, finished his coffee. 'It is clear to me now. I will pray to Allah for our success. That by His goodness and power He will help us succeed. I shall pray, too, for our people in Washington.'

'Your prayers will be needed.' For the first time there was disquiet in Hasim's voice. 'For this is a time of great danger. Though it is not the Americans we have to fear at this moment, but the Russians. They will feel threatened. They will know now we stole their formula and they will want revenge. They may even be tempted to crush us, destroy us with their missiles and bombs. In the coming hours, Moscow's reaction will decide everything.'

'What if the Russians take this into their own hands? What if they decide to strike back at us?'

'Then, Wassef, we are martyrs, and Washington is a wasteland.'

19

Moscow
12 November
1.30 a.m.

Ten miles from the Kremlin, in a thickly wooded forest, is Kuntsevo, one of the official dachas of the ruling President of Russia. In light snow, at exactly thirty minutes past one, a black Mercedes S600 swept in through the massive green gates and came to a halt outside an ivy-clad building that resembled an English country manor house. A worried-looking Vasily Kuzmin, seated in the back of the car next to his bodyguard, saw a clutter of official Mercedes already parked on the snow-dusted gravel. His bodyguard snapped open the rear door and Kuzmin moved quickly inside the dacha.

It was the same room in which Stalin had issued his orders for the final assault on Berlin in 1945, and where Andropov had planned the invasion of Afghanistan, thirty-four years later. A vast oval table dominated the centre, complemented by Bokkara rugs, polished antique furniture, a crystal chandelier. Of the seventeen men who stood around drinking coffee, waiting for Vasily Kuzmin, at least fifteen were his closest political allies. He greeted each of them in turn before they all took their seats at the table. 'Gentlemen, early this morning, no more than half an hour ago, I received the gravest news from the President of America.'

Referring to his notes, Kuzmin recollected every single detail of his conversation with President Booth, and the horrific manner in which the Americans kidnapped in Azerbaijan had met their deaths. 'I have summoned you here urgently not only to discuss the obvious matter of what has happened to our stolen formula,' Kuzmin said, grim faced, 'but because this dire threat by Abu Hasim and his al-Qaeda may pose the most serious menace to Russia's security.'

'How, Mr President?' the Interior Minister, Anatoli Sergeyev, asked.

'If this crazy fanatic Abu Hasim were to succeed in removing the Americans from the Gulf, it would open the way for him to create the strictly Muslim, pan-Islamic region that he's desired for so long.'

'Did you tell the American President about the theft of our formula?'

'No. I wanted to inform the Council of this grave situation first.' Kuzmin stared at the faces in the room. 'And I don't need to remind you, gentlemen, that a powerful, united Islamic front is not in our interests. Our entire south-eastern flank in central Asia is buffered by Muslim lands that are allied to the Russian Federation, a region vital to our country's defences. In turn, these lands border more Islamic countries, like Pakistan, Afghanistan, Kashmir, and Iran. Many of these states already see Abu Hasim as a hero, an Arab messiah. If he succeeds against the Americans, Muslims everywhere would be emboldened by his victory. Before we knew it vast regions of our Federation would be in danger of coming under his influence, taking up arms and baying for independence.'

'You're saying we are under threat also?'

'Exactly. Al-Qaeda's threat, in my opinion, has the potential to create the gravest crisis in our country's history. Very soon, we'd be faced by Islamic-inspired uprisings in our Muslim regions, massive civil unrest, and bloody guerrilla warfare. Our army would be hard stretched to quell such a magnitude of conflicts. Believe me, Anatoli, the war in Chechnya would seem like a minor skirmish by comparison. Nor do I need to remind you that the valuable oil and natural gas resources in Georgia, Tajikistan and Azerbaijan all pass through Russian pipelines. How long do you think that would continue if these Islamic territories rose up against us? We'd face economic ruin.'

The Security Council members looked horrified, for there was solid reasoning to Kuzmin's argument. Ten per cent of the Federation's population is Muslim, concentrated in central Asia and the Caucusus, territories of the highest strategic importance to Russia. Not only in the short term, because the oil and gas pipelines were critical to her fragile economic stability, but because their vast energy resources – which made even Saudi Arabia look deprived – had barely been exploited. At some point in the future they would become a substitute for the Gulf's oil and gas fields.

'The President is right,' Nikita Volsky, the Defence Minister, agreed. 'If al-Qaeda succeeds we could find ourselves facing a terrifying scenario. Today it's Washington that's under threat. Tomorrow it might be Moscow. That madman Abu Hasim could point our own nerve gas weapon at our heads, demanding we cease our influence in central Asia.'

Sasha Pavlov, the Justice Minister, jabbed a finger in the air in front of him. 'The only way to deal with people like that is with a heavy hand. We have a right to use force to prevent this danger developing on our doorstep. The Americans would do exactly the same if they were faced with violent rebellion, if armed insurgents in Hawaii or Puerto Rico demanded independence.

'I bear no ill-will against those of the Muslim faith who live within our borders,' Pavlov added. 'But these Islamic madmen are an entirely different breed. They can't be allowed to gain a position that would allow them to dictate to us, blackmail us, or threaten our citizens. I agree with the Defence Minister. If they win a victory against America, tomorrow it will be our turn to face their wrath. They would descend on us like a locust plague. We'll be vulnerable from the borders of Mongolia to the Caspian Sea.'

'And what do you propose to counter this threat, Sasha?' the Trade Minister, Boris Rudkin, asked. One of the few moderates on the Council, he was a middle-aged Muscovite with a large mole on his left jaw, a birthmark that press caricaturists had made much of over the years, amplifying its size totally out of proportion.

'Abu Hasim has stolen a powerful weapon of mass destruction from under our noses,' Pavlov answered. 'If he can threaten the Americans, he can do the same to us. Therefore it seems to me that what matters is destroying him and al-Qaeda before they can act.'

Rudkin had a habit of scratching his mole when worried or under duress. He was scratching it now. 'And what if Abu Hasim annihilates Washington?'

'That would be a tragedy. But it's a risk we have to take.'

'You're mad, Sasha. Totally crazy. We could end up sending the entire population of Washington to their deaths.'

'What would you rather, the destruction of the Russian Federation?'

The Finance Minister, Felix Akulev, another moderate, butted in. 'But we don't know for certain that Abu Hasim will pose us a threat.'

'For God's sake, Felix, he already does, and has for years. Didn't he send his top commander, Khattab, to lead the war in Chechnya? Support the Chechen fighters with arms and money? Didn't his comrades ravage our army in Afghanistan? And the FSB will let you have all the proof you need that Abu Hasim's mujahidin had a hand in the Moscow bombings. Do you honestly think this maniac won't take things a step farther now that he has our nerve gas? It would be the perfect irony. Being able to blackmail us with our own weapon.'

'Gentlemen, we're wasting time bickering.' Kuzmin turned to the head of the FSB. 'Igor, in your opinion, what are the chances of the Americans apprehending these terrorists in Washington?'

'Almost impossible. Time is not on their side. You can be sure Abu Hasim has planned his operation thoroughly because of the stakes. His people will have been given excellent covers. You only have to look at our own experiences to know how difficult it is to apprehend well-trained terrorists, especially in a crowded city. Have we yet caught all of the Muslim attackers responsible for bombing Moscow, years after the outrage? Or even rounded up all the Islamic guerrillas who still harangue our troops in Chechnya? The Americans cannot hunt down these people within seven days. And even if they did, the mujahidin operatives are fanatics. If they felt threatened, they'd detonate the gas, just as Abu Hasim threatened. I'd guarantee it. So the Americans have lost, no matter what happens.'

Kuzmin opened the envelope delivered to his office. 'I have here a list of Chechen prisoners in Russian jails. Most of them are hard-core Islamic rebels.'

'Surely you don't intend to release them?' Pavlov, the Justice Minister, asked.

'That decision is up to us. We may have to put it to a vote.'

'The army fought hard to capture these fanatics,' Pavlov argued. 'To set them free would be sheer madness. The first thing they'd do is rearm and start the Chechen war all over again with even more vigour.'

Kuzmin turned to Admiral Vodin, who commanded the Russian navy. 'Andrei? Your thoughts.'

'I agree. To release the prisoners would be crazy, a show of weakness. We might as well cut our own throats.'

'And what about the problem the Americans face?' Felix Akulev asked.

'The Americans! The Americans will always do what is best for them. What if the situation was reversed and we asked them to release those al-Qaeda terrorists who were jailed for blowing up the US embassies in Africa? Do you think they would consider our request? Not for a minute. When the hell did the Americans ever care about Russia? Look at what they've done to us in the past. They brought about the downfall of the Soviet empire. Helped our defeat in Afghanistan. And they knew our back was to the wall in Chechnya, yet they did nothing but criticise us over the war.'

'Mr President, there is something vital to consider here,' the Interior Minister interjected. 'The Russian people have not forgotten the loss of thousands of brave sons, brothers and fathers in the battle against the Chechens. If we release these prisoners, there would be public outrage. Our people would see the war as having been fought for nothing. I fear they would demand your immediate resignation.'

Kuzmin fell silent. Morosely, he picked up the FSB intelligence brief. 'An hour ago I read the latest reports from the FSB, and I'm afraid it's more bad news, along with the SVR's most recent intelligence. According to our agents in Afghanistan, Abu Hasim has established a number of new cells in central Asia and the

Caucasus. It seems their main objective is to mount spectacular terrorist strikes against the Federation. Furthermore, it's feared an alarming number of new Chechen terror cells have been organised in Moscow. The FSB believes that suicide bombing attacks are planned on civilian targets.'

The head of the SVR, Russia's foreign intelligence service, Misha Androsov, nodded. 'I have also seen the report just this afternoon, Mr President. What worries me is that now their friend Abu Hasim has the formula, the Chechens may not use just simple explosives but our own nerve gas. These Islamics didn't hesitate to use the gas to murder the kidnapped Americans. Their Chechen comrades would have even less hesitation using it against our troops and cities.'

Kuzmin's face twitched with outrage. 'The report also contained a reference to Nikolai Gorev, the man known as the Cobra, whom we suspect of killing Boris Novikov and stealing the formula. It's rumoured by one of our Chechen agents that Gorev travelled to Afghanistan six months ago in the company of Mohamed Rashid, one of al-Qaeda's top henchmen. The alliance of these two men has also been corroborated by our intelligence sources in Chechnya. It leads me to wonder if both of them aren't somehow directly involved in this monstrous threat in Washington.'

'What does the American President intend to do? Has he reached any decisions?'

'I asked him the same question,' Kuzmin told the Interior Minister. 'He intends pulling out fifteen per cent of his Gulf forces immediately.'

'The American President is an imbecile. He's already giving in to blackmail.'

'Or buying time, Anatoli. We'd probably do the same if we were in his shoes. But ultimately I fear he will have to agree to Abu Hasim's demands. The position he's in, military force is not a realistic option. The President himself made that clear.' Kuzmin looked across the table at General Butov. 'General, you have remained noticeably silent. What are your feelings?'

Yuri Butov was one of Kuzmin's most senior army commanders. At sixty-three he was a veteran of the wars in Afghanistan and Chechnya, and a much-decorated military legend. An impressive figure, well over six feet tall, with watery blue eyes and a mane of white hair, he carried himself bolt upright. His only son had been killed in the battle for Grozny, a loss that had aged the general at least ten years.

'I'm afraid feelings have nothing to do with it, Mr President, only facts. Abu Hasim stole from us the formula for a weapon of mass destruction. Let us be frank here. He may just as well have taken one of our nuclear warheads.'

'But getting the formula back will achieve nothing,' Kuzmin argued.

'That's not the point, Mr President. Rather, do we stand back and allow his criminal act against our country to go unpunished? Three months ago we didn't even know if our formula had been stolen, or who might have been behind its theft. Now we know, and have identified the guilty parties. I would suggest the time has come to administer the severest punishment. Having fought two wars against these Islamics, I've learned to my cost that they are capable of anything, madmen who think nothing of sacrificing their lives for their cause. How do you face that kind of fanatical sacrifice in an enemy, except by crushing him totally? The Interior Minister is right. The gas could be used as an ultimatum. Either we pull our armies out of the Muslim provinces, or they will use our own weapon against us, killing tens of thousands of our troops or wiping out our cities.'

Butov paused. 'A fundamental issue is at stake here. In 1979, the Soviet Union invaded Afghanistan to crush an Islamic rebellion, led by the same Abu Hasim and his like. We were defeated, and twenty years on there is no Soviet Union. What remains is being threatened by the same mujahidin forces. What began as an untreated wound has become a slowly spreading cancer. Are we to repeat the biggest mistake we made in Afghanistan by not crushing our enemy when we had the chance? Unless we wield the scalpel now, cut out this malignancy once and for all, then be assured that in less than five years, there will be no Russia.'

'What punishment would you suggest?'

'Annihilate them. If the Americans cannot act decisively, then we must. We have much more at stake here. Tens of millions of Muslims living within our borders, the militants among them growing bolder by the day. The only answer is to crush them completely, or face defeat and ruin.'

'In your professional opinion, Yuri, is a surgical strike against Abu Hasim possible? One that could kill him.'

'I believe so. But it would have to be swift and brutal.'

'How brutal?'

'Not a ground attack, because the Afghan terrain is too hostile. And a heavy nuclear strike is out, for obvious reasons. The fallout in neighbouring countries would win us no friends. However, we have powerful conventional bombs and missiles that can destroy with great precision. And low-grade nuclear devices which, if delivered by missile and primed for a ground-level burst, would contain the resulting blast and secondary damage to within perhaps ten square miles. A ten-kiloton warhead, for example, which would be the same size as the bomb dropped on Hiroshima.'

'You're suggesting we drop one these nuclear bombs on Abu Hasim's camp?'

'Anywhere near him would be sufficient, and he'd be vaporised.'

'What about his other camps?'

'Pick the major ones and carpet-bomb them, thick and hard. Use powerful, thousand-pound bombs. Hit the bastards with everything we've got. And I mean *everything*. Turn these camps into wastelands, with not a tree or a rock left standing or a single mujahidin left alive.'

Kuzmin pursed his lips in thought, then addressed Androsov, the head of the SVR. 'Misha, what is our latest intelligence on Abu Hasim? Can we locate him?'

'We keep a close watch on his mujahidin bases with our satellites, like the Americans. But out intelligence is even better, since the bases are nearer our borders. And from the handful of excellent Muslim agents we have in Afghanistan, we know in which of his training camps Abu Hasim has his command centre.'

'But can we be certain he'll be there?'

'One of our best agents is a senior figure in the regime in Kabul. Their intelligence always tries to keep a close watch on Abu Hasim's movements. This agent of ours has access to such information. I can request his urgent help to get us an exact fix on his whereabouts.'

'Could he do that?'

'I'm certain. In the past he's been reliable in the extreme.'

'How soon can we get this information?'

'The agent keeps in touch with a satellite radio transmitter. With luck, I could have news within hours.'

'Then see to it.' The President addressed the others. 'Gentlemen, I'm going to assume for now that we can get a fix on Abu Hasim's whereabouts. Which brings us to some decisions we have to make.'

Kuzmin called a vote. The first was on the question of the prisoners. It resulted in unanimous agreement against their release. The second vote concerned the question of direct military action, and Butov's suggestion: conventional carpet-bombing and the use of a single nuclear weapon. It came to the last two votes. 'Admiral Vodin?'

'I say yes.'

'Interior Minister Sergeyev?'

'Yes,' Sergeyev replied firmly. 'We finish this thing now, before it escalates. Before it tears apart the Federation and destroys Russia.'

Kuzmin counted sixteen votes in favour of Butov's action, and just two against: the Finance Minister, Akulev, and Trade Minister Boris Rudkin. The die was cast. He turned to the general.

'Do it,' he ordered. 'Destroy Abu Hasim.'

20

Five minutes after the Kuntsevo meeting had ended, General Yuri Butov was being driven at high speed by his military chauffeur towards the Moscow ring road. By 2.59 a.m., he had reached his destination, an austere granite building on the north-eastern outskirts of the city.

Taking an elevator five floors below ground level, he strode into the vast underground room that housed a secret command centre for Russian army headquarters. The chamber was thirty metres square, built to withstand the shock of a nuclear blast.

Butov's office was in a corner. The general sat, made an all-important phone call to an internal number, and simply gave the code word 'Storm Rising'. It activated a select group of two dozen high-ranking military officers on call day and night at a moment's notice. All over Moscow, men who were sitting down to meals with families or making love to their wives or girlfriends would hear their phones ringing and a voice at the other end would utter the code word, causing them to cease whatever they were doing at once and report to the command centre immediately.

As they received the calls, Butov was already planning the bare bones of the attack. Russia was still a superpower with a fearsome arsenal of weapons at her disposal. Thousands of nuclear warheads and ballistic missiles, and many hundreds of bomber regiments sited all over the Federation, could be deployed in an instant. Butov summoned his duty officer, who crossed to a large metal safe beneath a console table in the middle of the command room. He removed a large thick envelope marked 'Afghanistan' and brought it to the general.

Once a crisis was raging, Butov knew from experience, there

was little time for forward planning. The safe contained various sets of plans for a military strike against any nation likely to menace the Russian Federation. Inside the envelope were at least a dozen scenarios involving Afghanistan that her armed forces might have to react to. One included a punitive air strike against all of al-Qaeda's major bases in that country, drawn up during the height of the Chechen war, when Russian military intelligence suspected the terrorist leader of supplying arms and men to the rebels.

Butov opened the envelope. It contained mapped locations of al-Qaeda's eight principal camps – over twenty existed, but these eight were by far the most important – and the precise outline of an attack, using eighteen heavy bombers accompanied by fighter escorts. The bombers would strike in two waves, annihilating their targets. The air unit chosen was the 840th heavy bomber regiment in Solcy, outside Volgograd, which was equipped with Tu-160 'Blackjacks' and the Tu-95 'Bear', deadly and effective bombers suitable for long-range strikes. They would be protected on their journey by MiG-29 Fulcrum's from the 14th Fighter Wing based at nearby Zerdevka. Both air units were within three hours' flying time of the targets.

This option, Butov finally decided, would form the basis of the attack, but with necessary modifications, because there were still tactical problems to overcome. Kuzmin had ordered that the eight camps be struck at the same time, to heighten surprise. Also, one of the strike aircraft would have to drop an air-to-surface nuclear missile. The precise details of how to hit all the camps simultaneously would have to be worked out by the Commander of the Russian Air Force and a handful of his senior officers – already on their way to HQ – whom Butov would consult in order to fine-tune the plan, and make whatever alterations were needed. By the time the alerted officers were approaching the command centre, the general had finished scribbling his notes. He had just decided on the broad strokes of the first nuclear strike in over fifty years. One thing remained. A name for the operation.

The strategy was intended to destroy Abu Hasim and his bases.

Hammer them into oblivion. Operation Hammer struck him as entirely appropriate. Butov threw down his pen, satisfied. His phone buzzed. It was the duty officer. 'The Air Force Commander is on his way, sir. He should be here within five minutes.'

'Send him down the moment he appears.'

The Kremlin
4.30 a.m.

Vasily Kuzmin was in his Kremlin office. The telephone buzzed. 'Mr President, Misha Androsov and General Butov are here to see you.'

'Send them in.'

The double oak doors opened. Androsov, the head of the SVR, looked triumphant. 'Mr President, our Kabul agent confirms that Abu Hasim is at his main command post, forty miles south-west of Kandahar, and hasn't moved from there in the last twenty-four hours. We have the exact map co-ordinates.'

For a few seconds, Kuzmin hesitated. The arguments had been made, the vote agreed upon, but he was acutely on edge, and posed the question as if to reassure himself. 'You feel confident his information is correct?'

'I'd put my last rouble on it. I trust him implicitly.'

'General Butov?'

'Mr President, the attack is ready to proceed.'

Solcy, Russia
4.35 a.m.

Twenty miles south of the city of Volgograd, formerly Stalingrad, on a flat plain near the town of Solcy, are the headquarters of the 840th Heavy Bomber Regiment, one of over seven hundred military airbases scattered across the Russian Federation.

Three siren blasts roused the two teams of eighteen technician crew members on duty from their bunks. They raced along illuminated underground tunnels to their destination: the vaults that housed the nuclear armoury, for Solcy is one of two dozen bases where Russia's nuclear arsenal is stored. From one of the vaults the first of the three teams, overseen by an officer, carefully removed a silver ball the size of a small melon from its airless container and placed it on a specially made trolley. The ball was a plutonium core, one of many stored in the catacombs beneath the airbase. No sooner had it been placed on the trolley than the second team moved in, fitting the high-explosive cladding jacket that would detonate the core. Their job completed, the third team adjusted the bomb's pressure setting on their officer's instructions, fixing it for a ground-level burst to minimise its destructive radius and then wheeling it to the loading elevator twenty yards away, for delivery to the specially adapted warhead of a KH-102 missile.

At the same time, on the other side of the base in another underground tunnel, a dozen bomber-support crews were busily preparing over three hundred conventional thousand-pound bombs and missiles destined for the remaining aircraft chosen for the mission. The same three sharp siren blasts that had galvanised the technicians and support teams had alerted the crews of Russian air force pilots as they relaxed watching TV in their mess. Grabbing their helmets, they raced to a pre-assigned briefing room down the hall, where a wing commander was already waiting to give them their briefing.

It was short, and covered in exact detail the attack's planned route, the frequencies to be used, the security codes, and the co-ordinated strategy that would ensure that the mission was carried out with absolute precision. Even as the briefing proceeded, the underbellies of eighteen Tu-95 Bears and Tu-160 Blackjacks parked outside their hangars were being fitted with their cargo of thousand-pound bombs and missiles, all except one Tu-95 Bear: this was loaded with the single KH-102 nuclear missile meant to destroy Abu Hasim's lair.

Assigned to command this aircraft was Colonel Vadim Sukov. At thirty-seven, he was a veteran air force bomber pilot with over sixteen years' service who had flown in air campaigns in Afghanistan and Chechnya. So highly trained was Sukov to carry out his orders without question that it was only after the briefing was over and he was being driven in a covered truck to his aircraft, along with his flight crew, that the full and frightening realisation of what he was about to do hit him. This wasn't an exercise. He was actually going to fire a live thermonuclear missile on a mujahidin base in Afghanistan.

Three minutes later a grim-looking Sukov, strapped into his seat and having completed his pre-flight check, taxied to the runway threshold, the other aircraft lining up behind him. Cleared for take-off, Sukov released his brakes and applied power. The Tu-95 trundled down the lit runway, picking up speed, reaching the critical moment at which he pulled back gently on the stick and the heavy Bear rose into the night air. Sukov made a right turn on to a south-easterly course, heading towards his first marker, a beacon outside Astrakhan, on the Caspian Sea. On his port and starboard sides a pair of MiG Fulcrum escorts had already taken up their escort positions. Fifteen minutes later, at 05.11, he crossed the Astrakhan beacon. Sukov checked his Flight Management Computer for an estimate of when he would reach his target.

It calculated ninety-eight minutes exactly.

Moscow
5.12 a.m.

Boris Rudkin was in a state of shock. Lying in bed beside his wife in their apartment on Kempinsky Boulevard, the Trade Minister tossed and turned, unable to sleep. The phone call twenty minutes ago from the Kremlin had informed him that Operation Hammer was under way.

Rudkin's nerves were frayed. A nuclear bomb was about to be dropped on Afghanistan, a neutral country, and he had been one of only two Council members to oppose the attack. It both amazed and perturbed him, and said much about Kuzmin's aggressive style of government, his raging desire to make Russia once again a formidable world power.

But what if Kuzmin unleashed a holocaust by this action in

Afghanistan? What if Islamic terrorists, in retaliation, made it their business to destroy Moscow? If they could procure the formula for the nerve gas, it wasn't beyond the bounds of possibility. All it took was a handful of determined fanatics driven by an overwhelming desire for revenge. The prospect terrified Rudkin. He had three grown children, five adorable grandchildren. To think of them being gassed appalled him, and he was beside himself with dread. Finally, he sat bolt upright in bed. His wife snorted, roused from her sleep.

'Boris, in God's name, what's wrong?'

'Are there any cigarettes in the house?'

'Why should there be? You gave them up years ago.'

'Well, I need to take them up again.' Climbing out of bed, Rudkin dragged on his clothes.

'Boris! Where are you going?'

'To buy a pack of cigarettes.'

The Amoco filling station was open twenty-four hours. A couple of Moscow taxi-drivers were filling up at the forecourt pumps, but other than that the place was deserted. It was snowing, and Rudkin wore a heavy winter overcoat, his face muffled by a thick woollen scarf, so no one would recognise him. He bought a pack of Marlboro Lights from a pimply youth serving behind the hatch and climbed back into his car. His state driver and Mercedes were on call when needed, but Rudkin had used his own Volvo estate. He'd left his apartment by the back entrance and walked to the private underground carpark at the rear, so that the two ministerial bodyguards stationed outside his home wouldn't see him drive away.

Leaving the Amoco station, Rudkin drove for five minutes and pulled up outside Gorky Park. His hand trembled as he lit a Marlboro. He inhaled deeply, and immediately stubbed it out again, repelled by the taste. *Disgusting.*

After five years of doing without, why the hell had he bothered buying a pack? But he knew it was nerves. Rudkin was torn by indecision. His heart beat rapidly. He knew what he had to do, but had he the guts to do it? The phone booth was a couple of yards away. The night-light was out, broken or vandalised. Rudkin climbed out of the Volvo, stepped inside, and was greeted by an overpowering stench of urine. Some drunken bastard had pissed on the floor. He wiped the receiver with his sleeve and took a coin from his trouser pocket. As his hand lingered over the slot, he felt his legs shake. He withdrew his hand, began to turn away.

For God's sake, where's your courage? Rudkin reprimanded himself. He turned back, inserted the coin and punched the numbers.

Washington, DC
9.51 p.m.

'The caller rang the American ambassador's residence in Moscow.'

The Defence Secretary faced the President in the Oval Office. 'He said the bombers took off less than two hours ago, sir. Kuzmin's ordered eight of al-Qaeda's principal camps to be bombed into oblivion, including Abu Hasim's command post outside Kandahar.'

'Who gave us the information?'

'The caller didn't offer his name. But it had to be someone high up in Kuzmin's government. He knew about the decision to carry out the attack, and that Hasim had the nerve gas formula stolen in Moscow three months ago.'

'He gave no other details about the theft?'

'No, sir. But he suggested if we wanted proof of the attack we should try and monitor the aircraft using radar and satellites. I asked General Horton's help in doing just that.'

'And?' The President stared at the general, who accompanied the Defence Secretary.

'Eighteen heavy bomber aircraft took off from a Russian airbase at Solcy over an hour ago, Mr President,' the general answered. 'Our radar installations in Turkey and one of our AWACs picked them up. They were vectored heading south-east, on a direct course for Afghanistan. According to the Moscow caller, one of the bombers has an air-to-surface missle on board with a ten-kiloton nuclear warhead, to target Hasim's Kandahar command post. The rest are carrying conventional thousand-pound bombs and missiles. They're going to wipe the camps off the map.'

The President stood, dumbstruck. Placing one arm against the nearest wall, gazing out blankly towards the darkened lawns, he rested his forehead against his arm, as if he were going to throw up. When he finally spoke, his voice was hoarse with alarm. 'My God, Kuzmin must be *insane*. Doesn't he realise that an action like this may destroy Washington?'

'It seems to me he's made a choice between Washington and Russia's survival. Kuzmin probably thinks his oil and gas fields will be under threat next. I'd have to agree that it's a likely assumption. Kuzmin's obviously decided that a massive pre-emptive strike to destroy the enemy will prevent that from happening.'

'That doesn't allow the sonofabitch to condemn this city to death. Because that's exactly what he's doing.' The President turned to address Horton. 'General, how soon could our air force strike units in the Gulf intercept the Russian craft?'

'Even if they scrambled right now, our fighters wouldn't have enough time, sir. We estimate the Russians will reach their targets within forty minutes, maybe even sooner.'

'Could we shoot them down with long-range missiles from our Gulf destroyers?'

'Sir, there's no absolutely no guarantee that would work. We might not manage to take out all the aircraft. Some might still reach their targets. And our action could be tantamount to declaring war on Russia.'

'General, I'm not going to allow Kuzmin to trigger the destruction of this city. Alert whatever attack aircraft we've got nearest to the Russian bombers. Have them try to head for an intercept. And have our Gulf destroyers standing by for my further instructions.'

'Yes, Mr President.'

'I'm going to try and talk with Kuzmin.' The President reached for his telephone. 'John, I want everyone back in the conference room in case this thing turns ugly.'

Moscow
5.59 a.m.

The phone buzzed on Vasily Kuzmin's desk. Beside him lay a supper tray: hot vegetable soup and a pot of fresh coffee, but he had barely touched either, his stomach gripped by a knot of tension. The call from the White House surprised him, and he was instantly wary.

He spoke reasonable English and had no problem understanding the US President, nor the blunt tone, glacial as a Baltic wind.

'President Kuzmin, it has come to my attention that Russian bombers are on their way to attack Abu Hasim's bases in Afghanistan. My information is that the aircraft will reach their targets within the next thirty-five minutes. I cannot emphasise strongly enough that this would be the gravest act, a foolhardy enterprise that would jeopardise beyond repair the relationship between our two countries.'

Kuzmin was silent. How could the Americans have known? Had their radar picked up the aircraft? 'President Booth, may I ask where you got this information?'

'With respect, that isn't important. What *is* important is that you call off this attack *at once*. It will come to no good for both of our countries. Surely you must realise this?'

Kuzmin was irked. The American President sounded like a schoolmaster reprimanding an errant schoolboy. 'Mr President, I think it is *you* who must realise something. I can now inform you that an investigation by the FSB has revealed that the formula for a deadly nerve gas – code-named Substance A232X – was stolen from Russia. The culprits who carried out this grave criminal act are obviously these same fanatics who now threaten Washington. The same people who past experience has taught me want to destabilise and wreck the Russian Federation . . .'

'Mr Kuzmin, what's important right now is calling off the attack . . .'

'Let me finish, please. If Abu Hasim has his way and ejects US forces from the Gulf, we both know the entire Middle East will be swamped by a tidal wave of Islamic revolution. For Russia, this would be a catastrophe. In our central Asian regions are tens of millions of followers of the Prophet Mohammad. My country would be unable to prevent such an immense revolution from flooding across its borders. Russia would be terrorised, ripped apart. This I cannot and will not allow to happen. My country has a right to strike back at those who threaten its destruction. And please, don't tell me you would not do the same if the US found itself in our position.'

Kuzmin heard the deep sigh at the other end of the line before the American President replied. 'I'm not denying your right to punish al-Qaeda for this theft, Mr Kuzmin. I'm not denying that force may ultimately have to be used to preserve the unity of your country. But now is not the time for either punishment or force.'

'I totally disagree. To delay means only one thing – defeat. A decisive strike now will show these terrorists that their criminal actions will not succeed, or be tolerated.'

Kuzmin heard another sigh, even more exasperated. 'Mr Kuzmin, am I to understand that you will *not* call off this attack?'

'You understand correctly, Mr President.'

A long pause followed, and Kuzmin wondered whether the connection had been lost. Then President Booth's voice came back, cold and deliberate. 'Mr Kuzmin, I want you to be very clear about the consequences of your action, so let me be blunt. Like you, I have a duty to do my utmost to protect the citizens of my country from harm. To use extreme force, if necessary. Therefore, I must tell you that, as we speak, US fighter aircraft are on their way to intercept your air armada. Reluctantly, I have given instructions that they are to shoot down every last one of your aircraft the second they are within range.'

Kuzmin barely contained his fury. 'That would be a grave mistake. A blatant act of war. One that would bring swift retaliation, I can assure you!'

'Just as I can assure you that any retaliation you make will be met with an even greater force. US naval carriers in the Gulf armed with nuclear missiles are on stand-by at this very moment, ready to reply to any reprisal you may make.' The American President let the threat hang, allowing a pause before he carried on. 'Mr Kuzmin, we can crank this up as high as we want. But before this escalates into something both of us regret, I'd suggest you call off these bombers.'

Kuzmin fell silent. Were the Americans bluffing? Would they shoot down Russian aircraft? Were they rattling their missiles just as Reagan and Kennedy had done in the past? Kuzmin stared at the clock on his desk: 6.32. In less than nine minutes the bombers would be shedding their deadly loads. There was no time to reconvene his Council. Any decision to call off the attack would be his, and his alone. Beads of sweat glistened on his brow. He looked at the photographs of himself on the turret of the T-80 tank, and in the SU cockpit. He had forged his political image as a man who would never allow the further dissolution of Russia's power. A man of steel who would deal swift, harsh retribution to any enemy who threatened her sovereignty.

'You must be aware, Mr President,' Kuzmin said firmly, 'that the greatest danger facing Russia is from the forces of Islam. I cannot allow the day to come when al-Qaeda's terrorists will hold a gun to our heads, as they've done to you. Understand, therefore, that I cannot do as you ask. If I do not finish this now, then Russia is finished.'

'Mr Kuzmin, I don't know how much time exactly we have left . . .'

'You will *never* defeat these fanatics by giving in to them. My experience in Chechnya has taught me that. The only way is to crush them completely.'

'I'm well aware of your experience in Chechnya. But there are over half a million innocent citizens in Washington. Many of them may lose their lives if you call Hasim's bluff. That is something the American people would not tolerate. They would demand of me the harshest military retribution against your country. And I do mean the *harshest*, Mr Kuzmin. Because once those bombs of yours fall, and if Hasim carries out his promise and devastates Washington, then I, or whoever succeeds me if I die in the attack, shall hold you personally responsible. Is that what you want? To risk a war between our two countries? To risk the lives of millions of innocent people? And all because of some madman who threatens us *both*?'

Kuzmin loosened his shirt collar. The pressure was on him now. 'I am not attacking America. I am attacking terrorists who stole a weapon of mass destruction from Russia. A crime that cannot be allowed to go unpunished.'

'But Americans may very well die because of your action. And don't forget what's important here. We're *both* facing the same enemy. But we're not fighting him *together*. Instead, we're fighting each other. Don't you see? That's what Abu Hasim would want. To drive a wedge between us. And so far he's succeeded.'

Kuzmin remained steadfast. 'Because *you* have allowed him to succeed. Because *you* are prepared to withdraw fifteen per cent of your Gulf forces. You have given in to him already. How long can it be before you surrender completely?'

'My order of withdrawal was given for a good reason. To assure Hasim I took his threat seriously. But there are six days remaining, Mr Kuzmin. A lot can happen in six days. We may succeed in finding this device and foiling the attack. If we don't, and Hasim wins his game, then I make you this personal promise: I'll stand back while you bomb every one of his bases. Pummel them to dust for all I care. I'll probably even cheer you from the sidelines. But you must call off this attack *now*.'

Kuzmin felt cold sweat on his face. Beyond the Kremlin's north wall was the tomb of the unknown soldier. For him, it symbolised the sacrifice made to defend his country from enemy aggression. If he called off the bombers, how many more Russian soldiers would he condemn to die in the mountains of the Caucasus and central Asia, defending their country against the sword of Islam? Better to finish it here and now. But everything had depended on speed, on annihilating Hasim's camps and explaining why afterwards.

He could even have claimed that a nuclear weapon had been stolen by the Islamics, giving added weight to his reasoning for a pre-emptive bombing. He could have claimed anything *after* the event, and made it plausible. But he couldn't do that now.

'Like you, I have a family,' the American President went on. 'Right now, I'm looking at their photograph on my desk. Of my wife and son and daughters. I know they may well die because of your action. Look on your own desk. Look at the photographs of your family. Imagine how you would feel if they were about to die. You can have your justice, Mr Kuzmin. You can have every damned thing you want if you just wait.'

Kuzmin looked at the framed snapshot of his wife and daughters on his desk. How typical of the Americans to appeal to the heart, not the head. He massaged his temple with the fingers of his right hand. There was agony in that simple gesture, an agony he found impossible to shake off. The final decision had to be made. His desk clock read 6.40. Was it already too late? 'If I were to agree, there would be a precondition . . .'

'Name it. But for God's sake call off the attack *now*.'

Afghanistan

In the warm glow of the Tu-95 cockpit, forty thousand feet above Kandahar province, Colonel Vadim Sukov once again checked his bearings, scanned his instruments. In less than four minutes, he would release the KH-120 missile, and it would rapidly home in on its target co-ordinates twenty miles away. 'Arm cargo,' Sukov ordered, and pulled back on the throttles, reducing his speed.

'Cargo armed, sir,' came the almost immediate response from the bomb bay.

Sukov tensed. The ten-kiloton missile was now 'live', ready for delivery. Even at forty-thousand feet and twenty miles from the blast the crews would see the flash of the nuclear explosion, and the intensity could blind an observer. Special goggles would protect the crew's eyes. He slipped his pair on, relayed the instruction to his crew, then contacted his MiG escorts, their dark forms floating on his port and starboard sides, and ordered them to do likewise. A minute later, the other Blackjacks and Bears and their escorts peeled away to prepare for their bombing runs on their own designated targets. Sukov could pick them out as blips on his radar screen. '*Three minutes to missile release.*'

At 250 knots Sukov was rapidly approaching his objective. He positioned the throttles to near idle, his speed bled off, and he gave the command, 'Open bomb doors.'

Seconds later the bomb doors in the aircraft's belly whirred open and the Bear buffeted with the increased drag. '*Two minutes to missile release.*'

'Sir – sir, there's a call coming through.'

Sukov was distracted by the radio operator's voice in his earphones. 'From who, damn it?'

'Moscow command. *Endgame! Endgame!*'

'Disarm cargo! Disarm cargo at once!' Sukov screamed into his microphone, pulling back on the throttles, banking left. The aircraft began to turn, drifting away from the target. 'Cargo disarmed, sir,' the co-pilot called out.

Sukov wiped a glaze of sweat from his face and exhaled with relief. For whatever reasons, Operation Hammer had been stood down.

PART FOUR

11 November – 12 November

'The devastation of Washington will be total.'

21

Washington, DC
11 November
11.15 p.m.

In the United States, twenty-three hours had passed since al-Qaeda's threat had been delivered to the nation's capital. Darkness had fallen at just before 5.20 p.m. in Washington, and by 11 p.m., unaware of the charged telephone conversation between Vasily Kuzmin and the President of America, the FBI and the CIA, at their headquarters in Langley, Virginia, twenty miles away, were busy issuing secret orders to their station chiefs around the world to make a relentless effort to discover how Abu Hasim had acquired the nerve gas, how he might have constructed his device, and who among his supporters might be behind the effort to conceal it in Washington.

Sixteen miles away, at Fort Meade, Maryland, home to over thirty thousand employees of the National Security Agency, the same job was being done electronically. Using satellites and terrestrial communications stations covering every point of the globe, operating twenty-four hours of every day, and with 18 acres of computers underground, the NSA snatched millions of land-line and cellphone calls from the air and scoured transmitted e-mails, all in the sometimes questionable interests of America's security.

Be it a Chinese factory manager in Beijing making a private call to one of his customers, or an unsuspecting Italian politician enjoying an intimate phone conversation with his mistress in Rome, none was safe from the Agency's potent eavesdropping equipment. Stored on massive, powerful computers, the calls and e-mails were electronically filtered for certain programmed 'key' words that might identify them as worthy of investigation, before being sifted through and scrutinised by the Agency's analysts and cryptologists. Since noon that same day, months' worth of data stored on thousands of computer disks was being scrutinised yet again by the NSA, in the hope that it might throw up even the slenderest clue.

At Andrews Air Force Base outside Washington, extra nerve-gas 'sniffer' units – electronic devices that could detect the presence of a limited number of nerve agents and their component chemicals – were being flown in from specialist army chemical units around the country, along with army chemical weapons teams trained to use them. Over thirty all-weather helicopters equipped with night-vision cameras were already on their way to the capital, 'borrowed' from police forces in surrounding states, to bolster the FBI's own helicopter fleet. Once they arrived in Washington, their decals would be temporarily removed, and the fleet scattered to at least a dozen pre-selected landing strips, both public and military, so as not to arouse suspicion.

With such a massive search under way, every available FBI agent had been recalled for duty. Like most, Jack Collins always carried a pager and cellphone wherever he went. But that morning, when he met Nikki before the trip out to Chesapeake and the cemetery, he'd made a conscious decision to leave both at home. For at least one day in the year, he'd told himself, he was owed the luxury of forgetting about the Bureau. But when Nikki had driven him back to his apartment after dinner at her mother's he found a half-dozen calls on his answering machine, four more on his cellphone, and the same number on his pager. All were from Tom Murphy. He dialled Murphy's cellphone. It was answered on the first ring. 'Tom, it's Jack Collins.'

Murphy sighed. 'Jack, I've been trying to get you all day. Where the hell have you been? I need you here straight away.'

'What's up?'

'We'll talk in my office, Jack.'

Murphy didn't elaborate, but Collins could sense the urgency in his boss's tone, and wondered whether it had anything to do with the Union Station incident. He glanced over at Nikki, busily making coffee in the kitchen. She'd put Daniel to bed at her mom's, and they'd intended to spend the rest of the evening relaxing together, watching TV. 'I'm on my way. See you soon.'

When he told Nikki, he saw her disappointment. 'Is it an emergency?'

Collins tried to make light of it. 'It's probably nothing important, Nikki. Somebody at headquarters in a funk over nothing. But you know how it is. I've got to be there.'

'You want me to stay until you get back?'

'I may be a while. I don't want you waiting up half the night.'

After the visit to the cemetery that afternoon, Collins knew that Nikki had made an effort to be extra attentive. Even after their talk at Chesapeake she hadn't let her own disappointment show, and at her mom's her cheerfulness had been as evident as ever. Her unselfishness made him feel guilty. 'I'm really sorry about tonight, Nikki.'

'Hey, it's not a problem. You go do what you have to do.' He could still sense her disappointment, even though she was smiling. 'But call me at home later, OK?'

'Sure. I promise.' Collins kissed her. The kiss threatened to become an embrace. She winked up at him and smiled. 'Hey, I thought you had work to do. Come on, I'll walk you out to the car.'

In the West Wing, Paul Burton sat alone in a leather easy chair, overlooking the darkened White House lawns. He held a can of Pepsi in his hand, bought from the cold-drinks dispenser in the basement. The lights were off, except for the reading lamp on one of the side tables, and he gazed out blankly at the shadowed gardens. Accorded a rare few moments of quiet solitude, Burton was immersed in his thoughts. To many outsiders, it seemed that the White House was a dizzying place to work. Some of the brightest and best college graduates in America queued up to be staffers or interns, eager to forge a name for themselves in the most electrifying political capital on God's earth. Lured by Washington's glitz and power, they never really thought of the harsh demands their careers might ask of them. Long hours of hard work, weekends when you never got to see your family or friends; even the rare evenings you spent at home were likely to be interrupted by an abrupt summons to the White House to help deal with some kind of emergency. A Stanford graduate and former Marine officer, Burton had expected no less when he joined the President's staff as his Assistant for National Security Affairs. But of late, it seemed that he was living his life in the damned White House.

He hadn't seen his family since Friday. His wife Sally and their two young sons, Ben and Nathan, aged five and seven, had gone to her parents' home in Connecticut for a long weekend, and after the first Security Council meeting that morning he'd phoned and left a message on Sally's cellphone, telling her he was caught up in work and he'd contact her when he could. An established code for Sally not to phone him unless it was vitally urgent, and that he didn't know when he'd be home.

Burton sighed listlessly. He adored his sons. He'd discovered the joys of fatherhood for the first time relatively late in life at thirty-eight. There was innocent pleasure to be had from parenting that he'd never dreamed of. Sometimes, at weekends, he'd sleep with the boys in their room, telling them stories in the darkness, the storybook variety or the ones from his own childhood that they always wanted to hear. The Sunday before last, on his one day off, he'd spent most of the afternoon with Ben, who had dressed up in his Batman suit and insisted on his father playing Robin and wearing an old green curtain as a cape. They had charged around the garden for over an hour, Burton joining in his son's make-believe that they were Gotham City's dynamic duo battling against the forces of evil, until little Ben was exhausted, they flaked out under a tree, and Ben said, deadpan and breathless, 'It's hard work fighting baddies, isn't it, Dad?'

Burton recalled the innocent truism with a wry, fleeting smile. His years of bachelorhood had been fun, but the honest truth of it was that they paled by comparison to the love and pleasure he got from his children. And right now, that same love was causing him much anxiety.

His home was in Georgetown, barely two miles away. His boys attended school there. If Hasim's nerve gas were dispersed by design or accident, the lives of Sally and their sons would be in immediate danger. When he'd called her that morning he had desperately wanted to tell his wife to remain in Connecticut, but he remembered the President's admonition: no one moves their families out of DC, and no one gives the slightest hint that the city is under siege.

The door opened and the President came in. Burton hid his anxiety and moved to stand.

'Stay where you are, Paul.'

Strain lines creased the President's mouth as he sank into an easy chair. His energy seemed zapped.

'You spoke with Kuzmin again, sir?'

The President sighed, ran a hand over his face. Minutes after Kuzmin had stood down his bombers, both men had resumed their conversation in less charged circumstances, but not without hostility. 'I told the sonofabitch he almost gave me a heart attack. Told him again that had those bombs gone off there's no telling where it might have led. That his action was reckless in the extreme.'

'What did Kuzmin say?'

'There was no apology, if that's what you mean. No regret. And he made a precondition. If we don't neutralise the threat before the deadline's up, and have to withdraw from the Gulf, he says he retains the right to strike against Hasim, bomb al-Qaeda's bases to dust if need be. The same applies if in the meantime Hasim makes a direct threat against Russia. Kuzmin says there's absolutely no way he can allow Hasim's position of power to bring about the destruction of the Federation. And his country's prepared to suffer the consequences of any action Hasim might take, or that we might take against Russia in retaliation. Even if it means all-out war, he'll destroy Hasim and his networks.' The President ran his hand over his face again. 'The whole thing's a damned nightmare.'

'So we've got to find and neutralise the device within the time we've got left?'

'That's about the long and the short of it.'

'What about the nerve gas, sir?'

'Three months ago a former senior FSB officer turned businessman was murdered at his home in Moscow. His killer wasn't apprehended and there was no apparent motive. But then it turns out the victim had a copy of the nerve-gas formula in his safe – a research company he ran was involved in the production. It seems the formula was somehow copied by his killer.'

'Do they know who the culprit is?'

'Some guy named Nikolai Gorev, half Russian, half Chechen. Kuzmin's agreed to send us a translated copy of his file within the hour. Apparently he's been a thorn in Moscow's side for some time. A wanted Chechen terrorist who's got a grudge against Russia.'

'Why's that, sir?'

'He's totally deranged, according to Kuzmin. The kind of man who wants to spread chaos and anarchy, just for the hell of it. Not that I expected anything less from someone who'd help to hold a city of over half a million people hostage.'

'What's the connection to Hasim?'

'Through another terrorist named Mohamed Rashid, one of al-Qaeda's finest. I seem to recall his name appearing on CIA and FBI intelligence reports. Rashid's a bloodthirsty lunatic, an Islamic fanatic who's been implicated in the bombings of our embassies in Nairobi and Tanzania, and the attack on the *Cole*. Kuzmin says the man's also been involved in supplying arms and equipment to the Chechen rebels on al-Qaeda's behalf. And Russian intelligence says that Rashid and this guy Gorev travelled together to Afghanistan six months ago. He also seems to think it's possible they might be involved in Washington in some way. They've both got enough skill to carry out a mission of this sort. But we'll have to wait to see Kuzmin's full report, because right now I'm as wise as you are. But at least we've got a lead. That's something.'

'Why didn't Kuzmin make a public statement before now? Or inform the Western intelligence agencies privately? A theft of that kind is a serious international incident.'

'I asked the same question. Told the sonofabitch he owed it to us to let us know. I strongly pointed out that the very fact Russia had even formulated such a weapon broke the International Chemical Weapons Treaty. Kuzmin denies that, and said the gas already existed months before Russia became party to the treaty, and was kept top secret, but my guess is that's total bullshit. And he didn't explain what the murdered ex-officer was doing with the formula in his safe. He also says his intelligence people have been hard at work trying to crack the case, but they only learned in the last twenty-four hours that Gorev was involved, and were about to inform us. It's a lame excuse. But you know how secretive the Russians are. My guess is they didn't want us knowing about their nerve gas or the fact they had broken the treaty, and hoped they could hunt down those responsible and recover the formula before word got out.'

'But this guy Gorev may not even be behind the threat to Washington.'

'You're right. But as of now he's the only lead we've got, so for that we have to be grateful. Kuzmin made another demand. If Gorev's in Washington, he wants every effort made to apprehend him. And if he's exterminated in the process, so much the better.'

'Why, sir?'

'God knows. But it's a small price to pay if it helps save this city. One more thing. Kuzmin insisted on sending us one of his top intelligence people to help with the investigation and make sure we keep our end of the bargain. He'll be arriving in Washington in the morning. Apparently he's familiar with Gorev, can identify him if need be.'

'You think the FBI will see it as an intrusion?'

'In this instance, I doubt it. They'll take whatever help they can get. But we'll need to inform Doug Stevens about this straight away, so the Bureau will know what's happening.'

The President stood, glanced at his desk clock. ‘Shouldn’t our psychologists be here by now?’

‘They’re expected by 5 a.m. at the latest, sir. We’re having to fly two of them in from the west coast.’

‘I’ve asked Kuzmin for data on this A232X – that’s the codename for the gas – so projections can be made of possible damage to the District’s population if the device goes off. He assures me he’ll have one of Russia’s best chemical warfare scientists on a plane here with the information within the next twelve hours. Then our experts can immediately go to work on the figures.’

‘What about an antidote?’

The President was grim. ‘According to Kuzmin, there isn’t one.’

22

Moscow
12 November
7.20 a.m.

The Lada sedan carrying Major Alexei Kursk pulled up outside the private residence in the Ramenka district.

'Please wait here,' Kursk told the driver, and went up the walkway to the entrance, where a couple of armed militiamen stood guard either side of the front door. Kursk showed his ID, one of the militiamen rang the doorbell, and the major found himself being escorted into Igor Verbatin's wood-panelled study. The head of the FSB was standing by a coal fire, wearing a silk dressing gown, reading through a red-covered file. He turned as Kursk was led in. 'You may leave us, Georgi. Thank you.'

The bodyguard withdrew, shutting the door. 'Major Kursk, it was good of you to come so promptly, despite the hour. Take a seat. Can I offer you tea, coffee?'

Kursk sat in the nearest chair. 'No, thank you, sir.'

'No doubt you're wondering why I asked you here at such an early hour.'

'Yes, sir.' Kursk had been woken by the call at 6.50 a.m. Barely awake, but vigilant enough to be suspicious of his urgent summons to Verbatin's residence, he'd dressed and waited for the official car to arrive ten minutes later. Verbatin came to sit behind his study desk, made a steeple of his fingers, touched them to his lips. His voice softened almost to a whisper, hoarse with sudden anxiety. 'I'm afraid, Kursk, there's been another twist in the Novikov saga. And a very disturbing development at that.'

'Sir?'

'The formula we suspected of being stolen has been put to use. No doubt you're familiar with the name of Abu Hasim, the al-Qaeda terrorist?'

'Of course.'

In detail, Verbatin outlined the threat to Washington. When he had finished, Kursk was stunned. 'Hasim's message was delivered approximately twenty-four hours ago,' Verbatin added, rising from his chair. 'Needless to say, this doesn't bode well for Russia.'

'Sir?'

'Think about it, Kursk. Al-Qaeda has interfered in our Muslim regions in the past. The belief is they have designs on causing even more trouble in the future – indeed, Abu Hasim won't be happy until he has created a pan-Islamic superpower of some sort, encompassing all Muslim countries, and will do *anything* to attain his goal. The threat against the Americans is proof enough of that intent. After Washington, it may be Moscow's turn to suffer the same fate. Russia cannot tolerate that kind of intimidation from these mujahidin lunatics – if it is pursued to its logical conclusion, the entire Federation could crumble.'

'May I ask what the Americans intend?'

'To play along with al-Qaeda's demands for now. But obviously they will do their utmost to try to locate the device and hunt down the terrorist cell in their capital. However, with less than seven days, time isn't on their side.'

'Do they have any suspects?'

'Not yet.' Verbatin again picked up the file he was reading, slipped on a pair of glasses. 'But in that regard, we may have been able to help them.'

'Sir?'

'I've been reading through Nikolai Gorev's file again. It says here he speaks fluent English. While I'm not aware of any personal grudge he might harbour against the Americans, when you consider his involvement in the theft, his Chechen links and his non-Arab appearance, it struck me that a man like him might come in very useful to al-Qaeda in carrying out this deranged mission of theirs in Washington.'

Kursk's face darkened. 'You're suggesting Gorev might be in the US?'

'It cannot be discounted. Naturally, we passed the information on to the Americans, and the fact that Gorev was behind the formula's theft.'

'I see.'

Verbatin tapped the file. 'It's certainly not beyond the bounds of possibility that he's there now, playing a role in this monstrous threat. It's just the kind of dramatic plot that would appeal to Gorev's warped mind. Which brings us to why you're here, Kursk. You know the man better than most.' Turning to the world map on the wall, Verbatin tapped his finger on a point slightly inland on the East Coast of the United States. 'Have you ever been to Washington, Major?'

'No, sir.' Kursk shifted in his chair, had the feeling an axe was being sharpened and was about to fall as Verbatin turned back.

'But you speak fluent English. Or so I'm led to believe.'

'Reasonable, more like.'

'That will be sufficient, I'm sure. Since there's passable suspicion that Gorev could be in Washington, it has been decided that you will help the Americans. Aid them in finding these terrorists for the sake of co-operation between our two countries. And for the sake of our own national security.'

Kursk was bewildered. 'On whose orders?'

'President Kuzmin himself.'

'But my investigation here . . .' Kursk protested.

'Is suspended for now. It's imperative this threat be neutralised and the people behind it eliminated. We can't have Russia threatened next. There's another reason I want you in Washington, Major, and it's an important one, but we'll discuss that before you leave. As for Nikolai Gorev, if it turns out he's involved, personally I won't be happy until he's sent back to Russia in a body-bag. The man's a traitor of the highest order. And in this country, treachery is still punishable by death – a firing squad, no less. But a messy state trial would hardly be in our interests. Much better to try to finish this thing off-stage, with a bullet. Do you understand me, Major?'

Kursk balked. 'With respect, Colonel, I'm not a state executioner.'

'But you're a Russian citizen. Don't forget that. To what do you owe your allegiance? Your country and its survival, or this terrorist madman Gorev and the Islamic terrorists he may represent? Before I or the President are inclined to think otherwise, I'd suggest you cast no doubt on your loyalty.'

'How?'

'By helping run Gorev to ground if he's in Washington. Not only that, but finishing the matter once and for all by eliminating him. That's my final word on the matter. You'll be doing your motherland a great service. The man's been a thorn in our side for far too long.' Verbatin tossed the file aside with a flourish. 'Do as you're ordered, Kursk. Do your duty. Go home, pack your suitcase. You'll be on a specially arranged military flight to Washington leaving in just over an hour'.

Washington DC
11 November
3.30 p.m.

Mohamed Rashid stepped into the mosque. The Muslim place of worship was one of the District's oldest mosques, built almost forty years earlier, its gardens and buildings set within a railed enclosure. Small but elegant, with tiny windows, its façade was painted duck-egg blue, and a pair of solid double oak doors led inside.

Removing his shoes, he left them in one of the pigeonholes in the lobby and stepped inside. Like that of all mosques, the interior was completely open, devoid of chairs or benches, and bare of any icons. Rich carpets covered the floor, pillars soared to a gallery that ran around the interior, and quotations from the Koran were inscribed in wooden panels on the walls. It was one of over a dozen mosques that served the spiritual needs of Washington's Muslim community and was usually packed each Friday with devotees from the Arab countries and the far-flung outposts of the former Soviet Union. But it was Sunday, so there were few worshippers, barely twenty men, mostly elderly and white bearded, wearing frayed but spotlessly clean suits or kaftans: Chechens, Tartars, Turkmenis, Azerbaijanis. Gorev was late. Rashid despised the Russian, as much as he despised Karla Sharif. He had told them only what they needed to know. They knew nothing about the Americans kidnapped in Azerbaijan, or even his own true intentions if the US President failed to meet al-Qaeda's demands. The less they knew, the better.

Rashid moved into the mosque, sat cross-legged just inside the door, his back to the wall, holding a set of prayer beads. When he had prostrated himself and said his prayers to Allah and for his brother's soul, he sat up, perfectly still. Looking at the Muslim faces scattered around, and at the familiar quotations from the Koran inscribed on the walls, he felt at home here.

His real name was Saleem Rasham. He was born in Cairo, the eldest son of wealthy, professional parents, his father an eminent archaeologist, his mother a doctor. More fortunate than most, he attended Cairo's élite schools; by the time he was twelve he spoke fluent English and French. When his parents died that same year in a car crash in Luxor, he and his younger brother were raised by a brutal uncle in a squalid home near the Nile's west banks. To escape their uncle's brutality, he would take little Mahmoud and flee to the mosque, and it was there that both their politics were forged. Saleem joined the Islamic Brotherhood at seventeen, Mahmoud three years later. They fought together in Lebanon against the Israelis, and later joined the throngs of young Arab men who flocked to Afghanistan to fight the jihad against the Soviets, where Saleem earned himself a reputation for bravery, strategy and savagery in equal measure.

He was wounded many times, his right shoulder shattered by a Russian bullet. The doctors said he would never be able to use it again. Saleem learned to shoot with his left hand. He learned, too, that the only way to defeat the infidel was by following the path of al-Qaeda. The American missiles that rained down on the camps had killed Mahmoud and a dozen of their comrades. He had wept that day, the first time ever since his parents had died, and the night he buried Mahmoud's shattered body he had sworn his revenge.

He heard a movement behind him, and his hand reached instinctively for the pearl-handled knife in his pocket. He turned, saw Gorev standing there in his stockinged feet, his shoes tucked under one arm. 'You're late,' Rashid said. 'What kept you?'

'The traffic was bad. It took me a while to find my way.'

Rashid grimaced, put away his prayer beads. 'Come, we have work to do.'

Less than a mile from the limits of DC, at the window of a luxury penthouse apartment near tree-lined Wisconsin Avenue, Charles Rivermount took a deep slug from a crystal glass of thirty-year-old bourbon, savoured it, and swallowed. His tie loosened, the bourbon like honey in his throat, he took a pull on his hundred-dollar Panama cigar, blew out a lungful of smoke, and stared out at the darkening capital as if in a trance.

'Honey? Are you OK?'

Rivermount turned, his trance broken. A woman stood at the bedroom door, wearing a short, flimsy nightgown. She was almost half his age, thirty-two, slim and attractive, with short blonde hair. Sue-Beth Allen had been his mistress for two years. He kept the apartment for their use whenever they visited Washington, and they'd flown in on his private Learjet the day before Rivermount got the call to attend the crisis meeting at the White House that morning. He'd already had an important economics policy discussion to attend in the capital the next day, but the President had put it on hold until the crisis was resolved.

'Aren't you coming to bed, Charlie? You need some rest.'

'Sure, Sue-Beth. Just give me a few more minutes. I've got something on my mind.'

Sue-Beth Allen was the best thing that had happened to Rivermount's private life in recent years. They'd met at an oil-stock investment conference in Dallas. She was a secretary for an oil-company executive, bright as hell once you cut through her playful Southern charm – she was from Mississippi like himself – and they'd hit it off straight away. She'd kept him from going crazy in a bitter, joyless marriage, and for the first time in his life he'd experienced unbridled love and affection, and given it freely in return, all of which was why their affair had endured. She came over to join him, ran her fingernails across his back. 'What's the matter, Charlie? What is it that's got you so preoccupied?'

'Business, honey.'

'At the White House?'

Rivermount nodded. 'I've just got to think something through. A problem I can't tell you about. You mind?'

Sue-Beth shook her head. After two years of being the mistress of a vastly rich, dynamic man like Charles Rivermount, she'd learned to live with his frequent need for privacy to sort out his thoughts. 'I'll be waiting for you, you hear?' She kissed his neck, ran her nails down his back, moved back into the bedroom.

Rivermount watched her figure retreat with a pleasure that never seemed to diminish, then turned back to the panoramic window and let out a sigh. Half an hour ago his chauffeured Mercedes S600 had deposited him outside the luxury apartment block. He'd been escorted up to the penthouse by his Secret Service detail; two of them were still in the hall outside, two more in the lobby, another couple in the cars outside. No matter where he went, Rivermount, and Sue-Beth, could no longer count on their privacy.

Standing there, puffing on his fat Panama cigar, he was aware that everything about him suggested power and wealth – from his expensive Morton Brothers suit and tailored silk shirt, the hand-made English leather shoes and the solid gold Rolex watch, to the fleet of four private Learjets at his call twenty-four hours a day. To those who knew him in business – the wise ones at least – his good-old-boy Southern exterior was an act that hid a hard-nosed, crafty streak. At sixty-one, and despite the strain of overseeing branch offices in five American cities and six European capitals, he was still the chairman and sole owner of Rivermount

Arc Investments, one of America's largest and most successful private investment banking corporations.

It was no secret how Charles Rivermount had become wealthy: he did with other people's money what any other investment bank did – he invested in government securities, gilt-edged companies and public stocks and shares, only he did it much more successfully and with a canny eye on the trends and market shifts that can make or break any investment banker. His other success had been his interests in mining and oil and gas exploration, through a separate company, Rivermount Arc Exploration. His business achievements had led to his prestigious appointment as adviser to the President on economic affairs, and for a dirt-poor boy from Greenwood, Mississippi, who'd had to claw his way into business school, he'd done pretty damned well for himself.

He'd paid along the way, of course. A sham marriage, two mild heart attacks, a daughter who'd married a piss-poor trucker, and a thirty-year-old son who was hooked on cocaine. Despite Rivermount spending a small fortune on the best of Betty Ford Clinic treatments, and his tireless efforts to rescue him, the boy was a hopeless case.

Rivermount could admit to himself that he was partly to blame. He'd always been too involved in his business and too determined to succeed to spend much time with his family in the early years. For love, affection and parental effort, he'd substituted material things – cars, money, holidays, the best schools – to make up for his absence, and paid the price. He'd lost his son and daughter a long time ago; they were rebels who despised their father, and at times that deeply pained him. But he was as much a hostage to life as his children were.

Ever since his childhood, when he'd endured the grinding poverty of being one of a family of nine children on his father's hundred-acre dirt farm, he'd swore to himself he'd one day do better for himself. A passion for wealth and power over his own destiny had always driven him – as they still drove him at sixty-one, and he couldn't get away from that. *We are what we are.* You either accepted that, and did your best with it, or agonised about your role in life and drove yourself nuts.

Rivermount had long ago accepted himself for what he was: power hungry, driven by wealth and success. He still had scruples and values, issues that were important to him personally, but he could honestly admit that, more than anything, he wanted to be the richest, most powerful man in America. The deal he had going right now – if it panned out – would help him attain that goal, and so long as the nerve-gas crisis didn't take a wrong turn.

He looked at his watch. He could be recalled to the White House at any moment, and knew he ought to get some sleep while he could. He crushed out his cigar, flicked off the lights and went into the bedroom. Sue-Beth lay under the sheets in the darkness. He undressed, slid in beside her, and felt her warm, young body turn into his. 'I want you to do something for me, honey.'

'Sure, Charlie,' she said sleepily.

'This morning, before noon, I want you to pack your bags and fly down to Grand Cayman and wait for me there.' Rivermount kept a palatial fifteen-bedroom villa on the island, and his forty-million-dollar yacht, *Spirit of Mississippi*, was berthed there. He had two more, one in Cannes, another in Florida, all three yachts hardly ever used, except to entertain friends and business associates, including the Arab ones. Having Sue-Beth fly down to Cayman was as good an excuse as any to get her out of the capital. But he also had very important business for her to attend to on his behalf.

'You don't want me to stay here with you?'

'I'm going to be tied up day and night, honey. No point in you hanging around in the cold in Washington when you can be sunning yourself. I'll join you as soon as I can. Besides, Sheikh al-Khalid will be arriving in a couple of days and I want you to look after him. Soon as you get to the villa, call him in Riyadh and tell him I've been held up by urgent business in Washington. He'll understand, so you don't need to go into any details. When he arrives on Cayman, be sure he's got all the papers I'll need for the Saudi deal. And this is important

– when you call him, use the secure line. The one with the scrambler.'

'Why don't you call him yourself, Charlie?'

'I'd prefer you did it. Another thing. You'll find al-Khalid being very discreet during his visit – he'll be wearing Western clothes and will have only a small, private entourage with him, not like his usual fifty hangers-on. He wants his arrival kept very quiet this time, and so do I. He won't be staying at the villa, so when he flies in, you have the helicopter ferry him out to the yacht right away.'

'What's the matter, Charlie? Why all the secrecy?'

Rivermount never held much back from Sue-Beth. She'd become his confidante, his touchstone. But he'd drawn the line at top-secret NSC business, and especially *this* business, which could mean the biggest deal of his life. He and al-Khalid, and their Arab friends were sworn to the utmost secrecy. They had *big* plans, and *no one* could know what their intentions were. 'Just do what I ask, honey, and trust me on this one.'

Alexandria, Virginia
11 November
4.15 p.m.

Rashid drove his Explorer into the rear lot of a small disused warehouse, a five-minute drive from the Wentworth apartment block. The warehouse was near the old docks, a derelict area that had seen better days, and as Rashid climbed out of the jeep and went to unlock the double steel doors, Nikolai Gorev got out of the passenger's side and joined him.

'This way.' Rashid led the Russian inside the warehouse, shut the doors securely behind them, and flicked the light switch. Harsh neon light flooded the building, and Gorev saw a white Ryder van parked in the middle of the floor.

'Another of our boltholes. We may use this place if we have to store our cargo nearer the capital, but we'll see,' Rashid explained, and went to unlock the back of the Ryder. Two powerful Japanese

1,000cc motorcycles, a black Yamaha and a dark blue Honda, were propped up against the sides, along with three helmets with dark-tinted visors and three pairs of black motorcycle leathers. Two small black nylon backpacks sat near them, and a couple of wooden planks lay on the Ryder's floor, to manoeuvre the machines off the back of the van.

'Why the motorcycles?' Gorev asked.

'When it's time to leave Washington, or we have to make a quick escape, we may have need of them. I assume you've driven a motorcycle before?'

Gorev nodded. 'Often enough. It seems you've thought of everything.'

Rashid picked up one of the backpacks, threw it over. 'I like to be prepared. Here, one each.'

Gorev caught the backpack, opened it, and found three US army grenades, two incendiary devices, a compact Czech-made Skorpion machine-pistol, the 9mm version, and half a dozen loaded magazines. The Skorpion wasn't much bigger than his Beretta automatic, but Gorev knew the tiny Czech machinegun had a deadly reputation. 'What's the idea?'

'Extra protection, in case of trouble. The Skorpion's ideal in a difficult situation at close range. The grenades are added insurance. So keep them close to you at all times.'

'And the incendiaries?'

'In case you have to escape your apartment. Make sure you set them off, Gorev. The less evidence you leave behind for the police, the better. You understand me?' Rashid took the second backpack for himself, checked the incendiaries, Skorpion machine-pistol, magazines and grenades inside, closed it again, and slung the pack over his shoulder. He tossed Gorev an extra set of keys to the warehouse. 'Now you know where everything is, you'd better have these.'

'What about the safe house at Chesapeake? Shouldn't I take a look?'

'Karla will take you in the morning. It's at a place called Winston Bay. Just make sure you know how to find it again should anything go wrong. If your back's to the wall, it may be the saving of you. What about your Chechen friends and the rest of the equipment we need?'

'I have an appointment in Atlantic City this evening.'

'Good.' Rashid shut and locked the Ryder's doors. 'Any more questions, Gorev?'

'None that I can think of.'

Rashid nodded towards the door, all business. 'We'd better get on our way, I don't want you late for your appointment.'

23

Washington, DC
11 November
11.55 p.m.

When Collins entered the sixth floor of the Hoover building, it looked like bedlam. It was as if war had suddenly broken out and FBI Headquarters was the nerve centre of operations. He was promptly beckoned into Tom Murphy's office. 'Grab a seat,' Murphy said out of the side of his mouth before he resumed talking intently on the telephone.

Collins sat, noticed that beyond the glass wall that separated the outer open-plan offices everyone seemed to be in a state of urgency. Agents young and old worked on desktop computers or sifted through paperwork and files, dashed to consult colleagues or talked heatedly on telephones. Nobody seemed to be sitting still except him. Murphy got off the phone, agitated. 'We've got a dire situation, Jack.'

Being a New Yorker, Collins' boss was a straight talker, not the type to waste time on chitchat, and especially not this evening. There were no offers of coffee or banter; he came straight to the point. Five minutes later, when Murphy had explained the emergency, Collins was stunned. *So that's what the Union Station incident was all about.*

A scenario like this had been anticipated for years, but it didn't lessen Collins' shock. Experts had warned about it, predicted it. Some day, crazies or terrorists were going to attack a US city with a weapon of mass destruction. The public had become inured: counties Hollywood movies had used the scenario. But now it had finally happened. Knowing the sheer mountain of work that would lie ahead in any investigation of this kind, Collins took a deep breath, in frustration as much as in awe of the enormity of the threat.

Murphy said, 'You OK?'

Collins was pale. 'I guess the shock's still sinking in.'

'This is the one we've all been dreading,' Murphy said. 'The big enchilada. And I've got a lousy feeling it's going to be a hell of an uphill battle. It's barely started, but every man we've got is on the case, coast to coast.'

With the knowledge of an insider, Collins knew that the years of warnings and anticipation didn't mean that the US was any more prepared to counter a chemical, biological or nuclear attack. Indeed, the very opposite was the case. America's Achilles' heel was her vulnerability to just such a threat. Sheer size was a major part of it. No matter how many cops, coastguards and immigration officials policed the nation's borders, covering over three and a half million square miles of land and sea, they were impossible to guard thoroughly. Terrorists could still slip into the country using false papers or via thinly patrolled border routes from Canada, and melt into the sprawling, ethnically diverse towns and cities of America to carry out their attacks. And despite the experts' warnings, even the nation's capital was ill prepared. No one in the Bureau could ever forget the embarrassment sparked by the infamous Janet Reno incident.

In 1997, the US Attorney General, Janet Reno, invited over two hundred participants from the police and various federal agencies to the FBI's Washington headquarters, under the code-name Operation Poised Response, to take part in a 'war game' to see how they'd jointly handle a spectacular terrorist attack. One of the four scenarios examined was a chemical weapons strike on a Washington Redskins football game. The response was anything but poised. The meeting ended in inter-group squabbling and finger-pointing and Reno storming out in disgust. If two hundred of the city's top lawmen couldn't agree strategy, Collins wondered, what hope had the District's citizens?

'If the press get hold of this, we both know there'd be wholesale chaos on the streets,' Murphy went on. 'We're under strict orders to keep this thing under wraps. That's why I couldn't tell you the situation at the station, until I had clearance. Secrecy's absolutely imperative. The orders come from the President himself. Anyone disobeys, personally I wouldn't like to be in their shoes. They're off the case, pronto, and that'd be the least of their worries. They could kiss goodbye to career, pension and a lot more besides.'

Three copies, and only three, had been made of the two tapes, Murphy explained. The same number of copies had been made of the letter accompanying Abu Hasim's first video. Sets of each were stored in locked safes in the offices of senior Bureau personnel with the originals kept in a secure vault, so there could be no leaks.

Murphy stood, grim faced. 'Now that you're in the picture, we'll go take a look at the letter and videos. Then I'll get you filled in on where we are and what you'll be doing.'

In a darkened office, with the blinds down, Collins watched the silent dance of death. Saw twelve innocent men walk into a bare, white-walled room to meet their end in the most clinical, chilling manner he'd ever witnessed. When it was over and the tape finally clicked to a halt, Collins was overcome.

Bile rose in his throat. It was almost too much to take in. Obscene wasn't the word – it was a cold-blooded massacre, and his mouth twisted in anger. He had already seen the two video messages, heard the calm in Hasim's voice as he delivered his demands with not a trace of emotion. This was the same man whose acts of terror had sent Sean and countless other innocents to their deaths with the same kind of equanimity. Collins had an almost uncontrollable urge to take out his Glock automatic and drill the face on the screen. Murphy, sitting on the edge of the desk, holding the remote control, said, 'You OK, Jack?'

Collins nodded, seething with rage.

Murphy was a seasoned FBI agent, a man who'd witnessed countless victims of Mafia turf wars and ruthless drug barons, the nightmare aftermaths of air disasters, high-school shootings and bloody massacres carried out by crazed gunmen. But even so, his face was pale, his voice hoarse with raw emotion. 'I know how you feel. It's maybe the most terrifying, disturbing thing I've ever seen. Know what's really scary, almost impossible to imagine? That what happened to those fourteen guys could happen to a large portion of Washington's population. Men, women, kids. It just doesn't bear thinking about.'

Murphy flicked off the VCR, tossed the remote aside, opened the office blinds and went back to sit on the edge of his desk. There had been other terrorist threats and attacks against Washington that both men could recall: a threat to poison the city's water supply by right-wing extremists back in '92, an attempt to blow up the Capitol building by the Black Panthers decades before, a threat to blow up Congress by Patriot groups in the mid-nineties. But they all paled by comparison to this one. It was exactly the kind of spectacular terrorist threat the FBI had been dreading.

'The tapes have been gone over with a fine-tooth comb. Forensic threw up no fingerprints or other identifiable marks,' Murphy explained. 'The same with the Jiffy bag and typed sheets. But we've got the boys from Documents still working on the letters pages to see if we can trace their origin. If we could find out where they were bought, maybe we can get a lead.'

'What about witnesses?'

'No one was seen stashing the tape at the cemetery. And the video surveillance of the package being left in the locker at Union doesn't help us much. Maybe a man, but we're not sure – their face was covered with a scarf and the hood of their windcheater and they wore gloves. We've got some guys down there right now, questioning all Amtrak employees on duty that evening. The same with the private security firm that looks after the shopping-mall area of the station. But so far we've no witnesses who saw anyone leave the package. And it's pretty much a cert that the coins used in the ticket machine won't show up any prints, because the unknown subject wore gloves. We've had all the cash emptied from the ticket dispenser and we're checking every coin anyway.'

'What about the White House caller?'

'The experts are still trying to get a fix on him, but they've had no success yet. All they can really say is that it's likely he's of Arab origin.' Murphy sighed, got up off the desk. 'Not a great start, is it? And so far they're playing a clever game. However, we've had an interesting development that I'll tell you about in a minute. But first, let me reiterate something regarding security. Every man in the Bureau who knows what's happening is going to be tempted to move their loved ones out of danger, especially if the deadline draws close without a resolution. But if they do that, they risk blowing the lid off this whole thing. So nobody even hints to their families or friends that they ought to get out of town, understood? Those are the rules and they stay that way until we're told otherwise. And in case you're wondering, everyone at the White House obeys the same rules. The President included.'

At that moment, Collins' thoughts were not for the capital's millions of hapless citizens, or even for his own safety, but for Nikki. He couldn't even warn her to leave Washington.

'We need to tackle this as quietly as possible,' Murphy went on. 'And that's the damned difficulty. We can't have hordes of agents and uniformed cops stopping cars and pulling out passengers, searching for these people and their device. Either Joe Public's going to smell a rat, or we'll run the risk of maybe surprising one of Hasim's cell and they'll get rattled and press the button. We'll need to do it all discreetly. *Very* discreetly. Like we're walking on glass, every step we take. But we'll still need to cover ourselves so that if the public or press get an inkling that we've got a major investigation under way, and start asking serious questions, they get plausible answers.'

'So what do we tell them?'

'Nothing, unless we absolutely have to. And if we do, we've got a cover story.' Murphy explained about the fictitious stolen barrels of chloric acid. 'The acid's an industrial chemical used in the etching process. It's potentially hazardous, can cause serious pollution, burns, and even death if the fumes are inhaled. The plan is we'll be teaming up our guys with the city cops, one on one, in plainclothes. One agent, one cop. Only our agents will know what we're really looking for – the cops will be told its the chloric acid we're after. We'll be setting up as many of these two-man teams as we can, but there'll be a limit, obviously, or else we'll draw too much attention. But let me explain what we're up against.' Murphy crossed to a map of Washington and Collins followed him over.

'Over sixty square miles.' Murphy slapped a hand on the map. 'And that's just the District. We'll need to discreetly search the major towns and districts close to Washington, and the countryside as well, out beyond the borders with Virginia and Maryland. Farmhouses, barns, silos, storage depots, warehouses, deserted buildings of any kind. We're having a list drawn up, with the help of the tax authorities and relevant government agencies. We're contacting chemical suppliers all over the country, too, in case any of the nerve-gas components were bought Stateside. And agents are being dispatched to every cropdusting business across the nation, to check for anything suspicious.'

Collins knew that the task ahead was overwhelming. 'Have we got a name for the operation?'

'We're calling it Safe District.'

'What about the search for the al-Qaeda cell? Assuming there's more than one person baby-sitting the device.'

'As a starting point, we use our lists of Middle Eastern terrorist supporters.'

'But we've got hundreds, and that's just in the District alone.'

'And we'll need to put an undercover watch on every one,' Murphy answered. 'I don't care how many men it takes, it's got to be done, and quickly. Anyone suspicious, or anyone we suspect might be helping these crazies, we intensify our watch. Do it as prudently as we can. We reassess the situation in forty-eight hours. If by then we haven't produced anything, we narrow down the lists, or expand them, whatever. We'll also need our guys out on the highways in unmarked cars. Any pick-ups or trucks with heavy loads, or suspicious vehicles of any kind, we follow them, check them out, but from a safe distance. We don't go rushing in, weapons drawn. That's too much of a risk in any situation.'

'You said there'd been a development.'

Murphy nodded, came away from the map. 'This is where it starts to get interesting. The only piece of good news we've had so far. I got a call from the Assistant Director just before you got here. It turns out the formula for the nerve gas was stolen in Moscow. It's a new, top-secret chemical weapon – code-named Substance A232X – that the Russians developed, and it's got no antidote.' Murphy explained the circumstances of Boris Novikov's murder. 'The story is, the FSB investigation turned up a suspect on a security camera, who looked like he was tailing the victim weeks before his death. They're sending over two guys from Moscow – one a scientist who worked on the A232X programme who'll give us the lowdown on the gas and its likely damage projections. The other guy's an FSB officer who's going to help us with the hunt. They both arrive in Washington early today.'

Collins frowned. 'Why the co-operation?'

Murphy flicked his eyes to the ceiling. 'Orders from above. We take whatever help we can get.'

'So who's the FSB officer?'

'Name's Alexei Kursk. Rank of major. I'll want you to work with him, Jack. Give him all the co-operation you can. We'll muster a small team – Kursk, yourself, and one or two more agents. I'll go over the details as soon as we're through here.'

'So what's so special about Kursk?'

'He's familiar with the guy caught on camera, knows him from way back. His name's Nikolai Gorev, half Russian, half Chechen, a terrorist wanted by Moscow, heavily involved in the Chechen cause. They call him the Cobra. And there's another guy he's been seen with, whom Moscow thinks might also be a suspect. I better emphasise that the two suspects may not be same terrorists threatening Washington. But both of them have links to al-Qaeda, and Moscow seems to think they're pretty strong candidates for a plot like this.'

'Who's the other suspect?'

'Mohamed Rashid.'

Atlantic City, New Jersey
11 November
8.35 p.m.

The man was stocky, wore an expensive, well-tailored suit under a black leather jacket, and carried a silver-topped walking stick. He had a black patch over his left eye, and was accompanied by two armed bodyguards. On the man's instructions they remained a discreet distance away as he waited on the boardwalk, staring out to sea, smoking a cigar. The man's dark-windowed Mercedes limo was parked near the kerb.

'Hello, Ishim.'

Ishim Razan turned. He recognised Nikolai Gorev immediately. Razan grinned, displaying a couple of gold teeth. 'Well, if it isn't the Devil himself.'

Gorev smiled back, placed a hand on Razan's shoulder. 'It's good to see you, Ishim.'

The bar-restaurant was a block away, a dark, cavernous place with barely a dozen tables, a couple of electronic gaming machines and a kitchen at the back that filled the air with the pungent smells of garlic, spices, and coffee. A handful of bull-shouldered, fit young men sat at the bar, and when Gorev stepped in from the cold he heard a snatch of Chechen conversation. It died when the men turned to observe him enter, but their unwelcome stares vanished when they saw that he was accompanied by Ishim Razan and two of his bodyguards.

'Take a seat, Nikolai.' Razan picked a quiet table back from the window as his minders took another table near by, out of hearing distance.

As Gorev sat, he regarded Razan. He had changed. He no longer wore a Soviet paratrooper's uniform but an expensive leather jacket, and underneath it a well-cut suit of the finest cloth, an Italian designer label or from Fifth Avenue. The pale blue shirt was silk, complemented by a grey silk tie and solid gold cuff links. In his left hand he carried a silver-topped walking stick, which Gorev had heard was his trademark affectation. The Chechen had matured over the years: his hair had greyed a little at the temples, his face had filled out, but he was darkly handsome, groomed and polished, the only absurdity in his suave image the black patch that hid a missing eye. He sat down opposite Gorev and spoke in Chechen. 'It has been a long time, Nikolai. How did you know where to find me?'

'I've heard a lot about you over the years.'

'Good or bad?'

'Both.'

'And what else have you heard?'

'That Lieutenant Razan of the Hundred-and-fifth Airborne Division finally became tired of the endless jibes against his race and, having no chance of promotion, left the military. That he took to another kind of work, one much more profitable, and at which he has had great success.'

Razan laughed. 'You have heard much. Anything else?'

'That Ishim Razan is now the most feared, respected and powerful boss in the Chechen underworld in America. A man you can only encounter with shaking knees. That he has legitimate business interests in forestry, mining and property, not only in Russia, but also Europe and America. And that he has other, less public interests, in black-market diamonds and precious metals.'

A smile crept over Razan's face. 'I seem to recall that you had a certain reputation for being thorough in your intelligence-gathering, Nikolai. It's good to see it hasn't left you.'

'Your wife and family, how are they?'

'Healthy and well. I live in Salem, but Talina and the boys prefer the climate in Florida. I have a villa there, and join them mostly at weekends, or whenever I'm free. Life is good, Nikolai.' The Chechen plucked a thick cigar from his top pocket, lit it, blew a ring of smoke into the air. 'So, what's this stuff you said you needed so urgently?'

Gorev told him. Razan listened, raised his good eye, and for a moment he was mildly amused. 'You haven't been smoking those funny Arab cigarettes by any chance, have you, my friend?'

Gorev smiled. 'It's not my habit.'

'I know it must be for the Chechen cause, but what exactly are you up to?'

'Don't ask, Ishim. I'd trust you with my life, but I'd prefer you didn't get personally involved. The same applies for the equipment I need. I don't want to risk you attracting any unwanted attention from the police. A man like you must know of someone near Washington who can supply what I'm looking for, no questions asked. And I need to be sure they won't involve the police.'

Razan rubbed his jaw, reached for a notebook and pen inside his pocket, wrote something down, tore the page out and handed it across. 'This man can help you. He goes by the name of Benny Visto. He's at this address, on Fourteenth Street. He can provide anything you need, promptly and discreetly, but at a price.'

Gorev read the name and address. 'You're absolutely certain he won't involve the police?'

Razan smiled and stubbed out his cigar in a metal ashtray. 'Visto's a hardened criminal, Nikolai, and as vicious as they come. A man like him would never grass to the cops. But I'd tread carefully, old comrade. He's a nasty piece of work.'

It was cold on the Atlantic City boardwalk, the wind whipping up the waves. But it was a perfect evening for a walk, and Karla Sharif had parked her Honda Civic and now strolled along the wooden promenade. She wore a heavily padded windcheater, her hair tied back, and when she reached the middle of the boardwalk she stood looking out at the white-topped waves, the sea breeze washing her face, lost in her thoughts. Couples strolled along the boardwalk, some with small children, and she watched as a young mother stopped to button up her son's coat to keep him from the cold. The little boy was no more than four or five, with dark brown eyes and a head of curly hair. His mother's gesture made Karla think of winter afternoons when she would often walk with Josef along the old harbour at Tyr, pointing out the bright-coloured fishing boats, fussing at his scarf to make sure he kept warm, and the memory cut to her heart. She heard footsteps behind and turned as Gorev came over to join her. 'How did your business go?'

Gorev smiled. 'Just as I hoped. I got the information I needed. We can take care of it in the morning, after you show me the house in Chesapeake.' He lit a cigarette, cupping his lighter in his hands, and pulled up his collar against the breeze. 'I saw you from across the street. You looked miles away, Karla. What were you thinking, standing here?'

Karla was about to answer when suddenly a police car went by, cruising slowly along the promenade road, two uniformed officers inside. She noticed one of the officers glance in their direction and she turned away sharply, but Gorev stood there, unflinching, brazening it out until the car had passed. 'Relax, Karla, they can't possibly know who we are. And the last thing you want to do is look away suddenly. You of all people ought to know that. It's an act of the guilty.'

'I'm . . . I'm sorry, Nikolai. For . . . for a moment there I wasn't thinking.'

Gorev checked to make certain the police car had gone, saw it disappear round the corner. 'You're sure you're all right?' He searched her face, then tossed his cigarette into the white-topped waves. 'There's nothing on your mind you need to talk about? Nothing troubling you?'

'No. I'm sure.'

'You'd tell me if there was?'

'Of course.'

Gorev looked at her, uncertain whether she was telling the truth, but he let it go, and slipped her arm into his. 'Come, we don't want to hang about in case the police come back.'

24

FBI Headquarters
12 November
1.55 a.m.

In the grounds of the J. Edgar Hoover building is a small square, decorated with concrete flowerpots, a few evergreens and several park benches, a place where FBI employees sometimes take their lunch breaks, go for some fresh air, a smoke, or just to escape the claustrophobia of their offices. That cold twilit morning the square was deserted, the wind tossing the potted evergreens.

After his meeting with Murphy, Collins went down to the lobby and walked over to one of the benches, carrying an A4-size brown envelope. As he sat, his hands were shaking. Not from the cold or because he was still reeling after witnessing the macabre video, but because he was filled with a livid rage. In the months after the bombing of the USS *Cole*, the same name had cropped up, time and time again, in the intelligence reports compiled by the FBI, CIA and State Department: Mohamed Rashid, an al-Qaeda terrorist who had no scruples, a psychotic who killed without the slightest mercy, and who, the documents concluded, had masterminded the bombing of the *Cole*, among countless other terrorist outrages. Collins knew that intelligence reports were never an exact science, but with all the reports coming to the same conclusion, somehow he didn't doubt that they were true. Rashid had escaped the FBI dragnet that had resulted in the arrest of four other al-Qaeda terrorists who had taken part in the *Cole* attack.

He opened the envelope he'd taken from his desk. Inside was a grainy photograph of an Arab man. Taken from a distance, the shot was poor by any standards, even though it had been electronically enhanced: the man's face was blurred, slightly out of focus. It had been taken over five years ago at great personal risk by a Mossad agent, who had managed to secretly photograph a number of Islamic terrorists attending a meeting at a villa near Khartoum. It was also one of the few known photographs the FBI and the international intelligence community had of Mohamed Rashid. The man was a shadowy figure, cunning in the extreme, of whom few photographs existed, and this was about the best. Blurred and grainy as the image was, Collins remembered every perceived detail: the thin slash of the mouth, the curved nose, the dark, brutal eyes that hinted at a murderous savagery. He'd burned the face into his mind.

As he looked down at it again, his rage deepened. Collins tried to focus, force away the rage, replace it with cold determination. Murphy had assigned another Special Agent to work with Kursk and himself – a man named Lou Morgan, who worked in counter-terrorism and specialised in keeping track of Islamic terror groups. A Russian-speaking agent named Matt Flood would also be available to handle any translation, if needed. Their brief was to help apprehend Nikolai Gorev and Mohamed Rashid if they were on US soil. Collins guessed there was method in Murphy's choosing him: he had all the motive he'd need. If Rashid was part of the threat to Washington, he'd be hunting down the man who'd helped plan Sean's death. Collins heard footsteps, replaced the photograph in the envelope. A tall, athletic black man in his early thirties stepped out into the square from the lobby and came up beside him, rubbing his hands to keep out the chill. 'Man, sure is cold out this morning.'

Collins knew the agent who sat down beside him; years back, they'd worked together on a couple of cases. Lou Morgan was the son of a Baltimore insurance broker and didn't look remotely like a federal agent, a plus when it came to working undercover. His assignments took him all over the country, though he was usually primarily seconded to cases involving the District. Unkempt, with long black crinkly hair, he was unshaven, a pair of dark glasses stuffed into the pocket of his leather jacket, his Reebok sneakers scuffed and worn. 'You OK, Jack?'

'Sure. Just getting some air.'

'Saw you from the sixth-floor window. Thought I'd come down and break bread. They pulled me off a surveillance job up in New York. Flew me straight down here. Still don't know which end of me is up.'

'Murphy gave you the lowdown?'

Morgan nodded, took a pack of Marlboro Lights from his pocket, lit one, cupping it in his hands. 'Sure did. Jesus, it's almost too much to take in. This gas, it's got no antidote, right?'

'That's what they say.'

'I've got a brother living over near Dupont with a wife and four little kids. This thing goes belly up, there's no telling how it's going to pan out. I mean, I can't even fucking *warn* them.'

'Everyone's in the same boat, Lou.'

'Call me a cynic, but if push comes to shove I'll bet those guys in the White House are going to be calling relatives as far away as Seattle.'

'Think so?'

'Know so. Wouldn't you?' Morgan smiled, took a drag on his cigarette. A biting cold wind whistled across the square. Morgan shivered, the smile gone now as he said quietly, 'I was sorry to hear about Sean and Annie. Must have been hard to bear.' He hesitated before he added, 'You've been way down, huh?'

'Pretty far,' Collins acknowledged. 'But I've been climbing back up.'

'Just remember, friends are always there to give support, make the climb easier.' Morgan put a hand on Collins' shoulder. 'Ever you'd like to talk, say the word.'

Touched, Collins nodded.

Morgan took away his hand, stubbed out his cigarette with his sneaker, stood. Determination was etched on his face. 'If this guy Rashid's out there, we're going to find the sonofabitch, Jack. Rashid and whoever he's working with. Even if we've got to tear the District apart, brick by brick. I just want you to know that. These people are gonna have no place to hide.'

Chesapeake
12 November

It was a little before eight-thirty a.m. when Karla and Gorev reached the safe house at Winston Bay. It wasn't up to much, mostly clusters of beach cottages and summer homes, some with private jetties, and popular in summer. The rented cottage was on three acres, far enough away from any nosey neighbours, protected by a thick circle of pine trees that gave plenty of privacy and hid the property from the road.

'This is it,' Karla announced as they drove up the winding gravel driveway and pulled up beside a grey-painted, two-storey wood-and-brick cottage. When they climbed out she took a set of keys from under a rock beside the pine tree at the end of the veranda. 'If the traffic isn't bad, you can drive from Washington in forty-five minutes, Baltimore in even less. Come, I'll show you inside.'

The miniature American flag on the veranda pole, Gorev noticed, was a patriotic flourish in keeping with most of the Winston Bay homes they'd seen. Behind the cottage, fifty yards away, stood a wooden walkway and a boathouse that overlooked the watery vastness of Chesapeake Bay. Karla unlocked the front door. The cottage was pleasant: cream-painted walls, a stone fireplace, a telephone and TV, and three bedrooms, one of the wardrobes filled with an assortment of fresh clothes. There was a big open fireplace, a pile of logs stacked beside it. Gorev looked around the kitchen and found it well stocked with food and supplies. 'All the comforts of home. What's outside?'

'There's a car in the garage, if we need it.'

'Anything else?'

'A boathouse, and a private stretch of beach.'

'Let's go take a look.'

They strolled out to the garage adjoining the house. Gorev saw the grey Plymouth parked there, and then they walked down to the wooden boathouse. When he opened the doors he saw a Stratos powerboat inside. 'What's the idea of this?'

'The owner's gone abroad for a year. It came with the rental.'

The powerboat's blue-and-white paintwork was scratched and badly in need of a polish. Gorev examined the powerful 150hp Johnson engine with boyish admiration. It looked in good order. The tank was full of gas and he opened the fuel line, started the motor, let it run for a couple of minutes, then switched off, closed the fuel line again, and slapped the hull. 'It's a good machine. I'll say this for the Americans, they know how to build a decent powerboat. This thing will do fifty knots on the open waves. OK, I've seen enough.'

They stepped out of the boathouse, and Gorev closed the doors. The sun was shining out on the bay, the waters glistening, and he smiled over at Karla. 'How about we take a walk down to the beach?'

'Why?'

'Because I think we need to talk, Karla.'

'When I asked you earlier if there was something on your mind, you didn't tell me the truth, did you? What's troubling you, Karla?'

As they walked along the deserted beach, Karla pulled up her collar to fend off the cool breeze. 'So many thoughts, Nikolai.'

'Tell me.'

'About Josef, mostly.'

'I told you. This will all come right in the end. You have to believe that.' Gorev smiled at her. 'Where's the Karla I used to know? The one brimming with confidence, the one to whom nothing was impossible? With whom every man she met in Moscow fell in love?'

They came to some rocks and she went to sit on one of them, facing the sea. 'You exaggerate, Nikolai. But I'm sure there must be times when you remember what happened between us.'

'Of course. But I treated you badly. Let you fall in love with me, then left you.'

'It wasn't all your fault. I left Moscow of my own choosing.'

Gorev joined her, sat on the rocks, nodded. 'We were young then, Karla. And you did what you had to. You had a cause to fight for. You couldn't have stayed in Russia. I realised that a long time ago. Your place was with your people.'

She bit her lip, looked into Gorev's face. 'All those years ago in Moscow, sometimes it seemed as if I had two hearts. One that belonged to you, the other to my cause. I just wanted you to know that. You meant a lot to me, Nikolai.'

Something sparked between them, and for a moment it seemed that Gorev would kiss her, but he held back, smiled lightly. 'Maybe there's hope for me yet?'

Suddenly, Karla looked serious. 'There's something else I was thinking out on that boardwalk.'

'What?'

'That it all seems so unreal.'

'What does?'

'This. What we're doing. Threatening the lives of half a million people.'

'What's the matter? You're not getting cold feet, are you?'

'No. But I know that every time I walk in the streets I look at the faces I pass. And I wonder if I could go through with it. Could you do it, Nikolai? Kill innocent men, women, children? Would the end justify the means?'

'It's out of our hands, Karla. Better not even to think about it. And be careful. If Rashid heard you talking like that . . .'

'But Rashid will really do it, won't he? Can you really hate the Americans that much? That you'll let him detonate the bomb? Do it for him if it comes to it?'

Gorev shook his head. 'I can't answer that question, Karla. Not until it comes down to it. But I know what Rashid would say. He'll do whatever he has to. Whatever is necessary. He'd ask you when have the Americans ever cared for the Arabs, or the Islamic people, except to use them? And he'd be right. The Americans like to play the world's policeman, throw their weight around. They like to talk of justice, but it's a selective justice, to protect their position of power, their vested interests. They'll stick their noses into the Arab world only when it suits them, station their forces in the Gulf to protect their precious oil supplies, or invade Kuwait for the same reason, if their supplies are threatened. But they let your homeland, Palestine, bleed to death. And who can forget the invasion of Lebanon, when the Americans allowed the Israelis and the Lebanese Christian Militia to massacre almost eighteen thousand of your people in less than two months. The same Americans who stood by and did nothing when the Russians invaded Chechnya. Rashid will tell you that what we're doing will change all that, once and for all.'

'And you agree with everything Rashid and his friends do and say?'

Gorev shook his head. 'No, I don't, Karla. You think I like it when their bombs go off and innocents are maimed or killed? My heart bleeds, as much as the next man. But if I've learned one thing, it's that sometimes justice can only be achieved through violence.'

'But what if we have to detonate the bomb?'

Gorev looked towards the sea, shook his head. 'If the American President does as he is told, there won't be a need. He knows the rules, and the consequences, so it's all in his hands, not ours, Karla. But one thing's certain. If he tries to outsmart Rashid and his friends, or double-cross them, he'll pay.' He got up off the rocks suddenly, as if to end the conversation, held out his hand to her. 'And now we'd better get going. I think it's time I met our friend Visto.'

25

Washington, DC
12 November
10.25 a.m.

To those who know Washington, 14th Street is the city's red-light district, a seedy boulevard of burger and pizza joints, lap-dancing bars and strip clubs. The kind of place where anything illicit can be bought for cash: sex, an ounce of Colombian cocaine, a Saturday night special.

Near the corner of 14th and K Street that Monday morning, amid the hum of traffic and the flurries of litter, two transvestite hookers wearing stiletto heels and short leather skirts stood in the freezing cold, touting for business. In a store alcove near by, a couple of stressed-out junkies slipped twenty-dollar notes to a busy crack dealer.

Five storeys up, in the warmth of a penthouse loft, behind a plate-glass window, Benny Visto stood observing the scene the way the Emperor Nero might have observed Rome, as if it were all part of his private dominion, except that Visto was wearing dark Ray-Bans, smoking a charcoal-filtered Marlboro, and letting the warm, sweet tobacco smoke drift down into his thirty-five-year-old lungs.

In his white Tommy Hilfiger dressing gown, a silk grey scarf at his throat, a solid gold chain around his neck and a diamond stud in his ear, Visto made an imposing figure: half black, half Colombian, the broken nose adding a seedy grandeur. A closer inspection revealed a not-so-flattering picture, for the fruits of crime and dissipation showed clearly on Visto's fleshy body and arrogant face. But there was more there this morning – an annoyance with the world at large – and it didn't help his mood.

At eleven the previous night, one of his business ventures, a cash-rich brothel off K Street, had been raided by the metropolitan police. Not that Visto was in danger of being arrested himself. That was what the frontman was paid for. Much more serious was the twelve grand in the office safe which had been confiscated by the cops, the loss of on-going business, and the general motherfucking hassle.

He heard rap music blare as the kitchen door swung open behind him and a girl entered, carrying a cup of steaming coffee. She was Puerto Rican, sixteen, and wore one of Visto's dressing gowns over a white suspender belt and G-string, her eyes blotched, swollen from weeping. 'Can . . . can I get you anything, Benny?'

There was a nervousness in her voice, but Visto didn't look back, his attention drawn to two men he recognised as they crossed 14th, heading towards the entrance to his loft apartment in the street below. One of them was small and dangerous looking, his jet-black hair plastered back off his face. The other was well over six feet, with a hard face and big hands, his skull shaven to the bone. Without turning, Visto removed his Ray-Bans and said to the girl, 'Get me anything? Hey, that's fucking good, bitch. Seeing as you ain't fucking *given* me anything yet.'

The girl blushed. The truth was she had been unable to cope with some of the more bizarre demands Visto had made of her the previous night. 'I . . . I'm sorry, Benny.'

'Sorry like fuck!' There was a savage glint in Visto's eyes as he turned. The girl was frightened to death, shaking with fear. A delicious feeling of power, almost sexual in its intensity, flooded through Visto as he grabbed her hair, twisted it cruelly, pulled her face towards his. 'Next time, learn to do what you're told, bitch. You fucking understand?'

The young girl whimpered. 'Yes . . . yes, Benny.'

'Now haul your ass out of here, *pronto*.'

As the girl fled to the bedroom, Visto heard the doorbell ring. He crossed the loft to the steel-reinforced door, checked the peep-hole, unlocked the three sturdy locks, and stepped back. The two men he'd seen in the street came in. The tall, shaven-headed one was Visto's cousin, Frankie Tate, at six foot four all steroid muscle. The smaller man was Ricky Cortez, a Cuban. He had a barbed-wire tattoo around his neck and two more tattoos on his hands, a single letter on each of his fingers: LOVE on one hand, HATE on the other. His pit-bull eyes were constantly on the move, filled with a dangerous, restless energy. 'So what's the story?' Visto demanded.

'All the girls've been charged, Benny,' Cortez answered. 'And the cops got the premises boarded up. The attorney says this one's gonna cost, big time.'

'Fucking cops!' Visto snarled. 'Ain't they got nothin' better to do? Add to that, I'm down twelve grand. Ain't a good start to the fucking day, Frankie. What more good news you got?'

'There's a guy wants to see you, Benny. White dude. Came into the pool-hall down the street, said your name.'

'Cop?'

'Doesn't look like it.'

'Fuck's he want?'

'Man wouldn't say. Just that you might be able to help.' Frankie grinned, took a fold of banknotes from his pocket, handed them across. 'Said to give you this. Sign of his good faith. Five hundred bucks.'

Visto plucked the notes greedily from his cousin's hand, studied the ten fifty-dollar bills, and for the first time that morning he beamed, as he always did when money came his way. 'They look good, my man. I like it. Suggests there might be more where this came from. Get his ass up here and see what this motherfucker wants.'

Visto crossed to a drinks cabinet in a corner after Frankie and Ricky went out. Pouring a splash of bourbon into a cut-crystal glass, he suddenly felt in better mood. The prospect of money had made the dark clouds lift just a little. Maybe the morning wouldn't turn out so bad after all. Throwing five hundred bucks around, the dude had to have more. Might even provide him with a little diversion. He turned to some metal shelves lined with books, plucked out one with *Understanding Greek Philosophy* on the spine, settled himself into a leather chair by the window and replaced his Ray-Bans.

The door opened. Frankie and Ricky ushered Nikolai Gorev into the room, over to where Visto sat. 'This the dude, Benny.'

Visto looked up from his book. 'You got a name, mister?'

'Does it matter?'

Visto smiled, white teeth flashing. 'All right, honey. My time's limited, so let's get to it.'

'They tell me you're in the supply business.'

'Who tells you?'

'A friend.'

'Maybe this friend heard wrong.'

Gorev glanced at Frankie and Ricky. 'Could we talk in private?'

Visto grinned. 'Obvious the man here don't know the rules. You got something to say to me, you say it in the company of these brothers. Ain't no secret society here. Understood?'

'I need some equipment. Untraceable.'

'You don't say? What you got in mind?'

'For a start, I need a metropolitan police van. You know the type, I'm sure. The box shape the police bomb squad uses, complete with all the necessary police radio equipment. Also, I'll need three metropolitan police uniforms, with standard-issue sidearms. Nine-millimetre Glock pistols with regulation holsters, as well as two pump-action Browning shotguns.'

Visto peered over his Ray-Bans at his visitor and suddenly laughed out loud. 'Well stab me to death. The fuck you going to do, man? Start your own fucking police force?'

'Can you supply them?' Gorev asked flatly.

'Man walks in off the street, man I never saw before. Coulda walked straight out of a funny farm. Could even be an undercover cop for all I know.'

'Perhaps I made a mistake.'

Gorev turned to go, but Visto said, 'Hey, no need to get all upset. Chill, my man. Like, we got to establish some rapport here. See if we can work this out together.'

'Can you help me or not?'

'Maybe I can, maybe I can't. Visto's got friends who can get anything a man's heart desires, so long as he's got the cash. Uniforms and weapons, ain't no big problem. But if they got to steal a cop van, 'cause you need the genuine article, now that's something else. Stuff like that can draw some heavy flak. Every cop in town's gonna be sticking his nose up suspect ass. Visto's included.'

'I don't want you to steal a police van,' Gorev suggested. 'The last thing I need is for the police to be on the lookout for one of their stolen vehicles. But I'd like you to get me the same type model, and have it painted to look identical. Can you do that?'

Visto grinned over at Ricky and Frankie. 'The mans got his head screwed on. Van could be sprayed up to look just like the real thing, but with the actual *real* equipment inside. Radio and stuff. Less flak stealing those from the cops instead of the whole fucking van.'

'Can you do it?'

'Don't get into spray jobs personally, but I got associates who can maybe do that. Do it discreetly.'

'The van has to be painted regulation white. But with no markings, understand? Those must be supplied separately. I need the stick-on type.'

'Get your drift. You want the markings already made up and ready to stick on the van, whenever you want.'

'Exactly. Can it be done?'

'Don't see why not.'

'There can be no room for shoddy work or any error, Mr Visto. The job will need to be professional.'

'Wouldn't worry about that. The man I got in mind to do the work, he's the best. Guarantee you'll be pleased.'

'How much?'

'In total? A lot more than five hundred bucks. When you need all this stuff?'

'Within two days.'

'That's a rush job, man.' Visto puckered his lips, did some quick mental arithmetic. 'Job like that, having it done right, a man could be looking at the bones of twenty grand. You ain't got that kind of cash, or a substantial deposit, say ten grand, may as well walk back out the door and down those stairs.'

Gorev took an envelope from his pocket, removed a wad of five-hundred-dollar bills, splayed ten on Visto's coffee table. 'Five thousand on account. I can have another five thousand for you tomorrow. You get the rest when the equipment's delivered.'

The grin suddenly vanished from Visto's face, replaced by a look of pure greed. He plucked up the bills, studied them like a bank teller examining for counterfeit, then stuffed them in his dressing gown as the grin returned. 'Sounds good. I take it you won't get offended I don't offer you no receipt?'

'Just make sure you deliver. And on time.'

'Man pays cash up front, always gets his goods delivered on schedule. Visto takes great pride in that fact. But there are some things ought to be explained. Rules to keep you and me sweet. It turns out you're working for the cops on some undercover thing, or the cops ever come back on me, certain associates of mine would probably think your life wouldn't be worth a piece of shit. Understood, my man?'

'Understood.' Gorev handed across another envelope. 'Inside, you'll find exact details for the van's markings, their size, and all the paint colours. Please make sure your man follows my instructions exactly.'

'You're the boss.' Visto took the envelope. 'Seems like you've got everything pretty well planned. How'd you want to take delivery?'

'Somewhere outside Washington. But we can arrange that closer to the time.'

'No problem.'

Gorev turned to go, then hesitated, an infinitely threatening look on his face that Visto couldn't fail to register. 'One more thing. I keep my word, Mr Visto. Make sure you keep yours.'

Visto looked offended. 'Hey, really no need for that kind of attitude, man. Everything's cool. Visto always keeps to his word.'

Gorev held Visto's stare. 'The day after tomorrow, I'll expect the van, uniforms and weapons. Tomorrow evening, about six, I'll call here with the other five thousand, and to make certain there are no problems.'

'You got my personal guarantee there won't be, for sure, long as you make the rest of the deposit.' Visto thrust out a hand. 'Pleasure doing business. Frankie here will take you downstairs. God go with you, my man.'

Visto stood at the window, watching Frankie down in the street with the guy who'd left five grand deposit. 'Fucking dude threatened me, Ricky. You hear that?'

'Yeah.'

'Subtle, but still a threat nonetheless. Don't like that. Don't like that at all. Want you to do something for me, brother. Go out the back way. See where the dude goes when he leaves Frankie. Be quick about it, too. Ain't much time.'

'Sure, man.'

Ricky darted out the door and clattered down the back stairs. When he'd gone, Visto picked up his book again, riffled through the pages. He was still riffling through them five minutes later when Ricky came back, running up the stairs, almost out of breath. 'The dude got into a green Jap car, half a block away. Couldn't get the number, he left straight off.'

'On his lonesome?'

'Naw. Looked to me like there was a bitch at the wheel.'

Visto's brow creased in thought, and then he tapped the book in his hand. 'You ever hear of a man called Sclotus, Ricky?'

'Naw.'

'Sclotus, now he was a perceptive man. Lived way back, over in Greece, second century BC. Down in Lorton, serving my five, came across Sclotus in the library one day. Man's so wise he does my fucking head in. Know one of the things he said?'

'Naw.'

'Adversity never comes to a man without the promise of opportunity. Know what that means?'

'Naw.'

'Take this morning. I'm down twelve grand. Now I'm up five, with another fifteen on its tail. Maybe even the promise of more to come. With me, Ricky?'

Ricky shook his head.

'Man looking for ordnance like that, prepared to invest twenty grand, he's gotta be planning something heavy, something with a big fucking return. Now to me, guns and cops' uniforms suggests some serious business. Lots of possibilities there. A bank job maybe, or payroll heist, or some such form of liquid cash endeavour. Know what that means?'

'Naw.'

'Means maybe we got us a motherfucking golden opportunity here. Opportunity to grasp a piece of the action, so to speak. But first, we got to find out a little more about this dude and his bitch. Which is why I want you waiting across the street from the pool-hall when the man comes back tomorrow. See where he goes afterwards, find out what exactly we're dealing with here. But do it nice and discreet. You with me now, Ricky?'

Cortez grinned. 'I like it, Benny.'

Visto slipped on his Ray-Bans, grinned back. 'Thought you would, brother.'

26

Washington, DC
12 November
5.05 a.m.

'First of all, I'd like to thank you all for coming.'

Paul Burton regarded the three men and one woman who had joined him in the private room in the West Wing. They were the best brains in the business, had studied and probed the minds of some of the most wanted terrorists in the world. There was Professor Franklyn Ernest Young, head of the CIA's Psychiatric Affairs Section. Dr Janet H. Stern, a top New York psychiatrist and a recognised world expert on the behavioural psychology of terrorists, a woman who had written a half-dozen acclaimed books on the subject. Bud Leopold, a top FBI psychologist who had helped profile the Oklahoma bombers. Lucius Kane, a thirty-three-year-old blunt-talking CIA officer who was in charge of the Afghan desk, and who also had a Harvard degree in behavioural studies.

As soon as the experts were assembled in the room, Burton had outlined the threat and emphasised the absolute need for secrecy, before passing round copies of a twenty-two-page document entitled 'Abu Hasim: Personality and Behaviour Study'. The cover bore a 'Top Secret' stamp and the pale blue insignia of the CIA.

The origins of the document were no great secret to anyone present. For over forty years, the Agency had employed psychologists and behavioural analysts to study the personalities and behaviour of authoritative figures around the world. Put under the microscope were presidents and prime ministers, powerful business magnates, foreign politicians, top terrorists, religious leaders – people of significance whom the United States might have to consult, negotiate or come into conflict with, the idea being that the studies would help predict how such people would respond in a crisis situation that in some way involved the United States.

Each study involved considerable stealth, expense, travel and effort; agents were sent all over the globe to probe just a single aspect of a subject's character. It wasn't beyond the CIA's perseverance to send a covert Iraqi operative to the Tikrit district in northern Iraq, just to probe a peasant farm-worker who had attended school with Saddam Hussein when he was a ten-year-old, in order to learn more about the dictator's childhood. Or to seek out the former mistress of a dangerously right-wing Russian politician in Moscow, simply to get to know his sexual practices.

Every avenue of the subject's past and personality were relentlessly explored. Did he like girls or boys? Was he sexually aggressive? Assertive or placid as a child? Was he closer to his mother or to his father? Did he keep an animal as a pet, and was he cruel to it, or kind? Was he religious or irreligious? Sociable or a loner? How did the subject respond under duress? Endless questions had to be asked and answered before a profile was complete and the report written, only to be consigned to the CIA's Top Secret vaults until required, if ever.

Burton turned his attention to the folder on the man who was threatening to gas Washington and kill his wife and sons. He addressed Lucius Kane. 'Perhaps you'd like to start with the profile of Abu Hasim, Mr Kane? You're familiar more than most with the al-Qaeda, Hasim's activities and the character of the man. What's this study really saying about Abu Hasim?'

Kane cleared his throat, searching for the right words to convey his interpretation. 'What it's really telling us, sir, is that the man's a cult Islamic figure, a religious fanatic venerated by his followers. That he's a man who's both extremely cunning and capable of serious terrorist crimes. Someone who earnestly believes he's a saviour of the Islamic peoples, sent by Mohammad to rescue them from the evils of Western influence. A West he despises with an almost psychotic hatred.'

'You think he'll do what he says? Attempt to gas to death the population of Washington if he doesn't get his way?'

'Sir, the simple fact is, if Abu Hasim could, he'd destroy the *entire* United States, and without a shred of remorse,' Kane replied forcefully. 'Kill every man, woman and child in this country, and praise God afterwards. If I may be blunt, and with apologies to the lady present, he's not only mad, he's *extremely* fucking dangerous.'

12 November
11.05 a.m.

That Monday morning, the tourist crowds at the Washington Monument were thin on the ground, only a couple of half-empty tour buses in the parking lots. The sky was clear and blue, and half a mile away the White House rose up on Beacon Hill.

Karla Sharif and Nikolai Gorev arrived separately and sat on one of the benches. As they waited they saw Mohamed Rashid come down the path, scanning the few dozen tour bus passengers who'd stepped out with their cameras. Rashid took a video camera from his backpack and began to fiddle with it, the signal that it was safe to meet. He waited until he saw the return signal: Gorev opened a newspaper, pretended to read. Rashid came over, sat near them. 'Well?'

Gorev related his meeting with Visto. 'He'll get us what we need – the van, the uniforms, everything – within forty-eight hours.'

'How much?'

'Twenty thousand dollars.'

'Can he be trusted not to involve the police?'

'So I've been assured.'

'Let's hope you're right, Gorev. We'll need the van to move the chemical and device into the centre of Washington if we have to. There will be less risk of us being stopped in a police-type vehicle with proper markings.'

'What about the cargo and our two friends at the house?'

'I checked there this morning. There are no problems.' Rashid looked towards the distant White House with contempt. 'Everything now depends on the American President. On whether he has any intention of complying quickly with our demands. But we'll know the answer to that once I meet my contact.'

'When?'

'At noon, *inshallah.*' Rashid looked back at them. 'We'll meet afterwards. As soon as we know what the Americans' plans are, I pass on my report and Abu Hasim will decide our next move.'

Karla asked, 'And what if the news from the White House is bad? What if the Americans refuse to meet our demands?'

Rashid stood, fixed her with a steely look. 'Where's your faith, Karla Sharif? The American President will do exactly as we want of him. He has no other choice. What president in his right mind would condemn his own capital to death?'

27

'Mr Kane,' Paul Burton remarked grimly, 'you've painted an interesting but disturbing picture.'

For almost twenty minutes, the CIA's Lucius Kane had fascinated the others in the room with his account of Abu Hasim's life. The CIA report documented every important detail: Hasim's birth in 1957, as the seventeenth son of Sheikh Wahib Hasim and his eleventh wife, a Syrian woman; the fact that his father was one of the richest business magnates in the Middle East, a pious Sunni Muslim from the Yemen who had emigrated to Saudi Arabia at the turn of the twentieth century and begun the family business with a small construction company, destined to become an empire.

His father's friendship with the Saudi royal family was rewarded with the prestigious contract for the renovation of Mecca, Islam's holiest city, and that same friendship had eventually helped the Hasim family establish an industrial and financial conglomerate that built thousands of homes, military complexes, factories, roads and public buildings in almost every country in the Gulf. A conglomerate that had interests in international finance and banking, agriculture and irrigation, and exclusive rights to represent prestigious foreign companies such as Audi and Porsche.

The report also noted how his father had died in a plane crash in the early seventies, leaving behind no less than fifty-two sons and daughters, the fruit of twelve marriages, but even more impressively an industrial and financial estate worth over five billion US dollars, giving Abu Hasim an inheritance of over one hundred million, a fortune that he cannily invested, making himself even richer – worth over five hundred million dollars by some estimates.

It included details of how, after graduating from secondary school in 1973, Hasim made frequent trips to Beirut, the Lebanese capital, then a city of seedy and exotic nightclubs and bars. For several years he lived the life of the playboy, earning a reputation as a binge-drinking gambler who haunted the casinos of Beirut, often in the company of beautiful women. CIA sources pointed to his involvement in at least three drunken bar fights with other young men over attractive women, including bar-girls and dancers, and one woman believed to be a prostitute.

The report also pointed to Hasim's growing frustration within his family, his sense of being a black sheep, constantly in the shadow of an older brother who was his father's appointed successor, and his gradual realisation that he could not compete for his father's affection and gain authority in the family. And it pointed out how the black sheep finally found a cause in life, one that profoundly changed him, at the time of his enrolment at King Abdul Aziz University in Jeddah to study civil engineering, where he was introduced to the Muslim Brotherhood, which was to transform him into a hard-line Islamic fundamentalist.

There was an account of how, in 1979, when Soviet forces invaded Afghanistan, Hasim, like so many young Muslims enraged by the invasion, volunteered to fight with the mujahidin rebels against the Soviet invaders. Using his immense wealth and engineering skills, he provided financial and tactical support for the mujahidin cause, helped build field hospitals and training camps, provided care and money for the families of the rebels, all of which elevated him to hero status among his comrades.

And how, emboldened by a Muslim victory against the Soviets in Afghanistan, Hasim turned his attention to his homeland of Saudi Arabia. With growing paranoia, he considered the Muslim world to be dominated by the influences of the West, especially the United States, which he characterised as 'the Great Satan'. If the Soviets could be defeated, Hasim reasoned, then so too could the West, criminal infidels who pillaged Arab oil fields and eroded Arab culture.

The report also detailed the extreme version of Islam that

Hasim wanted to create throughout the Muslim world: the restoration to the Sharia, the strict Koranic law, banning women from schools and jobs, putting drinkers to the whip, stoning adulteresses to death, beheading murderers, cutting off thieves' hands, banning music, brothels and alcohol.

Even more terrifying was the long history of Hasim's terrorist actions, and the foundation of al-Qaeda, the Base, and his use of his wealth to aid Islamic countries and Muslim rebel groups: in Chechnya, Lebanon, Somalia, the Philippines, Pakistan and the Far East; his declaration of jihad, holy war, against the United States and the West, and the suicide bombing attacks by his supporters on US military bases and embassies.

'Basically,' Lucius Kane concluded, finishing his report, 'Hasim is a loner, an enigmatic and complex character, a fanatic. The vision that drives him is that of creating a united and powerful Islamic world, committed to the overthrow of the West's military and fiscal supremacy. He sees himself as a holy warrior, a kind of modern-day Saladin, the Muslim commander who liberated Jerusalem from the Crusaders, and he believes that God is one hundred per cent on his side, and is totally prepared to be a martyr for the Arab cause. He's learned in Afghanistan that perseverance, self-sacrifice and determination can work in defeating a superior military power. Knowing, as he must do now, that he has the US by the throat, he won't back off. He'll see this through to the end.'

'There's definitely no chance the guy could be bluffing?' Burton asked. 'You're absolutely sure he could go through with a chemical attack on Washington?'

'No question. Hasim's into sheer, in-your-face terrorism. You saw what al-Qaeda was capable of in Nairobi and Tanzania, and when they attacked the *Cole*. He means it all right. He'll do what he says if he doesn't get his way.'

Burton was about to throw the subject to the floor when Professor Janet Stern beat him to it. A petite, bird-like woman in her late fifties, her bleached blonde hair cropped short, she wore a black polo-neck sweater, black Lycra pants and chunky shoes.

With a pair of dark-framed glasses perched on her tiny nose, she reminded Burton of a feisty agony aunt from a New York glossy women's magazine.

'It's obvious as hell we're dealing with a religious zealot. And the kind of strict Islamic society Hasim wants to create suggests a powerful need for control. Lost as he must have been in a family of fifty-four, he has a deep-seated need to assert himself and prove his self-worth. He's also a guy who's had a love-hate relationship with his father, a man who was a powerful achiever and a fervent Muslim. Boys in particular are driven to compete with their fathers, and Hasim's no different.

'He wants to outshine that power, achievement and religious fervour, and make an even bigger impact than his old man. He's also punishing his family, loathes them for making him an outsider. Their friendship with the royal family, their business success, their upstanding position in Saudi society – everything they stand for he despises. He may have undergone a religious conversion, but he's still a rebel, and a competitive one. Realising his dream of returning to a Saudi Arabia that he's freed from the yoke of American and Western influence would prove his self-worth in a major way and eclipse his father's achievements. Subconsciously, that's really what drives him. He's trying to achieve something *significant*, something earth shattering in his life. And with his past record of serious terrorist crimes, that's what makes him very, *very* dangerous.'

'The time he spent in Beirut – drinking, gambling and whoring. I think that points to something.' Professor Franklyn Ernest Young, head of the CIA's Psychiatric Affairs Section spoke up. He was a large man with wild grey hair. 'Sure, a lot of wealthy young Arabs do that kind of thing – go abroad for R & R, sow their wild oats. But it seems to me that in Hasim's case, his father being strict and devoutly religious, it's like he was almost giving his old man the two fingers – saying to hell with you, buddy, I'll do it my way. It suggests Hasim has a desire to shock, to be unpredictable. The same with him going to fight in Afghanistan. Rich kids don't usually go off to fight wars. Yet he went and fought the Soviets –

that's pretty daring for someone from his background. And that kind of unpredictability and defiance, coupled with his religious fanaticism, makes him a difficult sonofabitch, someone who's unlikely to have any kind of meaningful dialogue with a perceived enemy like the United States.'

'The President's aim is to gain time to allow the FBI to try to find the device. Is there *any* way we can engage Hasim in meaningful discussion? Try to reason with him?'

'Not a chance.' Young shook his head forcefully from side to side. 'The guy's got us by the balls, and he knows it. He wants his demands handed to him on a plate. It's his way or nothing.'

'The only way you might get through to him is with religion,' Lucius Kane suggested. 'Through the Koran and God. That's the one angle that might work.'

'I don't buy that,' Professor Stern responded. 'For the most part, the Koran essentially preaches compassion, love and tolerance. Sensible, normal Muslims who abide by Mohammad's teachings don't plant bombs and try to gas hundreds of thousands of innocent people to death. No more than sensible, normal Christians who live by the Bible. But Hasim isn't in any way normal. The guy's a terrorist and a Muslim zealot, who practises an aberrant strain of Islam. A fanatic who reads into the Koran whatever he damn well pleases. He sees obscure meanings and takes his own interpretation. Quote him the Koran, and he'd quote it right back at you, with his own spin on it. Talk religion to him and you'd just be talking to a brick wall.'

'What if we threaten him?'

Bud Leopold, the FBI psychologist, shook his head vigorously. 'Won't work. The one thing you *can't* do is challenge him. At back of it all, the guy's unstable. Tell him we'll nuke him and his followers if he harms Washington, and he's just as likely to set off his device out of anger or defiance.'

'Then what are we supposed to do?' Burton was beginning to despair.

'Hasim's got nothing but contempt for the US. Trying to negotiate with him directly, even using an expert negotiator, would be a complete waste of time. He wouldn't listen. I'd say the only chance you've got is trying to talk to him through someone he'll trust. An intermediary whom he respects, or perceives as being on his side. Or at least understands where he's coming from.'

'But who?' Burton asked, with growing frustration. 'I can't think of any Arabs who'd be inclined to represent the US in talks and see things from *our* point of view. Especially someone Hasim would trust. Anyone he respects is likely to be a raving Islamic fundamentalist, like himself.'

'I can't think of anyone either,' Leopold answered. 'But I'm pretty sure it's the only way to go.'

The room fell silent. Burton looked at the others. 'Professor Young, Mr Kane? What do you think? Is it worth a try? Do I advise the President to go with this?'

Both men nodded, and Leopold said, 'Whoever it is we find, we'll have to try to brief them on exactly the right approach we'd like them to take if they agree to help.'

'And what approach would that be?'

'Absurd as it sounds, we've got to see it totally from Hasim's point of view at the very outset of any communication, by telling him he's right. That the US shouldn't be on Saudi Arabian soil. That it's been guilty of interference in the region. That we've been in the wrong and that we intend to help him find a solution and achieve his aims.'

'Should we *really* be saying that?'

'It's strategy. We need to make sure Hasim sees that we're taking him seriously. That way, he's more likely to engage in dialogue.'

'But will he listen?'

'Look at it this way. He's no longer the insignificant, black-sheep son who couldn't gain position within his family. He's a man who holds the future of the Arab people in his hands, who's got the most powerful president in the world securely by the balls. He's going to be on a high, to feel omnipotent, acutely aware of his own importance in all of this. The idea that the United States is going to be in an inferior position to him in any dialogue will appeal directly to his ego. Me, I think he'll talk.'

'Let's hope you're right.' Burton glanced at his watch. The meeting had gone on for almost three hours. Everyone was starting to look exhausted. 'Any more thoughts, anyone, before we finish? Professor Stern?'

Janet Stern was noticeably silent, her lips pursed in thought. 'There's something we're all forgetting here, and it's pretty vital. Sure, I agree with what Frank's said about the opening tactics to take. And I go along with using someone he trusts as an intermediary, assuming they'd co-operate. I've even got the feeling Frank's right that Hasim will talk. But back of it all, I've got a lousy suspicion we'd all be completely wasting our time.'

'Why?'

'Because we're missing an important point here. One that's the core of the damned problem.'

Burton frowned. 'And what's that?'

'Hasim's got a chip on his shoulder as regards America. No, not a chip, more like a damned plank. He *hates* Washington, and everything it stands for. Hates it with a psychotic intensity. To him, it's the root of evil, the head of the beast that has to be slain, the Great Satan. Whether his demands are met or not, that intense loathing isn't going to go away. And that's the big danger. In his heart and mind, no matter what the outcome of his threat or any negotiation, this guy really *wants* to gas the capital.'

28

Washington, DC
12 November
8.57 a.m.

Alexei Kursk watched in fascination through the Ford Galaxy's windscreen as the offices and hotels of downtown Washington sped past him in furious succession, like giant rows of simulated buildings in some vast, cosmic computer game.

'Five minutes more,' he heard the FBI driver at the wheel promise. 'Shouldn't take much longer than that.'

Kursk stared absently at the buildings flashing past. He was speeding headlong down elegant alleyways of granite and glass, catching glimpses of a metropolis he had never imagined he'd visit. It was three minutes before nine in the morning, and the streets of America's capital were crowded, but even the throngs of drivers and pedestrians were not bothering to give more than a passing glance at the two unmarked FBI vehicles as they raced west off the Capital Beltway from Dulles Airport towards the city, their sirens wailing.

Kursk was riding in the back seat of the first car. His first impression, once he entered DC, was that, apart from the ghettoes on the city's fringes, downtown Washington was strikingly attractive. Colonial façades. Dazzling white granite buildings, calculated to give a look of solid power. But what shocked Kursk were the homeless. Ragged bunches of mostly black men sleeping rough on the streets, huddled up on cold park benches or in freezing doorways. He had never imagined such blatant poverty in the most powerful capital on earth.

Kursk turned his thoughts to what lay ahead. He had little if no knowledge of Washington, no native feel for the city that was under siege. He would have to rely solely on the Americans for every shred of information. He also knew they'd have their work cut out. The main problem, Kursk appreciated, was that in a big, ethnically diverse city, a terrorist cell could easily hide. The Americans now had less than six days. To Kursk, it seemed utterly impossible that they could find the al-Qaeda cell, unless they had a lucky break.

The driver turned on to Pennsylvania Avenue, and the splendid grandeur of Capitol Hill came into view. Kursk wound down the window, dazzled by the sight, and for the hundredth time in the last nine hours he reflected on his predicament. What if Verbatin was right and Gorev was among the terrorists in Washington? And what if he succeeded in hunting him down? What then? If he did, Kursk harboured a secret hope that he might somehow be able to convince Nikolai Gorev to halt this madness. Perhaps it was a vain hope. But whatever transpired, he decided he had no intention of acting as a state executioner – no matter what the circumstances. The bonds between himself and Nikolai went too deep. He simply couldn't do it.

'We're almost there, sir,' the FBI driver said politely as the Galaxy sped along 7th Avenue and swung right on to 10th Street. 'Coming up right now.'

Seconds later, they reached the unmistakable fortress-like FBI Headquarters. Kursk had seen photographs of the J. Edgar Hoover building. 'Modern brutalism,' he remembered, had been one American architect's characterisation of the structure. It didn't look brutal so much as forbidding. The car suddenly swung left, and Kursk felt a tightening in his stomach as they dipped down into the yawning mouth of the Bureau's underground carpark.

Washington, DC
12.45 p.m.

Benny Visto was having lunch at the north end of 14th, Ricky and Frankie sharing the restaurant booth, the three of them enjoying plates of sand crabs with lobster sauce, when the two men walked in. Visto recognised them immediately, Feds from the Washington field office, and smelled trouble. The men came over. The taller of the two said, 'Benny. Long time no see. How's business?'

'What business you talking about, man?'

The Fed smiled. 'Tell your boys here to take a walk. We'd like a word.'

Benny dabbed lobster sauce from his lips with a paper napkin. 'Paid twenty bucks for these crabs, man. Like to enjoy them in peace. You spoiling my lunch.'

'It won't take long. We'd really appreciate your time.'

Visto sighed. It didn't pay to fuck with the Feds. They could make life difficult. He nodded to Frankie and Ricky. 'Take five. It's cool.'

Ricky and Frankie got up and went to the bar. The two men slid into the booth. Visto said, 'The fuck you gentlemen want?'

'We're looking for some people, Benny.'

'You always looking for something.'

'Arabs, Middle East types, looking for identity papers, weapons, whatever. Maybe even a safe house or storage facilities in or near the District.'

'Ain't heard of no Arabs looking for shit like that.'

'Maybe they're even screwing your girls.'

Visto grinned. 'What girls you talking about, man?'

'Then maybe they're screwing somebody else's girls. You with me, Benny?'

'Me, I'd figure Arabs wouldn't be interested in screwing no street chicks. They got money, prefer the high-class kind. Escort types.'

'Then how about you ask around for us? Put the word out on the street. Maybe someone heard something. If they did, we'd like to talk. Their information could be worth a lot of money.'

'Must be important, you guys throwing cash around.'

'It is. It's very important, Benny.'

Visto suppressed the temptation to smile. The day was only half over and already he saw another golden opportunity staring him in the face. 'Man wants something, he's gotta *give* something in return. Some of that old quid pro quo.'

The Fed sighed. 'What have you got in mind, Benny?'

'Friend of mine's got some girls who are pretty pissed off. Got a whole stack of charges lined up against them after the cops pulled off a raid on a certain therapeutic establishment near Fourteenth early this morning. Know that friend of mine would be pretty happy if the charges against his girls went away. Money got taken too. Twelve grand, cash. Friend's pretty sore about that. Pains me to see him so upset.'

'You put the word on the street, come up with something, I'll make sure the charges disappear and your friend's money is returned.'

'Sounds cool.'

The agent slipped a piece of paper under the table. 'You can reach me at this number, day or night. You hear anything, you holler.'

Visto took the paper. 'Like a stuck pig, my man.'

The two men stood. 'Enjoy your sand crabs.'

'Do my best.'

The Feds crossed to the door and went out. Visto picked up his napkin, dabbed his mouth, his mind engrossed as Frankie and Ricky came back. 'What the fuck those Feds want, Benny?'

'Looking for Arabs.' Visto pushed aside his plate and lit up a Marlboro Light, his brow furrowed in thought. 'Middle East types.'

'The fuck for?'

'Something's going down,' Visto explained. 'Something heavy. Feds throwing money around the street, giving me a number to call, night or day, there's got to be.'

Frankie said, 'So what you gonna do?'

'Don't owe those motherfuckers nothing, so it ain't my worry. But no harm in you boys keeping your eyes and ears open.' Visto grinned across the table. 'Even if it don't turn up nothin', could be worth a man's while stringing the Feds along, throwing them some bullshit story. Might mean getting back my twelve grand and my girls busy again.' The grin widened. 'With me?'

29

FBI Headquarters
Washington, DC
12 November
9.15 a.m.

The burly man at the head of the table introduced himself, authority flowing from his voice. 'Major Kursk, I'm Tom Murphy, head of the FBI's Counter-Terrorism Division.'

Kursk had sensed the tension the moment he entered the room. Of the four strangers who waited to greet him, each had a beleaguered look, stress showing in their eyes and around their mouths. Murphy had introduced his three agent colleagues in turn: Jack Collins, Lou Morgan and Matt Flood, a fluent Russian speaker who would act as translator, if needed. Kursk shook their hands. Each FBI man had his ID on a thin metal chain around his neck, and Kursk memorised the names. A few minutes of small talk had established that his fluency was sufficient for them to attempt to conduct their meeting in English. 'I believe you've already been made aware,' Murphy said, 'of the nature of the threat this city is facing, Major?'

Kursk nodded. 'Yes. I have.'

'Then perhaps I might begin by outlining what's been happening and where we are with the investigation.' Murphy patiently explained the sequence of events that had unfolded, from the tape being delivered to the Saudi diplomat, right up to the present. 'We had no suspects in our sights until we learned about the murder of Boris Novikov in Moscow and your investigation. So perhaps, Major, you'd like to fill us in with the details and we can go on from there?'

Kursk spoke for ten minutes, the interpreter helping when he faltered or searched for the correct English word. When he had finished, Murphy said, 'My information is that you're familiar with this Nikolai Gorev. May I ask how?'

Kursk explained, and was greeted by a silence so stony he could hear distant footsteps out in the hall. Murphy looked startled. 'I wasn't aware that your relationship had been that close, Major.'

Kursk noticed the agent named Collins stare over at him. It struck him that he might be seen by the FBI as an intruder, someone whose presence was less than welcome. Rivalry happened between police departments, never mind federal officers from different continents.

'It leads me to ask you a question,' Murphy went on delicately. 'One I feel I must ask. Assuming – just assuming – Gorev's in Washington along with Rashid, do you feel any conflict of interest in helping to hunt him down?'

Kursk stared unblinking at the faces around the table, hid the lie. 'No.'

Murphy nodded. 'I must apologise for asking, Major. But obviously in a case as sensitive and important as this, and with time not on our side, I need to feel certain that the commitment of everyone involved is one hundred per cent.'

'I understand.'

'Very well, then let's get down to business.' Murphy had a pad in front on him and picked up a pen. 'Mohamed Rashid we already know about. The guy's in the same league as Carlos the Jackal, as ruthless a terrorist as they come, with a list of charges against him a mile long. But what can you tell us about Gorev? We're interested in knowing the *kind* of man we may be dealing with. His strengths, his traits or weaknesses.'

Kursk gave a detailed account of Gorev's background before he removed a file from his briefcase. 'The file contains all the information you'll need, including Gorev's photograph, the best we have, taken by a Russian journalist in Chechnya a year ago.' He handed it across the table to Murphy. 'The file has been translated, naturally.'

'We'll have copies made.' Murphy accepted the file. He placed the head-and-shoulders photograph from the folder on the table for everyone to see. 'But please, go on.'

'About Nikolai Gorev I will say this. He's a total professional, who is a highly trained special forces paratrooper. From personal experience, I know he has absolutely no fear. As for his weaknesses, I know of none, except that he is easily angered by injustice, if you can call that a weakness. And you must never lie to him. To do so is fatal.'

Murphy tapped the photograph. 'Does he have any special habits we need to know about? Drug habits, sexual habits, which might cause him to seek relief if he was in Washington?'

'I know of none.'

'Any health problems that would require him to need special medication or the services of a doctor?'

'Again, I know of none.'

'Physical marks, handicaps or scars that might be noticed if Gorev was seen in public? Anything that stands out that might make it easier to identify him?'

'Gorev was wounded in battle in Afghanistan – a bullet wound to his right shoulder that left a scar. I believe that is mentioned in the file.'

Murphy finished jotting on the pad, sighed. 'OK, let me tell you how we're going to play this.' He stood, moved to a map on the wall, and briefly explained how the centre of Washington, DC, was broken down into four quadrants, speaking slowly and clearly so Kursk had time to understand. 'The name we've given the operation is Safe District. We've already put all our available agents in the city into one of three different teams, all co-ordinated from this headquarters. Call them teams A, B and C. Team A will be working with the Washington metropolitan police. It'll be their job to conduct systematic searches of every area in the District. For maximum use of resources, we'll be using pairs of FBI agents, Secret Service agents or plainclothes police, all working together. We're having lists made of buildings, boathouses and warehouses, likely places where the device and chemical may be stored. The owners will be contacted and asked about the rentals of their premises, if they've had any new tenants moving in recently, if they've noticed any suspicious movements by the occupants, and so on. As well as the searches in the District, we'll have another search going on in the outskirts, doing exactly the same kind of thing. This will be carried out by Team B.' Murphy pointed out the borders of DC, indicated Virginia and Maryland, making sure Kursk had a basic grasp of the geography. 'The kinds of places I'm talking about are Crystal City, Chevy Chase, Alexandria, Arlington . . .'

Kursk had no knowledge of these places, but he followed Murphy's finger as it pointed out the locations on the map.

'Then there's the third team, C. This will be made up of mobile units, of between three to four men. Kind of like flying squads, free to move around the chessboard at will. This group will act on tip-offs, hunches, any hot information we come across from informers or any other sources. They'll also be out on the pavements, handing out money to police and FBI informers, looking for information. Drug dealers and users, criminals, prostitutes, petty thieves, fences, hustlers, the kinds of people who know what's happening on the streets. The Secret Service will be doing the same thing, but we're working closely together, sharing information on informers and street sources and making sure nobody overlaps. We've already got these teams under way, working the pavements. They're asking about any new Middle Eastern kids on the block. Naturally, we'll have to ask them to go back over their beat and add Gorev and Chechens to the list. We're also working with Immigration to track down thousands of Arab-born illegals in this country. We've got to try and locate them, and establish what they've been doing. Again, we'll add Chechens to the list.'

Murphy paused. 'This will be the most intensive FBI operation ever carried out. The devil, as they say, is in the details. And I don't intend for us to overlook a single, minute detail. Are you understanding all I'm saying, Major? Or am I going too fast?'

Kursk shook his head. A word or two he hadn't grasped, but he'd got the gist of Murphy's plan. 'No, I understand.'

Kursk could see that the Americans were trying to cover every angle that he'd cover himself in similar circumstances. Offering money to street criminals seemed absurd, almost immoral. But

Kursk knew that it commonly paid off. There was really no such thing as honour among thieves. Criminals were in the business to make fast money, and where it came from didn't often matter. There were hardened gangsters he knew in Moscow who'd grass on their wheelchair-bound grandmother for the right money.

'You, Major Kursk, and Agents Collins, Morgan and Flood will work together as one of these teams, reporting directly to me. Agent Flood speaks fluent Russian if you have need of him, and Agent Morgan some Arabic. Agent Collins will be your team leader and you'll be working out of his office. Any questions anyone?'

There were none. Kursk guessed that the Americans had had their discussion time before he arrived. Murphy said briskly, 'Jack, if you'd have copies made of the files for you and the guys, and return the originals to me. Now, if you'll all excuse me, gentlemen, I've another meeting to attend.'

Murphy stood, addressed Kursk. 'I can speak for both myself and my men when I say that we appreciate your help, Major. If you need to talk with me at any stage about anything, don't hesitate.'

'One question. My firearm. Your people were to arrange the necessary authority for me to carry it in Washington.'

'That's all been taken care of, Major.' Murphy looked at the faces around the table. 'I'll leave you folks to get acquainted before you get under way. It's going to be a long hard slog ahead. So good luck to you all.'

They moved to Collins' office. Kursk noticed a single photograph on the desk. Of Collins on the front lawn of a suburban house, his arms around a smiling young man in naval uniform and a pretty dark-haired woman whom he supposed was Collins' wife. Kursk guessed the young man was their son.

'Take a seat, Major.' Collins was businesslike. He explained that it had been arranged for Kursk to stay in one of the apartments the FBI kept on 7th Avenue for visiting guests and police officers. 'Once we get through here, and if you need to unpack, Lou can show you to your accommodation.'

‘Thank you.’ Kursk sensed a distinct coldness in the American’s tone. ‘But I can do that later. I would prefer if we start work immediately.’

‘Good. I’ll have copies made of Gorev’s file, then we can make a start.’

Collins left the room. Morgan said, ‘Coffee, Major?’

‘Thank you.’

Morgan poured mugs from a percolator in the corner. ‘Are you long with the FBI, Agent Morgan?’

‘It’s Lou. Ten years.’ The black agent smiled as he handed Kursk a coffee. ‘It’s good to have you aboard, Major. You ever been to Washington before?’

‘Never. But please, call me Alexei.’ Kursk sipped his coffee, saw Collins disappear at the other end of the open-plan office beyond the glass-fronted door. ‘I have a feeling your friend thinks my presence here is unwelcome.’

Morgan shook his head. ‘Nothing to do with that, Alexei. Remember the terrorist attack on the USS *Cole* in the Gulf of Aden?’

‘Of course.’

Morgan nodded to the photograph on the desk. ‘Jack’s son was among the dead. He was barely nineteen, a navy seaman.’

A shocked Kursk regarded the photograph, picked it up. ‘I’m . . . I’m sorry.’

‘He was Jack’s only son. A tragedy like that can hit a man hard.’ Morgan put down his coffee. ‘Our intelligence tells us Mohamed Rashid helped plan the operation, chose the target, picked the people. All with Abu Hasim’s blessing. Seventeen young Americans died the day the *Cole* was blasted. Some of them no more than kids, barely out of high school. I guess that makes it personal for Jack. If Rashid’s out there, he wants him pretty bad. And that includes whoever’s helping him, old friend of yours or not.’

Kursk could think of nothing to say. Collins suddenly came back. He saw the photograph in Kursk’s hand. Kursk put it down, embarrassed. A look passed between them. Collins said,

'The copies are on their way. We'll have a read through them, then maybe you can answer any questions we might come up with. After that we'll drop your bags off at your apartment and take a drive out to Alexandria.'

'I'm sorry?'

'It's a district in Virginia, south of the Potomac river,' Morgan explained, indicating the area on the wall map, 'where a lot of Middle Eastern and Arab émigrés live. So it's one of the places we want to look. If Rashid or Gorev are in town there's always a chance they might be hiding out in a safe house somewhere in the area.'

'If they are,' Collins said to Kursk, 'you can be sure they'll be keeping a low profile. But they'll have to show their faces at some stage – maybe go to a store for food and supplies, visit a restaurant, buy gas if they're driving, take a taxi or public transport, or go for a walk in the streets.'

Collins removed an envelope from his drawer and took out a grainy black-and-white photograph, handed it to Kursk. 'This is one of the few shots we've got of Rashid, taken by a Mossad agent a few years back. It's pretty lousy, but it's all we've got to work with. We'll show the photographs of Rashid and Gorev to whatever FBI informants we've got in the district, have them keep their eyes open, just in case they make an appearance. After that, we'll find out what's been happening with the Arab suspects we're keeping a watch on, and see if anything's turned up.'

Kursk finished studying the photograph, handed it back. 'As you wish.'

Collins' desk phone buzzed. He picked it up. Kursk couldn't hear the caller, but he heard a hint of urgency in the reply. 'What's the address?'

Collins jotted something on his desk pad. 'OK, we're on our way.' He put the receiver down, tore off the scribbled note.

'You got anything, Jack?' Morgan asked.

'Maybe, maybe not. The list of warehouses our guys have been checking out – one of them's turned up something.'

Hundreds of warehouses had been visited since 8 a.m. that

morning, but without any initial success, as federal agents scoured the District and outlying regions in Virginia and Maryland for a likely hiding place for the device.

Morgan nodded. 'So what have we got?'

'The owner of a storage depot in Alexandria claims an Arab guy and a woman called to his office about five weeks ago, looking to rent a storage facility.'

'What happened?'

'They looked the place over, said they'd think about it, but never came back. We've got a couple of guys checking out the warehouse and questioning the owner. It might do no harm if we tagged along, showed him photographs of Rashid and Gorev.'

Morgan got up off the desk. 'I'll get a car from the pool, meet you guys downstairs.'

He headed out the door and Collins grabbed his jacket. Kursk said as delicately as he could, 'Your friend, he told me about your son . . .'

Kursk wanted to say more, if only to offer some words of sympathy, but he faltered as Collins fixed him with a stare that was almost frightening. 'One thing you better know, Major, and it's nothing personal. No matter what way you look at it, Nikolai Gorev's in the same boat as Mohamed Rashid. A terrorist linked to al-Qaeda. So I'll tell you something straight out, and for nothing. If they're both in Washington, and we find them, they're going to have a debt to pay.'

30

Washington, DC
12 November
8.15 a.m.

It was a scene that could have been repeated in millions of homes across America that morning. The TV was on, its volume turned up too high. Three-year-old Daniel Dean was watching the screen as he spooned in mouthfuls of Cheerios, while at the same time keeping his eyes totally fixed on the episode of *Pokémon* that blared from the set in front of him. Nikki Dean, sipping her coffee on the kitchen chair beside his, studied her son with tender fascination.

Daniel took his eyes off the set and his spoon fell to his plate with a clank. '*Pokémon* over now. Can I watch *Scoobydoo*?'

'Just for five minutes, Daniel. Then we've got to go.'

Her son flicked through the channels, and then his favourite cartoon dog came on. Nikki thought: *It's not that long ago he was a helpless infant. Now he's flicking channels, operating the video, going to preschool, talking, arguing, developing a mind all his own.* The previous night, lying in bed beside her son, stroking his hair, gazing down at his sleeping face and his sturdy, growing body, she had been overcome by a feeling of loss. Daniel was no longer a toddler; she was losing her baby.

Her thoughts strayed to her talk the previous day with Jack. The things she had wanted to tell him but hadn't. That she realised she'd come to a crisis in her life. That for the last couple of years she'd just tooled along with no real aim or purpose, just trying to be a good mother, keep her career going, put her failed marriage behind her. But lately she'd begun to feel it was time to put direction in her life. And she knew exactly what that direction should be.

A long time ago her mother had told her something, small words of wisdom she hadn't realised the truth of, not until she'd had

Daniel: *Life is about life.* It was about settling down, about filling your days with the mundane things of family, the rich storehouse of joy and love that opened up to you when you had children. If anyone had told her ten years ago, when she'd been ambitiously trying to forge a career in journalism, that having a baby would be the saving of her, she would have laughed at them. But she realised now that if she hadn't had Daniel in her life after she'd split from Mark, hadn't had the overpowering responsibility of a tiny infant who needed to be loved, cared for, fed and changed, she'd have been a basket case by now.

Direction, for her at least, meant a relationship, and it meant family. That was one of the things she hadn't admitted to Jack: she desperately wanted more children. And she couldn't wait for ever. She was suddenly aware of time racing on, that she didn't want herself and her son to be alone, but needed a solid, loving relationship – and soon, as much for Daniel's sake as her own. She just wasn't sure that Jack felt the same way.

He hadn't phoned her last night as he'd promised, and she wondered why. Had he just been too busy with work? Or had she said too much, scared him with her talk? She remembered the well-meaning advice she'd once been offered by a girlfriend: *If a man says he's not ready to commit, then believe him, and walk away.*

She finished her coffee. 'Daniel, we've got to go. It's time for preschool. And Mommy will be late for work.'

She had two interviews scheduled that day. One was with the Police Commissioner, to write a progress piece on the new Crisis Control Centre the metropolitan police had opened on Ecklington Place over a year before, and the other with Tony Gazara, the air traffic control manager at Reagan Airport. The airport story didn't interest Nikki much, but she'd been stuck with it. There had been two reported near-misses flying into Reagan in the last week and the *Post*'s editor wanted a piece on the ATC problem.

'Daniel, come on, honey.'

Daniel sighed, flicked off the TV, dropped the remote, dragged himself to his feet. 'Oh, OK.'

Nikki wrapped him up in his coat, hat and scarf, pulled on his Power Ranger satchel.

'Daniel . . . Mommy wants to ask you a question.' She hesitated, then said thoughtfully, 'Do you like Jack?'

A nod. 'Jack gave me a Power Ranger suit for my birthday.'

'Any other reasons?'

Daniel frowned, shrugged his shoulders.

'Would you like it if Mommy had a baby. If you had a brother or sister?'

'*No way.*'

'Why not?'

''Cause then I'd have to share my toys. Mom, can I bring my Power Ranger suit to school? Can we go swimming after?'

Her questions had made little impact – too much for a three-year-old, even one as bright as Daniel. All she could do was smile helplessly. 'I guess.'

'Thanks, Mom.' Daniel offered her a puckered kiss, scampered away. Nikki sat at the table, listening to the sound of her son's footsteps racing down the hall to his bedroom. How much time had she left? Five years, six? Maybe a little more, if she was lucky. Should she walk away now, cut her losses? She loved Jack Collins. And even if the relationship wasn't going the way she planned, walking out wasn't something she wanted to do. But sooner or later, she knew she'd have to make that choice.

Between 10th and 11th Street, a brisk ten-minute walk from the White House, is a tan-coloured modern building that serves as the headquarters of the United States Secret Service.

What began in 1865 as a tiny government agency created to suppress counterfeit currency in circulation during the American Civil War is now a service employing just over five thousand people: Special Agents, uniformed officers, and technical and professional support staff, with field offices in over a hundred cities across America and a dozen countries abroad, in places as diverse as Moscow and Bangkok.

Although the Secret Service's primary mission is to protect, and investigate threats against, the US President, Vice-President and their immediate families, as well as visiting foreign heads of state and other designated individuals, among them National Security Council members, their job isn't limited to 'taking a bullet for the President'. The Secret Service also investigates crimes that include the counterfeiting of US currency, financial and computer fraud, the false identification of documents, money laundering, and credit card fraud. Unknown to many, it has one of the most extensive libraries of inks and papers in the world – over eight hundred types of ink alone. So skilled are its experts that in the case of a written or printed note they can determine the likely country or region of origin of the paper it is written on, say when the paper was manufactured, and – from the ink sample – conclude when the letter was written accurate to within a day or two.

By 11.30 a.m. of the morning that Abu Hasim's demands were delivered to the White House, the Secret Service – like the FBI – had already kicked-started their intelligence-gathering. Scores of Special Agents from its Washington field office were on the streets, pumping their informers, offering substantial financial inducements for any information on Arabs looking to buy false or forged identification documents or stolen credit cards, or who had recently rented accommodation in the city. By two that afternoon, the Secret Service lab had also conducted its preliminary analysis of the written material accompanying the Jiffy bag delivered to the Saudi diplomat. It was determined that the address on the cover of the Jiffy had been written with a standard, mass-manufactured Bic blue-ink ballpoint pen, within four hours of its delivery. The page pinpointing the location of the left-luggage box at the Union Station had been written with the same pen, within the same time period, and by the same hand.

By midnight that night they would discover that the two typed pages of prisoner names had been printed by a Hewlett Packard 825c series inkjet printer, one of a large batch shipped from an HP distributor in the Philippines to seven Middle Eastern and Asian countries over a year before. The paper used had been manufactured six months earlier in a plant in Malaysia which supplied much of the Middle East and South-east Asia. The Bic, paper and the HP printer were mass-market products – nothing really distinctive about them, hard to track down to an individual purchaser, as was the Jiffy bag, a standard, easily purchased item that could have been bought in any one of many thousands of outlets in DC or its surrounding states. With luck, and time, they could eventually be traced – maybe to within any one of a few dozen or more stores – but not before considerable time and effort had been expended. But would a busy store assistant remember selling a single Bic pen, maybe a month or a year ago? Or a busy retailer keep account of every customer to whom he sold a box or ream of printer paper? The HP printer offered maybe the best prospect, but again, could its owner – who might be anywhere in the Middle East or South-east Asia – be tracked down before the deadline? And with no fingerprints on any of the material – apart from the Saudi diplomat's on the Jiffy – it was going to be a monumental uphill battle to glean any useful evidence.

Rob Owens, a tall, lean Pennsylvanian in his early fifties, and the Secret Service's Assistant Director of Protection, had been informed of the al-Qaeda threat at a private meeting with his Director at eight that morning, and was still recovering from the shock. The Secret Service's presidential protection detail had a roster of two hundred Special Agents, and their job was the most sought-after in the service. Since Abu Hasim's letter contained a direct threat to the President, it was going to be Owens's job to ensure the President's safety in the coming hours and days. Despite the advice that the President should not leave the White House, Owens would have every possible measure in place to try to evacuate him safely, and at short notice.

Failing that – in an emergency situation in which the device actually went off – then he might have no alternative but to use the basement bunker. Fitted with radiation, chemical and biological filtration systems, stocked with rations, biochemical decontamination suits, bunks, communications systems, and other necessities, the bunker had been built by the Army Corps of Engineers. It offered the President immediate sanctuary in the event of a sudden nuclear, biological or chemical attack. Owens was running through his 'to do' list – including making sure that he had a sufficient number of decontam suits and oxygen supplies stored in or near the Oval Office and the President's private quarters, ready for a hasty evacuation either to the bunker or for a dash across the lawns to the President's chopper – when there was a knock on his door, and a sad-faced, stocky man with a bushy moustache stepped into his office. 'You wanted to see me, sir?'

'Take a seat, Harry.'

The first thing you noticed when you looked at Harry Judd's face – apart from the mournful expression – was a deep, rutted cavity scar near the tip of his nose, about the size of a small fingernail. Owens always had a difficult time not looking at that deep scar – it begged notice, and made it look as if someone had bitten off a piece of Harry Judd's nose. At fifty-one, balding and just a touch overweight, Judd was a near-legend in the Secret Service, and had a rock-solid calm about him that was reassuring in a crisis.

As Deputy Assistant Director of Protection, he had served under four presidents and had been with the Secret Service over twenty-five years. He'd worked in field offices in Chicago, New York and Miami, on investigations into counterfeiting and credit card fraud, and had spent seven years on the protection shift before being promoted to his current position. He'd been on duty that day at the Washington Hilton when Reagan was shot – boy, did the Service learn from *that* one – and had the displeasure of taking one of Hinckley's .22 slugs, not in the nose but in the arm. The nose wound he'd suffered in Miami on a counterfeit case. Plastic surgery could have corrected the flesh rut, but Judd wasn't that kind of man – he hadn't an ounce of vanity. He always reminded Owens of a sad-faced bloodhound; a quick, intelligent bloodhound who lived for his job.

Judd had already been told of the al-Qaeda threat, and Owens gave him the list he'd made. 'We'll start with the decontam suits, Harry. Get them organised and in place. I've made a few suggestions about how we can keep them secure and out of view. But if you come up with anything better, well and good.'

Judd took the list, scratched the tip of his rutted nose, a habit which only drew more attention to his scar. 'Yes, sir.'

'Then I want you to do another check on the bunker. Make sure everything's in order and that we've got everything we need down there in case we've got to use it.'

'You're sure we'll have enough decontam suits?'

'We can get more if you think we'll need them. That's all for now, Harry. Get back to me if you think there's anything I've missed.'

Never in all his years of working with Harry Judd had Owens ever witnessed a shred of unease in the man. But he thought he sensed the angst in Judd's next question. 'Has anything turned up yet with the investigation?'

Owens shook his head. His own hope was that legwork on the street on the part of the Secret Service and FBI would crack the case, but there could be no guarantees. 'I'm afraid not. But I'm saying my prayers, Harry.'

A mile across Washington, a man stepped out into the Rose Garden.

'I need a few minutes alone. OK, fellas?'

'Sure.' The two Secret Service agents waited behind the French doors in the West Wing. As a member of the National Security Council, one of the President's most loyal advisers, a personal twenty-four-hour security detail was part of the territory for this man.

Alone, he strolled along one of the lawn's narrow concrete paths, lit a cigarette. The Rose Garden wasn't up to much, just a small patch of clipped grass and bushes and some white-painted wrought-iron furniture. A common misconception was that it was named because of the rose bushes that grew there, but the rose bushes were pretty thin on the ground; in fact the garden had been named after the matriarch, Rose Kennedy. The man took a deep breath, filled his lungs with air and tobacco smoke, and let out a troubled sigh. He'd been stuck inside the White House for almost twenty-four hours since the crisis meetings began, apart from a brief visit to his apartment, and badly needed some space to get his thoughts in order.

Strolling on the damp lawn, on this cold November morning, the question that had haunted him from the very start came back to haunt him again. Why was he doing this? Why was he helping a bunch of Islamic zealots put the lives of millions of his fellow Americans in danger? If he'd told anyone his reasons they would have thought he was crazy. Yet to him they were honourable reasons that could only change his country for the good and he was resolute about his aims. Nothing was going to change his mind. But he knew he was playing a dangerous game, and had to play it very cleverly.

He was scheduled to meet with his contact at noon, to pass on his information. First, he had to make the phone call. Using the White House lines was out of the question, as was a public pay-phone – his face was so well known from his interviews on TV and in the newspapers that it made it almost impossible for him to walk the streets without being noticed.

But he had a cellphone, tucked in his inside pocket. It was no ordinary cellphone, but what the police liked to call a 'clone'. The term had been explained to him. With some simple electronic equipment and a device called a Curtis unit, a thief or a technician could scan the airways for nearby cellphones. Once the unit detected one in the vicinity, it would 'read' the phone's ESN – Electronic Serial Number – and its mobile identification number, MIN, embedded in its circuits. The user could then implant the stolen ESN and MIN in his own cellphone. This meant he could then use the 'clone' free of charge – the calls were credited to the registered owner of the number. But even more importantly, it meant that any calls made on the 'clone' were virtually untraceable. With careful and minimal use, the clone could be used for weeks – even months – if the registered owner didn't carefully scrutinise or query his bills. He had been told that the two phones he and his contact were using had been cloned by an Arab technician in Washington, and he had been assured that with minimal use they were good for at least two weeks, after which the users' bills would arrive.

Standing on the cold lawn, he knew there was one other problem he faced – his Secret Service protection detail. How could he get rid of guys who lived in his ear every minute of every day? But he'd do it, he decided, and tossed away his cigarette. Somehow he'd get away from the White House, make his call, and meet his contact.

31

Washington, DC
12 November
10.35 a.m.

Collins had the siren on as they sped towards Alexandria. In the unmarked black Ford, racing out past the Pentagon towards the Leesburg Pike, they cleaved through the heavy traffic and reached Baileys Crossroads.

Collins sat in the front passenger seat, Morgan at the wheel, Kursk in the back. 'Some people call this area Little Arabia,' Morgan called out to Kursk over his shoulder, his voice almost drowned by the siren wall. 'A lot of folks from the Middle East seem to settle in either Alexandria or Montgomery County, north of DC. Don't ask me why. Birds of a feather, maybe. Iranians, Iraqis, Armenians, Lebanese, Afghans, Egyptians. You name it, they're here, man. All God's children.'

As they sped past a huge shopping mall, Kursk glimpsed a welter of carpet and Persian rug shops, massive chain stores and ethnic restaurants. Middle Eastern faces flashed by, some of the women dressed in veilless chadors, their men dark and swarthy, most sporting black leather jackets, and holding on to the hands of their handsome, brown-eyed children. They passed a restaurant called the Mount of Olives, and Morgan flicked off the siren and swung right off the main highway for a mile until they came to the entrance gates of a storage depot. 'Guess this is it.'

A billboard above the open gates said: *Abe's Storage Facilities. You can't ask for more when you store! Ask about our short-let specials!*

The site occupied about an acre, ringed by a fence topped with razor wire. Inside the fence was a two-storey warehouse built of breeze block, and beyond were dozens of big, brown-painted metal storage containers standing in parallel rows. Morgan drove into the parking area in front of the warehouse and braked. A dark blue Ford was parked near by, two casually dressed men standing beside it, one of them writing in a notebook. As Collins scrambled out, he recognised one of the FBI agents and went over, Morgan and Kursk in tow. 'Frank, what's the story?'

'The depot was on our checklist, Jack,' the agent said. 'When we questioned the owner, he remembered a couple who came by about five weeks ago. The guy said he was interested in renting storage for three months. He and the woman with him looked the place over. Neither gave a name. Told the owner they'd have a think about it and get back in touch but never did.'

'Descriptions?'

The agent consulted his notebook. 'He says the guy was definitely Arab, thirty-five to forty. About five-nine, a hundred and sixty pounds. Casually dressed, dark windcheater, jeans and sneakers. His hair was dyed a kind of blond, and he maybe had an earring. Apart from that he can't remember much more of the guy's description. The woman was about the same age. He wasn't sure if she was Arab or not – she didn't speak to him – but he says she could have been. Pretty, dark haired, possibly mid-thirties, maybe five-six, in good shape. Wore jeans, a brown half-length leather jacket.'

'Transport?'

'The owner's pretty sure they drove a dark green Honda Civic. He didn't take note of the plate, naturally. He'd no cause to.'

'They say what they wanted to store?'

'That's maybe the interesting part. Said they had some valuable household stuff and didn't want it messed with or stolen. The owner says most of his customers ask about security on the site, it's pretty much routine, but he thought the couple seemed overly concerned. They asked a lot of questions about how well the place was protected and exactly what kind of security he'd got in place. Like they wanted to be totally reassured no one would touch their stuff once it was locked up. That's about it.'

'So who's the owner?'

'Name's Abe Lacy. Elderly guy.' The agent smiled. 'He's

been pretty helpful, except he's cheesed off about us taking him downtown to see if we can get an ID on the couple.'

'Where's he now?'

'In his office. Said he had some calls to make first.'

'Mind if we have a quick word?'

'Sure. Be my guest.'

Collins, Morgan and Kursk stepped into the warehouse office. A thin, elderly man sat behind a battered desk, eating a pink-iced doughnut from a box of Dunkin' Donuts. His shirt was open at the collar, and his braces held up trousers that looked as if they were owned by someone a size bigger. He talked on the telephone as he chomped on his doughnut, and when he saw his visitors he said into the mouthpiece, 'Gotta go, Vinny. Got someone stepped into the office. Talk to you later, pal.'

'Mr Lacy?'

'Yeah, that's me.' The man put down the phone, wiped his mouth with his hand.

Collins showed his ID. 'Like to ask you a few questions.'

Lacy looked irritated. 'Hey, I just spent the last hour talking with your buddies, for Christ sakes. What's with you guys?'

'This won't take long, Mr Lacy.'

'Your friends said the same. Took an hour. Me, I got a business to run. And now my day's gone to fuck. I gotta go downtown and look at frigging mugshots of Arabs.'

'It's important, Mr Lacy. Otherwise we wouldn't be here. If you could just tell us again what happened.'

Lacy sighed, threw aside his doughnut, licked his fingers. 'I got good storage facilities here. People come by all the time to rent. People moving house, people got goods they want to keep safe. Costs them two hundred bucks a month for our biggest container. So this guy calls by 'bout five weeks ago. Says he needs storage. Got some stuff he wants to keep for maybe three months.'

'Did he say what kind, exactly?' Collins asked.

'Household stuff. But hey, what's it to me? Unless it's drugs, stolen goods, or he's stashing corpses in there, I don't want to know. He comes by here on the Friday. Arab guy, like I told your friends. Didn't give a name.'

'You're sure he was Arab?'

'Mister, this neighbourhood's a fucking bazaar. I know a towel-head when I see one. I told him the spiel, that I got the cheapest rates in town. You go elsewhere it's gonna cost you more. So the guy says he wants to see a container, the biggest one we got.'

'You show him?' Morgan asked.

Lacy nodded. 'The guy paces it out. Like he knows exactly how much space he's gotta have. Then he wants to know if we ever tamper with the stuff in the storage bays. I tell him no fucking way, or words to that effect. Once he pays, it's his private property, he's got the key. We keep a master in the office, sure, but unless it's an emergency and flames are coming out of the fucking container or the cops got a warrant to make me open it up, no one touches his stuff.'

'Go on, Mr Lacy.'

'Then he keeps asking about security, and if we got guards on the place. I tell him the place is alarmed, supervised twenty-four hours, seven days a week. That after close-up I got a private security company comes by on patrol, and they got German shepherds that frighten the fucking shit out of me. Guy seems happy enough. He goes to the car, comes back with the woman. Maybe mid-thirties, maybe a little more or less. Hard to tell, exactly. I gave your friends a description. Then they both look the container over, like they're trying to make up their minds.'

Collins took the photographs of Mohamed Rashid and Nikolai Gorev from an envelope. He handed Lacy the shot of Gorev first. 'You ever seen this guy before? He ever call by here, ask about storage?'

Lacy slipped on a pair of spectacles which he took from his shirt pocket. 'Naw.'

'Does he in any way resemble the man who called?'

'You're kidding. He don't look Arab, for Christ sakes.'

'Just thought I'd ask. Could this have been the man?'

Lacy took the grainy photograph of Mohamed Rashid, shrugged his bony shoulders. 'Hard to say. For a start, the guy I remember had dyed blond hair, maybe an earring. And this ain't exactly a fucking terrific shot, is it?'

'No, but think hard, Mr Lacy. Take your time, study the face. Try and think back.'

Lacy pondered, shrugged. 'Mighta been. Then again, might not. Really hard to say. I didn't get much of a look at his features. Besides, it was five fucking weeks ago.'

'You can't be more certain than that?'

'Naw. Sorry, pal.'

Lacy shook his head as he handed back the snapshot and Collins sighed. 'What about the woman, you get much of a look at her?'

'Seemed pretty, little I saw of her. Some of those Middle East gals are lookers, know what I mean? Big brown eyes and sexy figures, until they get past forty – start to pile on the lard and grow fucking moustaches.'

'So what happened after the couple looked the place over?' Morgan asked.

'Guy seemed undecided about something. He and the woman start whispering.'

'They spoke in English?'

'I couldn't hear. Then she walks back to the car and the guy says to me, "I'll think about it, and give you a call." Or words to that effect. I tell him to let me know as soon as he can 'cause I got people interested all the time. Guy never calls back. Didn't expect him to. Once a guy says he'll think about it, usually he already has.'

Collins glanced around the warehouse, stacked with wooden crates and boxes. A young Mexican-looking man in his twenties, wearing dirty overalls, had a box of tools out and was busy working on a fork-lift truck. 'Who's that?'

'Enrico. Looks after the place when I'm not here. Handyman, storeman, deputy manager, you name it.'

'Was he here the day the couple came by?'

'Naw. He was off that day. And for a couple of days before. His kid was sick. Had to take her to hospital.'

'Anyone else work here?'

'Yeah, Joey. He does the paperwork. It's his day off. But he only started two weeks ago. The guy he replaced quit three months back, left me in the shit.'

'Anything else you remember, Mr Lacy? Anything at all you can tell me?'

'Nothing. Unless you ever want to rent storage. I got the best rates in town.'

Collins smiled. 'I'll remember. The couple touch anything while they were here?'

'You mean like something they might have left their prints on?' Lacy shook his head. 'Look, I don't know what this is about, but your friends asked me that too. Told them I don't think so. I opened up the container for them, and the guy just walked in, paced around, and out. Didn't touch anything, far as I recall.'

'Has anyone been in there since?'

'Sure, lots. The can's been rented twice in five weeks. Got stuff in there now.'

'You said the couple drove a dark green Honda Civic?'

Lacy nodded. 'The woman drove, as I recall.'

'You see which direction they went after they left here?'

'Yep.' Lacy stood, stepped over to the window, pointed towards a crossroads. 'They hung a left at the crossroads, headed towards the District.'

Collins followed Lacy to the window, looked towards the crossroads. Scattered near the intersection were a few assorted stores, a gas station, a bank, and what looked like a doctor's surgery. Collins wondered whether any of them had security cameras pointed towards the road. But even if they did, after five weeks the tapes would probably have been erased. Still, he'd have to check. 'You got security cameras on the premises, Mr Lacy?'

'You Feds ever talk to each other? Your friends asked me that one too. I told them. I got two, but the cameras are just for show. Don't work. Never have.'

'Mind if we take a look around?'

'The fuck not? Next thing you know, they'll be running tour buses out of Tenth Street just to see Abe's Storage.'

'Which container did you show them?'

'Number fifty-three. Like I said, it's in use. The one beside it's empty. Same type, same size.' Lacy, irritated, stretched over to a wooden hook-board behind his desk, took down a set of keys. 'Enrico can show you. Me, I got some more calls to make before your buddies drag me downtown under protest.'

Collins looked over at Morgan and Kursk. 'You want to ask Mr Lacy anything else before we go take a look?'

Morgan said, 'You ever see the Honda drive by here before or after the couple called in? Maybe like they were looking the place over, checking it out?'

'Naw. Never saw them before.'

'Sure about that? Think hard, Mr Lacy.'

'I been doing nothing but thinking fucking hard ever since you Feds arrived. Believe me, I'd remember if I saw them before. Never did, or since.'

Collins looked at Kursk. 'You got all that, Major?'

'I think so.'

'Any questions?'

Kursk shook his head.

The storage container was halfway down the wire run. Enrico led the way, unlocked the two heavy padlocks on the bolts, top and bottom, and swung open the doors.

Collins, Morgan and Kursk stepped inside the metal container, their footsteps echoing. It took the three of them comfortably, with plenty of room to spare. 'What size are these things?' Collins called back to Enrico.

'Ten by twenty. Is the biggest container Mr Lacy got.'

Collins rapped on one of the metal walls. 'What would you fit in here? Typically?'

'Stuff from a house move. All the furniture, maybe. Or most of it, you pack it in good and tight.'

'That what most people put in here?'

Enrico shrugged. 'Sometimes firms use them. To store equipment, machinery maybe. Stuff they got no room for on their premises. They got lots of uses.'

They walked around the container for a couple of minutes, until finally Collins stepped back. 'OK, I guess we've seen enough. Thanks, Enrico.'

The two agents were still by their car, and Collins went over with Morgan, leaving Kursk trailing behind with Enrico as he padlocked the container.

'What do you think, Jack?' one of the agents said to Collins.

Collins shrugged. 'Hard to tell. Maybe it's something, maybe not. We'll have to wait and see how Lacy gets on with the mugshots, take it from there. You'll let me know straight away, Frank?'

'Sure. We'll go get him right now.'

As the two agents moved back to the warehouse, Collins looked over at Kursk. He was thirty feet away, chatting with Enrico, the two of them smoking cigarettes. After a few more minutes, Kursk left Enrico and came over. He tossed away his cigarette, nodded back towards the Mexican. 'He thinks he saw something.'

Collins frowned. 'What do you mean?'

'He thinks he saw the couple in the car drive by here, as if they were studying the warehouse.'

'I thought Lacy said Enrico was off that Friday?' Morgan pointed out.

Kursk nodded. 'He didn't see them that day. It was several days before.'

Collins shot a glance at Enrico. 'So what exactly did he see?'

'Something important.'

32

Washington, DC
12 November
11.58 a.m.

Mohamed Rashid walked for three blocks, towards Beacon Hill and the White House. The call to his cellphone had been brief. Once passwords had been exchanged he'd been given a time and a place for the meeting. One p.m. at H Street. The coded message meant Rashid needed to deduct an hour to get the true time of the meeting, which was noon. And he deducted two letters to give him one of the three designated meeting places near the White House that his contact had preselected in the preceding weeks. Only he and Rashid knew the locations. The reference to H Street meant they were to meet in the underground carpark on F Street.

When he reached F Street, Rashid entered the public carpark through the pedestrian entrance and went past the ticket machine and down the concrete stairwell to the first level. That Monday morning the carpark wasn't busy, and he saw the light grey Volvo parked near the emergency doors. The driver was seated inside, his face in shadow. Rashid had a newspaper under his arm, his signal that he wasn't being followed and the meeting was on. A second later he got the return sign: the Volvo's headlights flashed.

As he approached the car cautiously, his right hand was on the Glock pistol buried in his pocket. He couldn't see the driver's features – the man wore an overcoat, the collar pulled up, and a thick woollen scarf covered the lower half of his face. Rashid yanked opened the Volvo's rear door and climbed in.

Alexandria, Virginia
11.45 a.m.

'Let's go over it again, so there's no misunderstanding.'

They were in the unmarked Ford, Enrico in the back with Collins, who had spoken. Morgan and Kursk in front. There was an air of tension in the car as they drove through a warren of back streets towards old Alexandria. Not the well-kept, eighteenth-century tourist waterfront area of pretty, clapboarded town houses, but down near the harbour in a run-down neighbourhood. Kursk saw clutters of takeaway restaurants, ethnic stores and the blue-painted dome of a neighbourhood mosque rising up in the near distance.

'Wednesday I work late at the warehouse,' Enrico explained. He was still in his overalls and smelled of oil and grease. 'I had to take my daughter to the hospital the day before, so Wednesday I have to do work late to make up. When I finish, I drive out of the warehouse and lock the gates. It's about seven-thirty.'

'Go on,' Collins prompted.

'I was tired, man. Been working hard all day. So when I go to pull out into the traffic in my pick-up, I don't see this other car go by until I almost crash right into it. But the driver, see, she was looking in at the warehouse compound. The same with the guy she was with. Like they were checking it out, not watching the road. I slam on the brakes just in time and she swerved to miss me. It's my fault, but the woman, she didn't hoot her horn or get angry, just waved me on, no big deal. In this city, man, people get real mad you almost cause an accident like that, call you an asshole. But not this lady, she kept her cool. And she was a good looker.' Enrico pointed to Kursk in front. 'That's why I remember when your friend ask me if I ever seen a couple near the warehouse, driving a green Honda Civic. I remember the woman, for sure. Dark hair, very pretty. The kind of woman you notice. Know what I mean?'

'You're sure it was a guy with her in the car?'

Enrico nodded. 'No question. And it was definitely a green Honda Civic she drove. I remember real good, 'cause Friday I saw it again.'

'Tell me.'

'Friday, I go with my wife to pick up our daughter from the hospital in Fairfax. We drive back home to Alexandria. I take a left at Fairmont Avenue to stop and get a fill of gas. When I pay and walk back to my pick-up, that's when I see the green Honda again.'

'What time?'

'About one, maybe one-fifteen.'

'It was definitely the same Honda Civic?'

'I'm pretty sure. It was stopped at the lights, the same woman driving, maybe the same guy in the car with her, and when I pull out of the gas station I'm right behind them. She drives for maybe a quarter-mile and I'm still behind her, going in the same direction, towards Clifton Street, down near the harbour. After a little while, the Honda turns off and I see the couple drive into an apartment block. Then I see them get out of their car and walk towards the block, like they was going inside.'

'But you can't remember the block?'

'I only move here five months ago from Pittsburgh.' Enrico shrugged. 'I don't know this area too good. Most of the streets look the same.'

Collins opened the envelope, showed the photograph of Mohamed Rashid. 'Was this the man she was with?'

Enrico stared at the grainy photo, shrugged again. 'That's a pretty fuzzy shot, man. Is hard to say. I got a feeling the guy maybe had blond hair. And I really only remember the woman. I didn't see the guy too good. Just a glance, that's all.'

'But she was Middle Eastern looking, you're sure about that?'

Enrico shrugged. 'Maybe. But she could have been Latino. About thirty, maybe thirty-five.

Hard to say with women.'

Collins showed the photograph of Nikolai Gorev. 'What about this guy. You ever see him near the warehouse before?'

'Naw. Never.'

Collins sighed, put away the photographs and handed the envelope to Kursk as Morgan drove into a maze of narrow streets that led down to the harbour. The buildings were mostly old apartment complexes and shabby red-bricked town houses – a bustling, working-class neighbourhood, the pavements busy with kids and adults. 'Is around here somewhere,' Enrico said. 'One of these streets. You keep driving, man, maybe I'll remember the block.'

Washington, DC
12.11 p.m.

Mohamed Rashid stepped up out of the underground carpark and walked along F Street, his head reeling. For almost ten minutes he had sat in the back of the Volvo as his contact told him every detail of importance that had been discussed at the President's security meetings in the White House during the last sixteen hours. But two nuggets of information in particular had totally stunned Rashid.

He was still in shock when the Honda came round the corner on to F Street and pulled in next to him, Gorev in the passenger seat, Karla Sharif driving. As Rashid climbed in, Gorev saw that the Arab was livid, his face contorted with anger. 'What's wrong?'

Rashid ignored him. 'Drive,' he ordered.

Karla shifted into gear and pulled out from the kerb.

Alexandria, Virginia
12.25 p.m.

Collins was frustrated. They'd driven through the neighbourhood for forty minutes but Enrico was unsure which street the apartment block was on. They had seen no sign of a dark green Honda Civic parked in any of the blocks they passed. 'All these streets look the same,' Enrico protested. 'I can't tell which one.'

'Try and think back,' Collins told him. 'Do you remember

anything else on the street? A store near by? Another car? A house with a bright-coloured door, maybe? Anything that stood out? Anything at all?'

'No. But it wasn't down this far. I'm pretty sure, man.'

They were almost down at the old harbour, moving towards a neighbourhood of derelict waterfront warehouses and gritty red-bricked tenements. 'Which way did you enter the area?'

'I told you. From the south, off Cliften Street.'

Collins sighed aloud, caught Morgan's eye in the rear-view mirror. 'OK, let's go back, start again, and have another look. And this time, we take it real slow.'

33

Moscow
12 November

It was a little past 4 p.m. that Monday afternoon when General Yuri Butov's chauffeured Zil took a detour off the Moscow ring road. Instead of delivering him as usual to his home after his day's work at army headquarters, the Zil pulled up in the rear carpark of a bathhouse near the Moscow river. A private, members-only establishment, the bathhouse was a favourite haunt of senior cabinet officials and Kuzmin's inner circle.

Butov took a couple of towels from the heavily bosomed woman inside the door and went in. He made his way to one of the private chambers at the rear, undressed, and stepped inside. The room was filled with a fog of steam, but the general caught sight of Igor Verbatin, the FSB chief, sitting alone on one of the stone benches, naked except for a towel around his waist. Butov firmly closed the door and went to join him. 'Well?'

'You'll be glad to know that Major Kursk landed in Washington this morning.'

'And our nerve-gas expert, Professor Maslov?'

'He should be giving his talk at the White House this afternoon.' Verbatin shook his head in dismay. 'The Americans won't like what they're going to hear, Igor. The kind of damage they can expect if the device goes off will be truly awesome.'

'Don't remind me. I take it Kursk was made fully aware of his duty?'

'I'm certain he'll do his utmost to apprehend Gorev if he's involved in this.'

Butov filled a ceramic bowl with hot water. 'I meant his *other* duty.'

Verbatin nodded. 'We've provided Kursk with a cellphone and set aside a secure phone line, manned twenty-four hours, at our Washington embassy. Whatever vital developments there are in the hunt, the major will keep us informed.'

'Good.' Butov's face looked taut as he added some sprigs of mint to the steaming-hot bowl by his side. 'There's something important you ought to know. I met with Kuzmin before I came here.'

'How did he seem?'

'Unhappy.' Butov sponged his brow. 'Having to back down in the face of the Americans' threat has made him furious. Not only that, he's certain his change of heart weakened his leadership. In the cold light of dawn, it made him feel less resolute, and he didn't like that. So he's made a decision, Igor.'

'What kind of decision?'

Butov tossed his sponge into the bowl. 'We'll do our best to have our agents keep track of Abu Hasim's movements. We want to know precisely where the bastard is, so that next time we don't make any mistakes.'

'I'm not with you.'

'Kuzmin's made up his mind. If it appears Washington has to give in to these terrorists, we shall execute Operation Hammer as we originally intended, but do it swiftly, *before* the Americans are forced to withdraw their Gulf troops. Once that happens, the floodgates will already be opened and it will be far too late. That's not a situation we can tolerate.'

Verbatin frowned. 'But Kuzmin agreed to give the Americans until the deadline?'

Butov shook his head. 'Not if Major Kursk determines that they're running out of time and have no hope of winning their battle. Or if the terrorists are hunted into a corner and are threatening to set off their device. And there's another possible scenario that troubles Kuzmin. He has no intention whatsoever of releasing the Chechen prisoners, no matter what pressure the American President puts on him. But what if Kuzmin's refusal incites al-Qaeda to directly threaten Russia with a nerve-gas attack? That's probably the most dangerous situation of all.'

'Then what?'

'If any of those scenarios arise, we immediately destroy Abu Hasim and his al-Qaeda camps. But use more than one nuclear warhead this time.' Butov's face had a look of steely determination. 'Finish it once and for all.'

'But . . . what about Washington?'

'God help the poor bastards, Igor, that's all I can say.'

Alexandria, Virginia
12.48 p.m.

'They came *this* close to bombing the camps to oblivion. *This* close.'

Mohamed Rashid held up two fingers, centimetres apart. He was enraged, smoking furiously, pacing his apartment living room as he addressed Gorev and Karla Sharif. When they arrived back at the Wentworth he had explained everything of significance his contact had told him – the sense of impotence in the White House; the anger; the US President's decision to move fifteen per cent of American troops from the Gulf. But most importantly, the two things that had troubled Rashid above all – the bombing attempt by the Russians and their involvement in the FBI hunt. 'This changes everything,' Rashid railed. 'The Americans didn't heed the warning they were given not to attempt to find us. And now, to make matters worse for us, they know who they're looking for.'

'Your contact was sure about the Russian officer's name?' Gorev asked quietly. 'Alexei Kursk?'

'My source was certain. He wouldn't lie.' Rashid was fuming. 'He said the American President agreed to Kuzmin's demand that the Russians help hunt us down. He said this Major Kursk knows you. Who is he?'

Gorev took a pack of cigarettes from the coffee table, lit one anxiously. 'An old acquaintance.'

'You're certain it's the same man?'

'If it isn't, it's an incredible coincidence. Alexei Kursk is FSB. One of their top intelligence officers.'

'How does he know you?'

'A complex story. Let's just say we've known each other a long time.'

'I don't like it, Gorev.' Rashid was agitated. 'It smells of trouble.'

Gorev crossed to the window, drew on his cigarette as he looked out over the parking lot below. 'Don't fret about Alexei Kursk, he's the least of our concerns.'

'It wasn't Kursk I was concerned about. The FBI will now know who they're looking for.

They'll have both our descriptions plastered in every police station in Washington.'

'He's right, Nikolai,' Karla said. 'What can we do?'

Gorev came back from the window. 'There's not much we *can* do. Except be even more cautious, all of us.'

'It's a disaster.' Rashid was still furious. 'I'll need to inform Abu Hasim of the Russians' involvement and what they intend if the Americans fail. Our people in Afghanistan will need to take precautions. And so will we.'

'And what would you suggest?' Gorev asked.

'Exactly as you say. Be even more cautious. Keep our heads low. Go out only when we have to. The less we're seen on the streets, the better.' Rashid was grim as he stubbed out his cigarette, started to lead them towards the door. 'You'd better get back to your apartment, both of you, and remain there. I'll contact you later, after I've sent my message.'

Alexandria, Virginia
12.45 p.m.

They spotted the Honda Civic. A patch of dark green parked behind some trees in an apartment lot. Morgan pulled up across the street.

'What do you think?' Collins said to Enrico.

'Is hard to say, man. I can't see the car too good from here. Those fucking trees are in the way.'

Clusters of tall maple and oak dotted the parking lot, and Collins could just make out the green Honda behind the trees. A sign on the brick entrance wall said: *Wentworth Apartments*. They had passed the same block twenty minutes ago, but he was certain he hadn't seen the Honda. 'What about the block? You think this is it?'

Enrico scratched his head. 'I think so.' He scanned the surroundings, nodded. 'Must be, yeah.'

'You don't sound sure.'

'I'm pretty sure.'

Collins studied the apartment block. The Wentworth was red bricked, four storeys high. A short entrance road led directly into the complex, and about a dozen cars were in the parking area out front. The lobby, what he could see of it through the trees, looked empty. Collins thought for a moment. 'OK, Enrico, this is what I want you to do. Get out and walk over close to the Honda. Pass it by but make sure you take a good look and remember the plate number. When you get close to the block entrance, pretend like you've forgotten something. Tap your pockets, whatever. Then walk back close by the car again for a second look and come back here.'

Enrico was suddenly unsure. 'Hey, I don't even know who these people you're looking for are, man.'

'Terrorists,' Collins said honestly.

Enrico paled, shook his head. 'Hey, that's some heavy shit, man. I don't want to get involved with no fucking terrorists. *No way.*'

'I'm not asking you to. All I want is for you to identify the car and get the number.'

'Yeah? What if the guy or woman I saw come out? What if they go over to the car? What if they blow me away?'

'Now why would they do that?'

'They might remember me, just like I remembered them. If they see me, they might get suspicious.'

'If they show up, just walk away, nice and easy. Make your way back here. Give a wave, like we're here to pick you up.'

'You got it all figured out, ain't you? Except it's me who's being put in fucking danger, man.'

'There's no danger, not if you do it like I tell you.'

Enrico shook his head. 'Listen, I got three kids. I really don't want no fucking trouble.'

'There won't be. All you got to do is walk to the car, identify it, come back. Then you're out of it, OK? There's nothing to be afraid of, Enrico.'

'Easy for you to fucking say, man. You're still in the fucking car and I'm risking my ass.'

Collins flicked opened the door, patted Enrico's face. 'Listen to me. There's no risk. We'll be watching your back all the way. Just try not to look suspicious, OK?'

They watched Enrico stroll towards the parking lot, saunter up the driveway and disappear behind the bank of trees. Morgan anxiously lit a cigarette. 'If it's the car, how do you want to play it, Joe?'

'We have the plate checked out, take it from there. If it's them, we'll need to be damned certain. Put a twenty-four-hour watch on the place before we even think of moving in. I doubt they'd have the device in the apartment, but they may be able to trigger it remotely from a telephone.' Collins glanced at a tense-looking Kursk. 'You OK, Major?'

Kursk nodded. 'A word of advice, Agent Collins. If Gorev's in there, you'd better be well prepared.'

Morgan distracted them. 'Hey, Enrico's on the move again. Little man's doing OK.'

Enrico reappeared from behind the trees and walked towards the block entrance before he doubled back and passed the Honda a second time, giving it a sideways glance. He strolled back to the Ford, waving as he approached, and climbed in. 'Well?' Collins asked expectantly.

Tiny beads of sweat covered Enrico's face. 'Maybe I'm right, maybe I'm wrong, but to me it looks like the same fucking car, man.'

'You got the plate number?'

Enrico nodded.

12.55 p.m.

At the elevator, a troubled Gorev pushed the button and lit a cigarette as they waited for the doors to open. Karla put a hand on his arm. 'Perhaps Rashid is wrong. This man Kursk might not be the same one you knew in Moscow.'

'I doubt it, somehow. It makes perfect sense. Who better to help track me down than someone who knows me? I obviously slipped up badly in Moscow. Let's hope it doesn't jeopardise us all.' Gorev's face darkened. 'But the last thing I'd want is to have to come up against Alexei Kursk.'

'He's dangerous?'

'He's one of the FSB's best, but it's not for that reason. Alexei and I go back as far as I can remember. He's maybe the best friend I ever had. In fact, you met him in Moscow.'

Karla frowned. The elevator bell chimed, the doors slid open. Gorev stubbed out his cigarette in the ashtray by the doors, took her arm. 'Come, I'll explain on the way.'

Collins, sitting in the Ford, flicked off his cellphone. 'The car's registered to a Safa Yassin.'

'Arab?'

'Her licence says she's Lebanese born. Aged thirty-eight. Came here on a work visa four years ago.'

'Except that doesn't mean Bo Diddley. Could be a cover. Any previous?'

Collins shook his head and looked over at the green Honda, trying to make up his mind. 'No convictions, not even a parking ticket. The lady's clean.'

'What's her address?'

'Not here. Jackson Walk, over in Arlington.'

Morgan said, 'What's the matter, Joe?'

'Maybe the woman's straight. Maybe we're on a wild-goose chase here.'

'Yeah, and maybe we're not. So what do you want to do?'

'I think I need to take a closer look.'

'How close?'

Collins grabbed one of the two-way radios from the glove compartment, handed one to Morgan. 'I'd like to take a walk into the lobby. Find out if there's a caretaker or janitor. Ask him a few gentle questions about our friend, Safa, and show him the shots. See if he might recognise Rashid or Gorev. I'd like to be more certain we're on the right track before we think of escalating this.'

Morgan shrugged. 'Whatever you say.'

Collins said to Kursk, 'You got all that, Major?'

Kursk nodded.

'Lou, keep Enrico here company and stay by the radio.' Collins pushed open the rear door, slapped a hand on Kursk's shoulder. 'How about you and me take a walk to the lobby, Major?'

34

Alexandria, Virginia
12.52 p.m.

Collins strolled towards the Wentworth's lobby, Kursk beside him. They passed the green Honda Civic, and after he had double-checked the number plate, Collins glanced inside the car. There was no sign of any personal belongings on the seats, just an empty Starbucks coffee cup stashed in the driver's cup-hold. 'OK, let's take a walk inside.'

They wandered into a lobby that smelled of vanilla air-freshener. Elevators on the left, stairwell beside it. On the far right, Collins saw what looked like an office door, and knocked. An elderly black man with gentle, watery eyes came out. He wore a blue work coat, carried a broom and dust-pan. 'Can I help yous, gentlemen?'

'Are you the janitor?' Collins asked.

'Yes, sir.' The man smiled back. 'Sure am. Janitor, caretaker, general dogsbody, you name it.'

'What's your name, sir?'

'Sam Burke.'

'How long've you been working here, Sam?'

'Couple of years, maybe.'

'You know most of the people in the block?'

'Most, I guess.'

Collins showed his ID. 'FBI. I need to ask you a few questions. But it's kind of a delicate situation, Sam, so I'd like it if you didn't mention it to anyone. You understand what I'm saying?'

The caretaker's eyes lit knowingly, as if he'd just been asked to join a conspiracy. 'Yes, sir, I think I understand what you're saying.'

'The green Honda Civic parked outside. You know who owns it?'

The caretaker looked out towards the lot, shook his head. 'No, sir. I see the lady who drives it, coming and going here a few times, but can't say I know her. She doesn't live here, see. Just comes by to visit. Matter of fact, she came through here a little while ago, with the gentleman she comes by to see.'

'Is he Arab?'

'Yes, sir. I think he is. A Arab gentleman.'

'You know his name?'

'Not offhand. I can check if you want. All the names, they's on the wall here. Gentleman's in Apartment Twenty-three, I do believe.'

'Could you check that, please?'

'Sure thing.' The caretaker stepped back inside the office, ran a finger along a list tacked on the inside wall. 'Gentleman's name, it says here, is Omar Aziz. Yeah, he's in Apartment Twenty-three, all right. That's on the second floor. You take the elevator up, turn right when you come out. About seven, maybe eight doors down on the left, near the end of the corridor.'

'How long's he been living in the block, Sam?'

'Not long. A couple of months, maybe a little more.'

'Does he rent?'

'Yes, sir, I believe he does, like most folk here. Pretty much all rentals.' The caretaker looked from Collins to Kursk again. 'Is this lady or gentleman in some kind of trouble?'

Collins smiled. 'Not that I know of. We're just making some general enquiries. That's why I'd like you to keep this to yourself. It's very important nobody gets alarmed, Sam. Can I rely on you to do that? Keep this just between us?'

The caretaker nodded. 'Sure. You got it.'

'You know where Mr Aziz works?'

'Can't say I do. Man pretty much keeps to himself most times. Says hello once in a while, maybe, but that's about all.'

'Does he have a car?'

'Yes, sir, I believe he does. Blue Explorer. Usually parks it round the back lot.'

'You've got the photographs, Kursk?'

Kursk opened the envelope. 'Please . . . can you tell me if ever you see these two people before?'

The caretaker took the photographs Kursk handed him. He slipped on a pair of thick reading glasses, squinted as he studied Rashid first, then scratched his head. 'I don't recognise this gentleman. No, sir, I don't.'

'He doesn't look like Mr Aziz?'

'Mr Aziz don't look at all like this gentleman. He's got no beard, for one. And he's got short hair. Kinda fair, like blond coloured . . .'

'You're sure it's blond?

'Yes, sir. Maybe he dyes it.' The caretaker smiled. 'Guess he does. Not that that's any of my business . . .'

'And the second man?'

The caretaker flicked to the shot of Gorev, studied it closely, then stared back up at Kursk and frowned. 'Why, I do believe that could be the same man went by with the lady and Mr Aziz.'

'*When?*'

'When they came through the lobby 'bout twenty minutes ago.'

12.56 p.m.

The elevator doors opened. As they started across the lobby, Gorev halted in his tracks. He caught sight of the two men at the office door, one of them turned slightly towards him, in profile. It took Gorev no more than a split second to register Kursk. For a moment he was stunned to disbelief, then the blood drained from his face as he gripped Karla's arm.

'We've got company. The two men by the door. One of them's Alexei Kursk.'

Karla followed his stare, saw the two men standing in the door of the lobby office.

'Towards the stairway. Move, Karla!' Gorev whispered frantically. He took a firm hold of her arm, spun her round, and pushed Karla towards the stairwell as he reached for his Beretta.

The startled caretaker stared past his visitors and whispered, 'Why . . . that's the man now . . . and the lady.'

Collins and Kursk spun round in astonishment. They caught a glimpse of Gorev and the woman across the lobby before they pushed through the stairwell doors and the doors swung closed again. Collins had his Glock out in an instant. He raced across the lobby towards the stairwell, his heart pounding, a stunned Kursk behind him.

Reaching the second-floor stairwell, Gorev took up a position near the door, covering the stairs below. 'Warn Rashid,' he ordered Karla. 'I'll hold them off and meet you both round the back as quick as I can. Give me two minutes, no more . . . then get out of here. *Go, Karla!*'

There was a brief look of indecision on Karla Sharif's face. '*Go!*' Gorev urged.

She darted out into the corridor, and Gorev turned back towards the stairwell, heard a movement below, and cocked the Beretta.

Mohamed Rashid heard his doorbell buzz twice, then twice again. Frowning, he crossed to the security peep-hole, saw Karla Sharif outside in the hallway, and wondered whether she had left something behind. As he opened the door she pushed her way inside. 'There are police in the lobby, looking for us. *Get out now!*'

Rashid was stunned, but in an instant he had grabbed his nylon backpack and yanked out the Skorpion machine-pistol. 'Where's Gorev?'

'On the stairs, holding them off. We have to move quickly!'

Rashid grabbed her arm. 'How many police?'

'I only saw two.'

Enraged, Rashid cocked the Skorpion. 'Wait.' He turned, quickly checked the living room, took two incendiaries from his backpack, tossed one on to the couch and another on the carpet, and a second later came two snaps like firecrackers, the incendiaries bursting into flames. Karla checked that the way was clear, and they moved cautiously out into the corridor.

Collins pushed the stairwell door open a crack. Looking back at Kursk, he saw that the Russian had his pistol out – a Gyurza SR-1 automatic. Beads of sweat glistened on his face.

'Ready, Major?'

Kursk nodded. 'When you are.'

'Here goes.' Collins pushed open the door and moved cautiously into the stairwell, Kursk behind him. Tension braided the air and Collins' heart pounded. As they started to round the first bend in the stairs, two shots suddenly rang out. The noise in the enclosed stairwell was deafening. Then came two more shots, sending chips flying off the plaster walls above their heads.

'*Jesus!*' Collins fired twice up the stairwell in reply, and three shots answered in rapid succession, the rounds gouging the walls, ricochets whistling above their heads, and he and Kursk were forced to retreat back down the stairs into the lobby. Sweat beaded Collins' face. Across the lobby the frightened caretaker peered from the cover of the office door.

'Sam! What's out the back?'

'Car . . . carpark. Garbage area.'

'There a fire escape?'

'Yes, sir. There sure is.'

'Stay in the office and don't come out until I tell you to.'

'Yes, sir. Got no problem doing that.'

The caretaker disappeared into the office and the door banged shut. Collins flicked on his two-way radio. 'Lou? You there, Lou?'

A crackle, and then, '*Yeah, I'm here. Go ahead.*'

'They're in the building, Lou. Rashid, Gorev and the woman. They've got us pinned down at the ground-floor stairwell.'

'Jesus!'

'Get the call in fast, then cover the front.'

'Jack . . . listen to me, man, don't go doing anything crazy.'

'Get the call in, Lou! We need back-up.'

'Doing it now. Hang in there, Jack.'

Collins stuffed the radio in his pocket, wiped sweat from his face and turned to Kursk. 'Whoever's holding us off isn't going to stay up there for ever.' He nodded towards the lobby. 'I'll take a bet the others will try to make it out by the fire escape. How about you try and cover the back, Major?'

Kursk nodded, moved to go. Collins gripped his arm. 'Hey, just be careful, OK?'

Rashid led the way to the fire escape. They raced down the metal steps and across the rear parking lot to where Rashid's navy blue Explorer was parked. He yanked open the driver's door and Karla jumped in beside him, just as gunfire cracked somewhere deep inside the building. In panic, Rashid went to start the engine.

'What about Nikolai?'

'Forget him.' Rashid was frantic. 'We're getting out of here.'

'No, we're not leaving without him.' Karla moved to climb out of the Explorer but Rashid gripped her arm. 'Are you insane? We haven't got time!'

She pulled herself away, grabbed Rashid's Skorpion machine-pistol. 'I'm going back. Start the engine and wait for us.'

'You stupid bitch, you'll get us killed!' Rashid tried to stop her, but Karla jumped from the Explorer and raced towards the block's rear entrance.

Kursk reached the back door at the end of the lobby hallway. He jerked the handle, peered out, and saw an asphalt parking lot outside. It was deserted, apart from a half-dozen empty parked cars.

Which way was the fire escape? Left or right? He decided left, and stepped out cautiously. A corner of the apartment block jutted out from the main building and masked his view of the rest of the parking lot. As he stepped towards the corner a crackle of gunfire erupted from somewhere inside the block and he looked back, startled. It sounded as if Collins was still pinned down on the stairs. As Kursk started to turn round again he felt something hard prod his neck . . .

On the second-floor stairwell, Gorev slid a fresh magazine into the Beretta and checked his watch. He'd kept Kursk and the second man at bay for over two minutes. Karla and Rashid should have made it out the back by now. He noticed the smell of burning from along the corridor, and when he looked back saw a thin veil of smoke. *Time to move.* He shouted down the stairwell in Russian. 'Are you there, Alexei?'

No reply. '*Answer me!*' Gorev shouted.

A voice shouted back, in English. 'This is the FBI.'

Gorev thought: *It has to be the other man I saw in the lobby.* He shouted down the stairs, in English this time. 'I want to speak with Kursk. Get him for me!'

A pause before the voice came back. 'You want to talk, you talk to me. You and your friends do exactly as I say and no one's going to get hurt. Throw down your weapons, come down the stairs.'

Gorev thought: *The American must be alone. If Alexei was there, he'd have answered by now. He must have gone to get help or cover the back.*

Gorev tore open his backpack. He pulled out a grenade, yanked the pin and lobbed the grenade, which clattered down the stairwell . . .

Collins heard something rattle on the stairs. He twisted his body to get a better look, kept his Glock pointed up the stairwell, saw the grenade bounce towards him down the steps. There was a split second of indecision, a moment of cold, stark horror as he reached out, grabbed the grenade on its final bounce, and flung it back up the stairwell . . .

'Drop the pistol, or I'll kill you.'

A woman's voice spoke in English. Kursk dropped his pistol. It clattered to the ground.

'Raise your hands. Don't look round.'

Kursk raised his hands and the voice said, 'Move back inside.'

Kursk moved back to the rear door, went to open it. The moment he did so, the crack of an explosion erupted from inside the building and startled them both. Kursk seized the moment, spun round and grabbed the muzzle of the woman's machine-pistol, directing it away. He and Karla Sharif stared into each other's faces, struggling to gain control of the weapon. The Skorpion chattered. A burst sprayed the brick walls and the hot muzzle burned Kursk's hand, but he held on, tried to force the weapon from the woman's grasp. She held on to it fiercely, a strength in her that Kursk never could have imagined, and then something painfully hard jammed into his neck, and a familiar voice said, 'Let it go, Alexei. Let it go *now*.'

In the lobby, Collins staggered to his feet. His eardrums rang; his clothes were covered with fragments of plaster and wood. The blast had splintered the stairwell door, almost blown it off its hinges. The instant he'd thrown the grenade he'd flung himself bodily out the door, and a split second later the explosion had come, high up in the stairwell. The percussion had left him dazed. Suddenly a fire alarm went off, and the shrill sound of bells filled the lobby. '*Jack!*' Morgan burst into the lobby brandishing a Heckler from the car, holding it to his shoulder, prepared to fire. He stared over at the stairwell door. 'Jesus, are you OK, man? The fuck happened?'

'Grenade . . .' Collins was still in shock, his mind a fog.

'Help's on its way. Where's your weapon, Jack?'

Collins, still dazed, looked round for his Glock, couldn't remember where he'd dropped it. On the stairwell probably. Trying to move up the stairs again after Gorev was pointless. He would have taken the fire escape by now. The fog started to clear and a single thought entered his head: *Where the hell is Rashid?* Collins felt a sudden, powerful fury, a livid need for revenge.

Morgan said, 'You sure you're OK? Where the hell's Kursk?'

'The back way. Gone after the others. Give me the damned Heckler.' Collins frantically grabbed the weapon from Morgan and stumbled across the lobby towards the rear door . . .

Kursk let the muzzle go. The sound of a fire alarm could be heard inside the building. He turned round as the woman stepped away, brandishing the machine-pistol. Kursk saw a tense-looking Gorev holding a Beretta in his right hand, the barrel pointed directly at his face. 'Get over to the jeep,' Gorev ordered the woman.

Kursk stared at her, their eyes met for an instant, and then the woman raced away and disappeared round the corner. Gorev's face was pale, carved in stone, and Kursk noticed that he was clutching his side. 'You're a long way from home, Alexei.'

Kursk looked down. Blood dripped from a wound in Gorev's side, crimson spots spattered on the ground. Kursk noticed that his navy blue parka was stained with a slash of dark red. 'You need help.'

'I've suffered worse. But you can thank your friend. Tell him that from me.'

'What you're doing is insanity, Nikolai. You're only signing your own death warrants, all of you.'

'A matter of opinion.' Gorev raised his pistol. Kursk was white faced as Gorev aimed directly at his head, squeezed the trigger. At the last second Gorev turned the pistol away, fired into the nearby wall, sending brick chips flying. 'If I were you, Alexei, I'd keep my nose well out of this, for both our sakes. I'm telling you that as a friend. Otherwise, I'd hate to think where it all might lead. You and your comrade have overstepped the bounds already. Try and stop us, harm us in any way, and you'll turn this city into a graveyard. I mean that, Alexei. You're playing with fire.'

A navy blue Explorer roared up, growled to a halt, and its passenger door was flung open. Kursk saw the woman in the back seat, recognised the man that had to be Mohamed Rashid at the wheel, with blond dyed hair, cropped short. Gorev climbed in, still clutching his side, pulled the door shut and gave a grim salute through the rolled-down window. '*Dosvedanya*, old friend. And remember what I said, or else we'll both have the Devil to pay.'

The Explorer's engine revved, the tyres spun, and it tore away.

As the Explorer accelerated away, Collins burst out the rear door with the Heckler, Morgan behind him, brandishing his Glock. For a split second, Collins caught a glimpse of Rashid in the driver's seat. Kursk was in their line of fire and Collins screamed, '*Get down, Kursk!*'

Kursk, startled, saw the FBI men take aim. 'No! Don't shoot!' He moved to block the line of fire, but Collins barrelled past him, shoved him aside. 'Get out of the damned way!'

But as Collins and Morgan prepared to fire the Explorer screeched round the corner, put on a powerful burst of speed and was gone.

35

Washington, DC
1 p.m.

Sergei Maslov was astonished.

As he was sitting down with his wife to enjoy a breakfast of sausages and fried potatoes in their one-bed Moscow apartment, the knock had come on his front door. Two men he had never seen before produced FSB identity cards, instructed him to pack an overnight case, and assured Maslov's shocked wife Lara that her husband, the professor, was not being arrested but was required to attend a very important meeting outside Moscow and would be gone for two days, before whisking him in their car at high speed to the FSB's headquarters.

There, Maslov had been briefed for almost two hours by a half-dozen intelligence officials and senior chemists from the Defence Ministry before being sped away in a black-windowed BMW to Vnukovo airfield. Unceremoniously deposited in the cabin of a private American Learjet waiting on the tarmac, the thirty-nine-year-old scientist from Volgograd had been hurtled at over five hundred miles an hour across the darkness of the Arctic Circle.

Touching down at Andrews Air Force Base almost eight hours later, Maslov was met by a Russian embassy official and again whisked by car – this time part of a convoy of smoke-glassed Secret Service Chevrolet Jeeps and police motorcycle escorts – into the rear grounds of the White House. He was bundled along a narrow tunnel that ran into a basement of the East Wing, leading eventually to a small private room, crammed with high-powered computers, line-printers, scanners and at least a couple of dozen phone lines, along with a bubbling coffee-maker, a water dispenser, and a serving trolley laden with snacks and soft drinks: cans of Seven-Up, Fanta and Pepsi.

Disoriented from his hectic journey, and barely awake, Maslov met the twelve-strong group of US military officers and civilians, chemists and nerve-gas experts from the US Army Soldier and Biological Chemical Command who had been anxiously awaiting his arrival.

For almost two hours they had grilled him about Substance A232X, queried his figures and mathematical extrapolations, and between mouthfuls of coffee they had tapped his data into the computers, until finally the resulting print-outs were pressed into his hand and it was time for Maslov to be ushered into another room. He had never been to Washington before, let alone America, and certainly in his wildest dreams had never thought he would be a guest at the White House. But here he was, in a roomful of very important people: face to face with President Andrew W. Booth and his Security Council.

Maslov was overwhelmed. Tiny dew-drops of sweat began to form on his nose and forehead.

'Mr Maslov . . . Sergei . . . perhaps you'd like to begin, sir?'

Maslov nervously picked at the small gold earring in his left lobe, a trinket he'd worn since his student days at the Moscow Academy of Sciences, twenty years ago, when punk had been all the rage. The specialist interpreter by his side had been provided by the Americans, but Maslov doubted the woman would be needed. He spoke excellent English thanks to the time his father had served as Soviet military attaché in London. He was confident of his command of the language, had all the figures in front of him, knew the gist of what he wanted to say. He stood and faced the packed audience: the US President and his advisers seated at the table, senior chemical experts from the US Army standing around the walls.

'A nerve-gas attack on a big city like Washington, using a thousand litres of A232X, would have only one result – incredible human devastation,' Maslov began, trying to banish his anxiety by imagining he was addressing a class of students. 'However, I cannot say with total precision what such a weapon is going to do to your American capital. The fact is, there are no human studies for A232X, so everything I tell you is totally speculative. But what I can say is that the laboratory tests on animals I have witnessed suggest that the potential for death and injury is so great, so . . .' Maslov searched his mind for the right word, conscious of the female translator by his side, poised to see him through any difficulty. '. . . so immense, it is almost impossible to conceive.'

Seeing that he had engaged the attention of his audience, and with his confidence increasing, he walked over to the special map that had been set up on a trestle at the top of the conference table. It was a map of Washington, DC, showing the city centre and outlying districts. A series of three thick concentric circles in red, orange and green, drawn with indelible marker, fanned out from the capital's heart. Maslov was unfamiliar with Washington, but he knew exactly what the coloured circles meant, and that was enough.

'But what I have done – with the help of your colleagues – is to work out my best estimate of the human deaths and injuries such an attack would cause, based on our calculations. Since you don't know where the device is hidden, I have assumed for the purpose of this study a worst case-scenario – that it would be dispersed in optimum fashion, during a busy, near-windless day when the city's streets are heavily populated, near the centre of the capital, and from an ideal height – with the intention of causing maximum human damage.'

Maslov moved his finger in turn around each of the red, orange and green hoops. 'These three circles indicate the principal damage zones, in order of severity. Let us start with the red zone. If we assume it's rush hour, five-thirty p.m., on a typical working day, with people going about their usual daily business – leaving the office, waiting to catch a bus or walking to get to the metro, or perhaps driving home – and the device goes off, exploded by a carrier missile at a height of a thousand feet, the warhead containing one thousand litres of A232X . . .' Maslov again drew his finger around the red hoop: it touched the Union Station in the north, the National Mall down as far as 4th Street in the east, the edge of the Dwight D. Eisenhower Freeway in the south, and cut through Independence Avenue in the east. Capitol

Hill was bang in the centre of the hoop. 'Nobody inside this circle is going to survive. They will be gassed instantly.'

'Nobody?' the President asked, incredulous. 'Nobody at all?'

Maslov shook his head. 'No, sir. Even those people inside offices or homes will not be safe. Where windows are open, gas will drift into buildings. And even if they're closed, the gas will be sucked in by air-conditioning vents. Perhaps there may be small pockets of survivors – those who are deep underground, in basements or the metro system at the time of the attack – but not many. For everyone else within the circle . . .' Maslov clicked his fingers. 'They are corpses, just like that, virtually within seconds.'

Paul Burton was astounded. 'It seems incredible that a gas could do that.'

'You must remember, A232X is much more toxic than any other nerve gas,' Maslov replied. 'The actual killing dose is just 1.5 hundredths of a drop in the lungs. That's a minuscule amount, totally invisible to the naked eye.' Maslov paused. 'For example, in one test we conducted, a micro droplet one tenth the size of a pinhead caused a healthy German shepherd dog with a sixty-kilogram body weight to die within five seconds. You can take it that a perfectly healthy adolescent or child of the same physical weight would die within the same time if exposed to the same dose.'

Maslov paused again, let his chilling information sink in. 'What will happen is this: the victims might see the missile exploding. Then a foggy white gas cloud would appear overhead. There would be a faint unpleasant smell, like a mild rotting-fish odour. The victims would feel intense pain in their eyes, an unbearable tightness in their chest, as if a powerful band of steel had been placed around them. Bodily secretions would pour from their noses and mouths, and the victims would gasp desperately for air. They would suffer vomiting or diarrhoea, or both, and begin to twitch and convulse as their bodies went into spasm, quickly followed by loss of consciousness. Death would occur within seconds or minutes, depending on the how close they were to the device when it exploded. But in the case of the red zone, the sequence of symptoms would be almost non-existent, because almost everyone trapped inside this zone would inhale an overdose.' Maslov turned to the stunned, horrified faces staring up a him. 'They would perish immediately.'

Alexandria, Virginia
1.18 p.m.

Seven miles from the White House, Mohamed Rashid pulled up in the rear lot of the disused warehouse, a five-minute drive from the Wentworth apartment block.

He climbed out of the Explorer along with Karla and Gorev, quickly unlocked the warehouse doors, and they all moved inside. The white Ryder van was still parked there, and Rashid opened the back to reveal the pair of powerful Japanese motorcycles, a black Yamaha and a dark blue Honda, propped up against the sides. The rage hadn't left the Arab's face, and he slammed his fist on the van door. '*How?* How did they find us?'

'We'll worry about that later.' Gorev started to move, but then clutched his side and faltered, and Karla rushed to him. 'What's wrong?'

'Grenade shrapnel. My own fault. I wasn't quick enough to get out of the way of the blast.'

'Let me see.'

Gorev unzipped his parka and Karla saw that his left side sported a nasty gash, like a stab wound. His shirt was stained with crimson, and he looked in pain, beads of sweat on his face. Karla paled. 'You'll need a doctor, Nikolai. You've lost blood.'

'It's not as bad as it looks. A flesh wound. The bleeding's stopped, but give me something to patch it.'

'You better let me drive.'

'As long as you can manage.'

Karla took a scarf from her tote bag, and Gorev pressed it against his side. Rashid climbed into the rear of the van, ignoring

Gorev's state, and said angrily, '*Move*, both of you. We don't have time for this.'

A helicopter clattered somewhere in the far distance, galvanising them all. They worked frantically, manoeuvring the wooden planks into place and rolling down the machines, before Karla handed out the helmets and leather motorcycle gear. When they'd finished dressing, Rashid pulled on his helmet, tucked his Skorpion machine-pistol into his backpack, and hung the bag round his neck. 'Get away from here as fast you can.' Sweat drenched his face as he climbed on to the Yamaha, ready to make his escape. 'We'll use separate routes, and take special care you're not followed. We'll meet at the cottage. That's if we can make it before the police set up roadblocks.'

'And if we run into trouble?'

Rashid fixed Gorev with a cold stare, spat out his words. 'We're only small players in all of this. Nothing changes, no matter what happens to us. But I'll tell you this. The Americans will pay the price for their stupidity. I'll turn this city into a wasteland before I'm caught. You mark my words.'

He started the Yamaha, his mouth twisted in contempt. 'As for you, Gorev, you made a serious error. You should have finished the Russian when you had the chance. Don't *ever* make a mistake like that again.'

He snapped his visor shut, opened the throttle and drove the Yamaha over to the doorway. He inched his way out, glanced right and left, then gave the all-clear signal before he drove off.

Karla was tense as she mounted the Honda. 'Will you be all right?'

Gorev pulled on his helmet and climbed onto the pillion seat with difficulty, pain creasing his face. 'I've come through worse.'

'Rashid means it, doesn't he? He'll trigger the device if he's at risk of being caught.'

'I think you can count on it.' Gorev was grim. He snapped shut his visor. Karla did the same, then hit the start switch and the Honda purred into life.

Washington, DC
1.15 p.m.

'What about the next circle?' the President asked. 'I presume that represents the next wave of casualties?'

In the basement of the White House, Sergei Maslov had sensed a wave of animosity wash towards him from everyone in the room as they digested his words. He could understand why. He was, after all, a chemist who had worked on the nerve gas that could kill them all – their families, their friends, their fellow citizens.

'That is correct,' he replied. He turned to the map again, ran his finger around the orange circle, which encompassed the intersection of 12th Street and Jefferson to the west, the farther reaches of Capitol Street to the south, Lincoln Park to the east, and almost touched New York Avenue to the north. 'In this zone, in the immediate aftermath of the explosion, most victims will certainly inhale the gas, but in less extreme quantities – anything from the micro droplet necessary to kill them down to thousandths of a micron perhaps, enough to cause grave injury. By that I mean loss of muscle control, impaired lung and nerve function, acute breathing difficulties. Many survivors in this zone would suffer long-term serious illness. Victims with bad hearts, asthma or bronchitis would almost certainly perish. We are still talking about a hundred per cent casualty rate – or close to it – but the percentage of casualties who would die *immediately* diminishes to between fifty and seventy-five.'

'What about the survivors?' Charles Rivermount, assistant to the President on economic policy, pointed to the orange circle, inside which perhaps a million people would be trapped during the rush hour.

'Many of them will still die. You must realise that the aftermath of this attack would be like nothing in your country's experience. Chaos, and the massive numbers of injured, would overwhelm your emergency services, make it impossible for them to function properly. Ambulance crews would be prevented from moving into the area without wearing biochemical suits and breathing apparatus, making it difficult in itself to treat surviving victims lying in the streets. And the aid they could offer would be negligible.'

Listening to Maslov, Paul Burton was awestruck. In his mind's eye he saw not the red, orange and green circles but the living streets of Washington. Streets full of restaurants and cafés, galleries and shops. The guts of the city he had grown up in, studied in. The parks where he had played as a child and with his own sons. The city he loved because of its grandiose design, its cultural diversity, its elegance. Massachusetts Avenue, with its stately mansions. Capitol Hill, the icon of the nation. The bustling thoroughfares of Chinatown, with their smells of oriental spices. The Eastern market on 7th Street, where his mother used to take him as a kid to the Saturday farmer's mart to buy her fresh vegetables and fruit.

Nor did he take in the sheer volume of anonymous victims Maslov was speaking of. Instead he saw faces: cab-drivers, store-owners, waiters, cops, politicians, municipal and government workers. Close relatives, families and friends that he and his wife had known all their lives; Nathan's playmates and the infants in Ben's preschool. He saw the black neighbourhoods, the tenements in south Georgetown, the white-collar apartment blocks on Connecticut Avenue, the mansions of the rich out in Adams Morgan, and he knew that not a single home would be untouched by this tragedy.

'You're saying that it's *pointless* deploying our emergency medical response teams?'

Maslov nodded. 'In my opinion, they would be totally ineffective. There is no antidote for A232X. Many survivors will ultimately die, even if they get to a hospital.'

One of the army chemical experts spoke up. 'The chaos the professor spoke about is also going to be worsened by mass hysteria, sir.'

'Explain,' said the President.

'There's a medical phenomenon known as hysteria-induced

epidemic, a psychogenic illness, that comes into play. You have one person visibly sick and the people who see that person ill come down with the symptoms. The classic example is the Sarin gas attack on the Tokyo subway by the Aum Shinri Kyo cult. Twelve victims died and a thousand were injured, but almost five thousand people flocked to hospital complaining of symptoms. In the District, we'd be talking about a tidal wave of people swamping the few emergency medical services that might still exist.'

The bespectacled young Russian professor nodded his agreement, then turned to the third circle, in green. 'There is some hope, however, for those caught within the green zone.' The circumference around which he drew his finger touched the banks of the Anacostia river to the south, George Washington University to the east, Le Droit Park to the north, all the way out to Capitol Heights to the east. 'Here, casualties would be down to between fifteen and thirty per cent. But survivors would have to be moved out of the area quickly – in itself a major problem – to reduce the risk of inhaling gas particles.'

'How long would the gas remain in the air?'

'The A232X footprint – which is, in effect, the length of time trace particles linger in the atmosphere, on water or on man-made surfaces such as buildings or roads – is up to four months.'

Bob Rapp, the President's special adviser, standing at the back of the room, raised his voice. 'You're telling us America's capital will be uninhabitable for *four months*? How in hell is that possible?'

'Actually, it may even be longer, perhaps even six months,' Maslov suggested. 'Remember, you will have mounds of corpses on the streets – hundreds of thousands of unburied dead. The after-attack clean-up and the burials will take time. It would be safer not to commence any large-scale decontamination programme until the risk of exposure is reduced to near minimum. And there is also another risk to consider – typhoid or cholera outbreaks. People involved in the clean-up may be reluctant to enter the affected zones, for fear of putting their own lives in danger.'

'It seems to me,' a red-faced Mitch Gaines suggested, 'that if this device goes off, Washington will be turned into a total graveyard. Ruined, completely destroyed.'

'Your description is accurate,' Maslov agreed. 'And as I pointed out to your colleagues during our earlier discussions, there are other effects that you must consider, and which are as grave as the immense human casualties. This is a powerful weapon we're dealing with. It has the ability not just to destroy lives but to destroy a city in every conceivable way, most especially one like this.'

'What do you mean?' Katherine Ashmore, the Counsel to the President asked.

An army colonel from the Chemical Biological Rapid Response Team, standing against the back wall, responded. 'Ma'am, I think what the professor's trying to say is that by choosing Washington, these terrorists have picked the perfect target. Almost every government department has its headquarters in or near DC. Education, Health, Revenue, Treasury, the Federal Reserve which controls all banking operations in the United States. Then you've got the emergency and crisis management agencies, the military, the FBI, the CIA, the Pentagon, the Supreme Court, the Senate, the White House. Large numbers of employees and officials in all those departments, agencies and offices are going to be killed or seriously injured in an attack. That's going to affect our ability to function as a nation, apart from the massive problem of having to abandon the city for up to six months. But killing people isn't always the sole objective of even the most aggressive terrorists. Chaos and disruption are just as important. That's what this attack will ultimately achieve. If this country were a machine, Washington would be the main cog. If the cog were destroyed, the nation's infrastructure would grind to a halt. You'd have chaos and martial law, the economy damaged and society destabilised. Effectively, the United States government will have come to a virtual standstill.'

Maslov nodded agreement again. Silence engulfed the room. The deputies were still trying to take in the breathtaking tragedy the Russian scientist had painted; now they had to imagine another nightmare: bedlam reigning in every American city through lack of proper governance, law and order.

The President spoke. 'Professor Maslov, leaving aside those considerations for now, as frightening as they are, what's the bottom line here? How many deaths, how many casualties, maximum?'

Maslov riffled through his sheets – computer print-outs, models produced by complex programs that were virtually indisputable, spewed out by the American computers from the data he had supplied. Everything that would happen to Washington was on those pages. The effect on the city's medical services (less than five per cent operational), public utilities (totally defunct), police department (eight per cent effective), what percentage of pedestrians walking along Washington Avenue at rush hour would be killed (one hundred per cent), how many private dwellings and business premises would be uninhabitable in the aftermath owing to particle contamination (in excess of two hundred thousand) . . . On it went: the numbers of infants, children, adolescents and adult dead in each affected area within the three circles, the numbers of injured who would die within hours or days from lack of medical aid. A breakdown of the numbers of police, military, government officials, engineers, doctors, nurses and municipal workers who would survive or perish in each of the three zones.

A prophecy so chilling, so unthinkable, that Maslov, staring down at the cold black figures and adding them up, suddenly wished he were back in his grim Moscow apartment eating his breakfast, and not having to forecast the nightmare that lay ahead of the people in the room.

'For the conditions I have outlined, my estimate is that the total number of dead and injured in Washington, DC, would be just under a half million people.'

PART FIVE

12 November

'You have no option but to surrender, Mr President . . .'

36

Washington, DC
12 November
9.45 a.m.

Nikki turned her Toyota into the parking lot of Washington's Ronald Reagan National Airport. She had dropped Daniel off at preschool and had arrived in plenty of time for her interview with Tony Gazara, Reagan's air traffic control manager. Leaving her car, she walked to the ATC building and introduced herself to the receptionist, who made a call, and a minute later a tall, middle-aged man appeared, introduced himself as Tony Gazara, and led her up to his office on the top floor, with a panoramic view overlooking the aprons and runways. 'Take a seat, Miss Dean. Can I get you some coffee?'

'No, I'm fine, thank you. I've got another interview scheduled before noon, so I'd like to get straight to it, if you don't mind?'

'Sure. You know anything about ATC, Miss Dean?'

Nikki smiled, flicked open her notepad. 'Absolutely nothing, except every time I fly my life may depend on you people. Tell me about the near-misses. What happened?'

Gazara was immediately defensive. 'Look out of that window, Miss Dean. The thing of it is, we could have up to thirty thousand take-offs and landings a month at Reagan. Incidents like near-misses happen sometimes, like they happen at any busy airport. That's no excuse, of course, and I've got to tell you we had a lot of traffic on both those days. But our guys had everything under control. Sometimes the media blow these things out of proportion.'

'You think so?'

'I know so.'

'You're telling me people's lives weren't at risk?'

Gazara reddened slightly. 'As far as I'm concerned, ma'am, we run a tight ship here. We do a damned good job.'

'I'm not disputing that, Tony. The incident last Friday involved two civilian aircraft, is that right?'

Gazara nodded. 'Unusually, traffic was stacked that day due to bad weather, and there were pockets of heavy air turbulence in the airport vicinity. One of the planes was holding on stack, waiting to land, when it hit bad turbulence and dropped five hundred feet, breaching the two-thousand-feet separation between aircraft. No big deal really, and the pilots had everything under control at all times. But the regulations say a breach like that has got to be reported, and that's exactly what happened.'

'But what about the incident yesterday?' Nikki looked at her notes. 'The way I understand it, passengers on a Cessna private aircraft reported seeing a military transport aircraft come within a couple of hundred feet of their port side. The Cessna pilot had to take sudden evasive action that scared the hell out of his three passengers. And you're telling me nobody's life was in *danger*?'

Gazara was still defensive. 'We had a lot of traffic yesterday, most of it late scheduled. Most aircraft have something called TCAS, Miss Dean. That's Traffic Collision Avoidance System to you and me – think of it as a kind of airborne radar. What it means is, the pilot can tell if there's any danger of other aircraft in their vicinity, well before they see them, and an alert warning is announced in the cockpit. As a rule, small aircraft don't have such equipment – it's only mandatory for larger airplanes. But what made matters worse in this situation was that the military aircraft didn't seem to have its TCAS system working.'

'Why?'

Gazara shrugged. 'Maybe it was unserviceable, or switched off. But that's a question you'd have to address to the military. Either way, for whatever reason, their pilot wandered out of his flight envelope. Maybe he wasn't paying attention, maybe he didn't correctly hear his ATC instructions – I won't have all the facts until the FAA investigation is complete. But the moment our guys saw the trouble brewing on their screens they alerted the pilots to take action.'

Nikki glanced out the window. The aprons and runways looked

busy as hell. Beyond a line of US Air and Delta passenger aircraft, her eyes were drawn to at least seven huge green-painted military transporters sitting far out on the tarmac. 'Do you always get so much military traffic at Reagan, Tony?'

'Not at all. But don't ask me exactly what they're doing here. Some kind of exercise, I've been told. It's been going on like crazy since yesterday. Just came at us out of nowhere.'

Nikki spotted another military transporter taxiing in. And right behind it, another was touching down. Beside two of the parked transporters, troops in military fatigues were unloading dozens of sealed wooden boxes. Nikki thought: *There's a hell of a lot of military activity out there.* 'Those aircraft – what are they?'

Gazara followed the line of Nikki's finger, towards the apron where the soldiers were unloading. 'C-17s and C-130s. The military call them the workhorses of the air. They're used mostly to ferry men and equipment.'

'Was that the type involved in the near-miss?'

'Yes, ma'am. A C-130.'

'What kind of equipment are they moving? There sure seems to be a lot of it.'

Gazara shrugged. 'You'll have to ask the military, ma'am.'

Nikki was puzzled. 'Why wouldn't they use Andrews airbase? It's maybe only ten miles away.'

'Usually they do. But the word is, Andrews is busy as hell. They asked to divert their excess here.' Gazara stood, slid open a drawer in his filing cabinet. 'I've got some details of the near-misses right here. Then I'll answer any other questions you might have and let you get on your way.'

Maryland
2.10 p.m.

Thirty miles away, at Washington's second airport, Dulles International, the man who had the enormous task of administering DC had just landed from Heathrow.

Whisked through the VIP concourse, Mayor Albert Brown

emitted an irritated sigh as he sat in the back of his chauffeured Chrysler Le Baron limo speeding along the Eisenhower Highway towards the District. At fifty-one, a bald, handsome black American, he was a powerhouse of a man who oozed energy. That afternoon he wore one of his usual trademark three-piece suits and colourful bow ties. Beside him sat his deputy assistant, Sid Peterson, smoking a foul-smelling cigar, the source of Brown's irritation. 'Jesus, Sid, you want to choke me to death? Can't you find a better smoke than those Guatemalan firecrackers?'

'Sorry, Mr Mayor. Cigar bother you?'

Brown grunted, waved away a pall of grey smoke. 'So what the hell is it the President wants that I have to haul my ass back from London a day early? Can't he talk over the phone?'

Peterson cracked his window, let the slipstream suck out the smoke. 'Says it's urgent, Mr Mayor. And he'd like to talk in private.'

'Next you'll be telling me we're going directly to the goddamned White House.'

'No, sir. What I've been told, first he'd like to talk to you from your comms room.'

A floor above Brown's office at One Judiciary Square, in the private chamber that housed his personal gym equipment – the room accessed only by the mayor's security swipe card – was a battery of modern communications technology that allowed him to talk via a TV satellite link directly and securely to the White House. Brown was puzzled. If the President wanted to talk that urgently, he would have asked to see him at the White House. 'The hell's up, Sid?'

'I really don't know, sir. Guess we'll have to wait and see.'

Brown sighed, turned towards the limo's smoked-glass windows. 'Dynamic' was a word frequently used to describe Al Brown, and patience wasn't one of his virtues. Born in Los Angeles, the sixth son of a factory worker from the city tenements, Al Brown had suffered a harsh childhood of poverty which had given him an iron will. Graduating *magna cum laude* from Yale with a Bachelor of Arts in political science, he'd earned a doctorate from Harvard, and at only twenty-seven was appointed Deputy State Controller of Connecticut, with responsibility for managing the state's budget.

Later still came Washington, a position as Chief Financial Officer for the District of Columbia, and the tough mission of leading the then bankrupt nation's capital to financial recovery. Within three years, the resolute Brown had turned the District round, rescheduling loans, trimming municipal workers' excessive overtime bills, and discovering along the way the reasons why the District's books hadn't been balanced in the first place: his flamboyant boss had an abiding fondness for cocaine and expensive hookers that would eventually lose him his mayoral office.

Elected to replace him, Brown inherited a city in moral decline: corruption, poverty, filthy neighbourhoods, lousy schools, a drugs problem out of control, a spiralling crime rate and over a thousand homicides a year. But DC had always been a city with a grand vision – it was where George Washington had himself selected the site for the nation's capital on the banks of the Potomac. And the tenement kid from California had his own vision: safer streets, better education, clean and healthy neighbourhoods, affordable housing and health care. With three years of tough, aggressive action Brown had rescued the capital.

School standards were up, the streets were cleaner, corruption had diminished, crime and murder rates were down. With the help of tax breaks, billions of dollars' worth of private investment had started to pour in, run-down parts of the city were revitalised by developers, new business lured in. DC was no longer on the skids, but to finish his plan Brown needed the President to support another half-billion-dollar tax credit for the District. The President had been stalling.

As the car drove through the suburbs, Al Brown stared out through the smoked glass. He'd come to Washington with fear in his heart over the tough job he had to do, but he'd grown to love this city. The formal brick houses of Georgetown, the youthful and zesty Dupont Circle, the vibrant Adams Morgan, a hub of Latin American, African and other immigrants from around the world. For years, parts of DC had been neglected and abandoned, but now it was a vital, busy place, one of the wealthiest cities in America. The gritty industrial strips along New York Avenue were no longer an eyesore, but coveted by developers eager to build office space. The metro area was hopping with new nightclubs, restaurants and shops, and Washington had become a high-tech mecca: over half the world's Internet traffic now passed through DC.

Brown could reel off impressive figures: thirty-seven historic districts, more than fifty ethnic groups of every colour and creed, a city that was a magnet to twenty-one million visitors a year. But out there were the badlands of the Southeast – run-down, impoverished neighbourhoods with burnt-out stolen cars and graffiti-covered walls, where crack and crime still figured large.

It was problem areas like this, the decaying working-class districts and the metro pockets where homelessness was still a plague, which Brown wanted to tackle next. He could still remember the tenement days of his own childhood – the cries of hunger, argument and despair that woke him in the night. More than anything else, he wanted to help get these people out of their rut. But to do that, he needed the President's support.

The car cellphone buzzed, jolting Brown from his reverie. He turned from the window, grabbed the phone before Peterson could reach it. 'I'll take it.' He spoke a few words, then said, 'Thanks, Marion. Sure, I'll be there.' He ended the call, turned to Peterson. 'That was the President's secretary.'

'Yeah? She finally say what the man wanted to talk about?'

Brown's face lit up. 'No, she didn't. But forget about talking from my office. The President wants to see me right away. And it must be pretty important – he's set up a meeting at the White House.'

'Yeah?'

'Goddammit, Sid . . .' The glow expanded on Brown's face as the relentless rain beat against the window. '. . . I've got a feeling that maybe the man's going to see sense about our half-billion-dollar tax break.'

37

Chesapeake
2.38 p.m.

It was raining hard when Karla pulled up outside the cottage at Winston Bay. They climbed off the Honda, both drenched, and Karla found the key under the rock and let them in the front door. Gorev was still clutching his side, a look of discomfort on his face, and Karla said worriedly, 'Are you all right?'

'I've felt better. But at least the bleeding's stopped.'

'Let me see. I'll find something to dress the wound properly . . .'

'Later, Karla. We'd better get out of these wet clothes. Why don't you see what you can find upstairs for us both, and I'll get a fire going and see about something to dull this pain.'

Karla went upstairs and Gorev lit the fire, piling on the logs. As they blazed, he checked the temporary dressing Karla had applied, saw that the blood had congealed on the scarf and stuck to his wound, then went into the kitchen, found a bottle of vodka on one of the shelves, and took down two glasses. When he came out of the kitchen again, Karla was standing in front of the blazing logs, wearing a skirt and a sweater, and carrying a shirt and jeans. 'They're all I could find for you.'

'I'm sure they'll do.' Gorev poured vodka for each of them, handed across a glass. 'Here, drink it down, it'll steady your nerves.'

He saw the tension on Karla's face, and as she took the glass her hand was shaking. '*How* could the FBI have known where to find us?'

Gorev swallowed a mouthful of vodka, shook his head in disbelief. 'I've been asking myself the same question all the way down here. Was it luck, or something more than that? I've racked my brains but I can't think of a single mistake we made that led them to us. Can you? *Think*, Karla. Was there anything? Anything at all?'

'No. I was more than careful. Rashid too.'

'If the Americans knew where we were, they'd have had more men, and they'd have been far more careful before they made their move. I only saw two other men with Alexei. That tells me they had to have an element of luck.' Gorev shook his head again. 'But how has me confounded.'

Karla put her glass on the mantelpiece with a deeply troubled look. Gorev said, 'What's the matter?'

'There was a moment when I thought one of us might have to shoot your friend Alexei.'

Gorev's face darkened, and he lit a cigarette. 'To be honest, if it came down to it, I don't know what I would have done. But I don't think I could have harmed him, Karla. How could I? Alexei's been like a brother.'

'And what if there's a next time?'

'We'll have to make sure there isn't. From now on, we only go out when we have to, take no unnecessary risks. You can be certain the Americans will be searching everywhere, leaving no stone unturned.'

Karla's eyes were filled with anguish. 'But what's happened changes everything, Nikolai. Surely you see that? No matter how this turns out, whether we succeed or fail, there's going to be no way out of this for us, is there? The Americans will know who we are. And what good is it even if Josef is released? The Americans would find us, no matter where we tried to hide.'

Her face was white. Despair had crept into her voice, and she looked on the verge of tears. Gorev tossed his cigarette on to the fire, put out a hand, gently touched her arm.

'I've no answer to that, Karla. At least not right now.'

'But we're finished, aren't we? No matter what happens?'

'I didn't say that. There's always a way. If there's one thing I've learned, it's that anything is possible in this world.'

'Then what are we to do?'

'You're asking the wrong man. The next move's up to Rashid. But after what's happened I have a feeling he may have something unpleasant in store for the Americans.'

'What do you mean?'

'It's obvious now we can't hang around Washington for much longer without the risk of getting caught. It stands to reason Rashid will want to put pressure on the American President, make him see sense a lot quicker.'

'How?'

'Anything's likely where Rashid's concerned. And that's what worries me.' Gorev put down his glass. As he moved to pile another log on the fire, his face suddenly twisted in pain. He bent double, clutched his side again, his legs buckling as he collapsed in a heap on the couch.

'*Nikolai . . .*'

Karla moved to help him. Gorev was deathly pale as a surge of blood gushed between his fingers. 'Find something to stem the flow. *Quickly*, Karla.'

Karla hurried upstairs and came back with a bed-sheet and scissors. 'Let me look.'

She knelt, cut away part of Gorev's bloodstained shirt and removed the scarf, dabbed the flow from the wound, and paled when she saw a jagged piece of metal jutting from the flesh, still seeping blood. 'It looks more than a flesh wound, Nikolai. There's shrapnel lodged in the tissue. You'll need a doctor.'

'We'd be asking for trouble.' Sweat coursed down Gorev's face. 'You know that, Karla.'

'What if there's more shrapnel?'

'Worry about that later. Find some pliers or tweezers, or whatever you can to take it out. And get some hot water.'

'I might only make things worse . . .'

'For God's sake, don't argue, Karla.'

She went into the kitchen, boiled a kettle, came back with a basin of steaming water, then found a small pair of tweezers in her tote bag. 'It's all I've got.'

'It'll have to do. Tear up some of the sheet. And be ready to plug the wound when I tell you.'

'Nikolai, I can't do this.'

'If you don't I'll do it myself. Get ready.'

Karla cut strips off the sheet. Gorev parted the wound with his fingers so she could see the jagged metal splinter protruding from his flesh. 'Do it, Karla. *Now.*'

Karla gripped the metal with the tweezers and started to ease the shrapnel out. Gorev clenched his teeth. 'Get it over with. Pull harder.'

Karla gave a tug, the splinter started to move again, and then it was out. A stream of blood oozed from the wound, gushed on to the floor. 'Stem it, Karla. Quickly.'

She balled a cotton strip, stuck it into the gaping hole and kept it there, pressing hard. After a minute the cotton was soggy with blood and she replaced it with another, soaked in vodka to sterilise the wound, and finally the bleeding started to subside. Gorev grimaced. 'Bandage it up.'

She wrapped some cotton strips around his stomach, tied them tightly, and Gorev eased himself back on the couch. He looked weak, on the edge of exhaustion, his eyelids half open, the loss of blood showing on his face, which was racked by raw pain, glistening with sweat. Karla dabbed his brow. 'I've come through a lot worse. Don't worry, Karla.'

She tried to stand, but Gorev grasped her arm. 'Where are you going?'

'There has to be someone who can help.' Karla was ashen with concern. 'Rashid's people? Or your Chechen friend, Razan?'

'No.' Gorev was resolute, despite his agony. 'If the bleeding starts again, we'll think about it. But for now, let me rest.'

Fifteen miles away Mohamed Rashid turned his Yamaha off Highway 4. Thick forest lay on either side; he saw a placard that said *Picnic Area* and swung the motorcycle on to a narrow forest track.

He had left Alexandria far behind, crossed into Maryland, and there hadn't been a sign of anyone following him, on the road or in the air. He had escaped safely, of that he was sure, but he was still seething with rage, his anger like a living thing.

He drove into the forest for a couple of hundred yards and came to a deserted clearing with half a dozen rough-hewn log benches and tables. He was alone, no one to disturb him, and he switched off the Yamaha's engine and dismounted. He took his backpack and went over to one of the benches. Pine scented the air, and the woods were peaceful. He opened the backpack, lifted the laptop out of its carrying case and placed it on the bench in front on him.

How? How had the Americans found his apartment? The question rattled around inside his head, fuelling his anger. Logic told him it had to be chance, but this didn't dilute his feeling of rage. The first thing he intended to do when he returned to the cottage was alter his appearance. He had bought several different hair dyes in case of necessity: the blond hair would go, and so would the earring.

He connected the collapsible satellite dish to the port at the back of the computer, switched on, and after a few seconds the Windows program loaded. With its nickel-cadmium batteries, the laptop was good for five hours' solid use without having to be recharged, but he needed no more than five minutes. He aligned the dish, then typed an outline of his report, making sure to include everything in his message – the catastrophe that afternoon, and his recommendations about how to proceed next.

When he had finished typing the message, he scrolled through it a couple of times to make certain he was happy with the text, then hit the 'send' key and the signal was gone into the ether in less than two seconds. Nine thousand miles away in Afghanistan the coded transmission would be received almost instantly.

If the Americans picked up his seconds-long signal, they'd have a problem decoding it. Even with their most powerful computers, it would take them weeks at least to crack the code, the Pakistani programmer had assured al-Qaeda, and he had no reason to doubt the man, a brilliant cryptologist.

But what was more worrying, and more dangerous, was the time the transmitter was actually 'on air'. Receiving an incoming signal didn't pose the slightest problem to Rashid – it was simply being snatched from the ether, and no one could tell who it was being received by, or where. The dangerous part was when he was transmitting, or acknowledging a received signal. If the Americans were lucky, they could triangulate his signal with their computers and fix the exact location of his transmission. But they had to be *very* lucky and very fast, because his transmission was so brief. Even so, he had been instructed never to transmit from the same place twice, an instruction he had rigidly adhered to, altering his transmission locations every time by a minimum of ten miles.

He switched off the laptop. He was still seething. The day had been a disaster. But not a *complete* disaster.

If he had his way, the Americans would be given another harsh example of al-Qaeda's power. One that would make them agree to the demands immediately. As he began to pack away the computer he heard the crack of a twig behind him. Startled, Rashid reached into the backpack, gripped the butt of the Skorpion machine-pistol, cocked it but held it out of sight, down by his side.

Two hikers came out of the woods, wearing green rain capes and backpacks, a dark-haired girl and a blond young man – they looked like teenagers. Rashid wondered how long they'd been in the woods, observing him. The couple halted in their tracks, ten yards away, on the narrow trail that led towards the clearing. Rashid was in their path; they would have to move by him to pass.

They seemed uneasy about the presence of a stranger in the woods, and the girl suddenly grasped the boy's arm. He smiled nervously. 'Hi.'

Rashid nodded a reply.

The boy looked awkward, unsure of what to say next. He

glanced past Rashid, towards the picnic bench. 'That a laptop you got there, sir?'

Rashid nodded again.

'Hey, it's got a satellite dish, right?'

'Yes.'

'Looks cool.'

The couple started to move, but anxiety suddenly sparked in the boy's eyes when he noticed the machine-pistol by Rashid's side. 'Is . . . is that a gun, sir?'

This time Rashid didn't reply. He raised the Skorpion.

Chesapeake
2.55 p.m.

Karla stood at the kitchen window, staring out at darkening grey clouds and the drizzling rain. The weather didn't help her mood, and she turned away, sat at the table, her hand on her forehead, her mind a welter of confused thoughts.

Nikolai was still resting. Five minutes ago, when she'd felt his brow, it was burning, so she'd taken some ice cubes from the refrigerator, wrapped them in a tea towel, and tried to reduce his temperature.

When she went back into the kitchen to wring out the wet towel, the anguish suddenly hit her. She felt as if she were trapped in the middle of a nightmare, and she was filled with a terrible sense of dread. She knew that from now on she was a marked woman. The Americans would learn her identity after what had happened. They would find her, no matter how it turned out, no matter where she went – she would be hunted down, imprisoned, or even killed.

What would happen to Josef then? He'd already lost a father. Who would care for him? She loved her son with such intensity that the thought of him being left completely alone in the world, locked in a tiny cell for the next thirty years, caused her heart-wrenching agony. She wanted to cry, forced herself to hold back her tears.

For a few moments she entertained an insane thought: what if she called the police, gave herself up and told them everything? But if she did, she'd be condemning Nikolai to death, just as she'd be condemning Josef, and the mere thought of both those consequences filled her with such despair that it brought her close to breaking point.

She couldn't betray Nikolai any more than she could her own son. She had loved him once, deeply. She had always kept that part of her life in Moscow secret, even from her husband. She had made an effort to forget Nikolai when she returned to Lebanon to marry, and after Josef had been born, and as the years had passed, she had somehow managed to bury those cherished memories of the time they had spent in Moscow together in the back of her mind, but she had never forgotten him. How could she?

She had kept her secret hidden for a long time, but every time she looked at Josef's face, heard his voice, she was reminded of it. Her son had been conceived the last night she and Nikolai had spent together in Moscow. Two weeks later, after she returned to Tyr, she had married Michael. Her husband never knew, and she could never have brought herself to tell him. And so she had lived with the lie – Michael believing, until the day he died, that Josef was his son – and kept it hidden in the darkest chambers of her heart. But she knew that Josef's conception wasn't an accident of passion.

In truth, she had wanted Nikolai so much that having his child was the only way she could hold on to part of him. She had *wanted* to have his child, willed it to happen. And when she saw him again that day in Tyr, standing at her door, though so many years had passed and so much had changed, it had all come flooding back. It wasn't the same as Moscow – it could never be that – but she knew the tenderness was still there, and the shared spark they found in each other's company, and that a part of her cared deeply for him, always would. But could she tell him her secret? And what would it achieve after all these years?

She pushed the thought away, tried to concentrate on her

dilemma. She knew she was faced with really only one option: to carry on, and play her part.

It was the only chance that Josef would live and that he'd be set free. And even then it was a slim chance. But could she really do it? Could she help kill half a million people for the sake of her own son's life?

Her mind was tortured, and whatever it was that had kept her going went out of her then. Her shoulders sagged, and there was only anguish in her dark eyes as she slumped forward and buried her face in her hands, harsh sobs racking her body. *My darling Josef, what have I done?*

She heard a sound behind her, turned. Nikolai stood in the doorway. He lurched against the door frame, pale as death. She saw to her horror that he was bleeding again, crimson liquid dripping through his fingers where he was clutching his wound. '*Nikolai . . . !*'

As she rushed towards him, he collapsed.

38

Washington, DC
2.50 p.m.

'Mr President, you're looking marvellous! Absolutely terrific! Haven't seen you looking so good in a long time.' A beaming Al Brown bounded towards the President to grasp his hand, the praise flowing even as he crossed the room. 'You'll have to tell me what the secret is. Maybe I need to spend some time on that ranch of yours?'

The President shook the mayor's hand. Brown, now that he was up close, realised he'd definitely overdone the ass-licking. The President was lacklustre, red eyed from lack of sleep, as if he were under enormous stress. Distracted, he ushered Brown towards a black leather sofa. 'Take a seat, Al. Good to see you.'

The private room was next to the Oval Office. Informal and intimate, it was where the President sometimes liked to greet close friends or familiar visitors. A pair of polished Texas steer horns adorned a sideboard in the corner, and on the walls were photographs from the President's stint in the Texas Air National Guard, shots of him in uniform in the cockpit of an F-102 fighter, and with his family and friends. A steward brought them coffee and departed.

'Thanks for coming so promptly, Al.'

'My pleasure, Mr President.' Brown unbuttoned his jacket, reclined on the sofa. Relaxed and upbeat, his excitement undiminished, he smiled broadly. 'So, are we finally going to get your support on the half-billion dollars the District needs?'

The President's face tightened as he put down his coffee cup with a nervous rattle. 'The question of my support isn't why I wanted to see you, Al. I'm afraid it's something far more serious.'

Brown's disappointment was instant. His smile vanished, his eyebrows twitched with puzzlement. He set down his cup. 'Maybe you better explain, Mr President?'

'We've got a very disturbing crisis on our hands, Al. And it involves DC. Maybe the worst problem the capital's ever had to face.'

Deep worry lines were etched on the President's brow, anxiety suffused his voice. Brown shrugged, offered a broad grin to comfort the stressed man opposite. 'Hey, Washington's had its share of crises before, Mr President. It's always had to deal with one problem after another. But it's come through them all and survived. It'll come through this one, for sure.'

The President's eyes glazed with emotion as he stared back at Brown. 'You're wrong, Al. I'm afraid this is one problem the capital might not survive.'

Maryland
3.55 p.m.

At Fort Meade, between Baltimore and Washington, Major Chet Kilgore was having a lousy day. A former air force pilot with over three thousand hours in command of C-5 transporters, five years ago he'd found a new career with the NSA, the National Security Agency. After a week's leave in Florida he was on his first day back at work, and it hadn't been a good one.

To start with, two of the computer terminals on his watch had gone down with power supply problems, then a power glitch had hit his part of the building at lunch-time when a circuit breaker popped, requiring a system reboot. To make matters worse, his back was acting up – four badly slipped discs in his lower spine that he'd cracked in an auto accident and which frequently gave him hell, the reason why he'd had to quit flying in the first place. For the last half an hour he'd had to lie on the hard floor in his office to get some minor relief. He'd taken two Motrin pills, but the pain was only just starting to ease.

'Sir? You got a minute?'

'What's the matter, Joe?'

Sergeant Joe Romero turned from the word-processing program that was running on his desktop computer as Kilgore tottered over. 'Sir, that brief we had about any unusual transmissions out of the Washington area.'

'What about it?'

'I registered a burst-transmission intercept about half an hour ago.'

'Civilian traffic?'

'If it is, I haven't seen one like this before.'

'You got a clean snatch?'

'I think so, sir. I passed it on to Captain Donaldson to have it run through our computers. I gave him a call a couple of minutes ago. First indications are it's highly encrypted and he thinks it's going to be a tough bitch to crack.'

'Did you get a fix?'

'It was way too fast, sir. I can't even be sure where the hell it came from – Washington or Timbuktu. The burst was no longer than about two seconds.'

'Sounds interesting. OK, put a marker on the frequency, we'll pass it along, and if it turns up again we might get a fix.'

FBI Headquarters
Washington, DC
4.05 p.m.

The meeting at the Hoover building had been called by Matthew Cage, the FBI's Assistant Director. A tall man in his late forties, with handsome features, he had a shock of steel-grey hair.

Three people were present: Cage himself, Tom Murphy and George Canning, the head of the Washington field office. The Assistant Director, seated at the head of the table, was famed in the Bureau for his icy calm. Even in the gravest crises, the man was a rock of self-control. But after he had listened patiently to Murphy's briefing on what had happened at the Wentworth apartment block, Cage was livid. 'I can't believe the suspects just *vanished* into thin air.'

'Sir, we had choppers in the air within five minutes of Agent Morgan's call,' Murphy answered. 'Within twenty minutes, we had roadblocks in place up to a mile away, and over a hundred agents in the vicinity. Within forty-five we'd scoured every street, every alley, every public building. Our search is still on-going. We're expanding it block by block, house by house. My men did the very best they could, I want to emphasise that.'

'But so far there's been nothing?' Cage countered. 'No clues? No idea even in which direction the three suspects were headed?'

'No, sir.'

'*Christ*, Tom. We've got the biggest manhunt in the country's history under way – millions of dollars' worth of resources and manpower – and we let our quarry slip through the net. What do you think the Director's going to say? Or the President?'

'Sir, the call on the apartment block was a *very* long shot. A complete fluke. The guy from the storage facility wasn't in the least sure it was Rashid he spotted in the Honda that day. My men didn't expect trouble. But when it happened, they did everything they were supposed to – they gave it their best, put their lives on the line.'

'Long shot or not, we blew it, and it's a fiasco.' Cage, exasperated, tossed down the pen he'd been using to jot notes. His despondency pervaded the room. 'So where the hell are we now?'

'One of the terrorists set off a couple of incendiary devices in Rashid's apartment before they escaped. I believe it was a precaution on their part, to make it difficult for us to find any evidence. Fortunately, the fire department managed to get the blaze under control before it spread to the rest of the block, but the apartment was pretty badly damaged. My men are attempting to sift through what's left of it, sir, to see if they can turn up any clues, but it's going to take time.'

'How about the neighbours?'

'The neighbours hardly knew Rashid, even by sight. He kept to himself. The caretaker spotted him no more than a couple of times a week, and when he went out he'd usually take his car. He signed a year's lease three months ago. We're checking with the bank and landlord.'

'What about Gorev and the woman?'

'The caretaker spotted them enter the block twice in the past two days, and thinks maybe he saw the woman a couple of times before that in the last two months. The neighbours we've questioned say they never saw either Gorev or the woman before. And the few who witnessed the shooting from their windows couldn't tell us anything we didn't already know.'

'Do we have any idea who the woman is?'

'We're working on it, sir, and the address on her driver's licence is being visited by one of our teams as we speak. Oddly enough, Major Kursk suggested that he had the feeling he had either met or seen her somewhere before, perhaps in Moscow many years ago, in the company of Gorev. But he's not sure. Though if we can pull her prints from the car or the apartment, that may help us get a fix on her.'

'But we still don't know how they managed to escape?'

'No, sir, we don't. Within fifteen minutes of Morgan's call our choppers had spotted and tagged half a dozen vehicles similar to the navy blue Explorer, all within a five-mile radius of the apartment block. They were followed to their respective destinations by our ground units and observed, before each of the drivers and their passengers were checked out and questioned, and the Explorers thoroughly searched. But they all turned up clean – nothing suspicious about any one of them, or the vehicles. And every single passenger could account for their movements at the time of the shooting.'

'You think the three may still be hiding out in the area?'

'It's a possibility. We've sealed off all the streets within a mile radius of the Wentworth block. We're checking every vehicle and pedestrian going in and out of the radius, at the same time conducting a search within the perimeter. We're doing it slowly and methodically. If Rashid and the woman thought about renting storage only two miles away – assuming they intended to use it to store their device – then it's just as likely they may have rented somewhere else in the vicinity for the same purpose. We're questioning the owners of storage facilities, warehouses and depots in the area. But it's a sensitive operation, sir, and we're being cautious in the extreme. The problem is, if the three are still in the locality, and we locate them, we can't go in guns blazing. They might trigger the device.'

'But do you think they're still in there?' Cage persisted.

'You want my gut feeling? They escaped pretty quickly after the shooting, switched vehicles, and they've gone to ground. They're professionals. They'll have thought this through. Rashid's been in DC almost two months, the woman maybe for the same length of time, if the caretaker's anything to go by. They'll have organised safe houses, most likely a number of them, for use in an emergency.'

'Which means we're back at square one.' Cage was dejected. 'Isn't there *some* way we can speed up the investigation?'

'The word's already out on the street that we're looking for Arabs. I'd suggest we have our agents and the police revisit their informants. Show them photographs of Rashid and Gorev. Say they're wanted in connection with a serious crime and that they're armed and highly dangerous. We don't have to go into any more detail than that.'

Cage turned to George Canning, the head of the Washington field office. 'Have any of the informants turned up anything so far?'

'No, sir.'

'Would it help if we spread more money around? Put more pressure on them? Maybe both?'

'Most of these guys, if you come down hard on them, they shut up,' Canning answered. 'Then you're nowhere. And we've already spread a lot of money around. We put out any more and every criminal and crackhead in the country is going to be heading for DC, knocking down our door, sticking their paws out. The whole thing could get out of hand, turn into a farce.'

'OK, but do as Tom says. Beat the bushes harder. Have your men put the word out about Rashid, Gorev and the woman. Show their photographs. And make it clear these people aren't to be tangled with under *any* circumstances. This isn't a bounty hunt. It's information we're after.'

'Yes, sir.'

Cage addressed Murphy again. 'When Major Kursk confronted Gorev, did he get even the slightest feeling that he might listen to him?'

'No, sir, he didn't. The opposite, in fact.'

'Yet Gorev could have killed him but didn't.'

'I guess.'

'At least that implies Gorev may have a certain amount of respect or feeling for the man, if you can believe it. That if we got into a situation like this again, or we find Gorev, then Kursk just might be able to talk to him.'

'I really wouldn't like to count on it, sir. You ask me, it's a miracle the major didn't end up in the morgue.'

'Did Kursk give a reason for preventing Collins and Morgan from opening fire?'

'He claimed Gorev threatened to turn the city into a graveyard if he or the others were harmed. Kursk says he didn't want to risk them setting off the device.'

'You believe him? Or do you think he had another motive?'

'I guess we just have to take his word. But if what Kursk said is true, then maybe he did the right thing.'

'Keep an eye on him. If there's any doubt, I want him off the team. And to hell with President Kuzmin.'

Canning spoke up. 'Sir, there's another angle to consider here. Once al-Qaeda learn what's happened, they might feel their operation is under threat. It may ratchet things up a notch, and not in our favour. Maybe Abu Hasim's going to fear that this might not pan out the way he intends. He might even be tempted to cut his losses, say to hell with us, and just set off the device.'

'I'm well aware of that frightening possibility.' Cage's face displayed an uncharacteristic look of raw fear. 'I've got a meeting in five minutes with the Director before he reports to the President. I don't have to tell you they're both unhappy as hell. As far as they're concerned, this has turned out a complete disaster.'

'We did our very best, sir. We're still doing our very best,' Murphy offered. 'Most of my men, their lives are here in DC. It's where their families are, their friends and colleagues. They know damned well the enemy's at the gates, and that they're looking down the barrels of a shotgun. They know how big the stakes are. This isn't just an inanimate city under siege. It's their own lives, everyone close to them, everything they hold dear.'

Cage stood, acknowledged the answer with a crisp nod. 'Then let's all get back to work. The moment anything turns up, I want to know.'

39

FBI Headquarters
Washington, DC
4.45 p.m.

'How's the head?' Tom Murphy helped himself to a cup of coffee from the percolator in Collins' office and came over to join him.

Along with the FBI back-up teams, a paramedic squad had arrived at the Wentworth and offered to take Collins to the Alexandria Hospital, to have him examined by a doctor after the grenade blast. When he refused, they'd given him some pills to lessen the pain, but his eardrums still felt sore, his mind sluggish. 'Could have been a lot worse,' he answered. 'I'm lucky to still have it.'

'Wish I could tell you to go home and take the rest of the day off.' Murphy pulled up a chair. 'But we need every man we've got and I guess you probably wouldn't listen to me anyway.'

'How'd the meeting go?'

'I've had better.' Murphy sipped from his cup. 'Any news from Rashid's place?'

'Morgan's over there now. They're trying to sift through what's left of it, and check out any calls made from the phone. The Honda Civic turned up some prints on the wheel and dash, and some soil samples were found on the floor. Forensic's working on them now. They'll call as soon as they've got something.'

'What about the woman's address, the one on her driving licence, in Arlington?'

'Fake. The address is a house occupied by a retired Baptist minister in his eighties. He'd never heard of Safa Yassin, didn't know who the hell our guys were talking about. They checked with some of the neighbours, giving them a description of the woman, but none of them ever saw her either. Either anywhere near the house or on the street. They're still checking it out with the vehicle licensing authorities, but I wouldn't hold my breath.'

'And the search?'

'Still nothing,' Collins replied. 'They're gone, Tom. And we both know it.'

Murphy nodded and sighed. 'I guess we're back at square one.' He explained that FBI informants in the District would be revisited and shown photographs of Rashid and Gorev. 'But first we'll have the photograph of Rashid electronically altered to reflect his new hair colour and style, although I'm not sure it'll do us much good. Chances are he'll change his disguise again. And any pay-off from the streets, if there is one, might take some time to kick in, so let's hope the apartment or car turn up some clues, or we're going nowhere fast. Where's Kursk?'

'Morgan drove him over to his apartment. He's trying to try grab a couple of hours' sleep.'

'You heard what he told Morgan? That he had the feeling maybe he'd seen the woman with Gorev somewhere before?'

Collins nodded. 'Except he couldn't remember her name, or where. Which gets us nowhere.'

'We'll see what the prints turn up in the next couple of hours. If we don't get lucky, we'll have a photofit done. Between the janitor, you, Morgan and Kursk, we ought to come up with a reasonable description. You've still got your doubts about the major, Jack?'

'All I know is we'd have had a clear line of fire if he'd got out of the way. And it stands to reason his loyalties have to be divided. Gorev's an old friend. It's too personal with him, Tom.'

'And it's not with you?'

Collins didn't speak. Murphy said quietly, 'I didn't mean that the way it sounded, Jack. But you know, maybe Kursk did us all a favour. If you and Lou had opened up and taken out all three of them, without us first neutralising the device, God knows what might have happened. I'm not saying you lost it, Jack. But you should have kept yourself focused. This isn't just about Mohamed Rashid and your own personal revenge. It's about an entire city. Just try and remember that and keep it in perspective.'

'Are you dressing me down, Tom?'

'I'd prefer you saw it as well-meaning advice. I don't want any mistakes. We can't afford them.'

Collins started to answer the rebuke, but bit back his reply. 'What about Kursk?'

'We'll see how it goes. If there's really any doubt about him, I'll have him off the team and kept in the background.' Murphy stood. 'Meantime, you ought to get some sleep. You look like shit. Put you head down. I'll call if anything breaks.'

Murphy closed the door. Collins got up, snapped shut the office blinds. He felt angry at Murphy's rebuke. But he was right. He'd been too intent on his own revenge, and maybe it was clouding his judgment.

He felt exhausted. He'd gone for over thirty hours without sleep, and the pain killer was making him drowsy, but he fought the tiredness, rage still driving him on, no matter how hard he tried to suppress it, replace it with cold resolution. Every time he recalled the fleeting image of Mohamed Rashid escaping in the Explorer with Gorev and the woman, a wave of red-hot anger overwhelmed him. So close, and he'd lost him.

He came back to his desk, slumped into his chair. He hadn't called Nikki in almost twenty-four hours. She'd be wondering what the hell was wrong. He picked up the phone, started to make the call, but exhaustion flooded his body, overcame him like a tidal wave. He knew he couldn't fight it any more, and he let go of the receiver. As he went to lay his head on the desk, the phone buzzed.

Washington, DC
2 p.m.

Nikki Dean was pulled up outside a red-bricked building on Ecklington Place, north-west of DC.

The Crisis Control Centre the metropolitan police had opened over a year previously was in a gritty industrial neighbourhood near New York Avenue. Two years ago Mayor Al Brown had come up with the notion of relocating city government offices out of downtown DC and into the neighbourhoods they served. The move included the three main command centres of the metropolitan police, North, Central and East, the idea being that the increased presence of cops in crime-ridden working-class areas would give locals a better sense of security and help keep crime down.

Nikki had covered the centre's ribbon-cutting ceremony for the *Post*, and now her editor wanted a follow-up, to find out whether the mayor's venture had really made a difference. Her interview with the Police Commissioner had been arranged for 2.15, and as she parked her Toyota across the street she noticed activity in front of the building, uniformed cops and detectives coming and going. She approached the door. Two young rookie officers stood guard on the steps, barring her path. 'Can I help you, ma'am?'

Nikki showed her press ID. 'I've got an appointment with the Police Commissioner at two-fifteen. He's expecting me.'

One of the young cops looked at the other, handed back her ID and shook his head. 'I'm sorry, ma'am. We've got orders. No one's allowed inside the building, unless they're with the Met.'

'Orders from whom?'

'*Nikki!*'

She looked up and saw Brad Stelman come down the steps. He was tall and good looking, in his late thirties, with fair hair and a boyish grin. He ran the metropolitan police public affairs bureau, but before that he'd been a reporter with the *Post*. Nikki and he had worked together out of the same office, and he had personally organised her interview that afternoon. Stelman kissed her cheek. 'How's my favourite reporter?'

'Confused. What's going on, Brad? I thought I had an interview with the Commissioner. But these guys say I can't go in the building.'

Stelman said to the two officers, 'It's OK. I'll look after this. Miss Dean is an old friend of mine.' He turned back to her. 'How about I buy you a cup of coffee? There's a coffee shop across the street, we can talk there.'

'Why, what's the problem, Brad?'

Stelman smiled reassuringly, took her arm. 'No problem, Nikki, just a slight change of plan. I'll tell you over coffee.'

Washington, DC
4.50 p.m.

The studio apartment was two blocks from FBI Headquarters. It had a separate kitchen, a small living room with couch and coffee table, TV and video, a few shelves of well-thumbed books and magazines left by visiting FBI guests, and a double bed in a corner. Kursk lay on the bed, his arms under his head, the curtains closed.

He stared restlessly at the ceiling. He felt numb, as if he'd just recovered from an anaesthetic. His mouth was dry and a gloss of sweat glistened on his forehead. He'd lain there for two hours, tossing and turning, unable to sleep, his mind racked by the incident with Nikolai Gorev at the apartment block. He kept replaying every moment of the encounter, over and over again, until his mind was a jumble.

Finally, overcome with anguish, he got up off the bed, put his head in his hands. Why hadn't he moved when he heard Collins' command to get out of the line of fire? He knew Nikolai's warning had been part of it, but subconsciously he was aware it wasn't just that. He'd wanted to shield Nikolai. But he couldn't shield him again, knew that with certainty. It had gone beyond that, and the knowledge gave him a terrible hollow feeling in the pit of his stomach.

Something else had bothered him for the last two hours.

The woman he'd struggled with.

When he'd tried to wrestle the weapon from her and they'd stared into each other's faces, he'd had the uncanny feeling that he'd seen her somewhere before. He'd told Morgan about his intuition while Collins was being attended by the paramedics, but he couldn't remember where he'd seen her. He had racked his mind to recall when, where or how, but it was a blank.

Where had he seen her?

With her dark looks, the woman could have passed for a Chechen, but Kursk didn't think she was. She looked more Mediterranean, or Arab, as her fictitious identity implied. The thought had occurred to him that he may have seen her face among the FSB files of wanted international terrorists. Except he'd had the odd feeling his memory of her had to do with Gorev. He'd tried to remember, but it was no use. Nothing came.

He forced himself not to think of her face, to blank it from his mind. In a moment of stillness, perhaps it might come. He lifted his head from his hands, his mind aching, reassured himself that the FBI would scour the apartment and the Honda. Fingerprints were bound to turn up, and with them maybe a name, but then it struck him, a fleeting, sudden flashback that hit him like a sharp jab of electricity, gave him palpitations.

The phone buzzed. He picked it up.

'Major?'

Collins' voice. Cold and direct. 'Did I wake you, Kursk?

'I was already awake.'

'The search team found something over at Alexandria. Something important. They want us back there straight away.'

Kursk didn't reply. Collins said, 'Are you still there?'

'Yes, I'm here.' Kursk paused. 'The woman . . . I saw her before.'

'Morgan told me.'

'I remember where I saw her face.'

40

The coffee shop was busy for mid-afternoon. Nikki noticed that most of the customers were uniformed cops and detectives from the police building across the street, queuing for coffee and pastries to go. Stelman went to the counter and got two cups of coffee and came back to join Nikki at one of the stand-up tables near the window. 'So what's going on, Brad?'

Stelman waved his hand towards the window and the bustling activity outside the Crisis Control Centre. 'You mean all this?' He turned back to face her with an easy smile. 'Some bastard of a bureaucrat decided at the last minute that an emergency police exercise might be a good idea for the District, keep our cops on their toes.'

'What kind of exercise?'

'The usual kind of drill. Some imaginary disaster they've got to cope with. To tell the truth, I didn't get the exact details, but it's no big deal.'

'What about my interview?'

'That's why I came down to see you. It's been cancelled, I'm afraid. The Comish is pulling his hair out trying to run everything from the basement command room, and asked me to apologise. I know it's messed up your plans, Nikki, and I'm really sorry about that, but we'll arrange it again, and very soon.'

Nikki noticed a car pull up across the street. Three men who looked like detectives got out and entered the building purposefully. 'You're *sure* there's nothing more going on, Brad?'

Stelman looked puzzled. 'Like what?'

Nikki stirred her coffee. 'I was out at Reagan this morning, doing a piece on an ATC problem. The place was crawling with military uniforms. And I saw at least a half-dozen air force transporters being unloaded out on the aprons.'

Stelman frowned. 'So?'

'The guy from ATC I was interviewing didn't know what the story was, except he'd been told there was an army exercise going on. That Andrews was all clogged up and they'd requested to use Reagan for their overflow. It just seems kind of odd. First the military's conducting a drill, and now the cops.'

Stelman grinned, shook his head. 'Reporters are always looking for a conspiracy, Nikki. It comes with the territory – I was the same when I worked at the *Post.* Don't ask me what was going on over at Reagan, though I'm pretty sure it's nothing significant. Otherwise I'd have heard through the Comish. But I can tell you with my hand on my heart that what's going on at the command centre is just another run-of-the-mill, pain-in-the-ass exercise drill. Nothing more, nothing less.'

'But two at once?'

'Nikki, this is Washington, remember? Maybe the most important political and strategic capital in the world. We both know the military and police conduct exercises in the District all the time, and sometimes they never make the papers. Believe me, there's nothing sinister going on that I'm aware of. And if I knew there was, you'd be the first I'd call.'

'Maybe I should do a piece on this drill exercise?'

Stelman shrugged. 'Why not? Soon as it's all settled down, a couple of days from now, I'll make sure you get the details.'

Nikki tried not to make it obvious that she was studying Brad Stelman's face as he lifted his cup. She'd asked her last question deliberately, to see whether he registered any discomfort, but he didn't. She figured she'd know if he was lying; they'd been friends a long time.

The day she'd rung him to arrange the interview with the Commissioner, they'd caught up a little on what had been happening to them both. After he'd quit the *Post*, Stelman had gone to work in New York for almost a year, and had returned to DC only two months ago, to take up his new position with the Met. He was a decent guy, good looking with it, had a wry sense of humour that Nikki liked, and they'd always got on well when they'd worked together. More than that, if she was honest, she'd always been vaguely attracted to him. He had been divorced five years, with no kids. She'd always thought of him as a steady, trustworthy kind of guy, and when her marriage broke up he'd been one of the few colleagues she had confided in. She figured that, of all the people she knew, he'd be truthful with her.

He finished his coffee, seemed to sense her doubt. 'Look, if it puts your mind at ease, I can try and find out what was happening over at Reagan. I've got a buddy who's a senior officer at Andrews. I can give him a call, fish around a little.'

'Would you? I'd appreciate that, Brad.'

'Consider it done.'

Nikki reached for her diary. 'So when can we do the interview? Tomorrow?'

'Tomorrow the Comish has a full schedule. And that's the way it is pretty much up to Friday. Say next week some time. I'll call you later, firm it up.'

'You're sure you're not trying to fob me off, Brad?'

'You? Never.' Stelman laughed. 'And to prove it, how about I buy you dinner, to make it up to you for the interview?'

'I . . . I don't know, Brad. I'm seeing someone right now.'

'It's not an offer of marriage, Nikki.' Stelman smiled. 'Just two old friends catching up. You can fill me in on what's been happening at the *Post*.'

'If you put it like that.'

He handed her his card with his home number written on the back. 'Give me a call at home later, say about six, and I'll see what I've found out from my friend over at Andrews. Then maybe you can let me know when you're free for dinner. How's Daniel, by the way?'

'His fourth birthday's two weeks away. I've got a party arranged for thirty kids on my mom's back lawn. Any more than that, and I might have to borrow a couple of your experts from the Crisis Control Centre.'

Stelman laughed again, reached across to pat her hand in a friendly gesture. 'He's a terrific kid, Nikki. And he's lucky to have such a great mom. I'm pretty sure you'll be well able to cope. But if you need help, you've got my number.'

'Thanks for coming down to see me, Brad.'

'My pleasure. I better be getting back. But you finish your coffee here if you like, and I'll talk to you later, OK?'

'Sure.'

Stelman moved to the door, went out. Nikki watched him cross the street and go up the steps to the Control Centre. A thought entered her head, a thought that mildly upset her, and she reached for her bag, checked her cellphone. She'd switched it off when she'd arrived outside the police building, but there had been no missed calls in the meantime, or all that morning. Jack still hadn't tried to reach her.

Disheartened, she finished her coffee. She thought about phoning him, but decided to do it later. First, she'd have to get back to the *Post*, write up her report on Reagan, and then pick Daniel up from preschool.

Salem, New Jersey
5.05 p.m.

It was dark when Karla drove into Salem. Gorev was almost unconscious on the seat beside her, and when she felt his forehead it was ice cold. She was desperate until she found the address she was looking for, a couple of miles' drive from the town, along a tree-lined avenue of discreet, walled private mansions, out on the edge of the New Jersey countryside.

She drove up to a pair of solid steel gates. The property was surrounded by high walls on either side, and tall trees behind. A security camera with an infrared light was mounted on top of one of the stone entrance pillars, and she saw it swivel round to study her as she got out of the car. She went up to the intercom to press the button, and a few seconds later a metallic voice said in English, 'Yes? What do you want?'

'To see Ishim Razan.'

'Who's looking for him?'

'A friend of Nikolai Gorev's.'

'*Who?*'

'Just tell Razan I need his help. *Urgently*.'

A panel in the gates slid back and a pair of hard eyes inspected her. The gates swung open moments later and two tough-looking Chechen men came out. Karla saw at least another half-dozen armed guards in the darkness behind the entrance, near a wooden security hut. One of the guards held a shotgun in the crook of his arm; another rested his hand on his hip, ready to draw his weapon.

The two Chechens came towards her. They carried electric torches, and one of them flashed his light in her face, while the other man probed his beam around the Plymouth. They both saw the state Gorev was in, his shirt covered in blood. 'Who are you? What's going on here?' one of the Chechens demanded in English, his eyes slits of distrust.

Karla noticed that the men wore small ear receivers of the type used by professional bodyguards. 'My name isn't important. This man is a friend of Ishim Razan's and needs urgent medical help. His name is Nikolai Gorev.'

'What happened to him?'

'He's wounded.'

'Your bag. Hand it here.'

Karla handed him her bag from the car. The man searched it, looked at her driver's licence. 'Safa Yassin. That's your name?'

'Yes.' Karla was desperate. 'Please, he's losing blood . . .'

'Be quiet.' The man lifted his left hand and spoke something in Chechen into a wrist microphone connected to his earpiece. Karla saw that the second Chechen was already moving round to the back of the car, opening the boot and checking inside, before he knelt on the ground and peered under the chassis with a torch, then lifted the car's bonnet and did the same. He came back and nodded to the first man, who finished talking on his wrist mike, then said to Karla, 'A necessary precaution. Ishim Razan is a powerful man, and powerful men have enemies. My apologies, madam, but I must search you also. Turn round, please. Lift your arms.'

Karla turned, and the man's hands moved expertly over her body. When he found nothing, he quickly moved to Gorev, patted him down, and found the Beretta in his pocket. The Chechen turned back to Karla, his face hard. 'What's this?'

'It . . . it belongs to Nikolai.'

The guard's eyes narrowed with suspicion. 'Why did you come here?'

'There was nowhere else I could go. I couldn't take him to a hospital.'

The guard slipped the Beretta in his pocket, spun Karla round. 'Stay still. I want to search you again. Hold your arms out.'

The guard's hands probed Karla's body intimately for the slightest bulge.

'Please – Nikolai needs a doctor. Can't you talk to your boss?'

The man finished searching her, spun her round again. 'I already have.'

This time the Chechen had a pistol in his hand, and it was pointed at Karla's face. 'Get in the back of the car.'

He pushed Karla into the rear. His companion jumped into the driver's seat beside Gorev and started the Plymouth, which sped through the gates.

41

Washington, DC
4.45 p.m.

Around the corner from the famous Willard Hotel, at 529 14th Street, two blocks from the White House, are the headquarters of the National Press Club. At a quarter to five, Bob Rapp was about to give an interview to Jerry Tanbauer from the *Washington Times*. The venue was the Press Club taproom, a well-know hangout of hard-nosed international correspondents, journalists and reporters, but surprisingly it was nearly empty that late afternoon, with less than a handful of customers at the bar.

Rapp had known Tanbauer since the days they'd worked together at the *Times*. They were old friends, and the interview had originally been scheduled at the White House. Tanbauer wanted to do an in-depth piece on Rapp's role as press adviser to the President, and his elevation to the NSC, but that had been two days before the crisis had begun, and Rapp had decided that it might be best to keep Jerry Tanbauer well away from mansion territory. A gnome of a man in his early sixties with a bad prostate problem and an even worse wig, Tanbauer was an accredited White House correspondent, a veteran newshound who could sniff a story a mile off.

The President had cautioned his advisers to try to go about their business as normally as possible, and Rapp knew that if he'd cancelled his interview Tanbauer might have got suspicious, so he'd phoned his old colleague and told him he had a meeting at the Willard before the interview, and perhaps they might meet instead in the more casual atmosphere of the Press Club. Rapp thought the club venue was a good idea – at least he'd be seen out and about and behaving normally by some of Washington's press, no bad thing if he wanted to avoid arousing suspicion. Tanbauer didn't seem bothered in the least by the venue change, and he led Rapp to a quiet table at the end of the bar. 'Let me get you a drink, Bob. What will it be?'

'Soda and lime.'

'You're fucking kidding me. Since when are you on the wagon?'

Rapp shook his head, smiled. 'I'm not, Jerry, just trying to keep a clear head.'

'Important business at the White House?'

Rapp thought: *Is he fishing?* Tanbauer was *always* fishing, he decided, and laughed. 'Just too much Scotch last night. But hey, you go ahead.'

'Whatever you say, amigo.' Tanbauer laid his leather folder and palm-sized tape recorder on the table and scratched his groin, a hint of his troublesome prostate, not helped by a lifelong fondness for large quantities of single-malt whisky. 'I'll order the drinks, go take a leak, and then we can start, Bob. Be back in a sec.'

As Rapp took his seat, ten feet away at another table two of his Secret Service detail took up their positions. Rapp had got used to the protection. Not that he enjoyed the idea; he simply tolerated it.

The Press Club had once been one of his favourite haunts. He'd met Andrew Booth in the same taproom, after the then Texas governor had given a luncheon speech. Rapp had been impressed by the speech, but boldly suggested to Booth he could do better. The Governor smiled. 'Why don't you come work for me? To tell the truth, I could do with another writer, especially one of your calibre, Mr Rapp. I've long admired your work.'

Rapp had a sneaking admiration for the Texan governor, down-home as he was. He recognised a sharp mind behind the homespun philosophy Andrew Booth sometimes liked to dole out to the public. And a rare thing – at least for a politician eager for the power of presidency – he was a genuinely nice guy. There was an honesty about him, a willingness to listen to the opinions of others – worthless though those opinions might be – without a shred of condescension or arrogance. And that was the key as far as Rapp was concerned: Andrew Booth *listened.* Not only listened, but acted on good advice. That was the kind of man Rapp wanted as his president. After he started with the speeches, and Booth liked them enough to use them, they soon became friends. A friendship that culminated in Rapp's elevation to presidential adviser and a place on the NSC after Booth's election.

It was exactly the kind of career move Rapp had always secretly hankered after. He'd learned that a journalist's words changed very little – but by being close to power, by being able to influence the most powerful man on earth, he had an opportunity he never dreamed of. For over twenty years he'd been a reporter – eight of those spent as a war correspondent – and had twice been nominated for a Pulitzer for his reporting. He'd witnessed the worst of human savagery: in Northern Ireland, Angola and then his watershed, Lebanon.

The absolute worst, in terms of sheer brutality, had been Lebanon. He always remembered the day he'd walked through Sabra and Chatila and seen the terrible carnage inflicted by the Israeli-backed Phalangist militia after they'd attacked the impoverished Palestinian refugee camps. The butchery the Phalangists left behind them shocked him to the core. Kids, tiny babies, women, men, lying in alleyways and gutters, with their throats cut or their bodies ripped to shreds by bullets or blast bombs. He'd stepped into one ramshackle house and seen two pitiful corpses – an elderly man, clutching the body of a little boy no more than three or four, probably his grandson whom he'd tried to protect. Both bodies had their throats cut. He'd seen even worse that day, images that he could *never* forget, which still brought bile to his throat and tears to his eyes when he recalled them.

His reports on the attacks had earned him a Pulitzer nomination but he'd cracked afterwards. He'd had enough of war, and for a year after he returned from Lebanon he'd lived on pills, little white-and-yellow pills that helped him get through the nightmares. He'd mended slowly, but there would always be a part of him that could never be fully mended after Lebanon . . .

Rapp's cellphone buzzed, jolting him from his reverie. He

flicked it on, heard the familiar voice of Paul Burton. 'Bob, this is Paul. Something's come up. We need you back here straight away.'

'I'm just about to do an interview with Jerry Tanbauer.'

'*Jesus!* Is he with you now?'

'He's gone for a leak.'

'Whatever you do, don't give the guy any indication that you're rushing back here. You know the kind of guy Tanbauer is. He'd start to get suspicious.'

'Don't worry, I'll handle it. I'm on my way.'

Rapp flicked off his phone. His summons back to the White House meant there had to be a sudden development in the crisis. He just hoped it wasn't for the worse. Jerry Tanbauer came back with the drinks. 'Here we go. Soda and lime. You're going to poison yourself drinking this shit, Bob.'

Rapp stood, put away his cellphone. 'Jerry, my apologies, but I'm afraid we're going to have to leave the interview until another time.'

Tanbauer frowned. 'Like when?'

'I'll give you a call later. Maybe we can do it over the phone?'

'What the frig's the matter, Bob? You got trouble at the mansion?'

Rapp shook his head, hid the lie with a sad expression. 'Not at all. I just got a call from George Washington Hospital. An old friend of mine's been taken seriously ill. I've got to get over there right away.'

Salem, New Jersey
5.11 p.m.

The house was a mansion with a vast marble porch, double oak entrance doors, cathedral windows and tall stone columns. A huge water fountain gurgled away on the expansive, well-lit lawns. The moment the oak doors opened a couple of guards came out and the Chechen shouted an order to them. As the guards lifted Gorev out of the car, another voice barked, 'Handle him with care. He's someone I owe my life to, many times over.'

Karla saw a man step out on to the porch. He was stocky, in his forties, wearing a well-tailored suit, and his left eye was covered with a black patch. 'Forgive my men, but they're well paid to protect me. No one is above their suspicion, least of all a beautiful woman.' The man studied her face. 'My name is Ishim Razan. You say you're a friend of Nikolai's?'

'Yes.'

'You could pass for a Chechen, but you're not, are you? Or even Russian?'

'No.'

'No matter. Come this way.'

Karla followed Razan and his men down a long marble hallway to an annexe at the back of the house. It looked like a watch-room for the guards, with a couple of fold-up beds, a bank of TV security monitors, and a tiny kitchen. They had placed Gorev on a bed in a corner, and one of the guards took a first-aid kit from a drawer and gingerly began to examine Gorev's wound before checking his pulse. Razan said to him, 'Well, Eduard?'

'It looks nasty,' the guard replied. 'And he seems to have lost a fair amount of blood. How long has he been unconscious?'

'About twenty minutes,' Karla replied. 'He's been drifting in and out of consciousness for the last few hours, and it's got worse in the past while.'

'What exactly happened to him?' Razan said to her.

'He was injured by shrapnel. Please . . . he needs a proper doctor.'

'That much is obvious.' Razan frowned. 'How did this happen?'

Karla said nothing. Razan finally nodded and sighed. 'As you wish. The doctor's already on his way. Eduard here will manage until he arrives. He's skilled in first aid.'

'It's important the doctor is someone you can trust not to talk to the police.' Karla was anxious. 'Nikolai would want to be completely certain of that.'

Razan saw the concern on his visitor's face. 'Don't worry, I wouldn't deal with any other kind.' He put a reassuring hand on her shoulder. 'I've seen Nikolai live through worse. And you can take it from me, he's always had the Devil's luck.'

The doctor arrived ten minutes later. He was a large, middle-aged Russian with dark, sad eyes, a double chin and half-moon glasses that were held together with Scotch tape. His crumpled dark suit looked as if it hadn't been pressed in months, and he had the brown-stained fingers of a man who smoked incessantly. As if to prove it his suit jacket was smudged with grey patches of ash. He felt Gorev's pulse and said, 'What happened to him?'

They were still in the annexe at the back of the house. When Karla explained, the doctor took off his crumpled jacket and rolled up his sleeves. He scrubbed his hands at the sink, slipped on a pair of latex gloves, and carefully examined Gorev's wound, probing it with a finger.

Razan said to her, 'Don't let Arkady's appearance fool you. He's a true eccentric, but a thorough professional. Many years ago, before he came to work in America, he was a field surgeon with a Russian paratroop regiment, and saw service on the battlefields of Afghanistan. Trust me, he's an expert when it comes to this kind of thing. I've seen him bring men on their deathbeds back to life. Well, Arkady, what's the prognosis?'

The doctor looked up, his glasses perched on the bridge of his nose. 'It's bad enough, Ishim. At a guess some shrapnel is still lodged in the wound, and may have lacerated his gut. He's also lost a fair amount of blood. He'll need to be operated on, of course, and quickly.'

'Can you do it here?'

'I'd prefer to move him to a proper theatre, but if I really must.'

Razan nodded. 'It would be best.'

'Very well. But if we run into difficulty, we'll have to consider moving him. There's a private clinic in Atlantic City with a well-equipped theatre, run by a Russian surgeon. For a price, he can be relied on to keep his mouth shut.'

'As you wish.' Razan turned to his men. 'Make sure the doctor gets everything he needs. And bring one of the Mercedes round the front. Have it standing by, just in case we have to move the patient quickly.'

'Yes, Ishim.' One of the Chechen bodyguards left, while two of the others got to work, one of them drawing piping-hot water from the sink, the second man unfolding a small trestle table and covering it with a fresh white towel. The doctor opened his bag, laid out his instruments and began to fill a hypodermic with anaesthetic. 'This ought to kill any pain he's going to feel. But I'd prefer as few spectators as possible. So you may as well go for a walk, Ishim. This may take a little while.'

'Whatever you say.' Razan put a hand on Karla's arm, ushered her towards a back door that led out to the gardens. 'And now, Safa Yassin, or whoever you are, I think we need to have a talk.'

Afghanistan

Eight thousand miles away, the next day's dawn had yet to spread its yellow stain across the horizon. Unable to sleep, Abu Hasim had risen just after three a.m., and after his prayers he was seated cross-legged on the floor of his command post, dipping cuts of coarse bread into a bowl of milky goat's curd on the small wooden table in front of him, when Wassef Mazloum, his ravaged-faced commander, came in.

'Abu. A message has come. Tariq decoded it.'

Hasim remained seated as Mazloum handed him a sheet of paper, the decoded copy of Mohamed Rashid's signal from Washington. As he read it eagerly, Hasim's face muscles twitched. For a second or two he turned pale, then he flushed crimson. Suddenly he flung the page aside, sending it floating through the air, and then his hand swept across the table in a display of furious anger, the bowls of bread and goat's cheese scattering across the floor.

Wassef Mazloum stood there silently, unwilling to comment on his chief's sudden outburst. Hasim's teeth were clenched tight, and for several moments it seemed as if he was trying to summon all his strength to calm himself, breathing deeply and slowly until he was once again in control of his emotions. Finally, he raised himself from the floor, clutching the hem of his gown.

As he crossed to the mouth of his cave he had a distant gaze in his dark, brooding eyes. He stood there, scrutinising the horizon beyond his camp, where the tangerine light of the rising sun would soon spread like wildfire across the hills. Then he looked down into the moonlit valley, noticed a distance speck of black, a herd of goats grazing on a mountainside.

When he turned back to face Wassef Mazloum, the anger was gone, replaced by a frigid calm. His voice was soft, almost a hoarse whisper. 'The Americans think we are fools. But it is they who are the fools.'

'As you say, Abu.'

'They have attacked our cell, tried to destroy Mohamed and the others. They have been audacious, have not heeded the advice I gave them for their own good. Worse, it is obvious they are not treating our demands seriously. That must change, and change quickly.'

'Of course.'

'Get Tariq here. I wish to send an important message.'

'To whom?'

Hasim almost spat the words. 'The President of the United States.'

42

Washington, DC
5 p.m.

The White House situation room fell silent as the President took his seat. He waved Mayor Al Brown to the chair beside him as the regular members of the NSC crisis committee took their places at the table. The twenty-four-hour clock on the wall recorded the time: 17.00.

The President addressed the faces round the table. 'Gentlemen, I've given the mayor a briefing on the situation and we'll forgo our usual security procedures so he can join us. The reasons should be obvious. It's his city and his citizens who are under threat so it's only right he be here. So if anyone's got any objections I'd like to hear them now, before we start.'

No one registered their disapproval, and the President nodded to Doug Stevens, the FBI Director, to begin. 'Doug, let's hear your report.'

Stevens, with the uncomfortable air of a man who'd been asked to walk the gangplank, outlined in detail the events at the Wentworth apartment building. 'As it stands, the building's still sealed off. The apartment and the car are being examined by our forensic teams, and a square-mile section around the area has been cordoned and is being thoroughly searched. But as of now, Mr President, we've got no clues or leads as to where the occupants escaped to. However, I can assure you that my men are working flat out and using every means at their disposal to try and determine the whereabouts of the three terrorists involved. The good news is that two of them have been positively identified as the suspects Moscow came up with – Mohamed Rashid and Nikolai Gorev. I've got copies of their files, in case anyone would like to see them. We don't have an ID on the woman yet, but we're hoping her prints will turn up at the scene and give us something to work with.'

'What if the press get to hear about the search activity, or the shooting?'

'No doubt they will. But there's a million and one fob stories we can come up with, sir. I don't believe we're in jeopardy in that regard just yet.'

Charles Rivermount, beside himself with fury, chipped in. 'You're telling us these people just *vanished*?'

'They may still be within the cordon. That's why the search is proceeding slowly but thoroughly, and with due caution. Remember, if they're still in the area, and they feel threatened, these people could be tempted to trigger their device.'

'But they might just as easily have escaped your dragnet?'

'That's possible. But we won't know for certain until we complete the search, which should be within the hour.'

Rivermount was red with ire. 'The FBI costs our taxpayers billions of dollars. It's supposed to have the best and brightest lawmen in the country, employ the best experts in every field of criminal detection. But you're telling us your agents managed to corner the most wanted terrorist criminals on American soil, and *lost* them?'

'Mr Rivermount, the call to the apartment block was a long shot that unexpectedly yielded a result. My men did their utmost. Unfortunately they came up against a ruthless, heavily armed enemy.'

'Isn't that all part of the Bureau's job? Something they're supposed to be trained for? From where I sit, we blew maybe the best chance we had to apprehend this cell. And that smacks to me of gross incompetence.'

The FBI Director flushed. 'I greatly resent that remark, Mr Rivermount.'

'Gentlemen,' the President interrupted. His own anger had already been vented in a private confrontation with the Bureau's Director before the meeting began, and he didn't intend going down that road again. 'Let's not have this descend into bickering.

I can understand your frustrations. I share them, as does Mr Stevens. Mistakes have been made. The opportunity to apprehend these people has been temporarily lost. But let's move on and learn from these events. We now know for certain who two of these terrorists are. We also know how desperate and dangerous they are and what they're capable of.' He turned to Stevens again. 'Doug, assuming the worst and they escaped the net, where can they run to? What are they likely to do next?'

'They're bound to have more than one safe house, or people they can turn to for refuge in an emergency. Every known radical Islamic supporter and sympathiser in DC, Maryland and Virginia is already being watched around the clock. As of two hours ago, that watch has been intensified, their phone calls monitored, and their every movement scrupulously observed, in case our suspects might be in touch with any one of them for help. We're also having our agents revisit their street contacts to show photographs of two of the terrorists. Something else. It seems one of the terrorists – we think Gorev – was wounded in the shooting.'

'Badly?'

'We don't know, sir. Traces of blood were found on the first-floor landing that led all the way down to the rear of the apartment block. We're trawling every hospital, doctor and pharmacy in the metropolitan area, in case he seeks medical help. But as to guessing what our suspects might do next, I think we'll have to wait until our search of the area's complete. It's frustrating, I know, sir, but that's how it stands. But one guess I can make with near certainty. These people are going to be in contact with Abu Hasim. He's going to hear about what's happened. It's likely to make him feel threatened and angry. He's probably going to press his demands even more strongly.'

'I'm aware of that likelihood.' The President nodded, then turned to the head of the CIA. 'Dick, what do you have for us?'

'First of all, I should point out that our satellite reconnaissance has confirmed that all the Russians bombers returned to their base at Solcy, and their bombs have been returned to their stockpiles. We've no indication that Kuzmin's about to break his promise.'

'Good. And what about our efforts to make contact with Abu Hasim?'

'It's not looking promising. The best shot we had was with a man named Samar Mehmet. He's a retired Pakistani intelligence officer, someone the CIA had dealings with when we ran weapons to the mujahidin for use against the Soviets. He's still considered an old friend by Hasim. We asked him to make representations on our behalf.'

'Was he briefed on the situation?'

'Yes, sir,' the CIA chief replied. 'We requested he approach Hasim to open up a direct line of communication with us. We gave Mehmet a list of dedicated and secure satellite frequencies that can be used any time, night or day. Any transmission could be relayed directly here, to the situation room, in real time. Or Hasim could choose whatever method of communication he wishes. Unfortunately, Mehmet point-blankly refused to help. He doesn't want to be seen in any way as a CIA pawn, or a negotiator on our behalf.'

'The fact that he was briefed, doesn't that now make him a security risk? What if he talks to the international press?'

'We told Mehmet about Hasim's warning not to make the threat public. He won't leak it to the press, sir, I'm absolutely convinced of that – he wouldn't risk upsetting Hasim's strategy. But I'm also pretty sure that, despite his refusal, he'll let his old friend know that he was approached by us.'

'Did Mehmet at least give any indication of how he thought Hasim would react?'

The CIA chief was sombre. 'Off the record, he believes we'll be completely wasting our time. He thinks that if Hasim's gone this far he's not going to be swayed by arguments, especially from the White House. Being able to hold America to ransom is something Hasim's wanted desperately for many years. He's not going to want to relinquish his upper hand and he's not going to want to talk.'

'Does Mehmet hold out *any* hope at all?'

'Not really, sir.'

'Terrific,' the President said, deadpan.

'We'll try other avenues to make contact, sir. As many as we have to.'

Rebecca Joyce spoke up. 'What if we tell the Afghan regime what Hasim's up to? What if we tell them that the Russians are going to bomb their country to dust if Hasim doesn't call off his threat?'

'It still wouldn't stop Hasim,' the CIA Director answered. 'And even if the authorities attacked his camps and attempted to capture him, it wouldn't neutralise the threat. In fact, it would only exacerbate it. Hasim might feel cornered, enraged, and be tempted to explode his device. We'd be making a bad situation even worse.'

The President promptly cut in. 'Gentlemen, ladies, I'd like to move on. There're still a number of important issues to cover. Dick, have we had any luck trying to pinpoint communications from or to Hasim by his cell?'

'No, sir. We're scanning the airwaves over Afghanistan and the US every second, but so far we've got nothing.'

'General Horton, where are we with the fifteen per cent withdrawal of our troops from the Middle East?'

'It's under way, sir. The first transports should be lifting off from Saudi at nine p.m. this evening.'

As the President addressed the Council members in turn, Mayor Al Brown listened in stunned silence. He was still reeling after the private briefing thirty minutes ago, but now the reality of the President's frightening words hit home. Listening to the grim reports from around the table, he felt as if he were living a nightmare. When he could bear it no longer, he placed his palms flat on the table, the anger in his five-foot-six-inch body overflowing like lava. 'Mr President, I'd like to say a few words.'

'About what, Al?'

'The way to handle this.'

'You've got an angle?'

'Mr President, I've got an opinion. And for what it's worth, and with respect, I think some of these so-called experts here ought to shut the fuck up and listen to what I have to say.'

Washington, DC
4 p.m.

Three miles from the White House, Nikki Dean was waiting outside the preschool in Adams Morgan. She saw the doors open and Daniel come out with the other kids, carrying his Barney bag. He ran to her arms.

'How's my best boy? Did you have a good day?'

'OK, Mom.'

'Did you draw me a new picture?'

'Not today, Mom. Know what I saw?' There was a sudden infectious excitement in his voice.

'Tell me.' Nikki smiled as she led Daniel by the hand towards her Toyota. He always had something new to report after preschool: a new word discovered, a new game he'd learned to play, another new drawing of bright colours and incomprehensible squiggles to show her.

'Soldiers.'

'Really?'

'I saw them from the window. They's over there. Look, Mom.'

Daniel pointed across the street. One of the buildings opposite was a distribution warehouse, disused for months. Red bricked, surrounded by a wire fence, the loading bays were covered with litter, a crooked 'For Sale/To Let' sign nailed to one of the walls. Nikki noticed four army trucks and a Humvee personnel carrier parked at the bays, and two soldiers in fatigues standing inside the gates. 'Miss Elaine said they was *real* soldiers. Is they real soldiers, Mom?'

'I . . . I guess.' Nikki frowned, stopped by the kerb where she'd parked. 'Did Elaine say what the soldiers were doing there, Daniel?'

'No.' Daniel shrugged. 'She just said they was soldiers. Can we go see them, Mom?'

Nikki stared across the street. She'd passed the warehouse five days a week for almost a year, since Daniel began preschool, and she'd never noticed the military anywhere near the place. *Air transport planes at Reagan. Droves of cops at the Command Centre for a police exercise. And now the military using a disused warehouse in Adams Morgan.* 'Come with Mommy, Daniel.'

'Where we going?'

'Mommy wants to talk to the soldiers.' Holding Daniel's hand, Nikki crossed the street. The soldiers behind the fence looked over as she approached, offering them a smile. 'Hi. My little boy wanted to see you guys close up. Would you mind?'

'Not at all, ma'am.' One of the men, a black sergeant, smiled out through the fence, knelt down to face Daniel. 'What's your name, son?'

Daniel, bashful from the attention, clung to Nikki's hand, mesmerised. 'D . . . Daniel.'

'You want to be a soldier when you grow up, Daniel?'

'No, I want to be a Power Ranger.'

The sergeant laughed up at Nikki. 'Guess we just lost a recruit. Got a little boy myself. He loves the Power Rangers, too.'

'You mind me asking you guys what the army's doing at the warehouse?'

'It's part of an exercise, ma'am.' The sergeant stood.

'Really? What kind of exercise?'

'I'm afraid I can't say, ma'am. It's army business, you understand.'

'Which unit are you with?'

The sergeant exchanged a look with his comrade. 'I'm not at liberty to say, ma'am. It's no big deal, just all part of the exercise, you see.'

Nikki noticed the exchanged look, took note that the man wore no divisional flashes. 'I've never seen the army around here before. I couldn't help thinking it seemed kind of strange that you're using a disused warehouse in the neighbourhood.'

'Don't know about that, ma'am. We're just following orders.'

Nikki showed her press card. 'Actually, I'm a reporter. Is there someone I can speak with about this? I'm kind of curious if there might be a story in it.'

'I'm sorry, ma'am.' The sergeant studied the press card, suddenly even more wary. 'There isn't anyone around right now you could talk with. Tell you what, though, if you call the army public affairs office, I'm pretty sure they'd be able to help you.'

'Anyone in particular I can call?'

'Major Craig, ma'am. I guess he's the man to speak with.'

Nikki jotted the name in her notebook. 'Thank you, Sergeant. And thanks for talking with Daniel.'

'My pleasure, ma'am.' The sergeant winked at Daniel. 'So long, buddy. You ever change your mind about becoming a soldier, you let us know, OK?'

Washington, DC
5.30 p.m.

'First of all,' Al Brown began, 'Kuzmin was fucking right.'

The stunned faces around the situation-room table stared at DC's mayor. 'He should have bombed the sonofabitch to hell. The man's a wanted international criminal. An insane mass murderer, for Christ sakes. You ask me, the Russians had the right idea. Annihilate him!'

'Our first concern,' a red-faced General Horton answered, 'was for the citizens of your city, Mr Mayor.'

But Brown ignored the reply, his anger in full flow. 'The man's another fucking Carlos the Jackal. Another Qaddafi. Except maybe a million times worse. Abu Hasim's held this country to ransom for years. He's killed and terrorised innocent Americans, irrespective of race or creed. He's bankrolled every fanatical Muslim terror organisation you'd care to mention. His followers have bombed our embassies, our army bases, our naval vessels. Massacred our civilians as well as our military. This is a man who doesn't give a flying fuck for the value of a human life. Who's broken every civilised law under the sun.'

Brown carried on, crimson with fury. 'Who's used his personal fortune to help wage war in Chechnya, who's supported the Hezbollah and Hamas in Lebanon, Saddam Hussein in Iraq, and every Muslim fundamentalist lunatic in every country in the Middle and Far East which thinks of America as its enemy. And now he's threatening *my* city, *my* people. Listen, there's only one way to deal with a rabid dog like him and that's to put him down, *permanently*.'

Brown paused only to draw breath and then he was off again. 'But what do we do? We try to seize his bank accounts – without success. We try to pressure the Afghan authorities to find him and hand him over – without success. We bomb his camps in Afghanistan and try to kill him – without success. Can someone tell me what the fuck's going on here? We're the most advanced technological civilisation on this planet, with zillions of dollars' worth of weaponry and the best-equipped military at our disposal. And yet we still can't nail the bastard, even though we've been trying for years. Know what? We should be applauding Kuzmin right now. The man's got the right idea. Blow that province off the map. Solve the problem, zap the dirt-bag for good. But no, we're sitting around here like a bunch of fucking *schmucks*, and doing business with this asshole, giving in to his demands. Are we out of our fucking minds, or what?'

'There are innocent people in that region, Mr Mayor.'

'And there are innocent people in Washington. A lot more of them. Most of those diehard hillbilly tribes around Kandahar *support* Abu Hasim and his followers. That's why he's in hiding out there, for Christ sakes. How much fucking support do you reckon the guy's got in the District?'

'OK, so we nuke Hasim,' Katherine Ashmore, Counsel to the President, interjected. 'But what happens when we've got every Islamic country in the world crying out for our blood?'

'Islam? It's got *nothing to do* with Islam. That's the mistake you're making. Millions of this country's citizens are Muslims.

But they don't go around blowing people up, gassing them to death, or threatening a jihad just because their fucking next-door neighbour doesn't worship Allah. It's not *about* religion. It's about a madman. A crazy zealot who believes he's speaking for God. Know what's even crazier? We're listening to him. Worse, we're going to do what the asshole says. You ask me, we bomb the bastard. Then we tell the world what Hasim intended. That he wanted to wipe out this capital, massacre its population. Any sane person's going to know we were in the right.'

The room fell silent again. Al Brown, beads of sweat on his face, took a paper tissue from his pocket and dabbed his mouth. General Horton said quietly, 'Mr Mayor, the only way we're going to save your city is to find these madmen and their device.'

'Yeah? And what if we don't? What the fuck happens then, General? We'll still be up shit creek.'

The phone light flashed on the FBI Director's desk. In the heated exchange between the mayor and the general, the others barely noticed. The Director picked up, listened, and for several moments questioned the caller in a whisper, then said, 'Get back to me the moment you have anything else.'

When he put down the phone, he saw that everyone around the table had suddenly forgotten the argument and was staring at him. The Director's face was ashen. 'I can report that the search of the area around the Wentworth was completed less than a minute ago.'

'And?' the President asked.

'There's no sign of any device and all three terrorists have vanished.'

The President slapped his palm hard on the table, grimaced with disappointment. '*Damn!*'

'There's something else, Mr President,' the FBI Director went on. 'I've just been informed by the NSA that a message has been transmitted from Kandahar province by Hasim.'

'To whom?'

'You, sir. He wants to talk.'

43

Salem, New Jersey
5.40 p.m.

As the US President was being informed of the message from Kandahar, Ishim Razan was strolling along a gravel pathway, lined with manicured shrubs and miniature palms, Karla Sharif by his side. They had left the doctor to tend to Gorev, and Razan had dismissed his bodyguards. He plucked a cigar from his top pocket, lit it, blew smoke into the cold evening air. The dark gardens were lit by tiny lamps, the sky by stars.

'Safa Yassin. Is that really your name?'

'Does it matter?'

The Chechen shrugged. 'Names matter little at this moment. But there are other truths that matter very much.'

'Such as?'

'What exactly happened to Nikolai? And if someone harmed him, why?'

Karla shook her head. 'I mean no disrespect, but this is not your concern, Ishim Razan. Please . . . I can't tell you any more than that.'

'It's my concern if a friend of mine is in trouble.' Razan halted, regarded her. 'I'm not a fool, Safa Yassin. It's obvious there's much more to all this. Yesterday, Nikolai came to me looking for the name of a man who could supply him with a police vehicle, police weapons and uniforms. I asked myself why. What would Nikolai be up to on American soil? I couldn't find an answer. But I assumed that whatever it was it had to be for the Chechen cause and asked no questions.'

'But you're asking questions now.'

'Nikolai is an old friend. Someone I owe much too, not least my life. If he's in trouble, I wish to help.'

'You have already helped, Ishim Razan. By giving us refuge and having the doctor tend to Nikolai.'

Razan sighed. 'Does it have anything to do with the man whose name I gave Nikolai? The man named Visto?'

'No.'

'Then just tell me this. Are the police involved?'

Karla hesitated, bit her lip. 'Yes.'

Razan pursed his mouth in thought. Finally he nodded, took Karla's arm, and walked on in silence. They came to a trickling brook that ran through the garden, spanned by a tiny wooden bridge, a white wrought-iron bench beyond. They crossed the bridge and Razan gestured to the bench. 'Sit, Safa Yassin.'

Karla sat and pulled up her collar to keep out the chill of the cold night. Razan sat beside her. He looked up at the stars, blew a ring of smoke into the freezing air. Finally he said, 'Do you know how long Nikolai and I are friends?'

'No. He told me nothing about you.'

'Almost fifteen years. We were paratroopers together. He was the closest comrade I ever had. A fine officer, the kind any soldier would be proud to serve with. Courageous, trustworthy, someone who always kept his promises and expected others to keep theirs. And he has always been an honourable man, despite what the Russians say of him. To them, he's a turncoat, a traitor about whom they will say anything to slander his name. They call him a terrorist, but to the Chechen people he's a freedom fighter, a hero.'

'I know.'

'Have you ever been to Chechnya?'

'No.'

'Then you cannot know. The Chechen people hold him in the highest esteem. When the Russians invaded my country, when they came with their tanks and artillery and bombers to destroy my people and crush their spirit, Nikolai Gorev did more than anyone I know to protect them. He organised the evacuation of towns, risked his life to save them from Russian bombs, resisted the army with incredible bravery. Some, like me, those in the underworld, chose to remain outside the battle, helping the cause in any way we could. With the purchase of weapons, with money, by smuggling supplies. And that help is what I offer to you now. Anything I can do, any resources I have, they are yours. I do this for Nikolai.'

Karla didn't reply, looked back anxiously towards the house. Razan said quietly, 'Are you afraid for him?'

'Yes.'

'The doctor will do his best. He's in good hands.' Razan's cigar had gone out. He relit it, said quietly, 'Do you love Nikolai?'

'Once. Long ago.'

'And now?'

'I . . . I don't know.'

'I think you do.'

She turned to look at Razan. The Chechen gave her a half-smile. 'Among my blessings, I count seven sisters. With seven sisters, a man either gets to know women, or else he's doomed. I think you love him very much.'

'Perhaps.'

'Then why do you not allow me to help him?'

Karla regarded him. Beneath the tough face, beneath the dark, cunning exterior, there was a kindness she found touching. 'This is not your fight, Ishim Razan.'

'Then whose is it? Tell me that.'

Karla stood. 'Please. I've said too much already. Nikolai wouldn't want me to break a trust, even to you. I beg you not to ask me any more questions.'

The Chechen heard the hint of despair in her voice, saw her glance back again towards the house with a look of unease. He sighed, stood. 'Very well. Have it your way. But there is something I wish you to do for me, Safa Yassin.'

'What?'

Karla shivered, the chilly air biting into her bones as Razan took her arm. 'Come, it's getting cold. We'll go back to the house. I'll explain there.'

* * *

When they entered the back annexe, they found the doctor standing over the washbasin, scrubbing his hands, a cigarette dangling from his lips. Gorev lay unconscious on the bed, his stomach heavily bandaged. The doctor dried himself with a towel, came over. 'It's done. Fortunately, the operation wasn't as troublesome as I thought. The shrapnel nicked his gut but I've managed to clean out the wound and suture the laceration. There's no more shrapnel, so far as I can tell. But we'd need an X-ray to be certain.'

'How . . . how is he?'

The doctor saw Karla's concern. 'His pulse is steady enough. But he's quite weak, and a litre or more of blood would do him no harm. I've drawn a sample and will come back tonight to administer the transfusion.'

'His chances?' Razan asked.

'I wish all my patients were in such excellent physical shape.' The doctor smiled. 'He's not going to die, that's for sure. But he'll need to rest up.'

'For how long?' Karla asked.

'Several days at least.'

'That . . . that's impossible.'

'Not if you want him to make a full recovery. Have him on his feet too quickly and you risk disturbing the sutures, and God knows we don't want that.'

Karla went over to the bed. Gorev was in a deep sleep, his forehead covered in perspiration. She pulled up a chair beside him, wrung a cloth from a bowl of water by the bed and dabbed his brow. 'When will he wake?'

'When the anaesthetic wears off, in about an hour or two. But he'll still be groggy. I'd suggest no food for now, just water if he wants it.'

'He definitely can't be moved tonight?'

The doctor looked at Karla as if she were insane. 'Absolutely not. He needs rest, and lots of it.' He packed up his bag, turned to Razan. 'I've left some painkillers and antibiotics with Eduard. He's well capable of looking after the patient until I get back. In the morning, we'll review his progress.'

'My thanks, Arkady.'

The doctor grinned, suddenly invigorated, stubbed out his cigarette. 'No need. It was a thoroughly interesting evening. Like working the battlefields again.'

After the doctor had gone Razan led Karla to a drawing room at the front of the house. He poured a couple of malt whiskies from a Waterford crystal decanter, handed her a glass. 'Take it. You look like you could do with one.'

Karla took the crystal tumbler and Razan raised his drink. 'To Nikolai. Let's hope he makes a speedy recovery.' The Chechen swallowed his whisky, crossed to the window, looked out at the darkened lawns. 'Naturally, he'll remain here to recover, for however long he needs. He'll be safe and well looked after. You are free to stay with him.'

'That's not possible. Not tonight.'

Razan looked back. 'Then you may return at any time you wish. But try to take him from here without my permission and you risk my anger, Safa Yassin. Are you clear on this?'

Karla put down her glass. 'Have I any choice?'

'None. I value Nikolai's life too much. You still refuse to tell me what's going on?'

'I can't.'

'You're a stubborn woman, did anyone ever tell you that?'

'It has nothing to do with stubbornness. Nikolai would tell you the same.'

Razan came back from the window, picked up a telephone from a side table. 'Tell Yegori to come in here.'

Moments later the door opened. The Chechen who had forced Karla into her car entered the room, crossed to Razan. 'Ishim?'

Razan whispered something into his ear and the bodyguard left. Karla, puzzled, addressed Razan. 'You said there was something you wished me to do?'

Razan slapped his glass down. 'We'll get to that. You know

what still bothers me? There's something odd about all this, Safa Yassin. Something very odd indeed. My old grandmother used to say that whenever she felt a headache coming on she sensed trouble. And right now, my head's splitting.'

The Chechen bodyguard came back into the room, carrying a pair of cellphones and Gorev's Beretta pistol. He handed them to Razan, who said to Karla, 'The gun is Nikolai's, I believe?'

'Yes.'

'Take it.' Razan offered her the pistol. 'For all I know, you may have need of it.'

Karla slipped the Beretta into her pocket.

'Now I will tell you what I wish you to do. You refused my help, but again I offer it.' Razan handed Karla one of the cellphones. 'One each. If you need me for any reason, night or day, my number is stored in the cellphone's memory. You simply call. If Nikolai's condition worsens for any reason, and I need you, I do the same. Do you understand me, Safa Yassin?'

'Yes, I understand.'

'Good. Yegori will take you to your car.'

Razan was standing at the window minutes later, smoking a cigar, watching the red tail-lights of the Plymouth disappear down the driveway. He turned from the window as the door opened behind him and Yegori returned.

'You're clear about what you have to do?'

'Yes, Ishim. The men are ready.'

'Do it.'

44

Alexandria
5.30 p.m.

A sea of FBI tech vans and unmarked cars were parked all over the wire-fenced warehouse lot. It looked a frenzy of activity, and agents were positioned at the steel-mesh entrance gates to keep back the curious onlookers – a few dozen local kids and passers-by who stopped to gawk.

It was dark when Collins and Kursk drove up to the gates, and when they were waved into the warehouse parking area they saw Morgan over by an office door, hands on his hips as he watched a couple of crime-scene techs carrying in their equipment from one of the vans. He came over when he saw Kursk and Collins climb out of the Ford.

'Looks like this is where they disappeared to after the Wentworth.' Morgan jerked a thumb towards the warehouse. 'One of the search teams in the area noticed the front gates unlocked and decided to have a look around. The door into the office had been left open. They found the Explorer parked inside the bay, along with a white Ryder van.'

'They find anything in the vehicles?'

Morgan nodded. 'A couple of wooden planks and some discarded clothes in the van – two men's parkas and a woman's leather jacket. One of the parkas was bloodstained – looked like it got punctured by grenade shrapnel. There were also tyre marks on the ground that looked like the motorcycle variety. Seems like they must have had a bike or two stashed in back of the Ryder, all ready for a quick getaway. They sure had things planned real well, left nothing to chance.'

They moved over to the loading bay. The roll door was up and inside the warehouse they saw the dark blue Explorer and the Ryder. Crime-scene techs wearing latex gloves were working on both vehicles under the harsh electric glare of a half-dozen mobile arc lamps. Others were busy taking photographs, while a half-dozen techs wearing white disposable overalls were on their hands and knees, moving up the warehouse in a line, sweeping the floor for the smallest trace of evidence. 'Did the guys turn up anything else?'

'We found nothing in the clothes' pockets – no wallets, no papers, zilch. The Explorer's cab looked pretty clean inside, same with the Ryder. But the van had rental papers in the glove compartment in the name of Raoul Khan. Turns out it was hired six days ago in McLean, Virginia. We sent a couple of guys over to the Ryder office to question the female staff member who dealt with Khan. They called in a couple of minutes ago. She remembered the guy. From the description she gave, it sounds like it could have been Rashid.'

Collins looked over the warehouse. Apart from the Explorer and the van, it was bare as a bone. 'Who owns this place?'

Morgan consulted his notebook. 'Small company called Treasury Allied Properties in the District. Hired it out almost five weeks ago. A three-month lease to a guy named Ethan Nadiz who paid cash up front and said he wanted it for short-term storage. Our people are on their way to the company offices right now with photographs of Rashid and Gorev. Got a feeling in my water it'll turn out to be Rashid again. Man's got more aliases than I've had undercover.'

'Any witnesses see Rashid and the others drive in or out of here?'

'One so far. Guy who works in a furniture warehouse across the street says he thinks he saw the Explorer drive in here some time after two o'clock this afternoon. That fits with just about after they fled the Wentworth. But he was too busy to notice who was in the vehicle and he didn't notice them leave again. We're questioning folks and traders in the area – got a couple of dozen guys knocking on doors right now.'

'The store owner ever notice anyone come and go from here before?'

Morgan checked his notebook again. 'He had to come in early a couple of weeks back to do a stocktake. Five a.m., and he's getting out of his car and sees a guy driving out of the warehouse. Thinks it was the same Explorer. He barely got a glimpse of the driver but he thought maybe he could have been Arab. I showed him Rashid's photograph but the face didn't register. Still, my money's on Rashid. Seems like he's been a busy boy these past few weeks. And keeping his head low by coming in here at odd hours, hoping no one would see him.'

Collins stepped closer to the Explorer, where the techs were still working away, and peered inside, then moved over to the Ryder, Kursk following behind. There was nothing to see in either cabin. Both vehicles looked clean. 'What about the rest of the warehouse?'

'Empty apart from the trucks.'

'The office?'

'Looks like it hasn't been used. Nothing but a banged-up old table and chair and a couple of rusting filing cabinets, empty.'

'Did anyone check the building for chemical trace?'

Morgan nodded. 'One of the first things they did. The WMD guys went over it with their chemical detectors. Came up clean. Either Rashid and his friends didn't keep the stuff here, or it was too well sealed in its container to leave any marker.'

'Terrific.' Collins gritted his teeth, slammed a fist into the side of the Ryder in frustration.

'Know how you feel,' Morgan said. 'But at least we know how they got away.'

The White House
6.05 p.m.

'How long have we got?'

The President had temporarily abandoned the NSC meeting, left the conference room with a select group of his closest advisers, and moved to the Oval Office. As he took his place behind his leather desk, he had addressed the FBI Director.

'Just under two hours, sir,' Doug Stevens replied. 'He wants the link-up ready to go at bang on eight p.m., Eastern Standard Time, for a live two-way transmission, using one of the frequencies Dick's people suggested to Samar Mehmet.'

Six other people were crowded into the room: Dick Faulks, the head of the CIA; Paul Burton; General Horton; Charles Rivermount; and two of the President's other advisers, from whom he frequently took counsel: Mitch Gains, a former judge, and Bob Rapp, the long-time press adviser. The room crackled with apprehension.

'Despite his refusal to help, Samir Mehmet must have spoken to Hasim after all,' Faulks said to the President. 'I kind of figured he would.'

'What else exactly did the sonofabitch have to say?'

'That's it, sir. Only that he's going to talk to you,' Stevens replied.

The President ran a hand over his jaw, then looked at the circle of faces. 'You can bet what this is really about, can't you? Abu Hasim's already heard what happened. He's heard we almost messed up his operation. I don't believe he's really going to talk, at least not in any meaningful way. He's going to give it to us in the neck, tell us we're rattling him. He's going to rant and rave and then he's going to threaten us all over again. Tell us he'll wipe us all out if we don't play the game like he says. The damned sonofabitch . . .' The President suddenly pounded his knuckled fist on the desk, anger turning his face crimson. 'Doug, I'm going to have trouble with this. I'm going to have trouble not telling this major-league asshole what I honestly think of him.'

'You can't do that, sir,' Bob Rapp broke in. 'The last thing you want to do is anger Hasim. That's only going to jeopardise whatever chances you've got to convince him to give us more time, or even make him change his mind.'

The President took a handkerchief from his breast pocket, wiped his mouth. 'Bob, I don't hold out much hope of convincing him of *anything*. He's a mass murderer, a crazed terrorist killer of the highest order. A man who's got nothing in his heart but hatred for me and for the American people. He's not going to listen to a damned word I say.'

'Mr President, we've got less than two hours. That doesn't give us much time to prepare.' Mitch Gains was looking at his watch in near-panic. 'We need someone professional to help give us an angle on how to approach this, advise us on how to play it. Bob's right. The last thing we want to do is say the wrong thing and blow it. It's maybe the only opportunity we're going to get.'

'Who would you suggest?'

'We'll have to take whoever's closest,' Bob Rapp replied. 'Professor Janet Stern's only a couple of blocks away, staying at the Willard. And the CIA's Franklyn Young is in the Marriott, around the corner.'

'Get them here. Fast.'

Alexandria
5.40 p.m.

'The woman's name is Karla. That much I'm certain of. I don't remember her family name.'

'She's Chechen?' Morgan asked.

'Palestinian.'

Morgan took a pack of cigarettes from his pocket, frowned at Collins, then looked back at Kursk. 'So what's the connection to Gorev?'

They had left the warehouse, walked over by the perimeter fence. Far off, lights blazed in the District, the red beacon on top of the Memorial flashing in the darkness. Kursk paused to light the cigarette Morgan offered, and Collins answered for him. 'When Gorev served with the KGB, he taught at Patrice Lumumba University. Guerrilla warfare was one of his specialist subjects.'

Kursk nodded as he drew on his cigarette, said to Morgan, 'That's where he met her. Lumumba was no ordinary university, but a training school for terrorists. At that time, the KGB gave support to many revolutionary groups around the world. Some were offered places at the university, to train in terrorist warfare, and they came from many countries. The Italian Red Brigade, the Irish Republican Army, the PLO, the Japanese Red Army, revolutionaries from almost every part of Africa and South America. Among Lumumba's most famous graduates was Carlos Sanchez – Carlos the Jackal. But there were many others. Hundreds, if not thousands.'

'So where does this Karla fit in?' Morgan asked.

'She came with a PLO group. For many years they sent their most promising recruits to Lumumba, until Moscow decided to stop helping Yasser Arafat. But Karla, I believe, was one of their best.'

'You met her?'

'Just once, in Nikolai Gorev's company, at a party in Moscow. That's where I saw her. He introduced us.'

'How come you still remember her?' Morgan asked.

'I remember that for the last few months of her stay in Moscow she and Gorev became lovers. And when the time came for her to leave and return to the Middle East, Gorev resigned from the KGB. Soon after, he joined the army and was sent to fight in Afghanistan.'

Morgan raised an eyebrow, said a touch mockingly, 'Sounds like the man had a broken heart.'

'I can't say. And what the circumstances were of their parting I don't know. Nikolai Gorev wasn't the kind of man to talk about his private life. But I got the feeling she meant a great deal to him.'

'You're sure it's the same woman?'

'I'm certain. And seeing them both together makes me even more certain.'

Morgan took a drag on his cigarette, said to Collins, 'Abu Hasim supports anyone with a grudge against Israel, right? It's got to work the other way round, too. So I guess it makes sense a woman like her would be involved with Hasim. But how do we get some background?'

'Murphy's talking with the Israelis. If she's PLO, Mossad ought to have something on her. And he'll have Moscow try and dig up her file from Lumumba. Between the two, he ought to come up with something.'

Morgan, distracted, looked over towards the warehouse, then stubbed out his cigarette. An agent, talking on his cellphone, was holding up his hand and waving him over. 'Bet that's Murphy now, looking for an update. Be right back.'

Kursk drew on his cigarette, turned to look beyond the warehouse perimeter, towards the lights of the District. He was exhausted, guessed Collins felt the same. 'Are your people still checking the hospitals?'

Collins nodded. 'Gorev hasn't turned up at any of them yet, or in any of the doctor's surgeries that were visited.'

'I doubt he will look for medical help in such places. Not if it would risk attention from the police. Nikolai is no fool. If he needs a doctor, he will have found someone he thinks he can trust. A Chechen, or an Arab perhaps. Or a doctor who has dealings with the criminal world.'

'We're checking on all those too.'

Kursk nodded towards Washington's blaze of night-time lights. 'You can be certain he and the others will be even more careful after this. Only go out in public when they must. In such a big city, they will be even more difficult to find.'

'Are you giving up, Major?'

'No. But after tonight, there are only five days left. We had our luck, I think, by finding them once. From now on, it's going to be impossible. Don't you agree?'

Collins looked out at the darkened capital. 'You got a wife, Kursk?'

'Yes.'

'Kids?'

'A daughter. She is nine.'

'I've got a friend. A woman. She's got a three-year-old boy. I care about them both very much. Have you thought about how your daughter might die if she was in Washington and the device went off? Gassed to death like those men kidnapped in Azerbaijan? Maybe you ought to think about it, Major. You might be more eager to find Gorev and put him out of this game for good.'

'You think what I did was deliberate, to stop you killing him?'

Collins fixed the Russian with a stare. 'I don't know what to think, Kursk. If you did it for the right reason or the wrong. But you know the question I keep asking myself? How could anyone like Gorev square it with his mind to kill hundreds of thousands of men, women and kids?' He clicked his fingers. 'Snuff out their lives in cold blood, just like that.'

'I can't answer that question for him.'

'Then I'll answer it for you. Because he's an insane killer, pure and simple. A terrorist who hasn't got a shred of conscience, just like Rashid. The woman too, for all I know. And the sooner you accept that truth, the better we'll get along.'

'Gorev may be a lot of things, but he's not an indiscriminate killer, Agent Collins. Yes, he's killed in the past. But it's always been political, for the Chechen cause. I know him. He's not a mass-murderer. He's not some madman who'll destroy a city for the sake of it.'

'So what makes him tick? What drives him on in a situation like this? Why's he thrown in his lot with Rashid?'

'I can't say how or why he became part of this. But I can think of two good reasons. He wants his Chechen comrades released. Or else, somehow, he's been given no choice.' Kursk looked at Collins' face. 'There is a third, but it is doubtful. That he wants the same thing as you. Some kind of revenge.'

'I don't want revenge, Kursk. I want justice.'

'Isn't it sometimes the same thing?'

Collins was silent. Kursk tossed away his cigarette. 'May I say something?' He put out his hand. 'We end this now. Help each other. Not argue.'

Collins ignored the offered hand, went to speak, but Morgan caught his eye over by the Ford. He was waving at them. 'Get over here, Jack.'

Collins went over, Kursk behind him. Morgan finished talking on the radiophone, jumped into the Ford. 'Get in.'

Kursk got in the back as Collins climbed in the front passenger seat. 'What's up?'

'Some guy found the bodies of a teenage couple out at a picnic area in some woods in Maryland, about thirty miles from here. Both with multiple gunshot wounds.'

'What's it got to do with us?'

Morgan hit the ignition. 'It happened less than three hours ago, Jack. And here's the cherry. A witness saw a guy on a motorcycle drive out of the area in a damned big hurry.'

45

Washington, DC
6.35 p.m.

When the British Army under General Wade attacked Washington in 1814 and his rampaging troops torched the White House, the blaze was so intense that almost half the presidential residence was gutted. To this day, the blackened scorch marks may still be seen on the two-hundred-year-old mansion's original solid granite foundation posts, which were left exposed in the basement kitchens area, a reminder of a bitterly fought colonial war.

As the man stepped down into the cramped White House kitchens that evening, he paused for a moment to lean against one of the blackened granite posts and took a deep breath. A steward bustled past, dressed in a white waistcoat and dark pants, and carrying a silver tray. Behind him, a few seconds later, came a stocky, sad-faced Secret Service agent with a moustache, who looked to be on his way upstairs. He had a rutted scar on his nose, and the man instantly recognised him as Harry Judd, the Deputy Assistant Director of Protection. Judd paused for a second, the recognition mutual, and said politely, 'Good evening, sir. Can I help you?'

'No, thanks.' The man smiled back. 'Just getting a breath of air.'

'Of course, sir.' Harry Judd nodded and went out through a pair of swing-doors towards the stairs.

As soon as he was gone, the man glanced towards the kitchens, saw a white-hatted chef busily working over a stainless-steel worktop, too preoccupied to notice him. Making sure that Harry Judd was gone, the man turned right, slipped through another set of double doors, and found himself in the narrow East Wing delivery yard, deserted apart from some overflowing garbage bins.

There was a raw breeze, a hint of rain in the night air, but he ignored it, feeling the icy beads of perspiration on his face as he moved out into the dimly lit yard, knowing what had brought him here.

He had made a request to the President that he have a couple of minutes alone to mull over the impending meeting with Professors Janet Stern and the CIA's Franklyn Young, left the Oval Office, and taken the stairs down to the basement kitchens. But the request was a lie. Fifteen minutes ago, in the middle of the heated Oval Office meeting when the President had gathered his closest, most trusted advisers around him, the man had felt his cellphone vibrate discreetly in his inside breast pocket. After a brief pause, the phone had vibrated again.

The cellphone's throb had caused him a moment of near-panic that sent shock waves through his body. It was absurd: knowing that in the middle of the heated private gathering, listening to the President's tirade against Abu Hasim, he was the enemy in the camp, sharing the absolute confidence of the man he was betraying. He was perspiring heavily as he took the cellphone from his inside breast pocket. Switching it on, he checked the missed numbers in the green-illuminated window, to make absolutely certain that by some fluke they weren't wrong-number calls.

Neither were. His heart pounding, the man glanced above him. There were security cameras and listening devices almost everywhere in the White House, and at least one camera was positioned on the parapet wall high above the delivery yard. For all he knew, there might even be discreet microphones hidden around the walls. He was faced with a dilemma: he couldn't leave the White House at such a critical moment, but he knew that the two calls he'd received – two rings, followed by three more, both calls ten seconds apart – indicated that it was imperative he phone Mohamed Rashid.

He had thought about it frantically, reasoned that coming down to the kitchen yard was his best bet. To all intents and purposes his visit there was innocent: it wasn't unknown for White House staff to slip down to the yard area for a breath of air, a smoke, or even to make private calls from their cellphones. A gentle enquiry he'd made weeks ago to one of the Secret Service agents assigned to him had suggested that the yard wasn't bugged, but he couldn't rely entirely on that information, and he knew he'd have to make sure he kept the call he was about to make as brief and cryptic as possible, in case there really *were* microphones planted in the yard.

Turning his back on the parapet camera, he wiped the patina of cold sweat from his face and nervously punched in the number.

Harry Judd, the Deputy Assistant Director of Protection, descended a stairwell deep into the bowels of the White House. He'd been on duty all day with hardly a break, and had just scrounged a cheese sandwich and a cup of decaf coffee in the kitchens to keep him going.

When he came to the bottom of the stairs he halted outside a solid, smooth vault door. He flicked up the cover on the control panel on the wall to the left and punched in a six-digit code. Seconds later came a hissing sound as the airtight rubber seal around the door decompressed. Then the sixteen locking bolts disengaged with a clunk, and an electric motor whirred as the door swung open. It was eighteen inches thick, solid steel, and behind it was the President's bunker.

Judd stepped in. The lights came on automatically, and he moved to the centre of the room. It measured twenty-five square feet, its seamless concrete walls painted a cream colour. Around the walls were eight bunks, a couple of couches, and various metal cabinets in which were stored emergency equipment: first-aid kits, spare communications transceivers and batteries, a number of weapons and their munitions, decontam suits, oxygen, bottles, food ration packs, and more. As a temporary refuge in the event of a WMD – Weapons of Mass Destruction – attack, it had everything a small number of survivors might need to hold out for a couple of days, a week tops. Outside in the hall was another airtight steel door to an emergency evacuation tunnel that led up to a secret exit on the White House lawns.

The survivors could evacuate when it was considered safe to do so – assuming they came through the attack alive. There was a reasonable chance: the bunker's chemical, biological and radioactive filtration systems were claimed to be excellent, and had been verified as serviceable by a team from the Army Corps of Engineers that same afternoon, but until an actual WMD attack happened, you never could tell.

Judd took a good look around the room and made sure the seals on the metal cabinets were intact and unbroken. Everything was secure. He'd already checked the bunker earlier that day but he'd wanted to check it again, if only to reassure himself he had things under control, and despite the fact that the bunker room always gave him the creeps. It was cold, almost eerie. Standing there alone, under the low concrete ceiling, it felt to Judd like being in one of those pharaoh's tombs in Luxor that he'd visited with his wife Phyllis fourteen years ago when they'd taken a two-week vacation in Egypt – just before she'd upped and left him for a mild-mannered history professor over at Georgetown U who didn't have to work nights for a living, run alongside a limo, or risk getting his ass shot at by assassins.

Judd shivered. Being sealed up in a place like this wasn't his idea of fun. Still, he wouldn't be guaranteed a place in here anyhow. He'd be *way* down the list. Chances were, the device went off, he was a goner, like a lot of other folks in the White House who weren't on the A-list. As he stood there in the cold, unwelcome chamber, Judd ran a forefinger along the dented scar on his nose, and thought: *Whoever winds up down here, the President included, could be locking themselves into a burial chamber.* What if the filtration system went bust, or didn't do its job properly, or the rubber door seals leaked, allowing microscopic traces of the nerve gas to invade the room? Not enough to kill you instantly, rather slowly and agonisingly. Personally, Judd thought, he'd rather go quick – a deep sniff of the gas, a few seconds of intense pain, and then oblivion.

Way to go.

Judd stepped out of the bunker and punched in the code. The

solid metal door whirred back into place and the rubber seal hissed as it was repressurised.

Chesapeake
8.15 p.m.

Karla Sharif turned the Plymouth into the cottage at Winston Bay. As the headlights swept up the driveway and panned across the building, she thought she noticed a movement behind one of the downstairs curtains. The rain was coming down in sheets, and as she drove into the garage at the side she saw Rashid's Yamaha parked there. She was drenched as she went up on to the veranda and opened the door.

She got a shock when she saw Rashid. He looked different: his blond hair was dyed black, and the earring was gone. He had a surly look on his face as he stood just inside the doorway, clutching the Skorpion machine-pistol in his hand as he scanned the veranda. 'Where's Gorev? Why isn't he with you?'

'I'll tell you inside.'

Salem
8.30 p.m.

Ishim Razan was in the study of his New Jersey mansion, a glass of whisky in his hand as he watched the rain sweep across the lawns, lashing the tall cathedral windows. He wore a troubled frown as he stared at the drenching storm, his mind tortured by confusion. The door opened behind him and one of his bodyguards came in. 'Yegori called, Ishim.'

'And?'

'He says it's done.'

'What took him so long?'

'The weather was bad, and the woman drove a long distance. To a house in Chesapeake, over two hours away. Some place called Winston Bay.'

'Was she alone there?'

'Yegori can't be sure. The house is in its own grounds. He's going to need more time to have a look around. The men will stay in a motel near Chesapeake for the night, and Yegori says he'll check with you in the morning.'

Razan frowned, then nodded his satisfaction. 'How is the patient?'

'Sleeping. He ought to be fine until the doctor gets back.'

'Don't let Eduard leave his side for a moment. Understood?'

'Yes, Ishim.'

The bodyguard withdrew, leaving Razan alone again. For a moment or two he remained by the rain-lashed glass, his brow knitted in thought, his mind still confused. Then he made the decision. Putting his whisky down, he crossed to a table in the corner, picked up the phone and punched in a number.

Chesapeake
8.16 p.m.

'You *left* him there? Are you insane?'

'I had no choice. He needed proper medical attention.'

Rashid moved over to the window, opened the curtain a crack and peered out, as if to make sure Karla hadn't been followed. When he looked back, he was enraged. 'How do we know Razan can be trusted? You said he was suspicious, that he questioned you?'

'I told him nothing. He and Nikolai are old friends. Razan wanted to help him. That was his only concern. The Chechens wouldn't think of involving the police. Besides, what was I supposed to do, let Nikolai bleed to death?'

Rashid came away from the curtain, teeth clenched in anger. 'It would have been better if you had. A wounded man is a burden in battle, even you know that, Karla Sharif. Did the doctor give him medication? Drugs of any sort?'

'Yes.'

'What if Gorev's in a fevered state and talks? What if he says something that compromises us? Did you think of that?'

'You ought to know him better.' Karla was suddenly angry, Rashid's callousness goading her, and she added with contempt, 'You don't give a damn about Nikolai. Or anyone for that matter. Do you?'

'Nothing matters but our mission. If he dies, then so be it. *Inshallah*.'

'You know something, Mohamed Rashid?' Karla shook her head in disgust. 'You're a cold-hearted thug, with not even a shred of decency. I don't know how you can even bear to look at yourself in the mirror.'

Rashid stepped closer, until he was almost up to her face. The pearl-handled flick-knife appeared in an instant, too quickly for Karla to move, and the flat of the blade pressed hard against her cheek. Rashid gripped her hair, yanked it back savagely as he stared into her eyes. 'Remember who you are talking to, Karla Sharif. Remember who's in charge here and what your duty is. You've had your last warning. You will follow my orders and show me respect. Or do I have to carve my words into your face?'

Karla was defiant. 'I told you before. Don't threaten me. Not unless you really mean to use that knife. Now let go.'

Rashid's face twisted maliciously. He pressed the blade harder into her cheek, suddenly enjoying a delicious feeling of power. 'Any reason why I should?'

'Look down, Mohamed Rashid. See what's pointed between your legs.'

Rashid's expression changed. His eyes moved down in surprise, saw the Beretta that Karla had slipped from her jacket pocket pointed at his groin. The Egyptian gave a manic laugh, let go of her hair, and Karla pulled away.

'You know, I think I was right when we met in Tyr,' Rashid confessed. 'That in different circumstances, a woman like you might even excite me. When this is over, who knows? Maybe we can do something about that.'

'I'd rather lie with the Devil first.'

Rashid grunted, retracted the knife and slipped it into his

pocket, but Karla made no attempt to put away the Beretta. Rashid grabbed his jacket from the back of the chair, snapped his fingers, held out his hand in fury. 'Give me the car keys. I have work to do.'

'They're on the table. What work?'

'That's none of your business. But I'll tell you this. The Americans are going to wish they'd never crossed us this afternoon. For that, they're going to pay this night, and pay dearly.' Rashid picked up the keys, his mouth a vicious snarl. 'You will remain here until I return. In the morning, you will bring Gorev back to the cottage, no matter what condition he's in, and no matter what Razan says, you understand me? And you'd better pray that your stupidity hasn't jeopardised us, Karla Sharif. Because if it has, I'll keep my promise. I'll see to it that son of yours never sees daylight again.'

Rashid turned off the Suitland Parkway. Five minutes later he drove the Plymouth into the weed-covered driveway of the two-storey red-bricked house in Fulton Chase, in the District's South East.

The derelict rows of ghetto houses looked depressing in the rain, the wet streets deserted, and Rashid locked the car, raced up the front steps and rang the bell twice, allowed a three-second pause, then hit the bell twice again. A torn curtain twitched in the downstairs window, and a few moments later the front door opened. The big, rugged black man, Moses Lee, stood there, wearing a baseball shirt and jeans. For a second or two he didn't recognise his visitor, the earring gone, the blond hair dyed black, but then he grinned. 'See you got yourself some new hair. Surprised to see you so late, brother. You lock the car, like I been telling you?'

Rashid grunted. 'Where's Abdullah?'

'In the garage, where the man always is.'

The muddied grey Nissan van was still parked in the middle of the garage floor, and Abdullah sat guard on the wooden packing crate beside it, his pump-action shotgun resting on his lap. He stood as Rashid appeared with Moses Lee.

'We need privacy,' Rashid told Lee. 'Leave us.'

The black man shrugged. 'You're the boss. I'll be in the front room. Need me, just call.'

Lee left, cradling his Heckler and Koch, and Rashid crossed smartly to the Nissan van. Abdullah, seeing the purpose with which Rashid crossed the floor, and his altered appearance, sensed some kind of trouble and said, 'What's wrong?'

'There's something I need.' Rashid took the van keys from his pocket, pressed the alarm keypad, and the Nissan's lights flashed as the central locking disengaged. He swung open the rear doors to reveal the two sealed oil drums, their metal tops locked securely with metal bands. On the floor, attached by the slim cables connected to the drums, was the laptop computer. He climbed into the van with a sense of urgency, ignored the computer and drums, moved towards the back and located a black leather briefcase with brass combination locks.

Alarmed, Abdullah leaned into the van. 'Mohamed – what are you doing?'

'Shut up.' Sweat sparkled on Rashid's temples as he thumbed the combinations on the briefcase and flicked open the locks. Inside was an electronic timer and a twelve-volt battery, one of the flying leads from the timer connected to a detonator, embedded in a thick slab of Semtex plastic explosive. Taped to the corner of the briefcase was a remote control: a small, slim palm-sized black plastic box with a light-emitting diode battery indicator and an on-off switch, to trigger the explosive remotely, if need be, instead of using the timer. Rashid satisfied himself that the wires were not yet attached to the twelve-volt battery, or connected to the timer – that would have been dangerous anywhere near the chemical, but he would make the connections later, before it was time to set off his device. All he had to do now was make his call, and execute his plan. He had made all his preparations weeks before, in case they were necessary.

Fine beads of sweat appeared on Abdullah's upper lip, his face a worried frown. 'Mohamed – what's going on?'

'The Americans are about to learn a harsh lesson.'

46

7.32 p.m.

The Old Ebbitt Grill on 15th Street is two blocks from the White House. With its elegant nineteenth-century decor, casual atmosphere and private booths, the cosy bar and restaurant is a well-known District haunt, a favourite among theatre-goers, politicians and Secret Service agents alike.

It was just after 7.30 that evening when Nikki arrived at the restaurant. It was buzzing for a Monday night, and she saw at least two politicians at the bar whom she recognised. One of them gave her a wave, and she waved back. A waitress stood at the maître d's lectern as she approached. 'Can I help you, madam?'

'I'm here to meet Brad Stelman. He's booked us a table for seven-thirty.'

The waitress consulted her booking list, looked up with a friendly smile. 'Of course. If you'd please care to follow me.'

She led Nikki towards the back of the restaurant. Brad Stelman was already waiting, seated in one of the private booths. She had been just about to call him at six that evening as she'd arranged, to see whether he had any information from his air force friend at Andrews, but Stelman had called first. In a whispered tone, he'd asked to meet her urgently, suggested she join him that same evening for dinner at the Old Ebbitt, and before he hung up he told her not to call him back at home for any reason. Curious about why he had wanted to meet in person, and not talk on the telephone, she had left Daniel at her mother's, drove across town and parked her car in the underground lot on 14th Street.

Stelman was casually dressed in an open-necked shirt, jeans and sweater, and he stood when he saw her, smiled and kissed her on the cheek. 'I'm glad you could make it, Nikki.'

Despite the smile, Nikki thought she noticed tension around Stelman's mouth and eyes. 'Is everything OK, Brad?'

'Not exactly,' Stelman said flatly. 'But take a seat, Nikki.'

The waitress offered them menus, took Nikki's coat and left. 'What's wrong, Brad? Why all the secrecy?'

Stelman patted her hand in a friendly gesture, before shaking his head with a worried look. 'How about we order drinks first? I don't know about you, but I could do with a stiff Scotch. Then we'll talk.'

Maryland
6.45 p.m.

'How long have they been dead?'

''Bout four hours, we reckon.'

The dark woods a mile off the Maryland Highway were lit up with powerful arc lights. Yellow crime-scene tape was strung around the area, and the headlamps of police vehicles cut through the slanting rain like silvered knives. The Maryland sheriff, a big man with a pot belly and wearing a rain cape, had marched Collins, Kursk and Morgan through the trees until they came to a large, rain-sodden clearing with half a dozen wooden picnic tables, covered with sheets of protective plastic.

Near one of them, a waterproof tarpaulin had been placed over the corpses, and the sheriff had knelt and held it up, then shone his torch on the victims underneath. 'Sure had to be a cold-hearted bastard, whoever did it.'

The two bodies were lying close together. The fair-haired boy looked no more than seventeen; the dark-haired girl by his side even younger. One of the boy's arms lay flailed across the girl's chest, as if he had been trying to protect her. It was a pathetic, bloody sight, both of them machinegunned at close range. Collins' stomach churned, and as Kursk and Morgan studied the corpses he said to the sheriff, 'What about the witness you've got?'

'He's a local, lives in the nearest town. Name's Billy Sinclair.

Know him pretty well. He's a forest ranger. Been working these woods here 'bout fifteen years.'

'He's still around?'

'No, sir.' The sheriff shook his head and rain dripped off his hat. 'We sent him home after we took his statement. He was pretty distressed.'

'What exactly did he see and hear?'

'A guy wearing black leathers on a dark blue motorcycle. Maybe a Jap model, but he's not sure. Drove out of the woods at high speed just after Billy heard the shots. Had a satchel, or something like it, hanging around his neck. Dark colour, maybe black.'

'He's sure the motorcyclist was male?'

'Billy seemed pretty certain. Said the person's build didn't look at all like a woman's.'

'Did he get a look at his face?'

'No, sir, the guy had a black helmet on, and the visor was down.'

'You said the witness heard gunshots?'

'Two automatic bursts, one right after the other, that sounded like a machinegun. Less than a minute before the motorcycle sped away.'

'What time?'

''Bout two-thirty. He was just about to head home early.' The sheriff pointed behind him, towards a gap in the trees. 'There's a track over there that leads back to the main road from the picnic area. Billy was about thirty yards in off the track when he saw the motorcyclist shoot past, in a damned big hurry.'

'Did the killer see him?'

'Billy doesn't think so. He found the bodies a couple of minutes later, and got the call to us straight away. We got here within ten minutes, and I had a state-wide bulletin out less than five minutes after that, and passed it on to Virginia and DC.'

'What about the search locally?'

'We've got every available man on the lookout on every highway and minor road in the county for a dark-coloured motorcycle, any make or model, and with the bare description we had of the rider. The same goes for every town in the county within a twenty-mile radius. We even had a chopper up within an hour, doing a thermal check on the woods for miles around in case the guy was hiding out in the area, but so far we've turned up no suspects. Looks like our killer got clean away.'

'Did the witness say if he heard the motorcycle drive into the area? Or anyone else, maybe?'

The sheriff shook his head. 'Says he didn't. But whoever did it could have been here for a time before the shooting.'

'Have your forensic guys finished checking the area?'

'Not yet. The rain hasn't helped, but over there by that picnic bench they found a couple of single tyre marks and some smudged footprints they took mouldings of. It looked like the killer was standing over the bench, or sitting down at it, doing something.'

Collins looked over at the bench. A sheet of white plastic had been placed on the ground beneath it, and held down with stays. 'Anything else?'

'Twelve nine-mil shell casings right near the bodies.'

'You find any traces of fresh food on the bench?'

'Nope, nothing fresh. But there's lots of prints there, for sure, and it's going to take time to lift them all. We get lots of folks passing through, using this area.'

Collins stared down again at the two bodies, then scanned the surroundings. The rain dripped down through the trees; his hair and jacket were drenched. 'OK, we've seen enough for now.'

Kursk and Morgan stepped back and the sheriff let go of the tarpaulin and stood. 'You mind me asking why the Feds are interested?'

Collins moved towards the bench where the sheriff had indicated the tyre marks and footprints had been found. 'No reflection on your men, but I'd like to have our forensic people down to have another look.'

The sheriff looked suddenly irked by the Bureau's intrusion. 'The hell for?'

Collins turned to him. 'Because the deaths could be linked be a serious federal crime. Have the local press been here?'

'Been and gone.'

'The victims' next of kin?'

'We'll keep the parents away until we get the bodies to the morgue. They were too devastated anyway, like you'd expect.'

'One more thing, and it's important. You keep any mention of the Bureau out of the press.'

'Why?'

'Because if the killer gets to hear the Feds are sticking their noses in, it may have serious consequences. You've got to trust me on this. It's vital. A word gets out, it causes big trouble. You better tell your men.'

The sheriff frowned, shrugged. 'OK. Whatever you say.' He nodded towards the forensic van. 'I'll go have a word with my boys. If you need me, holler.'

With another frown, the sheriff moved off into the rain. Morgan said, 'What do you think, Jack?'

Collins scanned the clearing and the picnic benches. 'It's got to be one of them. The timing, not much more than an hour after the Wentworth, and the fact the killer drove a motorcycle. Then there's the automatic weapon, the nine-mil shells. It's just too much coincidence. The kids must have seen the guy's face, or interrupted something. But what? Whoever did this, they didn't stop for a picnic, that's for sure. They had to be up to something, maybe something important. Otherwise, why murder those two kids?' Collins glanced over at the covered teenagers' bodies. Angrily, he turned back to Kursk. 'So much for Gorev not being just another heartless killer. It looks to me like he's overstepped the mark again.'

'You can't be certain it was Gorev who did this.'

'Maybe not. But you can judge a man by the company he keeps. And in Gorev's case, that makes him guilty as sin, even if he didn't pull the damned trigger.' Collins' face was tight as he turned to Morgan. 'Get our forensic guys down here, pronto. Have them go over the scene again with a fine-tooth comb. And we better search the area for any hidden dumps or stashes, see if anything's been dug up around here.'

'Like what?'

'Your guess is as good as mine. Get our WMD guys down as well, with their sniffer equipment. Remind them to be discreet.'

'You think the chemical's been hidden around here?'

'Who knows? Then find me a map of Maryland. The bulletin went out about twenty minutes after the shooting. Whoever it was escaped on the motorcycle, maybe they just got lucky and managed to avoid the net without being spotted. But there's always a chance they had a safe house to go to, somewhere not too far from here.'

The White House
7.25 p.m.

'The one thing you can't do is criticise him. That's imperative. Tell Abu Hasim he's wrong, call him a crazy sonofabitch or a terrorist lunatic, and you risk blowing what may be our only chance of dialogue clear out of the water.'

Professor Janet Stern put down her coffee cup, leaned towards the President. His anxiety was obvious; there were dark rings under his eyes from lack of sleep. He wasn't sitting at his Oval Office desk, made from salvaged oak timbers from HMS *Resolute*, but on one of the couches, Stern perched beside him. The President's closest advisers were all back in the room, seated in a semicircle around the couch, along with the CIA's Franklyn Young.

'We're not exactly asking you to lick ass.' Stern gave a tiny flicker of a smile, and carried on. 'Though I guess it's coming close to it. But the idea here is to get a dialogue going. The first few minutes of contact are obviously vital, so any criticism of him on your part is going to be a negative. It's going to make Abu Hasim hostile, get his back up, make him even more determined to carry out his threat. So you've got to be *very* careful not to incite him by saying the wrong thing.'

'Janet's right, Mr President,' Franklyn Young added. 'We can't afford to balls this up. It's maybe the one chance we're going to get.'

'So what do I say to him? How do I approach this?'

'You tell him what he needs to be told. Like we told Paul earlier . . .' Stern glanced briefly at Paul Burton. 'Basically, you tell Hasim he's right. That you agree he's got a legitimate grievance. That you want to help him alleviate that grievance and achieve his aims. That you're taking him seriously and making progress in meeting his demands. But that you want to do this thing *together.* That way, maybe you have a chance of getting some kind of dialogue going. Try any other tack, like blaming him for the monstrous situation he's created, and I can guarantee the conversation will go nowhere.'

'You *really* think your kind of approach will work?'

'I can't guarantee it, Mr President. But you've got to trust us on this one. Abu Hasim's a terrorist. But he's also a zealot with a massive ego who believes he's got God on his side, and that he's the Arabs' saviour. You've got to stroke his ego. Tell him he's everything he thinks he is, right from the start, and he won't see you as antagonistic or threatening. You've also got to remember that Hasim's most prominent personality trait is that he's a loner. Loneliness can give terrorists a superiority complex. Zealots are prone to the same delusion. That same superiority complex causes them to believe they're a law unto themselves. In Abu Hasim's mind, crazed as it is, he's convinced of his own righteousness in threatening to destroy Washington. Absurd as it sounds, you've got to go along with that.'

The President was doubtful. 'If the guy's *that* far gone, what kind of hope do we have?'

'Very little. But it's all we've got. The important thing to remember is that you've got to try and use Hasim's traits to our advantage. As the guy's a loner, you've got to try and be his friend. Show him you're the person who can help him achieve his objective, find a solution to his problem. Flatter him. Play up to his opinion of himself as an Arab saviour. Try to use a soft, non-threatening tone of voice. And never give him the impression you don't take him seriously. That would be deadly.'

The President quickly jotted down some notes on a pad by

his side. He was conscious, like everyone else in the room, of the excruciating, rising tension, now that a live communication with Hasim was imminent. It had taken over thirty minutes to get Janet Stern and Franklyn Young to the meeting in the Oval Office. Less than fourteen minutes remained before the 8 p.m. deadline. 'Anything else?'

'Hasim's going to have a hard-on because he knows that he's got America by the balls,' Young advised. 'So he's going to feel all-powerful. We're hoping that might require him to let off some steam, to express his grievances, to get some anger out of his system. If that happens, that's your chance to gently agree with him, to flatter him and try and get on his side.'

'There's one other thing,' Stern added. 'And it's vitally important. Franklyn and I both agree that at the start, it's better you use an intermediary, and don't talk to Hasim directly.'

'Why the hell not?'

'Two good reasons,' Franklyn Young interrupted. 'One, you put a wall between you and the guy, which gives us time to think out our replies. In Hasim's mind, you're the man who can give him exactly what he wants, so you're the last person who should talk with him directly. The one thing you don't want to do is put yourself in a position where he can force you into a yes-or-no situation. That would mean we can't stall for time. You'd have no room to think, you'd have to reply immediately. And that's our second reason – our objectives here are to gain more time to help us find the nerve gas, and to try to negotiate with him. By using an intermediary, Hasim can't come at you head-on, so you've got a slight advantage.'

The President pursed his lips, still looked doubtful.

'It's a standard ploy used in hostage situations, Mr President,' Stern offered. 'A strategy that's known to get results. It keeps the hostage-taker tied up in dialogue with the negotiator, which gives us breathing space to work out our response and our strategy. That way, we gain time, and can try to steer the conversation in the direction we want it to go.'

'Except we're not talking about some criminal taking hostages in a bank heist. We're talking about an insane terrorist holding the lives of half a million people to ransom, for Christ's sake.'

'Exactly the same principles apply, Mr President. If the terrorist asks for something immediately, a negotiator can always stall him, tell him he has to refer to a greater authority to get him what he wants. And again, time is important here. It's a well-known fact that terrorists or hostage-takers become less and less sure of themselves as time goes by. In Abu Hasim's case, my hope would be that an intermediary may help make him feel a little less certain and in control. That's a situation we may be able to exploit to our advantage.'

'OK, we try it your way. So who do we use?'

'Normally, we'd be inclined to go for an older man,' Janet Stern replied. 'Someone even tempered, a listener, someone who'd enhance Hasim's sense of confidence, who might be seen as a kind of father figure. But Hasim had a love-hate relationship with his old man, so I'm not sure that strategy would work. And a younger man is out of the question – he might be seen as a threat, or as someone totally inconsequential, an insult even.' Stern looked at the faces gathered around her, and her gaze settled on Bob Rapp, the President's bearded press adviser.

'We thought Bob Rapp might be suitable. His name is well known internationally, and he's been a highly respected journalist as well as being seen as a man of influence and authority, someone who's considered to be very close to you personally. He's also slightly older than Hasim, but certainly not old enough to be thought by him as a fatherly figure. We also think he's got the right type of personality. Would you be prepared to accept the role of negotiator, Mr Rapp?'

Rapp was stunned. 'Of . . . of course. If that's what the President wants.'

'Is Bob acceptable to you, Mr President?'

The President nodded. 'Yes, he is. What about the incident at the apartment block? How do we play it? What excuse do we give?'

'Our best advice is to tell Hasim the truth. Or should I say the kind of truth that may mitigate any anger he might want to express. Tell him a mistake was made, but that you had no choice in ignoring his advice, that you had a half-million lives to protect. That surely he would have done the same if he was in your position. Then you tell him it won't happen again. That you're considering calling off the hunt for his cell.'

'But that's impossible,' the President retorted.

'Of course it is.' Stern pushed away her coffee cup. 'But remember, we're only buying time, Mr President. And attempting to get a dialogue going. There's no way you're going to call off the hunt, we all know that. Maybe Hasim will know it too. But you've simply *got* to tell him what he *wants* to hear. It's the only hope we have of moving this thing in the direction we want to go.'

'Very well. Anything else?'

'I'm pretty sure there's lots.' Young glanced at his watch. 'But it's all we've got time for, sir. Besides, if we keep going, you're going to get swamped. Keep it to what we've already told you. And we'll be right by your side during the transmission, ready to give you any advice we can.'

The President, conscious of the passing time, looked away from the two psychologists towards the others. 'I'm presuming Hasim may want to speak in Arabic. How are we handling that?'

'We've got two senior State Department interpreters, experts in Arabic, standing by in the situation room, Mr President,' Paul Burton replied. 'They're going to work in relays. Each time Hasim pauses to let us translate, one interpreter will give us the translation while the other takes over. That way, we'll have time to consider our response. We'll also be recording Hasim's words on tape, and have the recorder hooked up to a computer that will analyse his voice for stress and tension levels. And I'll have a line kept open to Vice-President Havers, so he can listen in on the entire conversation. God forbid, should anything go wrong and Hasim decides to trigger the device, the vice-president will know about it immediately, and can assume presidential authority.'

The President nodded, then anxiously glanced through his

notes and jotted a couple more, before looking up. 'How much longer have we got?'

'Four minutes.' Paul Burton, checking his watch, licked his lips with apprehension.

Everyone in the room started as a knock came on the door. Burton opened it, and General Horton almost burst into the room. 'My apologies for interrupting, Mr President. But we're all set to go. We've patched the satellite link into the situation room. Everything's ready for you to talk with Abu Hasim.'

47

Washington, DC
7.35 p.m.

'There's something going down, Nikki. Something *weird.*'

Nikki looked across as Brad Stelman raised his Scotch to his lips. The dining booth at the Old Ebbitt Grill was private enough for them not to be overheard, but there was such a buzz of conversation around them that no one could have eavesdropped. Stelman finished sipping his Scotch and put down his glass. Nikki had barely touched the Coke she'd ordered. 'What exactly do you mean?'

'I did like I said. Called my buddy who's a senior public affairs officer over at Andrews. Chewed the cud for a while, even arranged a squash game with him for next month. Then I pretended it was me who was at Reagan this morning and mentioned all the heavy military traffic. Asked him, very casually, what it might be about.'

'And?'

'That's when I get the first click in the back of my head that tells me something's wrong.'

'Wrong in what way?'

'Normally, the guy's pretty talkative. But as soon as I started asking questions about the Reagan traffic, I could almost feel him backing off over the phone. Like he didn't want to go there.'

Stelman was silent as a waitress appeared with the food they'd ordered: a steak and a smoked-chicken salad. When she had left, he carried on, both of them ignoring their food. 'So I persisted, kept asking. Then he says sure, he knows about it. The Reagan thing's all part of an exercise. Just standard military stuff, nothing to get worked up about. So I tell him I'm still doing some freelancing, apart from my job with the Met, and if I could talk to someone who might fill me in a little more, maybe I could even write a piece on it.'

'What did he say?'

'That he'd find out what he could and get straight back to me.'

'Did he?'

'No. But half an hour later, something else happens that makes me hear another click.'

'What?'

'I get a call from the Commissioner asking me to see him in his office. When I go in, he's all pally at first. Then he mentions he had a call from one of the senior brass he knows at Andrews. He'd heard about my enquiry into the exercise, wanted to know what it was about. He also wanted to know what was I doing moonlighting as a reporter when I was working for the Met. So I told the Comish what I told my officer buddy, gave him the same spiel. Told him I thought I'd try to keep my hand in with the newspapers, maybe write the odd story here and there. The Comish listens, all polite, then he says: "Brad, let me give you some advice, both as a friend and a boss. Forget about writing some piece on this military exercise. Forget about moonlighting as a reporter. The way I see it, either you're working for the Met, or you're not."'

Stelman took another sip of Scotch. 'Then he goes on about what a fine job I was doing. About how he wouldn't like to lose me, see me fuck up. But that he had certain rules to uphold, and one of those rules meant you couldn't compromise yourself by doing outside work that might involve a conflict of interest with my job. And the way he saw it, any kind of reporting was a conflict of interest.'

Stelman looked across at her. 'Of course, it's total bullshit, Nikki. Maybe he had a legitimate point about me reporting on the side, but I know the Comish – he's not one to tell you what to do in your spare time. Except now he's giving me a veiled warning. Telling me not to go poking my nose in somewhere it's not wanted. To back off.'

'But back off from what?'

Stelman shook his head. 'I haven't the foggiest, Nikki. But whatever it is, it's got the Comish rattled. I could see the guy was uncomfortable, maybe even troubled about something. Besides, there's no way he'd come down hard on me the way he did if it was something harmless. And no way my friend at Andrews would see fit to inform his superior about my enquiry if we were just talking about a harmless military exercise, that's for sure. There's got to be a lot more to this.'

'What did you tell the Commissioner?'

'What he wanted to hear. That it wouldn't happen again, that I'd forget about the story. Which he seemed pretty relieved about.' Stelman took another mouthful of Scotch, put down his glass, and Nikki saw his hand tremble. 'But then this evening something else happened. Something that really jinxed me. That's so weird, I just had to tell you.'

'What happened?'

'You're really going to think this is crazy, Nikki.'

Stelman was pale. Nikki frowned. 'Tell me.'

And Stelman told her.

Maryland
8.15 p.m.

The rain had eased. The dark woods were still lit by powerful arc lights, and a half-dozen more unmarked cars had arrived. The FBI teams had moved rapidly: forensic experts re-examining the crime scene, while a specialist group from the WMD unit got to work with their 'sniffer' equipment – hand-held chemical monitors – probing the homicide scene and the surrounding woods for traces of chemical agents.

As the teams worked away in the drizzle, Collins sat in the front of the Ford, Morgan beside him, Kursk in the back. Collins had the map of Maryland out. 'OK, let's go over what we think we've got. After the Wentworth, the guy switches to a motorcycle, drives out here. Why? If he's got a safe house in or near the District, and he's sensible, he's going to head there after the shoot-out and stay low. So a detour all the way out to Maryland isn't exactly logical. Unless he's stashed something in the woods he needs to retrieve or check up on. Or else, for some other reason, he's decided to stop en route to wherever it is he's going. Which might mean the safe house he's headed for isn't in DC. You agree, Major?'

Kursk nodded. 'It's possible.'

'We figure the killer had a head start of twenty minutes before the alert went out. But the guy's a professional and he's going to be careful, because he doesn't want to attract attention to himself by speeding. So let's say he's doing sixty miles an hour, tops. That puts him out almost twenty miles from here, say even twenty-five, maximum, before the cops start looking for him. Where could that put us on the map, Lou?'

From his notebook, Morgan tore out a blank leaf of paper, folded it over neatly. Using the paper as a rule, he placed it against the map's scale, and with his pen marked off a line on the top and then one at the bottom of the paper. The four-inch gap between the two lines represented a scale of ten miles. Collins shone the torch on the map as Morgan used the paper rule to mark off four points, each point twenty-five miles distant from the Maryland woods, then ran his pen around in a circle, touching each of the points.

Collins tapped a finger on the enclosed circle. 'I figure there's a chance our guy's still somewhere in here.'

'We're talking about a pretty big area, Jack.' Morgan studied the map. 'All the way from southern DC in the north to Prince George's County in the south. And from Alexandria all the way out towards the Chesapeake coast.'

'The killer could have gone farther,' Kursk suggested. 'Or escaped the police search, or changed transport. You will need to check if any vehicles were stolen within the circle.'

'We'll do that,' Collins answered.

'Or he could have taken a bus, a taxi or train.'

'We'll check that out, too. And I'll have a bulletin put out on the bike, see if it turns up abandoned. But my guess is he was heading away from DC, otherwise why come this far? Unless he'd got a stash here somewhere in the woods that he needed to retrieve. The nerve gas maybe, or weapons, whatever.' Collins turned back to Morgan. 'We'll need to get lists of rental properties – houses, apartments, even trailers – within the ring. Hotels, motels, guest-houses, too. These people could be staying anywhere. We'll keep it within the twenty-five miles to start with. Expand it out from there if we've no luck.'

Morgan looked despondent. 'That could take a long time, Jack. There's got to be thousands of rental properties alone, within a twenty-five-mile radius. Never mind hotels and stuff.'

'It's got to be done.'

'What about Islamic terrorist supporters, those living within the circle?' Kursk said.

'I'll have Murphy detail our people to go through the lists we've got, see what they can come up with. Doctors, too, with Middle Eastern or Chechen backgrounds.' Collins felt worn out, frustrated. It was another mammoth job, and Murphy would have to assign hundreds more men to carry out each of the tasks.

Kursk nodded beyond the rain-beaded windscreen, where the FBI teams were working the crime scene and searching the surrounding woods, the powerful beams from their torches knifing the darkness. 'I presume your men will let us know if the bloodstains are all from the victims?'

'Don't worry, Kursk, if there's any DNA trace suggesting that Gorev was here, we'll know about it.' Collins reached for his cellphone. 'I'll fill in Murphy, get things under way.'

'I sure could do with some rest. What do you think, Jack?' Morgan rubbed his eyes, exhausted. They had been working since eleven the previous night without sleep. Kursk had been awake even longer, almost forty-eight hours. Collins saw that the Russian could barely keep his eyes open.

'Soon as we're done here, we'll try and grab a couple of hours' rest.'

7.50 p.m.

'I got the feeling I was being watched after I left the office this evening.'

'Watched by whom?'

'I don't know, Nikki.' Stelman had a worried look as they sat in the booth in the Old Ebbitt.

'Then how can you be so sure?'

'About five, I'm heading home in my car. I notice another car following me close behind, a dark-coloured Chrysler sedan. Then it disappears in traffic and I don't think any more about it. Except ten minutes later I'm at home in my apartment, making coffee in the kitchen, when I glance down on to the street. I see a car parked opposite my apartment block. I'm pretty sure it's the same sedan. I see two guys inside. Then five minutes later, when I look again, the car's gone. So I go take a jog. I can't see the dark sedan anywhere. But jogging back I spot another car, parked farther up the street. Again, two guys inside. Like they're working a relay, watching me.'

'You didn't imagine it, Brad?'

'Nikki, I know what I saw. It was written all over these guys – they looked like professionals, either cops or Feds. And let's face it, the Comish's little talk was a warning. For whatever reasons, imagined or otherwise, I was convinced those guys in the cars were there for a purpose. To keep tabs on me.'

Nikki paled, glanced nervously around the restaurant. 'Were you followed here?'

'They tried to, but I shook them off. Parked over in Chinatown, took the subway.'

'They really tried to follow you?'

'Damned right they did. I spotted them behind me on the way through Chinatown. That's when I decided to take the subway. But they followed me down. It was the same two guys from the second car.'

'You're sure you lost them?'

'I'm sure, Nikki. I changed stations four times. The last time I saw them was at the Union, half an hour ago, just before I managed to lose them in the crowd. I changed lines twice again after that, to be certain.' Stelman tossed his fork down, his steak hardly touched, dabbed his mouth with his napkin. 'When I spotted the second car, I even began to wonder if my phones were being tapped. So I called you from a neighbour's phone. It's why I told you not to call me at home, just in case. I know it sounds like I'm being paranoid, Nikki. But I'm not, believe me. Just like I know now that you're not wrong about this. *Something* stinks.'

'I believe you.'

'The question is, where do you go from here?'

'I don't know.' Nikki frowned, shook her head. 'But there's got to be a story in it somewhere. And after what you've told me, my instinct tells me it could be a big one, some kind of conspiracy. Besides, there's something else I didn't mention.'

'What?'

Nikki explained about the army presence across the street from Daniel's preschool that afternoon. 'When I got home, I called the army public affairs office and got through to the Major Craig that the sergeant recommended I talk with. The major was polite, but he said he knew nothing about the exercise, which in his estimation probably meant it was no big deal. When I told him that I noticed the men were wearing no divisional flashes, and queried it, he asked for my name and number and said he'd get back to me by tomorrow if he found out something, or if he learned that the information was classified. But polite as he was, I got the feeling I'm not going to get anything out of him. I know when I'm being fobbed off.' Nikki paused. 'You're sure you don't know anything else about the police exercise, Brad?'

'Nothing other than what I've told you. And if there was something more ominous to it, the police brass are hardly going to tell me everything. I'm way down the chain, Nikki. Just a mouthpiece. Are you going to talk with your editor?'

Nikki thought about it, shook her head. 'No, I'll run with it alone for now. Until I've got something solid.'

'Look, Nikki, I know the last thing I need is to lose my job with the Met. But if you want me to help some more, I'll do it.'

'You've done enough already. I don't want you getting in any trouble.' Nikki smiled, reached her hand across and touched Stelman's affectionately. 'But thanks for the offer, Brad.'

'Still, if the Commissioner knows something – and I figure he's got to the way he reacted – then there's a good chance some of his senior officers know about it, too. Maybe I can dig around a little more.'

'Brad . . .'

'I'm still a reporter, Nikki, remember?' Stelman smiled back. 'Curiosity goes with the territory. But don't fret, I'll be careful.'

'What about the men following you?'

'Let me worry about them.' Stelman wrote on a slip of paper, handed it across. 'That's my sister's number over in Arlington. If you need to get in touch, call that number, but don't call me at home or on my cellphone, just in case those guys really do tap my lines. I'll try to get back to you as quick as I can from a pay-phone. Which tack are you going to take?'

'I wish I knew. My boyfriend's with the FBI. I think I'll try and talk with him first. See if he knows anything.'

Stelman frowned. 'Why didn't you do that before now?'

'Jack and I have an unwritten rule, we never talk about his work. But he got a call last night to report to FBI Headquarters – it seemed pretty urgent – and I haven't seen or heard from him since. Now it's made me think. If the cops and the army are involved in whatever this is, probably the Feds are too. Maybe that's why Jack hasn't called. Maybe he's been caught up in it.'

'Do you honestly think he'd talk if he was?'

'I guess not. But Jack's a straight and honest guy. I'd know if he was trying to mislead me, or cover something up. Even that could be a start.' Nikki wanted to make the call to Jack there and then, but she'd wait until she got outside. She checked the time – 8.20 – and reached for her bag. 'I've got to go, Brad. My mom's got a bridge club game at nine she can't miss. She's looking after Daniel until I get back – I couldn't get a baby-sitter at short notice. Thanks again for your help. I owe you. Look after yourself, OK?'

As she reached for her purse, Stelman put a hand on hers. 'Dinner's on me.'

'Then the next time's my treat.'

Stelman gave a hopeful smile. 'I'll hold you to it.'

Nikki stood, gave him a peck on the cheek. Stelman's hand touched hers, his voice full of concern. 'Just be careful, Nikki. And if you think you're getting in too deep, or there's trouble, you call me, OK?'

Maryland
8.20 p.m.

'The tests were all negative.'

'So that means the stuff wasn't here?'

'No, just that we can't detect any evidence of chemical, Jack. It could have been so well sealed that there wasn't a chance of even the slightest leakage. With the kind of nerve gas we're dealing with, that's highly likely, unless these guys want to risk killing themselves instantly. It's usually kept in binary form, and if you ask me they've got the two components kept separate and hermetically sealed in special airtight containers, or something like toughened glass. Maybe both, so there's no risk.'

Collins listened as the agent from WMD explained the results of their search of the woods. Beside him stood another agent, a forensic technician. They were all huddled around the Ford, including Morgan and Kursk.

'So it *could* have been here?'

'If you're asking for a professional opinion, Jack, I'd say no. Apart from animal burrows, we didn't find any earth disturbed in the woods, no secret hiding holes where the stuff might have been stashed. Not yet, anyway. But we'll carry on searching.'

'What if they kept it around here, well sealed, maybe inside something like a camper, but moved it on?' Morgan directed his question to the forensic technician. 'They'd need four-wheel transport to move so much liquid weight, right?'

'We found some tyre tracks fifty yards from here, but we've pretty much established they belonged to the witness's four-wheel-drive. We didn't find any others, Lou, apart from the motorcycle.'

'Has any other evidence turned up?'

The technician shook his head. 'Zilch. The local guys did a pretty good job. Didn't miss a thing, far as we can see. We're only going over their ground. But we'll carry on, just the same. Let you know if we find anything.'

'Thanks.'

'Sure.' As the two agents moved away, Morgan climbed into the driver's seat, Kursk into the back. Collins joined them in the front. 'What now?' Kursk asked, his voice weary, heavy with lack of sleep.

'You've got me there, Major. There's not much more we can do tonight.' Collins stared over at the grim crime scene, then nodded to Morgan. 'OK, Lou, let's get out of here and get some rest.'

Ten minutes later, Collins' cellphone buzzed. They were on Highway 4, heading back towards DC, Morgan at the wheel, Kursk in the back, already dozing. Collins, trying to rest, jolted awake. He flicked on his cell, heard the familiar voice. 'Jack . . . ?'

'Nikki . . . sorry I didn't call, but I've been busy as hell . . .'

'Jack, we need to talk.'

Collins heard the urgency in her voice, wondered whether it was some kind of emergency. 'What's wrong, Nikki? Are you OK? Is Daniel OK?'

'Daniel's fine, so am I. It's something else, Jack. But it's important. We need to meet tonight.'

Exhaustion flooded Collins' body. He ached for sleep, could barely stay awake, the highway lights a blur. 'Can't it wait until tomorrow, Nikki? I'm dead beat, honey. It's been a long day.'

'You sound like you haven't slept.'

'I haven't.'

'Since you left last night?'

'I guess not.'

There was a pause. 'I'm sorry for bothering you, Jack. I'm sure whatever you're doing has to be important . . .'

Collins heard concern in her voice, then there was another pause on the line, and when he didn't answer Nikki came back. 'But it can't wait, Jack. It just *can't*.'

'Nikki . . . please . . . tomorrow. We'll talk tomorrow.'

'It's got to be *now*, Jack. It's got to be tonight,' Nikki insisted. 'I'll meet you anywhere you want, but it's got to be tonight.'

48

Washington, DC
8.15 p.m.

On the sixth floor of the FBI's J. Edgar Hoover building, Thomas J. Murphy put down his phone. The head of the FBI's Counter-Terrorist Division was preoccupied with the discussion he had just had with a high-ranking Israeli intelligence officer over a secure line to Tel Aviv. The subject of their conversation was a young Palestinian woman named Karla Sharif.

In front of him, Murphy had the few sketchy details he had received in a confidential report from the FSB in Moscow half an hour ago, and which he had hoped the Israelis would be able to expand on.

Colonel Uri Rand in Tel Aviv, with typical Mossad efficiency, had done more than that: in a twenty-minute discussion he had given Murphy a highly detailed summary of Mossad's intelligence on the young woman. Not only that, but the contents of her file, along with her photograph, would be encrypted and sent to the Israeli embassy in Washington that very night, and, the colonel promised, would be translated and on Murphy's desk by 8 a.m. the next morning, hand-delivered by an embassy courier.

The Russians, too, had surprised Murphy with the speed and detail of their response. Scouring old KGB files, the FSB had discovered a Palestinian named Karla Dousad, linked to Nikolai Gorev, who had entered Moscow on 12 February 1983, then aged twenty, along with two dozen other Palestinians, for the purpose of collegial studies. Those studies, in reality, had involved a year at Patrice Lumumba University, where Karla Dousad had received KGB terrorist instruction. Her intensive course had included weapons training, bomb-making and operations planning, to name but a few subjects, and Murphy had absorbed the remaining details with mounting interest.

Karla Dousad's Palestinian father was an immigrant engineer in New York who had returned to Lebanon with his wife and daughter when she was twelve. A graduate of the American University in Beirut even before she travelled to Moscow, and fluent in French and English, Karla Dousad had proved herself one of the top Palestinian students the KGB had trained; their report mentioned a rumour that the infamous Carlos Sanchez – Carlos the Jackal – had been so impressed by her that he had wanted her for his own personal terror team.

The FSB also detailed a known relationship she had developed while in Moscow: with Nikolai Gorev, then a KGB instructor at the university. The two had often been seen in each other's company outside of classes; there were rumours among Gorev's KGB colleagues that the pair had developed an intense sexual relationship, and they had been observed spending weekends alone together at Gorev's apartment. Her training completed, Karla Dousad had immediately returned to Lebanon. Three months later, the report noted, Nikolai Gorev had resigned his KGB post and joined the army.

Just as interesting, from Murphy's point of view, were the gaps the Israeli colonel had filled in, where the Russian report had left off.

Karla Dousad's name had first cropped up in intelligence reports from Mossad's field agents as far back as 1982. Aged nineteen, she had joined the PLO in the aftermath of the Israeli-backed Phalangist militia massacres at the Palestinian refugee camps in Sabra and Chatila, and the Israeli-led excursions into Lebanon, which had left thousands of innocent people dead, including her own parents, and sparked a militant PLO backlash. Karla Dousad was among the thousands of enraged young Palestinians who were moved to join the PLO to exact revenge. According to Colonel Rand, she was suspected of having taken part in at least a half-dozen terrorist attacks against Israel, before being sent to Moscow to hone her skills.

That episode the Israelis knew little if nothing about, apart from the fact that Dousad had achieved a reputation as an excellent student while in Moscow, but they certainly knew what had happened to her in the aftermath: immediately after her return to Lebanon, she had married Michael Sharif, a schoolteacher and Palestinian activist, and moved to the outskirts of Beirut. She had given birth to a son, Josef, in the spring of the following year. Five years later her husband was killed in a massive car-bomb explosion that rocked Beirut and left twenty-five people dead.

Surprisingly, the promise she'd shown as a student had barely materialised after her return to Lebanon: for a time, her skills had been put to use training fresh PLO recruits, but especially after her husband's death it seemed that her involvement in the PLO cause had waned and she had disappeared entirely from the terrorist scene.

It didn't really make sense to Murphy: here was a woman who had trained to be the ultimate terrorist but had given up on her skills, and he wondered about that. Rather than spur her on to revenge, had her husband's death turned her from the terrorist path, or what?

'You think she's still in the game, Uri?' Murphy had asked the Mossad officer over the secure line to Tel Aviv.

'I don't think so, Tom. The word we got from our informers was that she no longer took part in terrorist activities or fraternised with known extremists, and was therefore no longer a threat. Exactly the reasons we halted our surveillance on her many years ago, and allowed her prison visits to her son. The consensus was she'd given up on the cause. It's not unknown for even hardened terrorists to have a change of heart. Do you mind me asking why you're interested?'

'Weird as it sounds, her name and some details about her cropped up in an investigation we're running. A false passport operation run by a couple of Lebanese-American businessmen.'

'That does seem most odd,' Rand suggested. 'Tell me more.'

'I will, just as soon as we've got to the bottom of it,' Murphy lied blatantly, his answer already prepared. The last thing he needed was to alert the Israelis to the threat, and he knew he was already on dangerous ground just by making enquiries. 'But don't fret, Uri, it really doesn't seem like anything Mossad should be worrying about.'

There was a slight pause on the other end of the line as the Israeli digested Murphy's reply. 'You'll let me know if it is?'

Murphy could sense the Israeli's bristling interest over the phone. 'You bet,' he lied again. 'But do me a favour. Is it possible that you can confirm if she's at her address in Tyr? Discreetly, I mean.'

'How soon do you need the information?'

'Straight away would be good.' Then Murphy laughed, intent on hiding his urgency with yet another lie in order not to give the game away. 'I'd like to get this thing wrapped before I go on leave tomorrow evening. I've got a golfing holiday planned in Florida.'

'Lucky you. Very well, I'll do my best to have the information for you by tomorrow.'

'Good talking to you, Uri. I appreciate your help.'

Five minutes after the phone call to Tel Aviv, a sober-looking Murphy finished reading through a clutch of papers and notes on his desk. He pushed himself to his feet, crossed to his office window, and mused again about what made a woman like Karla Sharif suddenly return to the terrorist fold after so many years of inactivity.

The Israelis had considered her no real threat, yet one telling detail from Tel Aviv had set alarm bells ringing in Murphy's head: Karla Sharif's last recorded visit to her son had been almost four months previously, on 21 July. She had been due to visit him again a month ago, on 21 October, but had not shown up at the prison. According to Rand's information, it was the first visit she'd ever missed.

The Israeli colonel had also promised to send her son's file, and had given Murphy the gist of his details over the phone: aged sixteen, Josef Sharif had been wounded while trying to smuggle explosives across the Israeli border with a Hamas comrade. Despite the seriousness of his crime, Mossad reckoned from his interrogation that he was probably a borderline Hamas supporter; a relative innocent led on by hardline peers and driven by teenage bravado.

Standing at the window, watching the blazing lights of DC, Murphy could understand Karla Sharif's initial reasons for joining the PLO. The Israeli-backed Phalangist massacres at the Sabra and Chatila refugee camps had been a shameful episode in Israel's history. If he'd been a young Palestinian and had witnessed the massacre of his parents and hundreds of his friends and neighbours – most of them entirely innocent – he'd have been tempted to take up a gun against the Israelis himself. He knew hardened military men who thought that whoever was responsible for that callous episode – everyone, all along the chain of command – should have been brought to trial at the Court of Human Rights. They were war criminals, no question. But the Israelis had never really admitted guilt or punished the offenders.

Murphy tried to focus on the dilemma that troubled him. Karla Sharif's reasons for joining the PLO he could certainly understand, but not her fresh involvement after so many years of being out of the game. He wondered whether her son's imprisonment, the continued unrest in the Palestinian Territories, or both, could have retriggered her interest. Her radical background, her son's imprisonment, her non-appearance at the jail and Kursk's identification of her pointed to only one thing in Murphy's mind: there was a damned good chance the FBI had their woman.

In Murphy's mind, it made sense for al-Qaeda to use someone like Karla Sharif: she spoke fluent English, had lived in America, had received top-class terrorist training, but had no recent connections to any terror organisation. In the US, she could probably blend in easily and pass for an American citizen.

He was convinced that Karla Sharif would not be at home when Mossad sent its agents to check. What nailed it for him and set his pulse racing was when he scanned through the copy of Abu Hasim's lists of prisoners which lay on his desk: a Josef Sharif was among those whose release the terrorists were demanding. There was a knock on his door, and one of Murphy's senior agents, Larry Soames stepped in, his sleeves rolled up, tie askew. He closed the door.

'Well, Larry?'

'Just thought I'd let you know. Our undercover teams have still turned up zilch. All the serious Islamic supporters on our lists are pretty much behaving themselves, not putting a foot out of line.'

'What about the cargo manifests?'

'Ditto. Zilch.'

Murphy grimaced. 'OK, go back another month. What about the stuff Collins asked for?'

'We're working on it, Tom.' Soames looked weary. 'Any more lists and they'll be coming out our asses. What's the news from Maryland?'

'Nothing yet. Collins said he'd get back to me if there's a lead.'

Soames nodded, moved to leave.

'Hang on. I'm not finished, Larry.'

Murphy crossed to the US wall map and stood there, hands on his hips. Palestinians were already on his roll-call of illegals. But he knew Karla Sharif could have entered the country in hundreds of different ways and using as many guises. The Wentworth's janitor had recalled first seeing her six weeks earlier. If she left Lebanon after 22 July and didn't turn up at the jail on 21 October, there was a likelihood she had entered the US some time between those dates. It was possible, but just as unlikely, that she had entered using her own name. Even if she had, it made sense that she would cover her tracks to avoid being found. At a guess, Murphy figured she would have used false documents and offered a misleading or fictitious address on her immigration forms, at whichever point she had entered the US. All of which would make it almost impossible to track her down, but Murphy had to follow the lead, see where it led.

'I want the immigration records for between 23 July and 17 October gone over again, and thoroughly. We'll need a breakdown of Middle East-born women who entered the country any time between those two dates. Confine it to the ages of between thirty to forty-five. Stick to the East Coast first and break them down into their respective nationalities. In particular I'm interested in the Lebanese-born, and especially if they're from a place called Tyr. That's spelled T-Y-R.'

Murphy grabbed a pen and notepad from his desk. 'Keep an eye out for this one.' He wrote the available details on a slip of paper: the name Karla Sharif, her date and place of birth, and her maiden name, Karla Dousad. 'It's a long shot, but she could have used either of those names. Then find out all you can using the name Karla Dousad – her parents were Palestinian immigrants, lived somewhere in New York where she was born. I'm going back over twenty-five years, but get everything you can – what schools she attended, addresses where she lived, and try to find out if she has any relatives in the US. And I want it done quickly, Larry.'

Soames raised an eye. 'She's hot?'

'Hot as hell. Get on it right away.'

7.59 p.m.

'We're ready to go live, Mr President.'

A hush descended on the conference room as the voice of the officer in the communications chamber next door filtered through the speakerphone. 'We're going to patch through the satellite radio link to Afghanistan in ten seconds.'

Around the table, tension showed on the faces of the President and his advisers, each acutely aware that they were about to hear the voice of the man threatening a half-million of their countrymen. 'Five seconds, Mr President. Four. Three. Two. One—'

A second later the hiss of soft radio static filled the room.

Bob Rapp looked anxiously over at Janet Stern, as if to seek confirmation that he could speak, and received an urgent nod.

'Mr Hasim . . . are you there?' Rapp's voice had a nervous tremor. One of the two State Department translators at once relayed his question, and the reply came seconds later.

'Yes, I am here. This is Abu Hasim.'

There was an unreal, metallic quality to the voice that filtered into the conference room over the secure, scrambled line: it sounded as if it came from a distant planet.

'Mr Hasim, this is Bob Rapp, one of the President's senior advisers. I'd like to make you aware that for the purposes of our conversation I have a translator from the State Department here beside me. He will translate your words into English, and mine into Arabic.'

'That is agreeable,' Hasim said, when the translator had finished. 'I am now ready to address your president.'

'Mr Hasim, sir,' Rapp answered courteously, 'the President first wishes me to assure you that your list of demands is being dealt with in the most serious and urgent manner. At this very moment, the President is conferring with his senior advisers as to how best he can assist you in meeting those demands and resolving this problem. For this reason, he has asked me to act as his personal liaison with you as we try to find solutions to the issues you've raised, and also to clarify with you some important issues of mutual concern. One issue, in particular, is the withdrawal of our forces from the Gulf within the remaining five days. This mass withdrawal within such a short timeframe will undoubtedly attract serious media and public interest. Yet you have warned that your demands be kept from the public. We need urgent clarification on that point, Mr Hasim. I would be grateful for your help in enlightening me as to how we can best go about a withdrawal.'

As the translator got to work, Rapp sat back from the microphone and anxiously licked his lips. He looked at Janet Stern and Franklyn Young, seated either side of the President. Both exchanged satisfied looks; Franklyn Young even offered him a smile. Rapp had slipped easily into his role of mediator. The President gave him a thumbs-up, and Rapp nodded his thanks.

A long silence ensued after the translator had done his work, and then Abu Hasim's voice came back. There was no mistaking the sharp tone, even before the translator had finished. 'Mr Rapp, I said I was ready to speak with your president. I ask you now, is he ready to speak with me?'

'Mr Hasim, as I explained, the President has asked me to liaise with you in this matter, so that we can first clarify several important issues. Meanwhile, he's working hard to find ways to meet your demands, sir.'

Rapp nodded to the translator.

'Your explanations are unnecessary,' Hasim replied seconds later. 'You have tried to make a fool of me. Tried to deceive me with your tactics. But I will not be deceived by the stupid tactics of you Americans. Tell your president that there will be no contact with me again on this frequency if he will not talk to me personally.'

The translator finished. Rapp said, 'Mr Hasim . . . ? Are you there, Mr Hasim?'

Janet Stern whispered, 'Keep him talking, Bob. Tell him anything you have to but keep the sonofabitch talking!'

'Mr Hasim . . . if you could just listen, please . . .'

There was another long silence, and then the voice that came back from the speakerphone was from the officer in the communications room. 'You're wasting your time, sir. He's cut the damned line.'

49

Mohamed Rashid turned the grey Plymouth across the George Mason Bridge, headed towards Arlington. The briefcase was on the floor behind his feet. At the exit for Arlington he turned the car off the highway and headed towards an apartment block a five-minute drive away. He had made a call from a public telephone on the way, and when he pulled up outside the block he saw the figure of a man waiting at the corner, his face in shadows. Rashid flashed the lights and the man walked towards him. He was in his twenties, slim as a reed, a young Saudi recruit he had trained personally. Without a word, the man slipped into the front seat, pulled the door shut.

'Is everything prepared, Tamir?' asked Rashid.

'Yes.'

'Where's the delivery truck?'

'Parked around the back.'

Twenty-five minutes later, Rashid drove the Plymouth through the near-deserted streets of Washington until he reached F Street, three blocks from FBI Headquarters. He pulled in midway along the avenue, directly across the street from a McDonald's restaurant.

Right behind him, the GM delivery truck halted at the kerb, Tamir at the wheel. The young Saudi climbed out, walked back to Rashid's Plymouth and got in beside him. Rashid had explained everything down to the last detail, and the man knew his fate, had trained for it, prayed for it. Rashid carefully reached down, lifted the briefcase from the floor and handed it over. The young man clutched it in front of him, stared down at the case as if it held some deep religious significance. His face was prickled with tiny droplets of sweat.

'Your moment has come, Tamir. You know exactly what you have to do.'

The man looked up, licked his lips, nodded earnestly. 'Yes, my brother.'

'May Allah go with you. This night, you will be a martyr in heaven.'

8.15 p.m.

'We need some calm here, people. Quiet down, everyone.'

In the situation room, the President called his shocked advisers to order. A babble of voices filled the air as everyone around the table tried to recover from the impact of Abu Hasim's blunt interruption of his transmission.

'Professor Stern . . .' the President's tone was bleak as he addressed the petite psychologist once the noise had died down. 'You're about the only one among us who doesn't look shocked by what just happened.'

'I guess I half expected it, Mr President. I know Franklyn and I suggested you use Mr Rapp as mediator. But in the back of my mind I had a feeling Hasim wouldn't fall for it. But we had to try. It's plain now he's not going to be duped, or easily swayed. This is going to be much harder than we thought.'

'It's obvious that Hasim's got a keen grasp of tactics,' Franklyn Young offered. 'Insane he may be, he's one sharp sonofabitch. We're facing an uphill battle.'

'What do you suggest we do?'

'Give it another five minutes, then try and talk to him directly.'

'And tell him what?'

'Exactly as we agreed,' Stern answered. 'Make him believe that you're taking him seriously. That you're working hard with your advisers to satisfy his demands. It might do no harm to say that you'd appreciate if he could still accept Mr Rapp as a personal mediator. That it would allow you to concentrate all your efforts on resolving his entire list of issues. But don't push it. Bring up the point about the Gulf withdrawal again. It's so vitally important we try to suck him into the conversation, get a dialogue going. And again – I stress this – don't anger him. Get him into an argument and you risk him cutting us off again. Maybe for good this time.'

The President pursed his lips tightly, finally nodded. 'OK, let's give it another shot.'

The President leaned towards the microphone. 'Mr Hasim,' he began immediately, once the line was open again. 'This is the President of the United States. Can you hear me?'

Hasim spoke, and the translator at the President's side relayed the reply. The terrorist's tone was calm, almost hushed. 'Yes, I can hear you.'

The President's face flushed red, evidence of his hidden fury that, as the leader of the most powerful country on earth, he was being forced to prostrate himself in front of a cowardly terrorist who'd destroy the American capital and kill hundreds of thousands of its citizens. 'Mr Hasim, I wish to assure you that the list of demands you delivered to me almost forty-eight hours ago has been given close and painstaking scrutiny by myself and my closest advisers, and that we are prepared to act on those demands. Before we proceed, however, I want to make it clear that I personally deplore your behaviour. No matter how great the differences that divide us – racial, religious or otherwise – and no matter how intensely you loathe this administration, or how great your hatred of the American people, their way of life and their core values, your decision to threaten to destroy this city and its population is a cowardly and inhumane act.'

The President's brutal honesty immediately sent everyone in the room into a panic. Janet Stern made an abrupt gesture that indicated 'stop', but the President ignored her, gritted his teeth and stabbed his finger at the translator. 'Interpret what I said!

Don't you dare change a damned word, you hear? I want this sonofabitch to know exactly how I feel.'

'Yes, sir.' As the translator did his work, Janet Stern shook her head in dismay. The President had gone his own way, disregarding everyone's advice. Still, she had a grudging admiration for the man. He had balls, and pride. And he'd been clever enough to let Hasim know from the very start that his ultimatum was being acted upon. Hearing that, Hasim would be less inclined to cut off the communication. But there was no telling *where* this conversation would go.

'You have a powerful weapon that threatens this nation, Mr Hasim,' the President continued, before Hasim even had a chance to reply. 'But understand that I, too, have at my disposal an array of weapons even more powerful that can annihilate you and every one of your followers, in Afghanistan or wherever else they may hide. If you force me to, and no matter what the consequences may be, I shall use my country's arsenal to destroy you. I want you to be aware of that, and to tell you that any president in my position would have been tempted to do exactly that the moment your message was delivered.

'However, I didn't, because I believe, like any sensible human being, that the first way to attempt to solve any conflict is through dialogue. I want you to know also that I have begun the process of acceding to your demands. There's a long list, and attending to it is taking up every moment of my time, which is why I ask that you allow Mr Rapp, whom you spoke with, to act as a conduit between us, so that I can devote all my energies to solving these problems, and with your help. For example, I have ordered that fifteen per cent of US troops leave Middle Eastern soil immediately. That withdrawal is already under way as we speak. But your stipulation that your threat must not be made public makes it extremely difficult for me order a complete pull-out of US forces in the region within the next five days without drawing massive media attention. That is one of the reasons why we need to talk, Mr Hasim. To find a way out of this dilemma.'

The President sat back from the microphone, sweat glistening on his forehead from the concentration he'd just exerted. As he dabbed his brow, he looked at Janet Stern and Franklyn Young. They each gave him a nod, confirming he was doing all right, but there was an ominous silence before Hasim answered through the translator.

'Mr President, I have not agreed to this talk to hear your threats. For too long America has used its superior power to intimidate the Arab world. It has ended now. We are equals. I will not be threatened.'

'Mr Hasim . . .' The President flushed. '. . . it's hardly you who's being threatened here. Let's not forget who began this.'

There was a pause as the translator got back to work, and then Hasim spoke again. '*Your* country began this. By using its power to abuse Arab nations and suppress their rightful place in the world. By its interference in Arab lands, where it is not wanted. And you are still abusing it by threatening me with your missiles. You shall not threaten me again, do you understand? Nor do I wish to hear your excuses. My demands require no further discussion, only action on your part. I have no intention of entering into a dialogue with you, or your administration. Not now, or in the future. I only wish to be assured that you are complying with all of my demands. Are you complying? Please answer yes or no.'

Hasim paused to allow the State Department translator to interpret his words. The President gritted his teeth, angered by the boldness of the man. 'Mr Hasim, it was not my intention to threaten you. Rather to make you aware of the tragic outcome if your device goes off and American citizens are harmed. You must understand the grave position it puts you and your followers in. That if you disperse this chemical, you and they will die also. Not only that, this nation is made up of many diverse religions and nationalities. There are many people of Arab blood, people from Afghanistan and your native Saudi Arabia among them. The vast majority of these people are God-fearing Muslims. They would also be among the victims of your attack. Surely, as a man of God, as a fellow Muslim, you are concerned by this? These people are your brothers, your sisters, and their children. I can't believe you'd want to see innocent fellow Muslims killed. Surely you understand my point?'

Hasim's reply, seconds later, was abrupt. 'I do not have to understand anything. If Muslims are to die, they will be martyrs to a holy and just cause. You have not answered my question. Are you complying with my demands?'

The President bit back his rage. 'Mr Hasim, I have no choice except to comply. But what guarantees can you give me that the bomb will be safely defused once your conditions are met?'

The translator spoke, and Hasim answered again. 'You will have my word, witnessed by Allah. The bomb is set to automatically detonate when the deadline chosen by me expires. Only I can deactivate it. When my demands are met, I shall relay to you its location.'

'And the problem of the media?'

'That is not my concern. Or how you remove your troops from the Middle East. Only that it is done, and by the time the deadline is due to expire.'

'Mr Hasim, America is a democracy. I am simply the head of a government. To withdraw within the timeframe you demand and without public explanation as to why would expose me to political and media enquiry. The American people would want to know *why* their troops are being withdrawn from the Middle East. As would her allies, including those in the Arab world. A withdrawal such as this is a mammoth military and political undertaking, and will have grave international repercussions, as I'm sure you're aware.'

Hasim's tone remained calm, almost without emotion. 'You are not listening, Mr President. Please do not waste my time with your speeches. I will not be drawn farther into this conversation. I will not enter into dialogue. Will you comply, yes or no?'

'Yes, Mr Hasim, I will comply. I'm trying to help you, but you're not making this easy. Surely there must be a way we can accommodate both our positions? What if we were to phase a withdrawal? Over several weeks? Wouldn't that be acceptable?

Your wishes will still be carried out. In the meantime, we can work together on how it can be done.'

There was a long pause before Hasim came back again. This time the calm had been replaced by an irate tone. 'As always, you Americans do not listen. I have told you my demands. I have told you I will not enter into dialogue. Yet you still attempt to cajole and bargain. Understand, I shall not bargain. You have vexed me by your attempts to negotiate, Mr President. But you have committed an even graver error.'

'What?'

'You have lied to me. I believe that you are not in the least serious about agreeing to my demands.'

A stark silence descended on the situation room as the translator delivered Hasim's reply, and the President turned to look at his advisers. Suddenly Hasim carried on. 'I do not believe that you intend to honour the commitment you just gave. And in asking me to help you, you are simply trying to buy time. I believe that you will use these remaining five days to try to locate the chemical device before the deadline expires. I know this is your hope, Mr President. But it is a vain hope. True, your FBI located and attacked members of one of my cells. By the grace of Allah, they escaped. But I have many followers hidden in the United States. You cannot hope to find them all, no matter how hard you try. And even if you found them, even if you killed them all, it would not prevent me carrying out my promise.'

There was a pause, and then Hasim continued. 'I say to you that fifteen per cent is not enough. Only by withdrawing every last American serviceman and fulfilling every one of my demands will you save your capital and its people. Yet you do not seem to understand this. Therefore, to impress again upon you my determination, and that of my followers, who are God's martyrs, I am forced to give you an example of our resolve, our willingness to die in order to bring ruin upon America. It will be the last example I offer, I promise you. After that, there will only be the destruction of your entire capital.'

The President, upon hearing the translation, felt a growing panic, and tried to interrupt.

'No, please, listen to me . . .'

The translation that came back was sharp and unforgiving. 'Interrupt me again and I shall immediately cease this communication, and for good. It is you who will listen to *me*, Mr President, and listen well. You and your advisers have brought this upon your own heads. You have now condemned innocent people to death by your vain hope and your intransigence. However, this last example I offer will allow you all to reconsider your position. It will focus your minds on what needs to be done, and impress on you all that there will be no more lies and false promises. By midnight, less than four hours from now, when you have witnessed and digested my warning, we will talk again. Until then, Mr President, may God have mercy on the souls you have condemned.'

50

Washington, DC
9.05 p.m.

'I'm tired, Mommy.'

'I know you are, honey, but this is important. Mommy's got to meet Jack. And you can have some pizza, and a strawberry milkshake. Wouldn't that be nice?'

Nikki stroked Daniel's hair and ushered him into the pizza restaurant on the corner of 10th and E Street. It was way past his bedtime and he was getting grumpy. She'd hated having to take him out with her so late, but she hadn't the heart to ask her mother to miss her bridge game and baby-sit – she'd done that too many times already and didn't want to abuse the favour – so instead of taking Daniel straight home she'd bundled him into her car and embarked on the ten-minute ride to the restaurant.

She took a seat by the corner window. When the waitress came, she ordered a coffee for herself and a small cheese-and-tomato pizza and milkshake for Daniel, then she diverted him with some crayons and a colouring book she took from his Barney bag.

'How about you show me what you can draw?'

As soon as Daniel was absorbed, scribbling on the pages, she looked towards the FBI Headquarters. Lights blazed in the building across the street, and she noticed several cars coming and going from the underground carpark. It made her think there was more activity than usual for this time of night – just after nine – or was she imagining it?

The district around the Hoover building normally quietened down after rush hour, and the same applied to the local bars and restaurants. She'd met Jack in this restaurant a couple of times during the busy lunch period, but this was the first time she'd ever been here in the evening, and the place was dead, barely half a dozen customers scattered around the tables.

She looked back towards the window. Jack had said he'd meet her at 9.15. For once he wasn't on time, and it was another twenty minutes before she saw the dark blue Ford pull up outside under a streetlamp. Jack was in the front passenger seat. A black man was driving, and there was another guy seated in the back who looked to be in his late thirties, tired faced, with Slavic cheekbones.

She watched Jack slam the door shut and tap the car's roof. The driver manoeuvred out from the kerb, hung a right, and disappeared down 10th Street, moving away past the FBI building.

The men were colleagues of Jack's, that much was obvious. Moments later he entered the restaurant. The first thing Nikki noticed were the dark rings under his eyes. He looked exhausted, pale and spent. She immediately felt guilty for having insisted that he meet her. He spotted her at the table, waved and came over, kissed her on the cheek. 'Nikki – I'm sorry I'm late, and about the last couple of days. I've been up to my eyes.'

He tousled Daniel's hair. 'You're up pretty late, aren't you? How's my cowboy?'

'I's OK, Jack.' Daniel toyed with his pizza, then went back to his crayons, and Nikki saw Jack give her a quizzical look. 'I had to bring him along, Jack. I couldn't get a baby-sitter.'

'That's OK. It's good to see you both.'

'You look dead beat.'

Collins slumped into the seat beside her, nodded, put a hand on hers. 'I'm pretty bushed. What's wrong, Nikki? What's so urgent?'

'Let me get us some coffee, then we'll talk.'

Washington, DC
9.54 p.m.

Tamir drove in the direction of Pennsylvania Avenue. His heart pounded in his chest, not from fear, but from excitement, yet despite this he felt a strange kind of calm. Death was only minutes away, and as he drove the truck he silently recited his prayers, the lines from the glorious Koran that offered him so much comfort: 'My prayer and my sacrifice and my life and my death are all for Allah. And death will come to him from every quarter, but he will not die.'

Thoughts intruded, of his family in Jeddah. He knew he would not see them again in this life, but this did not matter, and he pushed such earthly thoughts away. He was Tamir Salamah, and he was promised a place in heaven. He turned the truck right, on to Pennsylvania Avenue. Two more blocks and he would reach his destination.

Washington, DC
9.40 p.m.

'I want you to be honest with me about something, Jack. As honest as you can be under the circumstances.'

Nikki watched as Jack sipped the coffee the waitress had brought. He was barely able to keep his eyes open, but she could sense that he was wound up, on edge. He stared back at her, confused by her statement. 'Honest about what, Nikki? What circumstances?'

'I want to ask you something. I know it's going to sound like a weird question, but I don't know how else to put it.' Nikki leaned towards him, touched his arm. 'Jack, is there something going on in this city? Something . . . well, that maybe the public are not supposed to know about? That the Feds and maybe other law enforcement agencies want to keep from the public?'

She watched his face for a reaction. He frowned, instantly came awake. Nikki thought: *There's definitely a reaction.* It was the first time she had ever sensed raw nervousness in Jack, and for a moment he seemed almost frightened.

'What exactly are you talking about, Nikki?'

She looked at his face again. His faded blue eyes narrowed as they regarded her with an unmistakable look of caution. He looked even paler than when he'd stepped into the restaurant. 'It's a simple question, Jack.'

Collins frowned again. 'You've lost me, Nikki.'

'If you can't answer for security reasons or whatever, just say so, Jack, and I'll back off.'

'Nikki, I really don't know what you're getting at. What exactly did you mean when you said "something"?'

Nikki explained about her visit to Reagan, the police exercise, and about the troops near Daniel's playschool. She wondered about mentioning Brad Stelman being followed, but decided not to. 'It all seemed more than suspicious, Jack. I kind of felt like there was some kind of conspiracy going on around me. I know you don't like to talk about your work, and I know it's not my right to ask, but I felt I had to.'

'That's what this is about? It's the only reason why you wanted to meet me tonight?'

'I guess. Apart from telling you I missed you.'

Collins put down his coffee, shook his head. 'Nikki, I don't know what the cops and the army are up to. For that, you'll have to ask them. But you're right about one thing. I don't like to talk about my work. So even if there *was* something happening and the Feds were in on it, I couldn't say anything. But it this case I'll make an exception. There's nothing major going on that I know of, Nikki. Nothing at all.'

Nikki digested his answer. It seemed that he was telling the truth, but she couldn't be absolutely certain. And the fact that he'd seemed so cautious at first nagged her.

Why is he so cautious?

'Maybe I should be honest here, Jack. You want me to tell you what made me even more suspicious? You've been gone for almost twenty-four hours, without even a call. That's not like you, Jack. You always call. You always let me know you're all right. And when you didn't, it made me wonder if you were involved in what I think's going on. I'm a reporter, remember? And when reporters get feelings like that, they tend to act on them. So I need to get to the bottom of this, Jack. I really do.'

She studied his face. He looked uncomfortable, didn't reply. 'Jack, did you hear what I just said?'

'Yes, I heard.' He avoided looking at her, fell silent again, looked over at Daniel, who was starting to look sleepy as he toyed with his crayons.

'Talk to me, Jack. What's on your mind? Just tell me, and if you want me to keep it to myself, I'll do that.'

Again, he didn't reply. Nikki had never seen him so troubled, as if he were being tortured by something, or trying to fight some anguish deep within himself. And as he looked over at Daniel he seemed on the verge of breaking down. 'Jack . . . what's wrong?'

'Noth . . . nothing.'

'I don't think that's true, Jack.' She looked into his eyes, said it to his face. 'I think there's something very wrong. Something's worrying you deeply. And I'd like to know the truth.'

Washington, DC
9.57 p.m.

Tamir Salamah turned the truck on to 10th Street. On his right was the massive Hoover building, a sandstone monolith, his target. Fifty yards ahead was the entrance to the FBI's underground carpark. He had placed the briefcase in the back of the truck, in the middle of his deadly cargo. Beside him on the passenger seat was the remote control that would detonate the blast. He picked it up. The battery indicator light glowed red, indicating that it was active. All he needed to do was hit the on-switch and he would be vaporised in the explosion and enter heaven.

He pulled up in front of the Hoover building, rolled down his window and kept the engine running. A sign said: NO STOPPING. Stone bollards lined the kerb, a security measure meant to stop a car bomber from getting too close. But Tamir knew he was close enough. The second he halted the truck he saw two uniformed FBI officers emerge from the underground entrance and cautiously approach him. Their hands were on their pistols by their sides, and when they noticed Tamir's Middle Eastern features one of them spoke, a faint trace of nervousness in his voice. 'Hey, buddy, what you doing here?'

'I have a delivery to make.' Tamir positioned his finger on the remote control switch.

'I don't care what it is you've got to make, it says no stopping. Get this frigging truck out of here, right now. Can't you read the sign?'

'Yes, I can read the sign.' Tamir smiled and hit the switch.

Washington, DC
9.45 p.m.

'Nikki, I know I shouldn't be telling you this, but before I came here to meet you I was at a murder scene out in Maryland.' Collins faltered as he looked at her, wanted to say more, to tell her everything, unburden himself of the terrible secret that was causing him such heartache. Wanted to tell her to get out of DC with Daniel and her mom. And every time he looked over at Daniel's tiny face, watched the boy engrossed with his crayons, the heartache intensified. 'The victims were two kids, teenagers, a couple of years younger than Sean.'

Nikki put a hand to her mouth. 'I . . . I'm sorry to hear that.'

'They'd both been machinegunned to death.'

'Who . . . who did it?'

A look of pure loathing scoured Collins' face. 'A deranged killer. A lunatic. Someone we've got to catch, and pretty quickly, before he does it again. They've called every available man in on the hunt to find him. But he's no ordinary killer, Nikki, he's . . .' Collins faltered again, looked over at the FBI building, at the dozens of blazing lights, and thought about the desperate men and women tolling away inside, wanting to tell wives, husbands, families and loved ones what he wanted to tell Nikki, to leave DC as quickly as possible. But looking at those windows, seeing the burning lights, knowing the kind of dilemma his colleagues were facing, he fought the overwhelming urge to tell her everything, even though it tore at his heart. 'Nikki, I . . . I'm sorry. I can't go on with this . . . I just can't talk about it . . . It's too upsetting. Can you understand that?'

She reached over, put a hand on his, her voice full of concern. 'I understand. Is that the reason you didn't call?'

Collins gave a tired nod.

'You want to come home and rest a while?'

'I can't, Nikki. I've got to get back. I've got work to finish. Then I'll probably flake out at my desk.' Collins leaned forward. 'Look, I've said too much already. I could be in deep trouble simply for telling what I've just told you. Please understand something. It's important we get this guy, and damned quickly. But we've been ordered not to disclose a word about it to the public or press. There's a complete clampdown. And that's the way it's got to stay for now.'

'Why?'

'I can't answer that right now, Nikki. But believe me, it's vital. Any publicity, even just a hint, and you put more lives at risk. You don't want that on your conscience. So I've got to ask you to promise me you won't say a word. And I mean to *anyone* – colleagues, family, whatever. Otherwise I'm in deep trouble, and so are you, and a lot of other people.'

'I promise, Jack.'

Daniel had lost interest in his crayons, and leaned sleepily towards Nikki. 'I's getting tired, Mommy.'

Nikki hugged him close, rubbed his arm. 'It's OK, honey, we're going to leave very soon.'

Collins stroked Daniel's hair, then put his hand on Nikki's arm. 'Soon as I can, we'll take a few days away, you've got my word on that. You, me and Daniel. We could spend some time at the cottage, if you like. You could even head there tomorrow morning, and I'll join you as soon as I get free. Maybe you could even take your mom. It'll be just like the old times for her. What do you say?'

Nikki brightened. 'I'd love to, Jack.'

Collins felt a surge of hope. If he could get Nikki and her family out of DC without tipping his hand, he'd feel relieved. 'Soon as I get done, I'll join you. I promise.'

'But I can't go right now, Jack. I've got my work . . .'

'Take time off. Go sick. Whatever. You've been working hard. We both have. We need some time together.'

Nikki patted his hand. 'I know we do. But let's wait until we're both free. You just do what you have to do, Jack. I understand, really I do. And I give you my solemn promise that what you've told me won't go any farther than the two of us.'

Collins felt defeated. He couldn't force her to go Chesapeake. And he'd said too much already. If he pushed the issue any more, Nikki would get suspicious.

Daniel started to yawn again. 'I better go, Jack. Daniel's out of it. He ought to have been in bed long before now.'

'Sure. I'll walk you out.'

They finished their coffee and Collins took Nikki's arm, led her out the door as she held Daniel's hand. As they stepped on to a cold 10th Street, he said, 'You want me to carry Daniel to the car?'

'We'll be fine, Jack, I'm only parked two minutes away.'

'It's no trouble.'

'You better get back to the office. And try and get some sleep. But call me tomorrow if you can, OK?'

As Collins started to reply, he caught sight of a dark-coloured delivery truck parked right in front of the FBI building a hundred yards away across the road. It had halted beside the concrete security bollards. In the well-lit street, he saw two uniformed FBI men approach the truck and talk with the driver.

A split second later there was a tremendous explosion, like a massive clap of thunder, and an agonising pressure that sucked the air from Collins' lungs. The ground shook, and a violent orange flame mushroomed into the air. It seemed to Collins that one minute he was looking at the truck, with Nikki beside him, holding Daniel's hand, and the next thing a powerful blast of scalding-hot wind came hurtling across the street, followed by a wall of angry red flame.

Then there was another explosion as the pressure wave hit the restaurant, shattered the plate-glass windows and blew them off their feet, smothering them all in heat and darkness.

51

The White House
10.03 p.m.

The night was cloudless, the stars out, the rain gone. In the Rose Garden it was eerily quiet. The President wore an overcoat to keep out the chill, his face gaunt, his body plagued by fatigue. The confines of the situation room had proved too much to bear – in over twenty hours he hadn't slept or left the White House, and he desperately needed air, sucked in a deep, chilled lungful. 'What do you think, Bob?'

Bob Rapp, the man who had tried to act as his mediator, stood beside him. The President's advisers, the same five men and women who had joined him in the situation room when Hasim warned of an imminent attack, huddled around.

'There's no question he's going to hit. We can absolutely bet on it. But if he uses the nerve gas, we're fucked. No way can we keep a chemical attack from the press. Every reporter and news station will get to hear about it. Straight away, there're going to be banner headlines across the country, flash news reports, chaos on the streets.'

'Dick, what do you think the chances are he'll use the gas?' The President, his face growing more pallid, his mood depressingly sombre, addressed the CIA Director.

'Knowing the kind of warped mind Hasim has, I think it's possible. Maybe he's decided to use a small quantity, to raise the stakes. He also seemed anxious to stress the word martyr, sir. That suggests to me some kind of suicide attack. It can go either of two ways. He hits somewhere out of town, somewhere reasonably remote, with few casualties, to simply make a point. Or he hits a major target, with lots of casualties, to make a bigger point. Either way, I think we can count on serious damage, most likely with a bigger number of deaths than we witnessed on his tape. He's going to try to escalate this, make us see he's not bluffing. That he's capable of carrying out his ultimate threat.'

'My God, the man's a crazed lunatic. *Damn him to hell!*' The President's voice rose in frustration. Ten minutes ago, seconds after Hasim had cut the transmission, he had alerted the FBI Director and army chiefs of staff. A dozen chemical weapons teams were being deployed immediately to strategic locations in Washington, made up of FBI and army units. Everyone present was acutely aware of the seconds ticking by. That at any moment the attack could happen, killing unknown numbers of innocent civilians, not necessarily in the capital, but in any city or town in the US. To counter that possibility, army WMD units had been put on alert in every major city.

But it was crushingly obvious that the enemy had the advantage of surprise – the attack would come at a time and place of his choosing. Everyone with the President was conscious of their impotence: all they could do was wait, like sitting ducks, for it to happen.

'If he goes that far, how the hell are we supposed to keep this thing a secret? This city's going to go nuts. People are going to evacuate. And then where are we? Or Hasim? His threat's less effective. It doesn't make sense.'

'He's no fool, sir,' Rapp suggested. 'He's got to have figured out a way to carry out his attack in a way that fits in with his strategy. He's not going to blow this, not when he's got more than a glimmer of hope that we'll meet his demands.'

'Perverse as it sounds, I just hope to God you're right. Not that it's any consolation to the helpless victims that butcher's going to kill tonight. *Jesus*, I can't believe I'm saying that. I can't believe there's *nothing* we can do to prevent this attack . . .'

'There's not much, sir, except keep our people on alert and wait.'

The President took several deep breaths to calm himself, tried to marshal his thoughts. 'OK, two things we must do. First, I'll need to get on to President Kuzmin. We've got to be able to release *all* the prisoners. We're going to have to give Hasim something substantial, and quick.'

'But Kuzmin was adamant he's not going to agree to that, sir.'

'He'll damned well have to. We're caught between the Devil and the deep blue sea here.'

'We've got no leverage, sir.'

'Then we better think of some, and fast. The second thing, in case this all goes wrong, is that I want a doomsday study done immediately on how we're going to cope with the massive numbers of deaths and casualties that will result if Hasim's device goes off.'

'It's already being worked on, sir, by our military planners and FEMA. They promise me they'll have their strategies prepared in full by eight a.m.'

'I want a plan, gentlemen – no, not just a plan, but *the* plan – of how we're gong to deal with over a quarter of a million corpses and the hundreds of thousands of injured if the worst happens and this city's turned into a battle zone. And that's a very real possibility the way things are going. Let's make no mistake about it.'

The brutality of the President's chilling words sent a shiver down the spines of those around him. Just then a commotion erupted over by the West Wing's colonnaded walkway. Paul Burton burst through the French doors. He brushed past the Secret Service agents and rushed up to the President, breathless. 'It's happened, sir. Less than ten minutes ago . . . downtown.' Burton's face was a mask of alarm. 'There's been a massive blast.'

The President was ashen. 'Where, for God's sake?'

'FBI Headquarters.'

'How bad is it, Paul? How many casualties?'

Back in the Oval Office the President was behind his desk. His advisers had crowded into the room. An air of panic gripped them all, but in the midst of their alarm their attention was still on the

FBI Director, who had moved over to a corner, frantically talking on his cellphone to one of his senior agents in the Hoover building as he urgently sought information.

'We don't know yet, sir,' Burton replied. 'The FBI's sealed off the area. The first indications are there's been a suicide bombing, but the details are sketchy.'

'Was nerve gas dispersed?'

'We still don't know that yet. It's pretty crazy down there. No one seems to know exactly what's happening. All I got was that a truck exploded outside the Tenth Street entrance to the Hoover building.'

'*Jesus Christ!*'

When the FBI Director switched off his cellphone all eyes fastened on him as he came towards the President.

'Doug?'

'It's pretty bad, Mr President.' The Director's expression was bleak. 'A huge explosion. It's too early to give an exact estimate of casualties, but it appears that there may be dozens of dead, and many more serious casualties.'

The President's face was etched with concern. 'Was gas dispersed?'

'The first indications are no. But I can't be certain.'

'Then be certain. Get a chemical team in there, *fast*.'

'They're already on the scene, sir.'

'Then I want an answer, the second they've got one.' The President was pale as he turned to Paul Burton. 'And find out what's happening with our doomsday plan. Speed things up if you can. If this attack's anything to go by, it's damned likely we're going to need it.'

The President gritted his teeth, ran a hand over his face. His control over his anger was slipping away again, evidence of his frustration, his fury at being trapped in a seemingly hopeless dilemma. For a couple of moments, to those present, he seemed to be losing it, his hand trembling as it lingered on his face, as if he was close to breaking down, but when he took his hand away the trembling was gone, and there was a sudden steel in his voice.

'Bob, as soon as we get the answer from the chemical team, I want you to contact Abu Hasim again.'

'But he said midnight, sir.'

'I know what he damned well said.' The President slammed his fist on the desk. 'Just do as I say. I want to talk to that sonofabitch.'

Washington, DC
9.59 p.m.

Eight blocks from the White House, near the Potomac shore, Mohamed Rashid had heard the deafening explosion that ripped through 10th Street. He pulled into the kerb, rolled down his window, listened to the booming echoes of the blast as they raged through Washington's night-time streets like colossal claps of thunder. He saw cars pull in and puzzled pedestrians halt on the pavement look skyward.

Two minutes later, Rashid heard the first shriek of sirens, but by then he was already heading safely towards the Eisenhower Freeway and Chesapeake.

The White House
10.50 p.m.

The President switched on the microphone. He was back in the situation room. A flush of red seeped over his face, evidence of his anger. 'Mr Hasim, this is President Booth. Can you hear me?'

Hasim spoke, and the translator relayed the reply. Again, his tone was calm, almost courteous. 'Yes, Mr President, I can hear you.'

'Mr Hasim, what you have done tonight – murder yet more innocent Americans – is a barbaric act of terrorism that you shall one day pay dearly for. I want to assure you that this terrible crime you have committed will not go unpunished. No matter how long it takes, no matter what forces of law and order I have to muster to ensure that justice is done, no matter what the costs, financial or otherwise, I make you this solemn promise. That the perpetrators of this heinous act – you and your supporters – will pay for your callous actions.

'You have enraged me, Mr Hasim. You have awoken an anger in me I never thought possible. I want you to be fully aware of that, and that my resolve to punish those guilty of this outrage will not falter no matter how long it takes, no matter what effort it requires. Make no mistake, as sure as night follows day, you and they shall face American justice.' The President glared at the translator. 'Translate that, word for damned word. Leave nothing out.'

When the translator had finished, the President promptly carried on, unwilling to let Hasim reply until he had finished. 'I'm going to be honest with you, Mr Hasim. You may get what you want. You may have all your demands satisfied – our troops withdrawn from the Gulf, your prisoners released – but after this night you will *not* get away with the murderous atrocities you have inflicted on this nation, be they in the present or the past. Be clear about that. I will not be bowed or cowered by your threats, nor will the American people. You claim to be a soldier, Mr Hasim, so you must know that every battle has a price, both for the victor and for the vanquished. In that respect, whether you are victor or not, and no matter what power lies behind your threats, I have no doubt that the price of this battle will be your life.'

Again the translator interpreted the words, and again the President promptly carried on. 'I can be honest with you about something else, too. This evening, before we first spoke, I enlisted the help and advice of a number of experts, people who have an insight into your warped terrorist mind. They advised me on how to approach you, how to understand your psyche, how to use strategy to manoeuvre you into a dialogue. Their advice has been valuable, their insights, for the most part, correct.

'But from this moment on, Mr Hasim, I will have no use for their advice. From this moment on, I can see that any strategy I or my advisers might devise is pointless, and that the only way I might communicate with you is by employing the absolute truth.

Whether you accept it or not is up to you. But for my part, there will be no tricks, no guile, no posturing. Precious lives are at stake here. The innocent lives of hundreds of thousands of unknowing Americans – men, women and children – who sleep in their beds tonight unaware of this conversation, or of the real and terrifying threat that now hangs over them. Their lives are of paramount importance to me.

'For that reason, I want to assure you of my absolute candour in any dialogue we engage in. So, Mr Hasim, let us get down to business. The demands that you have set out are impossible for me to achieve within the time remaining. You of all people must know that. To withdraw all US forces from the Gulf in such a short time is a logistic impossibility. But tonight, the moment this transmission ends, I shall give the order to withdraw *all* American forces from the Gulf. Every prisoner you have asked to be released from American soil will be released, and transported to a country of your choosing. As to the remainder on the lists, you must understand that their fate is in the hands of other nations, and outside my control. Of course, I shall do my utmost to press for their release within the allotted timeframe. To convey to the foreign leaders involved how imperative it is they be handed over into your charge. If I fail, it will not be for want of trying, Mr Hasim. And that is as honest a response as I can give you.'

When the translator had finished, the situation room fell totally still. There was a long, worrying silence, filled only by the faint hum from the speakerphone. Those around the table looked at each other, wondering whether the transmission was still live, wondering whether Hasim had cut them off again after the President's enraged but honest comments, but then the Arab's voice finally came back, jolting them. Even before the translator had relayed his words, Hasim's fury was obvious, his tone agitated.

'You have spoken your piece, Mr American President. Now I will speak mine. When we communicated last, I made it clear that you will not threaten me. Yet you did so. You do it now again. Despite my warnings, despite my telling you that you no longer have that right. Yes, you are correct that many thousands of Americans may die. Yet you still risk their lives by your very arrogance, by your conviction that America is always right. What gives you this right, Mr President? What gives you the right to threaten me, as you have threatened thousands of Arabs in the past? You have no right, *no right whatsoever.*'

There was a brief pause, as if Hasim was trying to control his emotions, and then he carried on, his voice more subdued. 'Tonight in Washington you saw an example of my followers' martyrdom. Saw that they are willing to sacrifice their lives for a sacred cause. Those martyrs who are in your city right now will gladly meet the same fate if need be, will give up their lives without a moment's thought. Just as I am willing to die for the same cause, Mr President. But are you? Are the people around you? And even if you are, would countless numbers of your citizens be willing to die alongside you? The deaths inflicted tonight have been caused by you. By your lying, your intransigence, your vain attempts to trick and deceive me. I could have used my chemical weapon as an example to repay that deception, to show you and your government yet again the power that I possess. But no, I did not. Instead, I chose a less harmful way, and showed your citizens compassion, a compassion not merited by their president's deceitful words and actions.'

The President, his face crimson, was unable to contain his fury. 'Mr Hasim, you have murdered dozens of Americans this night, and yet you have the audacity to say you showed compassion? How dare you! There were innocent people in the street when your bomb exploded . . .'

Hasim's voice cut in harshly before the translator finished. 'You will be silent, Mr President! You will listen or I will cease this dialogue immediately!'

The moment he heard the translator's words the President bit back his urge to reply, but he was still crimson, his hands clenched on the table in front of him, his temper boiling, enraged by the gall of the man who threatened him.

Hasim continued. 'The point is, Mr President, I chose not to use my weapon. I chose also to give you a way to explain the explosion. You speak of your nation as if it were a unified people, but your nation is coming apart at the seams. There are many disaffected groups who could have been responsible for the explosion. Militia and patriot groups who have motive enough to attack your FBI. If you are wise, you will put the blame on them.'

There was a delay while the translator spoke, and then Hasim resumed. 'But enough, let us get down to business, as you say. You have said the prisoners in your hands will be released and my instruction in that regard is this – they will be all be flown by commercial airliner to an airport of my choosing somewhere in Afghanistan, and before my deadline expires. The details of the airport's location will be passed on to you by Samar Mehmet no later than two hours before the planes are due to land. As to the other prisoners, you say you have no control over their fate. That is untrue, Mr President. You have enormous power at your disposal, both military and financial, to influence these other states. I have no doubt you can use that power to its ultimate to ensure that *all* the remaining prisoners are released. Again, you will arrange that they are flown to Afghanistan in the same manner, and to an airport that will be disclosed to you two hours before the aircraft are due to land. Do you understand?'

'I told you, that's outside my control, Mr Hasim,' the President replied once the translator had finished. 'It's impossible for me to comply with that demand, at least for now. But my government is already conducting vigorous negotiations to have them released. This will take time and enormous effort. Already I have spoken with President Kuzmin about the release of those in Russian prisons, and I can assure you his initial reaction is very favourable. But I need more time.'

'You are lying!' Hasim's reply was instant and barbed. 'President Kuzmin is intent on keeping the prisoners. Furthermore, he has tried to destroy me by sending his bombers to attack my bases. Only by the grace of God, and your intervention, had he the sense to turn them back before it was too late. To prevent this from happening again, therefore, I wish you to make President

Kuzmin aware that if he attempts to destroy me once more, not only will Washington be destroyed, but I shall immediately order my followers to attack Moscow with the very same weapon. His capital city and its population will suffer the same fate.'

The President listened, stunned, to Hasim's translated answer.

'You see, Mr President, again you lie! You promised honesty, but you are not a man to keep your word. I can see now that any further dialogue between us is useless. From this moment on, I will not speak with you or your advisers again, not until all my terms have been fully complied with. And you will *not* make any attempt to contact me. To do so will be fatal.'

'Mr Hasim, you have my *solemn* word I will do my utmost to have the remaining prisoners released. But I need more than the five days remaining . . . I *need* extra time.'

'Your word is meaningless. Only actions count. You have no option but to surrender, Mr President. When will you realise that? And since you have broken your word, I now feel free to break mine. As of this moment, you no longer have five days.' Hasim paused. Everyone in the situation room waited, fearful of what he would say next. When he did speak his words chilled them all.

'From midnight you have thirty-six hours. Thirty-six hours in which to fulfil all of my demands or the device will explode.'

PART SIX
13 November

'Abu Hasim has won . . .'

52

Washington, DC
13 November
3.02 a.m.

In the early morning darkness, just after 3 a.m., a light burned brightly in the window of a sixth-floor office at 500 C Street, Federal Center Plaza.

Patrick Tod O'Brien, the man who occupied the office, was a big, burly, red-haired New Yorker in his early forties, with broad shoulders and heavy arms. A guy who looked as if he should have been a second-generation Irish-American working as a construction site foreman rather than a senior planning specialist with FEMA, the Federal Emergency Management Agency.

Deeply anxious, O'Brien threw down his pen. On the desk in front of him was a notepad, a Dell desktop computer, a thermos of coffee, and a photograph of his wife and two young daughters.

Turning away from the glare of his computer screen, he rubbed his gritty eyes and stared out of his window for distraction. Six floors down was a complex of deli shops, restaurants, a Holiday Inn, and a tiny square with wooden benches where O'Brien sometimes liked to take a packed lunch when the weather was good. But that early morning, the Plaza – home to dozens of US government departments including FEMA's headquarters – was deserted, a cold November wind whipping in from the nearby Potomac. The only activity was the occasional taxi pulling away from the Holiday Inn, with which – absurdly – the FEMA building shared a common entrance.

Very few guests who entered the lobby of the famous hotel chain would realise that one day their survival might depend on a man like O'Brien and the nine thousand full- and part-time FEMA employees in a dozen regional and area offices throughout America. Their job is one of the most daunting imaginable – to protect lives and property in the event of a major disaster striking US soil: hurricanes and tornadoes, floods and snowstorms, earthquakes and fire-storms, volcanic eruptions, an act of war or terrorism, be it a nuclear, chemical or biological attack. If disaster hits America on a grand scale, it is FEMA that co-ordinates the federal government response, and manages the messy job of post-disaster clean-up.

The Agency had proven its worth in dozens of critical disasters: in helping the victims of earthquakes in California, hurricanes on the Florida coast, tornadoes in the Midwest, raging snow blizzards, floods and wildfires in almost every state. O'Brien liked to think Agency staff were prepared to handle pretty much any disaster thrown at them, except maybe a hostile alien invasion. Besides, as his boss liked to jokingly point out, alien landings were a problem for Immigration.

The source of O'Brien's anxiety that morning was the special task he'd been given. Just before nine the previous evening he'd been summoned by a phone call to the eighth-floor office of FEMA's Director to be briefed on an urgent assignment: a disaster scenario to ponder. Emphasising that it was top secret, the Director wanted O'Brien's response by 8 a.m. the next morning. The scenario was this: what if Washington was hit by a large-scale terrorist chemical attack, using a deadly Novichok nerve gas ten to fifteen times more toxic than VX, and with no known antidote. The awesome power of the chemical, the likely method of its delivery, and its devastating potential in terms of human casualties had been outlined by the Director. O'Brien was astonished by the figures: *two hundred thousand injured, three hundred thousand dead.*

But managing disaster was O'Brien's job. He was used to dealing with horrifying scenarios in which the lives of hundreds of thousands, even millions, of people were at risk. Like certain of his colleagues – former military specialists – he had spent many years with the US Army, as a chemical and biological warfare expert. His task that day was to figure out how FEMA could respond: what measures it could take to minimise casualties before such an attack took place, and how to deal with both the survivors and the immense numbers of fatalities and injured in the aftermath.

A prime rule in managing a disaster was to try to have a firm plan already in place. FEMA liked to call it mitigation: taking sustained action to limit risk and damage to people and property *before* the event happened. For that reason, O'Brien's desktop computer was programmed with the outlines of dozens of disaster scenarios and the likely federal or state response. One of these was for a chemical attack by terrorists on Washington, DC. O'Brien had spent the remainder of the evening and early morning locked in his office, cut off from calls or visitors, studying the scenario using powerful software programs devised by FEMA and the US Defence Department.

Given the powerful toxicity of the nerve gas, O'Brien would adjust the programs accordingly: factoring in variables, modifying conditions, tweaking the figures, and then mulling over the projections. Then he would address the first big question he had to ask himself: could FEMA handle this emergency? And that was why he was deeply troubled. He still had some way to go before he completed his task, but deep in his gut he sensed he already knew the answer. *No.*

The damage figures were simply awesome. O'Brien sighed, turned away from his view of the Holiday Inn. Picking up his pen and the yellow legal pad, he looked back at the blue glare of his Dell screen. His task was Herculean. By morning he had to come up with an outline emergency plan for DC – to safely evacuate and decontaminate over one and a half million people, provide each one with food, shelter and any necessary medical aid, provide energy sources for heat and light, secure urgent hospital treatment for a *staggering* two hundred thousand injured victims, and maintain civil order.

And finally – a task so gruesome it made O'Brien shudder just thinking about it – figure out how to dispose of three hundred thousand dead bodies.

Chesapeake
7 a.m.

Karla awoke. She had slept badly, tossing and turning for the few hours she'd managed to rest, her mind still racked with worry over Nikolai. She dressed, went downstairs and made coffee.

Beyond the kitchen window the wind was gusting, the bay waters choppy. The cellphone Ishim Razan had given her hadn't rung all night, but she was still deeply anxious. She'd left the phone in her tote bag upstairs, and as she turned to fetch it and call Razan she started. Mohamed Rashid was leaning against the door frame, watching her. 'You woke early, Karla Sharif. What's the matter, couldn't you sleep?'

'I was worried about Nikolai.'

Rashid grunted. 'Come, there's something I want you to see.'

He went into the living room. Karla followed. He had returned after midnight, a look of satisfaction on his face, but he hadn't spoken a word to her before he went to his room. Now he turned on the TV, flicked to the NBC news channel.

A woman news reporter stood on a darkened Washington street. She spoke directly to the camera, and behind her, within viewing distance, was another street that looked like a war zone. It was cordoned off by dozens of uniformed police and lit by powerful arc lamps, and behind the police barriers there was a frenzy of activity: emergency rescue crews, fire department trucks, police vehicles, and fleets of ambulances. Karla saw wispy plumes of smoke rise into the air, and several of the buildings in the background looked badly wrecked or partly demolished. She caught the gist of the news report: FBI Headquarters on 10th Street had been ripped apart by a huge suicide truck-bomb explosion, and dozens had been killed or injured. Numbed by horror, she turned to look at Rashid, saw his face spark with triumph.

'I told you I'd teach the Americans a lesson.'

Karla, pale, said with disgust, 'Why? Why do it? Why kill those people?'

'Because action is the only thing these Americans understand. Now they've seen bodies on the streets, they'll take us seriously.' Rashid flicked off the TV with the remote. 'A pity I didn't kill more.'

Karla bit back her revulsion. 'Who drove the truck?'

'That's irrelevant.' Rashid tossed her the Plymouth's keys. 'Now, Karla Sharif, you will fetch Gorev. And I warn you, don't return without him.'

Five minutes later, as Karla turned the Plymouth out of the driveway, she fumbled in her tote bag on the seat beside her. She found the cellphone, scrolled to the stored number, and punched the dial button to call Ishim Razan. She didn't notice the black GM Savana van with tinted windows parked two hundred yards away, or the two Chechens inside watching her through a pair of powerful binoculars.

53

Salem
13 November
7.35 a.m.

Ishim Razan flicked off the cellphone. The call from Safa Yassin telling him she was on her way to New Jersey hadn't surprised him in the least. He had slept poorly, and when he had replaced the cellphone on the nightstand he climbed out of bed and slipped on a silk dressing gown.

Once he had showered and dressed, he went down the landing to another bedroom. When he entered, the room was in near-darkness, the curtains closed. One of his men was reclined in a chair, his feet resting on a footstool, a magazine open on his chest as he kept watch by Gorev's bedside. 'How's the patient?'

'He seems reasonable, Ishim, and his temperature's back to normal.'

'Did he wake during the night?'

'A couple of times.'

'And?'

'He was delirious, wanted to know where he was. Once I assured him he was in your safe hands, he drifted back to sleep.'

Razan moved over to the bed. Gorev was still sleeping; there was no sign of bloodstains on the fresh bandage around his stomach. Razan had ordered his men to move him to a guest room just before midnight, after the doctor had administered the transfusion. 'Take a break, Pashar. Go get some breakfast. I'll stay with him.'

When the guard had left, Razan felt Gorev's brow, then crossed to the window, drew back the curtains and opened out the windows, letting a burst of fresh air gust into the room, billowing the curtains. Gorev came awake groggily. Razan smiled, sat on the edge of the bed. 'For a man with a conscience, you sleep like a baby, Nikolai.'

Gorev pushed himself up, his face creasing with a twinge of pain. 'Ishim . . .'

'Take it easy. How do you feel?'

'Better than last night.'

'That's something, at least. My man has told you where you are?'

'I can just about recall. I must have been delirious.'

Razan indicated the pills by Gorev's bedside, a pack each of painkillers and antibiotics, and explained what the doctor had done. 'Don't worry, he can be trusted. You have the luck of the Devil, Nikolai, you know that? How many times is it you've been wounded and pulled through?'

'Too many.'

'All these heroics have to stop, old comrade, or you'll end up screwed down in a wooden box.'

'No doubt. It comes to us all in the end.'

'But it needn't come so soon.' Razan laid a hand fondly on Gorev's shoulder. 'Are you hungry?'

'Starving.'

Razan smiled. 'A pity. The doctor recommended only liquids for the next few days. I'll have the cook fix you something nourishing, to keep the hunger at bay.'

Razan started to get up. Gorev gripped his arm, said gratefully, 'Thanks, Ishim.'

'What are comrades for? If it hadn't been for you, my bones would be bleaching in the Afghan sun.' Razan grinned. 'Instead, I'm a successful Chechen gangster, the most feared man from Grozny, remember?'

Gorev managed a weak smile. 'Maybe I've a lot to answer for. Where's Karla?'

Razan frowned. 'You mean Safa, surely?'

'Yes . . . Safa.'

'On her way to see you. I told her you'd have to rest here for now.'

'I can't, Ishim. I've got things to do. And right this minute I need fresh air and to try to stretch my legs. You know me, I hate being cooped up.'

Gorev attempted to get up out of bed, his impatience obvious, but Razan put a hand firmly on his shoulder. 'Right now your recovery matters more. You can try a walk after breakfast, if you must. We can start with a gentle stroll in the garden. But try to leave and I might be forced to have my men restrain you.'

'You wouldn't dare, Ishim.'

'Try me. But we'll get to that discussion later. First, I'll fetch you something from the kitchen.' Razan stood, his tone sombre. 'And then, Nikolai, we need to have a serious talk.'

Washington, DC
13 November
8 a.m.

The President had barely slept, his body ravaged by tension. He had managed less than three hours, and as he entered the Oval Office he looked haggard. The FBI Director was already waiting. He started to stand. 'Don't get up, Doug.' The President slumped behind his desk. 'You wanted to see me.'

'We have the latest figures from the blast, sir. Thirteen confirmed dead and ten missing. Thirty injured, ten of them seriously. As for the explosive material, it was a mix of Semtex, ammonium nitrate and fuel oil. But Abu Hasim wasn't lying. We found no trace of nerve gas.'

The President sighed tiredly. 'If nothing else, at least there's that to be thankful for. What about the press?'

'We're telling them nothing except that our investigation is under way, but that we have suspicions it may have been the work of a right-wing extremist group.'

The President nodded. After his conversation with Abu Hasim, he and his shocked advisers had met for almost two hours, debating into the early morning, until they were all exhausted and the President had adjourned the meeting so that everyone could get some much-needed sleep – but only after they had reached a number of major decisions. One of them was that no blame for the explosion would be attached to any group external to the US, so as to avoid public and media suspicion.

'That's going to cause dismay and panic in itself, but it's still preferable to the alternative. What progress have you made with your investigation?'

'You mean the bombing, sir, or the hunt for the cell?'

'Both.'

'So far as we can tell, there was a single bomber. We caught the truck on our security cameras as he came in off Pennsylvania Avenue at nine-fifty-seven p.m., just moments before the blast. But what few human remains we scraped out of the mangled wreckage can't tell us for certain yet if the driver was alone.'

'What about the truck?'

'Rented a week ago from a Ryder office in Baltimore by a man named Sadim Takik. We've turned up nothing on him yet, but at a guess the name was probably an alias. Takik's driver's licence details we got from the rental office don't match with anything on our licensing databases, which suggests it was most likely a forged document. For now, the truck driver's real identity is a mystery. We can only assume he was one of the cell. And expendable, obviously.'

'And the hunt?'

The FBI Director explained the circumstances of the teenagers' murder in Maryland. 'We think the killer may have been one of the terrorists.'

The President's mouth pursed at the grim news. 'But you've got nothing solid?'

'No, sir. We're checking all hotels and rental properties, as well as those belonging to anyone of Middle Eastern origin, all within a twenty-five-mile radius, in case the suspect had a safe house in the area. But it's a big area, and it means another massive task, along with everything else we've got to contend with. It's going to take time, Mr President.'

'And time we don't have.'

'No, sir.'

The President, perturbed, looked away. For a long time, his hand on his jaw, he stared out beyond the White House lawns, as if trying to reach a decision. Finally, his hand fell from his jaw and he addressed Stevens. 'Doug, what are the real chances of ending this thing and apprehending the al-Qaeda cell within the next twenty-eight hours? Because that's all we've got left. Give me an honest-to-God answer.'

'Not good, Mr President.' The Director was gloomy. 'The Bureau's doing everything it can. Every man, every resource we've got is going into this. But the simple fact is, we haven't even covered a quarter of the ground we need to cover. Even if we were to pull in the police, military and National Guard on this, I still couldn't guarantee success. There's too much to cover, too many avenues to explore, in too short a time. If we had a couple of weeks, or even a month, to nail this down, maybe I'd be giving you a more hopeful answer. But as it stands, twenty-eight hours is impossible.'

'We're really up shit creek, aren't we?'

Stevens didn't respond. The President stood.

Stevens got up. 'What do you intend to do, sir?'

'The only thing we can. Start an immediate pull-out from the Gulf of all our personnel. But leave behind our equipment. Billions of dollars of military hardware gone to waste. Time permitting, we'll have a chance to destroy any sensitive material we can't take with us. But we'll try and leave that to the last minute.'

'When will you give the order, sir?'

'I've already given it. I'll be making my announcement to the Security Council in the next hour. General Horton's already got the pull-out under way. Our military transporters are en route to the Gulf right now, as well as chartered commercial aircraft from Europe. We're trying to spread out the chartered hire-ins, not use more than one or two aircraft from the same commercial company in case it gets noticed. As to whether we can complete the pull-out in time that's another matter.'

'What does the general think?'

'He doubts it. I'm going to inform the Gulf royal families about what's happening later this afternoon. They're all going to hit the roof, you can bet on that, and it's going to leave them damned worried about what might come next for their countries, but there's nothing we can do about that right now.'

'And the press?'

'We worry about the press later. We'll draft a presidential statement, but leave any announcement until we're past Abu Hasim's deadline and he's neutralised the device. That's if we can believe the sonofabitch will do as he says. Personally, I wouldn't trust him an inch. I still have grave doubts that he's going to keep his end of the bargain. Either he'll still set off the device – like Professor Stern said, he really wants to hurt us, no matter what the outcome of all this – or else, even when we comply with his demands, he won't tell us where the device is. He could probably keep it hidden for days, weeks or months if he wants to, just to have the threat still hanging over our heads.'

The President moved to the window. 'We'll have to have evacuation plans for the District in place, and ready to go. Our experts are working on it now, and we'll be discussing their recommendations at a meeting this afternoon, along with Al Brown. The mayor's as anxious as hell, as we all are, that we have something concrete in place to try and save as many citizens as we can.'

'What about Kuzmin? Is there any hope there?'

The President's mouth tightened as he shook his head. 'He still refuses to change his mind about the Chechen prisoners. That's when I last spoke to him, at one a.m. However, he's agreed to discuss the release with his own council and get back to me by this afternoon.'

'That's as far as he'll go?'

'I'm afraid so. As for the rest of the prisoners in Israel, Germany and Britain, we'll work on that problem today. And I've asked Dick Faulks to have his people in Pakistan provide Samar Mehmet with an electronic scrambling device for his phone, so any communication we have to make with him is kept secure.' The President glanced at his watch. 'If that's it, Doug, I've got some things to attend to before we start the meeting.'

Stevens said worriedly, 'There's one more thing, sir, and it's the real reason why I asked to see you in private before we went to the conference room.'

'Go on.'

'It's about the tape we made of your conversation with Hasim.'

'What about it?'

'I've gone back through the recording with Janet Stern, Franklyn Young and the CIA Director, and we think we've found something pretty disturbing.'

'The whole damned conversation was disturbing,' the President snapped.

'That wasn't really the context I meant, sir.'

'Then what did you mean?'

'In the heat of all that happened last night, there's something none of us latched on to, at least not immediately. But when we went back over the tape a number of times, and started to see what was between the lines, we really couldn't miss it. And it's got us all worried, sir.'

'What in the hell are you talking about, Doug?'

'There's something Hasim said that I'd like you to listen to again.'

54

Washington, DC
13 November
7 a.m.

George Washington Hospital is off Dupont Circle, a five-minute drive from the White House. It was still dark when Kursk climbed out of the grey cab at the front entrance.

At reception, he was told to take the elevator to the second floor. Stepping out, he found the crowded glass-fronted waiting room down the hall. Clusters of tired and anxious-looking men and women, some with young children, paced the floor or sat on benches around the waiting-room walls, some drinking coffee or soft drinks dispensed from a machine in the corner.

Morgan was among them, sipping coffee from a plastic cup as he talked with a distraught-looking grey-haired man in his mid-fifties, whose eyes looked red from crying and lack of sleep. Kursk waved. Morgan saw him and came out, closing the door. 'You managed to get some rest?'

'A few hours,' Kursk replied. 'And you?'

'Not a wink.' Morgan took a mouthful of coffee, ran a hand tiredly over his face, then jerked a thumb towards the glass-fronted room. 'Most of the folks in there have family injured in the blast. They've been waiting all night for news.'

Kursk glanced at the faces behind the glass. Husbands, wives, mothers, fathers, sons and daughters of the dying and injured. Kursk could only imagine their anguish as they waited expectantly to hear the fate of their loved ones. 'How many dead?'

'Thirteen, last I heard, with ten missing.'

'And injured?'

'Over thirty, some of them critical. Most are Feds, apart from a couple of security guards from an office building across the street, a few civilian pedestrians, and the people in the restaurant.'

Morgan nodded back towards the waiting room. 'That guy I was talking to just now, his daughter's been in theatre all night. She's twenty-six, with the Bureau only a year. When the bomb exploded she was in one of the second-floor offices that face Tenth Street. The poor guy's up the walls. She's his only daughter, and the doctors aren't hopeful.'

Kursk glanced at the man. He was pacing the floor nervously, running a hand through his hair, his face a tight mask of worry, like so many of the others in the room. If it had been Nadia who had been injured, Kursk knew he'd be totally distraught. 'How is Collins?'

'Lucky to be alive. He's concussed, got a few deep cuts, some cracked ribs. They want to keep him in for observation. Murphy went in to see him. I left them just a couple of minutes ago.'

'And his friend?'

'They wheeled her out of theatre a couple of hours back. The word I got, she's going to be OK. But her little boy's still in a bad way. He's got serious chest injuries and internal bleeding. They've got a level-one trauma centre in the hospital – that's why they brought most of the injured here – and a top surgeon is working on him right now. But the last I heard, it doesn't look good. He mightn't pull through.'

Kursk was uneasy, hardly knowing what to say. 'Can I see Collins?'

Morgan finished his coffee, crumpled the cup, tossed it in a garbage bin. 'Better wait here, Alexei, and I'll go see if Murphy's finished talking with him.'

Eight miles away, a tired-looking General Bud Horton, wearing his pyjamas, a cotton dressing gown and a pair of scuffed leather slippers, was busy pouring himself a cup of piping-hot Yemeni coffee in the kitchen of his home near Arlington, Virginia. The rich aroma of freshly brewed Arab coffee beans wafted around the room, and when Horton had finished pouring the treacly black liquid and had added two spoonfuls of white sugar – a luxury he allowed himself only at breakfast-time – he took his cup and moved into his wood-panelled study across the hall.

Pausing by his apple-wood desk, he stared out of the window at the pleasant, well-kept gardens. The house was a two-storey, detached, four-bedroom red-brick in a quiet, upper-middle-class neighbourhood, discreetly set back from the road and surrounded by tall Scots pines. It wasn't his family home – that was in Boston – but a government-rented property provided for the use of himself and his wife while Horton was in Washington.

Always an early riser, he had woken at 6.30 a.m., despite the miserable two hours' rest he'd managed, having returned home from the Pentagon at 4 a.m. after issuing his orders for the entire withdrawal of US army, navy and air force personnel from the Middle East. As he sipped his coffee thoughtfully, Horton looked at the shelves filled with his treasured tomes: his books on modern warfare and military history, studies of every general and military campaigner worth his salt, from Alexander the Great to Caesar, Napoleon to Patton. There were other subjects, too, most to do with Arab history, language and culture, which were his lifelong passions.

A West Point graduate, he'd been a young captain and a graduate engineer when he first saw action in Vietnam in 1968, and had twice been wounded and twice decorated for bravery. When the war in South-East Asia ended he'd won rapid promotion that later saw him the youngest officer ever to command the 19th Combat Engineers Battalion. Later still came a year at the US Army War College in Carlisle Barracks, Pennsylvania, a doctorate in military studies, and his appointment as General Commanding the 101st Airborne Division; and then what he regarded at the time as the pinnacle of his military career – Operation Desert Storm. But it wasn't to be the pinnacle, for subsequently, to crown it all, came his appointment as Chairman of the Joint Chiefs of Staff. Leaving aside his flawless military qualifications, Bud Horton had no need to wonder why the President had chosen him as Chairman; he knew the answer instinctively.

The job was in Washington – which meant liaising with government departments, military chiefs and politicians – and required the delicate skills of the seasoned diplomat, which not every general had. But Horton had those skills in spades. They were in his genes – his father, long dead, had been a senior and much-respected State Department attaché who'd spent most of his career in the Middle East. Somehow, Bud Horton had inherited his father's talent for diplomacy – he was a man who cultivated friendships easily, who had the innate ability to smooth ruffled feathers, broker deals and calm tensions.

Horton had also spent much of his young life in the Middle East. It was a part of the world his father had loved, and he'd inherited that same passion. The smell of the bazaar and the scorching heat of the desert were not alien to him. He looked behind him, put down his coffee, placed a hand on one of the pair of bronze Arab statues of Bedouin tribesmen on his study desk, given to him recently by his dear friend Wahib Farid, a Saudi minister. Bud Horton had been a pupil at the American School in Riyadh, where his father had served for eleven years, and spoke fluent Arabic – the only US general who'd served during Desert Storm who could do so – and counted among his many Arab friends a fair number of the Saudi intelligentsia and powerful palace officials, most of whom were his former school pals.

Those same connections had helped his government enormously during Desert Storm – easing frictions between the US and the Saudi royals and their military – and had no doubt aided Horton's career and led to his appointment as Chairman of the Joint Chiefs. He knew that many of his old Arab friends had mixed feelings about an American presence in the Gulf. And though they would rarely if ever voice their opinions in public, several of his closest friends would have agreed with the broad aims of a man like Abu Hasim: a Middle East free of any foreign military presence, the withdrawal of US support for Israel, and a solution to the decades-old question of a homeland for the Palestinians. Horton had his own strong feelings on each of those subjects – several of his intimate Arab friends knew where he stood – but in the military and around the conference tables in the White House he had wisely kept his opinions to himself. He checked his watch. He was expecting his private call from Saudi about now, and knew he'd have to be very *careful* what he said over the phone.

As he stood there, his hand caressing the cool, smooth bronze of the Bedou statue, the door opened behind him. Leila Horton was five years younger than her husband, the daughter of a Saudi diplomat, a woman with fine cheekbones and chiselled features who looked pretty even before she applied make-up. Bud Horton had fallen in love the moment he'd clapped eyes on her at a US embassy reception in Riyadh almost forty years ago, when he was a lanky nineteen-year-old. They had married five years later and she'd borne him two fine sons.

'Bud, you must hardly have slept. I heard you coming in about four.'

'I managed a couple of hours.' Horton kissed her forehead.

Leila touched his cheek with the back of her hand. 'It's that bad, my love?'

Her husband nodded. Leila Horton didn't enquire any further, but sensed his stress. 'When do you have to return to the White House?'

'Any time within the next hour. I'm expecting the call. You'll understand if I can't phone?'

'Of course, Bud. But if you can . . . I'll be out all day, but you can get me on my cellphone.' His wife kissed him, left him to his thoughts. Horton turned back to the window, picked up his coffee, finished it in one swallow, put down the cup shakily. There were few secrets he kept from his wife, but this was one of them. There was *no way* that he could tell Leila the truth. All he could hope was that he played his cards right and that they both survived the days ahead. But his mind was still tortured by the same dread that he'd felt since all this began. What if it all went somehow wrong? What if the device went off by accident, hundreds of thousands of people were gassed to death, and Washington was reduced to a wasteland? He shivered. And then the phone rang.

* * *

On the sixth floor of 500 C Street, Federal Center Plaza, Patrick Tod O'Brien was in despair. Busy in his office all night, over a mile from the FBI Headquarters and unaware of the explosion, he swallowed the last dregs of his coffee, and put down his cup. The problem he'd been given by FEMA's Director seemed almost unsolvable. To start with, he'd broken down the scenario into pre-disaster and post-disaster.

Pre-disaster, before the chemical attack actually took place, and knowing it was likely to happen, there would usually have been a lot FEMA could do. You rarely had the good fortune to know exactly *when* a disaster was going to strike – advance warning of maybe hours or a day or two at most with hurricanes, floods, or snowstorms, if you were lucky. Though with nature at the helm, things were always unpredictable: with earthquakes and tornadoes, they just hit, and you suffered the consequences. But properly forewarned, O'Brien could call on massive resources in FEMA's ten regional offices and get them to wherever the hell the calamity was going to strike.

And the National Emergency Response Team, ERT-N, a group of first-responding managers with a variety of expertise, could organise for specialist equipment, and whatever expert manpower was needed, to be rushed in. Positioning themselves close to the disaster zone, the experts would be ready to carry out their assigned tasks before disaster happened: sealing off and evacuating the area, liaising with the emergency services – fire and police departments, hospitals and emergency medical teams, and with the FBI, National Guard and any government agency they deemed appropriate.

But O'Brien was faced with serious problems – caused by two limiting conditions which had been outlined by his Director. One was that the actual threat could *not* be made public before the nerve-gas attack – thus giving no chance of moving potential victims as far away from the danger zone as possible. The second, an adjunct of the first, was that the emergency services must absolutely *not* be in evidence before the attack. They had to be close enough to react quickly – but they'd have to stand off, away from DC, until the nerve-gas device exploded and scattered its deadly load.

O'Brien hadn't questioned the two conditions, that wasn't his job, but they were sure as hell causing him a set of nightmarish problems. The vital period after a chemical attack – called the 'Golden Hour' – is the first sixty minutes, when you're trying to turn victims into patients. If you had to wait on the sidelines before an evacuation could get under way, if the city streets were clogged with dead and dying trapped in automobiles and buses, if the pavements and roads were littered with corpses and casualties, then your job was made infinitely more difficult. Emergency services couldn't just *drive* over the bodies of men, women and children lying in the streets or in vehicles; they'd have to clear away the dead, tend to and remove survivors. It would be a slow process, made worse by the fact that all emergency personnel working anywhere near the disaster zone would have to wear bulky, heavy-duty chemical protection suits and carry oxygen packs on their backs, which would slow their movements. Had he even any guarantee the suits would work? To move heavy buses, trucks and cars out of the path of the emergency crews, you'd also need an operation involving maybe hundreds of tanks and tow trucks. And because you couldn't get your emergency crews in quickly enough, then a lot more patients were going to wind up victims.

O'Brien felt frustrated. The conditions the Director had outlined meant that, pre-disaster, there was very little you could do. Except sit on the sidelines a safe distance away twiddling your thumbs, waiting for all hell to break loose, and hundreds of thousands of people to die. If that wasn't bad enough, then dealing with the post-disaster response, after the nerve-gas device went off, was a logistical nightmare.

Warning people once the attack happened wasn't the problem. Using FEMA's Emergency Alert System, O'Brien could plug into every major TV and radio station across America with pre-prepared event tapes. In the District, radio programmes could be interrupted and scrolled messages would appear across

TV screens, advising people of the attack and telling them what precautions to take – seek deep shelter, or get out of the city. And Washington, like every major American city, had an extreme-weather alert system – sirens placed strategically throughout the capital which warned people of approaching bad weather. People were accustomed to hearing the sirens going off – when hostile weather was imminent, and during monthly tests, carried out on the last Wednesday of every month. The sirens could also be used to alert the District to the attack. If the weather forecast wasn't extreme, then people hearing the sirens would have one of three reactions. They'd think it was either a test, or a malfunction, or they'd wonder what the hell was going on, and hopefully be wise enough to find out quickly what was happening and take cover.

But on a normal work day, with two million people in the District, if the device went off, killing three hundred thousand people, O'Brien would still be left with the daunting problem of what to advise the remaining one and a half million survivors and two hundred thousand injured to do. Not all of them could or would flee the city. They might not be physically able because of clogged streets, injured family members, or sheer panic, which always played a big part in survivors' reactions. O'Brien imagined an average District family unit – one like his own – which might with luck survive the attack. Father, mother, two small kids. Gripped by terror, fearful for the safety of their children, facing clogged roads and mass hysteria on the routes out of DC, the parents might decide that the best course was to seek shelter. Or they might have loved ones who were injured victims – his wife had elderly parents two blocks from their home in Georgetown – whom they might choose to stay with and help.

O'Brien had projected that at least a million people would manage to flee DC. It meant clogged roads and mass hysteria in the District and on the periphery – no way of avoiding that. But those fleeing would have to be kept moving in an orderly fashion on the roads and freeways – more difficult than might be imagined when survivors were still in panic mode. It also meant that field hospitals would have to be set up as close to the city as was safely possible, and medical teams, food, shelter and requisites – tents, cots, blankets – energy resources and decontamination areas would have to be on hand to provide for one million people or more. It was an awesome task.

And it still left the problem of trying to help another half-million survivors and two hundred thousand injured who'd have to seek shelter and take their chances in DC. The longer they stayed out in the open, the greater the chance that they'd inhale minute particles of nerve agent, carried on the air, blown by winds, or lingering on the clothing and bodies of the dead. They'd have to find secure shelter quickly.

But where in God's name could almost three-quarters of a million people find secure shelter?

O'Brien rose from his desk in dismay and crossed to the DC wall map. Amazingly, despite decades of Cold War and the threat of nuclear conflict, there were no public fallout shelters in the capital. Not *one* that O'Brien knew of – apart from the rumour of a shelter deep in the bowels of the White House. FEMA's DC staff could be moved safely outside the capital to oversee the disaster before it happened, but for ordinary citizens, it was a case of finding whatever deep hole they could crawl into – and praying.

But there *was* a subway system.

Marked with blue dots on the map were the District's thirty-two underground stations. Many were deep enough below ground to act as shelters. Minute chemical particles would be ingested into some of the stations, but not all would be contaminated, and O'Brien figured that the stay-behind survivors would have their best chance of remaining alive if they were instructed to head deep into the subway. But that posed yet another problem.

Survivors of the attack might not be reached for days, or longer. Which meant that food, water supplies and vital medical equipment would have to be secretly laid in. (How in God's name did you keep something like that secret? Subway workers and the personnel used to lay in the supplies would ask questions.)

Novichok also had a long footprint – four months or more – so gas particles would linger in the atmosphere, on water, on streets and buildings. The all-clear signalling that it was safe to move about the city wouldn't be given for a *long* time.

Which meant emergency search teams wearing protective chemical gear would have to go down into the bowels of the underground to rescue survivors. And once they'd been found, they have to get them into heavy-duty decontamination suits – the living, the sick, people with disabilities – move them above ground, and transport them out of the city to field hospitals and decontamination units. And so as not to clog up or overwhelm the field hospitals, aircraft would be needed to fly excess victims out to other cities for medical treatment. Rescue would be a slow, hazardous process.

Apart from the fact that O'Brien knew with chilling certainty that it would be impossible to procure the hundreds of thousands of decontamination suits that would be needed, there was another big dilemma.

Part of his difficulty, as in every disaster emergency, was getting responders and resources close enough to the problem, but not so close that they were a *part* of the problem: causing bottlenecks, congestion, adding to the chaos. In a situation like this, the rule was, you hit the disaster from the outside: drew, say, three concentric rings from the centre and worked your way in, circle after circle, dealing with the outer areas first, tidying up as you went, tending to the sick and injured and moving them out beyond the circles as quickly as possible, so that there were no bottlenecks to hold up progress. That was the rule. But in a situation like this all rules might be unworkable.

The reason: *Washington was no ordinary city.*

The White House, Congress, Senate and vital government agencies and departments were scattered all over the District. O'Brien foresaw there might be a need to prioritise the evacuation of these first. Their personnel might have to be put top of any rescue list, for reasons of national security. And high-priority papers, files and items vital to government would need to be secured and removed.

But maybe the biggest problem remained, and O'Brien had been leaving it until last. His head ached as he crossed over to the other wall and examined the US map. He focused again on DC. The damage figures projected two hundred thousand survivors, many with serious nerve-gas damage, and three hundred thousand dead.

Big question: *how in hell do you dispose of three hundred thousand corpses?*

Washington, DC
7.10 a.m.

Kursk sat in the waiting room. He was ravaged by exhaustion, but as he looked around at the family and friends of the injured – black and white, young and old, among them a couple of anxious wives with young children – his fatigue seemed unimportant.

The last eight hours had seemed a nightmare. As Morgan had dropped him off at the FBI apartment on 7th Street, they'd heard the roar of the explosion three blocks away. By the time they'd sped back to FBI Headquarters, 10th Street was in chaos.

Street lighting had been knocked out, fires raged in the darkness, and in the centre of the road huge plumes of smoke poured from the twisted and mangled skeleton of a truck. The front of the FBI HQ and several buildings across the street had been devastated by an enormous explosion, with hundreds of windows shattered. Part of the Hoover's façade had been blown away, and clumps of concrete were scattered everywhere. It looked like a scene from war-torn Beirut. And then came the screaming sirens of ambulances, fire engines and police cars.

Kursk followed a frantic Morgan into the FBI building via the undamaged Pennsylvania Avenue entrance, but rescue workers ordered them back. Then they picked their way through the mounds of street debris, Morgan flashing his ID at fire-fighters and police who blocked their path, until they reached the restaurant at the corner of 10th and E Street. Even before they got there, they saw the damage: the building's plate-glass windows had shattered, the façade and window frames were ablaze. A fire-fighting crew was hosing down the flames as dazed survivors were being led or stretchered out of a side entrance by paramedic crews. Collins, the woman and her child were among them.

All three were alive. Collins' face was covered with blood, and he was barely conscious as he was stretchered towards a fleet of ambulances. The woman and the little boy came next, and they looked much worse: the woman was comatose, bleeding from a severe head wound. The little boy was pitiful, his face and clothes lacerated, his eyelids closed and his breathing laboured. When his chest heaved and he coughed up blood, Kursk saw two of the paramedics exchange concerned looks that seemed to say: *This one might not make it.*

The ambulances sped off, and to Kursk the rest was a frantic blur: rescue workers escorted them to Pennsylvania Avenue, where survivors had been evacuated to an emergency holding point. Morgan got on his cellphone to his superiors, desperate to find out what he could about the blast. Legions of fire-fighting crews and police kept pouring into 10th Street. And then Kursk saw specialist FBI teams arrive, setting up powerful arc lamps and readying their equipment, preparing to comb the smouldering rubble and the mangled wreckage.

Finally, after 1 a.m., Morgan dropped an exhausted Kursk off at the FBI apartment before heading for George Washington Hospital. Kursk offered to join him, but Morgan shook his head. 'No point in us both waiting around the hospital. I'll call if I've got any news. Try and get some sleep.'

Morgan sped away in the Ford, blue light flashing. It was another hour before a restless Kursk could attempt to sleep – after thirty-six hours without rest his body was on the edge of collapse – but even so he kept waking in a cold sweat. Such a savage, indiscriminate act of violence as a massive truck bomb went beyond Nikolai Gorev's modus operandi. It wasn't like him. It wasn't the kind of tactic he'd used or condoned in the past.

But what if Collins was right? What if he'd finally overstepped the mark?

Morgan came back down the hall. With him was Murphy, the head of the Counter-Terrorist Division. Kursk stepped out of the waiting room. Murphy looked bleak, nodded. 'Major.'

'Can I see Collins? How is he?'

'A little rocky right now. Apart from the injuries he suffered, he's reasonably OK physically. But he's pretty shaken about what happened to Nikki and her son. He's hoping to speak with one of their medical team just as soon they're through. So maybe if you could give it a little while before you go see him?'

From the desolate look on Murphy's face, Kursk had the feeling he was about to hear bad news. 'Is something wrong?'

Murphy glanced anxiously at Morgan, then said to Kursk, 'I think we need to have a talk, Major. Something's happened you'll need to know about.'

55

Washington, DC
13 November

The two FBI agents hadn't slept in almost twenty hours. As they turned their unmarked Chevy Impala on to 14th Street, cruising past the lines of hookers and drug peddlers huddled in littered store alcoves to keep out of the cold, it was almost 2 am. Working non-stop since seven the previous morning, with coffee and junk food to keep them awake, they had scoured their beat all night, calling on pimps and petty criminals, putting out bait money to informers and showing the photographs in the hope of getting a lead on the three known suspects.

But like the other almost three hundred federal agents from the Washington field office scouring DC's underworld with the same purpose, they hadn't come up with a single worthwhile lead. The agent who was driving yawned. 'So who's next?'

His companion checked the list. 'Benny Visto.'

'That's what I like about this job – you get to keep the best of company.' The driver sighed, took an envelope containing the suspects' photographs from the side pocket of his seat and nodded to his colleague. 'OK, pull in near Visto's place and let's see what the little asshole's got to say.'

'What you mothers want, calling at this hour? Fuck's up, man?'

The FBI agent regarded the sleazy, tattooed figure of Ricky Cortez as he would a piece of shit. 'I need to talk with Benny. Get him for me.'

'Ain't here.' Cortez, standing at the open door, dressed only in jeans, pulled on his shirt.

'Where is he?'

'Don't know, motherfucker.'

'Talk to me like that again and that tongue of yours is going to be stuck up your ass.' The agent stepped into Visto's penthouse suite, his colleague behind him, hands on his hips, displaying the holstered Glock, just to let Cortez know they meant business. The suite was empty except for the Cuban and a young girl wearing a silk dressing gown who lay on Visto's bed. A hooker, the agent guessed, one of Cortez's fringe benefits. 'So where's Benny?'

'Tol' you. Don't know. Man's busy, comes and goes. Could be back early, could be back late. Benny ain't got no fixed schedule. He don't keep to no fucking timetable.'

The agent opened the envelope, held out the photographs. 'Ever see any of these people before, Ricky?'

Cortez glanced sullenly at the first shot, of an Arab, and didn't even bother to look at the rest. 'Naw.'

'Take a good look, Ricky.'

'The fuck for? I got some ass waiting, want to get back to bed.'

'*Look*, Ricky.'

Cortez, still sullen, barely gave the photographs a glimpse. 'Naw, ain't seen any of those mothers before.'

The agent glared back, put the shots back in the envelope. 'You've been real helpful, Ricky. How about you tell Benny to call me, soon as he gets back.'

Ricky's pit-bull eyes narrowed. 'The fuck for?'

''Cause it's important. And tell him if he doesn't, our deal's off.'

George Washington Hospital
Washington, DC
7.15 a.m.

Collins sat alone on the end of the hospital bed, wearing a gown, his ribs hurting, his head in his hands. His face was cut and bruised, covered with gauze and plaster to mask the stitches over his left eye and on his right cheek, and there was a bald patch where the doctors had cut the hair on his scalp to suture a three-inch head gash. Two of his ribs were cracked, his chest was tightly bandaged, and it hurt when he took a deep breath. His mind was a total blank as it struggled with the situation.

After the doctor and nurse had attended to him in ER, after they'd taken the X-rays and given him the painkillers, at about 3 a.m. he'd drifted off to sleep for a couple of hours, but not wanting to sleep, wanting only to know how Nikki and Daniel were. His mind fought the lethargic effect of the drug but his body couldn't. When he woke it was 5 a.m.. He was drowsy, in pain, and when the nurse came in he tried to get up out of bed, asking her about Nikki and Daniel.

'You stay right where you are, you hear?' The woman was friendly, but businesslike. 'They're in good hands. But you get some more sleep now. The surgeon's going to come by and talk to you later. You ain't doing anyone no good getting up out of that bed.'

He'd tried to sleep some more, but he kept waking, agonising over Nikki and Daniel, running the nightmare scene at the restaurant over and over in his mind. The powerful hurricane *whoosh* of the explosion raging in on them with a fierce intensity. The vaguely recalled sight of Nikki and little Daniel being blown off their feet by the force of the blast, before Collins struck his head and torso against something that felt like a concrete wall and was swallowed up by darkness, coming to in the hospital. He was still thinking about it when the door opened and Morgan appeared with Tom Murphy.

For half an hour, they filled him in on the events in the White House that led up to the explosion, and when Morgan left them alone to go get some coffee, Murphy explained about the new deadline, that the rules of the game had changed. Collins was even more shaken. *Thirty-six hours*.

'Right this minute it's closer to twenty-eight,' Murphy said dourly.

Collins thought: *We haven't a hope in hell.* 'Where have we got with the hunt?'

'Precisely nowhere.'

There had been many things to run down, but all of them had ended in blank walls, Murphy admitted. 'We'll try and trace the explosive materials used in the blast, but time's a constraint. There's zilch with the suicide driver's real identity, zilch from our people out trawling the streets. And the check on properties in the zone around the Maryland crime scene has drawn a blank up to now. Same with the hospitals and doctors – no one matching Gorev's description has shown up anywhere. And it's the same story with pretty much every avenue we've gone down – zilch.'

'What about Rashid's apartment?'

'He never used the phone line that was installed, and left nothing lying around that might throw us a lead. The guy was careful, very professional. He paid the rent in cash through a local bank, but didn't keep any account there. His Explorer turned up nothing either, except his prints, and Gorev's and the woman's. The names Rashid used when he bought the jeep and rented the warehouse were fakes. The same with the Ryder van. The only progress we've made is finding the woman's fingerprints on the Honda and the Explorer, which prove it's her.

'We got details on her background – she's American born of Palestinian parents, and went back with them to live in Lebanon when she was twelve. We've got two dozen agents from the New York field office checking out her family's old address in Queens and trying to find out if there are any relatives or friends Stateside she might still be in touch with, or tried to get in touch with recently. But my gut feeling is we'll be wasting our time. With her kind of background and training, I'm betting she wouldn't be dumb enough to expose herself by going anywhere near an old family address, or making contact with a relative in the US, unless she was in really deep trouble and on the run, and was faced with no other choice. She'd know they're the first places we'd look. But if any relatives or friends do turn up, we'll put them under watch.' Murphy sighed. 'Apart from that, we're pretty much nowhere.'

Morgan came back, and when he and Murphy left together, Collins sat there in despair. He knew that the difficulty of finding any terrorist cell was inversely proportional to its size: the smaller the cell the harder it was to find. And experience told him that this sort of case either cracked open in days or took weeks or months. Except they hadn't got months. They had twenty-eight hours.

It was the hopelessness of the situation, and the thought of Nikki and Daniel, which brought him close to tears. Which made him question what kind of people would be prepared to commit suicide by detonating a powerful truck bomb in the heart of a city. Who would murder innocent victims – maim a defenceless woman like Nikki and a three-year-old, helpless child like Daniel – just to make a point. But he knew the answer. The same kind of callous, brutal people who had killed Sean, and when he lingered on that thought, when it reopened the angry wound of his own bitter pain, his mind flooded with rage. He didn't just imagine the bruised and bloodied faces of Nikki and Daniel; he saw the dead faces of Sean and Annie, remembered the anguish and loss of their passing, the utter futility of their deaths. And remembering that loss, he could barely hold back the tears. Then the door opened again, and a doctor stepped in.

He wore a green paper gown and green booties over sneakers. The gown was bloodstained. He didn't look more than thirty-five. His face was dark with stubble, and the name tag on his gown said: Dr Bill Wolensa. Collins tried to stand but his legs felt weak. The doctor waved for him to remain seated and slumped into a chair at the end of the bed.

'I'm Bill Wolensa. I've been working on Nikki and Daniel.' He spoke without emotion, his voice flat, and Collins saw that the young surgeon was close to exhaustion. 'OK, the story is, Nikki's fine. She had a lacerated lower left arm, a couple of nasty cuts on her legs, and a few bumps and lacerations on her head that caused a fair amount of bleeding. As with you, the injuries caused some concussion. But we did a scan and there's no brain damage or serious cranial injury, so she's going to be OK. Nothing to worry about there.'

Collins felt a surge of relief. *Nikki's going to be OK.* 'Will there be any permanent damage?'

'I doubt it. The cuts and wounds were pretty routine, so they should heal OK. Right now, she's sleeping, but in a day or two at most and she'll be up and about, and on her way to being discharged.'

Collins nodded, afraid to ask the next question. The doctor sighed before going on. Collins thought: *Here's the bad news.*

'Her son, however, is a very ill little boy.'

Collins choked back his emotion. A knot of steel gripped his stomach. 'How ill?'

'He was thrown very hard by the force of the blast. That can happen when kids are caught up in an explosion – their body weight's so slight they get tossed around a lot more than an adult. Anyway, Daniel got thrown around pretty bad. He obviously struck his chest against something – maybe wood or metal, we can't be sure. All of his right-side ribs are broken, and three on the left side, so he had a failed chest. He can't breathe for himself and he's on a respirator. He arrived here with serious internal injuries and haemorrhaging, and pretty severe damage to the spleen and the large bowel. We had to remove part of the bowel, twenty centimetres, and part of the spleen, but we're undecided about removing the rest of it right now, even though it probably needs to be done.'

'Why?'

'His heart stopped right after he got here, most likely because of loss of blood volume. We got it going again, stemmed the haemorrhaging, and started replacing the blood loss. At the moment, he's stabilised, but he's weak and in a critical condition, so a serious op like taking out the rest of his spleen would be tough on his body. How he responds over the next eight to twelve hours is pretty much going to decide how we proceed, whether we remove the rest of the organ or not.'

'Would he live OK without it?'

'Sure. The spleen's an important part of the body's defence against infections, but people can get by without one.' Wolensa hesitated. 'The ribs, that's painful, but it's not life threatening. His chest took the main impact, and the spleen damage is the main problem. He has concussion, but we can't see any evidence of internal cranial bleeding. We'll be keeping a close watch on him over the coming hours.'

Collins' stomach tightened again. 'There's nothing else you can do?'

'Nothing, I'm afraid, until we see how he responds.' Wolensa stood, exhausted, leaned a hand against the wall. 'Mr Collins, I can imagine what you must be going through, and what the boy's mother is going to go through when she regains consciousness and hears about her son, but if the paramedics had got Daniel here five minutes later, I have to tell you, he'd be dead by now. So at least there's hope. The medical staff here are among the best, and I can assure you we'll be doing everything we possibly can. Not only for Daniel, but for all the others injured in the explosion.'

Wolensa rubbed his fingers into tired eyes, moved to the door, opened it. 'And now, if you'll excuse me, I still have to check on my other patients. It's been a difficult night, as you can understand. We've haven't just had Nikki and Daniel to deal with.'

'Can I see them?'

'No.' Wolensa shook his head. 'Both of them are in the critical-care unit right now. We don't allow visitors. The smallest infection can be lethal in the unit, and in Daniel's case, a damaged spleen can leave him open to infection. I'm sorry, but it would be too dangerous. Our staff are watching them constantly and are never more than a few feet away if things go wrong – and it's quite common for things to go wrong with seriously injured victims – so it's better if there's no one to get in the way.'

'When *can* I see them?'

Wolensa lingered at the open door. 'Give it another eight hours at least, then you can see Nikki. By then we ought to have moved her out of critical care. But the little boy . . . that may take a little longer.'

'Couldn't I just see Nikki right now?'

'Not a chance.'

Collins closed his eyes. Could he wait another eight hours? He had no choice.

'You're not the boy's father, are you?' Wolensa said. 'At least, that was what I was told.'

'No.'

Wolensa sighed again. 'Look, let me be frank here. The child might die. It's as stark as that. He's been through hell – he's wired up to a respirator, his body's been bruised, bloodied, battered and operated on, and he's heavily bandaged and got IV tubes and monitor wires hanging out of him. Would you want to remember him like that?'

Collins shook his head, distressed. 'What are his chances?'

'I'm not a bookie, Mr Collins. I never quote odds. And besides, they're irrelevant in this case. Either he makes it or he doesn't. I'm sorry for being so blunt, but that's how it is.' Wolensa suddenly looked behind him. A man stood in the open doorway. The doctor turned back to Collins. 'I think you've got a visitor waiting. I'll leave you in peace.'

Collins saw Kursk standing right outside the door. Wolensa started to leave then hesitated, a look of sympathy on his weary face. 'Look, if you really want, you can take a look at them through the glass front in the critical-care rooms. That's about the best I can offer right now.'

Kursk stepped into the room after Wolensa had gone. 'I heard what the doctor said about your friend's little boy. I'm sorry.'

Collins nodded grimly. 'Did Murphy fill you in?'

'Yes.'

'He says you were right about the woman. At least that's something. But we're still nowhere, Kursk.' Collins got up off the bed shakily, his chest hurting. He put a hand on a chair to support himself. Kursk went to help, but Collins said, 'No need, I'm OK.'

'You should stay in bed.'

'That's the last place I'm going to stay.' A steely look galvanised Collins' face. The door opened. Morgan came in, carrying a black plastic bag. 'I got them, Jack.'

Collins opened the bag, took out his bloodstained clothes. Kursk was puzzled. 'What are you doing?'

'First, I'm going to go home to change, have a shower, and try and get another couple of hours' rest. Then I'm going to get back to work. We've got twenty-eight hours to crack this thing. Maybe we haven't got a hope in hell of finding Rashid, Gorev and the woman, or stopping them in time. In fact, I'm pretty sure of it. But that doesn't mean we're not going to give it our best shot, right up to the deadline. Are you with us, Kursk?'

'Yes.' Kursk looked at him. 'What about your injuries?

'I can walk and talk, and that's enough. Give me ten minutes, then I'll meet you two out front.'

Morgan said, 'You sure you'll be OK, Jack?'

'Ten minutes.'

Kursk and Morgan took the elevator to the ground floor. As they came out into the lobby, Kursk said, 'Will you excuse me? I need to find a rest room.'

'Sure. I'll go get the car. Meet you outside when you're ready.' Morgan stepped out through the exit doors.

A minute later, having stopped off at reception, Kursk wandered along a hallway off the lobby until he found the rest rooms, but didn't step inside. For a second or two he hesitated, troubled by what he had to do, but knowing it was his duty. Then he took the cellphone from his pocket and punched in a private number at the Russian embassy.

Collins stood outside the glass-fronted window of the critical-care room. A couple of nurses were busy near Nikki's bed. She was sleeping. An enormous purple bruise covered the left side of her face, her head was bandaged, and a couple of drips were feeding into her left arm. The knot in Collins' stomach came back, tightened like steel.

Daniel was in another critical-care room off to the right, a curtain halfway round his bed. It was heart wrenching to see him, and Collins felt close to breaking down. The little boy was unconscious from the combination of drugs and injuries. Bottles and tubes ran into his veins, his chest and stomach were heavily bandaged, and his face and body were speckled with tiny cuts and a mass of dark, ugly bruises. An oxygen mask covered his mouth, he was wired up to a couple of monitors, and Collins noticed that his little chest barely moved as he breathed with the aid of a respirator.

He felt impotent, unable to do anything to help. A kind of catatonic numbness took hold, and as he stared from Nikki to Daniel he was unable even to pray. His mind sought the solace of emptiness, but the emptiness wouldn't come.

He thought of Sean, of the helplessness he had felt knowing that his son had died many thousands of miles away and he hadn't been there, that even if he had been there was nothing he could have done, just as there was nothing he could do now. He started to cry then, great convulsions of tears that shook his body and pained his chest.

When the tears subsided, when he had taken a couple of breaths to control himself, he knew two things with certainty: he wanted desperately for Daniel to live, didn't want Nikki to suffer the soul-numbing anguish of losing a child. And he wanted the people who had done this: he wanted Mohamed Rashid, wanted him and the others badly, the lust for revenge in his heart so savage that it went beyond all reason and truly frightened him.

Two minutes later, he was in the elevator, on his way down to the hospital exit.

56

Washington, DC
13 November
7.35 a.m.

How do you dispose of three hundred thousand corpses?

On Federal Plaza, Patrick Tod O'Brien was still stuck with the question as he studied the DC map. He thought perhaps they could entomb Washington, leave it as a monument to the dead, and go build a new capital. But he didn't believe that was a runner – you were talking about a national icon, a city of great historical and political importance. Turning it into some vast mausoleum wasn't really on.

And he foresaw other related problems in the aftermath: the entire centre of Washington – including hundreds of famous historical buildings and monuments – would have to be carefully cleaned of contaminants. O'Brien shuddered to think of the overall cost of this kind of disaster: you were talking about a clean-up costing billions upon billions of dollars, the biggest in America's history. But he had to get back to the question of the bodies.

They couldn't just leave three hundred thousand contaminated dead lying in the streets for long, not unless they wanted to risk plague, cholera or typhoid outbreaks. So the corpses had to be moved. And that meant transport. An awful lot of transport. And it meant body-bags, an awful lot of body-bags.

O'Brien's finger moved over the map, up to Boston to the north, then Baltimore and Philly to the east, and on to Chesapeake Bay farther south. He thought: *All those bodies, we can really only go one way.* They had to keep them far from the major cities to avoid spreading disease and contamination, move them out into the countryside to some holding area. And once there? He doubted that burning the corpses would be a runner. People –

including government – would have a thing about tossing human dead on to funeral pyres, as if they were infected farm carcasses, to be destroyed because of some deadly animal virus. So where did the bodies go after they reached the holding area?

To slow decomposition and help reduce the risk of disease, O'Brien considered moving the bodies up north, off the coast of Maine, where it was colder. What if they used container ships and naval vessels out of nearby Chesapeake Bay? Then they could either keep the bodies in cold storage until they could be properly buried or bury them at sea, which was a touch more humane. But first the victims would have to removed in an orderly fashion out through Maryland and Virginia to the bay. FEMA would have to mission-assign the Department of Transportation the horrendous task of ferrying them out of the city to the holding area. O'Brien was back to the transport problem again. Thousands of vehicles would be needed. Tractor trailers, Greyhound buses, private trucks would have to be commandeered. A survey would have to be made secretly of where the Department of Transport could get the vehicles.

And yet more questions reared their ugly heads: how many bodies could you fit in a five- or ten-ton truck, in a Greyhound bus, in a container ship or naval vessel? An immediate study would have to be made. Every single type of vehicle or vessel intended for use would have to be measured and the numbers of corpses they could carry per load calculated. And after use, because the nerve gas had such a long footprint, they would have to be either destroyed or mothballed for long periods to prevent spreading contamination.

The nightmare went on: judging by the figures he'd been given, O'Brien reckoned the DC police, fire departments and emergency services were going to be pretty much defunct. The President – assuming he survived – would have to invoke martial law. Whenever civil order broke down, you had mindless chaos in the streets: incidences of lawlessness, looting, robberies and murders shot through the roof. You'd need to marshal the National Guard as a temporary police force. But with high numbers of casualties in DC, Guardsmen among them, they'd have to be looking out of state to fill the gap.

O'Brien knew for sure that the scenario was far too big for DC alone to handle: with the emergency services defunct, vast numbers of seriously ill and traumatised survivors to cope with, FEMA would have to be looking to the governors of Virginia, Maryland, Cleveland, Philly and even New York for help – asking them to put their hospitals, emergency services, fire crews and National Guards at Washington's disposal once the attack was under way. Thousands of out-of-state Guardsmen would have to be deputised, and then federalised, making them custodians of America's laws. Even before that, FEMA would have to secretly secure the governors' discreet co-operation and assistance.

Something else worried O'Brien – he foresaw difficulties when it came to transporting massive numbers of contaminated, decomposing bodies over land to Chesapeake Bay. The state governors of Virginia and Maryland wouldn't like the idea of endless convoys of dangerous cargo being transported through their territory, for fear of contamination and disease.

Tough shit. FEMA's Director would have to advise that a presidential directive be signed into law.

Keeping everything under wraps until the attack took place, and yet at the same time having responders and emergency crews on stand-by ready for the event, was pretty much impossible, O'Brien figured. The best he could do to mask the truth behind the crisis would be to inform the crews involved that there was going to be a top-secret no-notice exercise, that they were on emergency call, and that all leave and vacation had been cancelled. Top-secret exercises were not uncommon.

But emergency crews weren't dumb: if they sensed a real threat, and if they had family or relatives in DC, they'd want to warn them, it was only human. It wouldn't be long before the District was in mass panic and there was total chaos in the streets. And what if the device went off *then*? The casualty figures could climb even higher. O'Brien sighed. The deeper you went into the problem, the messier it got. He knew FEMA would do everything possible to look after the victims, but the scenario was a recipe for *monumental* civil disaster.

Worse than that, thought O'Brien. *It's like Armageddon*.

A little after 7.45 he threw down his pen. He felt physically exhausted; his head throbbed. He'd had to deal with one of his most troubling and difficult assignments ever. True, he had the bones of a plan, the best he could come up with. He could roughly project how to try to cope with one and a half million unharmed survivors, two hundred thousand injured, and how to dispose of the corpses of three hundred thousand men, women and children. A massive amount of work remained to be done – he'd have to flesh out the plan, firm up the details. He also knew that having a plan was one thing, but in a crisis Murphy's Law was king.

Things went wrong, plans got messed up or had to be modified as you went along, and spanners got thrown in the works. And responders were human: large numbers of emergency personnel might crumple, mentally or physically unable to deal with the scale of such a staggering disaster – hundreds of thousands of dead, sick and injured. There was a good chance the plan could fall to pieces.

Troubled, O'Brien looked down at the photograph on his desk: of his wife of sixteen years, Helen, and their two young daughters. The most important people in his life. He loved them deeply. He felt a knot in the pit of his stomach, and a shiver suddenly went through him. He noticed that his hands were shaking.

He knew why. An assignment this secret – the Director had emphasised *top* secret – had to mean a realistic threat. And that worried the hell out of O'Brien. If this was for real, then Washington's citizens were in the deepest shit anyone could imagine.

The White House
8.45 a.m.

'OK, let me hear it again.'

'Yes, sir.' Doug Stevens, alone with the President in the Oval

Office, rewound the tape of the recorded conversation with Abu Hasim from the night before. 'If it's all right with you, sir, I'll go from just before he cut us off a second time, prior to the truck-bomb explosion. Then I'll play back the bit where you say you've spoken with Kuzmin about the prisoners – which was right before Hasim issued his new ultimatum.'

The President nodded. The FBI Director found the relevant segment on the tape, hit the recorder's play button, and adjusted the volume. Hasim's voice filtered from the speakers, and the translator's words followed on right behind:

'As always, you Americans do not listen. I have told you my demands. I have told you I will not enter into dialogue. Yet you still attempt to cajole and bargain. Understand, I shall not bargain. You have vexed me by your attempts to negotiate, Mr President. But you have committed an even graver error.'

'What?'

'You have lied to me. I believe that you are not in the least serious about agreeing to my demands. I do not believe that you intend to honour the commitment you just gave. And that in asking me to help you, you are simply trying to buy time. I believe that you will use these remaining five days to try to locate the chemical device before the deadline expires . . .'

Stevens pressed the stop button. 'Now we'll go to the part where you talk about Kuzmin, sir.'

Stevens fast-forwarded the tape, found the segment, hit the play button again. The President sounded crystal clear.

'. . . I have spoken with President Kuzmin about the release of those in Russian prisons, and I can assure you his initial reaction is very favourable. But I need more time.'

There was a brief pause before Hasim's voice interrupted, followed quickly by the translation: *'You are lying! President Kuzmin is intent on keeping the prisoners. Furthermore, he has tried to destroy me by sending his bombers to attack my bases. Only by the grace of God, and your intervention, had he the sense to turn them back before it was too late . . .'*

Stevens depressed the stop button, cutting off the tape. Turning to the President, he said, 'OK, three things bother me. One, how could Hasim have known about Kuzmin's bombing attempt on his bases? The aircraft flew in darkness, too high to spot visually. Al-Qaeda may have access to a limited radar capability in Afghanistan, and perhaps could have been told about a large number of aircraft approaching their bases, but how would they have known specifically they were *Russian* aircraft, and not American? And that their mission was to bomb al-Qaeda's bases?'

'Go on.'

'Two, how could Hasim have known you weren't exactly being truthful about Kuzmin's reply to your request about the prisoner releases?'

The President nodded. 'Yes, I thought about that. But what if he simply made a guess?'

'He could have. But it didn't sound like a guess to me.'

'Why?'

'The quickness of his response.' Stevens clicked his fingers. 'Hasim came back at you like that – instantly. And he made the accusation that you had lied to him with such raw vehemence that I think he knew the truth even before you stated that Kuzmin's initial reaction was very favourable. That's why his reply was delivered with so much contempt – he already knew Kuzmin's position. He *knew* you hadn't told him the truth.'

'What are you getting at, Doug? That there's a traitor – a mole – within Kuzmin's inner circle, someone who passed on the information to al-Qaeda?'

'Someone with Chechen sympathies? It's quite feasible, yes. I think it's something you're going to have to put to him as soon as you speak with him again.'

The President sighed. He was dreading making the call to Kuzmin to inform him of the 10th Street suicide bombing, Hasim's new deadline, and to discuss once again the prisoner issue. He knew the Russian leader wasn't going to like what he heard. Nor would Kuzmin enjoy the intense pressure the US President intended to subject him to in order to persuade him to sanction the release of the Russian-held prisoners – sparks were definitely going to fly. He'd scheduled his call to Moscow for just over an hour's time. 'OK, so it may be a very serious problem. But really it's Kuzmin's problem. For us, it changes nothing about our situation. We're still in a fix. We've still got no way out of this. And Hasim's device is going to go off unless we comply with his demands.'

'I appreciate that, sir, but if you could just bear with me a moment.' Stevens moved back to the tape recorder. 'Hasim guessed rightly you were trying to buy time, sir. That we were attempting to use the five remaining days to find the device. It's possible he's shrewd enough to guess at that, but it seemed to me he knew *exactly* what we were about – like it wasn't a guess at all, but he'd been primed beforehand about our tactics. And it's pretty obvious to me he had the suicide bomb in place, ready to go, and was going to have it set off, even before he accused you of lying to him. It was all part of his plan to put more pressure on us. But Kuzmin didn't know about our tactics, so far as I'm aware. Did he, sir?'

The President shook his head. 'No, I didn't tell him any of that.'

'Like I say, it could still have been a shrewd guess on Hasim's part that we'd try to stymie him. The same applies when we tried the ploy of using Bob Rapp as a mediator. He cottoned on to that pretty fast, too.'

'Where the hell's all this leading, Doug?'

'To my third and last point. If you'd just listen carefully to this portion of the tape, sir, because it's vitally important. It's what Hasim said when he talked about the prisoners in Russian jails.'

Stevens rewound the tape once more, hit the play button and Hasim's voice again invaded the room, the translator relaying his words:

'*. . . As to the others, you say you have no control over their fate. That is untrue, Mr President. You have enormous power at your disposal, both military and financial, to influence those other states.*

I have no doubt you can use that power to its ultimate to ensure that all the remaining prisoners are released.'

Stevens hit the stop button. The President looked up. 'So what's your point, Doug?'

'We keep tapes of all the conversations we've had in the situation room. When I heard the words in the third and fourth sentences, they rang a bell – I was sure I'd heard them before. So I went back through all the tapes. Those words you just heard are almost exactly the same ones Bob Rapp used when he talked to you during our second meeting in the situation room – "You have enormous power at your disposal, both military and financial, to influence those other states. I have no doubt you can use that power to its ultimate to ensure that all the remaining prisoners are released." Word for word, pause for pause, syntax for syntax, they're the same damned sentences that Bob used, all except the words "I have no doubt". And just to be sure, I double-checked with the translator and he sticks by his original interpretation of Hasim's words, phrase for phrase.'

The President sat upright, a curious look on his face as he stared at Stevens. 'Get to the point.'

'What I'm saying is this: Rapp utters two sentences, and then Hasim says pretty much exactly the same two sentences. Now to me, it seems that the chances of *that* happening are unlikely, but I'll concede it's always possible we could be dealing with a sheer coincidence. However, when you take *that* coincidence – I mean, Christ, it's like reported speech, as if someone overheard the words and repeated them – when you take that in conjunction with the other two points I've already made, about the bombers and about the prisoners, then to me it poses a very big and very worrying question we can't afford to ignore.' Stevens was ashen faced. 'What if Hasim's information came from *inside* the White House?'

57

Salem
New Jersey
13 November
10 a.m.

It was a cold, sunny morning, and Ishim Razan strolled along the gravel path that snaked through the mansion's gardens. Gorev walked beside him, and lit a cigarette. Razan said, 'Is it that bad, the trouble you're in?'

Gorev shrugged. 'It might be wiser not to ask, Ishim.'

'How do you feel?'

'Better, thanks to you. You have my gratitude.'

'It's not gratitude I want, Nikolai. An explanation would be enough.'

'Ishim . . .'

Razan put up a hand to silence Gorev's protest. They moved over the bridge spanning the stream, and when they crossed it Razan indicated the bench. 'Sit with me, if you can.'

Discomfort etched Gorev's face as he eased himself on to the bench, joining the Chechen. 'Why do I get the feeling I'm about to be cross-examined?'

Razan gazed out at the gardens. 'Last night, when your friend brought you here, I was concerned by what had happened to you. We're been through a lot together, Nikolai. And we have never lied to each other, not ever.'

'What's your point?'

'I was troubled. Not only by your injury, but also by the fact that your friend Safa, or whatever her name is, admitted the police were involved. Except she refused to tell me what you were both up to.'

'She was right, Ishim.' Gorev shook his head. 'This is really none of your business.'

'Except I made it my business.'

'What do you mean?'

'You're an old and valued comrade. You arrive here badly wounded – by a grenade no less – and barely conscious. So imagine my predicament. What am I to think? Did I need to make contact with our friends in Grozny and let them know? The whole affair was a puzzle. So after the doctor left, I made some calls to Chechnya.'

'Ishim . . .'

'I managed to get in touch with Hadik Selan, no less. I thought that if anyone knew what you were up to, it had to be one of the most senior resistance commanders.'

Gorev's face darkened. 'And?'

'Selan claimed to know nothing. He could think of no reason why you might be here. But Selan's as wily as a fox. Whether he was telling the truth or not is beyond me.'

'What else did he say?'

'Not much. The line was bad. Our talk lasted no more than a few minutes. But he suggested that if you needed my help in any way, I might offer it. Do you, Nikolai?'

'Not any more.' Gorev shook his head again, uneasy. 'Did you say my name over the telephone?'

'Why?'

'It may not have been wise, Ishim. The Russian listening posts in Grozny try to intercept Selan's conversations over the radio or telephone, as they do with every Chechen commander.'

'Don't you think I know that? And I'm wise enough not to compromise you or Selan in any way. Your family name wasn't mentioned. And Selan is as careful about what he says over the phone as I am.'

Gorev stood, his face troubled. 'No matter, it's done.'

Razan's frustration showed. 'What the hell are you up to, Nikolai?'

'I can't discuss it, Ishim. And believe me, the less you know the better. You may already have put yourself in danger by helping me. So I ask you not to tell anyone I was here. You haven't seen me. Understand? You can't betray me.'

'That would never happen. I'd protect you with my life if I had to, you know that.'

Gorev nodded, then looked at his watch. 'What time did Safa say she'd be here?'

'She ought to be arriving soon.'

'Then let's get back up to the house.'

As they crossed the bridge, Razan halted, put a hand on Gorev's arm. 'I have one more question.'

'No – no more, Ishim.'

'It has nothing to do with our talk. This woman, Safa, do you love her?'

'What's it to you?'

'It's a simple question, Nikolai. There's no trickery in my asking. You trust me, don't you?'

'More than any man I know.'

'Then tell me. For a start, is Safa really her name?'

Gorev hesitated. 'No. It's Karla.'

'Tell me about her. How did you meet?'

'In Moscow, at the university. It was another life, long before you and I served together.'

'She meant something to you back then?'

'More than I'd care to admit.'

Razan studied Gorev's face, then turned away, gazed towards some distant point on the horizon. 'Despite all your virtues, and the esteem I hold you in, you're a strange man, Nikolai.'

'In what way strange?'

'In my line of business, I've had to learn to be a good judge of a man's character. My life might depend on it. So I'm going to be honest with you. In all the years we've been friends, I never knew of a woman you truly loved. For you, there was never time. There were women along the way, of course, and quite a few of them loved you, I'm sure. And why not? You were always charming – a handsome, intelligent officer who commanded respect. It's easy to see how they found you attractive.'

'Ishim . . .'

'I don't say all this to embarrass you, only to help you understand yourself. Because you see, you could never really love in return. You were always too intent on other things – your work or a career or a cause. I'm sure the psychologists could make something of it: how the past can mould a man, how losing his parents at such a young age can sometimes make him reluctant to commit to any kind of relationship, because there's the fear of losing those he might love, yet again. It's so much easier to keep people at arm's length by committing to a career or a cause. There isn't the fear of rejection, of being let down.'

'What is this, Ishim? Some kind of amateur psychiatry?'

'Maybe it is, but hear me out. You see, I get the feeling that this Karla was entirely different where you were concerned. When it comes to feelings between a man and a woman, there is always the lover and the loved, we both know that. And while I get the impression that perhaps she loved you more than you loved her, she still had a place in your heart. She was important in your life. Perhaps more than you ever imagined?'

'Perhaps.'

'And on reflection, when it was over between you, it was only then you realised the truth. That you knew you should not have let her go, should have taken the risk and committed yourself. That she was a good woman, the kind a man would be proud to have as a wife. But at the time you didn't take the risk, did you?'

'No.'

'Tell me why.'

Gorev tossed away his cigarette. 'It's complicated, Ishim. Who knows? Maybe there's truth in what you said about my past, of being wary of pledging myself to someone. But Karla only came to Moscow for a year. When the time came for her to leave, we had to go our separate ways, and with good reason. She wasn't really free. She was engaged to be married, had a career and a cause that were important to her. You see, it's never simple, is it?'

'But I get the feeling she would have ventured everything to be with you.'

'Maybe you're right. But then I didn't, did I?'

'And is she free now?'

'Yes.'

'Do you love her?'

'Ishim, it's been so many years since Karla and I were together . . .'

'I'm an old friend, Nikolai. Don't look so embarrassed. And even if you haven't slept together in years, it's immaterial. Do you love her?'

'Yes, I love her.'

'Then can I give you some advice?'

'I get the feeling I'm going to hear it anyway.'

'When this business of yours is over, go live yourself a normal life. Settle down. Our time's too short, Nikolai, and with you, there's always been a battle. It's time you forgot the battle and smelled the roses.'

'And what about the cause?'

'There are always others to take up the torch. But you, you've fought too long and too hard, and at the expense of everything important in your life. Karla loves you. And from what you've told me, and my own intuition, I'm inclined to think she's loved you a very long time, and far more deeply that you could imagine. Except she's not the kind to say. With her, emotions run deep, but she doesn't wear her heart on her sleeve. She's a good woman, Nikolai. Take my advice, don't risk losing her a second time.'

'Those seven sisters of yours have a lot to answer for, Ishim. You're turning into quite a counsellor in your middle age, you know that?'

'I know, but don't dare tell my men.' Razan smiled faintly, then turned away as one of his guards appeared along the path. The man came over, whispered in Razan's ear, and his boss dismissed him. Gorev said, 'What's wrong?'

'Your friend has arrived. Let's not keep her waiting.' Razan nodded towards the mansion.

At the rear of the property, near the guards' security room, Gorev saw Karla step out. She waved, and he waved back. Then he turned, laid a hand on Razan's shoulder. 'You know I can't stay here, Ishim.'

The Chechen pursed his lips, nodded. 'There's an old saying: It comes as God wills. It applies particularly to men like us. However carefully you plan, one of these days someone turns up where they shouldn't. The gun that's never been known to jam does. That's what will kill you in the end, and me, when we least expect it. So whatever it is you're doing, I beg you, be careful, Nikolai.'

'I intend to be.'

'Then the rest, it seems, is in the hands of fate.'

Fifteen minutes later, Razan was in his study, smoking a cigar. He saw the Plymouth retreat down the driveway, Nikolai in the passenger seat, the woman driving. The door opened behind him, and the guard who had spoken to him in the garden came in. 'You sent for me, Ishim?'

'Tell Yegori and the men to call off their surveillance. Tell them it's over. They're to return from Chesapeake immediately.'

'Yes, Ishim.'

The guard left. Razan turned back to the window, watched as the Plymouth's red tail-lights disappeared out through the open gates. Whatever it was Nikolai and the woman were up to, he had the distinct feeling it was no longer any of his business.

58

FBI Headquarters
Washington, DC
13 November
8.15 a.m.

The streets around the Hoover building had been sealed off. Metropolitan police vehicles and barriers blocked the entrances, squads of police and FBI agents manned the boundaries, and no one was allowed to pass without a thorough check of their ID. Half a dozen fire tenders were still parked either end of the headquarters' 10th Street entrance, the crews helping to sift through the bomb debris, watched over by a couple of vigilant FBI forensic teams.

Kursk and Morgan pushed their way past the TV crews hanging around the cordon, and went up the steps and in through the undamaged passageway on E Street. When they got past the tight security check – ID verification, a metal detector arch and a body frisk – they took the elevator up to the sixth floor. The hallways were in chaos, with staff moving furniture from the bomb-damaged east side to hastily reallocated office space in the other three wings.

'I'm betting Jack won't get in until early afternoon,' Morgan said. 'He's going to need at least that much sleep. Help yourself to a coffee, Alexei. Meantime, I'll go see what's been happening.'

When Morgan had left, Kursk poured a cup of coffee from the percolator in the corner, then crossed to the window, looked down into the street. The embassy counsellor he had been instructed to contact had listened to his report of the previous night's events, as well as the state of progress of the FBI hunt, and Kursk knew that the moment he had hung up his information would be relayed immediately to Moscow.

As he stood there, he studied the massive blast damage on the opposite side of the street: the shattered windows and façades of office buildings, stores and restaurants. He grimaced, realised that whatever foolish glimmer of hope he had harboured of convincing Nikolai Gorev to halt this madness was gone. Nikolai was a dead man walking, no matter what way it turned out, whether the device went off or not. Kursk knew he would be hunted down relentlessly, wherever he tried to hide. Even if he were caught alive, the Russian charge of treason against him, alone, would ensure a harsh punishment: execution by firing squad.

Morgan came back, shaking his head. 'Murphy's tearing his hair out. Seems like we're going nowhere fast, except down a dead end.'

'What about the hospitals and private surgeries?'

'Our guys finished checking them out half an hour ago. Nobody matching Gorev's description turned up.'

Kursk put down his coffee. He went over to the wall map, studied it, his brow furrowed in thought. Morgan said, 'What's up, Alexei?'

'You checked all doctors of Chechen or Arab background in the search area?'

'Sure.'

'But not Russian.'

'Russians weren't on the list.'

'Perhaps they should have been.'

Morgan rubbed his jaw. 'See your point. It's also possible we're completely wasting our time here. Gorev might not have been wounded badly enough to even need a doctor.' He shrugged. 'But OK, I'll go mention it to Murphy, see what he says about tying up more manpower.'

As Morgan moved to leave, Kursk had another thought. It was a gamble, he knew – a hopeless gamble, and time was against him – but the more he considered it, the more he realised he had nothing to lose. He gestured to the telephone. 'I'd like to make a call.'

'Sure. Dial nine to get an outside line.'

Morgan left and closed the door. Kursk picked up the receiver and punched in the number.

Chesapeake
1.15 p.m.

It was turning cold out on Winston Bay that early afternoon, the wind blowing in ragged gusts as Gorev and Karla pulled up outside the cottage. On the veranda, Mohamed Rashid stepped out, glared at them both. 'So, you're back.'

Gorev slammed the Plymouth's door. 'I had a slight detour.'

Rashid grunted. 'So I heard. But you're still alive, I see.' He jerked a thumb. 'Inside, both of you. We need to talk.'

'What's wrong?' Gorev asked.

'There's been a change of plan.'

Washington, DC
12.02 p.m.

Harry Judd was a troubled man.

It was the FBI Director – seated beside Judd's boss – who troubled him. Or more to the point, what the FBI Director had to say. For thirty minutes, Judd had listened as Douglas Stevens spoke, and he could hardly believe his ears. He was still trying to get over the biggest shock in his Secret Service career when the Director finished. 'You're saying there might be a *mole* in the White House? Someone helping these terrorists?'

'Given the evidence, it's a distinct possibility,' Stevens replied. 'And I hesitate to use the word mole, Mr Judd. Traitor may prove to be the more apt word, despicable as it sounds.'

Judd had heard Stevens' 'evidence' and still found it incredible that al-Qaeda might have managed to plant a source of intelligence within the White House. 'If you don't mind me asking, sir, where do I fit in?'

'We want you to help try to find whoever it might be,' Rob Owens, the Assistant Director of Protection, answered. 'And we need to find them fast. You've got our full authority to use whatever means you have to, Harry.'

'This is a joint operation, right? The FBI and the Service working together.'

'Correct,' Stevens replied. 'Why, is that a problem, Mr Judd?'

Who are you kidding? Judd thought. It was definitely a problem. A long-standing rivalry existed between the Secret Service and the Federal Bureau; a mistrust that sometimes caused enough friction to generate sparks. The FBI had a presence in the White House, but it was mostly confined to running background checks on anyone applying to work there. As far as the Secret Service was concerned, the Feds were butt-heads – four-hundred-pound gorillas who liked to flex their muscles. And because of petty rivalries and jealousies, it wasn't uncommon for either party to refuse to disclose information to the other.

The FBI Director seemed to anticipate Judd's scepticism. 'Normally, the Bureau would be expected to take the lead, but in this case it seems likely the source may be operating principally on Secret Service territory, so we'll be working hand in glove. Don't worry, Mr Judd. At least this once, I promise you, everyone's going to singing from the same hymn sheet – there will be total and absolute co-operation between the Service and the Bureau. You have my solemn word on that.'

Judd would believe *that* when he saw it. 'So where do we start?'

The FBI Director started to pace the room. 'We'll begin by re-examining the background checks on every member of the National Security Council – everyone, obviously, except the President. Time's against us, so we can't afford to waste precious hours by working this investigation in stages. We'll go at it with all barrels. Straight away we also tap their phones – home and office numbers. We also watch their wives, girlfriends and secretaries. See where they go, who they talk to.'

Judd raised an eyebrow. 'We're talking about invading the privacy of some heavy hitters. Important people.'

'We're also talking about a possible serious breach of national security, Harry, so let us worry about that,' Owens told him.

'What about their e-mails?'

'We'll get a writ for those, if need be,' Stevens answered, but knew that such a requirement would only apply to personal computers that were the private property of individuals he deemed suspect. Most of the personal computers used by NSC members – especially those located in the White House or government buildings – had been paid for by the government, and as such were government property, so no writ would be needed. The Secret Service also had at its disposal the technical ability to hack into almost any computer, anywhere in the US. 'Trawl through them all in the last month. Any patterns or suspicious calls, we subpoena the phone company and find out where he or she phoned. If, within twenty-four hours, we've come up with nothing, we expand it out to everyone working in the White House – military personnel, every office worker, every Secret Service agent, right down the chain of hierarchy. But whoever it is, it stands to reason they had to have access to the situation room and/or the Oval Office, so we use that to narrow it down. How often are both rooms swept for bugs?'

The Secret Service carried out routine electronic countermeasures, checking the White House, Camp David and presidential vehicles and aircraft for ESIDs – electronic surreptitious intelligence devices. 'Every day,' Judd replied. 'Maybe even hourly, if we feel it's necessary. Especially if there's been access to any of the mansion's rooms by official visitors, foreign or otherwise. Or if the President has had guests staying over. It doesn't matter if it's his political buddies or a Hollywood star. No one's above suspicion. We sweep the rooms they've been in. The same applies if one of the secretaries gets a bunch of flowers delivered. We sweep the bouquet.'

Stevens turned to Rob Owens. 'I'm not doubting your thoroughness, Rob, but is it possible you could have missed a highly sophisticated listening device?'

'I really doubt it. The sweeps are very thorough, and the equipment we use is the best in the business.' Owens sounded confident, but then he immediately said to Judd, 'To be on the safe side, we better sweep the sit-room and Oval Office again, right away. But make sure it's done discreetly, when they're empty. We don't want to tip our hand. And you better examine the log books of our guys on NSC protection duty. Take particular note of any break in the patterns of the Council members' movements over the last few days. A hint of anything unusual, I want to hear about it.'

'Yes, sir.'

Owens got up from his chair. 'Report back here to me at six p.m. Or sooner if you've got something, Harry.'

Judd rose, scratched the hollow in his nose, hesitated before he said to the FBI Director, 'I've got a question.'

'Ask away.'

'You said run checks on *everyone* on the Council, except the President. I'm presuming you didn't mean yourself included?

Stevens shook his head. 'Even me, Mr Judd.'

Chesapeake
13 November
1.25 p.m.

'Thirty-six hours is insane. The Americans can never comply with all your demands in time.'

'They're already complying, Gorev.' Mohamed Rashid looked triumphant. 'They've started a complete withdrawal from Saudi and the Gulf. Whether they can meet our deadline is their problem. But by bringing it forward, we pressured them into seeing sense.'

'Like the bomb last night, is that what you mean?'

'It was a necessary warning, Gorev. And it worked, you can't deny that. You know as well as I do that the success of any mission depends on speed, aggression and surprise.'

Karla and Gorev stood in the centre of the living room. Gorev was angry. 'And whose idea was it to use the bomb?'

'Abu Hasim's. It was planned months ago, a necessary strategy in case we had need of it.'

'Are there any other strategies you haven't told me about?'

'Don't be smart, Gorev. And since when did you assume you had a right to know everything about al-Qaeda's plans? You shouldn't complain. It's got the kind of results you want. The Americans will release all their prisoners before the deadline – they'll be flown to Afghanistan – and it won't be long before the Russians and the others are forced to do the same. Now the Americans have seen how far we're prepared to go, they'll bring unbearable pressure on Kuzmin and the rest – use whatever means they have to save their capital before the deadline runs out. It's what you wanted, Gorev, isn't it? Your comrades set free. And you, Karla Sharif. Or don't you want your son back?'

'What if the others aren't released?'

'They will be. Where's your faith, woman? Don't you see what we've achieved? In the last two days we've gained more than in decades of struggle, but only by showing the Americans we mean business. Which is why we have to be prepared to see this through to the end – stand by our threat until the last second.'

Rashid reached for his backpack. 'Enough. You should both be grateful this has gone as planned.' He looked at Gorev. 'You have an appointment to keep with this man Visto.'

'This evening, at five o'clock.'

'You'd better take the motorcycle. I'll have need of the car later, and won't be back until late.' Rashid turned to Karla. 'Go with him, in case that wound of his starts to act up.'

Gorev reached towards the coffee table, picked up his Beretta, which Karla had returned, and checked the action. 'There's no need. She's been in enough danger already. And I'm able enough to drive alone.'

'It's not you I'm worried about, it's our operation. You'll do as I say. She goes with you. She can wait somewhere near by, out of harm's way, while you attend to our business.'

Karla touched Gorev's arm. 'It's all right, Nikolai. I'd rather go.'

Rashid undid the straps on his backpack, plucked out a wad of dollar banknotes, handed them to Gorev. 'The rest of Visto's money. Give him what you have to, the remainder when he delivers. And remember, watch yourselves. The Americans may have promised not to search for us, but we know that's a lie. Their police and FBI will still be on the lookout, you can depend on it. If you're stopped, challenged, or find yourselves in danger, get away from trouble as fast as you can. I don't want us compromised, not at this late stage.'

Gorev tucked the Beretta in his jacket pocket. 'Don't worry, I've no intention of being reckless.'

Rashid took an interstate map from the backpack. 'You'll tell Visto you want to take delivery of the equipment tonight.'

'Where do we store the van?'

'Here, in the garage. It ought to be perfectly safe until we have need of it.' Rashid unfolded the map. 'I'll show you exactly where I want Visto to make our rendezvous. And don't botch this, Gorev. Our plans may depend on it.'

59

Washington, DC
5 p.m.

Benny Visto lay half naked in bed. Beside him, wearing only a black G-string and stiletto heels, was one of the new girls who worked his stable.

She was nineteen, half Cuban, half Puerto Rican, with big breasts and a slim figure. His head propped on a pillow on the king-size, Visto watched as the girl's tongue moved down his belly in slow flicking movements. He was just beginning to enjoy himself when the door opened and his cousin Frankie came in. He grinned as his eyes settled on the girl. 'You keep doing that, you're going to catch something, Benny.'

'Told you not to disturb me. The fuck's up?'

'The dude's here. Let him in the backyard. He's on a fucking motorcycle.'

'What *dude*?'

'One who wants the van and other stuff.'

'Find Ricky. Have him haul his ass up here.'

'What about the guy?'

Visto got up off the bed, pulled on a silk dressing gown. 'Dude sure knows how to pick the wrong time.' He clicked his fingers at the girl. 'Get the fuck out. I got business.'

'S . . . sure, Benny.' The girl pulled on her clothes and left in a hurry. Visto plucked a small plastic bag of white powder from a sandalwood humidor. 'Motorcycle, you said?'

Frankie nodded.

'Get Ricky while I go take a look.'

Visto dressed and stepped into the kitchen at the back, overlooking the delivery yard below. It was enclosed by high stone walls and protected by a pair of sturdy metal gates. The blinds were closed and he opened them a crack and peered into the yard. The dude was standing beside a dark blue 1,000cc Honda, wearing motorcycle leathers and smoking a cigarette. Frankie came back, followed by Ricky.

Visto said, 'Take a good look, Ricky. You think that's the john in the photograph?'

Ricky studied Gorev's face through the blinds. 'Looks like him, Benny.'

'You're sure the Feds didn't say anything about what they wanted him for?'

'Naw. Just showed me the shots. The dude, another guy – an Arab – and some bitch. Maybe it was the one with him in the car last time? 'Cept I didn't get a good look.'

'Maybe.'

'You going to call the Feds like they asked, Benny?' Frankie said.

'Later. Want to take a good look at the dude first, then see the Feds' shots, make damned sure it's the same one they're looking for. If it is, then we try and find out from the Feds what he might be up to, and if it's worth our while turning him in, before we even think of telling them anything. No use showing our hand just yet.' Visto grinned. 'Could be a lot more opportunity than I thought.'

'What you mean, Benny?'

'Think about it, Frankie – maybe we've got a chance to double up on our profits. Get a piece of the dude's action, *and* a reward from the Feds. But let's see how it swings, play it cool for now.' Visto looked down into the yard again, rubbed his jaw as he studied the powerful Honda. 'Motorcycle like that, might make things a little tricky for you to follow him, don't you think, Ricky?'

The Cuban grinned. 'No trouble. I got it covered. The way I planned it, one of my guys is driving a Goldwing. We're using cellphones to keep in touch and do it like a relay. That way, any of us can drop back if he spots us tailing him, and another can take over.'

'How many fucking guys you got?'

Ricky's grin widened. 'Four, including me. I'm in a pick-up, Ronnie and Hector are in a car, and the other guy's on the Goldwing.'

'Sounds to me like a fucking convoy.' Visto nodded. 'OK, do your thing. Shouldn't be no more than ten minutes. Don't fuck up, hear?'

'Don't worry, Benny. He ain't gonna get away.'

Visto had a dangerous look as he patted the Cuban's scarred face. 'Better be right. Else you're gonna wish you were back behind bars. Got that, Ricky?'

'Sure.'

The Cuban left. Frankie said, 'Ricky ain't the fucking brightest. What if he loses him?'

Visto grinned. 'There's always the delivery later tonight, ain't there?' He dipped his thumb and forefinger into the bag, snorted a pinch of coke, felt the rush through his veins. 'OK, let's go see the man, show him what we got.'

Gorev tossed his cigarette away when he saw Visto come down the metal steps to the yard, followed by Frankie.

'Good to see you, man.'

'Have you organised everything I need?'

'We got the van. Had it painted today. Takes about twelve hours to bake dry. Have it by tonight, midnight at the latest, right on schedule.'

'What about the markings?'

'Made up just like you wanted. Ready to stick on.'

'And the rest?'

'Show the man the goods, Frankie.'

Frankie led the way inside the warehouse. He lugged two heavy grey plastic suitcases on to a trestle table, flicked one open. Inside, Gorev saw a collection of metropolitan police uniforms, complete with caps, and when he had inspected the items he nodded his satisfaction.

'They look good.'

'Ought to. They're the genuine article. Took a lot of trouble to get them.'

'What about the weapons?'

'Show him, Frankie. Make the man's day.'

Frankie opened the second suitcase. Inside were three police-issue Glock handguns, with leather belts and holsters, and two Browning twelve-gauge shotguns. Gorev checked each weapon thoroughly. 'Satisfied?' Visto said finally.

'I think you could say that.'

Visto rubbed his forefinger and thumb. 'Then how about I see some more cash?'

Gorev produced a wad of banknotes, handed them across. 'Another five thousand, as agreed. Count it if you like.'

Visto counted the money, greedily stuffed it in his pocket. 'Seems like we're on the homeward stretch.' He looked back at the Honda. 'I figure you won't be wanting to take the merchandise now. Not unless you're thinking of hitching a trailer to that machine of yours.'

'I'll take everything when you deliver the van.'

'Cool by me, so long as you got the other ten grand. So, where you want to do it?'

Gorev produced the interstate map and pointed to a town in Virginia, thirty miles south of Washington. 'There's a crossroads here, at Piedmont. You swing left and come to a Lutheran church. A half-mile down the road on the right there's a turnoff that leads into a forest track. Fifty yards along the track there's a clearing. You can't miss it. I'll be waiting at the clearing. I'd like you there at precisely ten-thirty tonight.'

Visto nodded. 'Sounds good.'

Gorev folded away the map, stuffed it in his jacket. 'It's been a pleasure doing business, Mr Visto.'

'Pleasure's all mine.'

Gorev crossed over to the Honda, Visto and Frankie behind him. As Gorev started to climb on, Visto said, 'Mind me asking something?'

'Ask away.'

'Man can't help wonder what you need all that stuff for. Cop-type van, uniforms, weapons.'

Gorev pulled on his leather gloves, fixed Visto with a dangerous stare. 'I'm sure you won't take it personally when I tell you that it's perhaps best you mind your own end of the business, Mr Visto. Otherwise there's likely to be a serious misunderstanding.'

'Don't follow.'

'Somebody's liable to get hurt. Badly.'

The threat registered instantly, and for a second or two Visto bristled, grinding his teeth in barely concealed anger, but then he suddenly laughed out loud. 'Hey, no sweat, man. No sweat at all.' He patted the motorcycle. 'Wouldn't like to lose my ten grand, so drive carefully, man.'

'I'll try to, Mr Visto.' Gorev eased himself on to the Honda, gunned it into life. He flicked down his visor and drove out through the gates. Frankie locked them and strolled back.

'What do you think, Benny?'

'What do I think? I think we've got ourselves one sassy son-of-a-fucking-bitch, that's what I think.' Visto's face twisted in a savage look. 'That's the *second* time the dude threatened me. Who the *fuck* he think he is?' He took another pinch of coke, inhaled deeply. 'Know what I say? Fuck the Feds. *Fuck them.* Me, I'm goin' to have that dude's ass. Know what else? That motherfucker thinks he can cut me out of this deal, motherfucker's got another think coming.'

60

Moscow
13 November

In lightly falling snow, at exactly 6 p.m. the Mercedes S600 carrying Vasily Kuzmin sped in through the massive gates of the Kremlin. The limo turned into a private courtyard, and when the convoy of vehicles protecting Kuzmin's car drew up, his bodyguards climbed out smartly and escorted him in through double oak doors.

Two minutes later Kuzmin was being led into the warmth of his office by Leonid Tushin, his private secretary. A log fire was blazing in the hearth. Kuzmin had been due to attend an important civic function in Kalinin that morning, and his car was speeding its way along the ring road to make the appointment when he'd got the call from Tushin. He immediately cancelled the engagement and returned to the Kremlin. He wanted absolute privacy for the phone conversation he was about to have. 'Well?' Kuzmin snapped at his private secretary.

'The American President is waiting on the line, sir.'

Kuzmin, in a sober mood, nodded. 'Put him through.'

Washington, DC
13 November

It was already dark as Gorev and Karla headed out of the city, taking 14th Street towards the bridge and Foggy Bottom, and then turning south-east on to Route 105. Ten minutes later, Gorev slowed, braked to a halt. Glancing in the side mirror, he kept his eyes on the dim headlights of a car that had pulled into a lay-by a hundred yards back. Karla thought there was something the matter with his wound, because he clutched his side as he leaned slightly to the right, but then he started to fiddle with something on the engine. 'What's wrong?' she said.

'There's a car stopped not far behind. Maybe it's my imagination, but I get the feeling it's been following us since we left the city.'

Karla was tempted to glance round, but Gorev said, 'Don't look back.'

'What do we do?'

'Carry on for now, see if I'm right.' Gorev shifted the Honda into gear again and pulled out. The road ahead twisted in a series of dangerous snake bends, with stands of trees on either side, but Gorev nonetheless suddenly increased power, taking the Honda up to seventy, rounding the bends sharply, noting that the headlights behind him matched his increase in speed. A quarter-mile farther on, Gorev rounded a tight curve in the road and immediately switched off all his lights, slowed, and swung left, pulling into a cluster of trees. He braked, turned off the engine and snapped up his visor. The car came round the curve and carried on, picking up speed. He caught a brief glimpse of the two men in the front, but he didn't recognise them. The car disappeared round the next bend.

'What do you think?' Karla asked.

'Hard to say.'

'But who could it be?'

Gorev frowned. 'Visto and his friends, maybe. I wouldn't trust his type, no more than he'd trust us. We'd better take another route to be on the safe side. Keep your eyes peeled, but don't look round. Use the mirror, Karla.'

Gorev turned the Honda round. He switched on the lights again, cut across the road, and drove back in the direction from which they'd come. Three minutes later they passed a gas station on the opposite side of the highway.

They didn't notice a powerful Goldwing motorcycle with a single rider that had pulled into the station forecourt seconds before they passed. A dark blue Ford pick-up had halted right beside it, the engine throbbing. Ricky Cortez was behind the wheel, the window rolled down, gritting his teeth as he watched the Honda go past just as he finished talking on his cellphone. He took the phone from his ear and called out to the Goldwing rider, 'Ronnie and Hector think the dude and his bitch might have twigged them. They're going to fall back a little. Get after the Honda and stay as far back as you can. We'll switch places every five minutes.'

'Sure, Ricky.' The Goldwing rider snapped down his visor.

'Keep in touch on the phone and don't lose them, you hear?' Cortez snarled. 'Fuck this up and Benny's going to have a fucking fit.'

The Goldwing rider nodded, revved, pulled out. He roared across the road, picking up speed rapidly as he followed in the direction of the Honda, and Ricky Cortez did the same.

Moscow
6.55 p.m.

Vasily Kuzmin slammed down the phone and rose from his desk. Crossing to the window, where snowflakes were brushing against the pane, he put his hands out as if in supplication, gripping either side of the window frame, then leaned forward and touched his throbbing brow to the freezing-cold glass.

The call from the American President had shaken him. First, the President had informed him of the devastation caused by the suicide bomber – a shocking, brutal act. Then he had spoken about the slow progress of the hunt. It was getting nowhere. No strong leads, apart from confirmation of the female terrorist's identity – a Palestinian graduate of Moscow's Patrice Lumumba, no less, and one of its best students.

To make matters even worse, then came the news of Abu Hasim's threat to Moscow on the issue of the prisoner releases – which alarmed Kuzmin so much his palms began to sweat and his heart race. *It's over*, he convinced himself. *The time has come to bomb al-Qaeda's bases to dust.*

'Mr Kuzmin,' the American President had said, his voice clear down the secure phone line, 'I know you made perfectly clear your intention to destroy Hasim's camps if he directly threatened Russia. But I'm asking you – pleading with you – to please hold back for now. We still have time to try to change the outcome of the situation.'

'Thirty-six hours is nothing, and even less remains,' Kuzmin replied forcefully, still reeling from the news. 'And your investigation is going nowhere. How can you have hope when there is really none? You are already withdrawing your troops from the Gulf . . .'

'Mr Kuzmin, I had no other choice. But it doesn't mean we're defeated. I need you to promise me that you won't attack the bases. And I *implore* you to help me by releasing the prisoners—'

'I can promise no such thing,' Kuzmin snapped. 'I already spoke with my council. We agreed unanimously that we cannot offer such a release . . .'

'But we're faced with a new situation here – a new threat, a new deadline.'

'Which will be urgently discussed by my council this very evening, *that* I can promise – but I can tell you now that they will never agree to any prisoner release. *Never.*'

There was a long silence at the other end, and Kuzmin heard the defeated sigh before President Andrew Booth spoke again. 'Mr Kuzmin, I am reluctant to again go down the road of using threats, of using the stick of my country's military might to convince you otherwise. That's not something I want to do, though I may yet be forced to.'

Kuzmin felt enraged again. He knew the Americans could always attempt to shoot down his bombers and risk all-out war, but they *couldn't* send a raiding party to Moscow and abduct the prisoners. He was about to cut in sharply, but Booth continued, 'However, I'd like to offer a carrot. A proposition, if you like. That in return for Russia holding back on its attack and releasing the prisoners—'

'When will you understand that the prisoner issue is not negotiable?' Kuzmin was still furious. 'As for your threats . . .'

'If you'd let me finish? What if, in return, my government offers a moratorium on our country's new missile defence system?'

Kuzmin fell silent. This was bribery of the highest order. The American's 'Star Wars' missile defence system was a massive problem for his government. If the US proceeded with their project it would mean that Russia, in order to ensure her defence, would have to spend billions of roubles trying to build a similar one – roubles it didn't have, and wouldn't have, not for many years, until the Russian economy was firmly on its feet. Kuzmin bit back his ire, let the silence settle a while longer, appreciating that it was a tantalising offer. 'I am tempted to ask for how long.'

'Three years.'

Kuzmin did not reply. He waited for the rest of the carrot, felt certain now that it was coming.

'Furthermore, Mr Kuzmin, your government is at present attempting to secure two major international loans, but with considerable difficulty. I can promise you that difficulty would at once disappear. The loans would be immediately guaranteed by the US government.'

Again, Kuzmin held back his reply. Was there more?

'In addition, you have my solemn promise that the US will desist from criticising your future actions and policies in Chechnya.'

Kuzmin pursed his lips. These were bold gestures, and very tempting, but would they be enough to sway his council? 'Mr President, again, I can promise nothing. My council must consider these . . . propositions of yours, along with everything else that has transpired. These are serious matters, and will take time.'

'I understand, Mr Kuzmin. But I need their response *today*. By midnight, Washington time, at the very latest. Otherwise, I can't make the deadline of the prisoner releases. Can you at least promise me that?'

'Very well. You shall have a final answer before then.'

Kuzmin let the coldness of the glass chill the headache brewing inside his skull. He reflected on the conversation with Andrew

Booth, and the questions it raised. What use was a moratorium on the missile defence issue if Abu Hasim succeeded, and then embarked on his plan to tear apart the Russian Federation? And if the prisoners were released, wouldn't the public outrage be enormous? Was such a deal worthwhile, if, as one of his own cabinet had suggested, it led to Kuzmin's own downfall?

Then there was the even more serious problem of Hasim's threat to deploy a nerve-gas device in Moscow if his bases were attacked. But what if Hasim were bluffing? What if he hadn't got another bomb in Moscow, or anywhere near it, and his threat was completely empty?

For several moments he reflected on Andrew Booth's dilemma. The man was desperate – the gestures he had offered were those of either a foolish man or an extreme optimist, or both. Kuzmin sympathised with Booth's plight, but he had his own country, his own people and his own agenda to consider, and they would take precedence. Still, the matter would have to be put to the vote.

Finally, he stood back from the icy glass, crossed to his desk and made a private phone call to the head of the FSB that lasted no more than three minutes. When he had replaced the receiver, he buzzed his private secretary.

'Mr President?'

'Arrange a security council meeting for eight-thirty this evening. Here, in the Kremlin. Do it promptly, Leonid. It's an extremely urgent matter.'

Chesapeake

Gorev turned on to the Chesapeake Beach road. They were three miles from Winston Bay and the rain had started to fall in a drizzle, coming in off the sea. Towards the southern end of the town, he swung in off the road and drove into the parking lot of a supermarket and liquor store. He switched off the engine, doused the lights. When Karla had climbed off, he removed his helmet, dismounted and scanned the road behind them.

'Did you see anything?' Karla asked.

For the last ten miles they'd stuck to the minor roads, taking every precautionary measure they could before swinging back on to the highway again. It was rush hour; the traffic had started to thicken as commuters began their journeys home from DC, and for most of the way there had been a fair number of vehicles on the roads, but Gorev had been able to weave in and out of the traffic. 'I'm almost sure I spotted a motorcycle behind us a few miles back, with a pick-up truck close behind, but I'm reasonably certain we lost them both.'

Karla took off her helmet and looked back along the road. 'I don't like it, Nikolai. What if it was the police or FBI?'

'They'd be a lot more professional, and by now they'd have had helicopters up, tracking us. No, my instinct tells me it's Visto.'

'But why would he have us followed?'

'A man like him puts his faith in no one but himself. I'd take a guess that he thought it might be prudent to try to find out a little more about who he's dealing with. Not that you'd blame a criminal for that, but it makes me wonder if he might get up to something more devious.'

'Like what?'

Gorev shook his head. 'God knows. Trying to cheat us in some way, or look for more money for his goods. We'll have to be on our toes when we take delivery of the truck and equipment tonight.'

'What if he goes to the police?'

'If Ishim said he won't, I think you can count on it.'

As Gorev started to mount the Honda, his face twisted in pain.

'What's wrong?'

'My side's acting up a little. It's nothing. I'll change the dressing when we get back.'

He saw the worry in Karla's eyes, put a hand gently to her face. 'Don't worry, I'm fine, I promise.' He pulled his helmet on as the rain started to come down more heavily. 'Now, let's get out of here and back to the cottage before we're both drenched.'

* * *

Ricky Cortez was livid. He swore as he pulled the pick-up in off the beach road at Chesapeake, the rain sluicing down. He'd driven up and down the road at least half a dozen times and seen no sign of the Honda or its passengers.

The Goldwing purred to a halt beside him, the rider climbed off, and seconds later the car drew up, Ronnie in the passenger seat, Hector driving. Ricky got out of the pick-up in a rage, strode over to Hector's car and lashed out with his boot, denting the door. 'You fucking assholes blind, or what?'

'Hey, watch my fucking car! I still got fucking repayments to make, man.'

'Fuck your car, and fuck you.' Ricky pulled a snub-nosed .38 revolver from his pocket, stuck it in through the window and up against Hector's nose. 'I told you on the phone to keep close behind. I told you to take the lead when me and the Goldwing had to drop behind. But no, you fucking lost them. You pair of assholes got any idea what Benny's going to do when I go back and tell him?'

'Hey, Ricky, go easy with the gun, man. There was too much traffic back there, we couldn't keep tagging them. The guy was doing some pretty fast weaving and I didn't have no fucking rocket strapped to my ass to keep up with him, man.'

Ricky, drenched by the rain, gritted his teeth, stepped back, kicked the car again. This time Hector kept his mouth shut, knowing Ricky's savage moods and where they could lead. The motorcycle rider started to move back to the Goldwing. Ricky turned on him. 'Where the *fuck* do you think you're going?'

'I thought we was going back home, man . . .'

'The fuck we are. We ain't finished yet. We're going to spread out, keep our eyes open. Try and catch up with these mothers again, even if we're out all fucking night, getting pissed on. I'll take the road south – you take the one back north.' He snarled at Hector and Ronnie, 'You two fucking assholes head inland. Anybody sees the dude and his bitch, they get in touch *straight away*, you hear?'

61

Washington, DC
13 November
11.55 a.m.

Nikki woke with a blinding headache. The room was a blur, her mind groggy as she tried to take in her surroundings. Then slowly her senses began to recover.

Her left arm throbbed. She saw that the lower part was heavily bandaged, and when she put her right hand to her brow she felt the dressing around her forehead. Her face and eyes seemed swollen, and a couple of drips fed into her left arm. She could remember the blast, the wall of heat and flame bursting towards the restaurant, could remember being blown off her feet by the incredible force, holding on to Daniel's hand, Jack beside her . . . and then blackness.

'*Daniel . . . !*' Her son's name came out in a scream as she was overcome by an appalling feeling of dread, her eyes filling with tears. What had happened to him? Was he alive, was he dead? '*Daniel . . . !*'

The next moment a nurse's friendly face was leaning over her, checking one of the drips in her arm. 'It's OK, honey. Your little boy's being looked after. You just rest for now. How are you feeling?'

'Where's my son?' Nikki dug her fingers desperately into the woman's hand. '*I want to see him now.* Where is he? What's happened to him?'

The nurse gently prised Nikki's hand away, her voice full of concern. 'The doctor's going to talk to you about Daniel, honey. I'll go get him right away.'

The White House
1.05 p.m.

Harry Judd stood in the centre of the Oval Office, hands on his hips, watching patiently as a Secret Service agent used a hand-held electronic detector to scour the room: checking the walls, the furniture, every item of equipment, the portraits on the walls, even the President's chair, desk and phones. After five minutes, the man switched off the device. 'Nada, as usual, Harry. We're squeaky clean.'

Judd had already checked the situation room. Every phone and socket, every wall, every chair. The table, the floors, the ceiling, the sound system, the TV monitors – every inch of wood and plaster, every single nook and cranny. All negative, as Judd had expected. But that didn't mean a bug *hadn't* been planted, which was a worrying option he had to consider.

Someone could have installed an ESID, removed it before the Secret Service carried out their electronic countermeasures, and then reinstalled it again afterwards. Except for that to happen someone had to have intimate knowledge of exactly *when* the rooms would be scanned, and that, Judd knew, would be pretty much impossible. Apart from the deliberate irregularity of the countermeasure sweeps, a number of people – from the Director all the way down to Judd himself – could order a specific room, or the entire mansion and its wings, swept on a whim or the merest suspicion.

No, he was pretty certain the rooms were clean. *Which means that whoever the source is, they aren't getting their information using electronic means.*

Judd nodded to his colleague. 'OK, Chuck, give it one more sweep, just to be absolutely certain. Then pack up.'

The man frowned. 'Are we looking for something in particular, Harry?'

Judd shook his head. *That* information he kept secret.

Washington, DC
12.20 p.m.

Collins woke. He'd slept fitfully, tossed and turned, his sleep disturbed by nightmares. When he checked his watch, he realised he'd been asleep for only four hours. He got out of bed, his legs feeling like jelly for the first few steps to the apartment living room. If he'd been able to think about it, he would have marvelled at the fact that he was still functional after only four hours' sleep in thirty-six. But what his mind didn't know his body did: he still felt shaky, on the verge of collapse.

The first thing he did was check his phone and cellphone for messages. There were none. Then he called the hospital. While he was waiting to be put through to the critical-care unit, it occurred to him that he should call Nikki's mother, tell her what had happened, in case she didn't already know: he'd do it before he left the apartment. A few moments later he was put through to a duty nurse, but she told him Nikki was still resting and that there was no change in Daniel's condition.

When he put down the receiver he was trembling. He looked in the mirror. His eyes were haunted, dark and bloodshot. He felt bands of tension across his chest and forehead, and his head throbbed with anxiety. He sucked oxygen deep into his lungs, slowed his racing heartbeat, then rubbed his temples, trying to calm his jangling nerves.

His tortured dreams had been of Nikki and Daniel, of Sean and Annie. And of facing Mohamed Rashid and exacting his retribution. For so long he'd felt no emotion. As if each tear he'd shed for his wife and son had carried away with it a small amount of feeling. But now he was feeling again, and with a malignant intensity. His life, and the people in it whom he loved, had again been ravaged by the same man. The need for revenge incited a cold rage in him that he knew only someone's death could assuage. He would control it, but it would also control him. He would not feel like a whole man again until he was purged of it. Only then could he find peace.

Ten minutes later he had showered, dressed and strapped on his gun. He grabbed his car keys, but before he headed to the lobby he called Morgan. His cellphone answered on the first ring. 'How you feeling, Jack?'

'I've got a headache you wouldn't believe.'

'Couldn't sleep?'

'Not much. Any news?'

'Our guys called at Karla Sharif's old address in New York and visited her former neighbours. It was so far back most of them could hardly remember the family ever living there, and those that did were sure they hadn't seen her around. She's got no relatives Stateside that we could find.'

'Anything else?'

'We turned up about two dozen properties in Maryland rented to Arab tenants, mostly families. They're all clean, and pretty much above suspicion, except for one Yemeni guy we pulled in for questioning who's been in the country about six months. The car in his garage turned out to be stolen. But he's scared shitless and being co-operative. It turns out he bought the car off a dodgy lot over in Baltimore. The guy's dumb, but he's no terrorist, Jack.'

'What about the cargo manifests, the ports and airports?'

'Still negative. There's a million ways they could have got their stuff in, Jack, we both know that. We could crack it, for sure, if we had the time and the manpower. But we haven't got either. It's getting to the stage where I'd give my left nut for a single good lead. Any word from the hospital?'

'There's no change, Lou. Where's Kursk?'

'Made a phone call about an hour ago and then disappeared. Haven't seen him since.'

'Where the hell did he go?'

'Didn't say. Just that he'd be back soon.'

George Washington Hospital
12.30 p.m.

'I'm Dr Bill Wolensa, Miss Dean. I operated on Daniel.'

The doctor wore an old Aran sweater, jeans and sneakers. He was unshaven, his hair ruffled, as if he'd just been roused from bed. He offered Nikki a faint smile, rubbed his stubble. 'Sorry about my appearance. It's been a hectic night and I've been trying to grab a few hours' sleep in one of the staffrooms down the hall.'

When the nurse had returned to tell her the doctor was coming, Nikki had insisted on getting out of bed. The nurse protested, but Nikki had her way. She sat on a chair, feeling shaky, the tubes still attached. Her nerves were fraught as Wolensa picked up her chart, studied it. 'You seem to be doing OK. You feeling all right? Don't worry about the facial bruises and the arm, they'll heal . . .'

'What about Daniel, Doctor . . . ?'

Wolensa put down the chart, pulled up the other chair, turned it round, sat. He rubbed his eyes with a thumb and forefinger before looking up. 'Not too good, I'm afraid.'

Nikki's heart sank. Her knuckles were bone white, gripping her gown as Wolensa explained everything. 'Your little boy's been through the mill. He's stable, but he hasn't really improved. It's the spleen we're worried about. We're monitoring him all the time and the one good thing I can tell you is that he hasn't got worse. But he hasn't got better either.'

Nikki put her head in her hands.

'Miss Dean . . . I told your partner, Mr Collins – I'm assuming he's your partner – that the paramedics got Daniel here just in time. Any later and we wouldn't have had any hope at all. So at least there's that to be grateful for.'

Nikki looked up, wiped her eyes. 'When can I see him?'

'I'm afraid that's impossible right now.' The doctor explained why. 'I'm really sorry, but it wouldn't be good for Daniel. Even if he woke and saw you looking in, he might only get upset that his mom couldn't be by his side. And it's him we have to think about, don't you agree?'

Nikki gave a weak nod. The doctor's answer didn't lessen her torment. She felt a desperate need to be with her son. 'What . . . what about Jack?'

'You mean Mr Collins? He had a couple of cracked ribs, some concussion, cuts and bruises. But otherwise he's going to be OK.'

'Can I see *him*?'

'I'm afraid he's not here.'

'What . . . what do you mean?'

'I spoke with him this morning, about seven. He was anxious to know about you and your son. Then it seems he discharged himself without consulting the medical staff.'

'Where did he go?'

'I've no idea. His concussion is still a cause for concern. Really, he should be in hospital.'

The thought crossed Nikki's mind that Jack might have returned to FBI Headquarters. 'Do you know what caused the explosion, Doctor?'

Wolensa shrugged. 'Only what one of the staff told me when they heard the latest news bulletin. It seems it was deliberate, a massive truck bomb that wrecked part of the Hoover building. No one's claimed responsibility. The FBI are speculating that it might have been a Patriot group. Some patriots. The survivors' injuries were horrific. There're at least thirteen dead and several others missing.'

'Please, Doctor, I *really* need to see Daniel. You can't understand the worry I'm going through . . .'

'I can only try to, Miss Dean.' Wolensa shook his head, sighed at the desperation in Nikki's voice. 'Perhaps later we can arrange for one of the nurses to let you see him through the glass, though only for a couple of moments. But right now, he's in good hands, I want you to know that, and we're doing our very best.'

Nikki was numb as Wolensa put a hand on her shoulder in an attempt to reassure her. She didn't feel encouraged, rather lost, and scared. Terribly scared. The doctor's hand fell away. 'If you'll excuse me now, I've got some other patients to check on.'

When he had left, Nikki slumped in the chair. She was too shocked to move. At that moment she just wanted to hold Daniel, feel his tiny body close to hers, smother him with love. Her anguish felt like a knife stuck in her chest, almost too much to bear, and she was close to breaking point. She suddenly understood the intensity of grief Jack must have felt when he'd lost Sean, and she wanted to cry, as much for him as for herself.

What had happened to Jack? Why had he discharged himself? Where had he gone? She fumbled on her bedside locker, searching for her cellphone to call him, but it wasn't there, nor were her clothes. She desperately wanted to call her editor, call anyone, tell them that her senses were screaming out that something was terribly wrong in this city and that people had a right to know. And she wanted to call her mother; she didn't want to upset her, but she had to tell her about Daniel.

She tried to concentrate, but she was agitated, her thoughts jumbled, interrupted by her concern for Daniel. She remembered the military activity at Reagan, and the warehouse near Daniel's preschool. She remembered the police exercise and Brad Stelman's suspicion that he was being followed, his fear that something odd was happening in the District. She remembered Jack's discomfort when she had questioned him. Above all, she remembered the horrendous explosion. They all added up in her tormented mind as in some way connected, telling her that something frightening *was* going on. What that something was she didn't know.

She thought: *I have to tell someone.* If she could find her cellphone she could call her editor. Tell him what she knew, get an investigative team working on it, and once they found out what was happening, plaster it all over the paper.

She was still agitated when the nurse returned, insisting she get back into bed. 'I . . . I need my cellphone. I have to call someone,' Nikki begged.

'I'll find it for you, honey. But for now, just do as I ask, or we're both going to get into big trouble.' The nurse guided her into bed. 'Your mom called, she's on her way over. She sounded pretty upset and wanted to see you, but the doctor says you've got to relax, so it's no use you being in a state, that won't do anybody any good. I'll give you something to help.'

The nurse made her swallow a couple of yellow pills with a glass of water. In a little while the sedative flooded Nikki's veins, overwhelmed her, and she closed her eyes and surrendered to darkness again.

62

Chesapeake
6.30 p.m.

At the cottage in Winston Bay the rain was still coming down in sheets. The Plymouth wasn't anywhere to be seen. When they went inside the cottage, Gorev piled a few logs on the fire and touched a match to some knots of old newspaper. As the logs started to blaze, he peeled off his motorcycle leathers and left them to dry.

'At least we've got the place to ourselves.' He removed his shirt, and Karla helped him change his dressing, while he examined the wound, before she put on a fresh bandage. 'The stitches seem all right and it hasn't bled again. It must be healing.'

'Has the pain gone?'

'Almost.' Gorev smiled. 'But a drink might help.'

Karla finished what she was doing, threw the soiled dressing on the fire, then went into the kitchen. She came back with the bottle of vodka and two glasses, placed them on the coffee table, and turned on the TV, flicking through the channels with the remote. Gorev said, 'What are you looking for?'

'News about the blast.'

'Don't torture yourself, Karla.'

She flicked the remote anyway, until she found the CNN news channel. A correspondent stood behind a police barrier near the end of 10th Street, microphone in hand, giving a live update on the damage to the FBI Headquarters and nearby buildings, his report peppered with details of the dead and injured.

As Gorev poured them each a vodka, he failed to notice the expression sweeping across Karla's face as she watched the TV. It remained there just an instant, a strange, distant gaze full of compassion and horror, fear and disgust. Gorev finished pouring, offered her a drink. 'Here, steady your nerves.'

'No, suddenly I don't feel like it, Nikolai.' Tension braided Karla's face as she flicked off the TV.

Gorev said, 'You look exhausted. Maybe you should try and sleep for a few hours?'

She didn't answer, crossed to the window, looked out at the rain lashing the glass, her face white. Gorev went to join her, touched her shoulder, gently turned her round. 'Tell me what the matter is.'

'I keep thinking about the people who were killed last night. Fathers, mothers, sons, daughters. It's just more senseless slaughter.'

Gorev put down his glass, looked into her face. 'You shouldn't blame yourself, Karla. It was Rashid's bloody handiwork, nothing to do with us.'

'Wasn't it? We're part of this too. There's no use saying we're innocent, Nikolai.'

'Don't lump us in with Rashid and his friends. We have different motives.'

'But it all comes down to the same thing in the end. Could you really live with yourself if Rashid sets off the device? We both know he's crazy enough to do it.'

'That's not going to happen. He'll follow his orders. Besides, the Americans have already agreed to the terms. We've won, we're getting what we wanted. And when the time comes, the device will be disarmed.'

'What if it goes off accidentally in the meantime? Have you thought of that? What if the streets are filled with thousands of dead and dying, something far worse than anything that happened last night? Would it have been worth it, Nikolai?'

There was a bitterness, an anger, in her voice Gorev had never heard before. 'What's got into you, Karla? Are you having second thoughts again?'

Karla shook her head, stress showing in her eyes. 'I really don't want to talk about it. Some day perhaps, if we ever come through this alive, but not now, not tonight.'

Gorev put a hand out to her face. 'I'm getting worried about you, you know that?'

'Don't be.' Karla took his hand away. 'And now, if you don't mind, I think I'll get some sleep.'

Washington, DC
1.15 p.m.

The Russian embassy on Wisconsin Avenue is one of the largest in Washington, a post-modern structure of glass and burnished steel, with banks of satellite communications dishes and aerials bristling on the roof. When the cab pulled up, Kursk paid the driver and approached the embassy's bullet-proof security booth. He showed his ID and passport, explained his business, and the guard on duty made a call to the main building.

As he waited, Kursk noticed a couple of private security vans parked in the embassy grounds, a handful of staff wheeling out trolleys laden with heavy cardboard boxes, helping to load them into the vans. The guard came back, handed him his ID and passport and pressed an electronic buzzer, opening the metal gate to admit him. 'You're expected, Major. First Secretary Lazarev will meet you in reception.'

Washington, DC
1.30 p.m.

Next on Harry Judd's list were the log books.

They were the records agents kept of their activities while on protection duty – the schedule of the protectee who was in their custody, the times, dates and places where the agents had accompanied them on official duty. But the agent logs divulged more than that – invariably they showed up the habits of the protectee, their routines, their absences, any unusual incidents. If any one of the NSC had strayed from their usual patterns of activity, then there was a good chance it would be revealed in the log books. Judd had a feeling that they might be the key.

He entered the drab, greystone Victorian-era, Old Executive Building across the street from the West Wing, where the Secret

Service had their White House bureau, and took the elevator up. Darlene, the down-to-earth Texan woman who ran the office, looked up, smiled cheerfully. 'Harry, how's it hanging?'

'No longer than usual, Darlene. The log books for the last month, I'd like to see them.'

'Which ones?'

'All of 'em.'

Washington, DC
1.31 p.m.

Vladimir Lazarev's office was bristling with activity when he led Kursk in. There was an air of controlled panic as a couple of embassy clerks grabbed armfuls of documents from Lazarev's filing cabinets and stacking them on trolleys out in the hall.

'You'll have to excuse us, Major. Things are rather hectic. Leave us, please.' Lazarev snapped his fingers, dismissing the clerks, then closed his door to ensure their privacy, gesturing Kursk to a seat.

'What brings you here, Major?' Lazarev, the First Secretary, was a Muscovite, a thin handsome man with busy blond eyebrows and a fondness for expensive Western suits. 'If I'm not mistaken, the agreement was that you passed me your information over our secure phone line?'

'I needed to discuss something urgent, in person.'

'You couldn't have chosen a worse time. It's bedlam here. So what is it, Kursk? Has there been a fresh development in the hunt?'

'I'm afraid not.' Kursk glanced towards Lazarev's filing-cabinet drawers. Several were pulled open, and stacks of files were lying on the floor. There was still bustle in the hallway outside, the sounds of staff moving trolleys along the corridor. 'You mind me asking what's going on?'

For a second or two Lazarev studied him as if he were completely mad, then he lit a Camel cigarette from a packet on his desk. 'In case you hadn't realised it, Kursk, there are less than twenty-four hours to the new deadline. For safety reasons, we're moving our staff and their families to our consulates in San Francisco and New York, along with important embassy documents. Too many things can go wrong, especially at this late stage. And Abu Hasim is a madman. Even if all his demands are satisfied, it wouldn't be beyond him to detonate his device.'

'Surely the press will get to hear of this?'

Lazarev shook his head, drew anxiously on his cigarette. 'No one working in this building is privy to what's really happening, except the ambassador and myself. Our Russian staff have been informed that important building work is being carried out over the next few weeks. We also spun them a story that there's been a security leak of epic proportions, and the embassy and their private homes will be swept for electronic listening devices. Naturally, they were instructed to keep the entire matter completely secret. It's caused a fair amount of upset, but it's as good an excuse as any, I suppose, and they may yet be grateful their lives were saved. Anyway, what can I do for you? You said it was urgent.'

Kursk explained. When he had finished, Lazarev's eyebrows rose and he stubbed out his cigarette. 'What the devil are you up to, Kursk?'

'I thought I made myself clear.'

Lazarev sighed. 'You're grasping at straws, Major. And isn't it a bit late in the day? If you had more time, perhaps it might be a worthwhile hunch to explore. But we're fast approaching the end of the line.'

'Can you help me?'

Lazarev shrugged, picked up his phone. 'Our resident SVR officer is Colonel Gromulko. He knows this city like the back of his hand, and anyone of importance. Let me give him a call.' Lazarev buzzed an internal number, spoke for a few moments, then replaced the receiver. 'Gromulko will see you in his office. I'll take you up there. But I have the feeling you're wasting your energy.' He wrote a number on a slip of paper, stood. 'If there's any change in the situation, or you run into trouble, call this secure number at our New York office. The line's manned around the clock. They'll pass on any message you have, directly to Moscow.'

Kursk rose. 'When do you leave?'

'We'll have the building emptied by six p.m. I'm booked on a flight to Moscow, leaving two hours later, along with the ambassador – the story is we've been recalled for urgent talks about our security leak. Our families flew out late this morning. I'm afraid I don't have much faith that this whole nasty business will have an agreeable outcome. Either way, and with a deranged lunatic like Abu Hasim involved, the feeling I get from Moscow is that it could turn into a massive human catastrophe, especially after what happened last night. So I think it's wise I get as far away from here as I can, don't you?' Lazarev's face was bleak as he led his visitor to the door. 'If you have any sense, Kursk, you'll do the same.'

Chesapeake
6.40 p.m.

Karla lay in the dark, listening to the rain outside. The window was open, moonlight flitting into the bedroom from between charcoal clouds, flashes of fork lightning far out on the bay. She heard the door open and Nikolai stood there. He said softly, 'Can I come in?'

'If you want.'

Her hair was tousled and there was something childlike about her face in the lunar light as Gorev went to sit on the end of the bed. He noticed that her eyes were wet. 'What's really the matter, Karla? Are you angry, hurt in some way?'

She shook her head. 'Just frightened.'

'Why?'

'What Rashid did last night, it's like a bad omen, as if there's much worse to come. More senseless death. More destruction.'

'Karla, that's just superstitious. You Arabs . . .'

'No, it's more than that, goes deeper. Maybe I've suddenly

realised everything about this is deadly serious. Now it's not a game any more. But it's not only that that makes me afraid. I have the feeling we're both doomed, no matter what the outcome. That I'll never see Josef again. But what can we expect? People like you and me, we can never escape our past.'

'What do you mean?'

'If you kill someone, or harm them, you pay a price for the wrong you do. It's a different price for different people. It doesn't matter if the killing or the wrong is just or unjust, you still pay the price. And there are a dozen currencies you can pay in. You might end up tainted or infected by the very people you hate. Or perhaps you are haunted by what you've done, or end up paying with your own life. I learned that lesson when my husband was killed. It was the price he'd paid for the wrongs he did for his cause. Just as I'm paying now for what I did.'

'And how do you think you'll pay for this?'

'I don't know. I hide behind my fragile piece of armour, telling myself that I had to do it, if only for Josef's sake.'

'I believe in what I'm doing. That's my armour.'

'And that's where we're different, Nikolai. But believe me, we'll both pay.'

'You want to forget about all this? Get out while you can?'

'Somehow I think it's gone too far for that. Where could I run?'

She tried to tell him everything, her fears, even her secret, but the words wouldn't come. What was the point? She had kept her silence for so long.

'What is it, Karla?'

She shook her head. 'Nothing.'

'You're not telling me the truth.' He saw it in her face then, a terrible fear, and it made her look very young and vulnerable. He touched her cheek, looked into her eyes. 'My poor Karla.'

Her arms went around his neck and she held him tightly. He moved under the covers beside her, and she pulled him close for warmth and comfort, and then suddenly, for no reason at all that made any kind of sense, she was crying, a deep sobbing that racked her whole body. 'Karla, what is it?'

She didn't reply for a moment and then she said, 'Do you want to know why I agreed to help Rashid?'

'Only if you want to tell me.'

She told him, and she was still crying when she had finished. In the darkness Gorev's face was white with anger, and then he whispered, 'It's all right, Karla. It's all right.'

He stroked her hair until her tears stopped. Then he held her gently, silent in the dark, until she finally fell asleep.

63

Washington, DC
7.45 p.m.

In the corner booth of a strip bar on 14th Street, wearing his Ray-Bans and sipping malt whisky, Benny Visto watched as two young women danced naked on a tiny stage. 'Good ass on that new chick.'

Frankie, beside him, swilled a beer. 'Want me to ask her over, Benny?'

Visto shook his head. 'Seems like little Ricky's back.'

The bar door had opened and Ricky Cortez appeared, looking like a drowned rat, his hair and clothes drenched as he dashed in from the rain. He saw Visto and Frankie, gave a nod, and scurried over to join them in the booth.

'Fuck you been doing, man?' Frankie grinned. 'Someone dump you in the Potomac?'

'It ain't funny, Frankie. So shut the fuck up.' Cortez gave Frankie a stare, then looked at Visto, the stare gone, replaced by fear. 'We lost them, Benny. The cunts disappeared. We followed them all the way to fucking Chesapeake. They twigged us – it was Hector and Ronnie's fault. That's the last time I work with those pair of assholes. They couldn't follow a fucking truck in two feet of snow.'

Visto put down his drink. 'You've displeased me, Ricky.' Slowly, he removed his Ray-Bans. 'Sent you on a job and you messed up. Warned you about that.'

Ricky saw Visto's eyes narrow, a look that Frankie liked to call the 'laser stare', always a sure sign of trouble. 'Benny, listen, I swear . . .'

Visto gave him a stinging slap across the face. The Cuban reeled back in the booth, clapping a hand on his jaw.

'Mess up again and you and me's going to have to part company. So just listen good. Man that I am, I'm going to give you a second chance. To redeem yourself, so to speak.' Visto took a map from his inside pocket and unfolded a sheet of paper on which was a hand-drawn diagram. 'Frankie here, now he's been more productive. Took a drive out to Piedmont, where we make the delivery, checked it out good. Made sure we're not walking into anything we can't handle. Man even drew us a diagram.' Visto stabbed the map with a finger. 'You know this place, Ricky?'

'Yeah, I know the crossroads.'

'What I want you to do is go get Hector again. Man might be useless at tailing but he's ace with a gun. Grab yourselves a couple of the silenced submachineguns we got stashed in his place. Get Ronnie, too, I'll want him to drive the van.' Visto again traced a finger on the diagram. 'Then take your pick-up and drive out past the forest, park a hundred yards beyond the entrance to the track, right here, in off the road. Make your way back to the clearing, right about here. Stay hidden in the woods and keep well out of sight. Be there by nine-thirty at least, an hour before the meet. If anyone shows up, you and Hector make fucking sure you keep your heads down and call me, otherwise just wait for me and Frankie to arrive. Got that?'

A slow grin spread across Ricky's face. 'I got it, Benny. What about the van?'

'Ronnie, he'll be at the wheel. We'll have the uniforms and stuff stashed in the back. Me, I'll be in Frankie's car. Ronnie will stick to our ass, but a safe enough distance behind in case the cops pull him over and find all the guns and shit.'

'So what happens?'

'Me and Frankie'll get to the clearing bang on time. I do the business and get the dude's cash. When it's time to boogie I'll shout, and you and Hector come out and cover him and whoever he's with. Leave the rest to me.' Visto handed Ricky the diagram. 'Better take this, make sure you know what you're doing. Give me a call on Frankie's car phone half an hour before the meet, let me know you're in place and everything's cool.' Visto fixed Ricky with another of his laser stares. 'No fuck-ups this time, Ricky, you dig?'

'Got it, Benny. For sure.' Ricky took the diagram, a vicious smile on his face at the thought of what lay ahead, then sidled out of the booth and headed for the door. Frankie drained his beer. 'What you gonna do if the dude don't play ball, Benny?'

Visto's jaw tightened with malice. 'Him and that bitch of his, they're gonna wish they never heard of Benny Visto, that's for sure.'

Washington, DC
2.30 p.m.

The restaurant off Dupont Circle specialised in Mediterranean food. The walls were covered with the usual photo gallery of famous Hollywood stars – Pacino, De Niro, Pesci – with a couple of limelight politicians, baseball players and Italian opera singers thrown in.

Seven years earlier the former Tuscan owner had sold the place lock, stock, and barrel, and retired to Miami to lie on the beach. The new owner – a thickset, muscular man in his early forties, with Slavic cheekbones, a limp and a badly fitting wig – had kept the photographs, the Mediterranean menu, and most of the clientèle.

That afternoon, at precisely 2.30, he was behind the bar checking some till receipts when the phone rang on the wall outside the kitchen. When he picked it up, the male caller didn't give a name, but he recognised the voice. A minute later the owner was in a foul mood as he put down the phone, pulled on his coat, then went into the kitchen and beckoned his chef. 'I've got to go out for an hour. Look after the place.'

'Where are you going, boss?'

'Mind your own fucking business.'

Washington, DC
2.45 p.m.

The park on Church Street, five minutes' walk from Dupont Circle, was empty that afternoon, apart from a few vagrants sitting on the benches, or wrapped up in sleeping bags to keep out the cold. Kursk was seated on one of the benches under a birch tree, dead leaves blowing around his feet.

He looked up as the man approached. The limp and badly fitting wig that were Viktor Suslov's trademarks were offset by an expensive suit and camel-hair overcoat. He sat down beside Kursk, but didn't offer his hand. 'It's been a long time, Major. Ten years at least.'

'I see you've finally bought yourself a decent suit, Viktor. Life must be good.'

Suslov shrugged. 'I can't complain.'

'Colonel Gromulko tells me you've done well since you quit working the black markets back home. A half-dozen restaurants. An import-export business. A wholesale jewellery outfit, to name but a few. I could go on, but the rest of it's highly illegal.'

Suslov grinned, lit a cigarette, cupping a gold lighter in his hands. 'Business is business. And besides, it's a lot more civilised here – the competition's less brutal. You have a falling out with someone and they don't throw a rubber tyre around your neck and set it alight with petrol, like the hard men in Moscow.' Suslov cocked his head. 'You're a long way from FSB Headquarters, Kursk. So what brings you to this neck of the woods?'

'I'm looking for a man, and I need your help. Or didn't Gromulko tell you?'

Suslov grimaced, shook his head. 'That bastard at the embassy told me nothing, except to meet you. He's the kind who can make life difficult if you don't keep in his favour. This man you're looking for, is he Moscow mafia?'

'No, but he's Russian. Half-Russian to be precise.'

'And the other half?'

'Chechen.'

Suslov sucked on his cigarette, tapped some ash. 'We don't get too many of those around these parts. A few, but most of them prefer to hang out over in Little Russia, New Jersey. You've heard of the place?'

'Yes, I've heard of it.'

'A lot of old hands from the Moscow underworld operate out of there. Russians, Chechens, Georgians, you name them, and into anything you'd care to mention – diamond smuggling, prostitution, drugs. So what's this man done? Killed someone? Run off with the Tsar's jewels?'

'I can't tell you that, Suslov. But he's an old friend. Someone whose welfare I'm concerned about. The man's name is Nikolai Gorev. He's been wounded and he's in trouble and I want to help.'

'And you think I can help you find him?'

'You've got connections. Our embassy friend assured me of that.'

'If you've got a name, why don't you go to the police?'

'The FBI are already involved. But I need to find Gorev before they do.'

'I don't understand.'

'You don't have to. Just that I need to find him, fast. I'm talking hours, not days. How many Russian and Chechen mobsters do you know of on the East Coast?'

Suslov shrugged. 'Close to a dozen big names.'

'Such as?'

'Dimitri Zavarzin, the diamond smuggler, and Matvei Yudenich, the big drugs tsar, to name but two. They flit between here and Russia to do their business. You probably ran into them back in Moscow.'

Kursk nodded. The FSB often had the unpleasant task of keeping Russia's gangland bosses in check, foiling their illegal operations, confiscating their property, and arresting their men. 'Yudenich is a nasty piece of work. A psychopath. He threatened to shoot me once, after I ruined one of his heroin deals.'

'Then you'll understand that people like Yudenich and the rest of them don't take kindly to enquiries from men like you. I can give you their names, how to contact them, sure, and you can go ask them, but if you take my advice you won't go messing with that lot. They'd have a tyre round your neck as quick as look at you.'

'I won't be doing the asking, Suslov. You will.'

'You must be fucking joking.'

Kursk shook his head. 'Make the calls and put the word around. Concentrate first off on the people who matter, the big mobsters, then work you way down the list. Give Gorev's name and explain what I told you. See if you get a reaction. Mention me by name if you really have to.'

'I could be nailing myself in a coffin doing that. There are mobsters I know who'd take the greatest pleasure in bumping off a nosey FSB officer, or anyone who's doing their bidding. What the fuck's in it for me?'

'A solemn promise. Gromulko tells me there's a file on you as thick as his arm. Crooked dealings with that import-export business of yours that the Russian tax authorities and Moscow police would like to chat with you about. Do as I ask and the file vanishes. Don't, and you'll be in cuffs and on a plane back to Moscow by nine o'clock tonight, helped on your way by the FBI.'

Suslov's mouth was tight with resentment.

'There's a number where you can reach me.' Kursk handed him a slip of paper. 'I'll expect your call no later than six o'clock.'

'That only gives me three fucking hours. What if I can't find this guy?'

'I don't think you want to know the answer to that, Suslov.'

64

Washington, DC
3.05 p.m.

Collins spent the best part of the afternoon checking around the offices of the teams working the District's streets, to see whether there were any leads he could follow up. Dozens had already warranted investigation.

That morning, just before ten, a known petty thief had fingered two young Arab-looking men he'd spotted buying heroin from a dealer on 14th Street. After following the men back to a Holiday Inn several blocks away, the thief had called his FBI contact. An undercover team had been dispatched, along with two technicians. With the hotel manager's help, the room next door to the Arabs' was taken over, their phone tapped, several 'scope' probes passed through some holes drilled in the walls to help observe the suspects, together with sensitive listening devices. The two men had taken the heroin and lain on their beds to enjoy their trip. Later, at lunch-time, when they left the hotel to visit a local grocery store, their room had been entered and searched, their personal belongings gone through, and their identities verified – the suspects were no more than the errant sons of DC-based Arab diplomats, indulging in some recreational drug-taking.

A small warehouse recently rented in Georgetown was watched by another undercover team from the Secret Service, and turned up a racket in stolen electrical goods run by a Palestinian immigrant and an American-born accomplice. A tip-off from a prostitute about the 'suspicious' occupant of a lodging house in the south-east district had led to the arrest of an escaped convict, on the run for over two years.

Then there were the tip-offs that deliberately wasted valuable time: people on the street with grudges or scores to settle, who wanted to make trouble for real or imagined enemies. Who wanted to ingratiate themselves with the FBI or Secret Service, or hoped for a pay-off for their 'help'. Pimps and hustlers, gang members, petty thieves and prostitutes had given numerous false leads, but they still had to be run down. Agents were still pounding the streets, trying to wheedle information, but up to now everything had drawn blanks. Everything and anything was turning up except the *right* information.

Outside the District, Collins knew that farmhouses, barns, silos, storage depots, warehouses and deserted buildings of any kind had been visited, and when investigated and cleared were scratched off the list that had been drawn up with the help of the tax authorities and government agencies. The same for chemical suppliers, farms that purchased larger-than-usual quantities of organophosphates, and cropdusting businesses. Almost eighty per cent of the list had already been cleared.

Within the twenty-five-mile radius of the teenagers' murder site in Maryland, occupants of rental properties had been discreetly visited by FBI agents posing as insurance salesmen or disguised as pizza delivery staff or telephone repair engineers, their job being to get a close look at the tenants and report back on anyone suspicious or remotely resembling the suspects.

Hundreds of Arab, Chechen and Palestinian illegals had also been tracked down, and their identities and activities established. Hundreds more remained on the register, dozens of whom were believed to be still unaccounted for in the District, or nearby Virginia and Maryland.

Most Bureau investigations, like this one, were methodical, plodding affairs. Pyramid shaped, they started from a wide base and proceeded up, by relentless investigation over weeks or months, to a summit point that produced results. But Collins knew the grim, disturbing truth, one that made him feel like a man waiting for the executioner's bullet. With so little time – hours, not weeks or months – there was absolutely no way they were going to get through everything before the deadline.

* * *

Tom Murphy came into the office just after 3 p.m.. His pallor was grey, his eyes bloodshot from lack of proper sleep, his shirt and tie askew. He poured a glass of water for himself and slumped into a chair. His voice shook.

'I've just had a meeting with the Assistant Director and the department heads. It's panic stations, Jack. Everyone's in a state of near-hysteria that we can't crack this. The Assistant Director's getting calls from the White House every half-hour, wanting to know what progress we've made, if we've any news. That tells you what kind of a state they're in over at the mansion.' Murphy took a couple of Tylenol from his pocket, swallowed them down with the water, massaged his brow. 'My head's fit to burst. This keeps up, they're going to carry me out of here in a box, long before midnight. Where's Lou and the major?'

'Lou's trying to grab some sleep in one of the offices. Kursk went out more than three hours ago and hasn't come back.'

'He say where he was going?'

'Lou said he didn't. Just that he'd be back.'

'Maybe you should call his apartment?'

The door opened and Agent Larry Soames appeared, clutching some sheets of computer print-out paper. 'Tom, you got a minute?'

'What is it, Larry?'

'We've got a problem. We've still got twenty-three Palestinian, Arab and Chechen-born illegals to try and locate, establish what they've been doing. We've also got a dozen more rental properties – three apartments, twelve houses – that turned up on the books of a small real estate firm in Prince's County that we missed earlier.'

'What's the problem?'

'Manpower, as usual.' Soames handed Murphy the sheets. 'There aren't enough bodies to get through all this shit before midnight.'

'Any of the illegals high priority?'

'At least four.'

Murphy studied the sheets, considered. 'Was the real estate agent shown the suspects' photographs?'

'That's the problem. The lucky bastard's where I'd like to be right now – sunning his ass in Bermuda. We spoke to his secretary over the phone, but she only joined the firm a couple of months back and didn't have anything to do with vetting the tenants, and says she hasn't seen any of them in the flesh, doesn't know if any of them are Arab. Most of the properties are along the Chesapeake coast, and a few are inland. She's given us a list of the tenants' names, but that means nothing – anyone can give an alias once they pay cash up front. We tried to get through to her boss at his hotel, had him paged even, but got no reply, either way. Which means we got to check all twelve.'

'How many more agents do you need?'

'At least a dozen.'

Murphy gave a frustrated sigh, stood and rubbed his throbbing forehead. 'All we've got to spare are eight guys who just finished working a double shift. Better put them on the rented properties.'

'It's not enough, Tom.'

Murphy turned crimson, his frustration exploding. 'I know it's not frigging enough, but Jesus, Larry, I'm not a frigging magician. I just can't make up the numbers, so you'll have to take what I can frigging give you and do the best with it, OK?' He ran a hand over his face, took a couple of breaths, trying to calm down, then turned to Collins. 'Jack, you and Lou take some of the illegals. Take Kursk with you if you can find him. Larry will fill you in. If something hot comes up in the meantime we'll get in touch. OK, Larry? Happy now?'

'Sure,' Larry said, deadpan. 'Ecstatic. I'm doing my frigging best too, Tom, you know. You're not the only one with frigging problems.'

As he went out the door, Morgan brushed past him, coming in. He yawned, scratched his head. 'What's got a bug up Larry's ass?'

'His temper's getting a little frayed, like the rest of us,' Murphy growled. 'You get some sleep?'

'Two hours on a floor with a coat over me.'

'That's two hours more than I've had. I've got a job for you and Jack. Larry will tell you.' Murphy started to leave, hesitated, said to Collins, 'With all that's been going on, I forgot to ask – how's Nikki and her little boy? Any change?'

Collins shook his head. 'I checked with the hospital just before you came in. I'll check later.'

Murphy put a hand on his shoulder. 'I know you're worried, Jack, but you can't do anything to help them. Our butts are to the wall, so maybe it's best you concentrate on the work. You'll be doing them both a favour.'

Washington, DC
3.35 p.m.

At the Old Executive Building, Harry Judd had spent two hours going through the protection-duty log books. The logs were sheets of computer-generated print-outs that were punch-holed and stored in black-covered loose binders.

Outside the White House, each protectee could have a half-dozen agents guarding them. Inside, protection was looser: usually down to a couple of agents slewing around the protectee in the background, but always near by, in case they were needed. If anything unusual was going to show up, Judd reckoned, it would most likely be during the closely guarded periods when the protectees were operating outside the confines of the White House.

Despite the plentiful cups of coffee Darlene brought him, by the end of the second hour Judd was getting bleary eyed reading through the hundreds of logs. He had a notebook by his side, and meticulously jotted down anything irregular he spotted. Protectees were human: like everyone else they had to stop for a leak, take detours home in case of family emergencies, or change schedules at the last minute.

But he did note that three of the NSC members had made several last-minute deviations from their external schedules. In the last month, Charles Rivermount had made three unscheduled stops at the Atlanta offices of his oil firm for urgent private meetings. Two of them, Judd noted, were with a Saudi sheikh named Nabil al-Khalid. The Arab name made Judd suspicious, and he noted that the last meeting with al-Khalid had been ten days earlier. As well as that, two days previously Rivermount had gone 'missing' for an hour. Rivermount, Judd knew, had a mistress, a Mississippi woman whom he kept in a privately rented apartment off Wisconsin Avenue. Secret Service agents had to allow for that kind of thing – whether or not they disapproved was immaterial, they were expected to use their discretion. The log noted that the agents protecting Rivermount had constantly remained near by – two at the end of the hallway outside the apartment, two in the lobby, two in a car outside. But Judd reckoned it wouldn't have been impossible for Rivermount, if he was determined enough, to slip out the back way for another rendezvous near by. Or, with his mistress's collusion, meet someone already waiting and hidden in the apartment.

Next was General Bud Horton. Unusual for a military man noted for being punctual, he had delayed official appointments on three occasions in the last two weeks. The delays were caused by private meetings in the home of another four-star general in Arlington. The agents on protection duty had remained outside the house, on Horton's instructions. Another incident had occurred when Horton – a man who hated being surrounded by 'civilian guards' – had insisted on leaving the White House alone, and out of uniform, after an NSC meeting twenty-four hours previously. Horton had said he needed air and wanted to go for a 'brisk walk'. The general sometimes had a short fuse – there had been other flare-ups Judd knew of, when Horton had complained bitterly about 'being baby-sat twenty-four hours a day and watched every time I go to the john'.

The third, and last, was Bob Rapp. He had an apartment on G Street, and on at least three occasions in the last month had insisted on entering another apartment block near by without his Secret Service protection detail accompanying him. Rapp, in his late forties, was unmarried, and a private man. Despite that he'd had public dalliances with several women over the years, although Judd had heard rumours that he was a closet homosexual. There was no overt evidence to prove it, but Judd knew that if rumours of this kind were made public they could destroy a man of Rapp's calibre and standing.

Judd didn't give a damn what the man did in his private life – that was his own business. His visits to the nearby apartment block were not part of a long-established pattern. Sure, Rapp might have a new boyfriend, but it would have to be checked out.

Judd jotted down the three names, details of the incidents, and noted the names of the agents working the duties. He was still reading through the logs when the phone rang on Darlene's desk, distracting him. 'Sure, he's here,' Darlene answered, and cupped the mouthpiece. 'It's for you, Harry.'

Judd crossed to her desk, took the receiver. 'Judd.'

'Harry, it's Rob. Making any progress?'

'Some. Got a few things I need to run down.'

'Good. Drop what you're doing and meet me down at headquarters straight away.'

'What's up?'

'Just get down here, Harry. It's about the FBI background checks. We've got something.'

65

Moscow

In the shadow of St Basil's Cathedral the chimes of the Kremlin clock were tolling 8.30 p.m. as the convoy of official cars filtered in below the east tower, then turned into the cobbled, snow-covered courtyard.

A weary Vasily Kuzmin, standing at his office window, hands behind his back, watched as the procession of vehicles began to disgorge their passengers, before the members of his council quickly made their way in through the set of double oak doors. Among them he spotted his feisty Interior Minister, Anatoli Sergeyev, the Justice Minister, Sasha Pavlov – a man known for his steely resolve – and the formidable, grey-haired General Yuri Butov, who had planned the attack on al-Qaeda's bases.

Kuzmin moved to his desk and picked up the leather folder that held his notes on the important matters he was about to discuss. A ripple of anxiety coursed through his body. It would be tough to attempt to convince men like these to change their minds: to accept the American President's carrot and agree to hand over the prisoners. In truth, Kuzmin couldn't even guess at the final vote. At that moment he wasn't even sure which way *he* would go. If there was a split vote, he might be forced to make the final decision himself. But if the decision went strongly against accepting the proposals – a very real possibility – then he knew with certainty that the order to bomb Hasim's bases into oblivion would be given once again, and probably that very night.

Tushin knocked. 'Everyone's here, sir.'

'Very good, Leonid. I'm ready to begin.'

Washington, DC
4 p.m.

Morgan was at the wheel as they drove towards Georgetown. Collins read through the computer print-out sheets on two illegals who still had to be accounted for: one was an Egyptian male medical student, aged twenty-five, the other a twenty-seven-year-old Palestinian female, a postgraduate student of English. Immigration had no record of their leaving the US after their student visas had expired in July, over four months ago. Both had attended Georgetown University and their given addresses were at cheap accommodations near the campus. It wasn't uncommon for foreign students to overstay their allotted time – chances were the two in question had broken the terms of their visas for entirely innocent reasons – but they still had to be found and accounted for. As Morgan drove along M Street, heading for the university, Collins said, 'Hang a right, Lou.'

Morgan frowned. 'The campus is straight on.'

'Take a turn for the hospital.'

'Jack . . . I know you're hurting, but you heard what Murphy said, man. Maybe it's best we just carry on. You can make a call . . .'

'I've got to see them, Lou. I've got to find out about Daniel. Please. Just do it.'

Minutes later, Morgan, silent, drove up to the entrance of the George Washington Hospital. He halted and Collins pushed open the door. 'I'll be as quick as I can.'

Moscow

The stormy meeting had gone on for even longer than Kuzmin had anticipated. Having outlined everything he'd discussed with the American President, he had broken the news of Hasim's threat to Moscow. The reaction of horror was immediately apparent on the assembled faces, and then all hell broke loose. Tempers flared and voices were raised; the anger, fear and bitterness in the Kremlin conference room were something to behold. It was the most heated meeting Kuzmin had ever sat through, and on three occasions he'd been forced to suspend the proceedings to allow tempers to subside, but it did no good.

'I told you,' Sergeyev, the Interior Minister railed bitterly. 'I told you this would happen. That it was only a matter of time.' He pointed a finger accusingly at the mole-blemished face of Boris Rudkin, the Trade Minster. 'You said Abu Hasim wasn't a direct threat to us. You said I was mad to suggest annihilating him. Now look where we are, Rudkin. We should have bombed the bastard when we had the chance, and worried about the consequences later.'

Rudkin, the moderate, was oddly silent, scratching his mole, looking under severe duress.

'And what if we had?' Finance Minister Akulev countered. 'What if Hasim was already capable of carrying out his attack? We might not be here but in the morgue, all of us.'

On it went. Arguments and counter-arguments, disagreements and harsh words, until Kuzmin, tiring of it all, deliberately raised a hand to interrupt, then shifted his gaze to General Butov, who was noticeably quiet. 'Yuri? You haven't voiced your opinion.'

'Like the Interior Minister, I expected this,' Butov answered, his anger barely controlled. 'But personally, I'm not convinced Hasim is ready to carry out an attack against Moscow. I think it's sheer bluff.'

'Why?'

'Because he would have used the threat before now. Informed us himself, at the same time as he was threatening the Americans. Also, most of the prisoners are jailed here. If Moscow was attacked, they'd be victims too.'

'You have a point.' Kuzmin open the file in his leather folder. 'And I'm inclined to agree. Just so as you're all aware, our intelligence hasn't the slightest indication of an al-Qaeda cell in the city. Isn't that true, Igor?'

'So far as we can ascertain, Mr President,' FSB chief Igor Verbatin acknowledged. 'But that's not to say our intelligence is completely infallible, or conclusive. Look at the Americans' experience. Had they any forewarning? Any credible intelligence to suggest an attack was imminent? Nor do we know if al-Qaeda would be capable of acting quickly in retaliation if we bombed their bases.'

Kuzmin sighed, looked at the others. 'Igor's right. Naturally, we'll intensify our intelligence-gathering to try and discover if the threat is a bluff or not. But that will take time and it still may not be conclusive. In the meanwhile, what are we left with? At this moment, I believe there are really only two options. We hold off our bombing, but we don't hand over the prisoners, either. Or we deal with the Americans, accept their offer.'

'But we agreed the prisoner issue wasn't negotiable,' Butov objected.

'Yet we have to admit that the Americans have made a solid and reasonable offer in return for their release.'

'But it's pure bribery,' Butov answered.

'Of course it is. But should we accept it?' Kuzmin paused. 'However, let us put that aside for now. There is also the unanswered question of how Abu Hasim *knew* we intended to bomb him.'

'Surely the American President isn't suggesting the source is one of us?' said Boris Rudkin.

'Whoever it is, obviously they have to be in a position of high authority. And the answer is no, President Booth is convinced that the source is in Washington, not Moscow.'

'Why?' asked General Butov.

'His FBI Director has taped evidence to suggest that information has been leaked by someone at high level within the White House.'

'That seems incredible.' The Justice Minister, Sasha Pavlov, looked shocked.

'It's certainly that,' Kuzmin answered, and his eyes swept around the faces in the room. 'But let me be blunt here, gentlemen.

I'm also convinced that someone in this room – for reasons of morals or fear – informed the Americans of our intention to bomb the al-Qaeda bases. As to who the culprit is, I'm certain I shall root him out – eventually.'

Kuzmin paused and let the threat hang, not at all certain that he would ever get to the bottom of the matter, but he had made his point, and for now that was sufficient. He looked pointedly at the solid hands of the gold Tsar Nicholas clock on the mantel of the ornate marble fireplace across the room: it was 11.50 already. After over three hours of intense argument and debate, and having slept poorly in the last forty-eight hours, he was physically and mentally exhausted.

'We've already overrun our time. We could spend the rest of our lives arguing the issues, but I believe the time has come to make up our minds as to whether we can accept this American offer and release the prisoners. I have deliberately avoided trying to influence you one way or another, even though your decision may also decide the fate of Washington. But that, I believe, is how it should be. So, General Butov, please, if you would do me the honour.'

Butov nodded, started taking the vote. 'Admiral Vodin?'

'I say no.'

'Interior Minister Sergeyev?'

'No,' Sergeyev replied firmly.

'Trade Minister Rudkin?'

'Yes.'

'Justice Minister Pavlov?'

'Yes.'

On it went. Kuzmin counted seven votes in favour, eight votes against accepting the American offer – including General Butov. The general turned to him. 'It's down to you, Mr President.'

Washington, DC
4.15 p.m.

Nikki had been moved into the main hospital complex. She was lying in a private single-bed room when Collins entered. The knot in his stomach came back the moment he saw her. She was no longer wired up to instruments or drips, but the enormous purple bruise that covered her right jaw hadn't subsided, and her face was still swollen. Her eyes were open but almost lifeless, staring at a television that wasn't on. A nurse had set a chair alongside the bed and Collins sat. He took Nikki's hand, and then her face turned towards his. Her eyes were full of tears. 'It's all my fault, Jack,' she whispered.

'What?'

'If I hadn't wanted to meet you last night . . . if only I hadn't been so damned persistent this wouldn't have happened. But I just had to see you, Jack . . . I was so impatient, I put my own curiosity before everything. I'm so sorry.'

For a moment Collins didn't know what to say. In her tortured mind, Nikki was blaming herself, but how could it have been her fault? 'I spoke with Dr Wolensa. He says Daniel's improved a little. His breathing's better, he's responding to the medication. Wolensa's more optimistic he's going to make it . . .'

'I know . . . but . . .'

'No buts.' He held her hand to his face, kissed it. 'He's going to be OK, Nikki. Daniel's going to be OK. So are you. That's all that matters right now. You have to hold on to that. Try and stay strong.'

Her hand closed on his like a claw. 'But I saw him, Jack. One of the nurses let me see him through the window . . . He looked so . . . beat up. So helpless . . .'

'I know.' He leaned forward to kiss her, but before their lips touched both of them started weeping. 'I love you, Nikki.'

Nikki wiped her eyes. 'Who did it, Jack? Who'd plant a bomb like that? Who'd want to kill and maim innocent people? Kids like Daniel. Who'd do that?'

Collins held on to her hand, shook his head.

'You know, don't you?'

'I . . . I can't talk about it, Nikki . . . Please.'

'Does it have something to do with what we talked about last night? It does, doesn't it?'

'Nikki . . . I'm begging you. What I said about it causing trouble if anything leaks out, I really meant it. It wouldn't be helping.'

'All that stuff we spoke about . . . the killer who machinegunned that young couple . . . it wasn't true, was it?'

'It wasn't a lie, Nikki. There's someone . . . someone deranged. He's got accomplices. We're trying to find them. That's all I can say. Please, leave it at that.'

For a moment Nikki stared back at him, studying his face, as if trying to read his thoughts, then she gave up, shook her head. 'Can I say one more thing? I remember the look on your face when you spoke about it in the restaurant. It was like a hatred it was so intense. It almost seemed like it was something deeply personal. Is it personal, Jack?'

Collins, reluctant to say any more, slowly let go of her hand. 'I don't want to go, but I've got to, Nikki.'

'I understand.'

'Do something for me? No more thoughts about it being your fault. No more of that crap, OK?' Collins stood. 'I saw your mom out in the hall. She was pretty emotional.'

'I know. She came over here as soon as you called her . . .'

'You think she'll hold up?'

'I hope so.'

'I'll have my cellphone on all the time. Call me when you want, or if you get any more news about Daniel. Will you do that?'

Nikki gave a nod. Collins leaned over, kissed her, and then he was gone.

Five minutes later, Nikki climbed out of bed. Her limbs ached, her head felt light, but she had made the decision to discharge herself, whether the hospital liked it or not. She'd already asked her mother to stay near Daniel, told her she might feel well enough to discharge herself later that afternoon, and she was to call her if there was any change in Daniel's condition, however small. Her mother had argued and disapproved of her leaving the hospital, but Nikki hadn't explained why she had to.

How could she? All she had was a strong intuition that something very, very strange and terrible was going on in the city, and she knew she had to find out what. She dreaded the thought of leaving her son's side, but just knowing that he had improved had given her hope, something to cling to.

Even thinking about that hope made her tearful, and she had to wipe her eyes. In a daze, she took her clothes from the closet in the corner and dressed. They were torn, peppered with dirt, and smelled of fire. She'd see her mother before she left, take a cab and change when she got back to her apartment. She made sure to take her cellphone and charger from the wall socket where she'd left it, and stuffed both in her pocket. Then she snapped open the door to her room and slipped out.

66

Chesapeake
7.30 p.m.

Gorev heard the sound of a car's engine pull into the driveway. He was barely dozing, his arms still around Karla. She was asleep, curled up like a child, her hair flailed across the pillow. He took his arms away from her gently and got up off the bed, his hand automatically reaching for the Beretta he'd left on the nightstand.

Crossing the landing to one of the front bedrooms, he peered though the curtain. The rain had stopped. He saw the Plymouth parked on the gravel outside the cottage, Mohamed Rashid climbing out, locking the door.

Gorev, overcome with anger, turned quickly from the window and started downstairs. He reached the bottom and was crossing to the door when it opened and Rashid came in, looking surprised to see him.

'Well, how did your meeting go with Visto?' Rashid noticed the Russian's livid expression. 'What's wrong, Gorev, is there a problem?'

'Nothing I can't handle, but we'll discuss that later.' Gorev jerked a thumb towards the living room. 'First, you and me need to have a little talk.'

The White House
4.15 p.m.

'So, have we got a damned evacuation plan, or what?'

Al Brown, the District's mayor, placed his balled fists on the vast walnut table in the Cabinet Room and stared across at Paul Burton. There were four people present: Brown, the President,

Paul Burton and Gavin G. Lord, the 'evacuation expert' for the capital.

They were seated in the sturdy brown leather chairs normally reserved for cabinet members, the names inscribed in neat brass plaques mounted behind each chair. Brown, his bald black head smooth and shining, and wearing one of his usual trademark three-piece suits and colourful yellow polka-dot bow ties, was obviously in no mood for pleasantness this afternoon, but his blunt, feisty language didn't offend the President in the slightest: he was well used to it. 'Well? Have we or have we not, Mr Burton?'

Burton, who had opened the meeting, gestured to Gavin Lord seated beside him, and picked up a heavy, blue-covered book from the table in front of him. Its title was: 'Crisis Evacuation Plan for Washington DC'. Compiled in 1996, it ran to over three hundred pages. 'I'll let Mr Lord answer that, but first of all I should point out that we already have a blueprint. This report is . . .'

'I read that report three years ago. It's not worth shit,' Brown retorted. 'I wouldn't give you two cents for it. Want to know what it's good for? All that shiny paper? Nothing. Not even for wiping your ass with.'

'I agree it's a little out of date, but there have been modifications since,' Lord offered, his face blushing. A tall, quiet-spoken man in his middle fifties, with a thin moustache, he had a shock of mousey grey hair and thick glasses. 'And it's basically an effective, well-thought-out plan.'

'Sure it is. If your balls aren't in a vice grip and you got all the time in the world to get your butt out of this city. Far as I recall, the quickest the report said that the capital could be evacuated was in thirty-six hours.'

'Well, yes . . .'

'We ain't got thirty-six hours, Mr Lord. More than likely we won't even have two hours. We've never dealt with a powerful chemical weapon like this before. The report doesn't take into account the kind of disaster we may have to face, nor the casualties we have to deal with, nor the speed with which we have to transport victims out of the affected areas and get them to emergency field hospitals . . . I could go on, you know?'

'Well, yes, I agree, but . . .'

'Mr Lord, like I said, that report there, as it stands, is not worth shit. What I want to know is, how the fuck do we clear out this city and in the quickest possible time?'

'I've spent a great deal of time studying that problem, Mr Mayor,' Lord answered.

'Then tell me. Give me a specific plan that will *work*. One that I can work *with* in case this thing goes belly up. Look, even if we find this device or that asshole Abu Hasim gets what he wants and tells us where it is, we know we're still not out of the woods. We may be faced with any number of situations: maybe the damned device is unstable, maybe Hasim decides to double-cross us and leaves it ticking away, or even if we find it maybe the experts decide there's a big risk involved in trying to disarm it. In each of those cases, it probably means we're going to have to evacuate the city rather than risk having the fucking thing blowing up in our faces.'

Silence muffled the room. Lord, unsettled by Brown's sharp language, fiddled nervously with the notes in front of him. The President gave him an encouraging nod. 'Please, go on, Mr Lord.'

'Firstly, if and when we commence our evacuation, we'll have to make all access to the city "one way" – that is, no inbound traffic except emergency vehicles, police and military transport. We'll principally use the highways and the subways for evacuation. Subway cars will run every few minutes from the District stations, working from the centre, out to the farthest points on the lines. They'll be organised in such a way that trains will be stacked up right behind one another, so that as one station fills up the carriages the train can speed straight to its end destination, but there's another one right behind it to take up the excess, and another behind that, and so on. Once they empty their human cargo, they'll be routed back along the return line to start all over again, but transporting their cargo in the opposite direction, so as not to waste time.

'Buses and trucks will be commandeered and all available military transport will be put to use. We'll be trying to keep traffic and people moving in an orderly and speedy fashion. People who aren't getting out in their own cars or under their own steam, those who are elderly, infirm or in hospitals, will be piled into whatever ambulances, buses and military trucks we can get, and trucked out of the city, like the others, to predetermined points outside the District, then we'll start all over again.

'Reagan Airport will also be used: civilian and military aircraft, police and private helicopters, and every private plane we can lay our hands on will be made available. We're assuming, obviously, that the device will be somewhere within the District quadrants. If it's not, or other areas are going to be affected, and we have to expand out, we can adapt our plans accordingly. I've already got adjustments ready in case of that situation. But the important thing in all this, obviously, is to maintain order.'

'How do we do that?' the President asked.

'We use predetermined routes for people to exit the capital. We assign certain areas to use certain freeways, and only in a certain direction. People living in the south-east of the District, for example, will be told to get on to the Eisenhower Freeway, going south-east. People in the north-east will be assigned a route going north-east, and so on. That way, we cut down on people driving off in any direction, causing traffic congestion.'

Al Brown raised a dubious eyebrow. 'You really think that in a situation like this, when people want to get themselves and their families out of this city fast, they're not going to take the route that *they* decide is quickest, and say to hell with any plan you might have?'

'We'll monitor the traffic closely, Mr Mayor. We'll have stewards along the route . . .'

Al Brown rolled his eyes, shook his head hopelessly. 'Mr Lord, in case you don't know it, there are people in this city who have guns. I'm not just talking about criminal types, punks and gangs, I'm talking about ordinary decent citizens who keep firearms for their own protection. You don't think that in a dire situation like this, when they want to get their asses out of town real quick, they're not going to use those guns to take any fucking route they want to? OK, so a steward stops them. They're not going to point that gun right up his nose and say "Fuck you, out of my way, asshole" and drive on their merry way?'

'Mr Mayor, I should have pointed out that by stewards I meant the police, as well as National Guardsmen . . .'

The President quickly cut in. 'Mr Lord, how will people know which route to take?'

'The way the FEMA plan works, sir, we broadcast our instructions over the radio and TV, and using mobile electronic message boards.'

'Not everyone's going to hear or see those messages.'

'But most will, Mr President. We'll make sure of that. And we'll already have had klaxons going off all over the city, warning people of a civil emergency.'

'What about the disabled, the infirm, who can't get out?'

Lord gave a helpless shrug. 'In cases like those, we just have to rely on their neighbours helping them to safety. It would be the same in any rapid mass evacuation, sir.'

'So what happens when we get these areas evacuated?' Al Brown asked. 'Where are we going to put the people? We can't just leave them out in the sticks or by the side of the highway, or at the end of a bus or subway line.'

'We'll have host areas set up in towns out in Maryland and Virginia. Again, much like the FEMA plan, we'll have organised tents, local schools, hotels, for temporary accommodation for the evacuees.'

Brown almost groaned. As always in his experience, plans on paper were dandy. Reality was a different fucking ball-game. 'Wait until the nice folks out in Maryland or Virginia hear they're going to play host to tens of thousands of black families from some of the District's worst drug-infested, crime-ridden ghettoes. Bet they're going to be real pleased.'

'Anything else, Mr Lord?' the President asked.

'I had thought we'd spend the next hour going through the plans in detail, Mr President. Which routes we'd use, the deployment of police and the National Guard, and so on. You might be interested in our figures for the traffic escape routes on the roads and bridges – using double lanes on each route, I'm estimating twelve hundred vehicles an hour can be progressed, with an average of four people per vehicle. Factoring in our ten major escape routes, we're hoping to move almost forty-eight thousand people an hour, and that's not accounting for those travelling on foot, by bus or subway, or in any emergency transport we provide. There's lots to cover. Like what we advise people to take with them when they evacuate: any cash they've got at home, and their personal valuables, a small amount of food and liquids, for example. I would also like to suggest the banks should be forced to close before the evacuation takes place, and that people are made aware of that in the transmitted bulletins.'

'What the hell for?' Brown asked.

'In an emergency, the first thing people tend to want to do is draw out their savings. We can't have that kind of pandemonium. Shutting the banks solves the problem. But if I could move on, sir. I'd like to spend some time going over a survey I had carried out from the air this afternoon, detailing our exit routes, and also give you precise evacuation details for the high-risk areas, get down to actual statistics and numbers in the evacuation zones, and also cover the predicted weather for the next forty-eight hours, which may be crucial . . .'

'What exactly is the forecast, Mr Lord?' the President asked.

Lord grimaced. 'Not good, from a safety point of view, sir. Clear skies, very light winds, no precipitation, mild temperatures. Conditions like that may be excellent for an evacuation, but they're damned near perfect for the dispersal of nerve gas.'

The President groaned. 'That's just great.'

'Mr Lord, if you don't mind,' Al Brown interrupted, his patience flagging, 'right now what I'm interested in is the bottom line here, and I still haven't heard it. How damned quickly can we evacuate? You said the plan had been improved on. But by how much?'

'By my calculations I think we can do it in eighteen, maybe twenty hours tops.'

'We won't *have* twenty hours.'

'I'm sorry, Mr Mayor. But I believe that's the absolute quickest it can be done.'

There was a knock on the Cabinet Room door. Paul Burton rose, went to open it, then stepped out of view to speak to someone in the hall outside. He was gone only a few seconds before he returned, closed the door, crossed back to the President, and leaned over to whisper in his ear.

The President's face paled, and then he rose from his chair with an air of gravity. 'Gentlemen, if you'll excuse me. I'm afraid something urgent's come up that requires my immediate attention.'

Chesapeake
7.40 p.m.

'You lied to me.' Gorev faced Rashid across the room.

'What if I did? If anything, Karla Sharif ought to be thankful that her son will be released. And don't tell me she doesn't want that, Gorev?'

'You're a liar, Rashid. She wasn't prepared to join us, even at that price. You forced her into it, threatened her son's life, and I was right all along. You conniving bastard.'

'I warned you before. You have no right to talk to me disrespectfully, Gorev.'

Gorev stepped closer to the Arab, stared at him, ignoring the reprimand. 'You used exactly the kind of persuasion I said you would. Embrace the cause or face your wrath. You don't deserve respect, Rashid. How do you look at yourself in the mirror? How?'

Rashid didn't flinch. 'Our mission is everything. Anything I have to do to accomplish it, I will. You think I care about a woman like Karla Sharif? She's a means to an end. As you are. As I am. We're simply pawns in this game. When will you realise that, Gorev?'

For a split second Gorev looked as if he would strike Rashid, his hostility at boiling point, but discipline got the better of him and instead of lashing out he went to grab his motorcycle leathers from beside the fire. 'And it's a game I'm getting rapidly tired of.'

'What are you saying, Gorev? You want out? You can't. It's too late for that.'

'I told you before, you'll get your pound of flesh. But after this, I'm finished with you and your lot. And don't think I haven't forgotten my promise. I told you if I found out you'd forced Karla into this you'd have me to answer to.'

'Is that another threat, Gorev?'

'Call it what you damned well want.'

As Gorev started to move towards the stairs, Rashid grabbed his arm. 'Let's put our differences aside for now, Gorev. Can't we do that at least? We're too close to the end of things, too close to getting everything we want. You said this man Visto was up to no good. That he tried to follow you. Maybe I should go along? This is too important a business to foul up. We may need the van and uniforms . . .'

'Forget it. Karla and I will handle it.' Gorev looked at Rashid's hand on his arm, then jerked it away. 'And I think I told you before – do that, and someone's liable to get hurt.'

Gorev's fist suddenly came up, struck Rashid hard across the jaw, and the Arab staggered back and hit the floor. 'That's something on account. The rest will come later, I can promise you that.'

As Gorev turned away, Rashid was up off the floor in an instant, his eyes livid. He had the ivory-handled flick-knife out and the blade sprung. Gorev turned, and in one swift movement the Beretta was in his hand, cocked, and pointed at Rashid's head. 'Try a move on me like that again and you won't live to regret it.'

Gorev skewered the Arab with a look of contempt, then lowered the Beretta and stormed up the stairs.

After he'd gone, Rashid stood there, enraged, still holding the knife in one hand, the other massaging his jaw. Hatred scoured through his veins. 'We'll see about that, Gorev,' he said through clenched teeth. 'We'll definitely see about that.'

67

Washington, DC
4.40 p.m.

For the first time in the last sixty hours, the President felt of a tiny surge of relief. It was almost as if someone had pulled a safety valve inside his head and released some of the incredible pent-up pressure, worry and distress that had built up over the last three days. Now there appeared to be a small light of hope at the end of the tunnel. It was hope at a steep price – he was having to give in to the brutal demands of insane terrorists – but at least in return he just might save the nation's capital and its citizens from terrible harm. Standing at the Oval Office window, looking out on to the lawns, he took several deep breaths.

'Mr President . . .'

He turned, faced the FBI Director, the only other person in the room. 'Sorry, Doug. I was lost there for a minute . . .'

'Now that Kuzmin's agreed to the prisoner release, what about the Israelis, sir? Surely they're going to be twice as difficult? Especially to get them to agree to a handover in time.'

The President shook his head. The call from Kuzmin telling him of the Russian council's positive decision was at least a good omen – suggesting that perhaps the District could be rescued after all. The Israelis would be difficult, he knew, but he was confident he could handle them. 'I've got our people working on it urgently, right this minute. At least this time we have powerful leverage.'

'Sir?'

'Our annual military aid package to Israel is due for approval next month.'

'You're going to put a gun to their head?'

'You're damned right I am. At this stage, there's no other way. Either they help us, or we stop helping them, and for good. The

Israelis badly need our support – their state can't function without it. And if I know the Israeli Prime Minster, he'll do as we ask. Sure, he'll rant, and stomp his feet, complain like hell, but in the end he's got a small price to pay – the release of a hundred and twenty prisoners for billions of dollars' worth of US aid.'

A sudden look of discomfort showed on Andrew Booth's face, as if the tiny surge of relief he'd just enjoyed was nothing more than a brief interlude, and he was dreading what was coming next. 'OK, Doug, let's get this business of our traitor done with.'

'Yes, sir. I'd like Rob Owens, the Secret Service Assistant Director, in on this. And Harry Judd. They're both waiting outside.'

'Get them in here.'

Maryland
10 p.m.

Benny Visto hated the countryside. He was used to the smell of gas fumes and traffic noise – fields and trees and all that rural shit weren't really his thing. He wrinkled his nose as Frankie, wearing a long raincoat, cracked open the driver's window in the Chrysler and a blast of country air swept in. 'The fuck you trying to do, man? Kill me? Put the fucking thing up.'

Frankie did as he was told. They had come off the highway five minutes earlier, the lights of quaint Maryland homes and farmhouses flashing past in the darkness, which did nothing to impress Visto. The van was tailing them, driven by Ronnie. The car phone rang. Visto flicked it on to speakerphone. 'Speak to me in gentle tones, my man.'

Ricky's voice came through. 'We're in place, Benny. Ready and waiting.'

'Anyone show up early, nosing around?'

'Naw. It's all clear.'

'Be there in half an hour. Anyone shows up meantime, or you run into problems, call.' Visto switched off the phone, grinned over at Frankie. 'Looks like we're all set up. You bring the stuff like I told you?'

'Sure, Benny, it's in the back, on the floor.'

Visto reached behind him, hefted over a black Reebok gym bag. He placed it in his lap, undid the zipper, and took out a lethal-looking French-made Mat submachinegun, fitted with a thick silencer. There were two snub-nosed .38 pistols in the bag, one each for him and Frankie, but Visto's attention was on the Mat, and he ran his fingers along the smooth, black barrel. 'Love this weapon. One burst, you cut a body in two. You know the plan, so leave all the talking to me.'

'Sure, Benny.'

'Then, when all the talking's done' – Visto patted the submachinegun – 'this little baby here's gonna have the last word.'

10.05 p.m.

Karla turned the Plymouth on to the narrow, deserted country road. She and Gorev were three minutes' drive from the rendezvous, but instead of coming from the east past the Lutheran church, Gorev insisted they take the longer route, circling round and cutting in back towards the road from the west. 'Turn off the headlights,' he told her. 'And keep your speed down. Take it nice and slow.'

Karla turned off the headlights and continued driving along the empty road, the forest on either side, the night-time landscape lit only by moon-wash. There were few homes in the area, a bare scattering of farms and detached properties, and their lights were some way off. When they were three hundred yards from the entrance to the forest track, Gorev said, 'Cut the engine. Coast on if you can, and pull in to the left. There should be a laneway.'

Karla did as he told her, and they both glimpsed the lane up ahead, cutting in to the left. The Plymouth started to slow, and they barely made it, coming to an abrupt halt when they had swung ten yards into the lane. Gorev climbed out.

'Where are you going?' Karla asked.

'The kind of man Visto is, I wouldn't put anything past him, especially after today.' Gorev took the Beretta from his pocket, screwed on the silencer. 'I'll go take a look. Stay here. Leave the lights off, and whatever you do don't start the engine again, unless it's an emergency. I'll be back as soon as I can.'

Gorev disappeared into the night, moving back down the lane towards the track that led to the forest clearing. Karla sat in the car in the quiet darkness, rolled down the window, her senses alert to any danger. It was fifteen minutes before Gorev returned. He yanked open the door, climbed in beside her again.

'Did you see anything?'

Washington, DC
4.45 p.m.

'We've got four names, Mr President. Every one of them, when we rechecked their backgrounds, had a Middle East connection that could make them in some way suspect.'

The FBI Director was seated on one of the Oval Office couches, the President standing over him, Rob Owens, the Secret Service Assistant Director of Protection and Harry Judd sitting on one of the other couches opposite. The President was sombre. 'That's the only criterion you used? A Middle East connection?'

'No, sir – Mr Judd can elaborate on several others later, but the Middle East thing jumped out at me as I went through their backgrounds. And it does seem to make a valid connection.'

'Go on.'

'All four are men. Charles Rivermount, General Bud Horton, Bob Rapp and Mitch Gains.'

The President was stunned. 'You're talking about four of my closest advisers, people whom I count as valued friends, and have done for years.'

'I realise that, sir.'

'There's got to be some mistake. What the hell makes them suspect?'

The FBI Director consulted his notebook. 'Let's start with

Charles Rivermount. One of his investment firms has major stock interest in two oil companies operating in Saudi Arabia. He also has close business links to this man.' Stevens handed across a photograph of an Arab, wearing traditional headdress. 'A Saudi sheikh named Nabil Rahman al-Khalid. Rivermount and he meet pretty regularly.'

'What the hell's wrong with that if they're in business together?'

'Al-Khalid's an extremely powerful, wealthy man, a distant cousin of Saudi's royal family. He's also been known to tacitly support Islamic fundamentalists financially in his home country, and the CIA has evidence that he's made secret and substantial contributions to several of al-Qaeda's so-called Islamic "charities", which are nothing but front organisations to funnel cash to their cause. But what's really interesting is that recently Rivermount's been trying to pull together the biggest oil deal of his life, and with al-Khalid's help. One that involves, over time, the sum of at least a hundred billion dollars. It's the deal of a lifetime for Rivermount, one he desperately wants.'

'I know Charles Rivermount. He's a patriot. He wouldn't sell out his country, never, not for any money.'

'He'll cheat on his wife, sir. Why not his country?'

The President didn't look affronted by the FBI Director's revelation; it was already common knowledge in the White House. 'That's his own business. Rivermount's wife likes to play the field herself. He found that out soon after the wedding. By mutual agreement, they remain married but both go their separate ways. You'll need something more convincing than that.'

'Which we've got, sir. Al-Khalid is one of those rich Saudis who'd be quite happy if the royal family were deposed by the Islamic fundamentalist movement in his country. No matter who's in power, they're going to have to sell their oil – the income from it is the only thing that keeps their country going. A man like Sheikh al-Khalid, with connections to the fundamentalists and al-Qaeda, could be well rewarded for his support, and become even wealthier, more powerful. He's got a lot to gain if the US quits the Gulf. Maybe Charles Rivermount has too.'

The President, unconvinced, pursed his lips. 'Who's next?'

'Mitch Gains, sir.' It was Rob Owens who answered.

'And what have you got on him?'

'His New York legal practice represents a number of wealthy Arab clients, whom Mr Gains counts as his close friends. He's also joint owner of four prime stud farms, one in Kentucky, one in Ireland, another two in the Arab Emirates. His partner in those ventures is an Arab businessman named Farid Sameika.'

'I know about Mitch's horse-breeding, and the Arab connection, but how does that place him under suspicion?'

'Farid Sameika's another contributor to al-Qaeda's Islamic "charities". He's also well known for his strong views on US policy vis-à-vis the state of Israel – he wants the US to stop supporting the Israelis. Put simply, Sameika hates the Jews, and refuses to do business with anyone who deals with them. Like I said, Mitch Gains and he are close friends – so there's got to be some meeting of minds.'

'Anything else?'

'Mr Gains has presidential ambitions, sir, which I'm sure you're aware of. I don't mean to be so blunt, but if al-Qaeda succeed, either by getting what they want or by destroying this city, you stand to suffer in the next election, Mr President. By that, I mean you'll most likely lose.'

'That's assuming I'm still alive,' the President reflected. He also recalled that he and Mitch Gains had had a recent falling out when he refused to nominate him as a future running mate for one of the very reasons Owens had outlined – Gains's stance on Israel. But he left that nugget out of the conversation; it was a private matter that he had dealt with personally. 'You included General Horton. Surely the man's above any kind of suspicion. He's a decorated 'Nam war hero, for God's sakes.'

'With an interesting past, which you're well aware of, sir. The general spent much of his young life in the Middle East. He mostly grew up there and was educated at the American School in Riyadh. His father served as a US attaché in Saudi for nine years, and later in Kuwait for another three. The general speaks fluent Arabic, has an abiding interest in Arab history and culture, and has many Arab friends and acquaintances. Even his wife's from Saudi. And he still visits the Middle East regularly – in a private capacity – at least three times a year, sometimes more.'

'Are you suggesting any of these friends of his might be supporters of al-Qaeda?'

'Not that we know of, sir. But that's not to say they're not. Our State Department people in Riyadh are in the process of evacuating the US embassy to meet the deadline so they can't help us out in that department right now, but we're working on it. Though we're not sure what motive the general might have, but there could be one, somewhere in his past.'

The President rubbed his jaw, lost for a moment in deep thought. 'You included Bob Rapp. Why?'

'He's a former reporter, and a much-respected one. He spent four years in the Lebanon as a war correspondent in the early to mid eighties. He was known to have mixed with Islamic radicals, even counted some of them among his friends. There was a rumour he even had a relationship with one of them.'

'Who?'

'A woman named Yelena Mazawi. She was a suspected Palestinian terrorist who was apparently killed by the Israelis during a raid on a PLO camp.'

'Bob was a reporter, for Christ's sake. Reporters are supposed to talk to radicals and terrorists. It's their job. And you said this relationship was a rumour. But even if it was true, is it possible Bob didn't know about her background?'

'It's always possible, sir. But some of the people he liked to talk to later became big names on the fundamentalist terrorist scene, sir. I should remind you that Rapp has also, on many occasions, vocally and in print, advocated a change of US policy towards Israel and the Arab nations.'

'I know he did. It's no damned secret. Bob and I have often spoke about that. But it was mostly in the past, when he was a much younger man. And for God's sakes, he's one hundred per cent American, and completely loyal to me.'

'There are other suspicions linked to these four men, sir.'

'Like what? Did the telephone taps turn up anything? Or scanning the contents of their personal computers, their e-mails?'

'Not as yet, sir,' Owens replied, and turned to Harry Judd. 'Harry, would you care to explain the rest?'

'Yes, sir.' Judd, ignored for the last fifteen minutes, cleared his throat, flicked open his notebook. 'Mr President, what's interesting – and coincidental – is that three of those four men – the exception being Mitch Gains – also turn out to have come to my notice when I checked back through the protection details' log books. There were several occasions when the suspects in question disappeared off our radar screen in the last few days and weeks, and under suspicious circumstances. I'd like to outline those circumstances to you, sir.'

For five minutes, Harry Judd gave precise details of each of the suspects' errant behaviour. When he had finished, he closed his notebook. 'The fact that Mitch Gains had a clean slate doesn't discount him. Maybe he was clever enough not to make any mistakes that might get a mention in the log books. But considering the behaviour and the background material we've just heard on these men, sir, I'm pretty much convinced that there's a strong chance one of these guys is our traitor.'

'Then how do you propose we smoke him out, Mr Judd?'

'I've got a plan, Mr President.'

68

Maryland
10.24 p.m.

Frankie swung left at the Piedmont crossroads, and they passed the Lutheran church. Ronnie was in the van, right behind them, keeping up. A half-mile down the road, Visto said, 'Hang a right.'

Frankie turned on to a forest track, heavily wooded either side. Fifty yards along the track they came to a clearing in the woods, their headlights sweeping across the thick clumps of trees. 'This is it,' Visto said. 'Pull in, switch off, and kill the lights.'

Frankie did as he was told, the engine died, and Ronnie pulled the van up behind them and followed suit, dousing his lights.

Visto stepped out of the car into almost total darkness. He carried a powerful electric torch in his left hand, but kept it switched off. The light wasn't bad, a lunar wash bathing the forest, the night clear, stars bright. Visto lit a cigarette, detected the fresh smell of pine in his nostrils, his ears assaulted by the utter stillness of the woods. 'You hear that, Frankie?'

'What?'

'Nothing. That's my point, man. It's like a fucking graveyard out here.'

He peered over towards the forest. Ricky and Hector were out there somewhere, lying in wait. A self-satisfied look crossed Visto's face as he drew hard on his cigarette. Everything was set up. He had one of the snub-nosed .38s deep in his pocket, and fingered the comfort of its cold, hard metal. Frankie had hidden the Mat underneath his long raincoat, the weapon dangling from a halter round his neck, ready for use, if need be. All Frankie had to do was open the coat, blast away and it was '*Hasta la vista,* asshole'.

'It's fucking cold out here, man,' Visto said, pulling up his coat collar, rubbing his hands.

'What time you got?'

Frankie tried to read his watch by the light of the moon. 'Looks to me like ten-thirty on the nail.'

'Someone's coming, Benny,' Ronnie called out.

Visto spun, saw the dipped headlights of a car turn in off the road, enter the forest track, approach the clearing. He tossed away his unfinished cigarette 'It's time to boogie.'

As Karla pulled in beside the van, Gorev said, 'Switch off the ignition, but leave the lights on.'

He went to get out of the car, and Karla worriedly put a hand on his. 'Be careful, Nicolai.'

'I intend to be. Just stay next to the car and be ready for any sign of trouble.'

Karla nodded, climbed out of the driver's seat, and Gorev left her standing there, crossed over to Visto. 'It seems you're right on time.'

'Always like to be prompt with my appointments. How you doing, my man? We all set to close this deal?'

'Whenever you are.'

'You got the rest of the cash?'

Gorev tapped his breast pocket. 'Right here, Mr Visto.'

'That's what I like to hear.' Visto jerked his head towards the van. 'Guess you'll want to take a final eyeball at the goods. Pretty sure you'll be pleased with the paint job.'

'I hope so, Mr Visto.'

'Know so. Then we can finish our business and we'll all be on our way.'

Visto opened the van's rear doors. He shone the torch inside and Gorev saw the suitcases Frankie had produced earlier that day. 'Mind if I take another look?'

'Be my guest.'

Gorev hauled out the cases, flicked them open and checked the uniforms and weapons.

'Everything looks in order, yet again. What about the markings for the van?'

A long cardboard box lay along one side of the van and Visto pulled it towards him and tore open the cardboard flaps, revealing a bunch of stick-on police decals. He picked one up, played the torch on it. 'Told you. You stick these on, the van here looks like the real thing. Happy?'

Gorev examined the rest of the decals. 'I think so.'

Visto replaced the flap on the box, stepped back from the van and shut the doors. Gorev held out his hand. 'The keys to the van, please.'

'Ronnie's got them. Give them here, Ronnie.'

Ronnie came over, handed the keys to Visto. As Gorev moved to take them, Visto held them out of reach, dangling in the air. 'Not so fast, sweetheart. First you and me need to have a little talk.'

'And what kind of talk would that be, Mr Visto?'

'Way I see it, you and me may be able to do some more business together.'

'What kind of business?'

'The kind between one brother in crime and another. See, all that hardware makes me figure maybe you're planning something big. Bank job, payroll heist maybe. Figure you might want the benefit of a business partner. Man like me has got access to all kinds of resources and expertise. Man like me could be a big help. Might be wise to take that help when it's offered. You with me?'

It seemed as if the penny had dropped for Gorev. He noticed Frankie move away from him slightly, fumble with a button on his overcoat. 'Your help won't be necessary.'

'Now why's that?'

'If you or your friends have any ideas in that direction, I'd suggest you quickly forget about them. You're treading on very dangerous ground.'

Visto's face was very white. 'Come again?'

'You might get hurt. If I could offer you some advice, Mr Visto.

Take the money I'm about to give you, leave the van, walk away from here, and forget about this conversation. That way, we'll both stay out of trouble.'

Visto gave a low chuckle. 'You know what you can do with your advice? Shove it up your lily-white ass.' The chuckle died, he took a step closer, skewered Gorev with a menacing look. 'Know what you need, mister?'

'What?'

'A lesson in manners. You need putting in place, and I'm just the man to do it.' Visto shook his head, looked back over at Frankie. 'I'll say this much for the dude, he's got some fucking nerve, talking to me like that.'

Frankie grinned. 'Man must be fucking crazy, Benny.'

'Crazy or not, I just hope the fuck he can back it up.' Visto switched his attention back to Gorev. 'Because if not, you and that bitch of yours are in deep shit, mister.' He glanced over at Karla, still waiting by the car. 'Matter of fact, might even take to screwing the bitch myself. Might enjoy that.'

Gorev said quietly, 'You know, there was a moment earlier today when I could have sworn somebody was following us. Still, nothing came of it. But now this business here, it's something much more disturbing.'

'What the *fuck* you talking about?'

'Your two friends hiding in the woods, waiting to surprise us. They're out cold, and will be for the next few hours. I have a feeling they're both going to need a doctor when they wake up.'

In that single frozen moment, Benny Visto knew he'd just made the biggest mistake in his life. 'Take him, Frankie!' he cried.

Frankie started to move, tearing open his raincoat. Gorev's right hand came up, holding the silenced Beretta. It spat once, hitting Frankie in the left shoulder. He spun with a cry, fell to the ground. Behind him Ronnie began to make a dash for the van but Karla already had him covered, grabbing the Skorpion machine-pistol through the Plymouth's open window, raising it in both her hands. Ronnie saw her aim and froze in his tracks. 'For fuck sake, don't shoot, lady, please. I'm not even armed . . .'

Gorev saw Visto wrench out a .38, but it was too late. He shot him once in the right arm. Visto staggered back, dropped the gun. '*Jesus* . . .'

Gorev kicked away the .38. He glanced back towards Karla, who was covering Ronnie and Frankie with the Skorpion, then moved over to where Frankie lay on the ground, clutching his wound, and tore the Mat submachinegun from around his neck. 'I'll take that.'

He removed the magazine, flung it into the woods, and tossed the submachinegun aside. Visto was still lying on the ground, a hand clapped to his bleeding arm. Gorev approached him. Visto said, 'All right, so I made a big fucking mistake.'

'Worse than that, you broke your word, Mr Visto. And where I come from, that's unforgivable.' Gorev raised the Beretta. 'In fact, there's a well-practised punishment for people like you.'

'For God's sake . . .'

Visto didn't get any farther because there was a dull thud as Gorev fired again. The bullet splintered Visto's right kneecap, shattering bone, and he screamed.

Gorev tossed him the envelope of money. 'Just so you know that I keep my word. Ten thousand, the final payment. And a word of warning, Mr Visto. You go to the police about this, and you and me will meet again. Only next time, it won't be a kneecap I'll shoot off, but something far more intimate. And that's just for a start. In fact, by the time I'm finished, I'm very sure you'll have need of an undertaker. Do we understand each other?'

'Yeah . . .' Visto clutched his knee in both hands, blood pumping between his fingers as he twisted in pain. 'Yeah . . . I understand.'

Frankie shook his head, watched as the van disappeared down the track, the man driving, the woman following right behind in the Plymouth. 'Who the *fuck* is that guy?'

'Get over here,' Visto cried out.

Frankie did as he was told, his right shoulder ablaze with pain, blood dripping down his fingers. Visto was still clutching his knee, the bleeding worse now, and there was a numbness in his wounded arm that frightened him. 'I don't know and I don't fucking care. Ronnie, get something to stop this bleeding . . . Frankie, give him a hand . . .'

'I'm fucking bleeding myself.'

'Do it, for fuck sake, before I pass out . . .'

'I'll find something, Benny.' Ronnie went to the car and came back with a rope from the trunk. While Frankie held the torch, Ronnie took a penknife from his pocket and cut up the rope, tied a length of it high on Visto's right arm, then another above his knee, examining the wounds with fascinated horror. The 9mm bullets had gone in one side and out the other. The kneecap had fragmented, splinters of white bone protruding through bloodied flesh and cartilage. Frankie's shoulder wasn't as bad – the bullet had barely chipped the bone, it was no more than a flesh wound – and when Ronnie had attended to him, he flashed the torch on Visto's knee again. '*Jeez*, it looks bad, Benny. Same with your arm. You'll need a hospital.'

'Like fuck I do.' There was sweat on his face and he was very white. 'You carry me into any hospital with a gunshot wound, they'll scream for the cops. I don't want no cops involved, you hear? Haul me up. Get me out of here.'

'What about Ricky and Hector?'

'Fuck them. Leave them where they are. It's their own fault, letting that dude surprise them. Assholes can walk home.' He swore as Frankie and Ronnie helped carry him to the Chrysler and manoeuvred him on to the back seat. 'Let's get the fuck away from here. Hurry up!'

'Where to, Benny?'

'Back to town. Take me to that private clinic. The one where I got that fucking quack to take care of some of the girls.'

'You mean Rotstein? He's a plastic surgeon, Benny. He does boob jobs.'

'He's a doctor, ain't he?' Visto said. 'Now get the fuck out of here, fast, before I fucking bleed to death.'

69

Washington, DC
5.15 p.m.

Kursk got out of the cab three blocks from the Hoover building and walked to 10th Street. He'd spent the rest of his afternoon aimlessly wandering around DC, hoping that Suslov would call. He hadn't. When he realised he hadn't eaten in almost eighteen hours, Kursk stopped at a sandwich bar, ate a thick roll with salami and salad, and drank two cups of hot coffee.

He couldn't help studying the faces of the people in the streets: mothers and fathers, school kids and teenagers, children in buggies, homeless beggars, cab-drivers, police officers – some of the hundreds of thousands of men, women and children whose lives were still in jeopardy. It felt surreal: he knew the terrible secret being withheld from them, the cruel death that could await them all, and yet he couldn't even warn them. How could Nikolai Gorev be part of such a terrible conspiracy, threaten to kill so many innocents? *How*?

Kursk combed through his memories, trying to understand, but there was nothing relevant in Gorev's character or distant past that revealed itself.

But one question returned to haunt him. Even if by some miracle he found his quarry again, could he kill Nikolai Gorev?

Kursk entered the busy Hoover building, passing through the tight security checks, his visitor's ID closely scrutinised, and went up to the sixth floor. Neither Collins nor Morgan was in the office, but Murphy was. He looked physically wrecked. 'We've been looking for you, Major. Another half-hour and I was going to put out a bulletin. You mind me asking where the hell you've been?'

'I had something to attend to.'

'Anything I need to know about?'

Kursk felt it was pointless telling Murphy until he found out whether Suslov had come up with anything. 'It was a personal matter.'

'Jack and Lou went to check out a couple of illegals, but I don't expect it to get us anywhere.' Murphy collapsed into a chair, ran a hand over his face, shook his head hopelessly. 'We're still looking at a blank wall, Alexei. We're not going to crack this in time, but I guess that's obvious. You mind me asking, have you got family?'

'A wife and daughter. Why?'

'Look, it's nothing personal. But maybe it's time you thought about getting your ass the hell out of DC.'

The White House
9.15 p.m.

Six blocks away the same thought would run through the minds of almost every one of the members of the National Security Council.

Like Kursk, they had a choice: they could leave the capital before the deadline and avoid the risk of anything going wrong after the time limit expired. Unlike Kursk, their President didn't have that choice, and it was this question that Mitch Gains brought up a few minutes after the Council took their seats in the situation room.

'What are you saying, Mitch?' the President asked. 'That I should quit Washington?'

'Sir, the Secret Service Director tells me that were the device to be set off, either deliberately or by mistake, between now and the deadline, there's no absolute guarantee that the bunker ventilation system can filter out the nerve gas. And even if they got you fitted out with a biohazard suit and oxygen supply, there's still no guarantee you could be brought out of here safely.'

'What are you proposing?'

'That before the deadline you allow the Secret Service to remove you to a safe place, sir.'

'One of the terms of Abu Hasim's letter was that I remain in the White House.'

'To hell with him. You've pretty much done everything that was asked of you . . .'

'But by leaving the White House I may be exposing all of you, and this city, to unwarranted risk. At this stage, that's not on.'

'But how the hell can Abu Hasim know, sir? The Secret Service can spirit you out of here without anyone knowing.'

Charles Rivermount spoke up. 'Mr President, Mitch is right. Nobody would know. I mean, without making too much of it, we all know about a certain ex-President who, with the help of his staff, could smuggle himself out of here without the press ever knowing, and whenever he damned well pleased. The man was being ferried in and out of here day and night, hidden in the back of a Toyota van, with a blanket over him – just so he could meet in secret with a certain young lady.'

The room erupted in nervous laughter, a welcome diversion considering the pent-up tension, but the President barely smiled. Looking at the faces around him, he paid particular attention to the four suspects: Charles Rivermount, Mitch Gains, General Horton, Bob Rapp. Each of them was laughing – Rivermount included – at the wisecrack. With disbelief the President thought: *One of you is a traitor.*

If it was Charles Rivermount or Mitch Gains, why would they condone him leaving the White House? To test his promise that he would keep his word, and then inform on him? Or for one of them to deflect any suspicion from himself? No matter, he had no intention of leaving the White House; and not because someone might inform on him. This was his place, whether it was a condition of Abu Hasim's demands or not. He wouldn't flee like a coward and leave millions of American citizens to their fate. Another thought struck him: even if he found his traitor, it wouldn't get Washington out of this mess.

'I'm sorry, but until this thing is over, my place is here, and that's final. So if we could move on, we've got some vital matters to discuss . . .'

Chesapeake
11.15 p.m.

Gorev and Karla pulled into the cottage driveway. Mohamed Rashid appeared on the veranda, and stepped down to the van as Gorev climbed out. 'Well, how was it?'

'All right.'

'They didn't try anything?'

'Far from it.' Gorev explained what had happened.

Rashid was deeply uneasy. 'This could mean serious trouble.'

'That's where I think you're wrong. You really believe he's going to tell the authorities he's in the business of supplying police uniforms and weapons? He'd be putting himself behind bars. Visto will settle his own scores, like any criminal, not take them to the police. But we've got plenty of breathing space – we'll be long gone by the time he's well enough to come looking for us.'

'Did you have to shoot him?'

'It's the only kind of response he understands. If I hadn't made my point, he'd have attempted to come after us tonight, tried to follow us here, I'm convinced of it.'

'How do you know he didn't?'

'We took the back roads, and checked behind us every mile of the way. I'm positive we weren't tailed.'

Rashid still looked uneasy as he went to inspect the van, getting into the cab. 'It's exactly what we need. Where are the rest of the things?'

'In the back. You'll find they're all in order. Visto kept his word about that.'

Rashid went round the back of the van, opened the door and, using a pencil torch, searched through the suitcases and the cardboard box of decals until he was completely satisfied. 'Good. It looks like we have everything. But I'm still not entirely happy about all this, Gorev. Something tells me we're on risky ground.'

'Look, Rashid, we did what we had to do under the circumstances. Whether you still use the van or not is your decision.'

Rashid grunted, nodded towards the garage. 'Get the van inside.'

'What about the car?'

Rashid held out his hand for the keys. 'I'll have need of it later.'

'For what?'

'That's my business,' Rashid said gruffly. 'In the meantime, you two better get your things together and then sleep while you can. Assuming there are no last-minutes hitches, and everything goes to plan, we'll be out of here long before noon.'

Washington, DC
5.55 p.m.

Kursk was alone in the office when his cellphone vibrated. 'Major? It's me, Suslov.'

'Well, Suslov?'

'I did like you asked. Called the big names first, worked my way down the list.'

'Did you get a reaction?'

'Yeah. Most of it hostile. The mafia hard men, they don't like people like me asking too many questions, least of all for the FSB. In fact, one of them accused me of being a snitch . . .'

'But did you find anything out, Suslov?'

'Not a fucking thing. They all said the same – they never heard of this guy Gorev. Didn't know who the hell I was talking about.'

'There must be more names you can try . . .'

'Kursk, believe me, I've tried them all. You don't want to destroy that file on me, fine, OK, but I've done my best. So do me a favour, Major – I don't want to talk with you, so don't call me again. Me, I don't want to wind up with a rubber necklace.' The line clicked dead.

Kursk, despondent, switched off his phone, crossed to the nearest desk. A terrible feeling of hopelessness gripped the pit of his stomach. His only hunch had led nowhere. Standing there, he turned towards the window, looked down at the police barriers and the pedestrians in the cold streets, and thought of his wife and daughter. He smiled to himself when he remembered the note little Nadia had left for him, reminding him to fix the kitchen sink; the childish hearts and flowers, and the dozens of kisses she'd drawn around the message, in bright pink marker.

In all the frantic, exhaustive chaos of the last few days, he hadn't even had time to call his family. He missed Lydia, missed Nadia, longed to see them. He would call them now. Maybe Murphy was right. Maybe it was time to get out of Washington.

70

The White House
11.15 p.m.

As the meeting in the situation room progressed, the President turned to General Horton.

'General, I believe you can report on the progress of our withdrawal?'

'Yes, Mr President. We're almost forty per cent complete.'

'We've only got twelve hours left, General . . .'

'I'm aware of that, sir. But as you know, we've got an additional slew of aircraft already arriving in the Gulf right now, both civilian and military. And three naval carriers are steaming on their way from the Indian Ocean, arriving in five hours' time. That will speed things up.'

'But will we make the deadline?'

'It's close, but we're hoping, sir . . .'

'Don't hope, just make sure we do. Speed it up more. Do whatever you have to.' The President turned to Bob Rapp. 'I believe the press have started asking questions, Bob?'

'Yes, sir. Jerry Tanbauer at the *Times* called me this evening. He'd heard that there was a large number of our troops being shipped back from the Gulf. I gave him the Christmas story, but that didn't really satisfy him.'

'So?'

'I pleaded ignorance, but said I'd find out what I could and get back to him tomorrow. That ought to stall him for now. But I believe the press office has already had calls from NBC and CNN late this evening. I'm pretty sure we can hold them off until tomorrow, right after the deadline, but any longer than that and there's going to be major speculation in the papers and over the airwaves. Several Middle East stations have already been making enquiries about the reason for the large numbers of troops being sent home.'

'So have the Saudis,' the Defence Secretary interrupted, speaking to the room at large. 'I informed the President that my office, as well as the State Department, had several frantic calls from Riyadh – both from the royals and their senior military people – wanting to know what was going on. There were other top-level calls from Kuwait, Bahrain and the United Arab Emirates. Publicly, the Arabs are saying nothing, but privately I guess it's no lie to say they're getting shit scared.'

The President nodded. 'I should also make you all aware that in the last hour all of the heads of the Gulf states have asked to speak to me personally about the matter. I've had it explained to them that I'll talk to each of them privately tomorrow, in the early afternoon, to explain the troop movements. Meanwhile, of necessity, I had to give them assurances that nothing unusual was happening. I had to lie, of course. But we have to keep them all on hold for now, for our own security. And the same rule still applies to everyone here – no one leaks anything to the press.'

General Horton said, 'Sir, the foreign press wires are going to be hopping during the night. What will we tell them?'

'We stall 'em. Stick to our original story for now, that this is a matter of seasonal leave. That the stable situation in the Gulf allows us to send large numbers of US servicemen and women home for the holiday period . . . nothing more than that.'

'But sir, before noon tomorrow they're going to find out that this is a *complete* withdrawal . . .'

'And not long after noon tomorrow, hopefully, when the device is located and we defuse it, they'll have our honest admission of what's happened. But not until then.' The President gestured to the FBI Director. 'Doug, I suppose I'm asking too much by hoping that we've got something by now?'

Doug Stevens shook his head solemnly. 'We're swamped, sir. We're still faced with the big problem of trying to keep the search discreet, and that's constraining us because we've had so much ground to cover. I know for certain we're not going to get through this investigation before the deadline. I'm sorry, sir . . . but it's just not physically possible. We'd need a lot more than twelve hours.'

The President, downhearted, made a steeple of his fingers, touched them to his mouth. 'We understand your predicament, Doug. But keep at it. We can't flag – not for a moment – even though we think the situation's hopeless.'

'Sir, what about the Israelis?' Katherine Ashmore interrupted.

'They're on board. I spoke with the Israeli Prime Minister. He'll have the prisoners in his jails flown to our staging point – a Russian airbase outside Sevastopol, on the Black Sea – in just under three hours' time, arriving at five a.m. President Kuzmin suggested this airbase both for his convenience and because of its proximity to Afghanistan. I should inform you that the British- and German-held prisoners will arrive at Sevastopol in the next two hours, as will the al-Qaeda prisoners from our own penitentiaries, and all will be held secretly at the base, under heavy guard. As we speak, President Kuzmin's prisoners are being boarded on to two Russian civilian aircraft at Moscow's Vnukovo airfield, and are scheduled to land at Sevastopol no later than four a.m. From there, they'll all be taken under guard aboard two hired-in 767 US commercial aircraft and flown to their final destination, once we learn that destination from al-Qaeda's point man in Pakistan.'

'Did you tell the Israeli PM about our Gulf withdrawal?' Rebecca Joyce asked.

'I told him everything, Rebecca. I had to. And with the proviso that he keep it entirely to himself. At least until after noon tomorrow. Naturally, the Prime Minister is deeply shocked, and seriously worried. He sees our withdrawal as a catastrophe for Israel. It puts his country in an impossible position, under immense threat.'

'What if he changes his mind? What if he has second thoughts, confides in his cabinet, and they consider that Israel would stand a better chance of surviving if he didn't release the prisoners? That way, we might be forced into a position where we couldn't meet al-Qaeda's demands, and so our troops would remain in the Gulf.'

'That point brings me to a vital piece of information you all need to be aware of. Mr Secretary, would you care to enlighten us?'

'Yes, sir,' the Secretary of Defence answered. 'Israel needs our aid, that's a given. But she'll need it even more from now on, without our US presence in the Arabian Peninsula. I suggested to the Israeli Prime Minister that to counter his fears we set up a number of temporary US bases on Israeli soil. He was in full agreement, and I've been working out the details with the help of General Horton. Our plan is that by midday tomorrow at least thirty per cent of our troops – among the last to be evacuated – will be moved to temporary bases in Israel. This move has helped to placate the Israeli PM just a little. In fact, we've already sent a forward group of two thousand men, part of our Gulf contingent, to help set up these emergency bases, and more troops are on their way this minute.'

Charles Rivermount frowned, raised his hand. 'Mr Secretary, correct me if I'm wrong, but I thought Abu Hasim said he wanted *all* our troops out of the Middle East. Israel's part of that region. Aren't we setting ourselves up for trouble here when Hasim finds out – as he surely will – that we've simply moved some of our forces to Israel?'

'Hasim said the *Arab* Middle East region,' the Defence Secretary replied. 'I need hardly point out that the Israelis are Jews, not Arabs. And if we want to get technical here, strictly speaking Israel is part of the Levant region.'

Mitch Gains said, 'Mr President, that kind of playing with words may not stop Hasim from seeing such a move as a serious breach of trust. It might even make him think that you're trying to dupe him. The sort of lunatic mind that he has, he might see it as an extreme provocation, one that could send him over the edge. He might well say to hell with it, and set off his damned bomb.'

'General Horton already made that point to me, and made it strongly,' the President replied. 'However, I've made my decision, and I intend sticking to it. If Hasim wants to argue the point, we'll cross that bridge if and when we come to it.'

'But, sir, aren't we stepping into a minefield? Al-Qaeda might think we've double-crossed them . . .'

The President raised a hand. 'I'm sorry, Mitch, but I'd like to wrap this up, and there are a couple of serious points I need to raise before I do.'

He turned to the faces around the table. 'Ladies and gentlemen, as I said, I'm not moving from here until this thing is over and done with, one way or another. The rest of you, however – for the continuation of national security – I'm ordering to leave Washington from ten a.m. tomorrow. Each of you will remove yourselves, and your immediate families if they're here, to outside of the District. You may invent whatever reasonable excuses you can think of – a surprise trip, a sudden emergency that requires you to leave with your family – anything, except, obviously, the truth. Nor are you to make your leaving look like a mass evacuation. You will each take a small number of personal belongings, use different routes, and will be driven and accompanied by a Secret Service escort.

'You will all rendezvous at an as yet undisclosed point outside Washington, from where you will be moved to a secure destination, along with members of our government and Senate – those who are in or near DC. They will be both advised of the situation and removed from the capital an hour prior to the deadline, but not before, and with the same conditions attached as apply to yourselves.'

'Would our destination be Mount Weather, sir?' Rebecca Joyce asked.

Mount Weather, in Berryville, Virginia, was a COG – Continuance of Government – facility, a billion-dollar tunnelled mountain site of over four hundred acres, run by FEMA. It contained a vast complex of secure underground bunkers designed to safely house the US President and his government in a national emergency. With its own dedicated water supply, communications facilities, utilities, bunks and sleeping quarters for up to two thousand people – and even its own crematorium – it was protected by a guillotine entrance gate and a thirty-four-ton metal blast door that was five feet thick, which took fifteen minutes to open or close.

'That's not yet decided, Rebecca. Ladies and gentlemen, I deeply regret that you are most definitely *not* allowed to include relatives and friends among those you take with you – *only* your immediate dependent family. Harsh as that sounds, you must understand that if you ignore my warning, you risk causing public suspicion and, ultimately perhaps, untold chaos in this city. Which, in turn, could lead to the terrorists panicking and exploding their device. I'm sure no one wants that horror on their conscience. If anyone attempts to break that rule, they'll be dealt with severely by me, or the Vice-President in my stead.

'So, to finish. I've arranged that all the prisoners will be ready to be transported from Sevastopol from seven a.m. tomorrow morning, EST, to be flown onward to their final destination. Once that has been accomplished, and our troop withdrawal is completed by the deadline, then hopefully the location of the device will be made known to us. But as a precautionary measure – in case Abu Hasim goes back on his word or something goes horribly wrong between now and then and the device explodes – I've ordered our emergency responder teams to be on twenty-four-hour stand-by.

'The responders haven't been told the reason why – just that a top-secret exercise is imminent. As of tonight, FEMA's pre-disaster recommendations are being put in place. Emergency medical supplies, food and decontamination suits will be secretly stored in locations throughout the District, in subway stations, in designated warehouses and depots, both close to and within the potential disaster zone. Emergency field hospitals, food stores, blankets, cots, field kitchens and temporary accommodations are being provisionally prepared and made ready to be rushed to strategic points outside the District. Our National Emergency Response Team has been put on alert, and is standing by, positioned in Virginia, Maryland and Pennsylvania. Vital government departments and their staff have already been targeted for priority evacuation, and high-priority papers, files and items essential to government will be secured and removed in the early hours of the coming morning.

'Our evacuation plans for the city – imperfect as they might be – are ready to go operational if they're needed. Despite our best efforts, if this thing goes belly up because some madman wants to destroy Washington no matter what concessions he wins, then at least I'd like us to be as prepared as we damned well can. Tomorrow morning, eight-thirty a.m., we'll meet back here again for one final conference before the deadline.'

The President rose. Everyone in the room stood, their faces sombre. 'Until then, let's all pray that this city gets safely through the night.'

The room was very dark, the only light the table lamp on the antique desk, with the array of flags behind it. The President sat in his leather chair, stared absently towards the Washington Monument. The Oval Office door clicked open. His Assistant for National Security Affairs, Paul Burton, entered. 'You sent for me, sir?'

The President gestured. 'Sit down, Paul.'

He looked over at Burton. His face had gained a few worry lives in the last few days. 'What do you think, Paul? Will Abu Hasim stick to his word?'

Burton thought for a moment, shook his head. 'I don't know, sir. My hope is that he will. That once he fulfils his ambition, gets what he's always wanted and humiliates us in the process, then he'll have no valid reason to renege on his promise.'

'I hope to God you're right. But do you think Hasim will think *I'm* going back on my word by bringing Israel into the equation? Will it provoke him?'

Burton gave a tiny fleeting smile. 'It's a clever move, sir, and a bold one. But I really can't gauge what his reaction will be. Only time will tell. But I'm pretty sure Abu Hasim will hear about it soon enough. Time enough to worry about it then, sir.'

The President sighed, rubbed his eyes with thumb and fore-finger. 'You know what really worries me? What Professor Stern said. That the likelihood is that this guy really *wants* to gas the capital, no matter what. You read all the FEMA report?'

'Of course, sir. Every word!'

'It's frightening reading. I keep thinking about the image of those dead bodies being transported out through the countryside of Virginia and Maryland – thousands upon thousands of truck-loads of them – and it chills me to the bone. Men, women, little children. Then the ships taking them up to the coast of Maine for burial. Our capital left like a ghost town . . . an entire nation with it's heart ripped out. It's almost inconceivable . . .'

Burton shook his head. 'You've done everything that was asked of you, sir. And what happens now isn't up to you. But you've got to pray it won't happen like that. That we come through this without harm or casualty.'

'I keep praying, Paul.' Booth shook his head in despair. 'But God help me, I keep seeing those images.'

For a moment Burton was silent, then he said quietly, 'Sir, Abu Hasim has won this battle. We all know that. But if it's any consolation, there'll be others. It's not going to end here.'

'Perhaps you're right.' The President glanced at his desk clock. It read 11.55. He rose. 'You better get some sleep. We all have an anxious day tomorrow.'

Burton stood. 'I thought you ought to know, sir. The press have been asking about your health. There have been quite a few calls this evening.'

'What did we tell them?'

'You had a bad flu bug. But you're on the mend, and ought to be continuing with your public engagements some time tomorrow.'

Andrew Booth was grim. 'That remains to be seen. I've talked to Vice-President Havers. Just so you know, if anything goes wrong within the next twelve hours, he's ready to assume presidential authority.'

When Burton had gone, the President swung his leather chair to face the lawns. Sitting there, in the dark silence of the room, he knew that Burton was right: Abu Hasim had won this battle. The most powerful country in the world had been defeated by a mad religious zealot with a weapon of mass destruction.

It galled him, made his heart a furnace. Already his mind was trying to figure out how to repay Hasim, how to recover the Gulf territory, but he knew that course was fraught with hazards. What if there were more devices planted in the US? At the first signs of any attempt to regain lost territory they could be triggered, this time without warning. He tried to concentrate on the next twelve hours. But his mind was assailed by the many things that could *still* go wrong.

What if Abu Hasim went back on his word, or upped his demands? What if, by some fluke, the device became unstable and exploded, or an errant signal set it off? What if the terrorists baby-sitting the nerve gas didn't like the idea of handing it over? The cold-blooded murder of the fourteen innocent Americans kidnapped in Azerbaijan, and the suicide blast at the Hoover building, had proved, if proof were needed, that terrorists like these were capable of anything.

And from what he could gather from the intelligence reports he'd read, a man like Mohamed Rashid was as insane and callous a murderer as his master. Would he follow his orders, do as his master told him once the terms of the letter were complied with? Or, in a moment of madness, would he – or Abu Hasim – decide to send hundreds of thousands more Americans to their deaths? Andrew Booth knew that Washington and its citizens were not out of the woods yet, not by a long shot.

Chilled by his alarming thoughts, he shook his head with dismay, his own words coming back to haunt him. *The lives of hundreds of thousands of people are in my hands. If I fail, many of them may die.*

They might still die, even if he *didn't* fail them.

As the clock on his desk struck midnight, there was one thing of which he was certain, although it was small consolation. He'd planted some bait tonight. At the behest of Harry Judd, he'd told an important lie during the NSC meeting, in the hope that one among the four suspects would take the bait, try to make contact with Abu Hasim, and in so doing reveal himself.

Before midday tomorrow, he might at least have found his traitor.

PART SEVEN
14 November

Resurrection Day

71

A little after midnight, a procession of six delivery trucks entered DC from the south, off the Eisenhower Freeway. Heading north, passing L'Enfant Plaza, they crossed the Mall until they reached Constitution Avenue.

From there, the trucks dispersed in pairs in three different directions: two heading east towards Union Station Plaza, two heading north towards Chinatown, and the final two moving east towards the Federal Triangle. Minutes later, six more delivery trucks entered the District from the direction of Chevy Chase, and from Tacoma Park in the north. By 5.30 a.m., a total of ninety-six special trucks would enter the District, with exactly the same cargo.

The contents of those eight dozen deliveries were known to their hand-picked military drivers and helpers, all of them dressed not in their military uniforms but in civilian overalls. Inside each truck were ten tons of sealed food rations, medical supplies and containers of fresh water. Over the course of the next five hours, the drivers and their helpers would offload and store their supplies in designated subway station storerooms, warehouses and depots all over the District.

As the cargo was being unloaded, senior emergency crew managers at underground offices in four secret command posts in military bases in Virginia and Maryland were already putting plans in place to safely evacuate and decontaminate over one and a half million of DC's population: to provide them with food, shelter, necessary medical aid, energy sources for heat and light, and to nominate hospitals for the treatment of up to three hundred thousand injured nerve-gas victims.

That same night, the National Emergency Response Team, ERT-N, whose members had been positioned at two of the four command posts, were carrying out their assigned tasks: drawing up lists of whatever specialist equipment and expert manpower might be needed, experts who would help seal off and evacuate the contaminated area, liaise with the emergency services – fire and police departments, hospitals and emergency medical teams – and with the FBI, National Guard and necessary government agencies.

Another specially picked technical team, based in Alexandria, had the task of ensuring that FEMA's Emergency Alert System was ready to be plugged into every major TV and radio station in DC, so that radio and TV programmes could be interrupted with pre-prepared event tapes, or scrolling messages that would appear across TV screens, advising people of an attack and telling them to seek shelter in subways or basements, or to get out of the city. Another group of technicians had the job that night of ensuring that the District's extreme-weather alert sirens were operational. But before carrying out their tests they were given one important condition – none of the sirens to be tested was to be set off, for fear of causing an alert. The technicians were instructed to disconnect the sirens, measure their coil resistance to ensure they were serviceable, and check the individual output circuit to the coils by measuring their voltage. If they passed both tests, the sirens were to be deemed to be in working order and reconnected; if not, they were to be replaced.

Washington's evacuation expert, Gavin G. Lord, flown by helicopter to one of the command posts in nearby Virginia, was already in the throes of a long and sleepless night, fine-tuning his plans and consulting other experts, determined to ensure that the exit routes he had chosen wouldn't cause bottlenecks or congestion. While he worked, a short distance away, in a half dozen offices down the hall, clusters of industrious men and women were busy labouring through their own sets of tasks.

The ugly questions of how many bodies you could fit in a five-or ten-ton truck, in a Greyhound bus, in a ship's container or in a naval vessel had already been answered. And so, unknown to thousands of registered businesses and individual owners of tractor trailers, buses, vans and truck fleets – living on the edges of DC and in nearby Virginia and Maryland – one group in the command post was adding the owners' names to a long list of people whose vehicles would be commandeered for the gruesome work of transporting hundreds of thousands of contaminated corpses out of the District. A squad from the same group had the job of drawing up a list of suitable sea vessels, both military and commercial, for shipping the corpses in sealed containers to an as yet unknown point, off the coast of Maine. Yet another had been given the task of compiling a list of likely sources – in the US and abroad – for over three hundred thousand body-bags.

Another crew – FEMA experts – was tweaking its plans and compiling lists of hospitals, emergency services and fire crews, in Virginia, Maryland and Philadelphia, that could be put at Washington's disposal if the attack was launched.

On it went, all through the night, the hard-working men and women in the command posts kept awake by grim resolve, anxiety and endless cups of coffee. And as they toiled away, the hearts of each of them were heavy with the same worry. If the device should go off, by accident or design, by midday, with the lives of up to two million people descending on the District at grave risk, they just hoped to God their plans worked and they would at least be able to save as many of them as possible.

At a quarter after midnight, Collins and Morgan arrived back at FBI Headquarters. They had tracked down the two illegals but produced no worthwhile leads. Immigration had got it wrong in one case: after three hours of slog, questioning his former landlord and several of his former room-mates, Collins and Morgan discovered that the twenty-six-year-old Egyptian medical student had graduated and actually been given a temporary work visa, had moved to San Francisco in mid-July and was working as an intern in a city hospital. Collins passed the man's name back to headquarters, who contacted the FBI's San Francisco field office, which followed up the request, and by 9 p.m. two agents had located the young doctor, thoroughly questioned him about his movements and background, and taken his name off the list.

The female illegal, a Palestinian postgraduate student of English, was still at large in DC, having overstayed on her visa, and after hours of interviewing campus staff and locating two of her fellow students, by 10 p.m. Collins and Morgan had finally found her at an address in Chevy Chase, where she had moved in with her American boyfriend. The young woman was obviously alarmed by the FBI visit, and willing to answer any questions. After accounting for her movements, and satisfying themselves that the student wasn't a likely terrorist or a supporter of any Middle East terrorist cause, Collins crossed her off the print-out and Morgan notified Immigration.

Back at the Hoover building, the investigation was speeding up in a frantic, last-ditch effort to locate the device and the three suspects. Throughout the late evening and all through the night, the FBI and Secret Service pulled out all the stops: thousands of tired and exhausted agents, some having had barely four hours' sleep in the last thirty-six, were pushing themselves to the limit, pounding the streets, putting a last-minute squeeze on pimps, prostitutes, informers, hustlers, drug dealers, pick-pockets and thieves, in a final desperate effort to ferret out even a sliver of information.

Along 14th Street, in the streets and alleyways off its main artery, and as far out as the high-crime-rate ghettoes of the north-east and the south-east, agents were kicking down doors, breaking up drug deals, or walking into gay clubs, bars and nightclubs, strip clubs, massage parlours and brothels, even interrupting prostitutes and their customers in the sex act, and showing them photographs of the three suspects.

In the District, since 1 p.m. the previous afternoon, two dozen FBI and army WMD teams in unmarked vans had been scouring the inner capital block by block, using chemical detection equipment. Working in pairs, and dressed as utility workers – either gas inspectors, electricity company technicians or telephone engineers – and carrying the proper company IDs, they entered building after building, paying particular attention to cellars, basements, underground garages, storage rooms and roof areas, probing the air for the slightest trace of a chemical 'signature'. They had found minute traces at dozens of locations – all harmless – from leaking air-conditioning and gas boiler units, from weak pipe joints feeding natural gas supplies, and in stores of industrial chemicals used for cleaning purposes, but none of the buildings had yet shown up any trace of organophosphate chemicals.

In the skies overhead Washington, as night fell, three Blackhawk helicopters fitted with 'hushed' rotors and kitted out with infra-red heat-detection and imaging equipment were making slow, mapped passes over suspect zones: the docks, the gritty industrial strips and several of the ghetto areas, in an attempt to 'see' with their infrared imaging equipment any suspiciously behaving or remote clusters of people, or even individuals, hanging out near deserted or suspect buildings, who might be terrorists at work.

It was little comfort to Tom Murphy that because of the intense agent and police activity over the last sixty-eight hours the crime rate in Washington had touched a record thirty-year low. After snatching two hours' sleep in his office, then calling his available men together and learning that the all-out effort had yet to produce a single worthwhile lead, he ordered them back to work with an irate dismissal.

Kursk had spent the best part of the evening in another office, helping two agents comb through a mountainous pile of shipping manifests, and took a break when Collins and Morgan appeared. 'Where the hell did you disappear to today, Alexei?' Morgan asked.

Kursk explained about his meeting with Suslov. 'Unfortunately, it came to nothing.'

'Guess that's another one bites the dust,' Morgan commented, shaking his head before he went to get a coffee.

'This guy Suslov,' Collins said, 'you really think he did what you asked?'

'He knows that Gromulko from the embassy is not the kind

to cross. Yes, I believe Suslov did as I asked. You friend and her little boy, how are they?'

'Improving a little. I'm going to call the hospital again, see if they're still OK.'

'At least you have some good news.'

'What about you, Kursk? Murphy tells me he thinks you ought to get out of Washington, just in case. He asked me to check the flights. There are none direct to Moscow, but there's a flight with United Airlines to Montreal at eight fifty-five a.m., with a connection to Moscow via London. If it was me, if I had family and I was in your position, I'd be taking that flight, Major. We've got little more than ten hours to go before the deadline. If we were going to get lucky, we should have turned up something by now.'

'What if I stay here for now? Help in whatever way I can for the next few hours?'

'There's nothing more you can do.' Collins shook his head. 'We're pretty much running out of road, Major. My advice is to go pack your bags and try and grab some sleep.'

'I'll have to clear it with Moscow.'

'Do that. And if you want, I can have a cab pick you up at seven-thirty to take you to the airport. Meantime, you're better off out of here. The tension's only going to get worse before midday.'

Kursk saw the strain on Collins' face, knew that every agent in the Hoover building was under the same stress. Most likely, they would remain in the capital until the bitter end, no matter what that end was to be. It was a sobering thought, and Kursk didn't envy them. He solemnly offered his hand. 'Good luck, Agent Collins. Perhaps I could see Lou before I go?'

'Sure. I'll go find him. Then let me call you a cab.'

'Thank you, but it's not far to the apartment, and I'd prefer to walk.'

At 1.45 a.m., Collins phoned Georgetown Hospital. When he was put through to the Critical Care Unit and asked after Daniel, the nurse confirmed that there had been some minor improvement. Daniel was still on a ventilator, but his breathing had stabilised, and twice that evening he had come awake briefly, long enough to establish that none of his senses had been impaired. Relieved, on the verge of tears, Collins asked about Nikki. The nurse put him on hold while she checked with a colleague, then came back on the line after a few minutes. 'Daniel's mom isn't here. But his grandmother's around. She's been here most of the day.'

Collins asked to speak with her. At first the nurse seemed a little irritated that he was holding up the line, but when he explained he couldn't get to the hospital she got Nikki's mother to come to the phone.

She was tearful, sobbing as she talked about Daniel's injuries. 'Jack . . . what's this world coming to? How could anyone maim a child like that . . . kill so many innocent bystanders? I don't understand it . . . Nikki and Daniel . . . what harm did they ever do to these people?'

'It's OK, Susan.' Collins tried to calm her. 'They're both going to be OK. It could have been a lot worse. You've got to think about that.'

The sobbing went on until Collins finally got her back on an even keel, and when she'd asked how he was, and enquired about his injuries, he enquired about Nikki.

'But Nikki's not here, Jack. I thought you would have known.'

'Known what?'

'She discharged herself.'

72

Washington, DC
14 November
12.05 a.m.

Harold Fellini Rotstein was a small, dapper man in his late fifties, with a fondness for bow ties and an even bigger fondness for women's breasts.

It was an affection that had enticed him into the plastic surgery business, at first specialising in boob jobs, but after botching operations on four young women in Miami, two of them rising film stars whom he'd implanted with leaky silicone cells, he'd been struck off the medical register. The court case had ruined him, cost Rotstein not only a small fortune but his right to practice. Still, he'd got over all that, changed his name, moved to DC, got himself a false medical diploma, and carried on as before, although these days his patients were mostly hookers, or transsexual males in the same business.

Tonight, Rotstein wished he'd got the hell out of the plastic surgery business. The reason was Benny Visto, lying on a table in Rotstein's private clinic, with half his knee blown off. Visto was one of the meanest, nastiest pimps Rotstein had ever had the misfortune to deal with. He'd had half a dozen of his girls endowed with impressive breast jobs, and while Rotstein appreciated the cash, he hadn't appreciated the buzz on his doorbell just after midnight, rousing him from bed in his apartment above his clinic, nor the unwelcome sight of the two wounded men which awaited him.

'He's in a bad way. He really needs a hospital, for God's sake.'

'Benny doesn't want no fucking hospitals.' Frankie Tate's voice was shaking as he clutched his wounded shoulder. 'He doesn't want no cops.'

'Listen,' Rotstein replied calmly. 'The gunshot wound to his arm is not a major problem, but his knee is. He needs a good surgeon, otherwise he may end up crippled. There's arterial damage – it may be that the bullet nicked an artery, which is why he's still bleeding. This is really a job for a specialist surgeon.'

'No, you listen, asshole.' Visto was trying in vain to raise himself from the table, his eyes barely focused. 'It says fucking surgeon on that fucking door of yours outside, don't it?'

'That's true, but it's not the point, Mr Visto. Your injuries require specialist medical equipment, a proper operating theatre . . .'

Frankie was leaning against the table with his good arm. He was in considerable pain, sweat pouring down his face, but he had the .38 out of his pocket in an instant, pushed the barrel against Rotstein's left cheek, and the doctor's eyes bulged in terror. 'Fuck the point. Just do what I say, and do it quick. Get working on fixing up Benny's leg, then take care of me. Or else you're going need some fucking surgery yourself, you hear, Rotstein?'

'Very . . . very well, but be it on your own head.' Rotstein, trembling, turned to Visto. 'I'll have to give you an anaesthetic, you understand this?'

'Give me anything you fucking want, but just get it fucking over and done with.'

His face beaded with sweat, Visto gritted his teeth, closed his eyes to the rivers of pain coursing through his leg. Rotstein went to a cupboard, and with trembling hands took down a syringe and a small bottle. He filled the syringe, inserted it into Visto's right arm. 'Try and relax, Mr Visto. In a couple more moments, you won't feel any pain.'

2.15 a.m.

Kursk reached the FBI visitors' apartment block on 7th Street, went up in the elevator, unlocked the door to his rooms, and switched on a table lamp. A bottle of Stolichnaya he hadn't opened was in his travel bag and he took it out, twisted off the cap and poured himself a large measure. He sat down, emptied the glass in one swallow and was about to pour another before he called the number he'd been given by Lazarev for the New York consulate when his cellphone vibrated. 'Kursk.'

'Major? It's Suslov.'

'I thought you said you didn't want to talk to me.'

'I don't. Except I got a call late tonight, from someone in DC who may have information about this guy Gorev. They heard I was asking.'

Kursk sat bolt upright. 'Who called you?'

'You don't know them, Major. I'll tell you when we meet. Can you meet me?'

'Wherever you want.'

'Take down this address. I'll see you there in half an hour and take you to see the guy. And Kursk . . .'

'What?'

'This is just between you and me. I don't want the FBI tagging along, or anyone from the embassy, you got that? I may be in enough trouble already.'

2.45 a.m.

Eight blocks away, at Dr Rotstein's private clinic, Benny Visto had taken a definite turn for the worse. Two hours after Rotstein had operated on his knee he'd lost consciousness. His blood pressure had dropped, his breathing had become laboured, and he'd started to bleed again, despite the doctor's best efforts.

Frankie, waiting in a room outside, his shoulder stitched and bandaged, went in when Rotstein called him. 'What the fuck's wrong?' he demanded.

'I've done my best, really I have.' Rotstein was nervous. 'But the bleeding has started again. I told you he should have gone to hospital.'

Frankie, alarmed, saw that Visto's face was covered with sweat and he was moaning, moving from side to side. He caught a glimpse of Rotstein lifting the dressing, shaking his head at the stitched-up pulp of Visto's knee, the tiny rivers of blood seeping though the sutures. Frankie turned away in disgust, bile rising in his stomach. 'How bad is it?'

'Very bad. There's a chance he may lose the leg. I did warn you . . .'

'Benny?' Frankie said.

Visto's eyes flickered open. For a moment he didn't seem to recognise his cousin. 'Fuck's going down, Frankie . . . ?'

'We have to get you to a hospital, Benny, you hear me?'

Visto gripped Frankie's wrist feverishly. 'No . . . no hospital, you hear? The cops been trying to get a bead on me for years. You want to hand me to them on a fucking plate? They find out about this, they'd be all over me . . .'

He fell back, eyes closed again. Frankie, desperate, turned to the doctor. 'For Christ's sake, ain't there a good surgeon you know? Someone you can get here to help? I'll make it worth their while.'

'It's not a question of money, Mr Tate, even if I could recommend someone, which I can't. I told you, we'd need a proper operating theatre . . . the right equipment. All I can really do is give him another injection to try and stop the haemorrhaging.'

'Then fucking do it.'

'But if that fails, I can't be held responsible . . .'

Frankie was livid. 'That's where you're wrong, Doc. If Benny goes, you go with him, you hear me? And that's a fucking promise.'

Kursk stepped out of the cab near Dupont Circle. The place looked deserted at that dark hour of the morning, just a handful of taxis flitting around the Circle. He headed towards P Street, not far from Suslov's restaurant, then turned a corner, following the directions he'd been given, until he came to an intersection, swung right and waited on the pavement outside a private red-brick town house.

He heard footsteps approach. A figure came out of an alleyway to the right, walking towards him. At first he thought it was Suslov, but when the figure got closer he saw the man's face under the flash of a streetlamp. He was young, big and burly, with a jagged, ugly scar on his left cheek. Kursk was immediately cautious. The man spoke in Russian. 'Major Kursk of the FSB?'

'Who are you?' Kursk's right hand lingered on a button of his coat, ready to reach for his automatic.

'That doesn't matter for now, Major. I have some information for you.'

Suddenly two more men rushed from the alleyway to Kursk's right. Before he had a chance to wrench out his handgun he felt a stinging blow to the back of his neck, and a jagged spasm of pain jolted down his spine. A car started up, moved out of the alleyway. It was black and shiny, a Chrysler, and its rear door swung open. Kursk was bundled roughly into the back. He tried to fight off his attackers and struggle free, but fists rained down, and then another blow struck him hard across the back of the neck and he blacked out.

73

Washington, DC
12.45 a.m.

The *Washington Post*, founded in 1877 on four sheets of rag paper that were destined to give birth to a powerhouse of newspaper publishing, has a long history of shedding light and truth on some of the darker corners of American politics. Down the decades, a wealth of US government cover-ups had been exposed by the *Post*'s reporters. Two of them, Woodward and Bernstein, had famously helped evict Richard Nixon from office, uncovering the President's involvement in the Watergate scandal.

Barney Redmond Woods, the night editor, was a grizzled, grey-haired man of fifty-six, a veteran who'd spent over thirty years in the newspaper business. He was sitting in his office that early morning, sipping from a mug of coffee, one of many he'd knocked back during his shift which had played havoc with his ulcers. The paper would be put to bed by 1.45 a.m.; half an hour later the presses would roll out the final edition, but far from being happy, Woods was strained. His shift ran from 3 p.m. to midnight, and he should have been home by now, unwinding with a triple Scotch and soda, but he was still stuck in his damned office.

'Nikki, you've got a hunch, that's all. You've got to give me something concrete if we're to run a story.'

Nikki, seated opposite, had been arguing her case with Barney Woods for the third time in the last two hours, until she was almost hoarse. It didn't help that she was in agony; her bandaged arm throbbed, her head ached, and every time she spoke her bruised face hurt like hell. Before leaving the hospital she'd forgotten to ask one of the nurses for some painkillers, and she was regretting it now. For the last four hours, since her medication had worn off, she'd felt the pain of every bump and laceration she'd suffered. When she'd looked at herself in the mirror in the ladies' rest room down the hall, she'd got a shock – with the dressing still around her forehead, together with her swollen face and bandaged arm, the treated cuts and tiny facial lacerations, she looked like someone who'd survived a head-on collision.

'There's smoke, sure, but where's the fire?' Woods argued. 'I need to see the fire, Nikki. And so far, I haven't seen any.'

Nikki thought: *He's right.* All she really had to go on was her intuition that something strange was happening in the District, but even that was leading her nowhere. She'd spent the last five hours on the phone: a half-dozen times she'd called the Police Commissioner, both at his office and at his home, to ask him directly about the police drill and explore her suspicions. The Commissioner obviously didn't want to talk with her; his wife didn't offer to say where he was or how Nikki could get in contact, and directed her, apologetically but firmly, to the metropolitan police public affairs office – Brad Stelman's domain – before she put down the phone. When she called police headquarters, she got the same fob-off – 'I'm sorry, ma'am, you'll have to call back tomorrow during office hours. There's no one here right now who can handle your query.'

She'd phoned the army public affairs office and asked to speak with Major Craig again. She was told that Craig was on leave, and was passed on to a Captain Torc, who listened politely as she again explained her query about the troop deployments in DC, but it got her absolutely nowhere. Torc insisted that Major Craig would have to deal with it, and that he'd be back in the office the following afternoon if she'd care to call back, or he'd have the major call her. The army was giving her the runaround again.

When she called the mayor's office, she got the same treatment – they didn't know anything about the police or army exercises and she'd have to contact their respective public affairs offices and direct her questions there. At the end of it all she was angry, frustrated and in agony without painkillers. The concussion she'd suffered didn't help; she felt lethargic, her head muzzy, as if she'd woken after a deep night's sleep aided by a double dose of sleeping pills. In between it all, racked by worry, she'd called her mother every hour at the hospital. Daniel was still stable – and he'd come awake twice. The news made her cry with joy and relief – but the fact that she wasn't near him right now was agony in itself. 'What about the bomb at the FBI Headquarters, Barney? What about that?'

'We ran the story yesterday, and we're still with it today, like every other goddamned newspaper, TV and radio station in the country. But the official line from the Feds is still the same – an obscure, unnamed Patriot group may be responsible.'

'What evidence have they offered?'

'Nikki, the blast only happened twenty-four hours ago and the investigation's barely begun. It's going to take the Feds time to get results. But I've got a dozen people working the story. Why the hell do you think I'm still hanging around here? If anything breaks, I want to know about it.'

'It's tied into it all somehow, Barney,' Nikki said in frustration. 'The troops deployed in DC, the military activity at the airport, the police exercise, the runaround I'm being given . . .'

Woods shook his head, stood, hitched up his trousers. 'That's not even a good conspiracy theory, Nikki. It's just a feeling, and there's nothing you can prove. Jesus, if I had a dime for every intuitive lead the people in this place have had over the years that turned out to be well wide of the mark, I'd be sunning myself on my own yacht in the Caribbean . . .'

'What about Brad Stelman? What about that?' She'd called Stelman at his sister's place. His sister said she hadn't heard from him since five that evening, when he'd called her from his office. Nikki left a message with her for her brother to call if he got in touch, then drove over to Stelman's apartment block, trying his cellphone and land-line numbers on the way, but got no response. She got no response either when she tried his apartment buzzer. After five minutes, almost paranoid, she'd checked the street outside for any men in cars or vans watching Stelman's block but saw no one suspicious. 'What about the fact he was followed yesterday evening? That he thought his phone was being tapped?'

'They're not facts, Nikki. Just Stelman's own intuition, until you can prove otherwise.'

'What if he's been abducted by the men who were watching him?'

'Nikki, the guy's only disappeared off the radar for the last eight, nine hours, for Christ sakes. How do you know he's been abducted? He could be anywhere. Getting laid, having a beer . . .' Woods shook his head. 'We've gone over it all, Nikki, and I know you think there's some kind of conspiracy, that something stinks in this town, but . . .'

'You don't?'

Woods sighed, came round his desk, placed a hand gently on her shoulder. 'Look, Nikki, I'm truly sorry about what happened to Daniel, just as I'm concerned about what happened to you. I also know you're under stress. And the fact that you left Daniel's bedside to come back here to work, in the state you're in, tells me you're sincere about this, and determined as hell, and maybe you've got something, something big. For what it's worth, frankly, I don't know what the hell to think. Maybe you're right. Maybe we're sitting on the biggest story we've had in years. But until we've got evidence, until we find out what the hell it is that might be happening, all we've got to give the reader is veiled hints. And that's not reporting, Nikki. It's speculation. And we can't hang a story on speculation.'

'My son's lying in a critical-care unit and thirteen people are dead. What more do you want, Barney? More bodies? What if there's another explosion, more people are killed? We owe it to this city to find out what's going on, we really do.'

Nikki's shoulders slumped; there was a thwarted look on her face. She was wearing herself down.

Woods, in response, ran a hand tiredly over his craggy face, collapsed into his chair. For a few moments he massaged his temples, then placed both his hands on the desk. 'OK, look, I'll tell you what I'll do. I'll get in touch with the mayor personally, and with a couple of senior cops I know in the Met. I'll throw out a line, tell them we're sniffing round a conspiracy story, big time – mention all the stuff you told me – and see what reaction I get. If I get the feeling they're worried, or trying to cover something up, we'll follow it up.'

'When will you call them?'

'Now, tonight. Al Brown's going to love me for ruining his sleep, so are my friends in the Met, but what the frig. In return, I'd like you to do something for me.'

'What?'

'Go back to the hospital. Go back to your little boy and stay with him. That's the only place you ought to be. I'll call you if I've got anything.' Woods checked his watch, thought for a moment. 'Maybe there's another angle I can try, too. I'll wake up someone else, a friend of mine who works at the White House. I had to call him anyway about something else, but I'll try throwing him the same line as the mayor and the others. I've known the guy for years. If I sense any hint that he's scared, or knows something he doesn't want to tell me, we'll take it from there. As for you, just get yourself back to the hospital.'

'First I've got to see if I can find Brad Stelman. And I've got some calls to make.'

Woods groaned. 'Jesus, I'm talking to a wall.'

There was something else Nikki had to do, but she didn't tell Woods. She would keep her word and divulge nothing of what Jack had told her, but she wanted to talk with him again. She was convinced that at the hospital he'd been on the edge of telling her the real truth about the case he was involved in. If she could just push him a little harder this time, maybe she could find out what that truth really was. Nikki stood. 'What's the story with your friend in the White House? Why do you have to call him?'

'The weirdest thing,' Woods said. 'I got a wire report tonight about a big number of our troops being shipped out of the Middle East, and no one seems to know a damned thing about what's going on.'

Washington, DC
4 a.m.

The man lay awake, unable to sleep. Getting out of bed, he pulled on a dressing gown, crossed to the bedroom window, stared out anxiously at the night-time lights of Washington. *So close to the end of things, and now this . . .*

He'd climbed into bed an hour ago, after making the call from his cloned cellphone and passing on his information about the transfer of US troops to Israel. He'd had to speak his message 'in clear', a potentially dangerous thing to do, but he'd simply had no alternative, and he'd kept the message brief and cut the connection immediately he'd finished. There wasn't time to arrange a meeting with his contact face to face – if he had insisted on leaving his home alone, without his Secret Service detail, he would have brought suspicion on himself. Making his call in clear language was slightly the lesser of the two risks – the cloned phone gave him a good degree of protection – but he hadn't slept since with worry, and he was fretting about Abu Hasim's reaction once he learned the news. This was a serious last-minute spanner in the works. A surprise twist no one could have anticipated. But one that could upset everything.

Question. Would Hasim demand that the President stick to the principle of their agreement and withdraw US troops entirely from the region, or would he accept the movement of a large percentage of those forces to Israel without argument? He felt strongly that Hasim would force the issue, insist on the troops being kept out of Israel, and that was what disturbed him. He knew Abu Hasim's personality. The news would make him furious. He would see the tactic as a treacherous move on the part of the US. More worrying, his rage would make him capable of anything – upping his demands or threatening to set off the device immediately. In his message the man had urged caution, but he was still deeply, deeply worried. This could lead anywhere. He put a trembling hand to his forehead.

So close to the end . . .

Something else troubled him. He had no doubt that Abu Hasim would want to respond to the President, and smartly. But by his doing so the question would inevitably arise in the White House as to how Hasim could have got his information so quickly. The man knew that in passing on the information there was a risk of his exposure. For that reason he had suggested to Hasim how to convey his knowledge of the troop movement to Israel without creating suspicion. He just hoped to God that Hasim had taken it on board. Otherwise he could find himself in peril.

His head throbbed. He crossed back to the bed, found the Tylenol in the nightstand drawer, and swallowed two without water. His dangerous journey would soon be coming to an end, but the end of things, he knew from experience, was always the difficult part. Eight hours remained, and he was certain he wouldn't be able to get back to sleep for any of them. Too many thoughts assailed him, too many fears racked his mind. True, he been guided by his hopes, his dreams, his vision. And he had remained steadfast, was resolved to see this through to the end, no matter what the personal cost. He simply had to; too much was at stake. *Nothing* would make him give in now. But he still shuddered, thinking of the eight traumatic hours that lay ahead. Fraught with hazards, they could endanger hundreds of thousands of lives. Shaking, he looked back at the clock on the nightstand.

4.10 a.m.

Resurrection Day had well and truly begun.

Washington, DC
3.50 a.m.

On the operating table in Harold Rotstein's clinic, Benny Visto lay very still.

'How is he?' Frankie demanded. He stood at the end of the table as Rotstein moved his stethoscope over Visto's chest.

'Alive, but only just, and in a very bad way.' Rotstein's voice was shaky. 'The bleeding seems to have started again.'

'What about that shot you gave him?'

'I . . . I didn't say it would work, Mr Tate. Trust me, I've done my absolute best.'

'You're telling me Benny's *dying*?'

'If he's not, he soon will be, unless you get him to a hospital.' Rotstein was trembling again. 'I'm sorry, Mr Tate, but—'

'Shut the fuck up.' In an instant Frankie made his decision, grabbed the doctor by the coat and pushed him towards the door. 'Get on the phone and call an ambulance.'

Rotstein was worried. An ambulance would cause all kinds of complications, including a visit from the police. 'But that will involve me with the law . . . and besides, Mr Visto said he didn't want . . .'

'What *I* want is for Benny to live. Now get out there and make the call.'

'What if you just drove him there yourself?'

'Do what I fucking told you, Rotstein!' Frankie shoved the doctor through the door. When he turned back to the table to stare at his cousin, he was shaking, his eyes wet. 'Tell you one thing, Benny,' he promised. 'I'll have the dude who did this. Swear to God I will, if it's the last fucking thing I do.'

Washington, DC
3.10 a.m.

The black Chrysler turned off Massachusetts Avenue and headed south towards the Capitol Beltway. It hit a pothole and Kursk started to come round, jogged awake by the bump. He was groggy, barely able to focus as the car passed the illuminated Capitol Building. His head spun, his voice was slurred. 'Who . . . who . . . are you. Where are you taking me?'

'Shut up,' a voice ordered in Russian.

Another voice laughed. 'Don't worry, Major, you'll know soon enough.'

In the darkness of the cab, in his groggy state, Kursk couldn't make out the faces around him, but he recognised the strong accents. Moscow hard men, all of them. Russians, not Georgians or Chechens. A chilling thought struck him through the fog: *Yudenich's men.*

Suddenly the car slowed to a halt at traffic lights. Kursk, in desperation, struggled to reach for the door. Hands grabbed at him from everywhere, a fist struck him in the face, and then someone yanked up his sleeve. 'Don't fight it, Kursk. You're finished anyway.'

A hypodermic jabbed his arm, and seconds later a powerful drug flooded his veins. Kursk lost it then; his eyes rolled in his head, his senses shut down, his body went limp, and he sank back in the seat.

74

Chesapeake
3.50 a.m.

Mohamed Rashid drove the Plymouth along the beach access road. He halted when he came to the end, switched off the engine. The wind was blowing in off Chesapeake Bay, the stars bright. He had driven south past Plum Point, fifteen miles from the cottage, and as he climbed out of the car his eyes searched the landscape.

The dark beach was deserted – no sound except the wind and water, and the clanking noise of the engine cooling. Not another person or car in sight, just as he had hoped. He'd chosen the site weeks ago, driven here half a dozen times to ensure it was isolated enough. Off to his right, a quarter-mile away, he saw the distant lights of the nearest house. It was too far away to be any threat, but he was determined to be more cautious after his confrontation with the couple in the woods. After five minutes studying his surroundings, listening for the slightest sounds of an approaching car, he moved back to the Plymouth.

His backpack was on the passenger seat. His transmission 'window' was between 4 and 5 a.m. He removed the laptop, opened out the satellite dish, connected it to the computer port, and ran the co-ax lead out, positioning the dish on the ground, metres from the car. Then he sat in the driver's seat, left the door open and switched on the computer. The screen came to life and the Windows program loaded. It took a few more moments to properly align the dish, then he typed an outline of his report, scrolled through it again until he was happy with the text, then hit the 'send' key. The signal burst was transmitted in less than two seconds.

The call to his cellphone over an hour ago from his White

House contact, and his news about the redeployment of troops to Israel, had unsettled him. So close to the end, and the Americans were playing tricks. It made him seethe. They were fools, playing with fire by being so devious, and he believed that Abu Hasim's reply would be fierce.

Rashid was confident he would receive the return signal at 7 a.m., his next receiving window. He would set up the laptop and dish back at the cottage. The reply would decide everything. He switched off the computer, folded away the sat dish, stored both in his backpack, and placed it on the passenger seat. He was wide awake, brimming with energy. Before he left the cottage he had mixed a little crystal meth in some coffee. Drinking the liquid had given him a surge of energy, enough to keep him wide awake for at least the next twenty-four hours.

Gorev's encounter with Visto troubled him. What if Visto went to the police? What if he gave them details of the police van and uniforms? To err on the safe side he should perhaps abandon his plan to use the police vehicle. But he would decide that later.

For now, his chief concern was the Israel issue. Because of it, the fools in the White House could yet destroy their own city. Strangely it didn't worry him. If he had to die to punish the Americans, then so be it if that was Allah's wish.

Washington, DC
3.45 a.m.

The black Chrysler exited off the Capitol Beltway. Ten minutes later it entered the back parking lot of a ramshackle warehouse in a grim industrial area five miles from DC. Kursk was still unconscious as the men dragged him from the back seat.

The driver and the front-seat passenger ran ahead, unlocked a pair of heavy-duty metal doors, moved into the warehouse and flicked some light switches. The building flooded with neon light. It was filthy, freezing cold, scattered with discarded wooden packing crates, and a single sturdy wooden chair was set under the harsh glare of one of the neon tubes. The men dragged Kursk inside, dumped him in the chair, secured his hands to the armrests with lengths of rope, and did the same with each of his ankles, fastening them to the chair's legs.

The scar-faced young man who had met Kursk off Dupont Circle casually lit a cigarette, then dug his hands into his pockets and tossed the service pistol, wallet and cellphone he'd taken from him on to one the packing crates. He said to one of this companions, 'Get the blowtorch ready and bring me the cosh from the car.'

'The others are here, Andrei.'

The scar-faced man turned, saw the dipped headlights as a couple of cars swept round the back of the warehouse and braked gently to a halt. A group of men climbed out of each vehicle. 'I think it's time to wake the major.'

FBI Headquarters
1.55 a.m.

Collins called Nikki's cellphone from the Hoover building. It rang once before she picked up.

'*Hello?*'

The line was bad, and Collins could barely hear her voice. 'Nikki, it's me. Can you hear me?'

'Wait a second – I've got to move near a window, the line's terrible.'

Moments later Nikki came on the line again, clearer. 'Can you hear me now?'

'I can hear you. What's going on, Nikki? I called the hospital . . .'

'Where are you?' Nikki interrupted.

'At the Hoover.'

'You've got to meet me, Jack. I'm at the *Post* right now, and I've got some calls to make and then I've got to go out for a while. Can you meet me in a couple of hours?'

'Nikki, I can't, honey. I'm right up to my neck. Just tell me what happened. Why did you discharge yourself? I thought you'd want to be with Daniel . . . is anything wrong I should know about?'

There was a pause. 'I can't talk about it, not over the phone,' Nikki said. 'But we have to meet, Jack. Please, it's *very* important.'

Collins sighed, instinct telling him Nikki wanted to tread the same ground they'd gone over in the restaurant last night. 'Nikki, if it's got to do with what we discussed, I told you, I can't go into it. Don't push it, please.'

Another pause, then Collins heard words that chilled him. 'You didn't tell me the truth, did you? You didn't tell me what's actually going on. This time we've really got to talk, Jack.'

Washington, DC
3.50 a.m.

Kursk came awake with a jolt as a fist crashed into his face. 'Wake up!'

Another blow struck him, a stinging slap to his jaw, and Kursk's head snapped sideways. He tasted blood in his mouth. His head lolled, his mind a fog, and it was a couple of moments before he started to come to his senses.

'Good. You're back in the land of the living.'

Kursk blinked, focused, saw the scar-faced young man standing over him with a companion, a half dozen others behind them. What Kursk saw next chilled him. The man's companion started to fiddle with the knobs on a portable blowtorch, rubber tubes running off it to an oxy-acetylene bottle near by. Scar-face had a leather cosh in his right hand. 'Can you hear me, Kursk?'

'Who . . . are you?'

'Never mind that. You remember the name Matvei Yudenich, no doubt?'

Kursk, still groggy, heard the name, had expected it, but said nothing.

Scar-face nodded to his companion. 'Let's see if we can jog his memory.'

The second man took out a cigarette lighter, touched it to the tip of the blowtorch and ignited the gas. The torch glowed red; then the red turned an intense blue. 'Start with his fingers, one at a time. We'll see if that loosens his tongue.'

As Kursk struggled, the man stepped forward with the blowtorch.

'*Wait!*'

A figure stepped out from the shadows. Blinded by the neon, Kursk couldn't see the man's face, but he heard the authority in his voice. 'Give me ten minutes. Alone,' the man said in Russian. Scar-face nodded. His companion doused the blowtorch, tossed it on the ground, and left with the others.

Slowly, the man who had spoken emerged farther out of the shadows. He took a handkerchief from his pocket, leaned across, dabbed blood from Kursk's mouth.

'Who are you?'

The man ignored the question. 'This business we're in, it's not a pleasant one, Major. And you've walked on dangerous ground. The men who brought you here, you know they mean to kill you? I can do nothing about that. But you've been asking questions, Major. And before you die, I'd like to find out why. You've been enquiring about a man named Nikolai Gorev.'

'Who are you?'

'My name is Ishim Razan.'

75

FBI Headquarters
Washington, DC
3.40 a.m.

Matthew Cage, the FBI Assistant Director, felt as if he'd aged ten years. His tanned, handsome face was washed out, creased with worry lines, his eyes red and gritty, testament to the restless twelve hours' sleep he'd had in just over three days. 'We've got to push even harder, Tom. We've got to beat the damned bushes with every stick we've got. And I mean beat the living daylights out of them. We've got just over eight hours left. Less than that if we're to be honest.'

Tom Murphy, in the chair opposite, thought: *What the fuck do you think I've been doing for the last three days?*

'With the greatest respect, sir,' Murphy said, 'we've beaten the bushes until there isn't a fucking leaf left. We've walked every street and alleyway in the District, put the squeeze on every petty criminal, pimp, pick-pocket, hooker and hustler we know of. Shone a light into every dark hole we could find. Searched every warehouse we deemed suspect, every building that might be used to store the chemical. Everyone's been giving it their *absolute* best – a hundred and fifty per cent. They're tired, they're washed out. I push them any harder, they're going to be ferrying our agents out of here on fucking stretchers.'

Cage slapped his hands on the desk in a gesture of hopelessness. He stood and paced the room, rubbing his neck, trying to alleviate his gnawing tension – so bad it felt as if his neck was going to snap. In the last two hours alone he'd had *six* calls from the White House, and four from his Director, asking after his progress. Their persistence was wearing him down. All he wanted this minute was to curl up in a bed, cover himself with a blanket and sleep for a week.

'You know what's galling?' Cage's jaw tightened as he gestured towards the District's lights. 'Those bastards are out there, somewhere. They're out there and we've got every resource we can muster – thousands of agents, tons of equipment, bags of money being doled out to informers – and we can't even get a whiff of them. What does that tell you?'

'How ineffective we are,' Murphy admitted tiredly. 'Or how good they are.'

'There's that. But by my reasoning, *somebody*'s got to be keeping their mouth shut. Somebody's got to *know* these people. Somebody's got to have seen or dealt with them, passed them on the street, served them in a gas station, sold them groceries, carried them in a cab, maybe done business with them. Terrorists can't live in a vacuum, and even if it means carrying people out of here on stretchers, you've got to push harder, Tom. If you've beaten every leaf off the bush, then pull the damned bush up by the roots. Look under every clod and rock. We're all tired, we're all washed out, we're all at our wits' end, but we've *got* to give it this last big push.'

Murphy, fighting his own fatigue, gave a silent nod. He'd worked tough investigations that took months, even years to crack. He was being asked to do the impossible – crack one of the toughest in just over eight more hours. True, he had manpower – every agent available – but he wished the guys on the executive floor could take time out and see for themselves what it was like working the salt-mines. Everyone on the case was living on their nerves, kept awake by coffee, fear and desperation. He'd had three men taken to hospital in the last four hours, suffering from exhaustion. Another had suffered a heart attack. No doubt there would be more casualties of the stress before the night was out. Murphy didn't feel so good himself, pains arcing across his chest, his legs like rubber; he wondered whether he'd make the next eight hours without collapsing. *Maybe I won't have to worry after that, maybe I'll be gassed to death anyway.* He thanked God that his ex-wife and his two sons were living over in Annapolis. The chances were they'd be safe there. But he knew he was doing *everything* he possibly could to crack this, didn't even bother to argue the issues again with Cage. 'Yes, sir.'

Cage picked up a notepad, studied the scribbled notes he'd made during the last phone call he'd received ten minutes ago. 'To top it all, we've got another serious problem on our hands.'

'What is it this time?'

'The White House has been getting calls from the press about our troops being pulled from the Gulf. So far, they've been able to long-finger them, by saying the President will issue a statement some time tomorrow on the matter, but inferring it's no big deal and the pull-out is just for the holiday season. However . . .' Cage paused, tapped his notepad. 'There's a woman reporter from the *Post* who's being very persistent in asking questions. She's been on to the mayor's office, hounded the Police Commissioner, talked to the army public affairs office. An hour ago, she even tried to get in touch with the Director himself. She called him half a dozen times and left a message for him to call her back, saying it was urgent. God knows how she got his private number, though I guess when you're a reporter with the *Post* you've got ways and means. But we think it might have been from a friend of hers, a public relations guy named Stelman, who works at metropolitan headquarters. She'd been plugging him for information about the police exercise. The Commissioner had to take Stelman aside tonight after he'd had him watched, and threatened to fire him on the spot if he helped her again in any way. Said he'd bring serious charges against Stelman if he divulged any more information to her. He's been told not to communicate with her in any way or he'll face the wrath of the Met.'

'Why the mayor and Commissioner? Or the Director? What have they got to do with the Gulf pull-out . . .'

'She's not been asking about that, Tom. Not her personally, at least not yet, but some other people at the *Post* have. She's more interested in the military operation in DC, and the police exercise, and she's been very persistent. She's been suggesting there's a cover-up, that there's more to the army and police exercises than is being admitted. The feeling is, she might know something. Or if she doesn't, she soon will, the way she's going. She's also been asking about the Bureau explosion. It's like she's pulling all the right strands together. If she goes public, then people are going to be running out of this city like there's no tomorrow. Which there won't be, not if Mohamed Rashid and his fiends see the streets emptying. Chances are, they'll think we're evacuating and press the button.'

'Where does that leave us?' Murphy asked worriedly.

'Those people at the *Post* don't give up until they've got to the bottom of a story, especially a cover-up. The White House thinks the woman poses a security risk, could blow this thing wide open, and they're worried as hell.'

'What are they going to do?'

'The Secret Service have got her address, her car licence number, her cellphone number. Somebody's been briefed to locate her. I wasn't told who they are and I didn't ask.'

'What's the intention?'

'Set up a meeting, on the pretence of having the kind of information she might be interested in.'

'And?'

'They put her away somewhere secure, for reasons of national security, until this thing's over, one way or the other.'

'Jesus, Matt, the *Post* would go wild with a story like that. Kidnapping one of their reporters? They'll tear the White House to shreds when they find out.'

'That's not my worry, Tom. God knows, we've got enough of our own.'

'So who's the journalist?'

'Her name's Nikki Dean.'

Washington, DC
3.55 a.m.

'You've heard of me, Kursk?'

'Tell me any state official in Moscow who hasn't.'

Razan brushed dust from one of the warehouse packing crates, sat, lit a cigar. 'So, Yudenich has an old score to settle? But then people like him always have. What did you do to him, Kursk?'

'Does it matter?'

Razan shrugged. 'I suppose not.'

'If this isn't your business, why are you here?'

'I heard you were asking questions. Yudenich heard too. Not that the questions you were asking mattered much to him. He saw an opportunity to settle a debt, nothing more. But to me, your questions mattered very much.'

'Why?'

'We'll get to that.'

'What about Yudenich?'

'He gets his pound of flesh, but I get to talk with you first.' Razan flicked ash from his cigar. 'Of course, you may have no reason to satisfy my curiosity, knowing that your death is a certainty. Perhaps all I can do on your behalf is ask that your passing be made less painful.'

'You and your kind, Razan, you make me sick. You take a life and it matters nothing.'

Razan shook his head. 'Don't label me with Yudenich. I'm not a bloodthirsty animal. But this isn't my business. Yudenich simply obliged me. Of course, I could ask him to forget about taking his revenge, but knowing Yudenich he wouldn't listen.' He shrugged. 'I doubt it will matter much, but perhaps I will ask anyway.'

'And in return?'

'You tell me why you're so interested in Nikolai Gorev.'

'You know him?'

'We served together as paratroopers, many years ago.'

'Do you know where he is?'

Razan shrugged, blew out a ring of smoke. 'Even if I did, I wouldn't tell you. Nikolai Gorev is one of the few men I respect, a hero to my people. I'd rather kill myself than betray him, especially to the scum of the FSB.'

Kursk's pulse quickened. 'You *do* know where he is, don't you?'

Razan ignored the question. 'You still haven't answered. Why were you asking after Gorev?'

'You wouldn't believe me.'

'Try me.'

'There's much more to this than you can know, Ishim Razan. Like you, Nikolai Gorev and I go back a long time.'

Razan frowned. 'What's that supposed to mean?'

'A long story. You can hear it if you want. But first I need your solemn promise you'll keep what I tell you a secret . . .'

Razan tossed his cigar on the floor, crushed it. 'I'm losing my patience, Major. And you're in no position to make conditions.'

'I need your word, Razan, if I'm to trust you.'

Razan considered, nodded. 'Very well, if it matters that much. You have my word.'

'Your *solemn* word.'

'As God is my judge. Now talk.'

76

On the fourth floor at Secret Service headquarters, between 10th and 11th Streets, a light blazed in Harry Judd's office. As he eased the telephone back in its cradle, he stood, lost in thought.

The call he'd just made had unsettled him. The truth was, he felt stunned, as if he'd been hit with a baseball bat. For the last eight hours, the four suspects on his list – General Horton, Mitch Gains, Bob Rapp and Charles Rivermount – had been subjected to the most intense surveillance anyone could imagine. In its attempt to find the White House source, Judd's plan had been simple – one of the oldest tricks in the book. You feed a single suspect false information and see if the information is made use of. If it comes back at you through another source, then you know who fed the source and you have your man.

In this case, there were four suspects, which made things more difficult. Each of them, of necessity, had been fed the same lie. But the same rules applied – whichever one made use of it was the guy you wanted to nail. However, actually *catching* the culprit in the act of passing on the information was how Judd hoped he was going to nab his man. He knew it wasn't going to be easy, but he had done his best to cover all the angles.

For a start, apart from their regular Secret Service protection detail – which had been primed about the surveillance – each suspect had a covert squad of eight men assigned to watch him. 'Watch' was hardly the word. Unknown to Rivermount, Gains, Rapp and Horton, their every movement and their every word was under scrutiny. Every e-mail they sent, every phone call they made, every person they met, every gesture they made in public was being noted and recorded.

Three men in each of the surveillance teams were riding in special vans – two vans to each suspect. These men were Technical Security specialists, and the vans were fitted with every high-tech, ultra-sensitive listening and recording device imaginable: directional and parabolic microphones, cellphone scanners, VHF and UHF receivers, infrared cameras. One van remained near each of the suspects' homes, the other followed them – at a safe distance – while they travelled in their official cars.

Not that there had been much movement that night, official or otherwise. All of the suspects had attended the scheduled 9 p.m. NSC meeting and all had left the White House by 1.30 a.m., escorted by the Secret Service details to their respective homes in the DC area. And all had made phone calls almost as soon as they returned home. General Horton two, Mitch Gains three, Rapp two, and Charles Rivermount six. All of the calls had been from their land lines, except four, which had been made on cellphones.

The men's respective land lines had been bugged since late the previous afternoon, but bugging a cellphone wasn't as easy. There were no exposed wires or wall phone sockets you could clip a bug into. If you got your hands on the cellphone, sure, you could bug it with a miniature ESID, but unless you employed the services of a pick-pocket forget it.

Still, there were other methods. All of the suspects had cellphones supplied by the White House – as NSC members, they were on twenty-four-hour call. Each of them also had individual cellphones of their own. Judd had got the numbers of each and every one and passed them on to the surveillance teams. He also had a dozen men down at the exchanges of the cellphone network providers – a court order always worked wonders – recording calls from each of the four NSC members, including their private mobiles. With the help of the network providers, who could triangulate the calls, Judd could also confirm roughly from where a call was being made, and its destination. As well as all that, the Technical Security specialists parked near each of the suspects' home were using directional scanners to listen in on cellphone frequencies, hoping to snatch any nearby dialogue, just in case one of the suspects was using a phone that wasn't officially registered to him.

Result: *Zero.*

Not a single one of the calls the suspects had made that night had contained a single mention of the lie that each of them had been fed. Of course, a message could have been passed on in code during a seemingly harmless conversation. For that reason, the recorded conversations were being picked over relentlessly, listened to again and again in case they contained some hidden meaning, some secret code. And the destination of the calls themselves had been traced – friends, wives, girlfriends, sons and daughters, relatives and, in the case of Charles Rivermount and Mitch Gains, business associates. None of the people who had been called – Judd had checked the list – was worthy of suspicion, except one. A call to Nabil Rahman al-Khalid, a business partner of Rivermount's. That particular conversation – lasting five minutes forty seconds, but which sounded harmless – was being given special scrutiny, but as yet it had produced zilch. No suggestion of a hidden coded message, or at least none that could so far be determined.

Then, at 2.56 a.m., Judd got a breakthrough.

One of the Technical Security specialist teams, scanning the airwaves outside a suspect's home, had snatched and recorded a brief but highly interesting ninety-three-second cellphone conversation. One of the team had sped back to headquarters with the recording. When Judd heard it, his blood ran cold. Then his shock was replaced by excitement, for by intercepting the call the Technical Security guys had hit on an invaluable tool that might just help in locating the terrorists. He'd immediately called Rob Owens, the Secret Service Assistant Director of Protection. Owens was rushing to headquarters right now.

Judd got no pleasure admitting it – but they had found their White House source.

Washington, DC
4.20 a.m.

It was very still in the warehouse, the silence overpowering. Ishim Razan's face was carved in stone, his shock total. For a few agonising moments the Chechen looked white as death, as if a terrible truth had dawned. The impact had sunk in, but he was still thunderstruck.

'I said you wouldn't believe me.'

Razan was at a loss for words. He flinched, as if he'd received a physical blow, managed to whisper hoarsely, 'You've told me everything?'

'Everything I know.'

The warehouse door slid open, a blast of icy air gusting into the room, and one of Razan's bodyguards stepped in from the cold. 'My pardon, Ishim, but Yudenich's men want to know when you'll be finished—'

'When I'm ready,' Razan almost barked. 'Tell them I'm not to be disturbed again.'

'Yes, Ishim.'

The man left. Razan stepped over to Kursk. His fingers trembled as he undid the ropes around his hands. 'So help me, I don't know why, but I believe you.'

'Then tell me what you know.' Kursk massaged his wrists, undid the ropes around his ankles.

'Two days ago, Gorev and a woman came to see me.'

'What was the woman's name?'

'Safa Yassin. Or so she claimed. But later Nikolai told me otherwise. He said her name was Karla. A Palestinian.'

'Why did they come to you?' Kursk stood, his pulse quickening.

'Nikolai was wounded. He stayed one night with me and left yesterday morning.'

'Was he badly wounded?'

'Enough to require a surgeon. He was bleeding heavily, a stomach wound, from grenade shrapnel. But he survived. The surgeon patched him up.'

'Where did he stay with you?'

Razan hesitated. 'New Jersey.'

'And then?'

'The woman came next morning and took him away.'

'Have you seen them since?'

'No.'

'Is that the truth, Ishim Razan?'

'Yes.'

'Where did the woman take Nikolai?'

Razan was silent. Kursk stepped over to where he stood. 'If you know, I beg you to tell me.'

Razan said nothing.

'I need to talk to Nikolai, convince him to end this. Will you help me find him?'

Razan, still in shock, seemed in torture as he turned away. 'You're asking me to go back on my word. To betray a man I owe my life to. To break my pledge to a hero of my people. Someone I consider a brother.'

'No more than I do. You think I wanted to hunt him down? But there are people out there tonight, innocent men, women and children, who know nothing of the danger they're in. At any second in the next eight hours they could be gassed to death. *All of them.* Could you live with that on your conscience, Ishim Razan? And without trying to persuade Nikolai to stop this insanity before something goes wrong. Could you?'

Still Razan said nothing. Kursk, in frustration, gripped the Chechen's shoulder, spun him round. 'What would you rather, Ishim Razan? Save one life, or half a million?'

77

Chesapeake
4.15 a.m.

Karla was woken by the sound of the sea. It was dark outside, the wash of the moon filtering into the room. When she reached out her hand for Nikolai, he wasn't there. Earlier, he'd come to her room again and lay beside her, stroking her hair until she fell asleep. Now she sat up in bed, was about to flick on the light when she saw him sitting silently in the dark, in a chair near the open window, smoking a cigarette, the only sound the lapping of the waves. Karla relaxed. 'You gave me a fright. I thought you'd gone. What are you doing?'

'Thinking.'

'About what?'

'Something Ishim Razan said to me.'

'Tell me.'

Gorev crushed out his cigarette, came over, kissed her forehead. 'It doesn't matter. You should try and sleep, Karla.'

'Tell me what Razan said.'

'He gave me some advice. That when my business was over, I should live a normal existence, settle down. Not that Ishim can talk, but I'm sure he meant well.'

'He told you that?'

'He seems to think that my whole life has been about battles and causes, not about living, and perhaps he's right.'

'It's not like you to admit that, Nikolai.'

'I know. Confusing, isn't it?'

'What else did he say?'

'Something I probably shouldn't mention.'

'What?'

Gorev hesitated. 'He thinks you've loved me for a very long

time, and far more deeply than I've ever known. That you were a good woman, and I shouldn't risk losing you a second time.'

He saw the look on her face then, a curiosity; and then another look, more sensitive, one that seemed to suggest she was close to tears. 'And what do you think?'

'The truth? I'm tired of it all, Karla. Tired of all the running, of constantly looking over my shoulder, wondering if the next man I meet will put a bullet in me.'

'What are you saying?'

'You remember that story by Pasternak? Where he says that the reason for our exploring is to arrive back where we started. And in so doing, we somehow discover who we are.'

'Yes.'

'He was wrong. We can never go back to where we started. And if we're wise enough, we can know who we are long before we reach the end. Do something for me, Karla.'

'What?'

'This will all be over soon. If it works in our favour, and Josef is free, and if it's not too late, be with me. Let's find somewhere quiet, not to start again, but to be together, make up for all those years we've lost. Josef too. There's a lot he needs to learn, and so much I can teach him. I don't want him wasting half his life by choosing the same path we did.'

'You mean that?'

'I mean it, Karla.'

Her lips trembled, and she suddenly started to cry. Her arms went around his neck and she clung to him. And then her mouth found his in the dark, kissed him, until she whispered, 'Make love to me, Nikolai. Really make love to me. The way it was in Moscow, the last time we were together. It's been such a long time since I felt loved like that.'

Gorev looked into her face, touched her cheek, felt a surge of emotion that was almost crushing. Then his finger traced the outline of her lips, and he kissed her, tenderly at first, then more fiercely, and drew her close.

Maryland
4.30 a.m.

At Fort Meade, headquarters of the National Security Agency, Sergeant Jimmy Nash frowned as he concentrated on the frozen snapshot image of a stream of electronic data that filled his desktop screen. Five minutes later, after tapping away at his keyboard and getting his calculations in order, he picked up the desk phone and called the watch officer. 'Major Sheehan? Nash here. Remember that burst transmission we put a marker on the other day? The highly encrypted code our guys are having trouble cracking.'

'What about it?'

'I registered another burst about twenty-five minutes ago, just like it, no more than two seconds long, on the same frequency.'

'Did we get a fix this time?'

'Yes, sir, we managed to get a good triangulation, got it right in a cocked hat.'

'Where the hell did it come from?'

'An area south of Plum Point, out along Chesapeake Bay.'

Washington, DC
5.05 a.m.

At Secret Service headquarters, things were moving fast. But not fast enough for Rob Owens, the Assistant Director, who was in a state of feverish excitement. Having listened to the tape of the intercepted cellphone conversation, he played it twice again, unable to believe his ears. White faced, he looked up at Harry Judd. 'When was the call made?'

'Two-fifty-six a.m.'

'From where?'

'We think the suspect's apartment, or thereabouts. We can pin it down to the exact floor, but not the *exact* apartment.'

'You sure it's him talking? Not someone else, a neighbour maybe?'

'To be absolutely positive I'm having a voice match done. We're trying to get our hands on a recording of an interview he gave on NBC about a month back. We should have it within an hour, and we'll see if they match. But me, I'm certain we've got our man.'

'What's the story with the phone he used?'

'We got the ESN and MIN numbers when we scanned the call.' Judd didn't have to explain that he meant the phone's Electronic Serial Number and the Mobile Identification Number embedded in its circuits, identifiers that could be scanned, along with the call; the Assistant Director knew as much about call-monitoring as he did. 'The cell's publicly registered to a doctor over in Georgetown. It's not even near the suspect's home.'

'And the number he called?'

'Publicly registered to an IBM engineer living out in Crystal City. I've run checks on both of them. They're native-born US citizens with no connection to any terror groups. The engineer's a retired US Navy officer with a list of citations the length of my arm. The doctor's squeaky clean, a paediatrician with not even a parking ticket to his name. An upstanding citizen who sings in the local Baptist choir, for God's sakes. But we've got a couple of teams watching their homes and listening out for any phone calls they make, on their land lines or cells, and we'll keep digging into their backgrounds and see if we come up with any dirt, though I've got a feeling in my water it'll turn up damn all. But if need be, we can get warrants and pull them in for questioning.'

'What do you think?'

'Gut feeling? We're talking cloned phones. Someone snatched their numbers – a clone's a perfect communication tool for a terrorist because of the untraceability factor, and the easiest thing in the world to do if you know how. We'll need to get a court order to get the doctor and engineer's bills from the phone company, check the listed calls, see if we can match any more calls between our suspect and the person's number he called.'

'Leave that to me,' Owens said. Despite the urgency, this had to be played by the book. America was a democracy, not a police state – though Owens knew folks who might argue otherwise – and if you wanted to check anyone's phone bills or investigate any calls they made, to keep it legal you had to have a court order.

'The other good news,' Judd said, 'is that we can get the network provider to maybe help us get a fix on the location of the guy he called. Again, we'll need a court order.'

Owens' excitement grew, and he nodded. 'I'm with you, go on.'

'Once the guy's phone is switched on, or he's talking on it, the provider can scan the call and triangulate his location. In a city, they can narrow the location down to a street, or even a building, because they've got base stations every couple of hundred yards, so they can tell you where the call's coming from to within maybe a hundred feet. After that, we've got the electronic equipment to narrow it down ourselves even farther. But if the guy our suspect called is out in the country, you could be talking about base stations every ten, twenty miles, or maybe even farther apart. It's more difficult to get a precise location for him. The closest maybe you could pinpoint his position is within ten or twenty miles. But if the cellphone's switched off, we won't be able to get a fix until he switches on again.'

Owens was still excited. 'It's something – a lead. The Feds are going to love you, Harry. I'll organise the court orders straight away.' He slipped the cassette from the recorder. 'You've got a copy of this?'

'Sure, I made a couple.'

Owens slipped the cassette into its hard plastic box, popped it in an envelope. 'As soon as you've got the voice match, we'll call the White House, but not before. I want our evidence hard as rock.' He was still stunned, shook his head as he held up the envelope. 'The President's not going to believe this, Harry. Jesus, this guy's one of his most trusted people.'

'I know.'

Washington, DC
3.15 a.m.

Nikki pulled up outside the Union Station, climbed out of her Toyota and locked the doors. The lights were on the Union's main hall, but the place looked eerily deserted, just a couple of cabs parked at the far end of the rank. The call to her cellphone at 2.45 a.m. had totally surprised her.

A man she didn't know, who said his name was Jacobson, and who claimed he worked for the mayor's office, said that he'd heard she had called Judiciary Square looking for information about the police and army exercises. If she wanted to meet, he had some startling information she might be interested in. He'd be outside the main entrance to the Union Station at 3.15 a.m. Nikki's pulse quickened. 'How . . . how will I recognise you?'

'I'll be wearing a pale raincoat and blue scarf. And Miss Dean, I insist you come alone. I don't want any newspaper photographers tagging along, and you tell no one about our meeting because this is strictly off the record, you understand? If you're not alone, our meeting's off.'

'I understand, but what kind of information do you . . .'

The line clicked dead before Nikki had a chance to finish the sentence. Puzzled, excited by the prospect of a lead, she'd grabbed her bag, made sure she had a spare notebook, and headed for the *Post*'s parking lot.

As she walked towards the station, she had her eyes fixed on the front entrance. She was too preoccupied to hear the car behind her, and then suddenly it cut in front of her. A dark blue Crown Victoria. Three big guys got out. They looked like detectives or Feds. Nikki recognised none of them as they approached. 'Nikki Dean?'

She was startled. Was one these the man she was supposed to meet? The one who had spoken wore a pale raincoat, a dark blue scarf. 'Who . . . who are you?'

'My name's Jacobson. You *are* Nikki Dean, right?'

'Yes.'

'Could you step over to the car, Miss Dean.'

Nikki studied the three men with apprehension, some instinct setting off alarm bells inside her head. Her heart beat furiously. 'I'm . . . I'm not stepping anywhere. Who are you guys?'

It happened quickly, before Nikki even had a chance to scream. One of the men grabbed her from behind, clapped a hand over her mouth. Nikki started to kick out in panic, but a second man got hold of her legs. They carried her bodily over to the Crown Victoria, the third man already opening the rear door. His two companions bundled her into the car. 'Gag her. Fast.'

As a scarf went around Nikki's mouth she tried to scream, but the gag tightened, and suddenly the Crown Victoria screeched away.

78

6 a.m.

At George Washington Hospital, Frankie Tate was in a state of agitation. They'd wheeled Benny Visto into ER from the ambulance at precisely 4.15 a.m., and Frankie was still anxiously waiting in the hall outside nearly two hours later, his arm throbbing like hell. A nurse came up to him, a little woman with a bust bigger than her ass. 'You're *sure* you don't want to see a doctor, sir? You look like you're in pain.'

She was annoying the hell out of him. 'I told you already, lady, no. Now keep the fuck away from me.'

The nurse withdrew, insulted, only this time looking as if she was going to call security. A second later the ER swung doors opened and a doctor came out, pulling a surgical mask off his face, his gown spattered with blood. Frankie recognised him – the guy had been with the emergency medical team who'd buzzed around Benny before they fast-wheeled him into theatre. 'Mr Tate?'

'How is he, Doc? Will he make it.'

'I'm afraid he's gone.'

Frankie stood there, numb, having feared the worst, but unable to take it in. 'He's . . . dead?'

'He passed away five minutes ago, Mr Tate. We did everything we could, but he'd lost a lot of blood and he'd got to us too late.'

Frankie was devastated, and a couple of tears started to run down his cheeks. He'd known Benny all his life. They'd been more brothers than cousins, ever since the days they were wild street kids hanging out together, and the loss hit him even harder than he'd anticipated. He was too stricken to see the two uniformed metropolitan police officers come out of a door near

ER and move either side of him, but the doctor did, and he gave the cops a nod, then put a hand delicately on Frankie's arm.

'Mr Tate, I'm sorry to have to bring this up right now, but your friend died from a gunshot wound, so naturally we've had to report it to the police. The officers here would like to ask you some questions.'

The White House
6.20 a.m.

'Sorry for waking you so early, sir.'

'I'm getting used to it, Paul.' The President, his hair tousled, dressed in his pyjamas and dressing gown, sipping from a cup of coffee his steward had brought, stood in the middle of the living room of his private quarters on the third floor of the White House. He'd gone to bed at 2.45 a.m. Of the less than four hours he'd spent in bed, he'd lain awake for three. 'Take a seat, gentlemen, and let's get this over with.'

FBI Director Douglas Stevens, Paul Burton and Richard 'Dick' Faulks, the CIA Director, had joined the President. He took a wing chair; the others chose the pair of settees near by.

'Samar Mehmet called half an hour ago from Islamabad, sir.' It was Faulks who spoke. 'He said he had an urgent message to pass on from Abu Hasim. It has do with the troop movement to Israel. There was no mention of the destination airfield yet for the prisoners, but it looks like our traitor took the bait.'

The President, tight lipped with anxiety, put down his cup and saucer, his hand shaking. There was a question he desperately wanted to ask, but he held back on it for now. 'First, tell me what Abu Hasim said.'

'Perhaps I should read it, sir?' Faulks suggested. 'Samar Mehmet translated Hasim's words into English, but he also gave it to us in the Arabic original, which we also had interpreted, so there could be no misunderstanding. Both translations agree.'

The President nodded, his tension rising as Faulks cleared his throat. 'The message reads: "To the President of the United

States, from Abu Hasim. When we last communicated, I promised we would not speak directly again. That remains my intention. However, information has come to my notice that requires this urgent communication, and your reply. Sources of mine in Israel have reported that numbers of US aircraft are now landing in that country. From this I have concluded that you are in the process of moving a significant quantity of your Middle East troops to Israel. If this is true, then it is *totally* unacceptable to al-Qaeda. It suggests to us yet another example of American deceit and dishonesty. Al-Qaeda will not accept US troops being moved to Israel, not under *any* circumstances. I wish to have clarification of this matter, sent through Samar Mehmet within an hour of your receipt of this message. If a reply is not received by that time, and to my satisfaction, then I must conclude that my information is correct and that you, Mr President, have decided to condemn your capital to immediate death by your action."'

Faulks looked up. 'The message ends there, sir.'

The President stood, exhaled a deep breadth. For the last four hours, scourged by apprehension, he'd tossed and turned in his bed, hoping that Doug Stevens had been wrong and that none of the four suspected men had betrayed him. But Stevens had been right and the message proved it. He felt crushed as he turned to Paul Burton. 'You made sure that none of our military aircraft landed in Israel?'

'Not a single one, sir. Not even the civilian ones we've hired in. Your orders were followed exactly to the letter. Most of our aircraft en route from the Middle East have landed in Germany and Britain.'

The President turned to Faulks. 'Dick, get a pen. Here's my response to Abu Hasim.'

Faulks took a pen and notebook from his inside pocket. 'I'm ready, sir.'

'Take this down. To Abu Hasim from the President of the United States. Mr Hasim, I do not know where you got this information, but I can assure you categorically that it is not true. No US troops are being sent to Israel, from the Middle

East or elsewhere, nor is that my intention. Several US aircraft, it is true, have landed there briefly, but only for the purpose of refuelling. These aircraft and the troops on board are taking off again immediately their refuelling is complete. They will not remain on Israeli soil. I repeat, they will *not* remain on Israeli soil. I am adhering completely to the terms of your letter. I trust you will adhere to yours. If you wish to communicate further regarding this obvious misunderstanding, I will be willing to furnish exact details, through Samar Mehmet, of the aircraft which have landed and taken off again.' The President nodded to Faulks. 'End it there, and have it passed on to Mehmet immediately.'

'I'll take a bet Abu Hasim's going to be scratching his head in confusion, sir,' Burton suggested.

'No doubt he will. Let's hope the answer satisfies him for now. But in theory we haven't put a foot wrong and that's what matters here.' The President turned to the question he was dreading. 'Now, what about our source? Have we got him?'

The FBI Director shot a glance at Faulks and Burton before answering. 'Sir, Rob Owens is waiting downstairs. I'd like him in on this to explain how—'

'*Have we got him?*'

'Yes, sir. We've got him.'

79

Chesapeake
6.45 a.m.

Gorev awoke. Karla was still sleeping, and he gently kissed her cheek, then climbed out of bed as quietly as he could, dressed in the dark, and went downstairs. He found Rashid in the kitchen, looking wide awake, the laptop on the table in front of him. The satellite dish was connected, positioned near the window, and as Gorev came in Rashid switched off the computer and began to disassemble the dish.

'I thought I heard you moving about.' Gorev gestured to the laptop. 'What's the idea? Is there something happening I should know about?'

'You'll learn soon enough. Where's Karla?'

'Upstairs.'

'You and she have renewed your old relationship, it seems. Unless I'm mistaken about the sleeping arrangements.'

'And what's it to you, Rashid?'

Rashid grunted, started to pack the laptop and dish in his backpack. 'Fetch her.'

'Why?'

'We have fresh orders.'

The White House
6.25 a.m.

'There's not a fragment of doubt?'

'No, Mr President. We've got our man. We compared our tape with the NBC interview he gave recently and confirmed it. The voices are a perfect match.'

The President was crushed. He had listened to the revelation, the tape of the cellphone conversation – a few brief words mentioning the redeployment of troops to Israel – and knew at once the identity of one of the voices he'd heard. But he asked the question anyway, to allay even the slightest technical doubt. Rob Owens, who had joined the others in the President's quarters, said, 'Would you like to hear the tape again, sir?'

'Once was quite enough,' the President said shakily.

'If more damning evidence is needed, we matched the second voice we caught during the two-way cellphone conversation. It was the voice of the caller to the White House who told us about the videotape at the cemetery which recorded the deaths of the men kidnapped in Azerbaijan. I just thought you should know that, sir. There's simply no question about the link between our man and the terrorists.'

The President, white faced, collapsed in his chair. His chest felt tight, his pulse raced. He could only shake his head. How could a man he'd known for so many years – a man whom he'd trusted enough to make him his adviser – betray him? Worse, how could he betray his country? The questions tormented him. He felt bile rise in his throat, perspiration run down his face.

'Are you all right, sir?' the CIA Director asked.

'No, I'm not.' The President forced himself to rise. '*Why?* Why in God's name would he help al-Qaeda? Why would he put the lives of hundreds of thousands of his fellow countrymen at risk? Be prepared to condemn them to death? *Why?* I can't understand it.'

Doug Stevens said, 'The only clues we have are the ones we turned up in his background check. But we're still digging, both the FBI and CIA.'

'Then dig faster, and as deep as you can. I want all you can get.'

'What do you intend to do about him, sir?'

'Is there a chance he might know where the terrorists are hiding out?'

Dick Faulks, the CIA Director considered the question. 'It's possible, but I doubt it. My feeling is al-Qaeda would want to keep him separate from the operation. To make contact, they'd use the cellphones, maybe secure meeting places or dead-letter drops, or possibly all three.'

'I'd agree, sir,' Stevens chipped in. 'It would only risk exposing their operation if he knew where the cell was hiding out, or even where the device was hidden. Al-Qaeda would keep that information to a close circle. Probably only the terrorists themselves know.'

'Then do we arrest him?' Paul Burton asked.

For a long time the President was silent. When he finally looked over at the others in the room they saw his anguish. He was close to tears, still unable to fathom the treachery of a man he'd trusted. 'No. Not yet. Keep watch on him for now. But I don't want any of this information made known to anyone outside this room. Is that understood? I intend bringing forward the final NSC meeting by an hour, to seven-thirty, so as to advise everyone of Abu Hasim's message regarding Israel. After that, I'll make a decision as to how I'll deal with him.'

'I think that's wise, sir,' Rob Owens advised, and explained about the cloned cellphones. 'If either man makes a call to the other in the coming hours, then there's a chance we can triangulate the calls and get a fix on both their locations. The most important one obviously being the terrorist contact at the other end.'

For the second time that morning the President was stunned. Not by bad news, but the first genuine glimmer of hope he'd had since the crisis began. 'You're saying we may be able to *find* the terrorists?'

'Or at least one of them. That's what we're hoping, sir.'

'There's also been another interesting development,' Faulks told the President.

'What?'

'The NSA over at Fort Meade picked up something called a burst transmission, almost two hours ago. It's an unusual, highly encrypted signal that they haven't been able to decode yet. They picked up a similar one recently but the transmission was so brief, no more than a couple of seconds, that they couldn't get a fix on its location. However, they primed their computers to latch on to the burst if it appeared on the airwaves again on the same frequency. When it did, they managed to get a fix to a specific area in Chesapeake Bay, south of Plum Point. They still haven't been able to decode the transmission, that's going to take more time. But the kind of signal we're talking about, so highly encrypted and non-military in source, is a little out of the ordinary. Fort Meade is suggesting we should look into it.'

'Are you telling me it might have come from the al-Qaeda cell?'

'It's too early to say, sir.' It was Stevens who answered. 'And obviously we can't mention it at the Council meeting or we'd be showing our hand. But I've ordered a surveillance team to be rushed to the area right away.'

Chesapeake
6.55 a.m.

When Gorev and Karla came down the stairs, Mohamed Rashid was standing by the fireplace, flicking through the TV channels with the remote.

'What's wrong?' Gorev said.

Rashid switched off the TV and tossed the remote aside. 'This morning I had news that the Americans had started moving troops from the Gulf into Israel.'

'News from whom?'

'My contact. Such an action by the Americans would go against the spirit of our demands. Except now, according to the signal I just received from Abu Hasim, the American President denies the move. He says US aircraft are landing in Israel, but only for refuelling.'

'I don't understand. What's going on?'

Rashid stepped away from the TV, a worried look on his face. 'Exactly, Gorev. What *is* going on? Abu Hasim has a suspicion that the Americans may be up to something. Either they're trying to confuse us in some way, deceive us, or else my contact's information was incorrect.'

'Is that likely?'

'I don't believe so. His information has always been reliable.'

'And what does he say now?'

'I haven't contacted him yet. But don't worry, I will. Except there's always a third possibility, as Abu Hasim has suggested. Our contact has been blown.'

'Does that put us in danger?' Karla asked.

'Don't worry, he knows nothing that can compromise us. Either where the nerve gas is stored or anything about our safe houses. And at this stage, he's outserved his usefulness.'

'So what's changed?' Gorev asked. 'You said there were fresh orders?'

Rashid moved to the table where he'd put his backpack and began sorting through his belongings, removing the Skorpion and checking that the magazine was loaded. 'The intention was that we'd load the chemical and device in the police van and move it into the centre of Washington if we had to. The likelihood of us being stopped in such a vehicle, wearing police uniforms, was remote. But I've made up my mind – it's too risky after your incident with Visto. For all we know, he could have told the police. Now we'll have to use another method.'

'But I thought the Americans were doing all you asked of them?' Karla said. 'Removing their troops, releasing the prisoners . . .'

'It seems they are. But after this, we can't be sure what they're up to. Our orders are to be prepared. So get your things together.'

'Why?'

'We'll join Abdullah and Moses at the safe house. If the Americans don't fully comply with the terms of our letter, we need to be ready to do our duty. If we need to, we'll have to risk using Abdullah's van to move the chemical closer to the capital.'

Rashid consulted his watch. 'Let's not waste any more time. I'll take the car. Gorev, you follow me on one of the motorcycles.

We'll both leave straight away.' He looked at Karla. 'You stay here and go through the house from top to bottom. Do a thorough job and make absolutely certain we've left nothing behind. When you're finished, take the other motorcycle and join us at the safe house. But I want you there no later than nine.'

Gorev was suddenly pale. 'I don't get it, Rashid. Why all the rush? The Americans still have until noon.'

'I told you, Abu Hasim is suspicious they may be up to something. It's made him angry, and wary. He wants to keep up the pressure. Make certain they concentrate their minds on fulfilling our demands and that they don't waste time trying to deceive us in any way. Which is why their President is about to be told of another change in our terms.'

80

Washington, DC

At 6.30 exactly, Tom Murphy was at his desk on the sixth floor of FBI Headquarters, his nerves in shreds as he drank sweetened black coffee to stay awake. He'd worked three straight shifts, with only a few hours of snatched rest in between, his blood pressure was way up, and he felt worse than shit. But as he used to point out to his ex-wife, that was sometimes a federal agent's lot, and only to be expected in an emergency. The difference being that the stress of *this* particular emergency was killing him.

With just over five hours left before the deadline's expiry, he knew he'd pushed his entire division to the limit, and didn't hold out the slightest hope of a breakthrough. Having failed to root out a single lead, he felt somehow personally responsible, crushed by a sense of defeat. Had he been a weaker man he would have given up by now, but Bronx-born Murphy was made of sterner stuff, and he was damned if he wasn't going to follow this all the way to the wire, even if it meant him being nailed into a casket.

Another thing that bothered him was the reporter. He'd agonised about telling Collins what had happened, but knew he couldn't. And wherever Nikki Dean was being held, she was incommunicado. Collins had tried to phone her and was worried about her safety – he'd told Murphy that half an hour ago, after he'd called the hospital and enquired about her son. The news was that the child had stabilised and was on his way to recovery. But still the abduction rankled Murphy. No doubt the poor woman was distressed and frantically wanting to see her son, but he didn't know how else the capital might be spared the immense danger of a mass exodus inspired by a media exposé if Nikki Dean uncovered the truth. And even if the *Post*'s presses couldn't roll out the word before the deadline, she could have turned to Washington's TV and radio stations. Still, he dreaded to think of the repercussions the woman's abduction might cause if this thing ended successfully. But there was no guarantee of that, of course, and by the time the deadline came his concerns might be totally irrelevant. By then everyone involved might be dead, himself included.

Five minutes later Murphy was about to pick up the phone when his door opened and the Assistant Director, Mathew Cage, burst into the room like a tornado. Murphy at once put up a hand defensively. 'I know what you're going to ask me, Matt, and I've pulled out all the stops. Believe me, I've got every agent available busting their ass—'

'Tom, listen up a minute.' Cage shut the door to ensure their privacy, and explained about the burst transmission that had been picked up by the NSA, and the cellphone intercept which, unknown to Cage, had been the work of the Secret Service.

Murphy was stunned, jumped up from his desk. 'Have we got co-ordinates?'

'Someplace south of Plum Point down in Chesapeake.' Cage handed Murphy the co-ordinates on a piece of paper, and both men crossed to study the wall map. 'I've already organised a couple of choppers to help with our surveillance. They'll have telemetry equipment on board to home in on the precise location, and as well as that Fort Meade's sending us blow-up maps of the area. That ought to help us pinpoint exactly the place we're looking for.'

Murphy frowned. 'But how the frig does Fort Meade know the cellphone conversation originated from one of the terrorists?'

'Don't ask me, but who the hell's complaining? If they're right, and can intercept it again, they may be able to get a precise fix. Now let's get a team down to Chesapeake, *fast*.'

'I'll get it moving right away.' As Murphy moved towards the door it burst open again and Larry Soames came in. 'Tom, you got a minute? It's important—'

'So is this. I need as many men as we've got, Larry. And I mean *right now*. Pull them off whatever you have to, this is urgent—'

'Tom, could you wait a second – we just had a call from the Met about a guy called Benny Visto.'

'*Who?*'

'He's a pimp and small-time crook who works out of Fourteenth Street. He died about forty minutes ago at George Washington Hospital, from bleeding as a result of a gunshot wound. The hospital got their hands on him too late.'

'What do you want us to do, send flowers?' Murphy was red faced. 'How the hell does that affect us?'

'He was shot by a man fitting Nikolai Gorev's description.'

Murphy gave Cage a quick look, then stared back at Soames. 'Go on.'

'Visto has a cousin named Frankie Tate, who's so cut up about his death he's singing like a canary. He told the cops a couple of our guys working the streets showed one of Visto's goons the photographs of two men we were looking for. They're holding him over at the Second District Station on Idaho Avenue.'

'What was the shooting about?'

Soames told him, and Murphy and Cage both frowned. 'A mock police van, uniforms and weapons,' Murphy said. 'What did they want the stuff for?'

'Tate thought they were going to use it for a robbery.'

'He's sure it was Gorev?'

'Damned sure. He said there was a woman with him. And the description he gave, it sounded like Karla Sharif.'

'Let's get this moving.' Murphy, galvanised, reached for the phone. 'And I'll need those men, Larry, right this instant. Where're Collins and Morgan?'

'On their way to interview Tate.'

81

Maryland
6.45 a.m.

In the early morning darkness, a GM Savana van with dark-tinted windows cut off the Eisenhower Freeway and headed south-east, on Route 4, past Andrews Air Force Base. The traffic was thin, and what little there was of it was headed into DC, but the Savana was going in the opposite direction, out into the Maryland countryside, towards the Chesapeake coast. Kursk sat in the middle row of seats, beside Razan. Two Chechen bodyguards occupied the back seats, and another guard sat up front with the driver. Razan said to Kursk, 'How many of them are there, apart from Nikolai and the woman?'

'One other man. There may be more. I don't know.'

'Who's the one you know about?'

'Mohamed Rashid. A wanted terrorist.'

'Dangerous?'

'He's a madman, capable of anything. You still haven't told me what you and your men intend.'

'I'll tell you when we get there.'

'Razan, this is dangerous—'

'No arguments. We'll do this my way.'

'What about my weapon, my cellphone?'

Razan shook his head. 'I don't want to put temptation your way. I warn you, harm Nikolai in any way and you're a dead man. And unlike Yudenich, I'm not open to negotiation. You've cost me a lot tonight, Kursk. More than you'd earn in a lifetime. Let's hope it's worth it.'

Kursk glanced at the traffic headed towards DC. In another couple of hours the highways would be crammed with commuters. Razan hadn't told him where they were going, but from the highway signs Kursk saw they were heading south-east, into Maryland. Was the chemical being stored this far out in the countryside? It didn't make sense. He knew that somehow, he *had* to get to a phone to alert the FBI. Razan and his men were in over their heads, likely to charge into a situation fraught with danger. Kursk felt sweat running down his back, his heart pounding anxiously. 'With respect, Razan, you and your men are not equipped to handle this. It's far too hazardous, and better left to the authorities—'

Razan cut him off. 'No. I told you, we deal with this my way. How much longer, Yegori?' The bodyguard in front looked round, shrugged. 'In this traffic? Half an hour, no more.'

Four miles behind Alexei Kursk in the Savana, a convoy of nine vehicles – a blue Dodge van, three Cherokee four-wheel-drives with dark-tinted windows, a Dodge intrepid, and four Ford Sables – crammed with almost forty FBI agents was speeding its way towards a beach area south of Plum Point, Chesapeake, barely fifteen miles from Winston Bay.

Within fifteen minutes of the FBI Director being informed by Fort Meade of the source co-ordinates of the encrypted burst transmission, the rapid-response team had been assembled, including agents from the FBI's Hazardous Materials Response Unit. As the convoy had set off, two specially adapted Blackhawk helicopters had taken off from Andrews Air Force Base and were by now fourteen miles ahead of the vehicles. Fitted with airborne FLIR – forward-looking infrared – systems, high-powered surveillance lenses and telemetry units to get a precise fix on the transmission's source location, one of the Blackhawks reached the target co-ordinates – a thin ribbon of access road that led down to a public beach area on Chesapeake Bay – at 6.58 a.m. In almost total darkness, the helicopter performed a single pass over the target area at a thousand feet, the passive thermal imaging equipment fitted to its belly scanning the road, the immediate surrounding area and the nearby beach for any human activity, before the pilot banked inland. As the co-pilot radioed the results to the FBI convoy, including a detailed description of the target location, the pilot headed inland for four miles to join the second chopper, waiting in a holding position at a thousand feet.

Forty-one minutes later, by the time the FBI convoy came to within a mile of the location, it was after dawn. The moon was still out, and a thin, wispy fog was rolling in off the bay. The convoy pulled in on a side road, and after a quick discussion the agent in charge decided that two of his team, one male, one female, should reconnoitre the source area. The couple got into one of the Ford Sables and drove the short two miles to the beach access road.

It was 7.39 a.m. The couple turned left off the main road, leaving their headlights on. They drove down the rutted beach access track for fifty yards, bumping through mustard-coloured rain puddles, until the driver halted and switched off the engine. He climbed out of the Sable and went over to the bushes to take a leak. At the same time he carefully scanned the road to left and right – noticing the nearest property a quarter-mile away along the headland.

When he had finished his business, he walked back to the Sable and beckoned the female agent to join him. She took a slim electric torch from the car, and together they walked down the track, arm in arm towards the beach, like a couple out for an early morning stroll. A thin veil of sea fog misted the shore, and the orange tint of sunrise painted the horizon.

As they walked, the couple scanned the deserted beach to left and right, chatting away aimlessly, their well-practised eyes studying the dunes for any sign of movement – for any sign of *anything* – examining every inch of beach in their sight. After ten minutes' walking, they turned back and walked in the opposite direction, applying the same scrutiny. Another ten more minutes and they gave up their covert search, dropped their roles of strolling lovers and raced back to the Sable, the driver breathless as he grabbed his radiophone. 'Sierra one to base. Over.'

'Base here, hearing you loud and clear, Sierra one. You see anything down there? Over.'

'Negative, base. The road's deserted. There's frigging *nothing* down here.'

The President entered the situation room at exactly 7.30. He had changed into a dark suit and grey silk tie, his face solemn as he went to take his seat at the head of the table. The fourteen exhausted men and two women in the room – their much-needed sleep shattered forty minutes ago before they were driven at high speed to the White House by their Secret Service protection details – felt a heightened sense of tension as the President gestured for them to be seated.

'Ladies and gentlemen, first of all I'd like to thank you all for getting here so promptly. I know you're all pretty worn out from so little rest, so I'd like to apologise for interrupting your sleep to urgently bring forward this meeting. However . . .' Andrew Booth paused, desperately trying to avoid settling his gaze on the man among them who'd betrayed him. 'There's been another disturbing twist in this crisis, and a very unsettling one at that. But before we get to discussing it I'd like to confirm a number of messages we received through our point man, Mehmet, in Islamabad, from Abu Hasim.' The President nodded to CIA Director Faulks. 'Dick, would you explain?'

'Yes, sir.' Faulks addressed the Council. 'At six-forty-five a.m., Mehmet phoned us the co-ordinates and location of a former Soviet military airfield near Herat, north-west Afghanistan, which is to be the drop-off zone for the prisoners. The airfield is less than three hours' flying time from our holding point in Sevastopol. As soon as we received the call, the order was immediately given for all the prisoners to be put aboard the two aircraft. They took off from Sevastopol twenty-five minutes ago, and are presently en route to the Herat airfield, with an ETA of nine-fifty a.m., Eastern Standard Time.'

'However,' the President interrupted, 'before that communication was received we had a previous message, at six a.m., in which Abu Hasim claims his al-Qaeda sources have confirmed to him sightings of US military aircraft landing at Israeli airfields in the last several hours. In his message, Hasim made it perfectly clear that he will he not accept this move under any circumstances. While it was not my deliberate intention, Hasim obviously thinks I've tried to deceive him. Even though he had made no such specific proviso in his original demands, or raised any prior objection to where we might reposition our troops outside of the Gulf, he now claims such a move to be a breach of faith and demanded my clarification on the matter.

'For that reason, I immediately informed Hasim by a return message that our troops will *not* remain in Israel, but will be withdrawn at once. In fact, to reassure Hasim, I told him that there had obviously been a mistake on his part, and that the aircraft were there only for the purpose of refuelling. So the bottom line here, ladies and gentlemen, is that shifting some of our Gulf troops on to Israeli soil is now out of the question.'

Katherine Ashmore frowned. 'But how will the Israeli PM react, Mr President? Or have you not told him?'

'Not yet. But as soon as our meeting's over, it's my intention to do so.'

'He's going to be furious, sir. He's going to think you went back on your word.'

'I've no doubt he will. But our hands are tied.'

'You'll stick to that position, Mr President?' Charles Rivermount asked.

'Yes, I will. As of this moment, all US troops have already left Israeli soil.'

'I meant will you stick to that position in the future?' Rivermount clarified. 'When this is over with. Or will they be moved back?'

'No they will not is the answer. But right this minute I'm not sure we'll have a future.' Andrew Booth paused to look gloomily at the faces around him. 'Ladies and gentlemen, I have an admission to make. I want you all to know that I erred seriously in my decision to send US troops to Israel. It was a gamble and it backfired. Those among you who counselled me to caution were right, because I've walked us deeper into trouble.

That was made very clear in the last message we received from Abu Hasim fifty minutes ago, when he provided us with the Herat airbase co-ordinates. For along with that message, Hasim altered his terms, and in a way that in my opinion may make it impossible for us to save this city.'

The faces around the table were stunned, and then Rebecca Joyce asked, 'Altered them how, sir?'

'He's reduced the deadline again.' The President's face was very white. 'We now have just over two hours to satisfy all of his demands, or at precisely ten o'clock the device will explode.'

82

Washington, DC
7.20 a.m.

'Yeah, that's them. That's the pair.' Frankie Tate ground his teeth in contempt, tossed the photographs of Gorev and Karla Sharif aside, and looked up at Collins and Morgan. They were in one of the interview rooms at the Metropolitan Police Second District Station on Idaho Avenue. 'I'm fucking positive it's them. Your buddies showed Ricky the photographs a couple of days back.'

'Why the hell didn't you report it then?'

'Hey, that wasn't up to me,' Tate snarled back at an angry Collins. 'That was Benny's decision.'

'Tell me everything. From the start.'

'And don't leave anything out,' Morgan advised. 'Otherwise, you go down for withholding federal evidence, Frankie.'

'Hey, listen, I want this asshole to pay for what he did to Benny.' Tate's face was scoured by hatred, and when he had explained everything in detail, Collins said, 'Where did Ricky and the others follow the couple to?'

'Until right before Chesapeake Beach – that's when the assholes lost the trail.'

'Where did he try to pick up the trail again?'

'Down along the coast a couple of miles.'

'Give me *details*, Frankie. Where exactly did Ricky look?'

'He said they tried all the parking lots in the apartment blocks and privates houses along the beachfront, and the north and south end of the town. One of the guys even went inland a couple of miles. They didn't see them nowhere.' Frankie tapped the photographs on the table. 'You ask me, they couldn't have just fucking *vanished*. They got to be down along there somewhere, man. Why else the fuck would they drive all the way out to Chesapeake?'

'Have you got *any* idea where they might have gone?'

'The fuck should I know?'

Collins sighed with frustration. Morgan's cellphone rang and he stepped outside to take the call. Collins turned back to Frankie. 'How much did they pay for the van and stuff?'

'Twenty thousands bucks.'

'Cash?'

'Yeah. The dude even paid Benny the remainder after he shot him, like it was a point of honour. Who the fuck is he?'

'A terrorist.'

Frankie was stunned. 'Jesus. The fuck didn't your guys say that from the start?'

'I want you to think hard, Frankie. Is there anything else you can tell me that might help us find these people?'

'I told you every fucking thing I know.'

The door snapped open again, Morgan beckoned Collins, and they stepped into the hall outside. 'You get much more from Frankie?'

Collins shook his head. 'They've got to be near Chesapeake Beach, Lou. It's even right in the area we figured after the murder.'

'What do you want to do?'

'Drive down, search the area for the white box van. It's a good marker, unless they've got it stashed in a garage out of sight.' Collins checked the time: 7.40. 'We've only got four hours. I'll go grab the car. And we better tell Murphy. We could do with some choppers in the air to look out for the van. What's with the call?'

'That was him. He says it looks like the transmission site's thrown up nothing, apart from some tyre marks and footprints. He's having the guys down at Chesapeake go through the rest of the rental properties in the area that haven't been investigated yet.'

Collins' expression was bleak. 'Any more good news?'

'We haven't got four hours, Jack.'

The White House
7.38 a.m.

The shocked faces around the situation room said it all. First to speak was Rebecca Joyce, hoarse as she addressed Andrew Booth. 'But we can't possibly make it by ten o'clock. Can't we reason with Abu Hasim?'

'He made it clear in his message that he's not open to negotiation. End of story.'

'But why's he doing it, sir?' Katherine Ashmore asked. 'He's going to get what he wants anyway, by midday. What difference will two hours make?'

The President was morose. 'He said it would concentrate our minds, as if for some reason they're not concentrated enough already. Of course, he's making an impossible demand, and the fact that he won't even contemplate a negotiation, especially when he's already so close to achieving his ends, really makes me question if we can trust him to keep his word. That maybe Janet Stern was right all along – that no matter what, Hasim is hell-bent on destroying Washington.'

'But can we make the deadline, sir?' Paul Burton asked.

'So long as there's the slightest chance we can save this city, we have to try.' Booth looked ruefully at the clock on the wall. It read 7.40. 'The prisoners have an ETA of nine-fifty a.m. So far, there hasn't been a delay. But I checked before I got here. There's a possibility that imminent head winds *could* delay their arrival at Herat.'

'Could the pilots be ordered to increase their speed?' Katherine Ashmore suggested.

'I've had that imperative radioed to the flight crews, that they *have* to reach Herat before ten a.m. However, of more immediate concern is the withdrawal. General Horton, what's your prognosis? Can we still make it in time?'

Horton looked doubtful as he pondered the question. 'Sir, at six-thirty there were still over five thousand troops to be evacuated. At seven-fifteen, my update was that the withdrawal would be complete by eleven-forty-five – and only by the skin of our teeth. A ten o'clock deadline is completely unrealisable.'

'Isn't there *any* way we can accelerate things?' A frantic note sounded in Andrew Booth's voice, perspiration beading his upper lip. 'Ferry our men by helicopter out to our Gulf ships, rush in more aircraft, pile more men into each flight, whatever?'

'Every available helicopter we've got in the region is already being used for that purpose. As for piling more troops on board the aircraft, there are weight restrictions for take-off which will limit that. Maybe if personal equipment was left behind – the troops' rucksacks and weapons ditched – we might be able to cram more of them in. But the bottom line is, we'd need extra aircraft *already* in the Gulf, ready to leave straight away.'

'We haven't got them?'

'The last seven passenger loads were scheduled to take off at eleven-forty-five. Those same aircraft are at present returning from our bases in Germany to take the final batches, and aren't due to land until nine-thirty. There's no way they could load up with men and their equipment and do a turnaround in less than half an hour.'

'We have to do *something*, General.' Katherine Ashmore sounded panicked.

'There are three more civilian cargo aircraft we leased to fly out some of our military equipment that are scheduled to land at nine a.m. If we ditch the cargo and cram the aircraft with troops, we might make it in time, but I can't offer any guarantees. For all we know, any one of the aircraft might encounter an unexpected technical problem, and then where are we? A last option is that we ask the Saudis for their help. Tell them we need a half-dozen military transporters right away.'

'You think they'd do it?'

'No questions asked? I doubt it. They'd want an explanation.' Horton looked at Booth. 'You haven't spoken to the Saudi royals yet and told them the real truth of our predicament, have you, sir?'

'No, I haven't, but they're expecting my call by noon.' The President took a handkerchief from his pocket, dabbed his face. 'Ditch whatever equipment you have to, just so long as we can get our troops the hell out of there.'

'But what about the extra aircraft we may need?' Horton asked.

'Use your influence with the Saudis, but on a personal level – the army and air force people you know, who can make it happen. Try and arrange for the aircraft to be on stand-by, in case they're needed in a hurry. If the Saudis press you for an explanation, tell them I'll provide them with one, but *after* we've got our men out. Radio our air-crews – make them aware that every minute counts and have them push hard for an earlier ETA. You've got my permission to do whatever you have to accelerate this, General. Any problems, let me know immediately.'

'Yes, sir.' Horton stood at once. 'If you'll excuse me, I'll get on it right away.'

As Horton left in a hurry, the President consulted the wall clock and stood abruptly, cutting the meeting short with a final address. 'Because of the grave danger the changed deadline poses, instead of your removal at ten a.m., I'm now ordering you to leave Washington at once. With the exception of General Horton, the chiefs of staff, Doug Stevens and myself, you will be taken to your homes by your Secret Service teams, where you will gather your families together and leave the capital immediately for your secure destination. Ladies and gentlemen, there's really nothing more I can add, except to humbly thank you for your help, your advice, your friendship and your courage in this agonising crisis that we've had to face together.' At that moment, Booth was overcome. 'May God protect us all.'

In a shaded corner of the Rose Garden, Andrew Booth sat alone at one of the white-painted wrought-iron tables. It was cold, the sun risen, an icy feel to the morning, but he needed the fresh air in his lungs, even though it did nothing to invigorate him, his mood more dispirited than ever. As he sat there dabbing his brow with his handkerchief, trying to calm his jangling nerves, one of the West Wing French doors opened and Doug Stevens came out. 'My apologies for disturbing you, sir, but there's something I need to . . .' He was suddenly aware of the sickly gloss of perspiration on Booth's face. 'Are you all right, Mr President?'

'No, I'm not, Doug.' Booth looked tortured. 'It makes me feel ashamed that I had to mislead the Council about the deployment to Israel. That's the first time I've ever lied to them. And look where it's led. I've put this city in even worse jeopardy.'

'When will you tell them the truth, sir?'

Booth had a pained expression. 'Right this minute, there isn't much point.' He put away his handkerchief. 'I've been advised that for safety reasons I'm being moved to the bunker room at a quarter before ten. There'll be a place reserved for you, Doug. I'd like you to join me as a precaution, in case this thing goes haywire.'

'Yes, sir.'

'What did you want to see me about?'

'I got word my men finished searching the Chesapeake site.'

Andrew Booth got to his feet. 'And?'

'It's just a remote dirt road near the beach, miles from anywhere.'

'They found *nothing*?'

'Some car tyre tracks and footprints that may have been left by whoever sent the message, but that's about all. They probably knew they'd put themselves at risk if we picked up their signal, so they got the hell out of there. We've stepped up the search in the Chesapeake Bay area, rechecking rental properties and hotels. My gut feeling is they may be somewhere in the vicinity of the site.'

The President was despondent. 'We're clutching at straws here, aren't we, Doug? There can't be much hope of finding our quarry within two hours.'

'The only slim chance we have is if our source calls his contact again, and we can get a fix on wherever he's phoning. But to be honest, maybe it's too late even to hope for that.' Stevens consulted his watch. 'We've been digging as deep as we can into his background, turning over every stone we can find. The report should be with me shortly, but that's not going to do us much good, apart from maybe helping us get a better grip on his motives.'

'So there's not a damned thing we can do?'

Stevens thought. 'If it was up to me, I'd confront the traitor. Face to face, just the two of you. Let him know his treacherous game is up and that he's not being evacuated from Washington with the others but will have to face the consequences of his treachery.'

'And?'

'Then appeal for his help. Tell him it's not to late to redeem himself, by giving us every assistance he can to try and find the cell and the chemical. He may be desperate enough to want to save his own neck, but I've no way of knowing. Of course, the question is, will he even have a clue where they're hidden? We could be wasting our time asking.'

'But you think it might be worth a try?'

'We've only two hours. What have we got to lose?'

83

Chesapeake
7.35 a.m.

It was light when the GM Savana cruised into Winston Bay. Kursk squinted through the tinted windows. The small beachside community was no more than a few clusters of cottages and summer homes, most with private jetties. A quarter-mile past the bay, Razan's driver turned on to a narrow slip road. A sparse forest lay to the left, the beach to the right. There were residences either side, large and small, most of them set discreetly back from the road, surrounded by wooden fences or banks of trees, some with 'Private Property' signs displayed at the entrances. Kursk noticed very few lights on, and guessed that most of them were summer homes.

'Where's the house?' Razan asked.

'Coming up on the right,' Yegori, his bodyguard, answered. 'Right there!'

As they drove past a bank of pine trees, Kursk saw the entrance to a property in its own private grounds, a winding gravel driveway leading up to it. He got a glimpse of a grey-painted two-storey cottage built of wood and brick. It was well away from its neighbours, and protected by a hedge of tall pine trees. He noticed a light on in one of the windows, an American flag on the veranda. The Chechen driver kept going, and when they had driven past Yegori said, 'How do you want to play it, Ishim?'

'Keep on for another hundred yards,' Razan ordered the driver. 'Then pull in and switch off the engine.' The driver did as he was told, pulled in off the road, killed the ignition. Kursk looked behind him, saw that the cottage appeared to back directly on to the beach and the watery darkness of Chesapeake Bay.

'Did you get a good look at the place last time, Yegori?' Razan asked.

'As much as I could.'

'What's around the back?'

'A private stretch of beach, and a jetty. A boathouse, too, I think.'

'Could you reach the rear of the cottage from the beach without too much trouble?'

'I reckon so.'

'What are you going to do, Razan?' Kursk was sweating.

'You'll see.' Razan nodded to his men, and Glock automatic pistols suddenly appeared in their hands, the two bodyguards in the back hauling MP-5 submachine-guns from under the seats. 'Yegori, take Pashar with you and cover the rear from the beach. Leave your cellphone on vibrate, and if you encounter any problems, call me. And remember, Nikolai and the woman are not to be harmed under any circumstances, but I want them apprehended. Whoever's with them is another matter. I'll leave that to your own judgment, but be careful, they could be highly dangerous.' Razan consulted his watch. 'What time have you got?'

'Seven-forty.'

'You've got exactly ten minutes to get in place, then I'll go in the front way with the others.'

'Yes, Ishim.' Yegori yanked open the door and a blast of salty air gusted into the dark cabin. The second bodyguard joined him from the rear, and the two men moved out into the morning light as the Savana's doors shut again. 'You still haven't answered me, Razan.' Kursk was growing more anxious by the second. 'What are you going to do?'

'Try and talk sense into Nikolai.'

'And if that doesn't work?'

Razan didn't reply, took Kursk's service pistol from his pocket, handed it across. 'For you own protection, nothing more. I warn you again – harm a hair on Nikolai's head and you'll never see Moscow again.' Razan consulted his watch, slid open the door, said to the driver, 'Stay here. The rest of you come with me. You too, Kursk.'

Maryland
8.15 a.m.

On Route 4, Collins had the siren on as they sped through the early morning traffic towards Chesapeake. Morgan was at the wheel, overtaking anything in their path, the Ford touching ninety-five as he kept his foot down on the clear stretches of highway. Fifteen miles from Chesapeake Beach, Collins cellphone buzzed. It was Murphy. 'Jack? Where are you?'

'Just past Melwood.'

'I've got the teams moving up from Plum Point, inland and along the coast, checking every rental property in the Chesapeake area that's left on the list. It's slow going and they've still got more than three dozen properties to get through, but I've got more men on their way right now to try and speed things up.'

'What about the choppers?'

'We've got two already sweeping up the coast and four more on their way. If they see anything like a white box-van, don't worry, I'll let you know. Keep in touch, Jack.'

The line clicked dead. Collins flicked off the cell, relayed Murphy's update to Morgan, then thought for a moment and shook his head. 'You know, it doesn't make sense, Lou.'

'What doesn't?'

'Rashid's a professional – he's not going to risk moving the chemical all the way up from Chesapeake. He's got to have it stashed nearer DC. Know what I think? Chances are he's not going to be around even if we find the hideout.'

'You're saying we're on a wild-goose chase?'

Collins grimly checked the time: 8.17. 'Probably.'

Washington, DC
8.17 a.m.

The man finished packing his Samsonite suitcase. He hadn't packed much, just the essentials: extra clothes, a washbag, and the few personal belongings he could cram into the single piece of luggage he was allowed. He guessed that he and the others were being taken to the massive government underground bunker at Mount Weather for their protection.

Alone in the bedroom, sweating heavily, he turned to stare at the cloned cellphone he'd left on the nightstand. He knew he had to risk calling Rashid, but he didn't have much time. To make matters worse, two Secret Service agents were in the living room next door, waiting for him to finish packing, and he'd barely had a private moment since they'd delivered him to his residence. As if to prove it, a knock sounded on the bedroom door. 'Come in.'

One of the Secret Service agents poked his head round. 'I'm sorry, sir, but we really have to rush things along.'

'I'll need a few more minutes.'

The agent sighed. 'But no more than that, sir, then we have to move.' When he withdrew, the man picked up the cellphone, was about to step into the bathroom to make his call when suddenly the door burst open again. He slipped the phone into his pocket, was surprised to see Harry Judd step into the room. 'Mr Judd. What are you doing here?'

'If you could come with me, sir.'

'I still need a few more minutes.'

'That isn't possible. Just come with me.'

'Very well.' The man gave in to Judd's abrupt tone, sensing the urgency, grabbed his jacket from the bed. 'Are you at liberty to say yet where I'm being taken, Mr Judd?'

'Yes, I am. Back to the White House, Mr Rapp.'

The White House
8.35 a.m.

The President's face was tightly drawn as he took the manila folder Doug Stevens handed him. They were in the living room of Booth's private living quarters, and he stared at the folder, held it in both hands. 'This is it?'

'Yes, sir,' Stevens replied. 'Every personal detail we could find out about Bob Rapp. And it makes for disturbing reading. But if you like, I can save time and fill you in?'

'Maybe you better.'

'You may recall I mentioned the young Palestinian woman, Yelena Mazawi, with whom we thought Rapp had a relationship while he was a correspondent in Lebanon?'

Booth nodded. 'You said she was a suspected Arab terrorist, killed by the Israelis. What about her?'

'Her relationship with Rapp went much deeper than we imagined.'

'What do you mean?'

'She was his wife.'

Stevens paused, registered the President's shock. For a few moments, Andrew Booth was speechless, and then he nodded for Stevens to continue.

'Not only that, the PLO "camp" where she was killed was called Sabra. You'll have heard of the brutal massacres at the Sabra and Chatila refugee camps, sir. They've gone down in infamy. The Phalanginsts, an Israelis-back militia, believed the camps were harbouring PLO guerrillas, so they stormed in and butchered all round them. They shot to death or cut the throats of every Arab they could find – men, women, and children alike. It was a heinous act, nothing but cold blooded murder, almost eighteen hundred people killed in a single day of savagery. Yelena Mazawi was visiting relatives when the attack happened, and was butchered like the rest. According to the Red Crescent report which catalogued each of the dead victims, she had her throat slit and bled to death.' Stevens paused. 'What's more she was eight months pregnant at the time.'

The President, stunned, said hoarsely, 'Go on.'

'Rapp went to pieces afterwards, just cracked up. Soon after he returned Stateside he spent six months in a psychiatric hospital.'

'And afterwards?'

'We've tried to put the rest together, sir, but some of it's fact, and some of it's conjecture on our part.'

'Tell me.'

'So far as we can ascertain, at least one of the young Arab radicals that Rapp associated with in Lebanon later became a senior figure in the Moslem Botherhood, and then al-Qaeda. What's interesting – and perhaps telling – is that he's a brother of Yelena Mazawi's. That's mentioned in the report, sir. Plus the fact that Rapp visited the Middle-East on several occasions over the years in a private capacity. Some months back he was also part of an official delegation that visited Istanbul, during which his Secret Service detail reported him inexplicably missing for almost two hours. It wouldn't surprise me if he met with an al-Qaeda contact, probably Mazawi's cousin.'

'*Why* did he betray us, Doug? What was his *real* motive? This country wasn't responsible for his wife's death.'

Stevens considered. 'If you want my honest opinion, I think for a long time Rapp's been a secret ally to the Arab cause. He's criticised US policy in the Middle East in the past, way before he joined your administration, and you knew about that. Obviously his feelings went far deeper and were far more personal and bitter than any of us imagined, though he's been careful enough to hide them.'

'But what did he hope to achieve?'

'I can only tell you what I suspect might have been his reasoning.'

'What?'

'That in some way he wanted to be a midwife to change.' Stevens shrugged. 'That's the only motive that makes sense. Looking back over the stuff he wrote years ago, it's plain he advocated strongly for a shift in our Middle-East strategic policy. That at the expense of our support for Israel, he felt the Arab nations were being deliberately kept in check, even downtrodden. And that it didn't matter to us if their just causes were being ignored – like Palestine – so long as we got our oil. Rapp believed passionately we were backing the wrong horse – that if we allied ourselves more favourably with the Islamic world we'd still have our oil, and a lot more Arab sympathy than we've endeared in the past.'

'Why didn't he advocate that policy more strongly? Why didn't he argue his cause with words rather than in a callous act of treachery?'

'Only Rapp can answer that question, sir.'

'Where is he now?'

'Downstairs. Harry Judd and a couple of his men are keeping watch over him.'

'Bring him up.'

Chesapeake
7.52 a.m.

Karla had gone through the cottage, checking all the rooms to make sure nothing was left behind. When she had finished, she packed her tote bag and changed into her motorcycle leathers. She still had a terrible feeling of dread in the pit of her stomach, and it wouldn't go away. All that kept her going was Nikolai's promise, words she had waited such a long time to hear, but even their comfort couldn't ease her anxiety. Being with him again had meant so much to her, but she knew she couldn't be at peace, not until this was over.

Before Nikolai had left with Rashid, they'd had a brief moment alone together in her bedroom. He'd looked into her eyes. 'Do you have any regrets, Karla?'

'None.'

'You're certain?'

'More certain than I've ever been.'

Then he'd touched her cheek, kissed her, and tried to put on a brave face, as he always did. 'All will be well, Karla. Don't worry, I'll see you later, my love.'

But there was something in his eyes, a troubling look she'd never seen before, which told her he was as ravaged by fear as she was, and after he'd gone, thoughts assailed her. *What if it goes wrong? What if Washington is destroyed, and hundreds of thousands of innocent people are massacred? What if I never see Josef again?* As she went to pick up the keys to the Honda, the front door suddenly burst open and two men rushed into the room, brandishing pistols.

It happened so quickly that Karla didn't see another two men slip in the back way. For a split, shock-filled second, she couldn't even react, and then they grabbed her from behind and a hand went over her mouth. As she struggled, the first two men rushed up the stairs, armed with MP-5s. Then Ishim Razan stepped in through the front door, followed by Alexei Kursk, both of them armed with pistols, and Karla could barely take it all in. She suddenly recognised the other intruders. *Razan's bodyguards.*

The men who had rushed upstairs came back down. 'She's alone, Ishim. The place is empty.'

'Let her go. Then keep watch outside.'

The bodyguards let go of Karla. They left, and then she was alone with Kursk and Razan. The Chechen indicated a chair. 'Sit.'

Slowly, in a daze, Karla sat, her heart beating wildly.

Kursk came over, pistol in hand, pointed the muzzle at her head. 'Where's Nikolai?'

84

The White House
8.45 a.m.

President Andrew Booth stood at a window in his private suite. The door clicked open. Booth turned as Harry Judd entered. He was accompanied by Bob Rapp, and an escort of two Secret Service agents who stood just outside the door, each with a hand resting on the holstered sidearms on their hips.

Booth nodded. Harry Judd withdrew, closing the door, and then the President was alone with Rapp. A crushing silence filled the room, the atmosphere charged with electricity. Booth came away from the window, and his eyes sparked with an intense rage as he stepped closer to his visitor. For an instant it seemed as if he was about to strike Rapp, but with a supreme effort he managed to suppress the urge. 'I believe Mr Stevens told you why you're here?'

Rapp gave a silent nod, his face expressionless.

The President slumped into a chair by the window. With a deep sigh, he looked towards the lawns, his knuckles white as he gripped the armrests. When he finally spoke, his voice was hoarse with emotion. 'Ten years ago I met a man I very much admired. A man I believed to be honest, decent and full of principle. A man who eventually became a friend. Not only a friend, but someone I chose as one of my advisers. An honour that I bestowed on him because I totally trusted his judgment, his loyalty, his integrity.' Booth paused, shook his head fiercely, his disbelief overflowing. 'But never, *never* in my whole life, have I been so completely wrong about someone.'

Rapp remained silent.

The President, close to tears, slowly looked back from the window, stared at him. 'Right this minute I'm not even going to ask you exactly why you betrayed your country and placed it in such jeopardy, why you aided an enemy bent on holding this capital to ransom, perhaps even destroying it. I'm not even going to question your personal motives, or ask if you were in some way compromised and forced into this. All that can come later. But right now, what's more important is that this city is faced with terrible destruction because Abu Hasim may have made it impossible for me to satisfy his insane demands on time. For all I know, that may have been his intention all along.' Booth paused, searched Rapp's face. 'Do you have anything to say to that?'

Rapp, still silent, avoided the President's stare, looked down at the floor.

Booth noticed that the man's body was trembling, beads of sweat glistening on his brow and upper lip. 'In just over an hour from now,' Booth continued, 'this capital and its entire population may be subjected to the worst terrorist attack in human history. If that happens, you will have to face the awesome consequences of your treachery, because if this city dies, you die with it. And so will I, probably. I don't know if that scares you or not, but it sure as hell scares me. But you know what scares me even more, what horrifies me?' The President, his eyes wet, looked towards the window, then directly back at Rapp. 'All the thousands upon thousands of unknowing, innocent people out there who could be dead before this morning's out. And I can do nothing about it.' He paused. 'But maybe *you* can.'

Rapp's face was deathly white. He finally looked up, spoke. 'What do you want me to do?' he asked hoarsely.

'Help me.' The President's voice was strained, pleading. 'Help me stop this thing, before it's too late.'

Chesapeake
7.55 a.m.

'Where's Nikolai?' Kursk repeated.

Karla was slumped in the chair, too dazed to reply. Her heart pounded wildly, and she was overwhelmed by her hopelessness. Kursk stood over her, still holding the pistol, and when she didn't answer Ishim Razan came over, put a hand on her shoulder. 'It's over for you, surely you know that? Why don't you tell us where he is?'

'I . . . I don't know.'

'I don't believe that, Karla Sharif.' Razan shook his head. 'No more than I believe you could willingly play a role in something so deranged. But I keep asking myself *why?*'

Karla fought back bitter tears, buried her face in her hands. 'You'd never understand.'

'Tell me,' Alexei Kursk said quietly, and put down his pistol. 'Tell me why you and Nikolai helped Rashid.'

She told him. It came in a gush of words, and when she had finished her eyes were wet. 'Where's Nikolai now?' Kursk asked.

'Gone.'

'Gone where?'

Karla shook her head, felt as if she was going to break down completely. For a moment it seemed that Kursk was about to lose his patience with her, but then he said gently, 'Is it because you feel you can't betray him?'

Karla wrung her hands in torment. 'How could I?'

'If you think I want to kill him, you're mistaken,' Kursk said. 'But Nikolai has to see reason. We both know he's not a man like Mohamed Rashid. He's not the kind who'd kill and maim half a million people just to make a point, or satisfy a blind hatred. He was driven to this, just as you were. But now it's time to end it. I think you know that, just as I think you know it's within your power to help me, to tell me everything. But you're torn between your conscience and your unwillingness to betray Nikolai. Isn't that so?'

Karla still didn't reply; Kursk's words had cut into her heart.

'Do Nikolai and your son mean more to you than an event that may cause such awesome tragedy?'

'I . . . I can't betray Nikolai. Don't ask me . . .'

'Then think of the faces of the people you've passed in the streets these last months. You're a mother, Karla Sharif. Think of the tens of thousands of women like you in Washington. Think of those who have sons or daughters and who are sitting down to breakfast with them this morning, or taking their children to school, or kissing them goodbye, unknowingly for the last time, because they may never see them again if the chemical is despersed. And with men like Mohamed Rashid and Abu Hasim, given their hatred for this country, you know that's a distinct possibility. Think of those women, Karla Sharif, and then think of the grief you've gone through and imagine what *their* grief will be like. Do you want to inflict such immense suffering on so many people?' Kursk leaned in closer, stared into her face. 'I know what Nikolai means to you. I know you don't want to betray him. But I have only one question. Could you live with your conscience if you don't?'

The White House
8.50 a.m.

The room was eerily quiet. The President, astonished by Rapp's silence, said angrily, 'I'm still waiting for an answer.'

'I can't help you.'

Booth was stupefied by his reply. '*Why?*'

'Because it's outside of my control. Nothing I could do or say would change anything. It's gone too far for that.'

'*Why* for God's sake?' Booth's anger erupted. 'Why put your country in jeopardy? Why help a bunch of terrorists hold this city hostage? What did you hope to achieve? Or were you forced into it in some way? Were you blackmailed or threatened?'

For the first time since he had entered the room, Rapp looked directly at Booth. 'No,' he replied quietly. 'Everything I did, I did knowingly.'

'Is that *all* you have to say?'

'You couldn't even begin to understand.'

'Couldn't I?' Booth, his expression livid, picked up the manila folder from the table nearby, thrust it at Rapp. 'I know about Yelena Mazawi. I know about the terrible personal grief you suffered. I know about your crack-up afterwards. I've learned more about you in this last hour from my intelligence sources than in all the years I've known you. Look if you want, it's all in there.'

Rapp took the folder, examined the pages. He turned paler, then let the folder fall on the table. 'Then you must have figured out why I did it?'

'Because you shared the same kind of goals as your radical Arab friends? Is that the reason? Because you thought you could somehow be a midwife to change? Or are you just insane?'

Rapp moved over to the window, looked out, his eyes misted. 'What I set out to do was inspired by a higher good.'

'You definitely must be crazy.' Booth was flabbergasted.

'Have you any idea what it's like to wade through a sea of corpses?' Rapp turned back and his voice suddenly trembled. 'Have you any idea what it's like to see eighteen hundred people lying dead in a river of their own blood, some of them people you knew, people you'd befriended? What it's like to find your pregnant wife dead among them? You weep and you shriek at the injustice of it, but you know it does no good, that it can never change anything. That day at Sabra, after the massacre, when I walked through the camp, when I found Yelena lying butchered in a gutter with her throat ripped open, I was overwhelmed. With despair, with anger, with a profound sense of injustice for the slaughter I saw around me, and I could do nothing about it. But from then on, it was easy to make up my mind where my allegiance lay. Easy to resolve to myself that if ever a time came when I could be an agent for change, to help Yelena's people, I'd willingly play my part for a cause I believed in.'

'Why not argue that cause with words instead of terror? Why, for God's sake?'

'Since when have words ever changed our foreign policy? I tried words in the past. They achieved nothing.'

'But why make innocent Americans pay for something they're not guilty of?' Booth said hoarsely. 'Americans didn't kill your wife and unborn child. Your country didn't commit that evil crime.'

'But American arms and missiles did.' Rapp had a tortured

look, his voice thick with agony. 'And when eighteen hundred Arabs perished that day, we didn't give a damn. What if it had been eighteen hundred Americans, or Jews, Mr President? Do you think this country would have stood up and taken notice? When it suits us, we can be so self-righteous. If Saddam Hussein invades Kuwait and puts our oil supplies in jeopardy, or some drug-dealing South American tin-pot dictator gets out of line, sure, we'll do something about it. But if a bunch of worthless Arabs get massacred? Where's our righteousness when that happens?'

'I can't answer for the past. I can't answer for something I'm not responsible for.'

'I'm not asking you to. But you have an opportunity to do something no US President has ever done before. To do the honourable thing. To correct the wrongs of the past.'

'By giving in to threat and blackmail? You're insane, Rapp. Totally insane if you can justify in your mind what you've done. What do you hope to achieve? Some kind of warped personal justice? Is that it? What the hell do you want out of this?'

'The same things Yelena would have wanted, no more, no less. Everything you heard on the tape.'

'Even if it costs hundreds of thousands of American lives? Even if it turns this city into a graveyard?'

'It doesn't have to go that far. It never did,' Rapp said with conviction. 'Not if you fulfil the terms of the letter. And that decision was never mine, but yours. You could have fulfilled them from the very start. But no, you put at risk a half million people against someone whom you have no leverage against, and who's prepared to die tomorrow.'

'That's your *last* word?'

'I don't have the last word, Mr President. You do. Me, I'm just a bit player, a messenger. It's outside of my control, and always was. And with or without me, nothing would be any different. The part I played is insignificant to all of this, or don't you see that?'

The President put a hand to his head, massaged it in a gesture of utter futility. He was acutely aware of the hopelessness of the situation, of Rapp's steadfastness, of the minutes fast ticking by as he looked at the clock on his desk. 'I can see this argument is going nowhere. That I'm talking to a wall.' Booth sighed with bitter frustration. 'Nevertheless, I'm going to ask you one last time. Will you *help* me?'

'I told you. I can't.'

85

In the South-Eastdistrict, Gorev turned the Yamaha into the front driveway of the house in Futon Chase. As he dismounted, Rashid drove up behind him in the Plymouth and parked on the street, keeping the garage entrance free. He climbed out, locked the car, went up the steps with Gorev, and knocked on the front door. This time it was Abdullah who answered, and when they stepped into the hallway Rashid said, 'Where's Moses?'

'Sleeping. He was on guard all night.'

'Wake him, we've got work to do,' Rashid said gruffly, and pushed past him towards the garage.

8.14 a.m.

The GM Savana swung on to Route 4 and the driver put his foot down, the engine snarling as it touched ninety. Kursk was seated in the middle row next to Karla Sharif, Razan on the other side. The early morning traffic was thick in the direction of DC, but the driver kept in the fast lane, flashing his headlights and sounding his horn at the cars in front. Kursk grimly checked the time. 'This is no longer something you and your men can handle, Razan. And if you want my advice, you're best staying out of it. I'll need to call for help, urgently. And I'll need a map, if your men have one.'

Razan considered, shot a nervous glance at Karla, and nodded. 'Just remember, if it's possible I don't want Nikolai harmed.'

Kursk held out his hand. 'My cellphone.'

Washington, DC
South-East District
8.30 a.m.

Rashid stepped over to the muddied Nissan. He took a set of keys from his pocket and pressed the button on the alarm keypad. The Nissan's lights flashed and the central locking disengaged. He swung open the rear doors, revealing the two sealed oil drums inside. On the floor next to the drums was the laptop computer, hooked up to the satellite dish receiver, placed near the front of the van, the laptop connected to the drums by slim electric cables.

Rashid climbed into the van. Gorev was anxious as he joined him in the back. 'What are you going to do?'

'Set the computer to trigger the detonator.' Rashid removed the hard plastic wallet containing the disk from his pocket. 'Time it to go off automatically two hours from now, at ten-thirty. Abu Hasim will give the Americans half an hour's grace, but no more.'

Gorev put a hand firmly on Rashid's arm. 'Do you have to do that right now?'

'Those were my orders, Gorev.' Rashid pulled his arm away. Sweat glinted on his temples as he opened the laptop and switched on. The screen flickered to life and the boot program loaded. When it had finished, Rashid opened the plastic wallet, slid out the disk, inserted it into the slit at the side of the laptop, and hit the enter key. When the disk had loaded, the prompt appeared on the top left-hand side of the screen: 'ACTIVE. TO PROCEED, ENTER PASSWORD'.

Rashid tapped in the password, *al-Wakia*, the screen cleared, and another command appeared: 'ENTER COUNTDOWN PERIOD'.

Rashid checked his watch, waited until the minute hand swept round to the half hour, typed the figures 02.00.00, then hit enter again.

Another line appeared on screen: 'COMMENCING COUNT-DOWN. TWO HOURS BEFORE DETONATION.'

The figure 02.00.00 he had entered was highlighted on the screen, and started to count down in seconds.

01.59.59

01.59.58

01.59.57

Rashid's face lit with triumph. 'It's done.' He looked back at Gorev. 'We'll get on our way once Karla arrives.'

'And then?'

'We leave the van near the centre of Washington. In a delivery yard on 15th Street belonging to a friend of Abdullah's. Then we make our way to Baltimore in the car. The computer will do the rest, detonate the drums when the time has elapsed, unless Abu Hasim decides otherwise.'

Gorev was uneasy. 'And what if the police or FBI stop us on the way into Washington? For all we know, they might decide to check every vehicle entering the city.'

'They'd be fools if they interfered with us. I'll trigger the nerve gas myself if I have to. All I'd have to do is re-enter the password, and make the computer fire the detonators immediately.' Rashid wiped the perspiration from his face with the back of his hand and climbed out of the van. When Gorev joined him, Rashid locked the rear doors, flicked on the alarm again, and the central locking engaged with a *clunk*.

Gorev was still troubled. 'It doesn't feel right, Rashid. This is not the way it was planned.'

'What's the matter, Gorev? Have you lost your nerve? Can't you face the reality?'

'I never thought it would go this far.'

'Well, it has.'

'Listen Rashid, you were supposed to give the Americans until noon.' Cold sweat broke out on Gorev's brow. 'What if you've made it impossible for them to make the deadline?'

'Then they've condemned their city to death.'

86

Washington, DC
8.16 a.m.

Five miles away, at FBI Headquarters, Tom Murphy was seated behind his desk, seething with hopeless frustration. The helicopters searching Chesapeake from the air, and the teams on the ground, scouring the coast and inland, had so far thrown up no sign of the terrorists' box-shaped white van. Twice in the last ten minutes the Assistant Director had called, urging Murphy to hurry his men, and reminding him – as if he needed reminding – of the fast-approaching deadline, just over ninety minutes away. Murphy, dabbing sweat from his face, had just picked up his phone to get another update on the Chesapeake search when the door burst open and Larry Soames came in, looking so flushed and agitated that Murphy at once jumped up, fearing the building was on fire. 'Tom, I've got Kursk on my line—'

'I thought he was on a plane for Montreal. What the hell's he—'

Soames cut across him, his voice bursting with strain and excitement. 'You're not going to believe this. He's found them . . . Kursk's found the sons of bitches.'

Four minutes later, after a brief but charged conversation with Alexei Kursk, a stunned Murphy told him to stay on the line and handed the phone to Soames.

A half-dozen more agents had crowded into Murphy's office to hear the news from a jubilant Soames, and Murphy pushed through them with fevered excitement and bounded over to the wall map, his pulse racing. Pandemonium was breaking out in the open-plan offices outside, people getting up excitedly from their terminals to come over to the office as word spread, but Murphy was oblivious to it all as he concentrated on the map, sweat breaking out on his face. He knew Fulton Chase on the edges of the South-East. It was a gritty, high-crime neighbourhood, five miles from the District.

'Dan, get on to the Haz-Mat guys,' Murphy yelled back at one of the agents. 'The same with the Army Technical Support Unit. Tell them I want back-up. I need them waiting on Virginia Avenue beside the Capitol Power plant in the South-East, standing by and ready to move. And tell those guys I want them in *unmarked* vehicles and in civvies. I don't want any indicators that will give them away, you hear? Do it *now*, Danny.'

'Right away!' The agent darted out of the office, which was getting crowded as more agents packed in and stood by the door, anxiously waiting to find out whether they were needed, or whether there was something – *anything* – they could do.

Murphy's mind was racing as he tried to think on his feet, without panic, without hysteria, but it wasn't easy. He had ninety minutes, maybe even less, and a hundred and one things to do, and each of them screamed for his attention. Kursk had said that Karla Sharif had told him Rashid intended moving the chemical closer to the District that morning, but she didn't know at what time – *Jesus, how did Kursk manage that coup?* – but Murphy didn't even dwell on the thought. He could find out later when he hooked up with Kursk. Now he was just so thankful for the breakthrough he felt like crying. Instead, he tried to focus on the problems he faced. So many things could go wrong, and if he made one false step it would all collapse.

Getting a team of his agents close to and even inside the safe house was going to take tremendous skill and cunning, but what frightened Murphy was it had to be done fast. Going in gung-ho was out of the question – it risked blowing the whole thing sky high. Any one of the terrorists might panic and set off the device prematurely. Above all, he had to be careful not to alert their suspicions. That was going to be a *major* problem. In certain parts of the South-East neighbourhoods, rife with crack and crime, the locals could smell any kind of intrusion from the law just by sniffing the air. And what if Rashid had people near the safe house keeping lookout, ready to warn them of any trouble? Even if he didn't, and Murphy flooded the area with agents, sure as hell they'd soon enough get spotted. Federal agents – especially droves of them – had a habit of sticking out like a sore thumb.

He knew he needed a rendezvous point, backed off from the safe house, where he could have his men standing by. Somewhere not too far away, but not too close, with good road access to the street the safe house was on, and as he frantically searched the map Murphy thought he found it, less than a quarter-mile from Fulton Chase. He made a quick decision, jabbed the map and roared, 'Does anyone know this area?'

Agents crowded around him. One of them spoke up. 'Yes, sir.'

'Then get over there as quick as you damned well can. Take a half-dozen men with you in unmarked cars – and I don't want lights flashing or sirens blaring. I need you to find someplace we can use as a temporary command post, somewhere we can park a lot of our vehicles so we don't attract too much attention, and I need you to find it *fast*. A service depot maybe, or a warehouse complex that's got a big and busy lot. You know anywhere like that around there?'

'Sure. There's a whole bunch of vacant industrial premises in the area. You'd have your choice, sir.'

'Find one that's right – *pronto* – then call me, and I'll have the Haz-Mat and tech support people hook up with us there. But nobody, and I mean nobody, goes anywhere near Fulton Chase or the damned house, and they wait until I get there. Is that understood? Now get going!'

As the agent barrelled out the door, followed by a handful of his colleagues, Murphy spun round, shouted over at Soames. 'Is Kursk still hanging on?'

'Yeah, he's still on the line.' Soames had the receiver pressed to his ear.

'Tell him not to hang up, I'll be with him in two minutes.' Murphy clicked his fingers at another agent. 'Chuck, I want a half-dozen of our best undercover people – all of them black. I'll want them to recon the street, and one of them to take a walk by the house and give it a look-over, so make sure they're the type who'd melt into the background in the South-East neighbourhoods, otherwise, if Rashid and his friends smell the slightest hint of trouble, we're in the shit.' Murphy mopped his sweating face with the back of his hand. 'And get two more dozen agents over to the South-East. Have them waiting near Garfield Park until they hear from me. And remember, I want everyone in unmarked vans and cars, you hear?'

'Got you.'

Murphy spun to address Soames again. 'Larry, have someone else hang on the line, and get in touch with Collins and Morgan. Tell them what's happening. Tell them Kursk wants us to meet up with him somewhere along Route Four, near Forestville, on the way in from Maryland. See if they can do it in the next fifteen minutes, and if they can, then they're to get their asses back to the South-East, pronto! Just as soon as we've got a rendezvous point, I'll tell them where we'll hook up.'

Breathless with excitement, Murphy reached across his desk, grabbed his cellphone with a trembling hand, and ferociously punched in the Assistant Director's number. It was answered after one ring. 'Cage.'

'Matt, we found them!' Murphy yelled. 'You can tell the President we found the bastards! They're in a house over in Fulton Park on the South-East. That's where they've got the chemical stored.'

Eight miles from Chesapeake, Collins' cellphone buzzed. He flicked it on, heard Larry Soames's voice, and what sounded like a mayhem of other voices in the background.

'Jack?'

'Go ahead, Larry.'

'Jack, I want you to listen to me . . .'

87

Washington, DC, South-East
8.48 a.m.

At the safe house, Moses Lee was drinking coffee, sitting on an easy chair by the front window, the MP-5 cradled in the crook of an arm, when Rashid came into the living room, followed by Gorev. 'How are you brothers doing?'

'You've been keeping a close watch on the street?' Rashid asked.

'Sure. I was on watch until midnight, then I grabbed some sleep and Abdullah took over. Now it's my frigging turn again.' Lee stood, his muscles bulging beneath the stretched cotton of his T-shirt, and gestured towards the window. 'Don't worry, it's all been real quiet. No cops in sight, no neighbourhood assholes bothering us.'

Rashid went over to the window, anxiously pulled back the filthy curtain, peered into the street, and said over his shoulder to Gorev, 'She should have been here by now.'

'Maybe she's caught in traffic?'

'She's on a motorcycle, Gorev. She shouldn't have that problem.'

'What if it broke down?'

'Then why didn't she call here? She has the number.'

A look of concern crossed Gorev's face, but he tried to shrug his anxiety off. 'Don't worry about Karla, she'll be here.'

Rashid frowned doubtfully, said to Moses, 'Keep a good lookout. If you see her arrive, let me know.' He checked his watch, turned back to Gorev. 'If she's not here in the next twenty minutes, we'll go without her.'

8.32 a.m.

Speeding north-west on Route 4 towards Forestville, twelve miles from the centre of DC, Collins was in a state of fevered anxiety. The strain under which he had been living for the last three days had got even worse since he'd heard the news about Kursk and the woman. He and Morgan had sped back from Chesapeake in a state of amazement. Collins' mind was on fire, his body taut as a coiled spring. *They'd found the safe house.*

But would Rashid still be there? What if he'd already left, moved the chemical? Even if he hadn't, how would they gain access to the house without alerting the people inside? And even if the device was still there, could they disarm it in time? What if the whole thing went haywire? He hoped to God Murphy had some kind of plan, but the more he thought about it, the more he realised how near impossible the situation still was, and how infinitely hazardous. He was convinced that Rashid was the kind of terrorist who, at the first sign of any kind of trouble, wouldn't have a single qualm about turning himself into a martyr and taking half the population of Washington with him.

Rashid. The hope of finding him again made Collins' pulse race, and he sweated as he stared fixedly ahead. Morgan drove like a madman, the speedometer climbing to over a hundred as he held the accelerator hard to the floor, the siren wailing as they sped along the fast lane, the engine growling. 'The mall's coming up on the right,' Collins yelled. 'Take the next exit.'

Morgan swung off the highway, and two minutes later they roared into the shopping-mall parking lot, where Murphy had arranged for them to meet Kursk. Parked in the forecourt they saw the Savana with dark-tinted windows, Kursk waiting beside it. He waved, then rolled open the Savana's rear passenger door, and a woman got out. Collins saw that it was Karla Sharif. She looked pale and drawn, and as Morgan went to pull up beside the Savana Kursk immediately rolled the passenger door shut again, and the vehicle revved and screeched away, heading out of the mall. Collins was confused, his mouth agape. 'What's going on, Kursk?'

The Russian yanked open the Ford's rear door, guided Karla Sharif into the back seat and jumped in after her. 'I'll tell you on the way.'

8.59 a.m.

The vacant warehouse was just off the South-East Freeway, a quarter-mile from Fulton Chase. It had been closed for business for almost four months, but that morning the unfenced parking lot was occupied by a half-dozen cars, two Dodge vans with dark-tinted windows, and at least two dozen anxious-looking federal agents.

A grey Ford Galaxy tore into the lot, sped towards the vehicles and jerked to a halt. Tom Murphy jumped out, lathered in sweat, the rear doors opening as three more agents climbed out behind him. Murphy ran over to one of his men and roared in near-panic, 'Where the fuck's Collins and Morgan? They ought to be fucking here by now!'

The man nodded past Murphy's shoulder as yet another unmarked FBI Ford suddenly screeched into the lot. 'They're right behind you, sir.'

There comes a time in every crisis situation, as a deadline looms and there's no obvious sign of a positive resolution, when panic sets in. No matter how hard law enforcement agents and hostage negotiators try to control the tense, final moments of a difficult situation – especially one that presents an extreme threat to human life – panic starts to rear its ugly head. Some negotiators like to call it 'deadline hysteria'.

As resolution nears and tensions climb high, exhaustion starts to factor into the equation, nervous fears arise, and stark terror begins to take over. Tom Murphy liked to compare such moments to a kind of hurricane. And as the storm whipped up, as the elements raged all around and people went crazy, he liked to employ a certain tactic: tell everyone around him to shut the fuck up, find a quiet place in the middle of the blizzard of activity, block his mind to the frantic immediacy of the deadline, and try to go through his checklist of 'things to do' in clear, calm, logical steps.

Except this morning it wasn't entirely working out that way. First of all, after a desperate, hurried talk with Karla Sharif, he had Collins, Morgan and Kursk take her into the rear of one of the vans to quiz her some more, get her to draw them a detailed layout of the interior of the safe house, give them names and descriptions of the people inside, and then keep her out of the way for now, because Murphy had two dozen agents buzzing around him, all waiting to be told what to do, or desperate to fill him in on the frantic activity that had been taking place in the last fifteen minutes while Murphy had been speeding to the rendezvous from headquarters. He jabbed a finger at one of his men. 'Dave, what's the story with our guys doing the recon?'

'We've got three of them on the street where the house is. One of them took a walk by the property two minutes ago. There's a grey Plymouth parked on the street and a black Yamaha motorcycle parked right in the driveway.'

'Any sign of activity?'

'Absolutely none. And all the curtains are closed, upstairs and down, so our guy couldn't see a thing inside.'

Murphy thought: *if the Plymouth and motorcycle are parked outside, what were the chances that the van was still in the garage? Had Rashid already moved it closer to the centre of the District? Please God, let it still be in there!* 'Tell those guys if they see anything move I want to know about it immediately. What's the house look like?'

'Two-storey, run-down. The same with most of the properties along the street.'

'What about the garage?'

'Our guy says it's got a metal pull-down door that looks solid enough. He thinks you're not going to be able to beat it down or break in from the outside without making a lot of noise. But we might be able to ram it.'

'No! That's too dangerous. If the chemical's still in there, we could set the damned thing off. Are the houses either side of the property occupied?'

'It looks like it.'

'Do *any* near by look unoccupied?'

'Unless we go knocking on doors, it's going to be hard to tell. You want our guys to do that?'

'No! I just want them to watch the damned house and do what they're supposed to do for now!' His face and shirt drenched with perspiration, Murphy turned to another of his men. 'What about our tech people, have they got their listening equipment set up yet?'

'They're doing it right now, Tom. They're in a van parked near the end of the street, out of sight of the house.'

'Tell them to stay there. I don't want them moving any closer, even if they can't pick up anything.' Murphy didn't know whether the directional listening devices in the tech van would help much, but it was worth a try. 'Did any of the guys on the street try and get a look near the rear of the house? I want to know if we can gain access the back way.'

An agent carrying a two-way radio spoke up. 'One of them is doing it right now. He's going to call me back. But he thinks if the other houses near by are anything to go by, there should be a small rear garden that backs on to the house behind.'

'For God's sake, tell him to be careful. They might have a lookout.'

'He's aware of that, Tom.'

Murphy was shaking inside with a mixture fear, exhaustion and nervous excitement, and knew that every agent around him was feeling the same turmoil. With barely an hour to go before the deadline, and no way of knowing when Rashid would move, tension electrified the air. His reserves of energy dwindling, Murphy was aware that deadline hysteria was starting to creep in.

'Then let me know as soon as he calls you.'

For the umpteenth time, Murphy wiped sweat from his face, then he raced over to the green van where the woman was being held and jumped in the back.

* * *

In the cramped cabin, Karla Sharif was seated between Collins and Morgan, with Kursk facing her. Perspiration dampened her face and she looked under enormous strain, her body trembling so much that Murphy wondered whether she was going to break down. 'We're going to need your help,' he told her urgently. 'We're going to need you to get us inside the house. Do you think you can do that?'

'I . . . I don't know.' Her eyes were terror ridden.

'Listen, lady, we haven't much time and you're the only hope we've got,' Murphy said. 'And Rashid's expecting you, right?'

'Y . . . yes.'

'Then we need to do it *fast.*' Murphy turned and snapped at one of his men, 'I want a wire on her! Get her wired up for sound, right now!'

'Tom,' Collins interrupted, 'we've got a problem here.'

'What?'

'They're expecting her to arrive on a motorcycle.'

'*What?*'

When Collins explained, Murphy groaned, hammered his forehead with the heel of his hand. 'Oh, Jesus . . .' In all the frantic activity, he hadn't even thought about *how* Karla Sharif was meant to travel up from Chesapeake. Where the fuck was he going to get an identical blue 1,000cc Honda at this stage? It was a *major* fucking spanner in the works, and he shook his head in total despair. 'Jesus, we're fucking screwed, Jack.'

'Maybe there's still a way we can get her inside.'

'*How, for Christ's sake?*'

Collins explained, and when he had finished everyone turned to look at Karla Sharif, who was suddenly very white as Collins said to her, 'The question is, do you think you can do it?'

88

Izzy Madek smacked his lips. After a busy ten-hour night shift, his ass glued to the seat of his grey metro cab, he was looking forward to a breakfast of scrambled eggs, some hash browns, a little bacon on the side, some crisp buttered muffins, and a cup of sweet hot coffee to wash it all down. He'd dropped off his last fare near the South-East Freeway and was cruising his ancient Buick towards his favourite breakfast stop off Minnesota Avenue when all of a sudden it happened. *'The fuck . . . !'*

He screeched to a halt. Two guys jumped out in front of the cab, one black, one white, both of them waving pistols. As Izzy slammed the brakes on hard, the white guy dashed over to the driver's-side window and flashed a gold badge. 'FBI! Get out!'

'The fuck have I done, man—!'

Collins yanked open the door, dragged Izzy bodily from the car. 'We need to borrow your cab.'

9.06 a.m.

Murphy had moved his command post to the end of the street, a hundred and fifty yards from the safe house. He was in the front of one of the Dodge vans, Kursk seated beside him, and both of them were lathered in sweat. 'Have we got everyone in place?' Murphy shouted to one of his men.

Wedged in the back of the cabin, a radio glued to his ear, the agent gave him the thumbs-up. 'We're all ready to go, Tom. Just give the word.'

Murphy made the sign of the cross, took a deep breath, and thought: *This is it. If I mess things up, half a million people could be victims inside the next few minutes*. He felt he was being crushed by the weight of the thought, but he'd tried to put everything in place, tried to cover every angle he could in the short time available. He'd considered trying to take over a couple of the houses across the street, entering them from the back and getting snipers in place to cover the front of the safe house, but it was too risky. Neighbours might see the activity and panic at the sight of heavily armed FBI agents swarming though their backyards; Rashid might be alerted, could have a lookout on that side of the street.

However, on Murphy's signal, six of his men, wearing Kevlar bullet-proof vests and armed with Heckler and Koch submachine-guns, were ready to scale the walls at the rear of the safe house and go in the back way. A dozen more were in another Dodge van right behind Murphy, ready to move as soon as he gave the word. He'd advised his agents of the interior layout of the house that Karla Sharif had provided – if he'd had enough time he'd have sent a couple of his people to study the interior of a similar property in one of the nearby streets, but the clock was ticking and he really didn't have that luxury. He was anticipating that the two other men along with Rashid and Gorev – an Arab named Abdullah, and an American black named Moses – would still be in the house, and would be heavily armed.

He had six black undercover agents on the street, two of them in a car fifty yards from the house, another two, the youngest of the bunch, dressed in baggy street clothes, loitering a little farther down the street, trying to look as if they were a couple of ghetto guys just chewing the cud. Four unmarked vans crammed with Haz-Mat people and chemical experts from the army Technical Support Unit were a block away, ready to race towards the safe house as soon as Murphy gave the order. A hundred more agents had arrived at the warehouse lot, his reserve waiting to be called on, and three helicopters were hovering over the South-East Freeway, all ready to rush to the scene if they were needed, like the half-dozen ambulances waiting in position just off the freeway, half a mile away.

As well as that, two expert hostage negotiators and two Arab translators were in the van behind Murphy, in case of a stand-off.

But Murphy doubted it would come down to that; gut instinct told him this was a do-or-die situation, with only two ways to go if Rashid was inside the house – either they killed him or he'd set off the device. Another thought troubled him: Karla Sharif. He knew she was in a high state of anxiety, barely hanging in there, completely on edge. She had been wired for sound with a one-way miniature transmitter, taped to her belly, the tiny microphone attached inside her blouse, which meant that Murphy would be able to hear – hopefully – what was being said inside the house. The signal level had been checked by his men – it was good, and he'd told Karla Sharif to try to keep her conversation in English when she entered the house.

Murphy thought: *I just hope to Christ she can carry this through and do exactly as she's been told.* Yet another question troubled him. *Can I entirely trust her? What if she changes her mind once she gets inside the house?*

He didn't even want to dwell on that thought. He mopped his face, took another look at the dilapidated red-bricked town house with his binoculars. Still he saw no movement. *Please God, be good to me this day.* He crossed himself again, removed his Glock automatic from his shoulder holster, made the decision. 'OK, we're going in. Get ready, guys.' The agents in the van started to finger their weapons nervously, the air in the sweaty cabin electric as Murphy flicked on the transceiver in his hand, pressed it to his mouth. 'Jack, we're all set up. Let's do it.'

Collins' voice came back on the radio. 'We're on our way.'

Five seconds later, Murphy saw the grey metro cab turn into the street from the other end. It moved slowly, hugging the kerb, moving towards the house. Murphy tapped the van's driver on the shoulder. '*Go!*'

The Dodge throbbed into life, then started to crawl down the street at five miles an hour.

* * *

The grey metro cab cruised up the street. Morgan was driving, moving at barely ten miles an hour, Karla Sharif in the passenger seat behind him. Hunched down on the seat beside her, wearing his FBI jacket with the gold letters embazoned on the back, Collins had his Glock in his right hand. 'We're almost there, Jack,' Morgan said. 'Another fifty yards. Get ready, man.'

Collins rolled his sleeve across his damp brow, stared up at Karla Sharif's face. He saw that her legs were shaking, and it was obvious she was having trouble keeping herself together. 'You're sure about what you have to do?'

'Yes.'

'Just try and remember what we told you, OK? Keep it clear in your mind.'

Karla Sharif was still shaking. Collins thought: *She's not going to be able to go through with this.* Some instinct made him reach out, forget his hostility towards her, touch her hand reassuringly. 'Remember, we're right behind you.'

'We're here!' Morgan slowed the cab and braked gently to a halt, just ten yards short of the red-bricked house. Collins kept his head well down, but managed to look up again at Karla Sharif. He could feel her fear – it was like a living thing, and her trembling had got worse. 'Take a couple of deep breaths,' he told her. 'Then step out of the cab and do like I told you.'

Karla froze. She was unable to move, just stared ahead, her lips quivering.

Morgan suddenly turned to her. 'Please, lady! Don't let us down. You've got to do it!'

She was on the verge of tears. 'Promise me something?'

'What?' Collins asked.

'Promise me you'll try not to harm Nikolai.'

'That's going to be up to him. Now please, you've got to go. Step out, do like I told you, and try and stay calm.'

Trembling, and with supreme effort, Karla forced herself to step out of the cab. She shut the rear door after her, opened her bag and came round to hand Morgan a hundred-dollar bill through his rolled-down window. He shook his head, as if he didn't have change, then the two of them pretended to talk for a few moments, until Karla turned and with shaking legs started to walk up to the house.

89

Moses Lee, watching from the front window, the MP-5 cradled in his hands, saw the grey metro cab pull up. He got to his feet, cracked open the net curtain a fraction, saw the woman step out of the cab, search in her bag to pay the driver, then saw the driver shake his head. The cabby said something to her, and then the woman turned away from the car and came up the path to the house, while the driver remained in the cab and kept his engine running.

Some instinct made Lee glance out into the street. For the past couple of minutes, he'd noticed two black guys, maybe fifty yards away, over on the other side. They wore street clothes – baggy nylon jackets, loose jeans and woollen hats – and as they stood there talking they seemed to be absorbed in their conversation. But was it his imagination, or did he notice one of them take a sly look towards the house a couple of times? Something else bothered him about the two young men: they seemed a little older than most of the guys you saw hanging out in the street. Not by much – the two were in their mid to late twenties maybe – but even that tiny inconsistency made him suspicious.

Added to that, ten minutes ago he'd noticed a sedan car go by with another two black guys inside. Nothing strange about that, but he was convinced that the car's passenger had shot a glance at the house as he drove past, as if he were giving it the once-over. Lee hadn't seen the car since, and the two things, taken separately, wouldn't have caused him any great concern. But taken together, they made him wonder whether there might be trouble, and triggered an alarm inside his head.

Lee frowned, just as Abdullah came into the room behind him, drinking coffee, cradling the pump-action shotgun. 'Tell your friend the lady's arrived in a cab,' Lee told him urgently. 'And tell him I got a feeling there's something weird going down out on the street.'

Karla walked up the path to the house. Her legs felt weak, her heart was pounding in hammer blows. She saw the curtain flicker in the downstairs front window and her anxiety soared. She was being watched, had expected it, but it heightened her fear.

She knew what she was supposed to do, had understood everything she had been told. She knew that she couldn't go back, but could she go through with it? Could she really betray Nikolai? Or had she done that already? She wanted this nightmare to be over, wanted desperately for it to end right here and now, and in her heart she knew there was no other way. All she could hope for was that she could she somehow save him. She fought back tears as she went up the steps, conscious of the transmitter taped to her stomach and rubbing against her skin, the miniature microphone clipped under her blouse.

She rang the bell. Her hand was trembling as she took it away. *'Whatever you do, don't let them see you're anxious or afraid. Tell them your excuse, that you need change to pay the driver. When you've got the change, return to the cab, pay the fare, then go back into the house, leaving the latch off and the door ajar.'*

'Can't I tell Nikolai?'

'Absolutely not! It's too risky. We don't know how he'll react. You'll have to do this alone.'

That was how she felt right now. *Alone.* And frightened, more frightened than she had ever been in her life. Suddenly the front door opened, but only by about six inches. Karla caught a brief glimpse of Moses Lee, standing just inside the hall, but he made no attempt to open the door fully and let her in. 'It's me,' Karla said, trying desperately to stop her voice from shaking.

'What's with the cab?'

'The motorcycle broke down.'

Silence. The door still didn't open. 'Why . . . why don't you let me in?'

No response. Karla thought: *There's something wrong, something terribly wrong.* She could sense it, her heart pounding faster. Then whispered voices came from inside the hall, and her spirits sank even farther. *They know. They know I've betrayed them.* And then the door suddenly opened and Lee's powerful black hand came out and pulled her inside.

'The *fuck's* going on?' Morgan said aloud.

'Why, what's happening?' Collins was still crouched in the back, on the opposite side, unable to see.

'Someone just dragged her inside the house. Don't move, Jack, whatever you do, *don't fucking move.*' Morgan flicked on the radio. 'Tom? They just pulled her inside the fucking house!'

'*What?*'

'Someone opened the door, pulled her into the hall, and the door closed. It's not right, Tom. The bastards must be on to us. You want us to go in?'

There was a pause, a long and desperate pause – Murphy had heard the exchange at the door through his earpiece but couldn't see what had happened – and then he said, 'No! I've got her on the wire. Don't do a fucking thing for now! Stay right were you are and don't do a fucking thing until I tell you!'

'What's going on?' Rashid faced Karla in the front room. He had the Skorpion in one hand, gripped her arm with the other. 'I asked you a question.'

'The motorcycle broke down. I had to take a taxi.'

'Broke down where?'

'A couple of miles from here. The engine cut out and I had to abandon it. That's what kept me.' Despite her fear, Karla tried to look defensive. 'Why all these questions? I've told you what happened.'

Rashid searched her eyes, animal caution written all over his face. Gorev, standing behind him, stepped forward, pulled his arm away. 'Let her go, Rashid. Karla's done nothing wrong.'

'Maybe not. But I don't like coincidences. Moses saw two men loitering across the street. Another two went by in a car a little while ago. He thinks they may have been watching the house.'

'Are you sure of that?' Gorev shot a look at Moses.

'It looked that way to me.'

'The two men on the street, where are they now?'

'Moved on. Haven't seen them since.'

'But they could have been harmless?'

'Sure. But me, I wouldn't like to take no chances.'

'Did you notice anyone follow you from Chesapeake?' Gorev asked Karla.

'No . . . I didn't see anyone. I was careful.'

Rashid was still suspicious. Sweat beaded his face as he looked over at Abdullah, who stood at the window, watching the taxi. 'What's happening?'

'Nothing. The cab-driver is still waiting.'

Rashid turned back to Karla. 'Why's he waiting?'

'I only had a hundred-dollar bill. He hadn't change. I need ten dollars to pay him.'

'Where did he pick you up – in the street or from a rank?'

'In the street.'

Rashid considered. 'And you're certain no one followed you?'

'I told you already. What are you getting at, Rashid?'

Rashid didn't reply, crossed to the window, looked out at the waiting cab and the black driver, then scanned the empty street. Gorev followed him and did the same. 'I think you're overreacting, Rashid. It's understandable. We're all on edge here. Let Karla pay the driver and be done with it. If he's made to wait any longer he'll only get suspicious. And then we could be in trouble.'

Rashid wiped sweat from his face. He seemed to consider for a moment, uncertain, and then nodded to Moses. 'Give her the money.'

Moses took out a wallet, handed over a ten-dollar bill. Karla took it, started to turn towards the hall, but suddenly Rashid gripped her arm again. 'Wait!'

'But . . . I need to pay the driver.'

'No, let Moses do it.'

90

In the Dodge van, Murphy heard it all. The voices, speaking in English, told him he was in *deep* shit.

'*Moses saw two men loitering across the street. Another two went by in a car a little while ago. He thinks they may have been watching the house.*'

And then, a little later: '*But . . . I need to pay the driver.*'

'*No, let Moses do it.*'

Panic gripped him. He knew that as soon as the guy called Moses walked down the path and peered into the cab he'd see Collins and realise what was going on. Worse, Murphy had no doubt from the tone of one of the voices – probably Rashid's – that the others inside the house would be watching, and that they were already highly suspicious. Three minutes ago he'd moved his undercover teams farther down the street, but he was still in the Dodge, and less than eighty yards from the house. What if Moses noticed the van? Would he suspect something? It was all going haywire, and Murphy knew he had only seconds to decide what to do. Had he really any choice? Frantically, he put the radio to his mouth. 'Lou, it's gone wrong. It's not the woman who's coming out, it's one of the others . . . the black guy, Moses!'

'*Shit! What do you want us to do?*'

'Take him down as soon he nears the cab. Then we're going in!'

In the front room, Karla was beginning to panic. She thought: *It's all going horribly wrong.* She watched as Moses checked his automatic pistol, slipped it into his trouser pocket and tossed his MP-5 and two spare magazines to Abdullah. 'Take these.' As

Abdullah took the weapon and magazines, Rashid said to him, 'Go cover the back entrance, and don't leave your position unless I tell you.'

Abdullah left the room, brandishing the MP-5, and Rashid went over to the window with the Skorpion, again studied the waiting cab through a crack in the curtains, and nodded to Moses. 'If you see anything suspicious, get back inside at once.'

'Sure, no sweat. Just you brothers make sure you watch my ass.' Moses went out into the hall, and Rashid said to Gorev, 'I'll cover him from the window. You take the garage. Make sure the doors are secure and stay there until I order you to do otherwise.' He tossed Gorev the keys to the Nissan van. 'Be ready to move the van if we have to.'

'You're sure you're not overreacting, Rashid?'

'We're not going to take chances. Do as I say, Gorev!'

Gorev cocked his Beretta. A look passed between him and Rashid, and then he turned and followed Moses out into the hall. As Karla moved to go after him, Rashid grabbed her arm. 'Where do you think you're going?'

'With . . . with Nikolai.'

'You stay here with me.' Rashid's eyes narrowed with suspicion. 'I don't know what it is, but there's something about this I don't like.'

Karla was near breaking point, desperately trying to hide her anxiety, feeling that any second now she was going to collapse. She thought: *I've lost my one chance to warn Nikolai.* At that moment she feared the worst; every last hope she had nurtured was dashed. Looking out the window, she saw Moses step out the door, start to walk down the path.

Rashid went to cover him, and cocked the Skorpion.

Moses Lee stepped out of the front door. He kept his eyes on the cab and the black driver, then started to walk slowly down the path. His instinct for danger was well honed, and halfway along the path something clicked inside his head. The driver was watching him approach – not just casually, but intently. *Too fucking intently*. Moses met his stare, and the man tried to avoid looking directly at him.

Another click.

Moses glanced quickly up and down the street. To his left, a dark green Dodge van was parked by the kerb, eighty yards away . . .

Another click.

Farther along, fifty yards away from the van on the other side of the street, were two more cars, the dark shapes of figures inside. He was damned sure one of the cars was the same sedan he'd seen from the window, ten minutes earlier . . .

Another click. At that precise moment, he knew with certainty there was trouble.

Fuck . . .

He dipped his hand into his pocket for the pistol, his gaze returning to the cab and the driver. The man was still watching him. At the same time his arm was moving across the seat, as if he was reaching for something, and then . . .

Moses saw another movement, but in the back of the cab this time. He noticed that the rear window was already rolled down, a white guy appearing, a gun in his hand . . .

Moses wrenched out his pistol, got off two quick shots at the figure in the back, and a split second later all hell broke loose . . .

In the cab, Morgan saw the front door open, and whispered to Collins, 'He's coming out, Jack! Wait until I give you the word!'

Morgan saw the big black man named Moses step out of the house and start to walk slowly down the path. He was well muscled, looked the kind who could handle himself, and Morgan sweated as he watched him approach the cab, taking his time, moving as if he was in no great hurry. As he walked, the man stared at him. Morgan turned his head away slightly, but kept trying to watch the guy as he came closer. He saw him look left, then right, and Morgan's heart was in his mouth as he saw the guy reach into his pocket . . .

'Jack, he's on to us!' Morgan screamed. 'Take him down!'

Collins came up from behind the seat, the Glock in his hand, just as Moses fired and two shots rang out, shattering the cab window . . .

Collins heard the crack of two gunshots and a double *zing*.

Two rounds whistled inches from his head – one through the open window, another punching a hole through the roof – and he frantically climbed out the far side of the cab, hit the ground, crawled towards the rear end of the car. At that same moment, the downstairs front window in the house shattered, and a burst of machinegun fire blazed, stitching the cab, punching holes in the metalwork, sending glass flying.

Morgan was trying to fire his pistol as he clambered out the driver's side when a round caught him in his right leg, and then another. He yelled, clapped a hand on his leg, dragged himself behind the cab as another burst of machinegun fire raked the chassis. Blood pumped between Morgan's fingers, but as Collins crawled towards him he yelled, 'I'm OK, Jack! Just get the bastards!'

'For Christ's sake don't move!' Collins crawled farther to the right, out of sight of the front window of the house, poked his head out from behind the cab and saw the black guy, Moses, reach the front door, spin round and fire again at the car. Collins aimed, fired twice, the bullets ripping into Moses' heart, punching him back against the doorway.

Another barrage of gunfire erupted from the front window, slamming into the cab, gouging chunks of concrete from the ground to Collins' left. But he was beyond reason now, in the grip of fury, filled with a fierce energy, and it spurred him on as he came out from behind the cab, ignoring the gunfire as he sprinted towards the house, emptying the Glock at the front window as he ran.

Suddenly the street came alive with FBI vehicles screeching to a halt, dozens of men piling out, and then the firing started, a steady stream directed through the downstairs front window of the house, shattering glass, sending brick chips flying. The flashes of gunfire from inside the house died, and when Collins reached the front door he stepped past the black man's body and flattened himself against the side wall. Even in his panicked state he was aware of the seconds ticking away, of the urgency, knew he had to get inside the house *fast*, and find Rashid.

Drenched with perspiration, he ejected the spent magazine from the Glock, slammed home a fresh one, and started to move into the hall . . .

In the front room, Rashid's face was a beacon of horror as he saw the events unfolding on the street. He was livid as he raised the Skorpion, the weapon bucking wildly in his hands as he fired through the front window, shattering glass, raking the cab with gunfire, his wrath almost like a living thing. As he continued to fire, vehicles were suddenly pouring into the street from every direction, tyres screeching, men clambering out, gunfire exploding from all sides, and in that instant Rashid knew that Karla Sharif had betrayed them . . .

'Bitch!' he screamed, and swung the Skorpion round, his face white with rage as he sought his target.

She was gone.

Then a hail of deadly gunfire poured in through the shattered front window, stitching the walls, sending plaster chips flying, and Rashid swore, crouched, and scuttled towards the garage like a man possessed . . .

Abdullah was covering the back entrance when he was suddenly startled by an explosion of gunfire from the front of the house. Two quick shots, then two more, followed by a crackle of sustained machinegun fire.

In a state of panic, he started to move from his position towards the front, but then remembered Rashid's orders. As he spun back round to cover the rear he saw three men in black bullet-proof Kevlar jackets and black helmets, carrying Heckler and Koch submachine-guns, clambering over the back wall. Abdullah brought up the MP-5, and it chattered in his hands . . .

The street outside was a scene of chaos. As soon as Murphy gave the order to move in, a dozen vehicles had poured in from both ends of the street and pulled up near the house. Heavily armed agents wearing Kevlar jackets piled out, taking cover behind the cars and vans as gunfire raked the street from the downstairs front window of the house.

Murphy and Kursk were the first to arrive as the Dodge screeched to a halt fifty feet from the property. They saw the flashes of gunfire from the downstairs window, and jumped out of the Dodge, crouched behind it. Morgan was lying behind the grey cab, thirty feet away, clutching his bloodied leg, as Collins sprinted towards the house, firing as he ran.

Murphy clutched his radio and screamed, 'We've got an agent headed for the front door – give him back-up! Direct fire towards the downstairs front window! I repeat – the downstairs front window! Take the shooter out!'

A savage barrage of fire was suddenly directed towards the front window by the agents in the street, and Murphy saw Collins reach the front door, flatten himself against the side wall, eject the magazine from his Glock and prepare to reload.

An agent with a radio in his hand dashed up to Murphy, breathless. 'We're being held off at the rear entrance, sir. We've got two men down, wounded by a shooter at the downstairs window.'

'I want him taken out *immediately*! Do whatever you fucking have to. And someone get a medic for Morgan!' Murphy didn't take his eyes off Collins for a second, saw him slam home a fresh magazine. 'What's happening with the wire?' Murphy yelled back at one of his men near the rear of the Dodge, who had a pair of headphones on. 'Can you hear anything?'

'No, sir, it's gone dead!'

'*Christ!*' As chaos raged around him, Murphy felt it was all falling to pieces, and one frantic thought dominated his mind:

We have to get inside the house – fast – and stop Rashid triggering the device.

Murphy hadn't a doubt in his mind that the Arab was crazy enough to do it – for all he knew the bastard might be doing it right now. It seemed that the firing from the front window had died, and he saw Collins start to move towards the front door, his Glock readied in both hands.

'Where's the back-up for Collins?' Murphy screamed. He turned away, directing his attention towards a group of agents crouched behind one of the FBI vehicles. Already some of them were moving out from behind their cover, cautiously starting towards the house, but to Murphy, frantic, no one was moving fast enough. 'I want us in that front door *now*! I don't want him going in alone!'

'Kursk's gone after him, sir!'

'*What?* Murphy turned, saw Kursk sprint towards the house, his pistol drawn, just as Collins started to move in through the front door . . .

Gorev had just checked the garage doors, made sure they were locked and secure, when he heard the first two shots. Then he heard another two, followed by a welter of crackling machinegun fire that came from somewhere inside the house.

His face drained, and he started to race back towards the kitchen, ignoring Rashid's order to remain in the garage, his Beretta at the ready, his only fear at that moment Karla's safety. He heard the screech of tyres outside in the street, and as he reached the garage doorway Karla came rushing in, stumbled into his arms, pushing him back, her fingers tightening on his flesh. Her face was distraught, totally panic stricken, and before Gorev could speak she cried, 'Don't go out there, Nikolai! Don't go out, or you're dead!'

The frenzy of gunfire continued inside the house, and then it was answered from outside, a crackling barrage that was so intense Gorev moved to push past her, wielding the Beretta in alarm, but Karla held him back. 'No, Nikolai, please . . . don't go!'

'What's going on . . . ?'

Gorev suddenly saw it then, saw the truth in her face, tears welling in her eyes, a terrible fear in her voice. 'It's over, Nikolai. It had to be, don't you understand? Give me the keys to the van. We have to stop Rashid!'

Gorev was suddenly white faced, hoarse with disbelief. 'What have you done?'

'For God's sake give me the keys—'

At that moment Karla heard racing footsteps, and knew she was too late. As she turned she let go of Gorev, saw Rashid storm in, the Skorpion in his hands, his eyes wild with hate, scoured with panic. 'She betrayed us, Gorev! The bitch betrayed us!'

A savage look lit Rashid's face with something near to madness, and then he lost it completely. In one quick movement he levelled the Skorpion and squeezed the trigger. The burst caught Karla in the chest, sent her flying back. Gorev was transfixed, his mouth agape, horror spreading over his face as he saw her hit the wall, a blush of crimson spreading across her upper torso.

'She was a traitor!' Rashid yelled. 'She tried to stop us! She deserved to die!'

'*NO!*' Gorev screamed, all sanity gone as he raised the Beretta, but the Arab still had the Skorpion in his hands and he squeezed the trigger again. Gorev took a burst of machinegun fire that almost lifted him off his feet, sent him staggering back. There was blood in his mouth and he was choking on it, but Rashid kept firing until he had emptied the magazine. Gorev's body twitched in an obscene dance of death, then it crumpled to the floor.

Rashid wasted no time. He moved towards the body, his face glistening with oily sweat as he knelt, fumbled for the Nissan's keys in Gorev's pocket, knowing exactly what he was going to do . . .

At the back of the house, Abdullah emptied the MP-5 through the window, then crouched down, ejected the magazine, and loaded another. He had seen more men trying to climb over the wall, others trying to direct fire towards him from several vantage points at the back. As he cocked the MP-5 and went to raise himself to aim again, a rapid burst of fire made him duck his head, and then a hail of lead drilled into the room, shattering the remaining windows, gouging the walls, forcing him to keep his head down.

He was bathed in sweat, knew the situation was hopeless. Then an object came hurtling through the shattered window. Abdullah got a brief glimpse of the stun grenade, before it exploded with a flash. The percussion stunned him, knocked him off his feet. Then an oblong canister clattered on the floor, trailing white smoke.

Tear gas.

The canister smouldered, began to fill the room with acrid smoke. Abdullah heard machinegun fire from the direction of the garage, put a hand over his nose and mouth, and darted out of the room . . .

Collins moved into the hallway, holding the Glock at arm's length. The firing from the street and the front room had stopped – he'd checked the room and it was empty – but from somewhere towards the back of the house he heard staccato bursts from a submachine-gun, and the noise of a blast filled the air as shouts came from the street outside. Kursk had stepped into the hall behind him, ten feet away, and was moving up to join him, his gun at the ready. As Collins stepped cautiously forward, he found himself in the empty kitchen. There was another door off to the left, half open. He ignored it, remembered he had to turn right, knowing this would lead him to the garage, knowing he had to get their fast. Kursk screamed, 'Behind you!'

Collins ducked and turned as an Arab wielding an MP-5 burst into the kitchen from the room to the right, his hand covering his mouth as white smoke billowed out the door behind him. Before Collins had a chance to aim, Kursk fired, hitting the man in the left side, then shot him twice again, hitting him in the head.

Collins stood, heard frantic noises in the hall as agents poured into the house. Tear gas began to seep into the kitchen, and as Kursk covered him he started towards the garage . . .

* * *

Rashid was in a frenzy. As he fumbled for the keys in Gorev's pocket, all hell was breaking loose inside the house, a welter of noise and gunfire that made it difficult for him to concentrate. Then he found the keys, stood, pressed the alarm pad. The Nissan's central locking disengaged with a clunk. As he went to yank open the Nissan's rear door he heard the shots in the kitchen, and brought up the Skorpion . . .

As Collins moved into the garage doorway, his hands outstretched, clutching the Glock, two things happened almost at once. He saw Karla Sharif and Gorev sprawled on the floor, their bodies twisted grotesquely . . .

And he saw Rashid . . .

He was frantically inserting a fresh magazine into the Skorpion, and as he brought up his weapon and cocked it, a look of madness lit up his eyes.

To Collins, in that single, stark moment of terror, everything seemed to happen in slow motion.

He fired once.

The first shot punched Rashid in the shoulder.

He lurched, and Collins fired twice again.

The second bullet caught Rashid in the chest.

The third hit him in the head, killing him instantly.

Everything was a blur to Collins after that. A frenzied blur of wailing sirens and noise and frantic bedlam, as agents rushed into the garage, Murphy behind them, screaming for the Haz-Mat team and the army chemical experts, and Kursk's voice, raised, shouting for an ambulance . . .

Epilogue

Washington, DC

It was almost one that afternoon when the President entered the Oval Office. Doug Stevens was already there, and he turned as the door clicked open. 'Mr President.'

'Doug.' Andrew Booth slumped into his chair. For the last two hours he'd been a recluse, had retreated to his private quarters, needing solitude to recover from the mind-crushing burdens he'd shouldered in the last three and a half days. And to reflect, after he'd said his prayers of thanks, on what he might do next.

Once he'd showered, shaved and put on fresh clothes, he'd sat alone for ten minutes at his bedroom window, staring out at the capital, close to breaking point, overwhelmed by relief that it was still there, unharmed, living and breathing, before his eyes, and that his nightmare of lines of trucks ferrying hundreds of thousands of bodies out to Maryland and Virginia had not become reality. 'You've got an update for me, Doug?'

'Yes, sir. The device has been totally disarmed and I've been assured that the chemical is in a safe condition. An army technical support unit is about to move it to a secure location and they'll have the removal completed by late this afternoon. Until that's done, our emergency evacuation plans will remain in place. But the word from the experts is we're pretty much out of extreme danger.'

'Thank God.' Booth clasped his hands together, as if in silent prayer. 'What's happening with the woman, Karla Sharif?'

'She's being operated on by a team of surgeons over at George Washington Hospital.'

'Will she make it?'

'I really can't say, sir. She's in a pretty bad way.'

'What did we turn up so far?'

'She was co-operative when we questioned her before we sent her in, and helped us fill in the blind spots.' Stevens explained the details he had to hand. 'The name for the operation was Resurrection Day. The Arab term is *al-Wakia*, I believe.'

'That stuff you said about her, you think it's true? That she was forced into it? That al-Qaeda threatened to kill her son if she didn't go along?'

'That's the way it appears. It seems she'd been an unwilling participant from the start, plagued by doubts all along, but she had little choice. And in light of what she did to try and stop Rashid, Major Kursk asked that you consider his special request, sir.'

The President reflected. 'Even if her explanation as to why she helped al-Qaeda is true, she still had a choice. And difficult and stark as that choice was, she made her decision. There has to be a harsh price for that.'

'What will we do about her, sir, if she pulls through?'

The President thought again. 'I don't want her name appearing on any reports into this affair. She gets no mention, you understand? After I've had time to reflect, we'll deal with this in our own way. As for the bodies of Gorev and Rashid, Dick Faulks made a suggestion they be cremated, and we have it done quietly, with no big fuss. No headstones, no nothing. I think that's wise.'

'Whatever you say, sir.'

'What about the reporter lady?'

'She was released from custody an hour ago.'

'Was she told the truth?'

'Yes, sir.'

'What's her mood like?'

'Hard to tell. She just seemed relieved she knew the truth and that it's all over. I guess we'll know in time if she's going to press charges. We might have trouble with that one, but that's another day's worry. Just like Rapp.'

Booth was solemn. 'What about her son?'

'The word I got, it looks like he's going to be OK.'

The President nodded. 'I've reconvened the Security Council for an hour's time to review everything we've got to hand.' He rose, some instinct making him turn and stare up at the seal behind his desk. The bald eagle, clutching its arrows, stared back. For several moments he studied the symbol of his office and his country. 'You know, I really didn't think we'd make it. I really feared that Abu Hasim would triumph in the end and decimate this city, no matter what the outcome. But it seems we've had our own day of resurrection.'

The President turned back. Stevens saw that Booth's eyes were wet. 'That'll be all for now, Doug.'

'What about Abu Hasim, Mr President? Surely we can't let him get away with what he's done? Aren't we going to make him pay?'

'Yes, we are.'

Nikki parked the car and Collins walked alone through the cemetery gates. The graveyard was empty, and he moved past the granite and bronze tombs to the small hill shaded by pines until he came to the headstone where he had laid his wife and son to rest. He placed the flowers on the grave, said the prayers and the words he wanted to say, the same words he always said – that he missed them, that he longed for them back, that their passing had left a terrible sorrow, an unending ache.

That nothing could replace them, *nothing*, not ever. His eyes swept over the smooth granite and the gold-leaf paint on the cold chiselled-words that inscribed his pain. *Until we're together again, I'll miss you, always.*

He would always come here and be haunted by their absence. There was no cure for his pain, and if truth to tell, he didn't want any. He never wanted to forget the sacredness of his memories with his wife and son. And though he knew his dreams would still reclaim him, he was aware now that they would do so less often. He would move on, make another life for himself with Nikki and Daniel. Not to forget his past, because he could never forget, but to make himself whole again, heal himself, and in so doing honour the memory of the two people he had loved and lost.

For a fleeting moment an image flashed before his eyes: the grainy photograph he would no longer keep, of the cold, hard face of the man who had helped take Sean's life. But then the image was gone and with it went the hatred, the rage, the vehemence that for so long had made a stone of his heart. On this day, at this moment, he simply wanted to remember.

When he had finished talking, when he had finished his whispered words to the dead, he touched the stone that bore their names. '*I miss you Annie, I miss you, Sean.*'

Then he turned and walked down the hill towards the gates where Nikki waited.

Afghanistan

As the sun rose over the horizon, Abu Hasim climbed up the hill. Clutching his gown and using his cane, he reached the top and unrolled his prayer rug. Facing south-west to Mecca, he invoked the name of Allah, the Master of the World, the All Merciful and All Compassionate, the Supreme Sovereign of the Last Judgment. Then he knelt, prostrating his body three times, touching his forehead to the ground each time, glorifying the name of God and his Prophet. His ritual over, Abu Hasim sat back on his rug, breathing heavily, staring out at the lofty pinnaces of ochre mountains that spread jaggedly across the horizon. There was no sound but the whisper of a gentle breeze.

All evening and morning he had waited anxiously for word from Washington. When the ultimatum had expired by three hours and no word had come, when he had received no news that the aircraft had landed with the prisoners, his triumph of the last few days had evaporated, replaced by a hollow feeling in the pit of his stomach, the sickening certainty that his gamble had failed.

By morning his fear had grown. He had no doubt now that the device had been found and neutralised. He would pay for his failure. The Americans would use all the technology at their disposal to try to locate him. Missiles would rain down on his camps, of that he was certain. Which was why he had moved his base fifty miles up the valley to a secret place, the deep tunnels bored into the rocks where no one ventured but him and his men. The Americans could look, but could they find him here? He turned as he heard a noise, saw Wassef Mazloum, his ravaged-faced commander, hurrying up the slope. When he reached the top, Mazloum handed him a folded slip of paper. 'A message came, Abu.'

'From whom?'

'Our friend in Islamabad. The Americans told him to give it to you.'

Abu Hasim rose, unfolded the paper, read the message. He face turned very pale, as if a cold hand had suddenly twisted deep inside his bowels. For several moments he stood there, beads of cold sweat on his brow, his gown blowing in the breeze. Then he turned to stare out at the desolate landscape, the parched, stony mountains that surrounded him like prison watchtowers, held out his hand and let the paper fall. It blew away, snatched by the wind. Abu Hasim turned, left his prayer rug on the ground where it lay, and walked down the hill.

Mazloum watched him go, until his eye caught sight of the piece of paper, blowing over the rocks. He had read the words, recalled the simple message. They were from the blessed Koran, a chilling prophecy for the Day of Resurrection:

There shall befall them the evil consequences of what they do, and they shall not escape. For their soul shall taste of death, and they shall be paid fully their reward, wheresoever they hide.

Moscow

The snow was falling heavily at Sheremetyevo airport the following day, the flakes swirling in a brutish, icy wind that blew in from the Russian steppes. An hour after his aircraft touched down, Alexei Kursk was in the back of a taxi as it drove towards Mazilov. He ached to see his wife and daughter again, but as the taxi rounded a bend and came to a bridge over the Moscow river, he said to the driver, 'Pull in here.'

The driver braked to a halt. 'Wait. I won't be long,' Kursk told him, and climbed out.

The glacial wind had died, but the snow still fell. Not far away he could see his home, the outline of the small, brick-built house on the river bend, the roof covered in white, a plume of wood smoke curling from its chimney. As the snow drifted down, his mind was flooded by memories. He and Nikolai on the steps of St Basil's Cathedral, both of them eighteen, the day they graduated from high school. And farther back, another memory, of two small boys, sitting on the riverbank, twelve years old, their arms around each other's shoulders. *We're blood brothers, remember?*

And the day Nikolai's father had been cremated, when they had walked across the fields until they came to the small rise where a willow tree overhung the banks, and Nikolai, desolate, had scattered his father's ashes on the water.

The willow tree was long gone. As Kursk stepped towards the middle of the bridge he looked down. There were icy patches near the embankments, but the water wasn't completely frozen, wouldn't be until late December; for now the Moscow river still flowed on its way to the sea.

Kursk took the parcel from under his arm. Unwrapping the brown paper from the ceramic vase, he scattered Nikolai Gorev's ashes. They drifted down to the cold water, falling with the flakes of snow, until they sank and were embraced by the depths of the great river. 'It's over now, Nikolai,' he said aloud. 'You're at peace.'

Kursk stood there, lingering for a few minutes until he had finished a silent prayer, and then he turned and walked back to the waiting car.

Florida

The white-painted house was on a hill, a private rented villa that looked out over the sea and the Florida coast. Not the same splendid views as her old house in Tyr, no sweeping gardens of olive trees, no scent of jasmine or bougainvillaea, but for several weeks now it had been her home.

It was a warm December day, and Karla Sharif sat on the veranda, staring out at the blue water. The armed FBI men who protected her never let her out of their sight, and one of them sat near her now, reading a magazine as he basked in the sun. That morning she had finished writing her letter, it was in her pocket now as she waited for her visitor to appear. The silver four-wheel-drive Explorer with black-tinted windows came up the hill ten minutes later. It braked to a halt on the gravel driveway, and when the passenger stepped out of the car he climbed slowly up the steps of the veranda.

He was a big man, tall and robust, and she remembered his name: Tom Murphy. The other FBI men stepped away to allow them their privacy, and as Murphy went to sit in one of the cane chairs near by he wiped his brow with the back of his hand. 'How's your health? Is it on the mend?'

Her wounds still hurt, her scars still livid, but they were healing. The doctors had warned her it would take months until her body had repaired and she would be right again. But the other wounds, the ones that would never heal, hurt her most. 'Thank you, yes.'

'I wanted to tell you we'll be moving you pretty soon,' Murphy said. 'For security reasons I'm not at liberty to say where, or when exactly you'll be departing. But soon you'll start your life again, with a new name and identity.'

Karla Sharif asked the question she was desperate for her visitor to answer. 'And my son?'

Murphy told her what he knew. That the Israelis had moved Josef to a different high security prison. A place where the prisoners were kept in solitary for their own safety, where he was watched twenty-four hours a day and kept separate from the other inmates.

'Do you think I'll ever see him again?'

A flicker of sympathy showed in Murphy's eyes. 'That's not up to me. I know Major Kursk made a request on your behalf that your son be released. But we'll have to wait and see. In time, perhaps, it'll be considered. But even if that happens, it will be up to him whether he wants to see you or not.'

Karla nodded, bit her lip. 'Will you do something for me?'

'If I can.'

'Will you see that Josef gets this?' She took the unsealed envelope from her pocket. 'It's a private letter to my son, but I left it open. I know that under the circumstances you'll have to read it.'

Murphy nodded, opened the envelope. He slid out the handwritten letter and took his time reading the pages. When he had finished, he looked thoughtfully out to sea, as if moved by the words he'd read, then finally he folded the pages and returned his gaze to Karla. 'I promise you it will be delivered.'

'Thank you.'

Murphy stood, slipped the envelope into his pocket. He didn't offer to shake her hand, even though for some reason he looked as if he wanted to, but gave a nod instead. 'We probably won't be seeing each other again, and I know it might seem odd me saying this, considering everything, but good luck to you.'

She watched as Murphy went back down the steps. When he reached the Explorer, he looked back at her one last time, then he climbed into the passenger seat and the four-wheel-drive swung round and drove back down the hill. She watched it go. When it had disappeared, she looked out towards the sparkling water. Her heart felt broken. Broken for the man she had loved, and for the son she couldn't be with. She remembered she had told Nikolai that she believed you paid a price for the wrong you do. It didn't matter whether the wrong was just or unjust, you still paid the price, just as Nikolai had paid, and she was paying now. The grief was unbearable. So many times during these last weeks she had wondered whether she should have told him her secret, but then what difference would it have made to him, or to her? In time she would no longer weep when she thought of him.

But she would always weep for Josef. She had told him everything in her letter, and how much she loved him. Told him he was still young, perhaps too young to understand or to forgive her for not telling him the truth about his past, but she hoped that some day he would find it in his heart to do so. She had his photograph by her bed. He was a fine-looking boy, tall and strong, and so much like his father. Every day, and every night before she slept, she prayed that some day she would see him again, and that they would be together. And however small or vain it was, she at least had that hope to cling to.

Acknowledgements

When I began writing Resurrection Day in earnest in the summer of 1999, I knew exactly what the book was to be about – a dramatic attack on American's capital, Washington, DC, by an al-Qaeda terrorist cell armed with a new and deadly weapon of mass destruction.

When I finished the first draft in late August 2001, I put it aside to mull over how I might cut down the manuscript, more sharply focus the story, and also make some headway on the next book. On September 11, I switched on my TV and like millions of others watched in horror as al Qaeda hijackers crashed into the Twin Towers and the most astounding act of terror in history unfolded.

While writing this novel I had a constant dread that al Qaeda might carry out a major terror assault on a US city. Having completed much of my research and interviewed many terrorist experts and listened to their opinions I had come to the stark conclusion that such an assault was not only possible, but imminent. The same experts also unanimously agreed that the terrifying scenario I intended to write about in my book, and which I outlined to them, was perfectly feasible. 'Yes, it could definitely happen,' they all said. 'But let's pray it never does.'

And then, on September 11, fiction became reality. Who can ever forget those extreme scenes of horror? Trapped victims hurling themselves from the World Trade Center's Twin Towers in final acts of suicidal despair. Lower Manhattan's soaring landmarks of steel and glass imploding, killing thousands of helpless innocents.

Since September 11, so much has happened that has changed

the world. But it is important to reflect that the al Qaeda attacks could have transpired in so many ways. If planned differently, they might have been even more massive in their scope and evil intent, the damage and the numbers of deaths even more horrifying. What if a biological or nuclear weapon had been used? Or the terrifying weapon of mass destruction I suggest in this book? After the events of September 11, extreme terrorist plots are no longer just the fantasy of thriller writers, but reality. We have come to live in the time of our fiction.

In the aftermath of the attacks, I genuinely believed my novel would not be published. It was too emotive a subject, the public's nerves were too raw, and I was convinced my publisher would have no appetite for a book whose subject matter was ripped from today's headlines. Unwilling to leave the manuscript aside, I carried on, for I still had facts to verify with the experts I had consulted.

But nobody wanted to talk. Doors that were once open were now firmly shut. The FBI, the CIA, White House staff, and the many authoritative US sources with whom I had spoken, simply stopped answering my calls. They were in shock, unwilling to talk; the premise of my book was too close to the bone and their national security was suddenly a very real concern. I had to use other means to reach my end – invoking a writer's fictional licence in minor instances where I couldn't verify the facts – but reached it was.

Resurrection Day was a massive undertaking, and there are so many people who helped adorn the tapestry of this book with the threads of their knowledge. Most requested that I not mention them by name, and after the attacks they expressed that view even more strongly. But I would like to thank them now, collectively, for their help and courtesy in answering my many questions – this book could not have been written without them. I would also especially like to thank my editor at Hodder, Carolyn Mays, for her enduring faith in this novel, and for her incredibly incisive editorial judgment. The reading public is too often unaware of the vital input editors may make – they're the quiet, unsung heroes of the business, toiling away in the background – and I'm deeply grateful to Carolyn for her invaluable advice, courage, and patience.

Resurrection Day is fiction, but in many ways it is a story of what *might* have happened had September 11th not transpired the way it did, and the al Qaeda attacks had taken a dramatically different course – one with an even greater potential for human death and disaster.

It is also the story of what may yet happen.

But let's pray it never does.